Satyajit Ray was born on 2 May 1921 in Calcutta. After graduating from Presidency College, Calcutta, in 1940, he studied art at Rabindranath Tagore's university, Santiniketan. By 1943, Ray was back in Calcutta and had joined an advertising firm as a visualizer. He also started designing covers and illustrating books brought out by Signet Press. A deep interest in films led to his establishing the Calcutta Film Society in 1947. During a six-month trip to Europe, in 1950, Ray became a member of the London Film Club and managed to see ninety-nine films in only four and a half months.

In 1955, after overcoming innumerable difficulties, Satyajit Ray completed his first film, *Pather Panchali*, with financial assistance from the West Bengal government. The film was an award-winner at the Cannes Film Festival and established Ray as a director of international stature. Together with *Aparajito* (The Unvanquished, 1956) and *Apur Sansar* (The World of Apu, 1959), it forms the Apu trilogy and perhaps constitutes Ray's finest work. Ray's other films include *Jalsaghar* (The Music Room, 1958), *Charulata* (1964), *Aranyer Din Ratri* (Days and Nights in the Forest, 1970), *Shatranj Ke Khilari* (The Chess Players, 1977), *Ghare Baire* (The Home and the World, 1984), *Ganashatru* (Enemy of the People, 1989), *Shakha Proshakha* (Branches of a Tree, 1990) and *Agantuk* (The Stranger, 1991). Ray also made several documentaries, including one on Tagore. In 1987, he made the documentary *Sukumar Ray*, to commemorate the birth centenary of his father, perhaps Bengal's most famous writer of nonsense verse and children's books. Satyajit Ray won numerous awards for his films. Both the British Federation of Film Societies and the Moscow Film Festival Committee named him one of the greatest directors of the second half of the twentieth century. In 1992, he was awarded the Oscar for Lifetime Achievement by the Academy of Motion Picture Arts and Sciences and, in the same year, was also honoured with the Bharat Ratna.

Apart from being a film-maker, Satyajit Ray was a writer of repute. In 1961, he revived the children's magazine, *Sandesh*, which his grandfather, Upendrakishore Ray, had started and to which his father used to contribute frequently. Satyajit Ray contributed numerous poems, stories and essays to *Sandesh*, and also published several books in Bengali, most of which became bestsellers. In 1978, Oxford University awarded him its DLitt degree.

Satyajit Ray died in Calcutta in April 1992.

* * *

Gopa Majumdar has translated several works from Bengali to English, the most notable of these being Ashapurna Debi's *Subarnalata*, Taslima Nasrin's *My Girlhood* and Bibhutibhushan Bandyopadhyay's *Aparajito*, for which she won the Sahitya Akademi Award in 2001. She has translated several volumes of Satyajit Ray's short stories, a number of Professor Shonku stories and all of the Feluda stories for Penguin Books India. She is currently translating Ray's cinematic writings for Penguin.

SATYAJIT RAY

THE COMPLETE
ADVENTURES OF FELUDA
I

PENGUIN BOOKS

PENGUIN BOOKS

USA | Canada | UK | Ireland | Australia
New Zealand | India | South Africa | China

Penguin Books is part of the Penguin Random House group of companies
whose addresses can be found at global.penguinrandomhouse.com

Published by Penguin Random House India Pvt. Ltd
7th Floor, Infinity Tower C, DLF Cyber City,
Gurgaon 122 002, Haryana, India

Penguin
Random House
India

First published by Penguin Books India 2000
This rejacketed edition published 2015

12 11 10 9 8 7 6

ISBN 9780143425038

Typeset in Sabon by Mantra Virtual Services, New Delhi
Printed at Replika Press Pvt. Ltd, India

CONTENTS

AUTHOR'S NOTE

I have been an avid reader of crime fiction for a very long time. I read all the Sherlock Holmes stories while still at school. When I revived the children's magazine *Sandesh* which my grandfather launched seventy-five years ago, I started writing stories for it. The first Feluda story—a long-short—appeared in 1965. Felu is the nickname of Pradosh Mitter, private investigator. The story was told in the first person by Felu's Waston—his fourteen-year-old cousin Tapesh. The suffix 'da' (short for 'dada') means an elder brother.

Although the Feluda stories were written for the largely teenaged readers of *Sandesh*, I found they were being read by their parents as well. Soon longer stories followed—novelettes—taking place in a variety of picturesque settings. A third character was introduced early on: Lalmohan Ganguli, writer of cheap, popular thrillers. He serves as a foil to Felu and provides dollops of humour.

When I wrote my first Feluda story, I scarcely imagined he would prove so popular that I would be forced to write a Feluda novel every year. To write a whodunit while keeping in mind a young readership is not an easy task, because the stories have to be kept 'clean'. No illicit love, no *crime passionel*, and only a modicum of violence. I hope adult readers will bear this in mind when reading these stories.

Calcutta
February 1988

Satyajit Ray

FOREWORD

My husband was always deeply interested in science fiction stories. It was not surprising, therefore, when he decided to write them for his children's magazine *Sandesh*.

One day, he told me that he wanted to experiment with stories other than the science fiction ones.

'What other kind?' I asked, although I knew the answer instinctively, since both of us were avid readers of detective stories. He didn't have to tell me, so he smiled and said ruefully, 'But there's a big snag . . .' I looked inquiringly at him. 'The magazine is meant for children and adolescents, which means I shall have to avoid sex and violence—the backbone of crime thrillers . . . you do realize the difficulty, don't you?'

I did, indeed. Still, I told him to go ahead and give it a try—I had so much faith in him!

He did. And that's how 'Feluda' was born and became an instant hit. Story after story came out, and they all met with resounding success. When they were published in book form, they became best-sellers. It was really amazing!

After finishing each story, he would throw up his hands and say, 'I have run out of plots. How can one possibly go on writing detective stories without even a hint of sex and hardly any violence to speak of?'

I couldn't agree with him more, but at the same time, I knew he would never give up and was bound to succeed at his endeavour. That is exactly what he did. He never stopped and went on writing till the end of his days. That was my husband, Satyajit Ray, who surmounted all difficulties and came out on top!

Calcutta
October 1995

Bijoya Ray

INTRODUCTION

One of my earliest recollections of childhood is of struggling to get two thick bound volumes from my father's bookshelf, with a view to using them as walls for my dolls' house. To my complete bewilderment, when my father saw what I had done, he told me to put them back instantly. Why? They were only books, after all. 'No,' he explained, handling the two volumes with the same tenderness that he normally reserved for me, 'these are not just books. They are bound issues of *Sandesh,* a magazine we used to read as children. You don't get it any more.' Neither of us knew then that *Sandesh* would reappear only a few years later, revived and brought to life by none other than Satyajit Ray, the grandson of its original founder, Upendrakishore.

That Satyajit Ray was a film-maker was something I, and many other children of my generation, came to know only when we were older. At least, we had heard he made films which seemed to throw all the grown-ups into raptures, but to us he was simply the man who had opened a door to endless fun and joy, in the pages of a magazine that was exclusively for us. This was in 1961.

In 1965, *Sandesh* began to publish a new story (*Danger in Darjeeling*) about two cousins on holiday in Darjeeling. The older one of these was Feluda, whose real name was Pradosh C. Mitter. The younger one, who narrated the story, was called Tapesh; but Feluda affectionately called him Topshe. They happened to meet an amiable old gentleman called Rajen Babu who had started to receive mysterious threats. Feluda, who had read a great many crime stories and was a very clever man (Topshe told us), soon discovered who the culprit was.

It was a relatively short and simple tale, serialized in three or four instalments. Yet, it created such a stir among the young readers of *Sandesh* that the creator of Feluda felt obliged to produce another story with the same characters, this time set in Lucknow (*The Emperor's Ring*), in 1966. Feluda's character took a more definite shape in this story. Not only was he a man with acute powers of observation and a razor-sharp brain, we learnt, but he also possessed a deep and thorough knowledge of virtually every subject under the sun, ranging from history to hypnotism. He was good at cricket, knew at least a hundred indoor games, a number of card tricks, and could write with both hands. The entries he made into his personal notebook were in Greek.

After *The Emperor's Ring,* there was no looking back: Feluda simply went from strength to strength. Over the next three years, *Kailash Chowdhury's Jewel* and *The Anubis Mystery,* the first two Feluda stories set in Calcutta, appeared, followed by another travel adventure, *Trouble in Gangtok.* Over the next two decades, Ray would write at least one Feluda story every year. Between 1965 and 1992, thirty-four Feluda stories appeared. *The Magical Mystery,* the last in the series, was published posthumously in 1995-96.

In 1970, Feluda made his first appearance in the *Desh* magazine, which was unquestionably a magazine for adults. This surprised many, but it was really evidence of Feluda's popularity amongst young and old alike. Between 1970 and 1992, nineteen Feluda stories appeared in the annual Puja issue of *Desh* (the others were published in *Sandesh,* except for one which appeared in *Anandamela,* another children's magazine). Pouncing upon the copy of *Desh* as soon as it arrived, after having artfully fended off every other taker in the house, became as much a part of the Puja festivities as wearing new clothes or going to the temple.

A year later, Ray introduced a new character. Lalmohan Ganguli (alias Jatayu), a writer of cheap popular thrillers, who made his debut in *The Golden Fortress.* Simple, gullible, friendly and either ignorant of or mistaken about most things in life, he proved to be a perfect foil to Feluda, and a means of providing what Ray called 'dollops of humour'. The following year (1972) readers were presented with *A Mysterious Case,* where Jatayu made an encore appearance. After this, he remained with the two cousins throughout, becoming very soon an important member of the team and winning the affection of millions. It is, in fact, impossible now to think of Feluda without thinking of Jatayu. Interestingly, the two films Ray made based on Feluda stories *(The Golden Fortress* in 1974, and *The Elephant God* in 1978) both featured Lalmohan Babu, as did the television film *Kissa Kathmandu Ka* (based on *The Criminals of Kathmandu)* made by Sandip Ray a few years later.

Ray had often spoken of his interest in crime fiction. He had read all the Sherlock Holmes stories before leaving school. It was therefore no surprise that he should start writing crime stories himself. But why did the arrival of Feluda make such a tremendous impact on his readers? After all, it wasn't as though there had never been other detectives in children's fiction in Bengal. The reason was, in fact, a simple one. In spite of all his accomplishments, Feluda did not emerge as a larger-than-life superman whom one would venerate and admire from afar, but never get close to. On the contrary, Topshe's charming narration described him as so utterly normal and human that it was not difficult at all to see him almost as a member of one's own family. A genius he might well be, but his behaviour was exactly what one might expect from an older cousin. He teased Topshe endlessly and bullied him often, but his love and concern for his young Watson was never in doubt. Every child who read *Sandesh* could see himself—or, for that matter, herself—in Topshe. Herein lay Ray's greatest strength. Feluda came, saw and conquered chiefly because each case was seen and presented through the eyes of an adolescent. Ray's language was simple, lucid, warm and direct, without ever becoming boring or patronizing, even when Feluda corrected a mistake Topshe made, or gave him new information. Added to this were his graphic descriptions of the various places Feluda and Topshe visited. Sometimes it was difficult to tell whether one was watching a film or reading a book, so well were all relevant details captured in just a few succinct words, regardless of whether the action was taking place in a small village in Bengal, a monastery in Sikkim, or the streets of Hong Kong.

It would be wrong to think, however, that it was smooth sailing at all times. Feluda and his team, like most celebrities, had to pay the price of fame. It was their popularity among adults that began to cause problems. Naturally, the expectations of adults were different. They wanted 'spice' in the stories and would probably not have objected to subjects such as illicit love or *crime passionnel*. Feluda's creator, on the other hand, could never allow himself to forget that he wrote primarily for children and, as such, was obliged to keep the stories 'clean'. Clearly, letters from critical or disappointed readers became such a sore point that Feluda spoke openly about it in *The Mystery of Nayan*, the last novel published during Ray's lifetime. 'Don't forget Topshe writes my stories mainly for adolescents,' Feluda says in the opening chapter. 'The problem is that these stories are read by the children's parents, uncles, aunts and everyone else. Each reader at every level has his own peculiar demand. How on earth is he to satisfy each one of them?'

The readers were suitably chastened. And Feluda's popularity

rose even higher. In 1990, when he turned twenty-five, an ardent
admirer in Delhi went to the extent of designing a special card to
mark the occasion. Ray is said to have been both amazed and greatly
amused by the display of such deep devotion.

By this time, Feluda had already stepped out of Bengal. In 1988,
the first collection of Feluda stories appeared in English translation
(The Adventures of Feluda, translated by Chitrita Banerji). This was
followed by my translations of the remaining Feluda stories, which
appeared in *The Emperor's Ring: The Further Adventures of Feluda*
(1993), *The Mystery of the Elephant God: More Adventures of
Feluda* (1994), *Feluda's Last Case and Other Stories* (1995), *The
House of Death and Other Feluda Stories* (1997), *The Royal Bengal
Mystery and Other Feluda Stories* (1997) and *The Mystery of the
Pink Pearl: The Final Feluda Stories* (1998). *The Magical Mystery*
was published in *Indigo,* a collection of Ray's short stories, in 2000.

Initially, Ray was hesitant to allow the Feluda stories to be
translated as he was unsure about the response of non-Bengali
readers. However, the two films he had made as well as the television
series made by his son had evoked an interest from other
communities. When he did finally give his consent, it was only to
discover that he need not have worried at all. The Three Musketeers,
comprising Pradosh C. Mitter, Private Investigator, and his two
assistants, were received with as much enthusiasm elsewhere in India
as they had been in Bengal.

Translating the Feluda stories has been a deeply fulfilling
experience for me. Some of the early stories took me back to my
early teens, when a ride in a taxi would cost one the princely sum of
one rupee and seventy paise, and a bearded foreigner in colourful
clothes was likely to be labeled a 'hippie' *(The Anubis Mystery* and
Trouble in Gangtok). More importantly, translating these stories gave
me a new insight into the author's mind and a chance to rediscover
his varied interests, ranging from music and magic to history and
hypnotism and, of course, cinema.

This definitive edition contains, in two volumes, all the Feluda
stories that Ray completed. Included are new translations (by me) of
The Golden Fortress, The Bandits of Bombay and *The Secret of the
Cemetery.* For the first time, the stories are arranged in chronological
order, and one can note Feluda's development from a totally unknown
amateur detective to a famous professional private investigator. Those

who have read them before may be pleased to find them all together in an omnibus edition. To those who haven't, one hopes it will give an excellent opportunity to get acquainted with a legend in Bengal, and catch a glimpse of the brilliant mind of its creator.

London   Gopa Majumdar
June 2004

CHRONOLOGY OF THE FELUDA STORIES

No	Name of story	Bengali title	Published	Written in
1	Danger in Darjeeling	Feludar Goendagiri	Sandesh	1965-66
2	The Emperor's Ring	Badshahi Aangti	Sandesh	1966-67
3	Kailash Chowdhury's Jewel	Kailash Chowdhury'r Pathar	Sandesh	1967
4	The Anubis Mystery	Sheyal-Debota Rahasya	Sandesh	1970
5	Trouble in Gangtok	Gangtokey Gandogol	Desh	1970
6	The Golden Fortress	Sonar Kella	Desh	1971
7	Incident on the Kalka Mail	Baksho Rahasya	Desh	1972
8	A Killer in Kailash	Kailashey Kelenkari	Desh	1973
9	The Key	Samaddarer Chabi	Sandesh	1973
10	The Royal Bengal Mystery	Royal Bengal Rahasya	Desh	1974
11	The Locked Chest	Ghurghutiyar Ghatona	Sandesh	1975
12	The Mystery of the Elephant God	Joy Baba Felunath	Desh	1975
13	The Bandits of Bombay	Bombaiyer Bombetey	Desh	1976
14	The Mystery of the Walking Dead	Gosaipur Sargaram	Sandesh	1976
15	The Secret of the Cemetery	Gorosthaney Sabdhan	Desh	1977
16	The Curse of the Goddess	Chhinnamastar Abhishaap	Desh	1978
17	The House of Death	Hatyapuri	Sandesh	1979
18	The Mysterious Tenant	Golokdham Rahasya	Sandesh	1980
19	The Criminals of Kathmandu	Joto Kando Kathmandutey	Desh	1980

No	Name of story	Bengali title	Published	Written in
20	Napoleon's Letter	Napoleoner Chitthi	Sandesh	1981
21	Tintoretto's Jesus	Tintorettor Jishu	Desh	1982
22	The Disappearance of Ambar Sen	Ambar Sen Antardhan Rahasya	Anandamela	1983
23	The Gold Coins of Jehangir	Jahangirer Swarnamudra	Sandesh	1983
24	Crime in Kedarnath	Ebar Kando Kedarnathey	Desh	1984
25	The Acharya Murder Case	Bospukurey Khunkharapi	Sandesh	1985
26	Murder in the Mountains	Darjeeling Jamjamat	Sandesh	1986
27	The Magical Mystery	Indrajal Rahasya	Sandesh, 1995-96	1987
28	The Case of the Apsara Theatre	Apsara Theatre'r Mamla	Sandesh	1987
29	Peril in Paradise	Bhuswargya Bhayankar	Desh	1987
30	Shakuntala's Necklace	Shakuntalar Kontthohar	Desh	1988
31	Feluda in London	Londoney Feluda	Desh	1989
32	The Mystery of the Pink Pearl	Golapi Mukta Rahasya	Sandesh	1989
33	Dr Munshi's Diary	Dr Munshir Diary	Sandesh	1990
34	The Mystery of Nayan	Nayan Rahasya	Desh	1990
35	Robertson's Ruby	Robertsoner Ruby	Desh, 1992	1990

Danger in Darjeeling

I saw Rajen Babu come to the Mall every day. He struck me as an amiable old man. All his hair had turned grey, and his face always wore a cheerful expression. He generally spent a few minutes in the corner shop that sold old Nepali and Tibetan things; then he came and sat on a bench in the Mall for about half-an-hour, until it started to get dark. After that he went straight home. One day, I followed him quietly to see where he lived. He turned around just as we reached his front gate and asked, 'Who are you? Why have you been following me?'

'My name is Tapesh Ranjan,' I replied quickly.

'Well then, here is a lozenge for you,' he said, offering me a lemon drop. 'Come to my house one day. I'll show you my collection of masks,' he added.

Who knew that this friendly old soul would get into such trouble? Why, he seemed totally incapable of getting involved with anything even remotely sinister!

Feluda snapped at me when I mentioned this. 'How can you tell just by looking at someone what he might get mixed up with?' he demanded.

This annoyed me. 'What do you know of Rajen Babu?' I said. 'He's a good man. A very kind man. He has done a lot for the poor Nepali people who live in slums. There's no reason why he should be in trouble. I know. I see him every day. You haven't seen him even once. In fact, I've hardly seen you go out at all since we came to Darjeeling.'

'All right, all right. Let's have all the details then. What would a little boy like you know of danger, anyway?'

Now, this wasn't fair. I was not a little boy any more. I was thirteen and a half. Feluda was twenty-seven.

To tell you the truth, I came to know about the trouble Rajen Babu was in purely by accident. I was sitting on a bench in the Mall today, waiting for the band to start playing. On my left was Tinkori Babu, reading a newspaper. He had recently arrived from Calcutta to spend the summer in Darjeeling, and had taken a room on rent in Rajen Babu's house. I was trying to lean over his shoulder and look at the sports page, when Rajen Babu arrived panting and collapsed on the empty portion of our bench, next to Tinkori Babu. He looked visibly shaken.

'What's the matter?' asked Tinkori Babu, folding his newspaper. 'Did you just run up a hill?'

'No, no,' Rajen Babu replied cautiously, wiping his face with one corner of his scarf. 'Something incredible has happened.'

I knew what 'incredible' meant. Feluda was quite partial to the word.

'What do you mean?' Tinkori Babu asked.

'Look, here it is,' Rajen Babu passed a piece of folded blue paper to Tinkori Babu. I could tell it was a letter, but made no attempt to read it when Tinkori Babu unfolded it. I looked away instead, humming under my breath to indicate a complete lack of interest in what the two old men were discussing. But I heard Tinkori Babu remark, 'You're right, it *is* incredible! Who could possibly write such a threatening letter to you?'

'I don't know. That's what's so puzzling. I don't remember having deliberately caused anyone any harm. As far as I know, I have no enemies.'

Tinkori Babu leant towards his neighbour. 'We'd better not talk about this in public,' he whispered. 'Let's go home.'

The two gentlemen left.

Feluda remained silent for a while after I had finished my story. Then he frowned and said, 'You mean you think we need to investigate?'

'Why, didn't you tell me you were looking for a mystery? And you said you had read so many detective novels that you could work as a sleuth yourself!'

'Yes, that's true. I could prove it, too. I didn't go to the Mall today, did I? But I could tell you which side you sat on.'

'All right, which side was it?'

'You chose a bench on the right side of the Radha restaurant, didn't you?'

'That's terrific. How did you guess?'

'The sun came out this evening. Your left cheek looks sunburnt but the right one is all right. This could happen only if you sat on that side of the Mall. That's the bit that catches the evening sunshine.'

'Incredible!'

'Yes. Anyway, I think we should go and visit Mr Rajen Majumdar.'

'Another seventy-seven steps.'

'And what if it's not?'

'It has to be, Feluda. I counted the last time.'

'Remember you'll get knocked on the head if you're wrong.'

'OK, but not too hard. A sharp knock may damage my brain.'

To my amazement, seventy-seven steps later, we were still at some distance from Rajen Babu's gate. Another twenty-three brought us right up to it. Feluda hit my head lightly, and asked, 'Did you count the steps on your way back?'

'Yes.'

'That explains it. You went down the hill on your way back, you idiot. You must have taken very big steps.'

'Well . . . yes, maybe.'

'I'm sure you did. You see, young people always tend to take big, long steps when going downhill. Older people have to be more cautious, so they take smaller, measured steps.'

We went in through the gate. Feluda pressed the calling bell. Someone in the distance was listening to a radio.

'Have you decided what you're going to say to him?' I asked.

'That's my business. You, my dear, will keep your mouth shut.'

'Even if they ask me something.? You mean I shouldn't even make a reply?'

'Shut up.'

A Nepali servant opened the door. *'Andar aaiye,'* he said.

We stepped into the living room. Made of wood, the house had a lovely old charm. All the furniture in the room was made of cane. The walls were covered with strange masks, most showing large teeth and wearing rather unpleasant expressions. Some of them frightened me. Apart from these, the room was full of old weapons—shields and swords and daggers. Beside these hung pictures of the Buddha, painted on cloth. Heaven knew how old they were, but the golden colour that had been used had not faded at all.

We took two cane chairs. Feluda rose briefly to inspect the walls. Then he came back and said, 'All the nails are new. So Rajen Babu's passion for antiques must have developed only recently.'

Rajen Babu came into the room. Feluda sprang to his feet and said, 'Do you remember me? I am Joykrishna Mitter's son, Felu.'

Rajen Babu looked a little taken aback at first. Then his face broke into a smile. 'Felu? Of course I remember you. My word, you have become a young man! How is everyone at home? Is your father here?'

As Feluda answered these questions, I sat trying to hide my

astonishment. How unfair the whole thing was—why hadn't Feluda told me that he knew Rajen Babu?

It turned out that Rajen Babu had worked in Calcutta for many years as a lawyer. He had once helped Feluda's father fight a case. He had come to Darjeeling and settled here ten years ago, soon after his retirement.

Feluda introduced me to him. He showed no sign of recognition. Perhaps the matter of offering me a lozenge a week ago had slipped his mind completely.

'You're fond of antiques, I see,' said Feluda conversationally.

'Yes. It's turned almost into an obsession.'

'How long—?'

'Over the last six months. But I've managed to collect quite a lot of things.'

Feluda cleared his throat. Then he told Rajen Babu what he had heard from me, and ended by saying, 'I still remember how you had helped my father. If I could do anything in return . . .'

Rajen Babu looked both pleased and relieved. But before he could say anything, Tinkori Babu walked into the room. From the way he was breathing, it appeared that he had just come back after his evening walk. Rajen Babu made the introductions. 'Tinkori Babu happens to be a neighbour of Gyanesh, a friend of mine. When this friend heard that I was going to let one of my rooms, he suggested that I give it to Tinkori Babu. He would have gone to a hotel otherwise.'

Tinkori Babu laughed. 'I did hesitate to take up his offer, I must admit; chiefly because of my special weakness for cheroots. You see, Rajen Babu might well have objected to the smell. So I wrote to him first to let him know. He said he didn't mind, so here I am.'

'Are you here simply for a change of air?'

'Yes, but the air, I've noticed, isn't as cool and fresh as one might have expected.'

'Are you fond of music?' asked Feluda unexpectedly.

'Yes, but how did you guess?' Tinkori Babu gave a startled smile.

'Well, I noticed your finger,' Feluda explained. 'You were beating it on top of your walking-stick, in keeping with the rhythm of that song from the radio.'

'You're quite right,' Rajen Babu laughed, 'he sings Shyamasangeet.'

Feluda changed the subject. 'Do you have the letter here?' he asked.

'Oh yes. Right next to my heart,' said Rajen Babu and took it out of the inside pocket of his jacket. Feluda spread it out.

It was not handwritten. A few printed words had been cut out of books or newspapers and pasted on a sheet of paper. 'Be prepared to pay for your sins,' it read.

'Did this come by post?'

'Yes. It was posted in Darjeeling, but I'm afraid I threw the envelope away.'

'Have you reason to suspect anyone?'

'No. For the life of me, I cannot recall ever having harmed anyone.'

'Do certain people visit you regularly?'

'Well, I don't get too many visitors. Dr Phoni Mitra comes occasionally if I happen to be ill.'

'Is he a good doctor?'

'About average, I should say. But then, my complaints have always been quite ordinary—I mean, no more than the usual coughs and colds. So I haven't had to look for a really good doctor.'

'Does he charge a fee?'

'Of course. But that's hardly a problem. I've got plenty of money, thank God.'

'Who else visits you?'

'A Mr Ghoshal has recently started coming to my house . . . look, here he is!' A man of medium height wearing a dark suit was shown into the room.

'Did I hear my name?' he asked with a smile.

'Yes, I was just about to tell these people that you share my interest in antiques. Allow me to introduce them.'

After exchanging greetings, Mr Ghoshal—whose full name was Abanimohan Ghoshal—said to Rajen Babu, 'I thought I'd drop by since you didn't come to the shop today.'

'N-no, I wasn't feeling very well, so I decided to stay in.'

It was clear that Rajen Babu did not want to tell Mr Ghoshal about the letter. Feluda had hidden it the minute Mr Ghoshal had walked in.

'All right, if you're busy today, I'll come back another time . . . actually, I wanted to take a look at that Tibetan bell,' said Mr Ghoshal.

'Oh, that's not a problem at all. I'll get it for you.' Rajen Babu disappeared into the house to fetch the bell.

'Do you live here in Darjeeling?' Feluda asked Mr Ghoshal, who had picked up a dagger and was looking at it closely. 'No,' he replied, turning the dagger in his hand. 'I don't stay in any one place for very long. I have to travel a lot. But I like collecting curios.' Feluda told me afterwards that a curio was a rare and ancient object of art.

Rajen Babu returned with the bell. It was really striking to look at. Its base was made of silver, the handle was a mixture of brass and copper, which was studded with colourful stones. Mr Ghoshal took a long time to examine it carefully. Then he put it down on a table and said, 'You got yourself a very good deal there. It's absolutely genuine.'

'Ah, that's a relief. You're the expert, of course. The man at the shop told me it came straight out of the household of the Dalai Lama.'

'That may well be true. But I don't suppose you'd want to part with it? I mean . . . suppose you got a handsome offer?'

Rajen Babu shook his head, smiling sweetly.

'No. You see, I bought that bell simply because I liked it, I have no wish to sell it only to make money.'

'Very well,' Mr Ghoshal rose. 'I hope you'll be out and about tomorrow.'

'Thank you. I hope so, too.'

When Mr Ghoshal had gone, Feluda said to Rajen Babu, 'Don't you think it might be wise not to go out of the house for the next few days?'

'Yes, you're probably right. But this business of an anonymous letter is so incredible that I cannot really bring myself to take it seriously. It just seems like a foolish practical joke!'

'Well, why don't you stay in until we can be definite about that? How long have you had that Nepali servant?'

'Right from the start. He is completely reliable.'

Feluda now turned to Tinkori Babu. 'Do you stay at home most of the time?'

'Yes, but I go for morning and evening walks, so I'm out of the house for a couple of hours every day. In any case, should there be any real danger, I doubt if I could do anything to help. I am sixty-four, younger than Rajen Babu by only a year.'

'Don't involve poor Tinkori Babu in this, please,' Rajen Babu said. 'After all, he's come here to relax, so let him enjoy himself. I'll stay in if you insist, together with my servant. You two can come and visit me every day, if you so wish.'

'All right.'

Feluda stood up. So did I. It was time to go.

There was a fireplace in front of us. Over it, on a mantelshelf, were three framed photographs. Feluda moved closer to the fireplace to look at these. 'My wife,' said Rajen Babu, pointing at the first photograph. 'She died barely five years after our marriage.'

The second photo was of a young boy, who must have been about my own age when the photo was taken. A handsome boy indeed. 'Who is this?' Feluda asked.

Rajen Babu began laughing. 'That photo is there simply to show how time can change everything. Would you believe that that is my own photograph, taken when I was a child? I used to go to a missionary school in Bankura in those days. My father was the magistrate there. But don't let those angelic looks deceive you. I might have been a good-looking child, but I was extremely naughty. My teachers were all fed up with me. In fact, I didn't spare the students, either. I remember having kicked the best runner in our school in a hundred-yards race to stop him from winning.'

The third photo was of a young man in his late twenties. It turned out to be Rajen Babu's only child, Prabeer Majumdar.

'Where is he now?' Feluda asked.

Rajen Babu cleared his throat. 'I don't know,' he said after a pause. 'He left home sixteen years ago. There is virtually no contact between us.'

Feluda started walking towards the front door. 'A very interesting case,' he muttered. Now he was talking like the detectives one read about.

We came out of the house. It was already dark outside. Lights had been switched on in every house nestling in the hills. A mist was rising from the Rangeet valley down below. Rajen Babu and Tinkori Babu both walked up to the gate to see us off. Rajen Babu lowered his voice and said to Feluda, 'Actually, I have to confess that despite everything, I do feel faintly nervous. After all, something like this in this peaceful atmosphere was so totally unexpected . . .'

'Don't worry,' said Feluda firmly. 'I'll definitely get to the bottom of this case.'

'Thank you. Goodbye!' said Rajen Babu and went back into the house. Tinkori Babu lingered. 'I am truly impressed by your power of observation,' he said. 'I, too, have read a large number of detective novels. Maybe I can help you with this case.'

'Really? How?'

'Look at the letter in your hand. Take the various printed words. Do they tell you anything?'

Feluda thought for a few seconds. 'The words were cut out with a blade, not scissors,' he said.

'Very good.'

'Second, each word has come from a different source—the typeface and the quality of paper vary from each other.'

'Yes. Can you guess what those different sources might be?'

'These two words—"prepared" and "pay"—appear to be a newspaper.'

'Right. *Ananda Bazar.*'

'How can you tell?'

'Only *Ananda Bazar* uses that typeface. And the other words were taken out of books, I think. Not very old books, mind you, for those different typefaces have been in use over the last twenty years, and no more. Apart from this, does the smell of the glue tell you anything?'

'I think the sender used Grippex glue.'

'Brilliant!'

'I might say the same for you.'

Tinkori Babu smiled. 'I try, but at your age, my dear fellow, I doubt if I knew what the word "detective" meant.'

We said namaskar after this and went on our way. 'I don't yet know whether I can solve this mystery,' said Feluda on the way back to our hotel, 'but getting to know Tinkori Babu would be an added bonus.'

'If he is so good at crime detection, why don't you let him do all the hard work? Why waste your own time making enquiries?'

'Ah well, Tinkori Babu might know a lot about printing and typefaces, but that doesn't necessarily mean he'd know everything!'

Feluda's answer pleased me. I bet Tinkori Babu isn't as clever as Feluda, I thought. Aloud, I said, 'Who do you suppose is the culprit?'

'The culp—' Feluda broke off. I saw him turn around and glance at a man who had come from the opposite direction and had just passed us.

'Did you see him?'

'No, I didn't see his face.'

'The light from that street lamp fell on his face for only a second, and I thought—'

'What?'

'No, never mind. Let's go, I feel quite hungry.'

Feluda is my cousin. He and I were in Darjeeling with my father for a holiday. Father had got to know some of the other guests in our hotel fairly well, and was spending most of his time with them. He didn't stop us from going wherever we wished, nor did he ask too many questions.

I woke a little later than usual the next day. Father was in the room, but there was no sign of Feluda.

'Felu left early this morning,' Father explained. 'He said he'd try to catch a glimpse of Kanchenjunga.'

I knew this couldn't be true. Feluda must have gone out to investigate, which was most annoying because he wasn't supposed to go out without me. Anyway, I had a quick cup of tea, and then I went out myself.

I spotted Feluda near a taxi stand. 'This is not fair!' I complained. 'Why did you go out alone?'

'I was feeling a bit feverish, so I went to see a doctor.'

'Dr Phoni Mitra?'

'Aha, you're beginning to use your brain, too!'

'What did he say?'

'He charged me four rupees and wrote out a prescription.'

'Is he a good doctor?'

'Do you think a good doctor would write a prescription for someone in perfect health? Besides, his house looked old and decrepit. I don't think he has a good practice.'

'Then he couldn't have sent that letter.'

'Why not?'

'A poor man wouldn't dare.'

'Yes, he would, if he was desperate for money.'

'But that letter said nothing about money.'

'There was no need to ask openly.'

'What do you mean?'

'How did Rajen Babu strike you yesterday?'

'He seemed a little frightened.'

'Fear can make anyone ill.'

'Oh?'

'Yes, seriously ill. And if that happened, he'd naturally turn to his doctor. What might happen then is something even a fathead like you can figure out, I'm sure.'

How clever Feluda was! But if Dr Mitra had really planned the whole thing the way Feluda described, he must be extraordinarily crafty, too.

By this time, we had reached the Mall. As we came near the fountain, Feluda suddenly said, 'I feel a bit curious about curios.' We were, in fact, standing quite close to the Nepal Curio Shop. Rajen Babu and Mr Ghoshal visited this shop every day. Feluda and I walked into the shop. Its owner came forward to greet us. He had a light grey jacket on, a muffler round his neck, and wore a black cap with golden embroidery. He beamed at us genially.

The shop was cluttered with old and ancient objects. A strange musty smell came from them. It was quiet inside. Feluda looked around for a while, then said, sounding important, 'Do you have good *tankhas*?'

'Come into the next room, sir. We've sold what was really good. But we're expecting some fresh stock soon.'

'What is a *tankha*?' I whispered.

'You'll know when you see one,' Feluda whispered back.

The next room was even smaller and darker. The owner of the shop brought out a painting of the Buddha, done on a piece of silk. 'This is the last piece left, but it's a little damaged,' he said. So this was a *tankha*! Rajen Babu had heaps of these in his house. Feluda examined the *tankha* like an expert, peering at it closely, and then looking at it from various angles. Three minutes later, he said, 'This doesn't appear to be more than seventy years old. I am looking for something much older than that, at least three hundred years, you see.'

'We're getting some new things this evening, sir. You might find what you're looking for if you came back later today.'

'This evening, did you say?'

'Yes, sir.'

'Oh, I must inform Rajen Babu.'

'Mr Majumdar? He knows about it already. All my regular customers are coming in the evening to look at the fresh arrivals.'

'Does Mr Ghoshal know?'

'Of course.'

'Who else is a regular buyer?'

'There's Mr Gilmour, the manager of a tea estate. He visits my shop twice a week. Then there's Mr Naulakha. But he's away in Sikkim at present.'

'All right, I'll try to drop in in the evening . . . Topshe, would you like a mask?' I couldn't resist the offer. Feluda selected one himself and paid for it. 'This was the most horrendous of them all,' he remarked, passing it to me. He had once told me there was no such word as 'horrendous'. It was really a mixture of 'tremendous' and 'horrible'. But I must say it was rather an appropriate word for the mask.

Feluda started to say something as we came out of the shop, but stopped abruptly. I found him staring at a man once again. Was it the same man he had seen last night? He was a man in his early forties, expensively dressed in a well-cut suit. He had stopped in the middle of the Mall to light his pipe. His eyes were hidden behind dark glasses. Somehow he looked vaguely familiar, but I couldn't recall ever having met him before.

Feluda stepped forward and approached him. 'Excuse me,' he said, 'are you Mr Chatterjee?'

'No,' replied the man, biting the end of his pipe, 'I am not.'

Feluda appeared to be completely taken aback. 'Strange! Aren't you staying at the Central Hotel?'

The man smiled a little contemptuously. 'No, I am at the Mount Everest; and I don't have a twin,' he said and strode off in the direction of Observatory Hill.

I noticed he was carrying a brown parcel, on which were printed the words 'Nepal Curio Shop'.

'Feluda!' I said softly. 'Do you think he bought a mask like mine?'

'Yes, he may well have done that. After all, those masks weren't all meant for your own exclusive use, were they? Anyway, let's go and have a cup of coffee.' We turned towards a coffee shop. 'Did you recognize that man?' asked Feluda.

'How could I,' I replied, 'when you yourself failed to recognize him?'

'Who said I had failed?'

'Of course you did! You got his name wrong, didn't you?'

'Why are you so stupid? I did that deliberately, just to get him to tell me where he was staying. Do you know what his real name is?'

'No. What is it?'

'Prabeer Majumdar.'

'Yes, yes, you're right! Rajen Babu's son, isn't he? We saw his photograph yesterday. No wonder he seemed familiar. But of course now he's a lot older.'

'Even so, there are a lot of similarities between father and son. But did you notice his clothes? His suit must have been from London, his tie from Paris and shoes from Italy. In short, there's no doubt that he's recently returned from abroad.'

'But does that mean Rajen Babu doesn't know his own son is in town?'

'Perhaps his son doesn't even know that his father lives here. We should try to find out more.'

The plot thickens, I told myself, going up on the open terrace of the coffee shop. I loved sitting here. One could get such a superb view of the town and the market from here.

Tinkori Babu was sitting at a corner table, drinking coffee. He waved at us, inviting us to join him.

'As a reward for your powerful observation and expertise in detection, I would like to treat you to two cups of hot chocolate. You wouldn't mind, I hope?' he said with a twinkle in his eye. My mouth began to water at the prospect of a cup of hot chocolate. Tinkori Babu called a waiter and placed his order. Then he took out a book from his jacket pocket and offered it to Feluda. 'This is for you. I had just one copy left. It's my latest book.'

Feluda stared at the cover. 'Your book? You mean . . . you write under the pseudonym Secret Agent?' Tinkori Babu's eyes drooped. He smiled slightly and nodded. Feluda grew more excited. 'But you're my favourite writer! I've read all your books. No other writer can write mystery stories the way you do.'

'Thank you, thank you. To tell you the truth, I had come to Darjeeling to chalk out a plot for my next novel. But I've now spent most of my time trying to sort out a real life mystery.'

'I do consider myself very fortunate. I had no idea I'd get to meet you like this!'

'The only sad thing is that I have to go back to Calcutta. I'm returning tomorrow. But I think I may be of some help to you before I leave.'

'I'm very pleased to hear that. By the way, we saw Rajen Babu's son today.'

'What!'

'Only ten minutes ago.'

'Are you sure? Did you see him properly?'

'Yes, I am almost a hundred per cent sure. All we need to do is check with the Mount Everest Hotel, and then there won't be any doubt left.'

Suddenly, Tinkori Babu sighed. 'Did Rajen Babu talk to you about his son?' he asked.

'No, not much.'

'I have heard quite a lot. Apparently, his son had fallen into bad company. He was caught stealing money from his father's cupboard. Rajen Babu told him to get out of his house. Prabeer did leave his home after that and disappeared without a trace. He was twenty-four at the time. A few years later, Rajen Babu began to regret what he'd done and tried to track his son down. But there was no sign of Prabeer anywhere. About ten years ago, a friend of Rajen Babu came and told him he'd spotted Prabeer somewhere in England. But that was all.'

'That means Rajen Babu doesn't know his son is here in Darjeeling.'

'I'm sure he doesn't. And I don't think he should be told. After all, he's already had one shock. Another one might . . .' Tinkori Babu stopped. Then he looked straight at Feluda and shook his head. 'I think I am going mad. Really, I should give up writing mystery stories.'

Feluda laughed. 'You mean it's only just occurred to you that the letter might have been sent by Prabeer Majumdar himself?'

'Exactly. But . . . I don't know . . .' Tinkori Babu broke off absent-mindedly.

The waiter came back and placed our hot chocolate before us. This seemed to cheer him up. 'How did you find Dr Phoni Mitra?' he asked.

'Good heavens, how do you know I went there?'

'I paid him a visit shortly after you left.'

'Did you see me coming out of his house?'

'No. I found a cigarette stub on his floor. I knew he didn't smoke, so I asked him if he'd already had a patient. He said yes, and from his description I could guess that it was you. However, I didn't know then that you smoked. Now, looking at your slightly yellowish fingertips, I can be totally sure.'

'You really are a most clever man. But tell me, did you suspect Dr Mitra as well?'

'Yes. He doesn't exactly inspire confidence, does he?'

'You're right. I'm surprised Rajen Babu consults him rather than anyone else.'

'There's a reason for it. Soon after he arrived in Darjeeling, Rajen Babu had suddenly turned religious. It was Dr Mitra who had found him a guru at that time. As followers of the same guru, they are now like brothers.'

'I see. But did Dr Mitra say anything useful? What did you talk about?'

'Oh, just this and that. I went there really to take a look at the books on his shelves. There weren't many. Those that I saw were all old.'

'Yes, I noticed it, too.'

'Mind you, he might well have got hold of different books from elsewhere, just to get the right printed words. But I'm pretty certain that is not the case. That man seemed far too lazy to go to such trouble.'

'Well, that takes care of Dr Mitra. What do you think of Mr Ghoshal?'

'I don't trust him either. He's a crook. He pretends to be interested in art and antiques, but I think what he really wants to do is sell to foreign buyers at a much higher price what he can buy relatively cheaply here.'

'But do you think he might have a motive in sending a threatening letter to Rajen Babu?'

'I haven't really thought about it.'

'I think I might have stumbled onto something.'

I looked at Feluda in surprise. His eyes were shining with excitement.

'What do you mean?'

'I learnt today,' Feluda said, lowering his voice, 'that the shop they both go to is going to get some fresh supplies this evening.'

Tinkori Babu perked up immediately. 'I see, I see!' he exclaimed. 'A letter like that would naturally frighten Rajen Babu into staying at home for a few days. In the meantime, Abani Ghoshal would go in and make a clean sweep.'

'Exactly.'

Tinkori Babu paid for the chocolate and rose. We went out

together. My heart was beating fast. Abani Ghoshal, Prabeer
Majumdar and Dr Phoni Mitra. As many as three suspects. Who was
the real culprit?

Tinkori Babu went home. Feluda and I walked over to the Mount
Everest Hotel. They confirmed that a man called Prabeer Majumdar
had checked in five days ago.

We were supposed to visit Rajen Babu in the evening. But it began to
rain so heavily at around 4 p.m. that we were forced to stay in.
Feluda spent that whole evening scribbling in a notebook. I was
dying to find out what he was writing, but didn't dare ask. In the
end, I picked up the book Tinkori Babu had given Feluda and began
reading it. It was so thrilling that in a matter of minutes, all thoughts
of Rajen Babu went out of my mind.

The rain stopped at 8 p.m. But by then it was very cold outside.
Father, for once, stood firm and refused to allow us to go out.

Feluda shook me awake the next morning. 'Get up, Topshe.
Quick!'

'What—what is it?' I sat up.

Feluda whispered into my ear, speaking through clenched teeth.
'Rajen Babu's Nepali servant was here a few moments ago. He said
Rajen Babu wants to see us, and it's urgent. Do you want to come
with me?'

'Of course!'

We got ready and were in Rajen Babu's house in less than twenty
minutes. We found him lying in his bed, looking pale and haggard.
Dr Mitra was by his side, feeling his pulse; and Tinkori Babu was
standing before him, fanning him with a hand-held fan, despite the
cold.

Dr Mitra released his hand as we came in. Rajen Babu spoke with
some difficulty. 'Last night . . . after midnight . . . I woke suddenly
and there it was . . . in this room . . . I saw a masked face!' Rajen Babu
continued, 'I can't tell you . . . how I spent the night!'

'Has anything been stolen?'

'No. But I'm sure he bent over me . . . only to take the keys from
under my pillow. Oh, it was horrible . . . horrible!'

'Take it easy,' said the doctor. 'I'm going to give you something to
help you sleep. You need complete rest.' He stood up.

'Dr Mitra,' said Feluda suddenly, 'did you go to see a patient last night? Your jacket's got a streak of mud on it.'

'Oh yes,' Dr Mitra replied readily enough. 'I did have to go out last night. Since I have chosen to dedicate my life to my patients, I can hardly refuse to go out when I'm needed, come rain or shine.'

He collected his fee and left. Rajen Babu sat up in his bed. 'I feel a lot better now that you're here,' he admitted. 'I did feel considerably shaken, I must say. But now I think I might be able to go and sit in the living room.' Feluda and Tinkori Babu helped him to his feet. We made our way to the living room.

'I rang the railway station to change my ticket,' said Tinkori Babu. 'I don't want to leave today. But they said if I cancelled my ticket now, they couldn't give me a booking for another ten days. So I fear I've got to go.' This pleased me. I wanted Feluda to solve the mystery single-handedly.

'My servant was supposed to stay in yesterday,' Rajen Babu explained, 'but I myself told him to take some time off. His father is very ill, you see. He went home last night.'

'What did the mask look like?' Feluda asked.

'It was a perfectly ordinary mask, the kind you can get anywhere in Darjeeling. There are at least five of those in this room. There's one, look!' The mask he pointed out was almost an exact replica of the one Feluda had bought me yesterday.

Tinkori Babu spoke again. 'I think we ought to inform the police. We can no longer call this a joke. Rajen Babu may need protection. Felu Babu, you can continue with your investigation, nobody will object to that. But having thought things over, I do feel the police should know what's happened. I'll go myself to the police station right away. I don't think your life's in any danger, Rajen Babu, but please keep an eye on that Tibetan bell.'

We decided to take our leave. But before we left, Feluda said, 'Since Tinkori Babu is leaving today, you're going to be left with a vacant room, aren't you? Would you mind if we came and spent the night in it?'

'No, no, why should I mind? You're like a son to me. I'd be delighted. To tell you the truth, I'm beginning to lose my nerve. Those who are reckless in their youth generally tend to grow rather feeble in their old age. At least, that's what has happened to me.'

'I'll come and see you off at the station,' Feluda said to Tinkori Babu.

We passed the curio shop on our way back. Neither of us could help look inside. We saw two men looking around and talking. From the easy familiarity with which they were talking, it seemed as if they had known each other for a long time. One of them was Abani Ghoshal. The other was Prabeer Majumdar. I glanced at Feluda. He didn't seem surprised at all.

We went to the station at half-past ten to say goodbye to Tinkori Babu. He arrived in five minutes. 'My feet ache from having walked uphill,' he said. I noticed he was walking with a slight limp. 'Besides,' he added, 'it took me a while to buy this. I know Rajen Babu couldn't go to the curio shop but they really did get a lot of good stuff yesterday. So I chose something for him this morning. Will you please give it to him with my good wishes?'

'Certainly,' said Feluda, taking a brown packet from Tinkori Babu. 'There's one thing I meant to ask you. If I solve this mystery, I'd like to tell you about it. Will you give me your address, please?'

'You'll find the address of my publisher in my book. He'll forward all letters addressed to me. Goodbye . . . good luck!'

He climbed into a blue first-class carriage. The train left.

'That man would have made a lot of money and quite a name for himself if he had lived abroad. He has a real talent for writing crime stories,' Feluda remarked.

We returned to our hotel from the station. But Feluda went out again and, this time, refused to take me with him. When he finally came back, it was time to go to Rajen Babu's house to stay the night. As we set off, I said to him, 'You might at least tell me where you were during the day.'

'I went to various places. Twice to the Mount Everest Hotel, once to Dr Mitra's house, then to the curio shop, the library and one or two other places.'

'I see.'

'Is there anything else you'd like to know?'

'Have you been able to figure out who is the real cul—?'

'The time hasn't come to disclose that. No, not yet.'

'But who do you suspect the most?'

'I suspect everybody, including you.'

'Me?'

'Yes. Anyone who has a mask is a suspect.'

'Really? In that case, why don't you include yourself in your list?'

'Don't talk rubbish.'

'I'm not! You didn't tell me that you knew Rajen Babu, which means you were not totally honest with me. Besides, you could have easily used that mask. I did not hide it anywhere, did I?'

'Shut up, shut up!'

Rajen Babu seemed a lot better when we arrived at his house, although he still looked faintly uneasy. 'I felt fine during the day,' he told us, 'but I must say I'm beginning to feel nervous again now it's getting dark.'

Feluda gave him the packet from Tinkori Babu. Rajen Babu opened it quickly and took out a beautiful statue of the Buddha, the sight of which actually moved him to tears.

'Did the police come to make enquiries?' asked Feluda.

'Oh yes. They asked a thousand questions. God knows if they'll get anywhere, but at least they've agreed to post someone outside the house during the night. That's a relief, anyway. In fact, if you wish to go back to your hotel, it will be quite all right.'

'No, we'd rather stay here, if you don't mind. It's too noisy in our hotel. I need peace and quiet to think about this case.'

Rajen Babu smiled. 'Of course you can stay. You'll get your peace and quiet here, and I can promise you an excellent meal. That Nepali boy is a very good cook. I've asked him to make his special chicken curry. The food in your hotel could never be half as tasty, I'm sure.'

We were shown to our room. Feluda stretched out on his bed and lit a cigarette. I saw him blow out five smoke rings in a row. His eyes were half-closed. After a few seconds of silence, he said, 'Dr Mitra did go out to see a patient last night. I found that out this morning. A rich businessman who lives in Cart Road. He was with his patient from eleven-thirty to half-past twelve.'

'Does that rule him out completely?'

Feluda did not answer my question. Instead, he said, 'Prabeer Majumdar has lived abroad for so long and has such a lot of money that I can't see why he should suddenly arrive here and start threatening his father. He stands to gain very little, actually. Why, I learnt that he recently made a packet at the local races!'

I sat holding my breath. It was obvious that Feluda hadn't finished. I was right. Feluda stubbed out his cigarette and continued, 'Mr Gilmour has come to Darjeeling from his tea estate. I met him at the Planters' Club. He told me there was only one Tibetan bell that had come out of the palace of the Dalai Lama, and it is with him. The one Rajen Babu has is a fake. Abani Ghoshal is aware of it.'

'You mean the bell that we saw here isn't all that valuable?'

'No. Besides, both Abani Ghoshal and Prabeer Majumdar were at a party last night, from 9 p.m. to 3 a.m. They got totally drunk, I believe.'

'That man wearing a mask came here soon after midnight, didn't he?'

'Yes.'

I began to feel rather strange. 'Well then, who does that leave us with?'

Feluda did not reply. He sighed and rose to his feet. 'I'm going to sit in the living room for a minute,' he said. 'Do not disturb me.'

I took his place on the bed when he left. It was getting dark, but I felt too lazy to get up and switch on the lights. Through the open window I could see lights in the distance, on Observatory Hill. The noise from the Mall had died down. I heard the sound of hooves after a while. They got louder and louder, then slowly faded away.

It soon grew almost totally dark. The hill and the houses on it were now practically invisible. Perhaps a mist was rising again. I began to feel sleepy. Just as my eyes started to close, I suddenly sensed the presence of someone else in the room. My blood froze. Too terrified to look in the direction of the door, I kept my eyes fixed on the window. But I could feel the man move closer to the bed. There, he was now standing right next to me, and was leaning over my face. Transfixed, I watched his face come closer . . . oh, how horrible it was . . . a mask! He was wearing a mask!

I opened my mouth to scream, but an unseen hand pulled the mask away, and my scream became a nervous gasp. 'Feluda! Oh my God, it's you!'

'Had you dozed off? Of course it's me. Who did you think . . .?' Feluda started to laugh, but suddenly grew grave. Then he sat down next to me, and said, 'I was simply trying on all those masks in the living room. Why don't you wear this one for a second?' He passed me his mask. I put it on.

'Can you sense something unusual?'

'Why, no! It's a size too large for me, that's all.'

'Think carefully. Isn't there anything else that might strike you as odd?'

'Well . . . there's a faint smell, I think.'

'Of what?'

'Cheroot?'

'Exactly.'

Feluda took the mask off. My heart started to beat faster again. 'T-t-t-inkori Babu?' I stammered.

Feluda sighed. 'Yes, I'm afraid so. It must have been extremely easy for him. He had access to all kinds of printed material; and you must have noticed he was limping this morning. That might have been the result of jumping out of a window last night. But what I totally fail to understand is his motive. He appeared to respect Rajen Babu a lot. Why then did he do something like this? What for? Perhaps we shall never know.'

The night passed peacefully and without any further excitement. In the morning, just as we sat down to have breakfast with our host, his Nepali servant came in with a letter for him. It was once again a blue envelope with a Darjeeling post-mark.

Rajen Babu went white. He took out the letter with a trembling hand and passed it to Feluda. 'You read it,' he said in a low voice.

Feluda read it aloud. This is what it said:

Dear Raju,

When I first wrote to you from Calcutta after Gyanesh told me you had a house in Darjeeling, I had no idea who you really were. But that photograph of yours on your mantelshelf told me instantly that you were none other than the boy who had once been my classmate in the missionary school in Bankura fifty years ago.

I did not know that the desire for revenge would raise its head even after so many years. You see, I was the boy you kicked at that hundred-yards race on our sports day. Not only did I miss out on winning a medal and setting a new record, but you also managed to injure me pretty seriously. Unfortunately, my father got transferred to a different town only a few days after this incident, which was why I never got the chance to have a showdown with you then; nor did you ever learn just how badly you had hurt me, both mentally and physically. I had to spend three months in a hospital with my leg in a cast.

When I saw you here in Darjeeling, leading such a comfortable and peaceful life, I suddenly thought of doing something that would cause you a great deal of anxiety and ruin your peace of mind, at least for a short time. This was my way of settling scores, and punishing you for your past sins.

With good wishes,

Yours sincerely,

Tinu

(Tinkori Mukhopadhyay)

The Emperor's Ring

ONE

I was at first quite disappointed when I heard Baba say, 'Let's have a holiday in Lucknow this year. Dhiru has been asking us for a long time to go and visit him.' It was my belief that Lucknow was dull and boring. Baba did say we'd include a trip to Haridwar and Laxmanjhoola, and the latter was in the hills—but that would be just for a few days. We generally went to either Darjeeling or Puri. I liked both the sea and the mountains. Lucknow had neither. So I said to Baba, 'Couldn't we ask Feluda to come with us?'

Feluda has a theory about himself. No matter where he goes, he says, mysterious things start happening around him. And true enough, the last time he went with us to Darjeeling, all those strange things happened to Rajen Babu. If Lucknow could offer something similar, it wouldn't matter too much if the place itself was boring.

Baba said, 'Felu would be most welcome, but can he get away?'

Feluda appeared quite enthusiastic when I told him. 'Went there in 1958 to play a cricket match,' he said. 'It's not a bad place at all. If you went inside the Bhoolbhulaia in the Burra Imambara, I'm sure your eyes would pop out. What an imagination those nawabs had—my God!'

'You'll get leave, won't you?'

Feluda ignored my question and continued to speak: 'And it's not just the Bhoolbhulaia. You'll get to see the Monkey Bridge over the Gomti, and of course the battered Residency.'

'What's the Residency?'

'It was the centre of the British forces during the Mutiny. They couldn't do a thing. The sepoys tore it apart.'

Feluda had been at his job for two years. Since he hadn't taken any leave in the first year, it wasn't difficult for him now to get a couple of weeks off.

Perhaps I should explain here that Feluda is my cousin. I am fourteen and he is twenty-seven. Some people think him crazy, some say he is only eccentric, others call him just plain lazy. But I happen to know that few men of his age possess his intelligence. And, if he finds a job that interests him, he can work harder than anyone I know. Besides, he is good at cricket, knows at least a hundred indoor games, a number of card tricks, a little hypnotism and can write with both hands. When he was in school, his memory was so good that he had memorized every word in Tagore's 'Snatched from the Gods' after just two readings.

But what is most remarkable about Feluda is his power of deduction. This is a skill he has acquired simply by reading and regular practice. The police haven't yet discovered his talents, so Feluda has remained an amateur private detective.

One look at a person is enough for him to guess—accurately—a number of things about him.

When we met Dhiru Kaka at the Lucknow railway station, Feluda whispered into my ear: 'Is your Kaka fond of gardening?'

I knew that Dhiru Kaka had a garden, but Feluda could not have known about it. After all, Dhiru Kaka was not a relative; Baba and he were childhood friends.

'How did you guess?' I asked, amazed.

'When he turns around,' said Feluda, still whispering, 'you'll see a rose leaf sticking out from under the heel of his right shoe. And the index finger of his right hand has got tincture of iodine on it. Possibly the result of messing about in a rose bush early this morning.'

I realized on the way to Dhiru Kaka's house from the station that Lucknow was really a beautiful place. There were buildings with turrets and minarets all around; the roads were broad and clean and the traffic, besides motor cars, included two different kinds of horse-drawn carriages. One, I learnt, was called a tonga and the other was an ekka. If Dhiru Kaka hadn't met us in his old Chevrolet, we might have had to get into one of those.

Dhiru Kaka said, 'Aren't you now glad you came to this nice place? It's not filthy like Calcutta, is it?'

Baba and Dhiru Kaka were sitting at the back. Feluda and I were both sitting beside the driver, Din Dayal Singh. Feluda whispered again, 'Ask him about the Bhoolbhulaia?'

I find it difficult not to do something if Feluda asks me to do it. So I said, 'What is the Bhoolbhulaia, Dhiru Kaka?'

'You'll see it for yourself!' Dhiru Kaka laughed, 'It's actually a maze inside the Imambara. The nawabs used to play hide-and-seek in it with their queens.'

This time Feluda himself spoke. 'Is it true that you cannot come out of it unless you take a trained guide with you?'

'Yes, so I believe. Once a British soldier—oh, it was many years ago—had a few glasses and laid a wager with someone. Said no one should follow him into the maze, he'd come out himself. Two days later, his body was found in a lane of the maze.'

My heart started beating faster. 'Did you go in alone or with a guide?' I asked Feluda.

'I took a guide. But it is possible to go alone.'

'Really?'

I stared. Well, nothing was too difficult for Feluda, I knew. 'How is it possible?'

Feluda's eyes drooped. He nodded twice, but remained silent. I could tell he would not speak. His eyes were now taking in every detail of the city of Lucknow.

Dhiru Kaka was a lawyer. He had come to Lucknow twenty years ago and stayed on. He was, I believe, fairly well known in legal circles. He had lost his wife three years ago, and his son was in Frankfurt. He lived alone, with his bearer, Jagmohan, a cook and a maali. His house in Secunder Bagh was a little more than three miles from the station. The main gate bore his name: D. K. SANYAL, MA, BLB, Advocate.

A cobbled driveway led to a bungalow. His garden lay on both sides of the driveway. I spotted a maali working with a lawnmower as we stopped at the front door.

Baba said after lunch, 'You must be tired after your journey. I suggest we start our sightseeing from tomorrow.' So I spent the whole afternoon learning card tricks from Feluda. 'Indians have fingers that are far more flexible than those of Europeans,' Feluda told me, 'so it's easier for us to learn tricks that require sleight of hand.'

In the evening, we went out to the garden to have our tea. As we sat under a eucalyptus tree, cups and saucers in our hands, a car drew up outside the main gate. Feluda said, 'Fiat,' without even looking. This was followed by footsteps on the driveway, and a gentleman in a grey suit appeared shortly. He was fair, wore glasses and most of his hair was grey. Yet, it was clear that he was not very much older than Baba.

Dhiru Kaka rose with a smile, his hands folded in a namaskaar. 'Jagmohan, bring another chair,' he said. Turning towards Baba, he added, 'Allow me to introduce a special friend. This is Dr Srivastava.'

Feluda and I had both risen by this time. Feluda muttered under his breath, 'The chap's nervous for some reason. He forgot to greet your father.'

Dhiru Kaka continued, 'Srivastava is an osteopath and a genuine

Lucknowwalla.'

I heard Feluda whisper again. 'Do you know what an osteopath is?'

'No.'

'A doctor who specializes in problems of your bones.'

An extra chair arrived and we all sat down. Dr Srivastava picked up Baba's teacup absentmindedly and was about to take a sip when Baba coughed politely. Dr Srivastava started, said, 'I am so sorry,' and put it down.

Dhiru Kaka said thoughtfully, 'You seem a little preoccupied today. Are you thinking of a difficult case?'

Baba intervened at this point.

'You are talking to him in Bengali, Dhiru. Does he understand it?'

Dhiru Kaka laughed, 'Understand it? Good God—why don't you quote a few lines from Tagore, eh, Srivastava?'

Dr Srivastava appeared a little uncomfortable. 'I know a little Bengali,' he confessed, 'and I have read some of Tagore's works.'

'Really?'

'Yes. Great poet.'

Perhaps they would now start a great discussion on poetry, I thought. But Dr Srivastava picked up his own cup this time with an unsteady hand and said, 'Last night a daku came to my house.'

Daku? What was that?

The next words Dhiru Kaka spoke explained it. 'You mean a dacoit? Heavens, I thought they existed only in Madhya Pradesh. How did one get into Lucknow?'

'Call it a dacoit or an ordinary thief. You know about my ring, don't you, Mr Sanyal?'

'The one Pyarelal had given you? Has it been stolen?'

'No, no. But I do believe the thief came to steal it.'

Baba said, 'What's this about a ring?'

Dr Srivastava turned to Dhiru Kaka. 'You tell him.'

Dhiru Kaka explained, 'Pyarelal Seth was a famous, wealthy businessman of Lucknow. A Gujarati by birth, he had lived in Calcutta for some time. So he had a smattering of Bengali. When his son, Mahabir, was about thirteen, he went down with some serious ailment affecting his bones. Dr Srivastava cured him. Pyarelal's wife was no more, and the first of his two sons had died of typhoid a few years earlier. So you can imagine how grateful he must have felt to Dr Srivastava for saving the life of his only remaining child. Before he died himself, he gave a very expensive and valuable ring to Dr Srivastava.'

'When did he die?'

'Last July,' said Srivastava, 'three months ago. He had his first heart attack in May, which nearly killed him. That was when he gave me the ring. Then the second attack came in July. I went to visit him. It was all over in no time. Look . . .'

Srivastava brought out a blue velvet box from his pocket. It was slightly bigger than a matchbox. The evening sun fell on its content as he lifted the lid, and a bright, glittering rainbow dazzled our eyes.

Dr Srivastava looked around briefly before pulling the ring out of the box.

A huge white stone gleamed in the middle. It was surrounded by several smaller red, blue and green ones.

I had never seen a ring so exquisitely beautiful.

I gave Feluda a sidelong glance. He was scratching his ear with a dry leaf of eucalyptus, but his eyes were fixed on the ring.

'It must be very old,' said Baba. 'Is there a history behind it?'

Dr Srivastava replaced the ring in the box, put it back in his pocket and picked up his cup once more.

'Yes,' he said, 'there is indeed. This ring is more than three hundred years old. It once belonged to the Emperor Aurangzeb.'

Baba's eyes widened.

'You don't say! You mean *the* Aurangzeb? Shah Jahan's son?'

'Yes. But the story I've heard goes back to when Aurangzeb was still only a prince. Shah Jahan was the Emperor, trying to conquer Samarkand. His forces kept getting defeated. Once he sent his men under Aurangzeb's command. Aurangzeb was badly injured in the attack. He might have died, but an army officer saved him. Aurangzeb took this ring from his finger and gave it to his officer as his reward.'

'Goodness, it's incredible!'

'Yes. Pyarelal bought this ring in Agra from a descendant of that army officer. I don't know how much he paid for it. But I have had the stones examined. That big one is a diamond. So you can imagine its value.'

'At least two hundred thousand,' said Dhiru Kaka, 'if it was Jahannan Khan's instead of Aurangzeb's, even then it would fetch about a hundred-and-fifty thousand rupees.'

Dr Srivastava said, 'Now you know why I am so upset after

yesterday's incident. I live alone, you see, and I have to go out at all hours to see my patients. I could, of course, tell the police. But what if I did, and then someone attacked me? You never can tell, can you? I had, in fact, once thought of keeping the ring in a bank. But then I felt it would not be the same. I mean, I like showing it to my friends. So I kept it in my house.'

Dhiru Kaka said, 'Have you shown it to many people?'

'No. I got it only a few months ago. And those who come to my house are all my friends, people I trust. I haven't shown it to anyone else.'

It was beginning to get dark. The top of the eucalyptus tree shone in the remaining sunlight, but that would fade away soon. I looked at Dr Srivastava. He seemed oddly restless.

'Let's go in,' said Dhiru Kaka, 'we need to think this over.'

We left the garden and went into the living-room. Feluda didn't appear to be interested at all. He pulled out a pack of cards as soon as we had all sat down, and began to practise a new trick he had learnt.

Baba was not a great talker, but when he did speak, he chose his words carefully. 'Why,' he now asked, 'are you assuming that the thief came simply to steal your ring? Wasn't anything else stolen? After all, he—or they—might have been just petty thieves, interested in plain cash.'

Srivastava said, 'Well, let me explain. Thieves and burglars don't often strike in our area chiefly because of Bonobihari Babu. Besides, Mr Jhunjhunwalla is my next-door neighbour, and Mr Billimoria lives next to him. Both are very rich. You can tell that just by looking at their houses. So why should a thief come to my humble abode?'

'If your neighbours are rich,' said Dhiru Kaka, 'they must have made arrangements to guard their wealth. A petty thief wouldn't risk breaking through heavy security. After all, big money isn't his game, is it? I suspect if he could lay his hands on five hundred rupees, it would keep him going for six months. So I'm not surprised that they broke into your house, and not your neighbour's.'

Dr Srivastava continued to look doubtful. 'I really don't know, Mr Sanyal,' he said. 'I feel convinced they were after that ring. They opened a cupboard in the room next to mine. All its drawers were pulled out. There were other valuable things and enough time to grab them. Yet, when I woke suddenly, they ran away without taking a single thing. I find that odd. Besides—'

Srivastava stopped abruptly, frowning. After a few moments of silence, he said, 'When Pyarelal gave me that ring, I got the impression that he was just trying to get rid of it. For some reason he didn't want to keep it in his house any longer. And—'

He stopped again and frowned once more.

'And what, Dr Srivastava?' asked Dhiru Kaka.

Srivastava sighed. 'I went to see him after his second attack. He tried to tell me something, but couldn't. But I heard one thing clearly.'

'What was that?'

'He said it twice—"a spy. . . a spy. . ."'

Dhiru Kaka rose from the sofa.

'No, Doctor,' he said, 'it doesn't matter what Pyarelal said. I am convinced it was just an ordinary thief. Perhaps you haven't heard, but the barrister Bhudeb Mitra's house was recently burgled, too. They got away with a radio and some silver. But if you're feeling nervous about keeping the ring in your house, please feel free to leave it with me. I shall put it in my Godrej almirah and it'll be quite safe. You can collect it when you get over your nervousness.'

Srivastava looked visibly relieved. His lips spread in a smile.

'That is exactly what I came here to propose, but couldn't bring myself to say it. Thank you very much, Mr Sanyal. I shall feel a lot easier in my mind if you keep the ring.'

He took the ring out of his pocket and handed it to Dhiru Kaka, who went straight into his bedroom with it.

At this point, Feluda opened his mouth. 'Who is Bonobihari Babu?' he asked.

'Pardon?' Dr Srivastava was still slightly preoccupied.

'Didn't you just say that houses where you live were safe from burglars because of one Bonobihari Babu? Who is he? Someone in the police?'

Srivastava laughed, 'Oh, no, no. He has nothing to do with the police—but he gives us a special protection that's even better than what the police could give. He's quite an interesting character. His ancestors were zamindars in Bengal. When they lost their land, Bonobihari Babu went into business. He began exporting animals.'

'Animals?' Baba and Feluda spoke together.

'Yes. Animals from here are often needed in Europe, America or Australia for their zoos, circuses and television. Many Indians are in this business. Bonobihari Babu made a lot of money, I believe. He retired about three years ago and came to Lucknow, together with some of his animals. He bought a house not far from mine and turned it into a zoo.'

'How very strange!' Baba exclaimed.

'Yes. What is special about this zoo is that all its animals are very . . . very . . . how shall I put it . . .'

'Vicious?'

'Yes, yes. That's it. Most vicious.'

I had heard that Lucknow already had a very good zoo. Animals were kept out in the open there, on a man-made island. But what was this about a private zoo?

Srivastava continued, 'He has a wild cat. And a hyena, an alligator and a scorpion. You can hear some of these animals even from a distance. Thieves don't dare come our way!'

Feluda now asked the question that was trembling on my lips.

'Is it possible to see this zoo?'

Dhiru Kaka returned at this moment and said, 'That's simple. We can go any time. Bonobihari Babu is a most amiable man, not vicious at all!'

Srivastava rose to take his leave. 'I must go now. There is a patient I need to see.'

We went with him up to the main gate to see him off. He said 'good-night' to everyone, thanked Dhiru Kaka again and drove off in his Fiat. Baba and Dhiru Kaka began walking back to the house. Feluda took a cigarette out of his pocket and was about to light it when a black car shot past us and disappeared in the same direction as Dr Srivastava's car.

'Standard Herald,' said Feluda, 'I missed the number.'

'What would you do with the number?'

'It looked as though that car was following Dr Srivastava. Can't you see how dark it is on the other side of the road? That's where it was waiting. The driver changed gears in front of our gate. Didn't you notice?'

Feluda turned towards the house. It was at least fifty yards from the gate. I could tell, for I have often run in hundred-yards races in school. The light in the living-room was on. I could clearly see through the window. There were Baba and Dhiru Kaka, going into the room. Then I looked at Feluda. He was staring at the open window. The frown on his face and the way he bit his lip told me that he was worried about something.

'You know, Topshe—'

I am not really called Topshe. My name is Tapesh, but Feluda has changed it to Topshe.

'What?' I asked.

'I shouldn't have allowed this to happen.'

'What are you talking about?'

'That window should have been closed. You can see everything that goes on in that room from the gate. An ordinary bulb might have made a difference; but Dhiru Kaka has got a fluorescent light, which makes it worse.'

'So what if you can see everything?'

'Can you see your father?

'Just his head. He's sitting in a chair.'

'Who was sitting in that chair ten minutes ago?'

'Dr Srivastava.'

'He stood up to show the ring to your father, remember?'

'Yes. I don't forget things so quickly.'

'If someone was watching from the gate, he could quite easily have seen him do it.'

'Oh no! But why do you think there might have been someone?'

Feluda stooped and picked up a tiny object from the cobbled path. Silently, he handed it to me. It was a cigarette butt. 'Look at the tip carefully,' said Feluda.

I peered at it closely and in the faint light from the street lamp, saw what I needed to see.

'Well?' said Feluda.

'Charminar,' I replied, 'and whoever was smoking it was also chewing a paan. One end is smeared with its juice.'

'Very good. Come, let's go in.'

That night, before going to bed, Feluda asked Dhiru Kaka to show him the ring again. The two of us had a good look at it. I had no idea Feluda knew so much about stones. He turned the ring round and round under a table lamp and kept up a running commentary: 'These blue stones that you see are called sapphires. The red ones are rubies and the green ones emeralds. The others, I think, are topaz. But the real thing to look at, of course, is this diamond in the middle. Not many would have had the privilege of actually holding such a stone in their hand!'

Then he slipped the ring on to the third finger of his left hand and said, 'Look, my finger is the same size as Aurangzeb's!'

True, the ring fitted perfectly.

Feluda stared at the glittering stones and said, 'Who knows, this ring could have had an intriguing past. But you know what, Topshe—I am not interested in its history. Whether it had once belonged to Aurangzeb or Altamash or Akram Khan is not important. We need to know what its future is, and whether—at present—it's being chased by an admirer. If so, who is he and why is he so desperate to get hold of it?'

Then he removed the ring from his finger, gave it to me and said, 'Go now, give it back to Dhiru Kaka. And please open those windows when you return.'

TWO

The next day, we left for the Imambara after an early lunch. Baba and Dhiru Kaka went in the car. Feluda and I both chose to ride in a tonga.

It was great fun. I had never ridden in a horse-drawn carriage before. Feluda had, of course. It was his view that a bumpy ride in a tonga was very good for one's digestion.

'Dhiru Kaka has such an excellent cook that I can see it's going to be difficult not to indulge myself,' he said, 'so I think an occasional ride in a tonga is a good idea.'

Bumping through new and unfamiliar streets, we finally reached a place that the tongawalla said was called 'Kaiser Bagh'.

'See how they've mixed Urdu with German?' Feluda remarked.

Most of the well-known Mughal buildings were around Kaiser Bagh. The tongawalla began pointing them out: 'There's Badshah Manzil . . . and that's Chandiwali Barradari . . . and that's called Lakhu Phatak . . .'

The path led through a huge gate. 'This is Rumi Darwaza,' we were told. Beyond the Rumi Darwaza was 'Machchli Bhawan', which is where the Burra Imambara stood.

I gaped, speechless, at its sheer size. I had no idea a palace could be so massive.

We had spotted Dhiru Kaka's car from our tonga. We paid the tongawalla and went to join the others. Baba and Dhiru Kaka were talking to a tall, middle-aged man.

Feluda laid a hand on my shoulder and spoke under his breath:

'Black Standard Herald!'

True enough, there was a black Standard Herald parked next to Dhiru Kaka's car.

'Look at that fresh mark on the mudguard!'

'How do you know it's fresh?'

'It's white paint, can't you see? That car must have brushed against a newly painted wall or a gate. If the car wasn't washed this morning, that mark could well have got there last night.'

Dhiru Kaka greeted us, 'Come and meet Bonobihari Babu, the man with a zoo in his house.'

Surprised, I raised my hands in a namaskaar. Was this indeed that strange man? He was fair, about six feet tall, sported a thin moustache and a pointed beard and wore gold-framed glasses. The whole effect was quite impressive.

He thumped me on the back and said, 'How do you find the capital of Laxman? You do know, don't you, that in the ancient times Lucknow was known as Laxmanavati?'

His voice matched his personality. 'Bonobihari Babu was going to Chowk Bazar,' said Dhiru Kaka, 'he stopped here only because he saw our car.'

'Yes,' said the gentleman, 'I usually go out in the afternoon. Most of my mornings and evenings have to be devoted to the animals.'

'In fact,' said Dhiru Kaka, 'we were planning to descend on you. These two are very interested in seeing your zoo.'

'Good. You're welcome any time. Why don't you come today? I am always happy to receive visitors, but most people are too scared to step into my house. They think the cages I've put my animals in are not as strong as those in a regular zoo. If that was the case, how do you suppose I have survived all these years?'

Everyone laughed at this little joke, with the only exception of Feluda. He leant closer to me and muttered, 'The man's reeking with *attar*. Attempt at hiding the smell of animals, probably.'

The Standard, as it turned out, did not belong to Bonobihari Babu, for I saw him call his driver from a blue Ambassador and give him a couple of letters to post. Then he said to us: 'You'll see the Imambara, won't you? We can go back to my place afterwards.'

'Are you coming in with us?'

'Yes, why not? I've been in it just once before. That was in 1963, two days after I arrived in Lucknow. Time I saw again what those nawabs could get up to.'

We passed through the gate and began walking across a large courtyard towards the main building.

'Two hundred years ago,' said Bonobihari Babu, walking by my side, 'Nawab Asaf-ud-Daula built this palace. He wanted it to outshine all the buildings in Agra and Delhi. So a competition was held among the most well-known designers and architects. The best design was selected—and you can see the final result. It may not be as beautiful as some of the other Mughal buildings, but it is certainly the number one as far as the size of a palace goes. No other palace in the world has such a large audience hall.'

A whole football stadium could fit into this, I thought, staring at the hall. But that wasn't all. Outside, there was a massive well. The nawab had clearly thought big. The guide told us the well was used for punishing criminals. They were simply thrown into it, and no one ever saw them again.

But what took my breath away was the Bhoolbhulaia. Little passages ran in all possible directions. No matter where I went or what corners I turned, it always seemed as though I was back where I'd begun. All passages were identical—walls on both sides, a low ceiling and, in the middle of the wall, a tiny niche. The guide said that when the nawabs played hide-and-seek with their queens, oil lamps used to burn in those little niches. The thought of flickering lamps in those spooky little passages gave me goosepimples.

Feluda, I noticed, kept very close to the wall. But I couldn't understand why he was lagging behind all of us. Then I got totally absorbed in the excitement of going through the winding maze and had forgotten all about him, until I heard Baba exclaim: 'Oh, where is Felu?'

I turned around quickly. Feluda was nowhere to be seen. My heart missed a beat. However, only a few seconds later, he reappeared after Baba called out to him. 'If I were to walk so fast,' he said, 'I couldn't possibly get an idea of how the maze is designed.'

The door at the end of the last passage in the maze opened onto the huge roof of the Imambara. It had a wonderful view. One could see practically the whole of Lucknow from it. There were a few other people already on the roof. One of them—a young man—came walking towards Dhiru Kaka, smiling.

'Mahabir!' Dhiru Kaka exclaimed, 'When did you arrive?'

'Three days ago. I always return to Lucknow at this time of the year. I'll go back after Diwali. I have two friends with me, so we're out sightseeing.'

'This is Pyarelal's son,' said Dhiru Kaka, 'he lives in Bombay. He's an actor.'

I looked at Mahabir. He was staring at Bonobihari Babu as though he had seen him before.

'Have we met before?' asked Bonobihari Babu, echoing my thoughts.

'Yes, I think so,' Mahabir replied, 'but for the life of me I can't remember where.'

'I met your father once. But you were not here then.'

'Oh. I see,' said Mahabir, embarrassed, 'I must have made a mistake. Sorry. Well, I must get back to my friends. Namaskaar.'

He left. He must be younger than Feluda, I thought. A good-looking man, and very well built. Perhaps he was interested in sports.

Bonobihari Babu said, 'It might be a good idea to go to my place now. If you must see the animals, it's best to do so in daylight. I haven't yet been able to arrange lights in their cages.'

We paid the guide and went down. A staircase ran from the roof straight to the ground floor.

Just as we came out of the gate, I saw Mahabir and his friends get into the black Standard.

THREE

It was nearly 4 p.m. by the time we reached Bonobihari Babu's house. It was impossible to tell from outside that the house contained a mini zoo. The animals were all kept in the back garden.

'This house was built about thirty years before the Mutiny by a wealthy Muslim merchant,' Bonobihari Babu told us. 'I bought it from an Englishman.'

The house was obviously quite old. The carvings on the wall were typically Mughal.

'I hope you don't mind having coffee. There's no tea in my house, I am afraid,' said Bonobihari Babu.

I felt quite pleased at this for I wasn't allowed to have too much coffee at home. But we had to see the animals first.

The living-room led to a veranda, behind which sprawled a huge garden. Individual cages for the animals were strewn all over this garden. There was a pond in the middle surrounded by tall iron spikes. An alligator lay in it, sunning itself lazily. Bonobihari Babu said, 'Ten years ago, when I found it in Munger, it was only a baby. I kept it in a water tank in my house in Calcutta. Then one day I discovered it had slipped out and swallowed a kitten!'

Little pavements ran from the pond to other cages. A strange hissing noise came from one of them. We left the alligator and made our way to it.

A large cat, nearly as big as a medium-sized dog, stared at us through bright green eyes. It had a striped body and was really more like a tiger than a cat.

'This comes from Africa. An Anglo-Indian dealer in animals in Calcutta sold it to me. Even the Alipore zoo doesn't have a creature like this.'

We moved on from the wild cat to look at a hyena, then a wolf and then an American rattle-snake. I knew it was extremely poisonous. An object like a long, narrow sea-shell was attached to its tail, not different from the kind of shell I had often collected on the beaches of Puri. The snake shook its tail slightly as it moved, dragging the shell on the ground, making a noise like a rattle. In the western states of America, it was this noise that warned people of the movements of a rattle-snake.

We saw two other creatures that made my flesh creep. In a glass case was the large and awful blue scorpion of America. In another was a spider, sticking out its black, hairy legs. It was probably as big as my palm, with all my fingers spread out. This, I learnt, was the famous Black Widow spider from Africa.

'The poisons of the scorpion and this spider are neuro toxins,' Bonobihari Babu said. 'What it means is that one sting from either can kill a human being.'

We returned to the living-room and sat down on sofas. Bonobihari Babu himself took a chair and said, 'Often, in the silence of the night, I can hear the hyena laugh, the cat hiss, the wolf cry and the snake rattle. It makes a rather strange chorus, but it helps me sleep in peace. Where would I find a better battery of bodyguards, tell me? But then, if an outsider did break in, none of these captive animals could really do anything. I have a different arrangement to take care of that. Badshah!'

A massive black hound bounded out of the next room. This was Bonobihari Babu's real bodyguard. Not only did Badshah protect his master, but he also made sure that no harm came to the animals in the zoo.

Feluda was sitting next to me. 'Labrador hound,' he said softly, 'the same breed as the Hound of the Baskervilles!'

Baba had been silent throughout. Now he said, 'Tell me, do you really enjoy living with these wild animals in your house?'

Bonobihari Babu took out a pipe and began filling it. 'Why not?' he replied. 'What's there to be afraid of? There was a time when I used to go hunting regularly, and my aim was perfect. But I never killed anything except wild animals. Once—only once—did I kill a deer. I was simply showing off to an American friend, trying to prove how good my aim was, and the deer was about a hundred-and-fifty yards away. I felt such bitter remorse afterwards that I had to give up hunting altogether. But animals had become a part of my life. So I went into the business of exporting some of them. Then, when I retired, having a zoo in my house seemed only natural. The good thing about living with these animals is that they don't pretend to be anything other than what they are—vicious and venomous. But look at man! One who appears to be totally good and honest may turn out to be a first-rate criminal. You can't really trust even a close friend these days, can you? So I've decided to spend the rest of my life in the company of animals. I don't meddle in other people's affairs, you see. I keep to myself. So what others think or say about my lifestyle doesn't matter to me at all. But I've been told that my little zoo has been responsible for keeping burglars at bay. If that is true, I must say I've unwittingly done some good to the whole community.'

This last remark made me first look at Dhiru Kaka, and then at Feluda. Could it be that Bonobihari Babu didn't know about the attempted theft at Dr Srivastava's house?

I didn't have to wait long to get an answer. Dr Srivastava himself arrived almost as soon as Bonobihari Babu's bearer appeared with the coffee and some sweets.

After greeting everyone, Dr Srivastava said to Dhiru Kaka, 'A boy fell from a tree and broke his arm, not very far from where you live. I went to your house after seeing him. Your bearer told me you hadn't returned. So I came straight here.'

Dhiru Kaka gave Dr Srivastava a reassuring look, to indicate that his ring was safe.

Srivastava appeared to know Bonobihari Babu quite well. Perhaps friendliness among neighbours ran more easily in small towns.

'Bonobihari Babu,' he said jokingly, 'your watchmen are getting slack.'

Bonobihari Babu seemed taken aback.

'What do you mean?' he asked.

'A thief broke into my house the day before yesterday, and none of your animals made a noise.'

'What? A thief? In your house? When?'

'At about 3 a.m. No, he didn't actually take anything. I woke suddenly, so he ran away.'

'Even so, I must say he must have been an expert to have escaped Badshah's attention. Why, your house can't be more than a couple of hundred yards from mine! Whoever it was must have walked past my compound. There is no other way!'

'Never mind,' said Srivastava, 'I just wanted you to know what had happened.'

The sweets were still lying on our plates. 'Have some of these,' Bonobihari Babu invited, 'these are called *Sandile ka laddoo* and *gulabi reori*. These and *bhoona pera*—all three are a speciality of Lucknow.'

I wasn't too fond of sweets, so I paid little attention to these words and began watching Bonobihari Babu closely. He seemed a little thoughtful. Feluda, however, was busy stuffing himself. Having eaten two laddoos already, he stretched out a hand and pretended to wave a fly away from my coffee-cup. Before I knew it, he had picked up a laddoo from my plate with supreme nonchalance.

Rather unexpectedly, at this point Bonobihari Babu turned to Srivastava and asked, 'Hope you still have the Emperor's ring?'

Dr Srivastava choked. Then, pulling himself together with an effort, he covered the sudden fit of coughing with a small laugh and said, 'Good God—you haven't forgotten!'

Bonobihari Babu blew out smoke from his pipe.

'How could I forget? Mind you, I'm not really interested in such things. But you don't often get to see something so remarkable, do you?'

'Oh, the ring's quite safe,' said Dr Srivastava, 'I am aware of its value.'

Bonobihari Babu stood up. 'Excuse me,' he said, 'it's time to feed my cat.'

We took our cue and rose with him to take our leave.

On our way out we saw a man carry a bag into the house. A

powerful man, no doubt. His muscles were bulging under his shirt. His name was Ganesh Guha, we learnt. He had apparently been with Bonobihari Babu for a long time, right from the days of animal exporting. He now looked after the zoo.

'I couldn't have managed without Ganesh,' Bonobihari Babu told us. 'That man knows no fear. Once the wild cat clawed him. He stayed on, despite that.'

'It was really a pleasure to have you,' he continued, as we got into our car, 'do come again. You're going to be in Lucknow for some time, aren't you?'

'Yes,' said Baba, 'but we might go to Haridwar for a few days.'

'I see. Someone told me of a twelve-foot python that's just been found near Laxmanjhoola. As a matter of fact, I was toying with the idea of going there myself.'

We dropped Dr Srivastava at his house. Just as he got out of the car, a sudden strange, eerie howl coming from Bonobihari Babu's garden startled us all. Only Feluda yawned and said, 'Hyena.' Heavens—so this was the famous laugh of a hyena? It chilled my blood.

'Yes, that noise often gave me the creeps,' Dr Srivastava said through the window, 'but now I've got used to it.'

'You didn't have any further problems last night, did you?' Dhiru Kaka asked.

'No, no. Nothing,' Dr Srivastava laughed.

It was nearly dark by the time we got home. From somewhere in the distance came the sound of drumbeats. 'Preparations for Ram Lila,' Dhiru Kaka explained.

'What is Ram Lila?'

'Oh, it's a north Indian performance held during Dussehra. The whole story of the Ramayana is staged as a play. It ends with Ram and Lakshman galloping across in a chariot and shooting arrows at a colossal effigy of Ravan. The effigy is filled with gunpowder. So, when the arrows hit it, it bursts into flames. Crackers burst and rockets fly . . . and, eventually, the mighty Ravan is reduced to ashes. Oh . . . it's a spectacle worth watching!'

'Dr Srivastava came while you were out,' Dhiru Kaka's bearer told us as we got home, 'and a sadhubaba. He waited for about half-an-hour and then left.'

'Sadhubaba?'

It was obvious that Dhiru Kaka had not been expecting a visit from a holy man.

'Where did he wait?'

'In the living-room.'

'And he wanted to see me?'

'Yes.'

'Did he actually mention my name?'

'Yes.'

'That's strange!'

Dhiru Kaka thought for a minute, then suddenly rushed into his bedroom. We heard him open his Godrej almirah, which was followed by an agonized cry: 'Oh no! Disaster!' Baba, Feluda and I ran after him.

Dhiru Kaka was standing with the small blue velvet box open in his hand, his eyes bulging. The box was empty.

He stared foolishly into space for a few seconds. Then he flopped down on his bed with a thud.

FOUR

It seemed cooler the following morning, so Baba told me to wrap a muffler round my throat. I could tell from his frown and preoccupied air that he was deeply worried. Dhiru Kaka had left the house very early in the morning without telling anyone where he was going. After yesterday's incident, he had said only one thing over and over: 'How will I now face Srivastava?'

Baba had tried to comfort him by saying: 'But it wasn't your fault! How were you to know the thief would turn up in your absence dressed as a sadhu? Why don't you go to the police? Didn't you say you knew Inspector Gargari?' So it could be that Dhiru Kaka had gone to inform the police.

Baba said over breakfast: 'I had thought of taking you to the Residency. But perhaps it's best that I stay in today. You two can go out for a while, if you like.'

I nearly smiled at this, for Feluda had already said he'd like to explore the place on foot and I had decided to join him. I knew what he had in mind was something other than just aimless walking. His eyes had taken on a steely glint since last night.

We left shortly after eight.

As soon as we were out of the house, Feluda said, 'Let me warn you, Topshe. If you talk or ask too many questions, I'll send you back. Just keep your mouth shut and walk by my side.'

'But what if Dhiru Kaka informs the police?'

'So what if he does?'

'Suppose they catch the thief before you?'

'No matter. I'll change my name, that's all.'

Dhiru Kaka lived on Frazer Road. It was a quiet street, with houses which had large gardens on either side. It led to Dupling Road. Unlike Calcutta, all roads in Lucknow were clearly marked.

There was a paan shop at the corner where Dupling Road joined Park Road. Feluda ambled towards this shop.

'Can I have a *meetha* (sweet) paan?' he asked.

'Yes, babu, I'll make you one with special masala,' said the paanwalla.

'Thank you.'

The paan was duly handed to him. Feluda paid for it, put it in his mouth and said, 'Look, I am new to this town. Can you tell me where can I find the Ramakrishna Mission?'

'Ramakrishna Mishir?'

'No, no. Ramakrishna Mission. I've heard that a great sadhu is visiting Lucknow and is staying at the Ramakrishna Mission.'

The paanwalla shook his head and muttered something I couldn't catch. But we got some information from another source.

A man with a huge moustache was lying on a string bed nearby, singing merrily and beating an old rusted tin. He now stopped singing and said, 'Would that be a bearded sadhubaba? Wearing dark glasses? Yesterday I spoke to such a man. He asked me where the nearest tonga stand was, and I showed him.'

'Where is it?'

'Five minutes from here. Just after that crossing, you can see a whole row of tongas.'

'Shukriya,' said Feluda.

'That was "thank you" in Urdu,' he said to me as an aside. I had never heard the word before.

The eighth tongawalla we asked admitted that a bearded, saffron-clad man had indeed hired his tonga the previous evening.

'Where did you take him?'

'Istishan,' said the tongawalla.

'You mean the railway station?'

'Yes, yes.'

'How much do you charge to get there?'

'Seventy-five paise.'

'And how long does it take?'

'Ten minutes.'

'If I pay you a whole rupee, can you get us to the station in eight minutes? Now?'

'Why, have you a train to catch?'

'Yes, the best train in the world. The Imperial Express!'

The tongawalla grinned, foolishly and said, 'All right. I'll get you there in eight minutes.'

On our way, I asked a little hesitantly, 'Do you think the sadhu is still waiting at the station clutching that ring?' At this, Feluda glared at me so furiously that I promptly shut up.

A little later, he asked our driver, 'Did the sadhubaba have any luggage?'

The driver thought for a minute and said, 'Yes, I think he had a case. But not a large one.'

'I see.'

On reaching the station, we began asking all the likely people who might remember having seen the sadhu. But those at the ticket booth or the gate couldn't help; nor could the porters. The manager of a restaurant at the railway station said, 'Are you talking about Pavitrananda Thakur? The one who lives in Dehra Dun? He arrived only three days ago. He couldn't have gone back so early. Besides, he always travels with a huge entourage.'

At last, the chowkidar of the first-class waiting-room said he had seen a man who fitted our description.

'Did he sit here in the waiting-room?'

'No, he didn't.'

'Well?'

'He went into the bathroom. He was carrying a small case.'

'What happened then?'

'I don't know, babu. I didn't see him after that.'

'Were you here throughout?'

'Yes. The Doon Express was about to arrive. There were a lot of people here. I didn't leave the room at all.'

'Perhaps you didn't notice him again.'

'Well—all right, perhaps I didn't.'

But the man looked as though what he really wanted to say was that if the sadhubaba had come out of the bathroom, he would certainly have seen him.

If that was the case, where had the sadhu disappeared?

We came out of the station. Here, too, stood a row of tongas. We got into one. I was beginning to look upon these contraptions with a new respect. The last one had taken exactly seven minutes and fifty-seven seconds to reach the station.

I couldn't help asking another question as we set off. 'Did the sadhubaba simply vanish in the bathroom?'

'Yes, he might have done,' said Feluda. 'Sadhus and sannyasis in the olden days could disappear at will—or so I've heard.'

I knew he wasn't serious, but he spoke with such a perfectly straight face that it was impossible to tell.

A funny noise greeted us as we reached the main road. It sounded like a band, and it was coming closer. Bang, bang, twiddle-dee-dum!

Then we saw it was a tonga like ours, with the difference that this one was decorated with artificial flowers, balloons and colourful flags. The music was coming from a loudspeaker, and a man wearing a fool's cap was throwing great fistfuls of printed paper at people.

'Advertisement for a Hindi film,' Feluda said.

He was right. I could see, as the other tonga went past us, that a brightly painted poster was pasted on its side. The film was called *Daku Mansoor*. A couple of handbills landed in our tonga, and with them, came a white sheet of paper, screwed into a ball. It hit against Feluda's chest and fell on the floor.

'I saw the man who threw it, Feluda,' I yelled, 'he was dressed like an Afghan. But—'

Before I could finish speaking, Feluda had picked up the piece of paper, clambered down and started to run in the man's direction. I simply watched with amazement the speed at which he ran, despite jostling crowds, without colliding into anyone.

The driver, by this time, had stopped the tonga. I could do nothing but wait. The music from the loudspeaker had grown faint, although a few urchins were still busy collecting the handbills. Feluda returned a few moments later, panting. He jumped into the tonga, gestured to the driver to start, and said, 'He managed to escape only because I wasn't familiar with the little alleyways of this place!'

'Did you actually see him?' I asked.

'How could I have missed him when even you saw him?'

I said nothing more. If Feluda hadn't already seen the man, I would have said that although he was dressed like one, the man was remarkably short for an Afghan.

Feluda now took out the screwed-up piece of paper, smoothed it out and read its contents. Then he folded it three times and put it in his wallet. I did not dare ask what was written on it.

We returned home to discover that Dhiru Kaka had come back, and with him was Srivastava. The latter did not appear to be too upset by the loss of his ring. 'That ring had a jinx on it, I tell you,' he said, 'it caused trouble everywhere it went. You were lucky it was stolen in your absence. Suppose they had broken into your house at night? Suppose they had turned violent?'

Dhiru Kaka smiled at this.

'That would have made more sense,' he said. 'This man simply made a fool of me. It is this that I find so hard to accept!'

'Stop worrying, Dhiru Babu. That ring would have gone, anyway, even if I didn't part with it. And please don't go to the police. That would make matters worse. Whoever it was might try to attack you again!'

All this while, Feluda was leafing through a copy of *Life* magazine. He now laid it aside, leant back in the sofa and asked, 'Does Mahabir know about this ring?'

'You mean Pyarelal's son?'

'Yes.'

'Well, I don't know for sure. He used to be in Doon School. Then he joined the military academy, but left it eventually and went off to Bombay. Now he's become an actor, I believe.'

'Did Pyarelal approve of his son acting in films?'

'He never mentioned anything to me. But I know he was very fond of his son.'

'Was Mahabir in Lucknow when Pyarelal died?'

'No, he was in Bombay. He arrived as soon as he heard the news.'

Dhiru Kaka said, 'Good heavens, Felu, you are asking questions like the police!'

'He's an amateur detective, you see,' Baba explained. 'He has a positive . . . er. . . knack in these matters.'

Dr Srivastava looked at Feluda with undisguised surprise.

'That's good,' he said, 'very good indeed.'

Only Dhiru Kaka remarked, a little dryly, I thought: 'And the thief took something from the very house where we have a detective staying! That is regrettable, isn't it?'

Feluda made no comment. Instead, he turned to Srivastava and asked another question.

'Is Mahabir earning enough from films?'

'I don't know about that. He went to Bombay only two years ago.'

'He does have plenty of money, doesn't he? I mean . . .'

'Yes. Pyarelal left him all his property. Acting in films is more or less just a pastime for him.'

'Hm,' said Feluda and picked up the *Life* again.

Srivastava suddenly looked at his watch and exclaimed, 'My God, is that the time? I forgot all about my patient! Sorry, you'll have to excuse me.'

Dhiru Kaka and Baba went out with him. Feluda dropped the magazine on a table and asked, 'Where would you like to go—the moon or Mars?'

'At this moment,' I replied, 'I'd like to do just one thing.'

Feluda paid no attention to me. 'I've just seen a picture of the surface of the moon in that magazine. It didn't seem very interesting. I feel curious about Mars.'

I rose from my chair. 'Feluda,' I said, 'what I am curious about is that piece of paper in your wallet.'

'Oh that! Here, look!'

He flicked the neatly folded paper towards me as though he was playing carrom. I opened it and found just two words: Watch Out!

The writer had used a red liquid of some kind. It wasn't ink. What could it be? Feluda must have guessed what I was thinking, for he said: 'Sometimes, after a paan has been stuffed with masala, some of its juice overflows on to the stalk. Those words were written with the red juice from a paan.'

I brought the paper close to my nose. It smelt distinctly of paan.

'But who could have written it?'

'I don't know.'

'Why should anyone tell you to watch out? You didn't steal the ring!'

Feluda burst out laughing.

'The culprit doesn't get warnings and threats, silly! They are given to the culprit's enemy. And a detective is always an enemy. So whoever chases a criminal has to risk his life!'

My heart beat faster and my throat started to go dry. I swallowed hard and said, 'In that case, we should perhaps take some steps to protect ourselves.'

'And who told you I haven't taken those steps already?' said Feluda and took out a small round tin from his pocket.

'Denticare,' it said.

Why, it was only a tin of toothpowder. I had seen my grandfather use it years ago. Surprised, I asked, 'What would you do with tooth-powder, Feluda?'

'Don't be silly! It's not toothpowder.'

'What is it then?'

Feluda widened his eyes, stretched his neck and proclaimed proudly, 'It's Powdered Thunder!'

FIVE

That night, after dinner, Feluda said suddenly, 'Topshe, what do you make of all this?'

'All what?'

'Everything that's happened so far.'

'Why, you should know! You're the detective! Besides, how can I draw any conclusions until we find out who that sannyasi was?'

'But surely certain things are quite clear? For instance, the fact that the sannyasi went into the bathroom and didn't come out. Now that is pretty revealing, isn't it?'

'What does it reveal?'

'Can't you figure that out?'

'Well, all it can mean is that the chowkidar wasn't paying enough attention.'

'No, no, you ass!'

'What, then?'

'If the sannyasi had indeed come out, that chowkidar would definitely have seen him.'

'You mean he never did?'

'Do you remember what he was carrying?'

'Look, I wasn't . . . oh yes, he had a small attaché case.'

'Have you ever seen a sannyasi with an attaché case?'

'No, can't say I have.'

'Well, I think that's distinctly suspicious.'

'What do you suspect?'

'That sannyasi was no more than a non-sannyasi just like you and me. And his normal clothes were in that attaché case. The saffron robe was a disguise. Possibly the beard was false, too.'

'Oh, I see. You mean he changed into different clothes, stuffed his robe into the case and came out looking totally different. No wonder the chowkidar couldn't recognize him!'

'Yes, now you're talking!'

'But who threw that piece of paper at you?'

'Either the fake sannyasi himself, or one of his men. He must have heard us making enquiries at the station, so he decided to give us a warning.'

'All right. But are there any more mysteries?'

'There is no end to them, my boy! Who followed Dr Srivastava in that black car? Who was watching us from the gate, smoking a Charminar and chewing a paan? Was it the same sannyasi, or was it someone else? What "spy" did Pyarelal talk about? Why does Bonobihari Babu keep wild animals in his house? Where had Mahabir seen Bonobihari Babu before? How much does he know about the ring?'

I lay awake that night, thinking these things over. Feluda was scribbling something in a blue notebook. Then he put it away and went to bed at half past ten. Soon, he was fast asleep.

Drums beat in the distance. Oh yes, Ram Lila. I heard an animal at some stage—it might have been a dog or a jackal, but it sounded like a hyena.

Why was Feluda puzzled by Bonobihari Babu's wild animals? One didn't always have to do things for a specific reason, did one? People had strange hobbies. So perhaps keeping wild animals was just a hobby for him?

It's difficult to tell when I fell asleep; nor can I tell what woke me. It was still dark. And everything was very quiet. The drums were silent, as were the animals. All I could hear was Feluda breathing heavily in his sleep next to me and the alarm clock ticking behind my head. Then my eyes fell on the window.

Normally, I could see a fair bit of the starry sky through the open window. Tonight, something blocked most of it.

As the last remnants of sleep cleared from my eyes, I realized with a shock what it was. A man was standing outside at the window, holding its bars, and staring into our room.

My heart stood still. Yet, I couldn't take my eyes off that figure. The room was utterly dark and the starlight outside was not good enough to see the man's face. But I could make out that the lower half of his face was covered by a dark cloth.

Now he put a hand through the bars in the window. But no, it wasn't just his hand. He was holding a rod.

A sweet, yet strong smell hit my nostrils. I was already breathless with fear. Now my limbs began to go numb.

I tried to muster all my will power. Then slowly, without moving my body, I stretched out my left arm towards Feluda. He was still asleep.

My eyes hadn't moved from the window. The man was still holding the rod and that smell was getting stronger. I began to feel giddy.

At this moment, my hand brushed against Feluda's waist. I gave him a nudge. Feluda moved slightly and his bed creaked noisily with the movement. In that instant, the man vanished from the window.

'Why are you poking at me?' asked Feluda sleepily. I swallowed and tried to speak.

'Window,' I managed.

'What about the window? Who's . . . God, what's that smell?'

Fully awake, Feluda jumped up and ran to the window. He stared out of it for a few moments, then turned back to me.

'Tell me exactly what you saw.'

I was still finding it difficult to talk. 'A man . .' I croaked, 'with a rod . . . inside . . .

'Did he stretch the rod out into our room?'

'Yes.'

'I see. He must have had chloroform dabbed on that rod. He wanted us to faint.'

'But why?'

'It could be a different thief. May be he thought the ring was still in our house. Never mind. Go back to sleep now, and please don't tell you father or Dhiru Kaka about this. They'll only get nervous and spoil all my work.'

The next morning, both Baba and Dhiru Kaka appeared more relaxed. The police had been informed and Inspector Gargari had already started working on the case. So it wasn't likely that there would be any further problem.

I sent up a silent prayer for Feluda. Dear God, don't let the police win. Let it be Feluda who finds the ring. May the full credit go to him, not the police.

Baba said, 'I'm thinking of taking you out today to a few other places.'

We decided to leave after lunch. But before a final decision could be taken on where we should go, Bonobihari Babu turned up at the house. It was he who eventually settled the matter.

'I had to come when I heard of the daylight robbery,' he said. 'If only you had a hound, Dhiru Babu, this wouldn't have happened. A well-trained pedigree hound would have taken just five seconds to figure out what the sadhu's intentions were. But what's the use of offering you advice now? The damage is done! Never mind. Have one of these,' he added, unwrapping the small packet he was carrying, 'these are the best paan in Lucknow. Banaras is the only other place where you can find such good quality paan.'

I began to feel slightly uneasy. If Bonobihari Babu stayed for too long, our plans for the afternoon would be spoilt. But he asked at this point, 'Are you planning to go out or will you stay in?'

Baba said, 'Well, these fellows haven't seen anything except the Imambara. So I was thinking of taking them somewhere else.'

'Haven't you seen the Residency?' Bonobihari Babu asked me. I shook my head.

'Then allow me to show it to you. You won't find a guide like me. I have a thorough knowledge of the Mutiny.'

Then he turned to Dhiru Kaka and said, 'There is only one thing I'm feeling curious about. Where did you keep the ring? In a chest?'

'No, I haven't got one in my house. The thief took it from my Godrej almirah. The key, of course, was in my pocket. He must have used a duplicate.'

'I believe he left the box behind?'

'Yes.'

'Very strange! Was the box in a drawer?'

'Yes.'

'And you searched the drawer thoroughly, I presume?'

'Every inch of it.'

'You could check for fingerprints, couldn't you? I mean, on the handle of the almirah and that little box . . . ?'

'That wouldn't help. Both are full of my own fingerprints.'

Bonobihari Babu shook his head and said, 'Pyarelal was a strange man. He didn't even bother to have the ring insured. And the person he gave it to was just as foolish. However, I hope he's now learnt a lesson.'

We didn't get the chance to take a tonga this time. All of us got into Bonobihari Babu's car. Feluda and I sat in the front.

As we were passing through Clive Road, Bonobihari Babu asked us, 'Did you ever think you'd get involved in such a mysterious event in Lucknow?'

I shook my head. Feluda chuckled.

Baba spoke for him. 'Felu is thrilled to be here,' he said, 'because he's very interested in such things. He's an amateur sleuth, you see.'

'Indeed?' Bonobihari Babu sounded both surprised and pleased, 'It's an excellent way of exercising the brain. Well, Felu Babu, how far have you got?'

'I've only just started.'

'I don't know what you'd call a mystery. But certainly I am mystified by many things.'

'What do you mean?' asked Dhiru Kaka.

'Well, how do you suppose that sannyasi got hold of a duplicate key? Besides, your house wasn't totally empty. How could he go into your bedroom knowing that the bearer and the cook were in the house? In any case, one little thing has always worried me.'

'What is that?'

'Did Pyarelal really give that ring to Dr Srivastava, or did Sri—?'

'What are you saying, Bonobihari Babu? Surely you don't suspect poor Dr Srivastava!'

'Why not? Everyone is under suspicion until this matter gets cleared up. And that includes you and me. Isn't that right, Felu Babu?'

'Certainly. We mustn't forget that Dr Srivastava and that sadhu had both gone to our house that evening,' said Feluda.

'Exactly!' Bonobihari Babu seemed to grow positively excited.

Baba spoke a little haltingly. 'But . . . if Srivastava had indeed used unfair means to get hold of that ring, why should he give it to us for safe keeping? And then why should he steal it again?'

Bonobihari Babu laughed out loud. 'That's simple! His house was burgled. So he got frightened and passed the ring on to you. But temptation didn't leave him, so he stole it back, fooled the real thief and killed two birds with one stone!'

I began to feel quite confused. How could an amiable gentleman like Srivastava be a thief? Was Feluda in agreement with what had just been said? Or had his suspicion fallen on Dr Srivastava only after Bonobihari Babu began speaking?

In fact, he hadn't finished. 'Srivastava is a nice enough man, I agree,' Bonobihari Babu went on. 'But just think for a minute—he's built his own house, stuffed it with expensive furniture and he certainly lives in style. Now, how could he have done that? I mean, how much does he earn as an osteopath in a small town like Lucknow?'

Dhiru Kaka said, 'Who knows, perhaps his father left him some money?'

'No. His father was just a clerk in a post office in Allahabad.'

At this point, Feluda suddenly asked something completely irrelevant.

'Have you ever been bitten by any of your animals?'

'No, never.'

'What is that mark on your right wrist?'

'Oh ho ho—you do have sharp eyes, I must say! That mark normally stays hidden under my sleeve. It's the result of fencing. My opponent's sword scratched my wrist.'

The Residency was really worth seeing. It was a beautiful place—there were trees everywhere and, amidst them, a few broken old British houses, all built in the mid-nineteenth century. On the trees sat large groups of monkeys. Lucknow, I had heard, was well known for its monkeys. Now I could see for myself what these creatures could get up to.

A few street-urchins were firing stones at the monkeys from their catapults. Bonobihari Babu went across and gave them a nasty earful. Then he returned to us and said, 'I cannot stand cruelty to animals. Unfortunately, there's plenty of it to be seen in our country.'

I had read about the Sepoy Mutiny. Going through the Residency made those events pass through my mind like pictures on a screen. Bonobihari Babu, in the meantime, had begun his commentary.

'During the time of the Mutiny, Lucknow was ruled by the

Nawab. The British forces were all stationed in the Residency here. Henry Lawrence was their Commander-in-Chief. When trouble started, most of the other British men and women in Lucknow went and took refuge in a hospital. Sir Henry fought bravely, but was eventually killed by the sepoys. What happened to the British after that is obvious from the state of this building. If Sir Colin Campbell hadn't arrived with reinforcements, heaven knows what greater horrors the British in Lucknow would have had to endure . . . This was their billiard room. Just look what those cannon balls did to it!'

Baba and Dhiru Kaka had gone for a walk since they had both seen the Residency before. Only Feluda and I were inside, totally engrossed in what Bonobihari Babu was saying, and looking at the remains of the broken buildings, all built two hundred years ago. Suddenly, through a hole in the wall, something came flying in. It shot past Feluda's ear, bumped against the opposite wall and fell on the ground with a thud. It turned out to be a stone.

In the next instant, I saw Bonobihari Babu pull Feluda sharply to one side, just as another stone came in and fell on the floor. There was no doubt that both had been thrown with a catapult.

Bonobihari Babu, despite his age, moved with remarkable agility. He jumped through a bigger gap in the wall and landed on the grass outside. Feluda and I joined him almost immediately. We all saw a bearded man running away. He was wearing a black coat and a red fez cap. Feluda rose to his feet without a word and ran after him. I was about to follow, but Bonobihari Babu pulled me back, saying: 'You are still only a schoolboy, Tapesh. It's better that you stay out of this.'

Feluda returned in a few minutes.

'Did you catch him?' asked Bonobihari Babu.

'No,' said Feluda, 'I was too far behind. He got into a black Standard car and fled.'

'Scoundrel!' Bonobihari Babu muttered. 'Come on now, we'd better get out of here.'

A little later, we met Baba and Dhiru Kaka. 'Why are you panting, Felu?' Baba asked.

'Perhaps he should give up being a sleuth,' said Bonobihari Babu, 'I think a goonda's after him!'

Both Baba and Dhiru Kaka began to look rather alarmed when they heard our story. But, in the end, Bonobihari Babu laughed. 'Don't look so worried,' he said, 'I was only joking. Those stones were actually meant for me, not Felu. Didn't you see me yell at those boys? It was simply their way of paying me back.' Then he turned to Feluda and said, 'Even so, Felu Babu, I would say that you really must be more careful. After all, you are young and new to this place. Why get involved in something that doesn't concern you?'

Feluda remained silent. We began walking back to the car.

'Was it really him they were trying to hit? Or was it you?' I whispered to Feluda.

'Do you think he'd have taken it so quietly if he was their target? Wouldn't he have screamed the roof down—or what's left of it?'

'I agree with you.'

'But I've got hold of one little thing. That man dropped it.'

Feluda took out a small black object from his pocket. It was a false moustache. One side still showed traces of gum. He put it back in his pocket and said, 'Bonobihari Babu knows very well those stones had been thrown at me.'

'Then why didn't he say so?'

'Well, either because he didn't want us to get worried, or . . .'

'Or what?'

Feluda didn't reply. Instead, he inclined his head, snapped his fingers and said, 'The plot gets thicker and thicker, Topshe! You're not to disturb me at all!'

He did not speak to me again that day. On returning home, he spent most of his time either pacing up and down in the garden or scribbling in his blue notebook. I took a quick look at what he'd written when he went out into the garden; but I couldn't read a single word, for the script used was something I had never seen before.

SIX

Feluda got into the tonga and said to the driver: 'Hazratganj.'

'Where is that?' I asked.

'It is the Chowringhee of Lucknow. There's lots to see in this town, beside royal palaces. I want to look at the shops today.'

Yesterday, from the Residency, we had gone to Bonobihari Babu's house for coffee, and taken a look at all the animals once more—the hyena, the rattle-snake, the spider, the wild cat and the scorpion.

While having coffee in the living-room, Feluda had looked at a locked door and said to Bonobihari Babu, 'I had noticed it was locked the last time we were here. Where does it lead to?'

'Oh yes—it's just a spare room. I've kept it locked ever since I moved in. Didn't want to take the trouble of having it cleaned, you see.'

'In that case, the padlock on it must have been recently changed—for it isn't rusted at all.'

Bonobihari Babu's smile did not falter, but he gave Feluda a very sharp look.

'Yes,' he said, 'the old one got so rusty that I was obliged to change it.'

Baba changed the subject. 'We were thinking of going to Haridwar and Laxmanjhoola,' he said.

Bonobihari Babu lit his pipe and blew out a pungent-smelling smoke.

'When would you like to go?' he asked. 'If you leave the day after tomorrow, I can come with you. I told you about that twelve-foot python, didn't I? I really must take a look at it. Besides, our sleuth has turned so active that it might be a good idea for all of us to go out of town for a while.'

Dhiru Kaka said, 'I cannot do that quite so easily. But there's no reason why the three of you can't go. Felu and Tapesh mustn't go back without having seen Laxmanjhoola.'

'If you come with me,' said Bonobihari Babu, 'I can arrange for you to stay at a dharamshala I know; and get a car to take you to Laxmanjhoola from Haridwar. I know a lot of people there. Now you must decide what you want to do.'

We decided to go with Bonobihari Babu on Friday, which was the day after tomorrow. Even a couple of days ago, I would have been quite pleased to have Bonobihari Babu accompany us. But the incident at the Residency had made me feel doubtful about the man. But Feluda didn't seem to mind, so I told myself not to worry.

This morning, Feluda said, 'I've run out of razor blades. Let's go and get some.' And so we were out in a tonga, going to Hazratganj. Apparently, you could get anything you wanted in Hazratganj.

Feluda had been totally silent since yesterday regarding the matter of the ring. When he had gone for his bath this morning, I had tried to read his scribbles once more, but they still didn't make any sense. One or two letters appeared to be English, but the rest were all totally strange.

Sitting beside him in the tonga, I couldn't contain my curiosity any longer, and told him what I'd done. He was furious at first. 'What you've done is despicable!' he said sternly. 'Why, one could call you a criminal!'

Then he relented a little.

'You could never read those words,' he said more amiably, 'because you don't know the script.'

'What script is it?'

'Greek.'

'And the language? Is that Greek, too?'

'No, it's English.'

'Where did you learn to write in Greek?'

'A long time ago, when I had just joined college. Some of those letters, of course, I had learnt in my maths class. You know, things like alpha, beta, gamma, delta, mu, pi, upsilon. I learnt the others from the Encyclopaedia Britannica. If you write something in English using Greek letters, it sounds like a code. No one could possibly make any sense of it!'

'How would you spell Lucknow in Greek?'

'Lambda upsilon kappa nu omicron upsilon. The letters "c" and "w" do not exist in Greek, so the spelling would be LUKNOU.'

'And how would you spell Calcutta?'

'Kappa alpha lambda kappa upsilon tau tau alpha.'

'Good heavens—it would take an hour to spell just three words!'

Hazratganj wasn't exactly Chowringhee, but it had some nice shops. We paid the tonga off and began walking.

'Look, Feluda, there's a stationery shop. They'll have blades.'

'Wait. There's something else I need to do.'

Feluda suddenly stopped before a shop. 'Malkani & Co., Antique & Curio Dealers', its signboard proclaimed in large letters.

One look at the showcase outside told me it was a shop that sold old things. Inside, it was packed with ancient jewellery, carpets, clocks, furniture, chandeliers, framed photographs and heaven knows what else.

A silver-haired gentleman in gold-framed glasses came forward to greet us.

'Do you have any jewellery dating back to the Mughal times?'

'No, I'm afraid not. But I could show you shields and armours of that period. Will that do?'

Feluda picked up an *attardaan* (perfume container) and turned it in his hand. 'I had seen some old jewellery in Pyarela's house,' he remarked casually. 'He was a regular customer here, wasn't he?'

The man seemed taken aback.

'Who? Which Pyarelal are you talking about?'

'Pyarelal Seth. The one who died a few months ago?'

Mr Malkani shook his head and said, 'No, he never bought anything from us, although ours is the biggest shop of this kind in Lucknow.'

'I see. In that case he must have bought those things in Calcutta.'

'Probably.'

'Who are your biggest buyers here?'

It was obvious from Mr Malkani's expression that he didn't have too many big buyers.

'Well,' he said, 'tourists from abroad sometimes buy things from us at a good price. Among the locals is Mr Mehta who buys a few things occasionally; and there's Mr Pestonji, who's one of my oldest customers. He bought a real Persian carpet only the other day for three thousand rupees.'

Feluda suddenly pointed at a barge and asked, 'Isn't that from Bengal?'

'Yes, Murshidabad.'

'Just look at it, Topshe. Isn't it beautiful?'

It was. Made of ivory, it was perfect in every detail. A nawab sat on its roof under a canopy, smoking from a hubble-bubble, courtiers sat by his side and, before him, stood a group of musicians and dancers. Sixteen oarsmen were rowing and one man sat at the rudder. Besides these, there were guards and messengers and every other personage necessary in a royal entourage. I couldn't take my eyes away.

'Where did you get that?' Feluda asked.

'Mr Sarkar sold it to me.'

'Which Mr Sarkar?'

'Mr B. Sarkar who lives in Badshah Nagar. He, too, has occasionally bought a few things from me. He's got a good collection.'

'I see. Well, all right then. You've got a nice little shop here. I'm glad to have seen it. Thank you.'

'Good day, sir.'

We came out of the shop.

'That means Bonobihari Sarkar frequents these shops,' said Feluda. 'I had had my suspicions all along.'

'But he said he wasn't interested in such things!'

'If he wasn't, how could he tell at one glance whether a stone was real or fake?'

A shop called The Empire Book Stall was next door to Malkani & Co. Feluda wanted to buy a book on Haridwar and Laxmanjhoola. So we went in, and found Pyarelal's son, Mahabir.

Feluda whispered softly, 'I can see he's buying a book on cricket. Very good.'

Mahabir was standing with his back to us. Feluda went up to the man behind the counter and said, 'Do you have anything by Neville Cardus?'

Mahabir spun round immediately. I knew Cardus had written some very good books on cricket.

'Are you looking for a particular book?' asked the bookseller.

'Yes, the one called *Centuries*.'

'No, I'm afraid we don't have that one. Shall I show you some other book?'

Mahabir came forward with a smile. 'Are you a cricket enthusiast?' he asked.

'Yes. So, apparently, are you!' Feluda replied.

Mahabir looked at the book he was holding.

'Yes,' he said, 'I had ordered this one. It's Bradman's autobiography.'

'Oh, I see. I've read that one. A brilliant book!'

'Who do you think was a greater cricketer—Ranji or Bradman?'

Soon, both were involved in an animated discussion. After a few minutes, Mahabir said, 'The Kwality restaurant isn't far from here. Why don't we sit down and have a cup of tea?'

Feluda agreed. The three of us trooped into the restaurant. I ordered a Coca-Cola and the others asked for tea.

'Do you play yourself?' Mahabir asked.

'I used to,' Feluda said. 'I have played here in Lucknow. How about you?'

'I was in the first eleven at the Doon School. My father, too, was a good player in school.'

A shadow passed over his face. Feluda began pouring the tea.

'You must have heard about the ring,' he said.

'Yes,' Mahabir replied. 'I went to visit Dr Srivastava. He told me.'

'Did you know your father had that ring and that he wanted to give it to Dr Srivastava?'

'My father had told me a long time ago that he wanted to give something of value to Srivastava for making me well. I did not come to know what it was until after his death. Dr Srivastava himself told me.'

Then he looked straight at Feluda. 'Why are you taking such an interest?'

Feluda smiled. 'It's . . . just a sort of hobby.'

Mahabir sipped his tea and said nothing.

'Who else is there in your house?' Feluda asked quietly.

'An old aunt and some servants.'

'Have they been with you for some time?'

'All from even before I was born. Pritam Singh, our bearer, was with my father in Calcutta, thirty-five years ago.'

'Did your father have any other articles like that ring?'

'I don't know. In fact, I had quite forgotten about this interest my father had. He began collecting antiques when I was very small. I opened an old chest only the other day. There were some other things of that period, but none as valuable as the ring.'

I sipped my Coca-Cola through a straw. Mahabir paused, then lowered his voice. 'Pritam Singh told me something rather strange.'

Feluda waited for him to continue. Mahabir looked around carefully and leant forward, still speaking softly.

'He said he had heard my father scream that morning before he had his second attack.'

'Oh?'

'Pritam Singh didn't, at first, pay much attention since my father used to suffer from backache, and often cried out in pain while rising from a chair or his bed. Yet, he would never allow anyone to help him up. Pritam Singh thought it was his backache that was bothering him again that morning. But now he says he might have been mistaken because apparently my father had screamed very loudly.'

'Do you happen to know if anyone had visited your father that day? Can Pritam Singh remember anything?'

'That's something I've already asked him, but he cannot say anything definitely. Father did occasionally have visitors in the morning, but Pritam can't now recall whether anyone in particular had visited him that day. When he eventually went into my father's room, he found him in pretty bad shape; but he was alone. Pritam

then rang Dr Srivastava as the doctor who normally treated
Father—Dr Graham—was away in Allahabad, attending a
conference.'

'And what about the spy?'

'Spy? What spy?' Mahabir sounded profoundly startled.

'Oh, clearly you haven't heard this one. Your father had started to
tell Dr Srivastava about a spy, but died before he could finish
speaking.'

Mahabir shook his head, 'I had no idea. And I cannot imagine
what my father could possibly have had to do with a spy!'

I had just finished my drink and twisted the straw when I noticed a
tall and hefty man having tea at the next table, staring at us. He rose
and came forward as he caught my eye.

'Namaskaar,' he said to Feluda, 'hope you remember me?'

'Yes, of course.'

I hadn't recognized him at first, but now I could. We had seen this
man in Bonobihari Babu's house. He was supposed to be in charge of
the zoo. Today, he had a piece of cotton stuck on his chin, held in
place by two strips of sticking plaster. Perhaps he had cut himself
while shaving.

'Do sit down,' Feluda invited. 'Meet Mahabir Seth. This is Ganesh
Guha.'

Now I noticed a scratch on his neck, although it was clearly an old
one.

'What happened to your chin?' asked Feluda.

Ganesh Babu picked up his cup from the next table and joined us.
'Don't remind me!' he winced. 'I'm surprised my whole body hasn't
been torn apart. You know about my job, don't you?'

'Yes. But I thought it was a job you'd taken on willingly.'

'You're joking! I do it because I have to—simply for the money. I
was once the keeper of a tiger in a circus. But that tiger was drugged
most of the time. I tell you, compared to the animals I handle in
Bonobihari Babu's zoo, that tiger was little more than a baby! The
wild cat clawed me the other day, and now the hyena slaps me on the
chin! I couldn't take it any more. So I told Mr Sarkar this morning I
had made up my mind. I want to go back to that circus. He agreed to
let me go.'

'What!' Feluda sounded surprised. 'You've given up your job?
Why, we were at your zoo only yesterday!'

'Yes, I know. And no doubt many other people would like to go and visit my zoo. But I am clearing out! I'll go straight to the station from here and buy myself a ticket to Howrah. Then I'll soon be home, away from it all. The thing is—' he stooped and spoke into Feluda's ear, 'That man is not . . . as straightforward as he might seem.'

'You mean Bonobihari Babu?'

'He was all right, I guess, until he laid his hands on something. Then he lost his head.'

'What thing?'

'No, I've already said too much!'

Ganesh Guha dropped a few coins on the next table and disappeared.

Feluda turned to Mahabir and said, 'Have you ever seen Bonobihari Babu's zoo?'

'No. I'd have liked to have seen it, but my father was dead against the idea. He hated the kind of animals that zoo is reported to be filled with. In fact, the sight of a cockroach would have given him palpitations! But now . . . yes, I think I'll go and see it.'

Mahabir snapped his fingers at a waiter. Feluda had already offered to pay, but Mahabir would not let him. Well, I thought to myself, a film actor was supposed to make a lot of money. So paying for a cup of tea and a cold drink couldn't hurt him much.

After paying the bill, he took out a packet of cigarettes and offered it to Feluda. I noticed they were Charminars.

'How long are you here for?' he asked.

'Tomorrow we're going to Haridwar for a couple of days, but after that we're here until next month.'

'Are you all going to Haridwar?'

'No, Dhiru Kaka cannot get away. So we three are going, and possibly Bonobihari Babu. He's going to look for a python in Laxmanjhoola.'

We went out of the restaurant.

'I have a car,' Mahabir offered, 'I could give you a lift.'

'No, thanks,' said Feluda. 'We can ride in a motor car any time in Calcutta. A tonga is a new experience, and an enjoyable one!'

Mahabir took Feluda's hand and clasped it warmly. 'It really was a pleasure to meet you,' he said. 'Let me tell you just one thing—if I get evidence that my father did not die a natural death and that someone was responsible for it, I will not rest until I have tracked down the criminal and settled scores with him. I may be young, but I did spend four years in the Military Academy. I have a licensed revolver, and I am a crack shot . . . good-bye!'

He crossed the road, got into his black Standard and drove off.

Feluda simply said, 'Bravo!'

Yes, the plot had certainly thickened. There appeared to be a puzzle within a puzzle, a maze within a maze.

We began walking in search of a tonga. Feluda didn't really need blades, I realized.

SEVEN

We had to take the Doon Express to get to Haridwar. It left Lucknow in the evening and reached Haridwar at 4.30 a.m.

When Baba had mentioned a possible visit to Haridwar before we left Calcutta, I had been pleased. Puri was the only holy place I had seen. So the thought of seeing another was quite exciting. But now, after all this hullabaloo over the stolen ring, I did not feel like leaving Lucknow.

Feluda, however, had not lost his enthusiasm. 'You'll see how interesting it is to go from Haridwar to Hrishikesh and then to Laxmanjhoola. The river is different in each place. The further north you go, the stronger it gets. In Laxmanjhoola, it gushes with such powerful turbulence that it's practically impossible to have a conversation by its side.'

'Have you been to all these places?'

'Yes, I went to all three after my last visit to Lucknow.'

Dhiru Kaka himself drove us to the station. Almost as soon as we had moved into our coach with our baggage, Dr Srivastava turned up. Nice of him to have come to see us off. But no, a coolie was carrying his suitcase! We stared at him. 'I had asked Dhiru Babu not to tell,' Dr Srivastava laughed, as the coolie put the suitcase down. 'He knew I wanted to go with you. Gave you a surprise, didn't I?'

Baba seemed very pleased.

'Good,' he said. 'I didn't think you'd be able to come away, or I'd have asked you myself.'

Srivastava dusted one corner of a seat and sat down. 'To tell you the truth,' he said, 'I've tried not to show it, but I have been upset by the loss of Pyarelal's gift. So I thought, getting away from it all might do me some good.'

Bonobihari Babu arrived within five minutes, with rather a lot of luggage. He greeted everyone with a smile and said, 'Stand by now for a spectacular event. Pavitrananda Swami is travelling in this train. His followers are coming to bid him farewell. Witness their devotion!'

A plump, saffron-clad figure arrived a little later, long hair flowing down his shoulders. He was accompanied by dozens of people with garlands in their hands. He got into the first-class coach next to ours. A few others crowded round the doorway. Presumably, all these were his devotees.

There were just five minutes left before the train's departure. We had all climbed into our own carriage. Dhiru Kaka was standing on the platform, chatting with Baba through an open window, when one of the men in saffron detached himself from the group and came walking towards Dhiru Kaka, a big smile on his face, his arm outstretched.

'Dhiru? Do you remember me?'

Dhiru Kaka stared dumbly for a few seconds, then with a shout of joy strode forward and nearly hugged the other man.

'Ambika! Is it really you? Goodness—why are you wearing these clothes?'

'Why, I've been in saffron now for seven years!'

Dhiru Kaka introduced him.

'Ambika and I were classmates in school. We last met each other about fifteen years ago.'

The guard blew his whistle. The wheels creaked into motion and we heard Ambika Babu tell his friend, 'I went to your house the other day. You weren't in, so I waited for nearly half-an-hour. Didn't your bearer tell you?'

We couldn't hear what Dhiru Kaka said in reply, for the train had gathered speed.

Amazed, I looked first at Feluda, and then at Baba. Feluda's brows were knitted in a deep frown.

'Very strange!' Baba said.

'Had you been suspecting that gentleman of having stolen the ring?' asked Bonobihari Babu.

'Yes, but obviously that must now be ruled out. But then who took the ring? Where did it go?'

The train clanked out of the platform. I stared with unseeing eyes at the minarets on top of the station. They were beautiful, but I was in no mood to admire them. All my thoughts were confused. What was Feluda thinking? Was he feeling a little embarrassed? After all, he had run all the way to the station to trace the sadhubaba.

But if the man we just saw talking with Dhiru Kaka was a perfectly genuine sannyasi, who was that other man with an attaché case? Had he been loitering outside Dhiru Kaka's house the same evening? If so, was it because he knew about the ring, or was there a different reason? And who had thrown that piece of paper at Feluda with 'Watch Out!' written on it?

Was Feluda asking himself the same questions? I looked at him again and found him deeply engrossed in reading his blue notebook with the Greek scribbles and, occasionally, making further notes.

Bonobihari Babu suddenly turned to Dr Srivastava and asked, 'Tell me, Doctor, were you the last person to see Pyarelal alive?'

Dr Srivastava was in the process of taking out oranges from a bag.

'Yes,' he replied, offering them to everyone, 'I was certainly by his bedside when he died. So were his widowed sister, his bearer and another servant.'

'Hm,' Bonobihari Babu said gravely. 'Were you informed after he suffered the attack?'

'Yes.'

'Do you treat ailments of the heart as well?'

'There is no reason why an osteopath cannot look at a heart patient, if need be. Besides, his own doctor—Dr Graham—was out of town that day. So they called me.'

'Who did?'

'His bearer.'

'Bearer?' Bonobihari Babu raised his eyebrows.

'Yes. Pritam Singh. He's been with the family for years. A very sensible and trustworthy man.'

Bonobihari Babu took the pipe out of his mouth and popped a piece of orange into it.

'You told us Pyarelal gave you that ring after his first attack. When he had his second, you were called, but he died.'

'Yes, that's right.'

'Was anyone else present in the room when you were given that ring?'

'How could that be, Bonobihari Babu? One doesn't give away precious and valuable things in front of an audience. Besides, you know what kind of a man Pyarelal was. He would never have wanted to publicize a noble deed. Do you know how many charities he supported secretly? He donated very heavily to hospitals and orphanages, yet it was never reported in the press. He wouldn't allow it!'

'Hm.'

Srivastava stared at Bonobihari Babu.

'Do you have . . . reservations about what I've just said?' he asked.

'The thing is, you see,' said Bonobihari Babu, 'I do think it would've been sensible if you had got someone to witness the event. Such a valuable object changed hands, and yet no one can testify . . .'

Srivastava was still staring, speechless. Then he burst out laughing.

'Tremendous!' he exclaimed. 'This really takes the cake. What you're implying is that I stole the ring from Pyarelal, then I gave it to Dhiru Babu, and then I went along and stole in back! Wonderful!'

The expression on Bonobihari Babu's face did not change. 'You acted sensibly,' he said coolly, 'I would've done the same. You took the ring over to Dhiru Babu to keep it safe from the burglar who had broken into your house. Then you took it back and thought the burglars wouldn't attack your house again. Tell me, Felu Babu, I am not too bad at detection, am I?'

Feluda shut his notebook and began peeling an orange.

'Surely,' he asked, 'there are plenty of witnesses to testify that Dr Srivastava did indeed save Mahabir's life?'

'Yes, there probably are,' Bonobihari Babu had to admit.

'In that case, it is my belief that no matter how valuable that ring was, its value could not have been more than that of a child's life. If Dr Srivastava did steal that ring, he is certainly an offender. But those who are now after it are real criminals; and dangerous ones, at that.'

'I see,' Bonobihari Babu said gravely, 'you don't believe that Srivastava has still got the ring, do you?'

'No, I don't, because I have evidence to the contrary.'

Everyone in the coach was silent. I stared at Feluda. Bonobihari Babu was the first to speak.

'May I ask what evidence it is?'

'Yes, you certainly may, but you won't get an answer, for the right time to discuss it hasn't yet come.'

I had never heard Feluda speak with such authority. Bonobihari Babu spoke again, with a hint of sarcasm in his voice, 'Let's hope I live to see the day!'

'It shouldn't take long,' Feluda said. 'There is only that matter of the spy to be cleared up.'

'Spy?' asked Bonobihari Babu, surprised. 'What spy?'

Dr Srivastava spoke this time.

'I think Felu Babu is referring to Pyarelal's last words. Just before he died, he did say the word "spy". In fact, he said it twice.'

Bonobihari Babu's frown went deeper.

'Strange! A spy in Lucknow?' Then, pipe in hand, he stared at the floor. 'Yes, it could be . . . I did suspect . . .' he muttered.

'What?'

'No, never mind. I may be wrong.'

Clearly he did not wish to talk about it. In any case, we had reached Hardoi, so our conversation came to a halt.

'A cup of tea might be a good idea,' said Feluda and went down on to the platform. I joined him for I couldn't see the point in sitting inside a train when it was standing at a station.

Just as I climbed down from our coach, another man in saffron clothes turned up from somewhere and got in.

'This is reserved,' said Bonobihari Babu quickly, 'there's no room.'

'Please, sir,' pleaded the man, 'allow me to travel up to Bareilly. Then I'll go elsewhere. I won't disturb you at night.'

Rather reluctantly, Bonobihari Babu made room for him to sit.

'These sannyasis will drive me mad,' said Feluda, waving at the chaiwalla.

The man with the tea came running. 'Would you like some?'

'Yes, why not?'

Feluda asked the others, but they all declined.

I was soon handed an earthen pot, filled with hot, steaming tea. I shifted it from one hand to the other, waiting for it to cool, and said, 'If Dr Srivastava turns out to be the thief, I shall be very upset.'

'Why?' Feluda asked, casually sipping the hot tea.

'Because I like him—he seems such a nice man!'

'You're a fathead! Haven't you read whodunits? The person who appears to be the least suspicious always turns out to be the culprit.'

'But this is not a story.'

'So what? Don't writers base their stories on what they see in real life?'

This annoyed me very much.

'In that case,' I asked, 'when Dr Srivastava came to our house with the ring, who was watching him from the gate and smoking a Charminar?'

'That might have been the burglar—or his accomplice.'

'You mean to say, Srivastava is a criminal and so are the burglars, which would make everyone a villain because Ganesh Guha said Bonobihari Babu wasn't simple, either!'

Feluda took another sip. But before he could reply, another screwed up piece of paper came flying, hit him on the forehead and fell into his earthen pot.

Feluda retrieved it instantly, scanned it and glanced at the crowd on the platform. Then we heard the guard's whistle. There was no time now to look for the person who threw it.

Before getting back to our compartment, Feluda looked once more at what was written on the paper and showed it to me before screwing it up again and throwing it away on the track.

It said: 'Watch Out!' and the words were written with the same red juice of a paan.

The thrilling and mysterious affair of the Emperor's ring had not been left behind in Lucknow at all. It was travelling with us.

EIGHT

It was getting dark. The lights in the train had just come on. We were speeding on our way to Bareilly.

There were seven people in all. Feluda and I had one berth, Baba and Srivastava had another and on the third sat Bonobihari Babu and the sannyasi. Bonobihari Babu had placed a large trunk and a wooden packing crate on the bunk over the berth Baba and Srivastava were sharing. A stranger was sleeping in the berth over mine. He was all wrapped up in a sheet. All I could see were his toes. He had not stirred since we left Lucknow.

I looked around. Bonobihari Babu was sitting crosslegged, smoking his pipe, Srivastava was reading the *Gitanjali,* and Baba looked as though he was trying very hard to keep awake. He kept rubbing his eyes as he tried to sit up straight.

The sannyasi didn't seem interested in us at all. He was turning the pages of a Hindi newspaper. Feluda was singing a song in Urdu, tapping his feet to the rhythm of the wheels:

Jab chhor chaley Lucknow nagari
Kahen haal ke hum par kya guzri.

He hummed the rest of it. I could tell he didn't know the words beyond the first two lines.

Bonobihari Babu spoke unexpectedly.

'How do you happen to know this song of Wajid Ali Shah?'

'An uncle of mine used to sing it,' Feluda replied. 'He was a very talented thumri singer.'

Bonobihari Babu inhaled deeply, stared out at the red western sky and said, 'Nawab Wajid Ali Shah was an amazing man. He was both a singer and a composer. He composed the first Indian opera—very much in the style of Western operas. But he was not a warrior. So the British took Lucknow, and the Nawab left for Bengal. His last days were spent in Matiaburuz, where all the Muslim tailors of Calcutta now live. What was most interesting was that Wajid Ali got together with Rajen Mullik, who was well known for his wealth, and planned the first zoo in Calcutta.'

He rose to his feet and opened his trunk. Then he took out a tape-recorder.

'Allow me to play some of my favourite music,' he said. He lifted the top and pressed a key. Something inside the recorder began whirring.

'If you really wish to enjoy this music, look out of the window.' I did. In the quickly gathering dusk, I saw a whole jungle rush past our window, and from its depths came the harsh cry of a wild cat. Or so it seemed.

'I have kept the volume low,' said Bonobihari Babu, 'so it would seem as though the sound was coming from afar.'

The cat was followed by the hyena. It was fascinating. The train was tearing through a jungle, and it seemed as though the hyena's laugh was coming from outside, echoing through the trees. Then came a different sound.

'Kir-r-r-r-r-r kit kit! Kir-r-r-r-r-r kit kit!'

My heart beat faster. Even the sannyasi had sat up and was listening intently.

'Rattle-snake,' Bonobihari Babu explained. 'That noise might frighten you, but the snake makes it simply to let the other animals know of its existence, so that it doesn't get trampled on.'

'You mean it wouldn't normally attack man?' Baba asked.

'No, not normally. But then, nor would any other snake. But if it was cornered or provoked, most certainly it would turn aggressive. For instance, if it was held captive in a small room and you happened to be in it, I'd say your chances of being attacked would be pretty strong. There is one other thing. These snakes can see in the dark.'

He switched the recorder off, and said, 'Unfortunately, the other inmates of my zoo are not represented here. Two of them—the spider and the scorpion—are, of course, totally silent. Now if I get that python, I'm going to record its hiss.'

'It felt weird to hear those sounds,' said Baba.

'Yes, it must have done. But it is different for me, you see. What you just heard, to my ears, is sweeter than music. Since I cannot take my animals with me when I travel, I carry their voices—so to speak.'

The train pulled in at Bareilly. A waiter came in with our dinner, and the sannyasi left.

Having finished what was on his own plate, Feluda coolly helped himself to a leg of chicken from mine.

'Chicken is good for the brain when it's being exercised so much,' he said by way of explanation.

'I see. And am I not exercising my brain?'

'No. For you the whole thing's no more than a game.'

'So where have you got to, with all your brain power?'

Feluda lowered his voice, so that only I could hear what he said. 'I have got an idea which spy Pyarelal had tried to talk about.' He refused to say any more.

The train left Bareilly.

'We have to get up at four in the morning,' said Baba. 'It's time for bed, I think.'

Bonobihari Babu switched the lights off.

'I shan't sleep,' he said. 'But rest assured, I'll wake you before we get to Haridwar.'

I stretched out on one half of our berth, leaving the other for Feluda. Looking out of the window, I could see the moon. It seemed to be travelling with us.

What were we going to do in Haridwar? The moon, for some odd reason, made me think. There was plenty to see in Haridwar, I knew. But if we came away simply after a look at the Ganges and the temples, it would all be rather tame. Something had to happen. I wanted something exciting to happen.

The train was making such a racket. How could anyone sleep in this? But, of course, people did. It was strange. If, at home, there was a constant clanking noise and someone kept shaking my bed, would I ever be able to sleep a wink? I had to ask Feluda.

'If a particular noise goes on for a long time,' he replied, 'the ears get used to it; so after a point, it doesn't disturb. And the rocking actually helps one to sleep. Haven't you seen babies being rocked to sleep? As a matter of fact, if the noise or the movement stopped, you'd wake instantly, which is why, very often, one wakes when a train stops at a station.'

Feluda was right. Soon, my eyes grew heavy with sleep and I began to see things. For a minute, I thought the man who was sleeping on the upper berth climbed down and moved around in the compartment. Then I heard a laugh—it could have been a man or a hyena. But there was no time to think for I was lost in the Bhoolbhulaia, going crazy trying to find my way out. Each time I turned a corner, there was a huge spider blocking my way and staring at me through green, luminescent eyes. Then it lifted one of its large hairy legs and laid it on my shoulder. At that moment, I opened my eyes and found Feluda shaking me by the shoulder.

'Get up, Topshe. Here's Haridwar!'

NINE

'Panda? Would you like a panda?'

'May I have your name, babu? Where are you from?'

'This way, babu. Which dharamshala are you booked at?'

'You will go to the temple of Baba Daksheshwar, won't you?'

I had no idea the group of pandas waiting on the platform would surround us like this, even though Feluda had warned me of the possibility. These pandas apparently kept huge ledgers that held records of one's ancestors—those who had visited Haridwar, that is—going back several hundred years. My great-great-grandfather was supposed to have left home to become a sannyasi. He had spent a long time in Haridwar. Perhaps one of those ledgers contained his name and address, or maybe even his handwriting? Who could tell?

'There is no need for a panda,' said Bonobihari Babu, 'that would only add to the confusion. Let's go to Sheetal Das's dharamshala. I know the place. We could be together, and the food's not too bad. It's just a matter of one night, anyway. Tomorrow we leave for

Hrishikesh and Laxmanjhoola.'

A coolie picked up our luggage. We came out of the station and hired three tongas. Feluda and I got into one, Baba and Dr Srivastava got into another and Bonobihari Babu took the third. It was still dark.

'A holy place,' said Feluda, 'is always dirty. But once you're by the river, it feels quite pleasant.'

Our tonga rattled along the lanes of Haridwar. Not a single shop was open yet. There were men sleeping on string beds by the roadside wrapped in blankets. Kerosene lamps flickered here and there. A few old men went past, metal pots in hand. They were going to the river, Feluda explained. They would stand immersed in waist-deep water and wait for sunrise, chanting hymns to welcome a new day. The rest of the town was still asleep.

Bonobihari Babu's tonga was leading us. It stopped in front of a white single-storeyed house, with large pillars. This clearly, was Sheetal Das's dharamshala.

There was a courtyard as we went in through the gate. Corridors ran round its sides and the rooms stood in neat rows.

A man from the dharamshala came out and took our luggage in. We were about to follow him through a door when another tonga came and stopped at the front gate. The sadhu who had travelled with us up to Bareilly climbed down from it.

I tugged at Feluda's sleeve.

'Look, it's the same man! The one in the train . . .'

Feluda gave the man a sidelong glance and said, 'Do you mean to say even this man is a suspect?'

'Well, this is the second time . . .'

'Sh-h-h. Not a word. Let's go in.'

Baba, Feluda and I were given one room. There were four beds in it. The occupant of the fourth bed was fast asleep.

Bonobihari Babu and Dr Srivastava were given the room next to ours. The sadhu joined them.

By the time all of us had had a wash and tea had been ordered, it was fairly bright. A number of people were now awake and the whole place had become quite noisy. I now realized what a wide variety of people were staying at the dharamshala. There were Bengalis, Marwaris, people from Uttar Pradesh, Gujaratis, Maharashtrians—all contributing equally to the general cacophony.

'Are you thinking of going out?' asked Baba.

'Yes, I'd like to go to the river,' Feluda said.

'All right. I'm going with Bonobihari Babu to arrange two taxis for tomorrow. And if you're going anywhere near a market, get an Eveready torch. After all, this is not a place like Lucknow. A torch may come in handy.'

We left. Feluda said the place was too small for a tonga ride. It was better to walk.

I soon began to feel the difference in temperature. Haridwar was definitely cooler than Lucknow and, possibly because it was so close to a river, covered by a misty haze. 'It's more smoke than mist,' Feluda said, 'the smoke comes from *angeethees*.'

We stopped to ask our way a little later. 'Half a mile from here,' we were told.

A different cacophony greeted us from a distance even before we reached the river. It turned out to be groups of bathers. Besides, hawkers and beggars lined the path running to the river bank, and they were no less noisy.

We pushed through the crowd and made our way to the steps that led to the edge of the water. The scene that met my eyes was one I have never witnessed since. It was as though a carnival was being held by the riverside. Bells pealed within a temple that stood by the steps. A Vaishnav sat singing a bhajan near the temple, surrounded by a group of old men and women. Cows, goats, dogs and cats moved about freely, in happy conjuction with the humans.

Feluda found a relatively quiet spot on the steps and we sat down. 'If you want a glimpse of ancient India,' he said, 'just watch the scene below.'

The whole thing was so different from Lucknow that I nearly forgot the stolen ring. Did Feluda feel the same way, or was his mind still working on the case? I looked at Feluda, but didn't dare ask him. He was taking out his cigarettes and a matchbox from his pocket with a contented air. This was clearly good opportunity to have a smoke since he couldn't when Baba was present.

He put a cigarette between his lips and pushed open the matchbox. Something flashed brightly.

Startled, I asked, 'What was that, Feluda?' By then, he had shut the box again.

'What was what?' he asked, apparently taken aback.

'That . . . object that's in your matchbox. I saw it flash.'

Feluda cupped his mouth with both hands to light his cigarette and inhaled. Then he blew the smoke out and said, 'Matchsticks have phosphorus in them, don't you know? That's what flashed in the sun.'

I couldn't ask anything further, but that seemed an unlikely story. Matchsticks didn't glitter in the sun!

We stayed by the river a little longer and then went to see the temple of Daksheshwar. By the time we were out of the temple, buying a torch in a stationery shop, it was nearly ten-thirty. But no matter what we did or saw, I simply could not get the matchbox out of my mind.

Somehow, I felt convinced what I had seen shining in the sun was the diamond in Aurangzeb's ring. If Feluda had said it was a coin, I might have believed him. But his tale of phosphorus in matchsticks was pure nonsense, and I knew it.

But what if it was the ring? Did the burglars know Feluda had it with him? Was that why they were threatening him and trying to hurt him? Why, they had even tried to chloroform us!

Feluda, however, appeared quite unperturbed. He was humming, quietly. 'There is a raga called Khat,' he stopped at one point to explain, 'it has to be sung in the morning. What I am humming is the same raga.'

I wanted to say, 'Keep your ragas to yourself. I am not interested and, in fact, I am very cross with you. Why did you tell me a lie?' But I couldn't utter these words for we had reached the dharamshala. I decided to tackle Feluda on the subject in the evening.

Baba, Bonobihari Babu and Dr Srivastava were sitting on the veranda, talking to another gentleman, who was wearing a dhoti and kurta and appeared to be another Bengali.

'We've arranged a couple of taxis,' Baba said upon our arrival, 'and we're leaving tomorrow morning at six. Bonobihari Babu knew those fellows, so we've been given a concession.'

The Bengali gentleman, called Bilash Babu, was from Allahabad.

He turned out to be a palmist. Bonobihari Babu offered his palm and asked, 'Is there any chance of my being bitten to death by an animal?'

Bilash Babu ran a clove on the lines of Bonobihari Babu's hand and said, 'Why, no! It looks like a natural death to me!'

My eyes fell on the palmist's feet. They were distinctly odd. The big toe on each foot was longer than the others by at least half-an-inch. I could have sworn I had seen these feet—or feet like these—quite recently. But where might that have been? I simply couldn't remember.

Bonobihari Babu gave a sigh of relief.

'Thank goodness!' he said.

'Why do you say that? Are you a shikari? Do you go tiger hunting, or what?' Bilash Babu seemed puzzled.

'No, no,' Bonobihari Babu replied, 'but it's just as well to make sure. A cousin of mine once got bitten by a mad dog. You know, purely out of the blue. The poor chap died of hydrophobia. So I thought . . .'

'Did you use to live in Calcutta?'

'Good heavens, is even that written in my hand?'

'Yes, so it would seem. And . . . are you interested in collecting antiques?'

'Antiques? Who, me? Oh no. It was Pyarelal who did that. I am interested in animals.'

'Are you? Is that why you were talking about getting bitten? But . . .'

'But what?' Bonobihari Babu asked eagerly.

'Have you recently been under stress?'

'How recently?'

'Say in the last thirty days?'

Bonobihari Babu laughed.

'No, sir. I have not a care in the world, and I haven't been worried. My only anxiety is about whether I shall find that python tomorrow in Laxmanjhoola.'

Bilash Babu looked as though he would have liked to have peered at his palms a little longer, but Bonobihari Babu withdrew them abruptly and yawned.

'The truth is,' he said, 'I don't really believe in palmistry. Please don't mind my saying this, but I don't think what we make of ourselves has anything to do with the lines on our hands. The only thing I believe in is man's own strength and his ability to succeed.'

So saying, he rose and went into his room.

My eyes went once more to Bilash Babu's feet.

But no, I still could not recall where I had seen them.

TEN

I didn't get the chance at all that day to speak to Feluda about his dazzling matchbox.

Baba wanted us to go to bed early since we had to be up at the crack of dawn the following morning; but by the time we finished dinner and were able to go to bed, it was past 10 p.m.

As I got into bed, I could hear someone snore very loudly through the communicating door between our room and the next.

'Bilash Babu,' said Feluda briefly.

'How do you know?'

'Why, he was snoring in the train yesterday. Didn't you hear him?'

In the train? Was Bilash Babu in the train with us? Of course! One little piece of the jigsaw puzzle fell into place.

'Those big toes!'

Feluda gently patted my shoulder.

'Good!' he said.

Yes, that was right. Bilash Babu was the man who had lain on the upper berth, wrapped in a sheet from head to toe. But I had seen his toes.

It was now time to ask Feluda the question that had been bothering me all day. But I had to wait until Baba was asleep. I could tell by his movements that he was still awake.

The dharamshala was gradually falling silent, as was the whole town. It was the beginning of winter, so people would, in any case, retire early. It was dark inside our room, but a light from the courtyard outside fell on the threshold. What was that noise under the bed? A rat or a mouse, probably.

Baba was now asleep. I could hear his deep, regular breathing. Turning to Feluda, I whispered, 'It was the ring, wasn't it?'

Feluda said nothing for a few moments. Then he sighed and whispered back, 'All right. Since you have guessed it already, there's no point in hiding things from you. I have had the ring from the very first day. When all of you—including Dhiru Kaka—had gone to sleep, I saw that his trousers were hanging from a rack. I knew the keys of his almirah were in one of its pockets. So I took them out, opened the almirah and removed the ring. I didn't take the box deliberately, so that there would be no doubt that only the ring had gone.'

'But why?'

'Because I knew that would only provoke the real thief. And then it would be easier to catch him.'

'Does it mean that the sannyasi had turned up simply to steal the ring?'

'Yes, but it wasn't Ambika Babu. It was the other fake one, who had an attaché case in his hand. He must have had the shock of his life when he saw another sannyasi in the living-room! I bet that's when he went to the station and changed his clothes.'

'Who is this fake sannyasi?'

'I have my suspicions, but not enough evidence—yet.'

'You mean you've been carrying that ring in your pocket all these days?'

'No.'

'What did you do then?'

'I kept it in a safe place.'

'Where?'

'In the Bhoolbhulaia. In one of those little niches.'

Good God! What a clever mind! Now I could see why he had disappeared in that maze for a few minutes.

'But how could you have gone back to find it? You didn't know how the maze had been built? I mean, its plan . . .'

'I had made an arrangement for that. You may have noticed that the little finger on my left hand has a long nail. I had scratched numbers with it on the walls of those passages. The ring was in the seventh passage. I went back before leaving Lucknow and took it out. I didn't like the idea of the ring lying there while I went out of town.'

My heartbeat grew faster again.

'What if those burglars suspect that you've got the ring?'

'So what? They couldn't prove it. Anyway, I don't think they're clever enough to guess where the ring is.'

'In that case why are they threatening you?'

'Because they haven't given up hopes of getting hold of it. And they know very well that I am capable of ruining all their plans.'

'But—' my throat was so badly parched I could hardly speak, 'you might be in great danger!'

'Felu Mitter thrives on risks and danger.'

'But—'

'No more buts. Go to sleep.'

Feluda yawned and turned to his side.

The dharamshala was now totally quiet. A dog barked somewhere. The snoring in the next room continued non-stop. I could not get the matchbox and its content out of my mind. One had to marvel at the courage Feluda had shown. If it wasn't for what he had done, the ring would have been stolen and the thief would have got away with it.

'Kir-r-r-r-r-r kit kit kit! Kir-r-r-r-r-r-r kit kit kit!'

From the next room came the faint noise of the rattle-snake; but it sounded as though it was coming from a distance. Bonobihari Babu must be listening to his favourite music. Strangely enough, this funny noise soon soothed me to sleep.

Baba had set the alarm on his travelling clock for 5 a.m. I woke a little before it went off. It did not take us long to get ready after a cup of tea. 'We needn't worry about taking food,' said Dr Srivastava, 'there are shops at the foot of the bridge in Laxmanjhoola that sell very good puri-subzi.'

We were all wearing our woollens. Laxmanjhoola was further up in the hills and was bound to be cooler.

The two taxis arrived at a quarter to six and stopped by the front gate. Bilash Babu came out and joined us. It turned out that he, too, was going to Laxmanjhoola and would travel with us. As I stood debating on which car to get into, Bonobihari Babu said, 'Three in each car, obviously. I could tell you some interesting stories about animals, Tapesh. Would you like to join me?'

'Yes, why not? I'm sure Feluda would like to come along, too.'

Feluda didn't seem to mind. So Bonobihari Babu, Feluda and I got into one taxi and Baba got into the other with Dr Srivastava and Bilash Babu, who seemed to have struck up a friendship already.

Bonobihari Babu placed the wooden packing crate on the front seat beside the driver. 'For my python, if I can find it,' he said. Feluda sat in the middle in the back seat. I sat on his left and Bonobihari Babu went over to his right.

Both cars left at 6.15. Five minutes later, we were out of the main town and into the open countryside. The hills rose before us. If I looked out of the right window, I could catch an occasional glimpse of the Ganges. My heart suddenly felt light. Bonobihari Babu, too, appeared to be in a good mood, for he was humming under his breath, possibly at the thought of his python.

Feluda, however, did not utter a word. What was he thinking? Was the ring still in that matchbox in his pocket? There was no way of telling, for I knew he wouldn't smoke before Bonobihari Babu.

The other taxi was right in front of us. I could see Bilash Babu talking to Dr Srivastava. Perhaps the latter had seized this opportunity to have his palm read.

'The roads aren't dusty because of the early morning dew,' said Bonobihari Babu. 'But very soon, you'll see that other car throw up clouds of dust. I think we ought to let them go ahead. Driver, will you please slow down a bit?'

The bearded Sikh driver reduced the speed of our taxi and the distance between Baba's car and ours grew considerably.

I had wanted both cars to travel together, never mind about the dust. But I didn't dare say anything to Bonobihari Babu. When would he start on his stories?

There was a car behind ours, apparently in a hurry to overtake us. Annoyed by its honking, Bonobihari Babu said to the driver, 'This will drive me mad. Let it go, driver. Give way.'

The driver very obediently moved a little to the left and an old-fashioned Chevrolet taxi shot past us. Its passenger leant out of the window and gave us a quick look.

I recognized him instantly—it was the sannyasi from the train!

ELEVEN

It had already been decided that we would first go to Laxmanjhoola, spend most of the day there and stop at Hrishikesh on our way back. To tell the truth, I wasn't too keen on going to Hrishikesh, which I knew would be crowded and dirty like any other holy place. Only the river was likely to be a little different.

Bonobihari Babu was now singing the same Urdu song Feluda had been singing in the train:

Jab chhor chaley Lucknow nagari
Kahen haal ke hum par kya guzri . . .

He stopped abruptly and asked, 'Have you heard of Jim Corbett?'
'Yes.'

'He killed man-eaters in these valleys, but like me, he understood animals and loved them. I have always admired him for that.' Bonobihari Babu started singing again.

Our car sped towards Laxmanjhoola through the hills. On our right, the river occasionally showed itself through stretches of dense jungle. The sky was clouding over. The breeze seemed to grow cooler each time the sun got blocked out by a cloud.

I began to think about the stolen ring again. I had learnt quite a few things in the last few days, but there was such a lot that still remained unexplained. Why did Mahabir think Pyarelal's death had not been a natural one? Why had Pyarelal screamed? Which spy had he tried to talk about? Was it someone we knew, or was it an outsider?

All these thoughts chased one another in my mind, as I glanced about idly. My eyes suddenly fell on the rear-view mirror. I saw Feluda in it, looking intently in front of him. I turned my head. He was staring at the driver. My eyes turned automatically in the same direction. Then my heart seemed to stand still. On the driver's neck, between his turban and shirt-collar, was a long scratch.

We had seen someone recently with an identical mark.

It had been Ganesh Guha.

I looked at Feluda again. He was now gazing out of the window. I had never seen him look so grim.

Sitting with us in the Kwality restaurant, Ganesh Guha had said he had left his job and was leaving for Calcutta the same day. Today he was dressed like a Sikh and taking us to Laxmanjhoola. What could it mean? Then it occurred to me that this taxi had been arranged by Bonobihari Babu himself. Oh God . . . in that case . . . ?

I could think no more. My head began to reel. Where were we going? Was it Laxmanjhoola or was it somewhere else? What did Bonobihari Babu intend to do? He appeared calm enough and certainly did not look as though he had any ill-intent.

At this point, he startled me by speaking abruptly.

'We shall now turn left. There is a path that goes through the jungle. Then we'll come to a house where I expect to find the python. Let's just have a look now, then we can collect it on our way back. All right, Felu Babu?'

'Yes, fine,' said Feluda with remarkable composure. But I couldn't help ask, 'Didn't you say the python was in Laxmanjhoola?'

Bonobihari Babu burst out laughing.

'And who,' he asked, 'told you this is not Laxmanjhoola? Howrah doesn't simply mean the Howrah Bridge, does it? It means a whole region. Laxmanjhoola begins from here. The bridge over the Ganges is more than a mile from here.'

Our car took a left turn into the jungle. The path, covered with overgrown wild bushes, was virtually invisible.

I noticed that the driver didn't even wait for instructions. He drove as though he knew where he was going.

'How do you find this place, Felu Babu?' Bonobihari Babu asked. His voice sounded different. There appeared to be a suppressed excitement behind those simple words.

'Beautiful!' said Feluda and gently pressed my right hand with his left. I knew it was his way of saying—'Don't be afraid, I'm here.'

'Have you brought a handkerchief, Topshe?' asked Feluda. I wasn't prepared for such a question at all. So I could only stammer, 'H-h-andkerchief?'

'Don't you know what it is?'

'Yes, of course. But . . . I forgot to bring one.'

Bonobihari Babu said, 'Are you worried about the dust? It's not going to be all that dusty in here.'

'No, it's not the dust,' Feluda replied and stuffed a handkerchief into my pocket. I totally failed to see why he did this.

Bonobihari Babu's tape-recorder was lying on his lap. He now switched it on. A hyena started laughing amongst the trees.

The jungle was getting denser and darker. In any case, the sun was probably hiding behind clouds. I wondered where Baba's car might be. Could they have reached Laxmanjhoola already? If anything happened to us, they wouldn't even get to know. Was that why Bonobihari Babu had allowed them to go ahead?

I tried to muster all my courage. Although I had every faith in Feluda, something told me every bit of his own courage and presence of mind was about to be tested.

Our car was now crawling along in deep jungle. Bonobihari Babu had turned the recorder off; nor was he singing himself. All I could hear was a cricket and the crunch of leaves under the wheels.

After about ten minutes, through the tree trunks and other foliage, we saw a house. Who on earth could have built a house in a place like this? Then I remembered an uncle of mine who was a forest officer. He was supposed to live in a house in the middle of a forest, with just tigers and other wild animals for company. Perhaps this was a house like his?

As we went closer to the house, I realized it was made of wood and had been built on a raised platform. A wooden staircase went up to the front door. It was clearly very old and certainly didn't look as though anyone lived in it.

Our taxi stopped before this house. 'I don't think Pandeyji is at home,' said Bonobihari Babu, 'but let's go in and wait since we have travelled all this way. He may have stepped out only for a few minutes to gather firewood or something. He lives alone, you see, and has to do everything all by himself. But, like me, he's not afraid of animals. So come in, both of you. You've seen fake sannyasis, haven't you? Now you'll see a perfectly genuine one and perhaps learn something about how he lives.'

The three of us got out of the car. I cannot tell how I might have kept my nerve if it wasn't for Feluda's reassuring presence. In fact, his unruffled calm made me wonder if the whole thing wasn't just my imagination—what if the driver was an ordinary Sikh and Bonobihari Babu was telling the truth and this house did contain a sadhu called Pandeyji who had a twelve-foot python?

We walked towards the staircase, crunching dry leaves under our feet. Then we climbed up the steps and went in.

The room we walked into was not much larger than a railway compartment. There was another door that probably led to a second room, but it appeared to be locked from the other side. There were two small windows on the opposite wall, through which we could see the trees. The platform on which the house stood was no higher than a man of medium height.

Bonobihari Babu's tape-recorder was hanging from his shoulder. He put it down on the floor and said, 'You can see how simply he lives.'

There was a broken table, a bench with an arm missing and a tin chair. Feluda went across to the bench and sat down. I did the same.

Bonobihari Babu started filling his pipe. Then he lit it, put the match out, threw it out of the window and sat down on the chair, after having tested its strength by pressing its seat. 'A-a-a-a-h!' he sighed with pleasure and began puffing at his pipe, filling the whole room with smoke.

'Well,' he said after a while, in a low but clear voice, 'Felu Babu—can I have my ring back, please?'

TWELVE

'*Your* ring?'

I could tell that Feluda was quite taken aback by the question. Bonobihari Babu did not reply. He only stared at Feluda, the pipe hanging from one corner of his mouth, a little smile on his lips. The crickets outside were silent.

'Besides,' Feluda continued, 'what makes you think I have got it?'

Bonobihari Babu spoke this time.

'I had my suspicions throughout. I knew it couldn't have been stolen by an outsider. No one could have simply walked into the house and taken something from Dhiru Babu's bedroom without anyone having seen or heard anything. I found that impossible to believe. But although I suspected you, I didn't have any evidence to prove my theory. Now I do.'

'And what is that evidence?'

Silently, Bonobihari Babu picked up his tape-recorder and, placing it once more on his lap, switched it on. It froze my blood to hear what I did.

'It was that ring, wasn't it?' spoke my own voice from the machine.

'Since you have guessed it already, there is no point in hiding things from you . . '

Bonobihari Babu turned the machine off with a click. 'I had left it under your bed last night before you returned to your room,' he said. 'I couldn't, of course, be sure that you would indeed talk about the ring. But since you did, I couldn't miss such an opportunity to get what I wanted What better evidence would you need, eh, Felu Babu?'

'But how can you claim that the ring is yours?'

Bonobihari Babu put the recorder on the table, crossed his legs and leant back in his chair.

'In 1948,' he said, 'that is, exactly eighteen years ago, I bought that ring from the Naulakha Company in Calcutta. It cost me two hundred thousand rupees. I got to know Pyarelal soon after this. He didn't tell me he was interested in antiques, but I did show him the ring. The look on his face on seeing it made me instantly wary. Two days later, it disappeared from my house. The police were informed, but they couldn't catch the thief. Then I came to Lucknow, and so did Pyarelal. I learnt that he had had the ring all these years only when Srivastava showed it to me. I don't suppose Pyarelal thought he would survive his first heart attack. So he got rid of what he had stolen many years ago. But then he recovered, and I went to see him. What I had thought was that if he admitted to the theft, I could perhaps get the ring back from Srivastava. I'm sure he would have agreed, and I was even prepared to offer him some compensation. But do you know what happened? Pyarelal simply denied the whole thing. In fact, he went so far as to say he had never seen the ring in my house in Calcutta!'

Feluda broke in at this point, not a trace of fear in his voice, 'I would like to ask you something, Bonobihari Babu, and I hope you'll give me an answer.'

'No, you tell me first if you've got the ring with you now, or have you left it somewhere? I want to recover myself what is my own!'

'Oh?' said Feluda, speaking with undisguised scorn. 'How come then that you didn't hesitate to get other people to steal the ring for you, or even have me followed and threatened? That henchman of yours—Ganesh Guha, isn't it?—is dressed like a Sikh taxi driver today. I believe he was the fake sannyasi, wasn't he? You got him to break into Srivastava's house and follow his car the next day. But then he was told to keep an eye on me. Throwing stones at me at the Residency, trying to chloroform both of us, showering threats on me—all these were his doings, weren't they?'

Bonobihari Babu smiled, 'One cannot possibly do every little thing oneself, can one? An assistant can be very useful, you know. Besides, Ganesh is strong and healthy and has spent years handling wild animals. So I knew he'd be good at this reckless game. And I have to say this—if he has done anything wrong, it is only because I asked him to. What you have done, Felu Babu, is far worse. You are hanging on to something that doesn't belong to you. It is mine, I tell you, and I want it back. Today! Now!'

He practically shouted the last few words. I was still trying hard to stay calm, but my hands began to feel clammy.

Feluda's voice sounded cold as steel when he spoke.

'What use will that ring be to you, Bonobihari Babu, when you are charged with murder?'

Bonobihari Babu rose from his chair, trembling with rage.

'What . . . what impudence! You don't know what you're saying. How dare you!'

'I dare because I believe I see a murderer before me. Now will you tell me a bit more about the spy Pyarelal had mentioned? You appeared to know something about it.'

Bonobihari Babu smiled drily and said, 'There's nothing to explain. It's all quite simple. I had set a few men to follow him around to find out more about the ring. I'm sure that's what he meant.'

'And what if I tell you the word "spy" had nothing to do with your secret service?'

'What do you mean?'

'You went to visit Pyarelal the morning when he had his second attack, didn't you? You saw him before the attack came on.'

'So what? Are you implying that the very sight of me would give him a cardiac arrest? I had visited him often enough, even before that particular day.'

'Yes, but that day you were not empty-handed.'

'Empty-handed? What are you getting at?'

'You went armed with a box. In that box was an inmate of your zoo—that huge, poisonous African spider—the Black Widow. Isn't that right? What Pyarelal had tried to say was "spider", but he couldn't complete the word. So "a spider" became "a spy" . . .'

Bonobihari Babu suddenly went pale. He sat down again.

'But . . . but what could I have gained from showing him the spider?' he asked.

'You were probably unaware that the sight of a cockroach gave him palpitations. Your intention was probably just to frighten him into handing the ring over to you. But the whole thing took a nasty turn, didn't it? Pyarelal's fright caused a heart attack, leading to his death. Now who is responsible for it but you? And you sit there and tell me you had bought the ring in Calcutta. What if I tell you it was Pyarelal who had shown it to you eighteen years ago and, ever since then, you had wanted to get hold of it? In that room in your house—which you said you always kept locked—there are many more old and valuable objects stashed away. And the purpose of the zoo is to ward off burglars and robbers. Would you deny any of this?'

'May I,' Bonobihari Babu said gravely, 'ask you what else you happen to believe?'

'Yes, you certainly may,' Feluda replied, equally gravely. 'It is my belief that you will never again lay your eyes on the Emperor's ring, and your future will bring you your just desserts.'

'Ganesh!' Bonobihari Babu's shout rang through the air like a gunshot.

Ganesh Guha entered the room, carrying the packing crate.

Bonobihari Babu collected his tape-recorder and began backing out of the room.

'Cover your face!' Feluda told me. I did not stop to question why, and did as I was told, using the handkerchief I had been given.

Feluda took out another handkerchief from his pocket and, with it, the little tin of toothpowder.

Ganesh Guha, by this time, had placed the crate on the floor and lifted its lid. Just as he was about to retrace his steps, Feluda opened the tin in his hand and threw a handful of powder at both Ganesh Guha and Bonobihari Babu. Then he quickly covered his own face.

Through my handkerchief, I got the faint smell of a familiar object: black pepper.

It is difficult to describe the effect it had on the other two. Their faces were distorted with pain, which was followed by incessant sneezing and screams of agony. Bonobihari Babu stumbled out of the room, rolled down the stairs and landed on the ground outside. Ganesh Guha didn't fare any better, but he managed to pull the door shut behind him, thereby blocking our own escape.

Now my eyes went to the open crate on the floor. A snake was slowly raising its head from it, making the same terrifying noise I had heard before.

'Kir-r-r-r-r kit kit kit . . . Kir-r-r-r-r kit kit kit!'

I began to feel strangely lightheaded. Unable to move my limbs, I could only feel Feluda help me stand up on the bench before climbing on it himself.

I realized for the first time what terror could do to one. My eyes refused to move from the snake. Or it could be that the snake really did have the power to hypnotize. Before my petrified eyes, it slid out of its box, shook its rattle and seemed to glance around. Then it fixed its gaze on us, and began to move steadily towards our bench, wriggling sideways on the door, making a constant rattling noise. I appeared to be its immediate target.

I could feel my vision getting blurred. The snake was coming closer, and all I could do was stand there, rooted to the spot. Then, when it was only about a couple of yards away, it suddenly felt as though the house we were in was struck by lightning. There was a loud explosion, a flash of light—and a smell of gunpowder.

And the snake?

The head of the snake was crushed and severed from its body. The rattle shook a couple of times and was still.

At this point, I passed into oblivion.

I regained consciousness to find myself lying on a durrie under a tree. My head and forehead felt cold and damp. Clearly, someone had sprinkled water on me. My eyes slowly focused first on Dr Srivastava and then on Baba.

'How do you feel, Tapesh Babu?' said a vaguely familiar voice. Startled, I turned my head and saw Mahabir. But why was he wearing saffron clothes?

'I travelled with you up to Bareilly,' Mahabir grinned, 'and yet you didn't recognize me!'

He must be a talented actor. And he was wearing excellent make-up. In a long, flowing beard, he had truly been unrecognizable. Besides, he had changed both his voice and speech.

'Now you've seen how good my aim is. Actually, I began to feel doubtful about Bonobihari Babu the day we met at the Bhoolbhulaia and he denied ever having seen me before. The truth was that he had often visited our house in Calcutta and spoken to me a number of times. Once he and my father had a row over that ring. I recalled that event only a few days ago.'

'When we couldn't spot your car,' Baba added, 'we reversed ours and followed the tyre marks into the jungle. But it was Mahabir's idea.'

'And what happened to those two?'

'They have been adequately punished. Felu's powdered thunder had the most remarkable effect on both. Now they're being looked after by the police.'

'Police? How did the police get involved?'

'Why, they came with us! Bilash Babu is actually Inspector Gargari, you see.'

How very strange! Who would have thought that that palmist was really a police inspector? I had no idea the mystery of the Emperor's ring would end like this.

But where was Feluda?

A light flashed in my eyes again. But there was no loud noise this time. I saw Feluda standing at some distance, wearing the ring on his finger. He was turning it around in the sunlight that seeped through the leaves, and reflecting the light straight into my eyes.

I thought quietly to myself: if anyone had emerged a winner in this whole business truly like an emperor, it was none other than Feluda.

Kailash Chowdhury's Jewel

'See how you like my card.'

Feluda fished out a visiting card from his wallet and held it before me. It said: PRADOSH C. MITTER, PRIVATE INVESTIGATOR. Feluda was clearly trying to publicize what he did for a living. And why not? After his success over the missing diamond ring that had once belonged to Emperor Aurangzeb, he was fully entitled to tell everyone how clever he had been. But, of course, he didn't really have to worry about publicity. A lot of people had come to know about the case, anyway. In fact, Feluda had received a couple of offers 'already, but he didn't accept them as they were not challenging enough.

He put the card back in his wallet, and stretched his legs on the low table in front of him. 'It looks like I shall get the chance to exercise my brain during this Christmas break,' he said casually.

'Why? Have you found a new mystery?' I asked. Feluda's words had made me quite excited, but I didn't show it. He took out a small box from a side pocket and helped himself to some supari from it. 'You appear greatly excited,' he observed.

What? How did he guess? Feluda explained even before I could ask. 'Are you wondering how I knew? It isn't always possible to hide your feelings, you know, even if you try. Little things often give one away. When I made that remark about working during this Christmas break, you were about to yawn. My words made you close your mouth abruptly. If you were truly indifferent to what I said, you'd have finished your yawn in the usual way, without breaking it off.'

Once again I was startled by his powers of observation. 'Without being able to observe and take in even the minutest detail, no one can claim to be a detective,' Feluda had often said to me. 'Sherlock Holmes has shown us the way. All we need to do is follow him.'

'You didn't tell me why you will need to exercise your brain,' I reminded him.

'Have you heard of Kailash Chowdhury, of Shyampukur?'

'No. There are so many famous people in our city. I cannot have heard of all of them. I am only fifteen!'

Feluda lit a cigarette. 'His family owned a lot of land in Rajshahi. They were zamindars. But they also had property in Calcutta, so they moved here after Partition. Kailash Chowdhury is a lawyer. He used to go on shikar and, in fact, became quite well-known as a shikari. He even wrote two books on the subject. Sometime ago, an elephant went mad in the Jaldapara Reserve Forest and began creating such havoc that Kailash Babu was called in to kill it. His name was mentioned in almost every paper.'

'I see. What has all this to do with your brain? Is there a mystery regarding Kailash Chowdhury?'

Instead of giving me an answer, Feluda took out a letter from the front pocket of his jacket and passed it to me. 'Read it,' he said. I unfolded the letter and read what it said:

Dear Mr Mitter,
I decided to write to you after seeing your advertisement in the *Amrita Bazar Patrika*. I should be much obliged if you could come and meet me at the above address. I am sending this letter by express delivery. It should, therefore, reach you tomorrow. I shall expect you the day after, i.e. on Saturday, at 10 a.m.
Yours sincerely,
Kailash Chowdhury.

'But it's Saturday today!' I exclaimed. 'And nine o'clock already!'

'You're improving everyday. I am very glad to note that you remember days and dates so well.'

A sudden doubt raised its head in my mind. 'This letter speaks only of meeting you. What if he objects to an extra person?'

Feluda took the letter back from me, and folded it carefully before replacing it in his pocket.

'He should not, as you're a young boy. He might not see you as sufficiently important to object to. But if he does, we'll pack you off to another room. You can wait there while we finish our talk.'

My heart began beating faster. I had been wondering what to do in the Christmas holidays. Now it seemed as if I was in for a very interesting time.

We got off a tram near Shyampukur Street at five minutes to ten. Feluda had stopped on the way to buy a book written by Kailash Chowdhury. It was called *The Passion of Shikar*. He leafed through it in the tram, and said, as we got down, 'God knows why a brave man like him needs to see a private detective!'

Kailash Chowdhury's house, 51 Shyampukur Street, turned out to be a huge old mansion. A long drive led to the main house. There were gardens on both sides, marble statues and a fountain. We passed these and made our way to the front door. There were footsteps on the other side within thirty seconds of pressing the bell. One look at the man who opened the door told me it was not Kailash Chowdhury. No brave shikari could have such a mouse-like appearance. He was a man of medium height, rather plump, possibly no more than thirty years old. His eyes held a look of childlike innocence. In his hand was a magnifying glass.

'Whom would you like to see?' he asked. His voice was as mild as his appearance.

Feluda took out one of his cards and handed it to the gentleman. 'I have an appointment with Mr Chowdhury. He asked me to come here.'

The man cast a quick glance at the card, and said, 'Please come in.'

We followed him down the hall, up a flight of stairs and were ushered into what looked like a small office.

'Please have a seat. I'll go and inform my uncle,' he said and disappeared.

We took two old chairs with arms that faced an equally old table, painted black. Three sides of the room were lined with glass cases filled with books. On the table I noticed something interesting. Three fat stamp albums were stacked one on top of the other, and a fourth was lying open. Rows of stamps had been carefully pasted in it. A few loose stamps lay in a cellophane packet, together with the usual paraphernalia of stamp collectors: hinges, a pair of tweezers and a stamp catalogue. Now it was clear why the man who met us at the door was carrying a magnifying glass. He was obviously the collector of these stamps.

Feluda, too, was looking at these objects, but before either of us could make a remark, the same man returned and said, 'Uncle asked you to wait in the drawing room. He'll join you shortly.'

We were taken to the drawing room. It was a large room, with a chandelier, oil paintings, marble statues and a great number of vases that were strewn all over. Everything in it bore the mark of life during the Raj, at least life in an affluent household. On the floor was the skin of a Royal Bengal tiger, and from the walls stared four heads of deer, two cheetahs and a wild buffalo.

Nearly ten minutes later, a middle-aged man entered the room. He seemed pretty strong and agile for his age. His features were sharp, and he sported a thin moustache. He was wearing a red silk dressing gown over a pyjama-kurta.

We rose to our feet and said, 'Namaskar.' Mr Chowdhury

returned our greeting, but raised his eyebrows slightly on seeing me.

'This is my cousin,' Feluda explained. Mr Chowdhury took the smaller sofa next to ours, and asked, 'Do you carry out your investigations together?'

Feluda laughed, 'No, not really. But Tapesh happened to be involved in all the cases I have handled so far. He's never caused any trouble.'

'Very well. Abanish, you may go now; and see if you can arrange a cup of tea for these people.'

The stamp-collector was standing near the door. At these words, he disappeared inside. Kailash Chowdhury looked at Feluda, and said, 'I hope you don't mind, but I'd like to see the letter I wrote to you. Did you bring it?'

Feluda smiled. 'Is this to make sure I am the right person? Here's your letter, sir.'

Mr Chowdhury glanced briefly at the letter, said 'Thank you', and returned it to Feluda.

'One has to be careful in these matters, I'm sure you understand. Anyway, I assume you know a little bit about my work. I am known as a shikari.'

'Yes, sir. I did know that.'

Mr Chowdhury pointed at the heads of various animals on the walls and said, 'I killed all those. I learnt to use a rifle at the age of seventeen. Before that, as a child, I had used airguns and killed small birds. I am not afraid to fight anyone—or anything—if I can face my opponent, if I can see him. But if the adversary is a secret one . . . if he doesn't come out in the open . . . what does one do?'

He paused. I could feel my heart thudding faster again. The details of a mystery were about to be revealed, but Mr Chowdhury was beating about the bush so much that the suspense was getting higher every minute. A few seconds later, he resumed speaking. 'I didn't expect you to be so young,' he said. 'How old are you?'

'Twenty-eight.'

'I see. Well, I could have gone to the police. But I don't really have a lot of faith in them. Instead of helping, they usually make a total nuisance of themselves. Besides, I respect the young. So you may well be the right person for the job. I think an old head on young shoulders can achieve a lot more than an entire police force.'

He paused again. Feluda seized this opportunity to ask quickly, 'If you could tell me what the problem is . . .?'

Silently, Mr Chowdhury took out a piece of paper from his pocket and passed it to Feluda. 'See what you can make of it,' he said. Feluda unfolded it. I leant across and read what was written on it:

Do not make things worse for yourself. You must return what does not belong to you. Go to Victoria Memorial on Monday, and leave it under the first plant of the first row of lilies that faces the south gate. This must be done by 4 p.m. Do not try to inform the police, or go to a detective. If you do, you will end up exactly like the animals you killed on your shikar.

'What do you think?' Mr Chowdhury asked gravely.

Feluda stared at the note for a few moments. Then he said, 'The writer tried to mask his handwriting, for the same letters have been written in different ways. And he wrote on the top sheet of a new pad.'

'How can you tell?'

'If you write on a pad, the leaves below the top one always carry a faint impression of what is written on the upper sheet. It may not be legible, but it is there. This sheet is absolutely smooth.'

'Very good. Can you tell anything else?'

'No, it's impossible to say anything more simply by looking at it. Did this arrive by post?'

'Yes. The postmark said Park Street Post Office. I got this note three days ago. Today is Saturday, the 20th.'

Feluda returned the note to Mr Chowdhury and said, 'I would now like to ask you a few questions, if I may. You see, I know nothing about your life, except the tales of shikar that you wrote.'

'Very well. Go ahead with your questions. But please help yourself to the sweets before you begin.'

A bearer had come in a few minutes earlier and placed a silver plate before us, loaded with sweets. Feluda did not have to be told a second time. He picked up a rasgulla and popped it into his mouth. 'What,' he asked after a while, 'is this object that doesn't belong to you?'

'Frankly, Mr Mitter, I cannot think of anything like that at all. Everything I possess in this world, including things in this house, were either inherited or bought by me. Everything . . . except. . .' he stopped abruptly.

'Except what?'

'Well, there is something that's both valuable and tempting.'

'What is it?'

'A stone.'

'A precious stone?'

'Yes.'

'Did you buy it?'

'No.'

'Did it belong to your forefathers?'

'No, I found it in a jungle in Madhya Pradesh. There were four of us. We chased a tiger into the jungle and finally killed it. Then we found this ancient and abandoned temple. The stone was fixed on the forehead of the statue of the deity. I don't think anyone even knew of its existence.'

'Were you the first to see it?'

'Everyone else saw the temple, but yes, I was the first to notice the stone.'

'Who else was with you?'

'An American called Wright, a Punjabi called Kishorilal and my brother, Kedar.'

'Is your brother also a shikari?'

'He used to go on shikar with me sometimes, but now I don't know what he does. He went abroad four years ago.'

'Abroad?'

'Switzerland. Something to do with making watches.'

'When you found the stone, what happened? Didn't any of the others want to take it?'

'No, because none of us realized its value then. I came to know only when I had it assessed by a jeweller in Calcutta.'

'Who else got to know?'

'Not many people. I haven't got many relations. A couple of friends know about it, I told Kedar, and I think my nephew Abanish is aware of its value.'

'Do you keep the stone here in your house?'

'Yes, in my bedroom.'

'Why don't you keep it in a bank locker?'

'I did once. The very next day, I was almost run over by a car. Oh, I had a narrow escape, I can tell you. That made me think if I was separated from the stone it would bring me bad luck. Yes, I know it's superstition. Nevertheless, I brought it back from the bank.'

Feluda had finished eating. I could tell from the way he was frowning that he had started to think. He wiped his mouth, drank some water and said, 'Who else lives in this house?'

'My nephew, Abanish, and three old servants. Then there's my father, but he's very old and almost totally senile. One of the servants spends all his time looking after him.'

'What does your nephew do?'

'Nothing much, really. His passion is philately. He's talking of starting a shop to sell stamps.'

Feluda was quiet for a few moments, as if he was trying to come to a decision about something. Then he said slowly, 'Would you like me to find out who wrote that note?'

Mr Chowdhury seemed to force a smile. 'I am getting old, Mr Mitter. I can do without anxiety and tension. And it isn't just that note. Last night this man rang me. I couldn't recognize his voice. He said if I didn't place that object at the specified time and place, he'd come into my house and cause me bodily harm. But even so, I am not willing to part with that stone. Besides, this man cannot possibly have a legitimate claim on it. He's just hoping to frighten me by his threats. A crook like him ought to be punished. You must work out how.'

'There is only one thing that I can possibly do. I must go to Victoria Memorial on Monday and keep an eye on the lilies. This man has got to turn up.'

'He may not come himself.'

'That shouldn't matter. If we can catch whoever comes hoping to collect the stone, it won't be difficult to find out who is really behind the scene.'

'But the man might be dangerous. When he turns up at Victoria Memorial and discovers I have not placed the stone under that plant, God knows what he might do. Can't you do anything to find out who he is before Monday? I mean, there's that note and the phone call. Isn't that enough?'

Feluda got up and began pacing. 'Look, Mr Chowdhury,' he said, 'this man has said you'd get into trouble if you went to a private detective. Now, whether or not I take any action, you might be in trouble already. So really, you must decide whether you want me to go ahead.' Mr Chowdhury wiped his face with a handkerchief, although it was quite cold inside the room. 'You, and this young cousin of yours . . . well, you don't appear to be investigators. This is an advantage. I mean, people may have heard your name, but how many know what you look like? No, I don't think there's much chance of you being recognized as the detective I have hired. If you are still prepared to take this job, I will certainly pay you your fee.'

'Thank you. But before I go, I would like to see that stone.'

'Sure.'

All of us got up. The stone was kept in the wardrobe in his bedroom, Mr Chowdhury said. We followed him upstairs. A marble staircase went up to the first floor, ending at one end of a long, dark corridor. There were rooms on either side of the corridor. I did not actually count them, but at a guess there were at least ten rooms. Some of them were locked. There was no one in sight. The slightest noise sounded unnaturally loud in the eerie silence. I began to feel uneasy.

Mr Chowdhury's bedroom was the last one on the right. When we were more or less half way down the corridor, I suddenly realized that the door to one of the rooms was ajar. Through a small gap, a very old man was peering out, craning his neck to look at us. His eyes were dimmed with age, but as we got closer, I was shocked to notice the expression in them. The old man was staring with murder in his eyes. But he said nothing. I now felt positively scared.

'That's my father,' Mr Chowdhury explained hurriedly, continuing to walk. 'I told you he was senile, didn't I? He keeps peeping out of doors and windows. And he thinks everyone neglects him. That's why he looks so cross most of the time. But I can assure you every effort is made to make sure he's all right.'

The bedroom had a huge, high bed, and the wardrobe was next to it. Mr Chowdhury opened it, pulled out a drawer and took out a small, blue velvet box from it. 'I bought this box from a jeweller just to keep the stone in it,' he informed us, and opened it. A glittering stone lay inside, about the size of a litchi, radiating a greenish-blue light.

'This is a blue beryl. It's usually found in Brazil. There cannot be many of these in India, and certainly none of this size. I know that for a fact.'

Feluda picked up the stone, held it between his forefinger and thumb and looked closely at it for a few moments before returning it to its owner. Mr Chowdhury put it back in the drawer, then took out his wallet from his pocket. 'This is an advance payment,' he said, offering five crisp ten-rupee notes. 'I'll pay you the rest when this business is cleared up. All right?'

'Thank you,' said Feluda, accepting the money. This was the first time I saw him actually being paid for his services.

'I will need that note you were sent, and I'd like to speak to your nephew, please,' Feluda said, as we climbed down the stairs. The phone in the drawing room started ringing just as we reached the last step. Mr Chowdhury went quickly to answer it, leaving us behind. 'Hello!' we heard him say. This was followed by silence.

When we entered the drawing room a few seconds later, Mr Chowdhury replaced the receiver and sat down quickly, looking pale and frightened. 'It. . . it was that same voice!' he whispered.

'What did it say?'

'It simply repeated the same threat, but this time it was more specific. He actually said he wanted what I had found in an abandoned temple.'

'Did he say anything else?'

'No.'

'And you didn't recognize the voice?'

'No, all I can say is that it was a most unpleasant voice. Maybe you'd like to think again about taking on this case?'

Feluda smiled. 'I have finished thinking,' he replied.

We left the drawing room soon after this and made our way to the room of Mr Chowdhury's nephew, Abanish Babu. We found him closely examining something on a table with a magnifying glass. As we entered the room, he swiftly covered the object with one hand and got to his feet.

'Come in, come in!' he invited.

'I can see that you are very interested in stamps,' Feluda remarked. Abanish Babu's eyes lit up. 'Yes, sir. That's my only interest in life, my only passion. All I ever think of are stamps!'

'Do you specialize in any one country, or do you collect stamps from all over the world?'

'I used to collect them from wherever they happened to be, but of late I've started to concentrate on India. I had to sift through hundreds of old letters to get them.'

'Did you find anything good?'

'Good? Good?' Abanish Babu began to look ecstatic. 'Are you interested in this subject? Will you understand if I explain?'

'Try me,' Feluda smiled, 'I don't claim to be an expert, but like most other people, I was once keen on collecting stamps, and dreamt of acquiring the famous ones. You know, the one-penny stamp from the Cape of Good Hope, the two-penny from Mauritius and the 1856 ones from British Guyana. Ten years ago their price was in the region of a hundred thousand rupees. Now they must be worth a lot more.'

Abanish Babu grew even more excited. 'Well then,' he said with gleaming eyes, 'well then, I'm sure you'd understand. I'd like to show you something. Here it is.' He took his hand off the table and revealed the object he had been hiding. It turned out to be a very old stamp, detached from an envelope. Its original colour must have been green, but it had faded almost completely. Abanish Babu passed it to Feluda.

'What? What can you see?' he asked eagerly.

'An Indian stamp, about a hundred years old. It has a picture of Queen Victoria. I've seen such stamps before.'

'Have you? Yes, I'm sure you have. Now then, take another look through this magnifying glass.'

Feluda peered through the proffered glass.

'Now what do you see, eh?' Abanish Babu asked anxiously.

'There is a printing error.'

'Exactly!'

'The word is obviously POSTAGE, but instead of a "G", they printed a "C".'

Abanish Babu took the stamp back. 'Do you know how much that stamp is worth because of that error?'

'How much?'

'Twenty thousand.'

'What!'

'Yes, sir. I've checked with the authorities in UK. The catalogue does not mention the error. I was the first person to find it.'

'Congratulations! But . . . er . . . I wanted to discuss something else with you, Abanish Babu. I mean, something other than stamps.'

'Yes?'

'Your uncle—Kailash Chowdhury—has a valuable jewel. Are you aware of that?'

Abanish Babu had to think for a few moments before replying, 'Oh yes, yes. I did hear about it. I know nothing about its value, but it's supposed to be "lucky", or so my uncle said. Please forgive me, Mr Mitter, but of late I have been able to pay no attention to anything except my stamps.'

'How long have you lived in this house?'

'For the last five years. I moved here soon after my father died.'

'Do you get on with your uncle?'

'Which one do you mean? I have two uncles. One of them lives abroad.'

'Oh? I was speaking of Kailash Babu.'

'I see. Well, he is a very nice man, but . . .'

'But what?'

Abanish Babu frowned. 'For the last few days . . . he's been sort of . . . different.'

'How do you mean? When did you first notice this?'

'Two or three days ago. I told him about this stamp, but he paid no attention at all. Normally, he takes a great deal of interest. Besides, some of his old habits seem to be changing.'

'How?'

'He used to take a walk in the garden every morning before breakfast. He hasn't done that for the last couple of days. In fact, he gets up quite late. Maybe he hasn't been sleeping well.'

'Do you have any particular reason to say this?'

'Yes. My bedroom is on the ground floor. The room directly above mine is my uncle's. I have heard him pacing in the middle of the night. I've even heard his voice. I think he was having an argument.'

'An argument? With whom?'

'Probably Grandfather. Who else could it be? I've even heard footsteps going up and coming down the stairs. One night, I got up and went to the bottom of the stairs to see what was going on. I saw my uncle coming down from the roof, with a gun in his hand.'

'What time would that have been?'

'Around two o'clock in the morning, I should think.'

'What's there on the roof?'

'Nothing except a small attic. It was full of old papers and letters, but I took those away a month ago.'

Feluda rose. I could see he had no further questions to ask.

Abanish Babu said, 'Why did you ask me all this?'

Feluda smiled. 'You uncle has a lot on his mind at this moment. But you don't have to worry about it. Once things get sorted out, I'll come and have a look at your stamps. All right?'

We returned to the drawing room to say good-bye to Mr Chowdhury.

'I cannot guarantee anything, obviously, but I would like to say one thing,' Feluda told him. 'Please stop worrying and leave everything to me. Try to sleep at night. Take a sleeping pill, if necessary; and please do not go up to the roof. The houses in your lane are so close to one another that, for all we know, your enemy might be hiding on the roof of the house next door to keep an eye on you. If that is the cast, he may well jump across and attack you.'

'You think so? I did go up to the roof one night, but I took my gun with me. I'd heard a strange noise, you see. But I couldn't see anyone.'

'I hope you always keep your gun handy?'

'Oh yes. But mental tension and anxiety can often affect one's aim. If this business isn't cleared up soon, God knows what's going to happen to mine.'

The next day was Sunday. Feluda spent most of his time pacing in his room. At around four, I saw him change from his comfortable kurta-pyjama into trousers and a shirt.

'Are you going out?' I asked.

'Yes. I thought it might be a good idea to take a look at the lilies in the Victoria Memorial. You can come with me, if you like.'

We took a tram and got off at the crossing of Lower Circular Road. Then we walked slowly to the south gate of the Memorial. Not many people came here. In the evening, particularly, most people went to the front of the building, to the north gate.

We slipped in through the gate Twenty yards to the left, there stood rows of lilies. The blue beryl was supposed to be kept the next day under the first row of these. The sight of these flowers—beautiful though it was—suddenly gave me the creeps.

'Didn't your father have a pair of binoculars, which he'd taken to Darjeeling?' Feluda asked.

'Yes, he's still got them.'

'Good.'

We spent about fifteen minutes walking in the open ground surrounding the building. Then we took a taxi to the Lighthouse cinema. I got out with Feluda, feeling quite puzzled. Why did he suddenly want to see a film? But no, he was actually interested in a bookshop opposite the cinema. After leafing through a couple of other books, he picked up a fat stamp catalogue and began thumbing through its pages. I peered over his shoulder and whispered, 'Are you suspecting Abanish Babu?'

'Well, if he's so passionately fond of stamps, I'm sure he wouldn't mind laying his hands on some ready cash.'

'But. . . remember that phone call that came when we were still at Mr Chowdhury's? Abanish Babu could not have made it, surely?'

'No. That was made by Akbar Badshah. Or it may even have been Queen Victoria.'

This made me realize Feluda was no longer in the right mood to give straight answers to my questions, so I shut up.

It was eight o'clock by the time we got back home. Feluda took off his jacket and threw it on his bed. 'Look up Kailash Chowdhury's telephone number in the directory while I have a quick shower,' he said.

I sat down with the directory in my lap, but the phone started ringing before I could turn a single page. Considerably startled, I picked it up.

'Hello.'

'Who is speaking?'

What a strange voice! I had certainly never heard it before.

'Who would you like to speak to?' I asked. The answer came in the same harsh voice: 'Why does a young boy like you go around with a detective? Don't you fear for your life?'

I tried calling out to Feluda, but could not speak. My hands had started to tremble. Before I could replace the receiver, the man finished what he had to say, 'I am warning you—both of you. Lay off. Or the consequences will be . . . unhappy.'

I sat still in my chair, quite unable to move. Feluda walked into the room a few minutes later, and said, 'Hey, what's the matter? Why are you sitting in that corner so quietly? Who rang just now?'

I swallowed hard and told him what had happened. His face grew grave. Then he slapped my shoulder and said, 'Don't worry. The police have been informed. A few men in plain clothes will be there. We must be at Victoria Memorial tomorrow.'

I didn't find it easy to sleep that night. It wasn't just the telephone call that kept me awake. I kept thinking of Mr Chowdhury's house and all that I had seen in it: the staircase with the iron railing that went right up to the roof; the long, dark veranda with the marble floor on the first floor, and the old Mr Chowdhury peering out of a half-open door. Why was he staring at his son like that? And why had Kailash Babu gone to the roof carrying his gun? What kind of noise had he heard?

Feluda said only one thing before switching off his light, 'Did you know, Topshe, that people who send anonymous notes and threaten others on the telephone are basically cowards?' It was perhaps because of this remark that I finally fell asleep.

Feluda rang Kailash Chowdhury the following morning and told him to relax and stay at home. Feluda himself would take care of everything.

'When will you go to Victoria Memorial?' I asked him.

'The same time as yesterday. By the way, do you have a sketch pad and pens and other drawing material?'

I felt totally taken aback. 'Why? What do I need those for?'

'Never mind. Have you got them or not?'

'Yes, of course. I have my school drawing book.'

'Good. Take it with you. I'd want you to stand at a little distance from the lilies, and draw something—the trees, the building, the flowers, anything. I shall be your drawing teacher.'

Feluda could draw very well. In fact, I knew he could draw a reasonable portrait of a man after seeing him only once. The role of a drawing teacher would suit him perfectly.

Since the days were short in winter, we reached the Victoria Memorial a few minutes before four o'clock. There were even fewer people around today. Three Nepali ayahs were roaming idly with their charges in perambulators. An Indian family—possibly Marwaris—and a couple of old men were strolling about, but there was no one else in sight. At some distance away from the gate, closer to the compound wall, stood two men under a tree. Feluda glanced at them, and then nudged me quietly. That meant those two were his friends from the police. They were in plain clothes, but were probably armed. Feluda knew quite a lot of people in the police.

I parked myself opposite the rows of lilies and began sketching, although I could hardly concentrate on what I was doing. Feluda moved around with a pair of binoculars in his hands, occasionally grabbing my pad to make corrections and scolding me for making mistakes. Then he would move away again, and peer through the binoculars.

The sun was about to set. The clock in a church nearby struck five. It would soon get cold. The Marwaris left in a big car. The ayahs, too, began to push their perambulators towards the gate. The traffic on Lower Circular Road had intensified. I could hear frequent horns from cars and buses, caught in the evening rush. Feluda returned to me and was about to sit down on the grass, when something near the gate seemed to attract his attention. I followed his gaze quickly, but could see no one except a man wrapped in a brown shawl, who was standing by the road outside, quite a long way away from the gate. Feluda placed the binoculars to his eyes, had a quick look, then passed them to me. 'Take a look,' he whispered.

'You mean that man over there? The one wearing a shawl?'

'Hm.'

One glance through the binoculars brought the man clearly into view, as if he was standing only a few feet away. I gave an involuntary gasp. 'Why . . . this is Kailash Chowdhury himself!'

'Right. Perhaps he's come to look for us. Let's go.'

But the man began walking away just as we started to move. He was gone by the time we came out of the gate. 'Let's go to his house,' Feluda suggested, 'I don't think he saw us. He must have gone back feeling worried.'

There was no chance of finding a taxi at this hour, so we began walking towards Chowringhee in the hope of catching a tram. The road was heavily lined with cars. Soon, we found ourselves outside the Calcutta Club. What happened here was so unexpected and frightening that even as I write about it, I can feel myself break into a cold sweat. I was walking by Feluda's side when, without the slightest warning, he pulled me sharply away from the road. Then he leapt aside himself, as a speeding car missed him by inches.

'What the devil—!' Feluda exclaimed. 'I missed the number of that car.'

It was too late to do anything about that. Heaven knew where the car had come from, or what had possessed its driver to drive so fast in this traffic. But it had disappeared totally from sight. I had fallen on the pavement, my sketch pad and pencils had scattered in different directions. I picked myself up, without bothering to look for them. If Feluda hadn't seen that car coming and acted promptly, there was no doubt that both of us would have been crushed under its wheels.

Feluda did not utter a single word in the tram. He just sat looking grim. The first thing he said on reaching Mr Chowdhury's house was: 'Didn't you see us?'

Mr Chowdhury was sitting in a sofa in the drawing room. He seemed quite taken aback by our sudden arrival. 'See you?' he faltered. 'Where? What are you talking about?'

'You mean to say you didn't go to Victoria Memorial?'

'Who, me? Good heavens, no! I didn't leave the house at all. In fact, I spent all afternoon in my bedroom upstairs, feeling sick with worry. I've only just come down.'

'Well then, Mr Chowdhury, do you have an identical twin?'

Mr Chowdhury's jaw fell open. 'Oh God, didn't I tell you the other day?'

'Tell me what?'

'About Kedar? He's my twin.'

Feluda sat down quickly. Mr Chowdhury's face seemed to have lost all colour.

'Why, did you . . . did you see Kedar? Was he there?' he asked anxiously.

'Yes. It couldn't possibly have been anyone else.'

'My God!'

'Why do you say that? Does your twin have a claim on that stone?'

Mr Chowdhury suddenly went limp, as though all the energy in his body had been drained out. He leant against the arm of his sofa, and sighed. 'Yes,' he said slowly, 'yes, he does. You see, it was Kedar who found the stone first. I saw the temple, but Kedar was the one who noticed the stone fixed on the statue.'

'What happened next?'

'Well, I took it from him. I mean, I pestered and badgered him until he got fed up and gave it to me. In a way, it was the right thing to do, for Kedar would simply have sold it and wasted the money. When I learnt just how valuable the stone was, I did not tell Kedar. To be honest, when he left the country, I felt quite relieved. But now . . . perhaps he's come back because he couldn't find work abroad. Maybe he wants to sell the stone and start a business of his own.'

Feluda was silent for a few moments. Then he said, 'Do you have any idea what he might do next?'

'No. But I do know this: he will come and meet me here. I have stopped going out of the house, and I did not keep the stone where I was told to. There is no other way left for him now. If he wants the stone, he has to come here.'

'Would you like me to stay here? I might be able to help.'

'No, thank you. That will not be necessary. I have now made up my mind, Mr Mitter. If Kedar wants the stone, he can have it. I will simply hand it over to him. It's simply a matter of waiting until he turns up. You have already done so much, putting your life at risk. I am most grateful to you. If you send me your bill, I will let you have a cheque.'

'Thank you. You're right about the risk. We nearly got run over by a car.'

I had realized a while ago that one of my elbows was rather badly grazed, but had been trying to keep it out of sight. As we rose to take our leave, Feluda's eyes fell on it. 'Hey, you're hurt, aren't you?' he exclaimed, 'your elbow is bleeding! If you don't mind, Mr Chowdhury, I think Tapesh should put some Dettol on the wound, or it might get septic. Do you—?'

'Yes, yes,' Mr Chowdhury got up quickly. 'You are quite right. The streets are filthy, aren't they? Wait, let me ask Abanish.'

We followed Mr Chowdhury to Abanish Babu's room. 'Do we have any Dettol in the house, Abanish?' Mr Chowdhury asked. Abanish Babu gave him a startled glance.

'Why, I saw you bring a new bottle only a week ago!' he said. 'Don't tell me it's finished already?'

Mr Chowdhury gave an embarrassed laugh. 'Yes, of course. I totally forgot. I am going mad.'

Five minutes later, my elbow duly dabbed with Dettol, we came out of the house. Instead of going towards the main road where we might have caught a tram to go home, Feluda began walking in the opposite direction. Before I could ask him anything, he said, 'My friend Ganapati lives nearby. He promised to get me a ticket for the Test match. I'd like to see him.'

Ganapati Chatterjee's house turned out to be only two houses away. I had heard of him, but had never met him before. He opened the door when Feluda knocked: a rather plump man, wearing a pullover and trousers.

'Felu! What brings you here, my friend?'

'Surely you can guess?'

'Oh, I see. You needn't have come personally to remind me. I hadn't forgotten. I did promise, didn't I?'

'Yes, I know. But that's not the only reason why I am here. I believe there's a wonderful view of north Calcutta from your roof.

I'd like to see it, if you don't mind. Someone I know in a film company told me to look around. They're making a film on Calcutta.'

'OK, no problem. That staircase over there goes right up to the roof. I'll see about getting us a cup of tea.'

The house had four storeys. We got to the top and discovered that there was a very good view of Mr Chowdhury's house on the right. The whole house—from the garden to the roof—was visible. A light was on in one of the rooms on the first floor, and a man was moving about in it. It was Kailash Chowdhury's father. I could also see the attic on the roof. At least, I could see its window; its door was probably on the other side, hidden from view.

Another light on the second floor was switched on. It was the light on the staircase. Feluda took out the binoculars again and placed them before his eyes. A man was climbing the stairs. Who was it? Kailash Chowdhury. I could recognize his red silk dressing gown even from this distance. He disappeared from view for a few seconds, then suddenly appeared on the roof of his house. Feluda and I ducked promptly, and hid behind the wall that surrounded Ganapati Chatterjee's roof, peering cautiously over its edge.

Mr Chowdhury glanced around a couple of times, then went to the other side of the attic, presumably to go into it through the door we could not see. A second later, the light in the attic came on. Mr Chowdhury was now standing near its window with his back to us. My heart began beating faster. Mr Chowdhury stood still for a few moments, then bent down, possibly sitting on the ground. A little later, he stood up, switched the light off and went down the stairs once more.

Feluda put the binoculars away and said only one thing: 'Fishy. Very fishy.'

He didn't speak to me on our way back. When he gets into one of these moods, I don't like to disturb him. Normally, if he is agitated about something, he starts pacing in his room. Today, however, I saw him throw himself down on his bed and stare at the ceiling. At half past nine, he got up and started to scribble in his blue notebook. I knew he was writing in English, using Greek letters. So there was no way I could read and understand what he'd written. The only thing that was obvious was that he was still working on Mr

Chowdhury's case, although his client had dispensed with his services.

I lay awake for a long time, which was probably why I didn't wake the following morning until Feluda shook me. 'Topshe! Get up quickly, we must to go Shyampukur at once.'

'Why?' I sat up.

'I rang the house, but no one answered. Something is obviously wrong.'

In ten minutes, we were in a taxi, speeding up to Shyampukur Street. Feluda refused to tell me anything more, except, 'What a cunning man he is! If only I'd guessed it a little sooner, this would not have happened!'

When we reached Mr Chowdhury's house, Feluda saw that the front door was open and walked right in, without bothering to ring the bell. We crossed the landing and arrived at Abanish Babu's room. The sight that met my eyes made me gasp in horrified amazement. A chair lay overturned before a table, and next to it lay Abanish Babu. His hands were tied behind his back, a large handkerchief covered his mouth. Feluda bent over him quickly and untied him.

'Oh, oh, thank God! Thank you!' he exclaimed, breathing heavily.

'Who did this to you?'

'Who do you think?' he sat up, still panting, 'My uncle—Kailash Mama did this. I told you he was going crazy, didn't I? I got up quite early this morning, and decided to get some work done. It was still dark outside, so I switched the light on. My uncle walked in soon after that. The first thing he did was switch the light off. Then he struck my head, and I fell immediately. Everything went dark. I regained consciousness a few minutes before you arrived, but could neither move nor speak. Oh God!' he winced.

'And Kailash Babu? Where is he?' Feluda shouted.

'No idea.'

Feluda turned and leapt out of the room. I followed a second later.

There was no one in the drawing room. We lost no time in going upstairs, taking three steps at a time. Kailash Chowdhury's bedroom was empty, although the bed looked as though it had been slept in. The wardrobe had been left open. Feluda pulled a drawer out and found the small blue velvet box. When he opened it, I was somewhat surprised to see that the blue beryl was still in it, quite intact.

By this time, Abanish Babu had arrived at the door, still looking pathetic. 'Who has the key to the attic?' Feluda demanded. He seemed taken aback by the question.

'Th-that's with my uncle!' he said.

'OK, let's go up there,' Feluda announced, grabbing Abanish Babu by his shoulders and dragging him up the dark staircase.

We reached the roof, only to find that the attic was locked. A padlock hung at the door. Anyone else would have been daunted by the sight. But Feluda stepped back, then ran forward and struck the door with his shoulder, using all his strength. On his third attempt, the door gave in noisily. A few old rusted nails also came off the wall. Even I was surprised by Feluda's physical strength.

The room inside was dark. We stepped in cautiously. A few seconds later, when my eyes got used to the dark, I noticed another figure lying in one corner, bound and gagged exactly like Abanish Babu. Who was this? Kailash Chowdhury? Or was it Kedar?

Without a word, Feluda released him from his bondage and then carried him down to the bedroom. The man spoke only when he had been placed comfortably in his bed.

'Are you . . . the . . .?' he asked feebly, staring at Feluda.

'Yes, sir. I am Pradosh Mitter, the detective. I suppose it was you who had written me that letter, but of course I never got the chance to meet you. Abanish Babu, could you get him some warm milk, please?'

I stared at the man in amazement. So this was the real Kailash Chowdhury! He propped himself up on a pillow and said, 'I was physically strong, so I managed to survive somehow. Otherwise . . . in these four days . . .'

Feluda interrupted him, 'Sh-sh. You mustn't strain yourself.'

'No, but I have to tell you a few things. Or you'll never get the whole picture. There was no way I could meet you personally, you see, for he captured me the day I wrote to you. He dropped something in my tea, which made me virtually unconscious. He could never have overpowered me in any other way.'

'And he began to pass himself off as Kailash Chowdhury from that day?'

Kailash Babu nodded his head sadly, 'It is my own fault, Mr Mitter. I cannot blame anyone else. Our entire family suffers from one big weakness. We are all given to exaggerating the simplest things, and telling tall stories for no reason at all. I had bought that stone in Jabalpore for fifty rupees. I have no idea what possessed me to tell Kedar a strange story about a temple in a jungle, and a statue with that stone fixed on its forehead. He swallowed the whole thing, and began to eye that stone from that day. He envied me for many reasons. Perhaps he could not see why I should be so lucky, so successful in life, when he appeared to fail in everything he did. After all, we were identical twins, our fortunes should not have been so very different. Kedar had always been the black sheep—reckless and unscrupulous. Once he got mixed up with a gang that made counterfeit money. He would have gone to jail, but I managed to save him.

'Then he went abroad, after borrowing a great deal of money from me. I was glad. Good riddance, I thought. But only about a week ago, I came back home one day and found the stone missing. I never imagined for a moment that Kedar had come back and stolen it from my room. I rounded up all the servants and shouted at them, but nothing happened. Two days later, I wrote to you. Kedar turned up the same evening, and returned the stone to me. He was absolutely livid, for by this time, he had learnt that it had no value at all. He had been dreaming of getting at least a hundred thousand for it. He said he needed money desperately, would I give him twenty thousand? I refused. So he waited till I ordered a cup of tea, then managed to drug me and carry me up to the attic. When I woke, he told me he'd keep me there until I agreed to do as told. In the meantime, he'd pretend to be me, and he'd tell my office I was on sick leave.'

'He obviously did not know you had written to me,' Feluda added, 'So when we turned up, he took ten minutes to write a fake anonymous note and then gave us a cock-and-bull story about an imaginary enemy. If he didn't, he knew I'd get suspicious. At the same time, my presence in this house or in his life was highly undesirable. So he tried a threat on the telephone, then got in a car and tried to run us over.'

Kailash Chowdhury frowned. 'That makes perfect sense,' he said. 'What doesn't is why he left so suddenly. I did not agree to give him a single paisa. So why did he leave? Surely he didn't leave empty-handed?'

'No, no, no!' Shouted a voice at the door. None of us had seen Abanish Babu return with a glass of milk. 'Why should he leave empty-handed?' he screamed, 'He took my stamp! That precious, rare Victorian stamp has gone.'

Feluda stared at him, wide-eyed. 'What! He took your stamp?'

'Yes, yes. Kedar Mama has ruined me!'

'How much did you say it was worth?'

'Twenty thousand.'

'But—' Feluda turned to Abanish Babu and lowered his voice, 'according to the catalogue, Abanish Babu, it cannot possibly fetch more than fifty rupees.'

Abanish Babu went visibly pale.

'The Chowdhurys are prone to exaggerate everything to make an impression,' Feluda continued, 'and you are their nephew. So presumably, you inherited the same trait. Am I right?'

Abanish Babu began to look like a child who had lost his favourite toy. 'What was I supposed to do?' he said with a tragic air. 'I spent three years going through four thousand stamped envelopes. Not one of them was any good, except that one. Oh, all right, it wasn't much, but people believed my story. I got them interested!'

Feluda started laughing. 'Never mind, Abanish Babu,' he said, thumping his back, 'I think your uncle is going to be suitably punished, and that should give you some comfort. Let me ring the airport. You see, I had guessed he might try to escape this morning. So I rang Indian Airlines, and they told me he had a booking on their morning flight to Bombay. I began to suspect your uncle only when he said he couldn't remember having bought a new bottle of Dettol just a few days ago.'

The police had no problem in arresting Kedar Chowdhury; and Abanish Babu's stamp was duly returned to him. Feluda was paid so handsomely by Kailash Babu that, even after eating out three times, and seeing a couple of films with me, he still had a substantial amount left in his wallet.

Today, as we sat having tea at home, I said to him, 'Feluda, I have been thinking this through, and have reached a conclusion. Will you please tell me if I am right?'

'OK. What have you been thinking?'

'It's about Kailash Chowdhury's father. I think he knew what Kedar had done. I mean, maybe a father can tell the difference between identical twins. Perhaps that's the reason why he was throwing such murderous glances at his son.'

'That may or may not be the case. But since your thoughts appear to be the same as mine on this subject, I am hereby rewarding you for your intelligence.'

So saying, Feluda coolly helped himself to a jalebi from my plate.

The Anubis Mystery

'Who rang you, Feluda?' I asked, realizing instantly that I shouldn't have, for Feluda was doing yoga. He never spoke until he had finished every exercise, including *sheershasan*. He had started this about six months ago. The result was already noticeable. Feluda seemed a lot fitter, and openly admitted that yoga had done him a world of good.

I glanced at the clock. Feluda's reply came seven and a half minutes later. 'You don't know him,' he said, rising from the floor. Really, Feluda could be most annoying at times. So what if I didn't know the man? He could tell me his name, surely?

'Do *you* know him?' I asked impatiently. Feluda began chewing chick-peas which had been soaked overnight. This was a part of his keep-fit programme.

'I didn't know him before,' he replied, 'but I do now.'

Our Puja holidays had started a few days ago. Baba had gone to Jamshedpur on tour. Only Ma, Feluda and I were at home. We didn't plan to go out of town this time. I didn't mind staying at home as long as I could be with Feluda. He had become quite well known as an amateur detective. So it shouldn't be surprising at all, I thought, if he got involved in another case. My only fear was that he might one day refuse to take me with him. But that hadn't happened so far. Perhaps there was an advantage in being seen with a young boy. No one could guess easily that he was an investigator, if we travelled together.

'I bet you're dying to know who made that phone call,' Feluda added. This was an old technique. If he knew I was anxious for information, he never came to the point without beating about the bush and creating a lot of suspense. I tried to be casual. 'Well, if that phone call had anything to do with a mystery, naturally I'd be interested,' I said lightly.

Feluda slipped on a striped shirt. 'The man's called Nilmoni Sanyal,' he finally revealed, 'He lives on Roland Road, and wants to see me urgently. He didn't tell me why, but he sounded sort of nervous.'

'When do you have to go?'

'I told him I'd be there by nine. It's going to take us at least ten minutes by taxi, so let's go!'

On our way to Roland Road, I said to Feluda, 'But suppose this Mr Sanyal is a crook? Suppose he's called you over to his house only to cause you some harm? You've never met him before, have you?'

'No,' said Feluda, looking out of the window. 'There is always a risk in going out on a case like this. But mind you, if his sole intention was to cause me bodily harm, he wouldn't invite me to his house. It would be far more risky for him if the police came to know. A hired goonda could do the job much more simply.'

Last year, Feluda had won the first prize in the All India Rifle Competition. It was amazing how accurate his aim had become after only three months of practice. Now he possessed a revolver, although he didn't carry it in his pocket all the time, unlike detectives in books.

'Do you know what Mr Sanyal does for a living?' I asked.

'No. All I know about the man is that he takes paan, is probably slightly deaf and tends to say "Er . . ." before starting a sentence.' I asked no more questions after this.

We soon reached Nilmoni Sanyal's house. The meter showed one rupee and seventy paise. Feluda gave a two-rupee note to the driver and made a gesture indicating he could keep the change. We climbed out of the taxi and walked up to the front door. Feluda pressed the bell. The house had two storeys. It didn't appear to be very old. There was a front garden, but it looked a bit unkempt and neglected. A man who was probably the chowkidar opened the door and took Feluda's card from him. We were then ushered into the living room. I was surprised to see how well-furnished it was. It was obvious that a lot of money had been spent on acquiring the furniture and paintings, flower vases, and old artefacts displayed in a glass case. Someone had arranged these with a great deal of care.

Mr Sanyal entered the room a few minutes later. He was wearing a loose kurta over what must have been his sleeping-suit pyjamas. His fingers were loaded with rings. He was of medium height, clean-shaven and looked as if he had been sleeping. I tried to guess his age. He didn't seem to be more than fifty. 'You are Mr Pradosh Mitter?' he asked. 'I had no idea you were so young.' Feluda smiled politely. Then he pointed at me and said, 'This is my cousin. He's a very intelligent boy, but if you'd rather speak to me alone, I can send him out.'

I cast an anxious glance at Mr Sanyal, but he said, 'No, no, I don't mind at all. Er . . . would you like some tea or coffee?'

'No, thanks.'

'Very well then, allow me to tell you why I asked you to come here. But before I do so, I think I ought to tell you something about myself. I'm sure you've already noticed that I am reasonably wealthy, and am fond of antiques and other beautiful things. What you may find difficult to believe is that I wasn't born rich. I did not inherit any money; nor have I got a job, or a business.'

Nilmoni Babu stopped, and looked at us expectantly.

'Lottery?' said Feluda.

'Pardon?'

'I said, did you win a lottery?'

'Exactly, exactly!' Nilmoni Babu shouted like an excited child. 'I won two hundred and fifty thousand rupees in the Rangers Lottery eleven years ago. I have managed—pretty well, I must admit—all these years on the strength of that. I built this house eight years ago. Now you may wonder how I fill my time, do I not have an occupation at all? The thing is, you see, I have only one main occupation. I spend most of my time going to auction houses and buying the kind of things this room is filled with.' He waved his arms about to indicate what he meant. Then he continued, 'What happened recently may not have a direct connection with these objects of art in my collection, but I cannot be sure about that. Look—' he took out a few pieces of paper from his pocket and spread them out. There were three pieces in all, with something scribbled on them. A closer look showed me that instead of words, there were rows of little pictures. Some of them I could recognize—there were pictures of owls, snakes, the sun and the human eye. Others were more difficult to figure out. But the whole thing seemed familiar somehow. Where had I seen something like this before? In a book?

'These look like hieroglyphics,' said Feluda.

'What?' Nilmoni Babu sounded amazed.

'The form of writing used in ancient Egypt. That's what it looks like.'

'Really?'

'Yes, but it is extremely doubtful that we can find someone in Calcutta who might be able to tell us what it means.'

Nilmoni Babu's face fell. 'In that case, what shall I do? Someone has been mailing a note like that to me fairly regularly over the last few days. If I cannot have these read or decoded, it's going to be really worrying . . . what if these are warnings? What if it's someone threatening to kill me?'

Feluda thought for a while. Then he said, 'Is there anything from Egypt in your collection?'

Nilmoni Babu smiled slightly. 'I wouldn't know, and that's the truth. I bought these things only because they were beautiful, rare and expensive. I have very little idea of where they originally came from before they reached the auction house.'

'But all these things appear to be perfectly genuine. Nobody'll believe you're not a true connoisseur!'

'Er . . . that is simple enough. Most auction houses do their homework properly and have every item valued by an expert. So if something is expensive, you can safely assume that it is genuine. My greatest pleasure lies in outbidding my rivals, and why not, since I do have the means? If, in the process, I happen to collect something really valuable, so much the better.'

'But you wouldn't know if any of this stuff is Egyptian?'

Nilmoni Babu rose and walked over to the glass case. He brought out a statuette from the top shelf and gave it to Feluda. It was about six inches long. Made of some strange green stone, it was studded with several other colourful stones. What was most striking was that although its body had a human shape, its head was that of a jackal.

'I bought this only ten days ago at an auction. Could this be Egyptian?'

Feluda glanced briefly at the statuette, and said, 'Anubis.'

'Pardon?'

'Anubis. The ancient Egyptian god of the dead. It's a beautiful piece.'

'But,' Nilmoni. Babu sounded apprehensive, 'do you think there's a connection between this. . . this Anubis and those notes I've been receiving? Did I make a mistake by buying it? Is someone threatening to snatch it away from me?'

Feluda shook his head, returning the statuette to Nilmoni Babu. 'That is difficult to say. When did the first letter arrive?'

Last Monday.'

'You mean just after you bought it?'

'Yes.'

'Did you keep the envelopes?'

'No, I'm afraid not. Perhaps I should have kept them, but they were ordinary envelopes and the address was typewritten. The post mark said Elgin Road. That I did notice.'

'All right,' Feluda rose. 'I don't think we need do anything right now. But just to be on the safe side, I suggest you keep that statue somewhere else. Someone I know got burgled recently. Let's not take any chances.'

We came out of the living room and stood on the landing. 'Can you think of anyone who might wish to play a practical joke on you?' Feluda wanted to know.

Nilmoni Babu shook his head. 'No. I've lost touch with all my friends.'

'What about enemies?'

'Well . . . most wealthy people have enemies, but of course it's difficult to identify them. Everybody behaves so well in my presence. What they might do behind my back, I cannot tell.'

'Didn't you say you bought that piece at an auction?'

'Yes. At Aratoon Brothers.'

'Was anyone else interested in it?'

Nilmoni Babu suddenly grew agitated at this question. 'Mr Mitter,' he said excitedly, 'you have just opened a whole new aspect to this case. You see, I have a particular rival with whom I clash at most auctions. He was bidding for this Anubis, too.'

'Who is he?'

'A man called Pratul Datta.'

'What does he do?'

'I think he was a lawyer. Now he's retired. He and I were the only ones bidding for that statue. He stopped when I said twelve thousand. When I was getting into my car afterwards, I happened to catch his eye. I did not like the look in it, I can tell you!'

'I see.'

By this time, we had come out of the house and were walking towards the gate.

'Do a lot of people live in this house?' Feluda asked.

'Oh no. I am quite alone in this world. I live here with my driver, mali and two old and trusted servants, that's all.'

'Isn't there a small child in this house?' Feluda asked totally unexpectedly.

Nilmoni Babu stared for a few seconds, then burst out laughing. 'Just look at me! I forgot all about my nephew. Actually, I was thinking only of adults in this house. Yes, my nephew Jhuntu happens to be visiting me. His parents are away in Japan. His father runs a business. Jhuntu has been left in my charge. But the poor child has been suffering from influenza ever since he arrived. But what made you think there might be a child in my house?'

'I noticed a kite peeping out from behind a cupboard in your living room.'

A taxi arrived for us at this moment, crunching gravel under its tyres. It was thoughtful of Nilmoni Babu to have sent his servant out to fetch it. 'Thank you,' said Feluda, as we got in. 'Please let me know if anything suspicious occurs. But at this moment there's nothing to be done.'

On our way back, I said, 'There's something rather sinister about that statue of Anubis, isn't there?'

'If you replace a human head with the head of an animal, any statue would look sinister.'

'It's dangerous to keep statues of old Egyptian gods and goddesses.'

'Who told you that?'

'Why, you did! A long time ago.'

'No, never. All I told you was that some of the archaeologists who dug up old Egyptian statues ran into a lot of trouble afterwards.'

'Yes, yes, I remember now . . . there was a British gentleman, wasn't there . . . what was his name?'

'Lord Carnarvon.'

'And his dog?'

'The dog wasn't with him. Lord Carnarvon was in Egypt. His dog was in England. Soon after he helped dig the tomb of Tutankhamen, he fell ill and died. It was discovered later that his dog, who was thousands of miles away, died mysteriously at the same time as his master. He had been in perfect health, and no one could ever figure out the cause of his death.'

Any mention of Egypt always reminded me of this strange story I had heard from Feluda. That figure of Anubis might well have come from the tomb of some Egyptian pharaoh. Didn't Nilmoni Babu realize this? Why did he have to take such a big risk?

At a quarter to six the next morning, the phone rang just as I heard our newspaper land on our balcony with a thud. I picked up the receiver quickly and said 'hello', but before I could hear anything from the other side, Feluda rushed in and snatched it from me. I heard him say 'I see' three times, then he said, 'Yes, all right,' and put the phone down.

'Anubis disappeared last night,' he told me, his voice sounding hoarse. 'We've got to go there, at once!'

Since there was a lot less traffic so early in the morning, it took us only seven minutes to reach Nilmoni Babu's house. He was waiting for us outside his gate, looking thoroughly bemused. 'What a nightmare I've been through!' he exclaimed as we jumped out of our taxi. 'I've never had such a horrible experience.'

We went into the living room. Nilmoni Babu sank into a sofa before either of us could sit down, and showed us his wrists. It was obvious that his hands had been tied. The rope had left red marks on his skin.

'Tell me what happened,' said Feluda.

Nilmoni Babu took a deep breath and began, 'I took your advice and kept that Egyptian statue with me last night, right under my pillow. Now I feel it might have been simpler if I'd left it where it was. At least I might have been spared this physical pain. Anyway, I was sleeping peacefully enough, when suddenly I woke—no, I couldn't tell you the time—feeling quite breathless. I realized instantly that I had been gagged. I tried to resist my assailant with my arms, but he was far too strong for me. He tied my hands behind my back, took the statue of Anubis from under my pillow and disappeared—in just a few minutes! I didn't get to see his face at all.' Nilmoni Babu stopped for breath. After a brief pause, he resumed, 'When my bearer came in with my morning tea, he found me in my room, my hands still tied behind my back, my mouth gagged. By that time I had pins and needles all over my body. Anyway, he untied me, and I rang you immediately.'

Feluda heard him in silence, looking rather grim. Then he said, 'I'd like to inspect your bedroom, and then take some photographs of your house, if I may.' Photography was another passion he had developed recently.

Nilmoni Babu took us upstairs to see his bedroom. 'What!' exclaimed Feluda the minute he stepped into the room. 'You didn't put grills on your window?'

'No, I'm afraid not,' Nilmoni Babu shook his head regretfully. 'This house was built on the same pattern as foreign bungalows. So the windows were left without grills. And sadly, I have never been able to sleep with the windows closed.' Feluda took a quick look out of the window and said, 'It must have been very simple. There's a parapet, and a pipe. Any able-bodied man could climb into the room with perfect ease.'

Feluda took out his camera and began taking pictures. Then he said, 'Many I see the rest of your house?'

'Yes, of course.' Nilmoni Babu took us to the next room. Here we found a bundle lying on the bed, completely wrapped in a blanket. A small boy's face emerged as he removed part of the blanket and peered at us through eyes that seemed unnaturally large. The boy was obviously unwell.

'This is my nephew, Jhuntu,' said Nilmoni Babu. 'I had to call Dr Bose last night. He gave him a sleeping pill. So Jhuntu slept right through, without seeing or hearing anything at all.'

We glanced briefly into the other rooms on the first and the ground floor, and then we came down to look at the garden and its surrounding areas. There were three flower-pots just below the window of Nilmoni Babu's bedroom. Feluda began peering into these. The first two yielded nothing. In the third, he found an empty tin. 'Does anyone in this house take snuff?' he asked, lifting its lid. Nilmoni Babu shook his head. Feluda put the tin away in his pocket.

'Look, Mr Mitter,' said Nilmoni Babu, sounding openly desperate, 'I don't mind losing that statue so much. Maybe one day I'll be able to buy another. But what I can't stand is that an intruder should get into my house so easily and subject me to such . . . such . . . trauma! You've got to do something about this. If you can catch the thief I'll . . . I'll . . . give you . . . I mean . . .'

'A reward?'

'Yes, yes!'

'Thank you, Mr Sanyal, that is very kind of you. But I was going to make further investigations, anyway, not because I expected to be rewarded, but because I find this case both interesting and challenging.' Now he was talking like famous detectives in well-known crime stories. I felt very pleased.

After this, Feluda spent the next ten minutes talking to Nilmoni Babu's driver, Govind, his servants (Nandalal and Panchu) and his mali, Natabar. Sadly, none of them could tell us anything useful. The only outsider who had come to the house, they said, was Dr Bose. He had come at around 9 p.m. to see Jhuntu. After he had gone, Nilmoni Babu had gone out to buy some medicines from the local chemist. That was all.

We left soon after this. On our way back, I suddenly noticed that our taxi was not going in the direction of home. Where was Feluda taking me? But he was looking so grave that I didn't dare ask him.

Our taxi stopped outside a shop in Free School Street. 'Aratoon Brothers—Auctioneers', said its signboard, each letter painted in gleaming silver. I had never seen an auction house before. The sight of this one astounded me. Who knew so many different things could be collected under one roof? Somewhere among these various objects, Nilmoni Sanyal had found his Anubis. Feluda finished his work in just two minutes. The auction house gave him Pratul Datta's address—7/1 Lovelock Street. Were we going to go there now? No, Feluda told the driver to take us home.

When we sat down to have lunch later in the afternoon, I was still trying to work things out, and getting nowhere. Please God, I prayed silently, let Feluda find a clue or something, so that he had something concrete to work on. Otherwise, he might well have to accept defeat, which I would find totally unbearable.

'What next, Feluda?' I asked him.

'Fish curry,' he replied, mixing his rice with dal, 'and then I shall have vegetables, followed by chutney and dahi.'

'And then?'

'Then I shall wash my hands, rinse my mouth and have a paan.'

'After that?'

'I shall make a phone call and then I intend having a siesta.'

I saw no point in asking anything further. All I could do was wait patiently for him to make the phone call. I knew he would call Pratul Datta, so I had already taken his number from the directory.

When Feluda finally made the call, I could hear only his side of the conversation. This is how it went:

Feluda (changing his voice and sounding like an old man): 'Hello, I am speaking from Naktola.'

'My name is Joynarayan Bagchi. I am interested in antiques and ancient arts. In fact, I am writing a book on this subject.'

'Yes. Yes, I've heard of your collection, you see. So I wondered if I might go and see what you've got?'

'No, no, of course not!'

'Yes, thank you. Thank you very much indeed!'

Feluda put the receiver down and turned to me. 'He's having his house whitewashed, so he's had to move things around. But he's agreed to let us have a look this evening.'

'But,' I couldn't help asking, 'if he's really stolen the statue of Anubis, he's not going to show it to us, is he?'

'I don't know. If he's an idiot like you, he may. However, I am not going to visit him just to look for a stolen object. I simply want to meet the man.'

True to his word, Feluda went to his room after this to have a nap. He had this wonderful knack of catching a few minutes' sleep whenever necessary. Apparently, Napoleon had had this knack, too. He could go to sleep even on horseback, and wake a few moments later, much refreshed. Or so I had heard. I decided to pass the afternoon by leafing through one of Feluda's books on Egyptian art. Only a few minutes later, however, the phone rang. I ran to the living room to answer it.

'Hello!' I said.

There was no immediate response from the other side, though I could make out that there was someone holding a receiver to his ear. I began to feel uneasy. 'Can I speak to Pradosh Mitter?' asked a harsh voice after a few moments.

'He is resting,' I replied, swallowing once. May I know who's calling?'

The man fell silent again. Then he said, 'All right. Just tell him that the Egyptian god is where he should be. Mr Mitter needn't concern himself with the movements of Anubis. If he continues to meddle in this matter, the consequences may well be disastrous.' With a click, the line went dead.

I sat foolishly—heaven knows for how long—still holding the receiver in my hand. I finally had the sense to replace it only when Feluda walked into the room. 'Who was on the phone?' he asked. I repeated what I had been told by the strange voice. Feluda frowned and clicked his tongue in annoyance.

'You should have called me.'

'How could I? You always get cross if I disturb your siesta.'

'Hm. What did this man's voice sound like?'

'Harsh and gruff.'

'I see. Anyway, it's time now to get ready for Pratul Datta. I was beginning to see light, but now things have got complicated again.'

We got out of a taxi in front of Pratul Datta's house at five minutes to six that evening. We were both dressed for our parts—so cleverly disguised that I bet even Baba could not have recognized us. Feluda looked like an old man, about sixty years of age, sporting a wide moustache (liberally sprinkled with grey), with thick glasses perched on his nose. He was wearing a black jacket with a high neck, a white dhoti, long socks and brown tennis shoes. It took him about half-an-hour to get ready. Then he called me to his room and said, 'I have a few things for you. Put these on quickly.'

'What! Do I have to wear make-up as well?'

'Of course.' In two minutes, I had a wig on to cover my real hair and, like Feluda, a pair of glasses to hide my eyes. Then he took out an eyebrow pencil and worked on my neatly trimmed side-burns until they began to look untidy and overgrown. Finally, he said, 'You are my nephew. Your name is Subodh. Your only aim in life is to keep your mouth shut. Just remember that.'

We found Pratul Datta sitting in the veranda as we went in through the gate. His house must have been built thirty years ago, but the walls and doors and windows were gleaming after a new coat of paint.

Feluda bowed, his hands folded in a 'namaskar', and said in his thin, old-man voice, 'Excuse me, are you Mr Pratul Datta?'

'Yes,' Mr Datta replied without smiling.

'I am Joynarayan Bagchi, and this is my nephew Subodh.'

'Why have you brought him? You said nothing about a nephew on the phone!'

'N-no, but you see, he's recently started to paint and is very interested in art, so . . .' Mr Datta said nothing more. He rose to his feet.

'I don't mind you looking at things. But I had had to put everything away because of the whitewashing; and now every little piece has had to be dragged out. That wasn't easy, I can tell you. As it is, I've been going berserk with the workmen pushing and shoving all my furniture all day. The smell of paint makes me sick. I'll be glad when the whole thing's over. Anyway, come inside, please.'

I didn't like the brusque way in which he spoke, but once inside his drawing room on the first floor, my mouth fell open in amazement. His collection seemed larger than Nilmoni Babu's.

'You seemed to have gathered a lot of things from Egypt,' remarked Feluda.

'Yes. I bought some of these in Cairo. Others were bought locally.'

'Look, Subodh, my boy,' Feluda said, laying a hand on my back and giving me a sharp pinch quite unobtrusively. 'See all these animals? The Egyptians used to worship these as gods. This owl here, and that hawk over there—even these birds were gods for them.'

Mr Datta sat down on a sofa and lit a cheroot. I don't know what possessed me, but I suddenly found myself saying, 'Uncle, didn't they have a god that looked like a jackal?'

Mr Datta choked. 'This cheroot,' he said after a while, still coughing. 'You can't get good quality stuff any more. It never used to be so strong.'

Feluda ignored this remark. 'Heh heh,' he said in his thin voice, 'my nephew is talking of Anubis. I told him about Anubis only last night.'

Mr Datta flared up unexpectedly. 'Anubis? Ha! Stupid fool!'

Feluda stared at him through his glasses. 'I don't understand,' he complained. 'Why are you calling an ancient Egyptian god a stupid fool?'

'No, no, not Anubis. It's that man. I've seen him before at auctions. He is an idiot. His bidding makes no sense at all. There was a lovely statue, you see. But he quoted a figure so absurdly high that I had to withdraw. God knows where he gets that kind of money from.'

Feluda said nothing in reply. He glanced around the room once more, then said 'namaskar' again. 'Thank you very much,' he added, moving towards the door through which we had come. 'It was really very kind of you. It's given me a great deal of pleasure, and my nephew . . . heh heh . . . has learnt a lot.' On our way downstairs, Feluda asked one more question, very casually. 'Do you live alone in this house?'

'No,' came the reply. 'I live here with my wife. I have a son, but he doesn't live here.'

We came out of Mr Datta's house and began walking, in the hope of finding a taxi. It was remarkably quiet outside, although it was not even 7 p.m. There was no one in sight except two small boys who were out begging. One of them was singing Shyamasangeet; the other was playing a *khanjani*. As they came closer, Feluda began humming the same words:

Help me, Mother
for I have no one
to turn to . . .

A few minutes later, we reached Ballygunje Circular Road and spotted an empty taxi. Feluda stopped singing and shouted, 'Taxi!' so loudly that it screeched to a halt almost immediately. As we got in, I caught the driver give Feluda a puzzled look. He was probably wondering how a shrivelled old man like him could possibly have such powerful lungs!

When the phone rang the next morning, I was brushing my teeth. So it was Feluda who answered it. When I came out of the bathroom, he told me that Nilmoni Babu had just called to say that Pratul Datta's house had been burgled last night. All the cash had been left untouched. What was missing was a number of old and precious statues and other objects of art, the total value of which would be in the region of fifty thousand rupees. The theft had been reported by the press, and the police had started their investigations.

By the time we reached Pratul Datta's house, it was past 7 o'clock. Needless to say, this time we went without wearing any make-up. Just as we stepped in, a man of rather generous proportions, wearing a policeman's uniform, emerged from the house. It turned out that he knew Feluda. 'Good morning, Felu Babu,' he greeted us, grinning broadly and thumping Feluda on the back, 'I can see that it didn't take you long to find your way here!'

Feluda smiled politely, 'Well, I had to come, you see, since it's my job.'

'No, don't say it's your job. The job is ours. For you, it's no more than a pastime, isn't it?'

Feluda chose to ignore this. He said instead, 'Have you been able to work anything out? Is it simply a case of burglary?'

'Yes, yes, what else could it be? But Mr Datta is very upset. He told us something about an old man and his nephew who came to visit him yesterday. He thinks they're responsible.'

My throat suddenly felt dry. Perhaps Feluda had been a bit too reckless this time. What if—? But Feluda remained quite unperturbed. 'Well then, all you need to do is catch this old man and his nephew. Simple!' he said.

'Well said!' returned the plump police officer. 'That's exactly the kind of remark an amateur detective in a novel might have made.'

'Can we go into the house?' Feluda asked, determined not to take any notice of the jibes made by the officer.

'Yes, yes, go ahead.'

Pratul Datta was sitting on the same veranda. But he was clearly far too preoccupied to pay any attention to us. 'Do you want to see the room where all the action took place?' asked our friend from the police.

'Yes, please.'

We were taken to the drawing room upstairs. Feluda went straight to the balcony and leant over its railing. 'Look, there's a pipe. So gaining access was not a problem at all.'

'True. In any case, the door couldn't be closed because the paint was still wet. So really it was something like an open invitation.'

'What time did this happen?'

'At 9.45 p.m.'

'Who was the first to realize—?'

'There is an old servant. He was making the bed in that other room over there. He heard a noise, apparently, and came here to have a look. The room was totally dark. But someone knocked him out even before he could switch on the light. By the time he recovered sufficiently to raise an alarm, the thief had vanished.'

Feluda frowned. I had come to recognize this frown pretty well. It usually meant a new idea had occurred to him. 'I'd like to speak to this servant,' he said crisply.

'Very well.'

Mr Datta's servant was called Bangshalochan. He still appeared to be in a state of shock. 'Where does it hurt?' Feluda asked him, for he was obviously in pain.

'In the stomach,' he croaked.

'Stomach? The thief hit you in the stomach?'

'Yes, sir. And what a powerful blow it was—I felt as though a bomb had come and hit my body. Then everything went dark.'

'When did you hear the noise? What were you doing?'

'I couldn't tell you the exact time, Babu. I was making the bed in Ma's room. She was in the next room, doing her puja. There were two beggar boys singing in the street. Ma told me to give them some money. I was about to go, when there was a strange noise in this room. It sounded as though something heavy was knocked over. So I came to see what was going on, and . . .' Bangshalochan couldn't say anything more. It seemed that the thief had broken into the house only a couple of hours after we had gone. Feluda said, 'Thank you' both to Bangshalochan and the officer, and we left.

Feluda began walking without saying a word. His face was set, his eyes had taken on a glint that meant he was definitely on to something.

But I knew he wasn't yet prepared to talk about it. So I walked by his side silently, trying to think things through myself. Sadly, though, I got nowhere. It was obvious that Mr Datta was not the burglar who had attacked Nilmoni Babu. He seemed strong enough—and he had a deep voice—but somehow I couldn't imagine him climbing a pipe. A much younger man must have done it. But who could it be? And what was Feluda thinking about?

We continued to walk, ignoring every empty taxi that sailed by. After sometime, I suddenly realized we were standing quite close to the boundary wall of Nilmoni Dabu's house. Feluda began walking straight, with the wall on his left. After a few seconds, we realized the wall curved to the left. We made a left turn to follow it. About twenty steps later, Feluda stopped abruptly, and began inspecting a certain portion of the wall. Then he took out his small Japanese camera and took a photograph of that particular section. This time, I, too, peered closer and saw that there was a brown imprint of a hand. All that was visible was really two fingers and a portion of the palm, but it was clear that it was a child's hand that had left the mark.

We retraced our steps, making our way this time to the main gate. We pushed it open and went in. Nilmoni Babu rushed down to meet us. 'This may sound awful,' he told us when we were all seated in his living room, 'but I must confess today my heart is feeling a lot lighter. Yes, I do feel better knowing that my biggest rival has met with the same fate. But . . . where did my Anubis go? Who took him? You are a well-known detective, Mr Mitter. Are you still totally in the dark, even after two cases of burglary?'

Instead of replying, Feluda asked a seemingly irrelevant question. 'How is your nephew?'

'Who, Jhuntu? He's much better today, thanks. His temperature's gone down.'

'Do you know if he has any friends? I mean, is there a child who might climb over that boundary wall to come in here and play with Jhuntu?'

'Climb over the wall? Why do you say that?'

'I found the impression of a child's hand on the other side of the wall.'

'Was it a fresh mark?'

'That's difficult to say, but it can't be very old.'

'Well, I have never seen a child in this house. The only child who visits us occasionally is a small beggar boy. But he comes in through the gate, usually singing Shyamasangeet. He does have a good voice, I must say. However, there is a guava tree in my garden. So maybe that attracts little boys from time to time—I really couldn't say.'

'Hmm.'

Nilmoni Babu changed the subject. 'Did you learn anything new about the thief?'

'The man has extraordinary strength. Pratul Datta's servant was knocked unconscious with just one blow.'

'Then it must have been the same man who attacked me.'

'Perhaps. But I am concerned not so much with his physical strength but with the way his mind functions. He seems to have remarkable cunning.'

Nilmoni Babu began to look sort of helpless. 'I hope your own intelligence can match his cunning, Mr Mitter. Or else I must give up all hope of ever finding my Anubis again,' he said.

'Give me two more days. Felu Mitter has never been defeated. No, sir, not yet.'

We left soon after this. As we were walking down the driveway towards the front gate, we both heard a strange noise, as though someone was tapping on a glass pane. I turned around and saw a small boy standing at a window on the first floor. It was he who was tapping on the window pane. 'Jhuntu!' I said.

'Yes, I've seen him, too,' Feluda replied.

Feluda spent the afternoon scribbling in his famous blue notebook. I had learnt by now not to worry about what he was writing, for I knew whatever he wrote in his notebook was written in English, using Greek letters. I couldn't read it even if I tried; and certainly Feluda wouldn't tell me if I asked. In fact, he had stopped talking to me completely. I did not disturb him. He needed time to think. But he was humming a song under his breath. It was the same song that we had heard the beggar boy sing.

At about 5 p.m. Feluda broke his silence. 'I am going out for a few minutes,' he said. 'I have to collect the enlargements of my photograph from the studio.'

I was left all alone. Days were growing shorter. It grew fairly dark in less than an hour after Feluda left. The studio wasn't far from where we lived. Why was Feluda taking so long to come back? I did hope he hadn't gone somewhere else without telling me. Maybe his photos weren't ready, and he was being made to wait at the shop.

The sound of a *khanjani* reached my ears, which was followed immediately by a familiar song:

Help me, Mother
for I have no one
to turn to . . .

The same boys were now singing in our street. I went and stood near the window. Now I could see both boys. One of them was playing the *khanjani* and the other was singing. He really did sing well. They were now standing in front of our house. The one who was singing stopped and raised his face. 'Ma, please give us some money, Ma!' he cried. I took out a fifty-paisa coin from my wallet and threw it out of the window. The boy picked it up just as it landed at his feet with a faint chink. Then he put it in his shoulder bag, and walked on, picking up the song where he had left it.

I stared after him, profoundly puzzled. Our street wasn't particularly well-lit. But when the boy had raised his face to beg for money, I had seen it quite clearly. There was an uncanny resemblance between his face and Jhuntu's. No, I must have made a mistake, I told myself. Even so, this was something I had to tell Feluda the minute he got back.

He returned at half past six, looking cross. I had been right in thinking he'd had to wait in the shop. 'I'll make a dark room of my own and develop my own prints from now on,' he declared. 'These studios simply cannot be trusted to deliver on time.'

He spread out all his enlarged prints on his bed and began studying them. I could wait no longer, so I told him about the beggar boy. Feluda's face did not register any surprise. 'There's nothing odd about that,' he said.

'Isn't there?'

'No.'

'In that case, this whole business is more complicated than I thought.'

'Yes, that's true.'

'But do you actually believe that that young boy is involved in the burglaries?'

'He may well be.'

'But how can a boy of his age and his size be strong enough to knock people out?'

'Who said it was a young boy who attacked Nilmoni Babu and Bangshalochan?'

'Wasn't it?'

Feluda did not answer me. He went back to examining his photos. I found him looking carefully at the enlarged version of the photograph he had taken only this morning of the imprint of a hand on Nilmoni Babu's boundary wall.

'You told me once you could read palms,' I said jokingly. 'Can you tell me how long the owner of that hand will live?'

Feluda didn't laugh, or make a retort. He was frowning again, deep in thought. 'What do you make of this?' he asked suddenly. His question startled me.

'What do I make of what?'

'What you saw this morning, and what you're seeing now.'

'In the morning? You mean when you took that photo?'

'Yes.'

'It was the impression of a child's hand. What else was there to see?'

'Didn't its colour tell you anything?'

'Colour? It was brown, wasn't it?'

'Yes, but what did that mean?'

'That the boy had something smeared on his hand?'

'Something? Try to think, try to be more specific'

'Well, it might have been paint, mightn't it?'

'All right, but where could it have come from?'

'Brown paint? How should I know—no. wait, wait. I remember now. The doors and windows of Mr Datta's house were all painted brown!'

'Exactly. You caught some of it on your sleeve that day. If you look at your shirt, you'll probably still find it there.'

'But . . .' I began to feel a bit dazed, 'does that mean the person who got paint on his hand was the burglar who stole into Pratul Datta's house?'

'Yes, there's a possibility. But look at the photo again. Can you spot anything else?'

I tried to think very hard, but had to shake my head in the end.

'It's all right,' Feluda comforted me, 'I knew you wouldn't be able to spot it. If you had, I would've been very surprised—no, in fact, I would have been shocked.'

'Why?'

'Because that would have proved that you are no less clever-than me.'

'Oh? And what have you spotted, Mr Clever?'

'That this is more than just a complicated case. There is a sinister angle to it, which I have realized only recently. It is as horrific as Anubis himself!'

Feluda rang Nilmoni Babu the next day.

'Hello? Mr Sanyal? . . . Your mystery has been solved . . . No, I haven't actually got that statue, but I think I know where it is . . . Are you free this morning? . . . What? . . . He's worse, is he? . . . Which hospital? . . . All right. We'll meet later. Thank you.'

Feluda replaced the receiver and quickly dialled another number. I couldn't hear what he said for he lowered his voice and practically whispered into the telephone. But I could tell that he was speaking to someone in the police. Then he turned to me and said, 'Get ready quickly. We're going out. Yes, now.'

Luckily there wasn't much traffic on the roads since it was still fairly early. Besides, Feluda had told the driver to drive as fast as he could. It took us only a few minutes to reach Nilmoni Babu's street. Just as we reached his gate, we saw him driving out in his black Ambassador. There didn't seem to be anyone else in the car apart from Nilmoni Babu himself and his driver. 'Follow that car!' shouted Feluda. Excited, our driver placed his foot on the accelerator. I saw Nilmoni Babu's car take a right turn. At this moment, Feluda did something completely unexpected. He took out his revolver from the inside pocket of his jacket, leant out of the window and shot at the rear tyres of the Ambassador.

The noise from the revolver and the bursting of tyres was absolutely deafening. Then I saw the Ambassador lurch awkwardly, bump against a lamp-post and come to a standstill. Our taxi pulled up just behind it. From the opposite end came a police jeep and blocked the other side.

Nilmoni Sanyal climbed out his car and stood glancing around, looking furious. Feluda and I got out of our taxi and began walking towards him. From the police jeep, the same plump officer jumped out.

'What the hell is going on?' demanded Nilmoni Babu when he saw us.

'Who else is with you in the car apart from the driver, Mr Sanyal?' Feluda asked coldly.

'Who do you think?' Nilmoni Babu shouted. 'Didn't I tell you I was taking my nephew to the hospital?'

Without a word, Feluda stepped forward and pulled the handle of one of the rear doors of the Ambassador. The door opened, and a small child shot out from the car, promptly attaching himself to Feluda's throat.

Feluda might have been throttled to death. But he wasn't just an expert in yoga. He had learnt ji-jitsu and karate, too. It took him only a few seconds to twist the child's wrists, and swing him over his head, finally throwing him down on the road. The child screamed in pain, which made my heart jump into my mouth. The voice wasn't a child's voice at all. It belonged to a fully-grown adult. It sounded harsh and raucous. This was the voice I had heard on the telephone.

By this time, the police officer and his men had surrounded the car and arrested Nilmoni Babu, his driver and the 'child'.

Feluda straightened his collar and said, 'That imprint of his hand had made me wonder. It couldn't be a child's hand, for it had far too many lines on it. A child's hand would have been much more smooth. However, since the size of the palm was small, there could be just one explanation for it. The so-called "child' was really a dwarf. How old is your assistant, Mr Sanyal?'

'Forty,' Nilmoni Babu whispered. His own voice sounded different.

'You thought you were being very clever,' Feluda went on. 'Your plan was flawless, and your acting good enough to win an award. You told me a weird tale of warnings in hieroglyphics, then staged a robbery, just to remove suspicion from yourself. Then you had Pratul Datta's house burgled, and some of his possessions became yours. Tell me, the boy we saw in your house was the other beggar boy, wasn't he? The one who used to sing?'

Nilmoni Babu nodded in silence. 'Yes, that boy used to sing,' Feluda continued, 'and the dwarf played the *khanjani*. You never had a nephew at all. That was another story you cooked up. You've kept that boy in your house by force, haven't you, to help you with your misdeeds? I know that now, but it took me a while to figure it out. The boy and the dwarf were sent out together. The dwarf disappeared into Pratul Datta's house, leaving the khanjani with the singer, who continued to play it. The dwarf was obviously powerful enough to tackle Bangshalochan. It was a wonderful plan, really. I've got to give you full marks for planning all the details, Mr Sanyal.'

Nilmoni Babu sighed. 'The truth is,' he said, 'that I had become obsessed with ancient Egypt. I have studied that period in some depth. I couldn't bear the thought of Pratul Datta hanging on to those pieces of Egyptian art. I had to have them, at any cost.'

'Well, Mr Sanyal, you have now seen where greed and temptation can lead you. There is just one more thing I need to ask you for.'

'What is it?'

'My reward.'

Nilmoni Babu stared at Feluda blankly.

'Reward?'

'Yes. That statue of Anubis is with you, isn't it?'

Nilmoni Babu slipped his hand into his pocket rather foolishly. Then he brought it out, clutching a four-thousand-year-old statue of Anubis, the Egyptian god of the dead. The stones it was studded with glittered in the sun.

Feluda stretched an arm and took the statue from Nilmoni Babu. 'Thank you,' he said.

Nilmoni Babu swallowed, quite unable to speak. The police officer pushed him gently in the direction of the jeep.

Trouble in Gangtok

ONE

Even a little while ago it had been possible to stare out of the window and look at the yellow earth, criss-crossed with rivers that looked like silk ribbons and sweet little villages with tiny little houses in them. But now grey puffs of cloud had blocked out that scene totally. So I turned away from the window and began looking at my co-passengers in the plane.

Next to me sat Feluda, immersed in a book on space travel. He always read a lot, but I had never seen him read two books—one straight after the other—that were written on the same subject. Only yesterday, back at home, he had been reading something about the Takla Makan desert. Before that, he had finished a book on international cuisine, and another of short stories. It was imperative, he'd always maintained, for a detective to gain as much general knowledge as possible. Who knew what might come in handy one day?

There were two men sitting diagonally opposite me. One of them was barely visible. All I could see was his right hand and a portion of his blue trousers. He was beating one of his fingers on his knee. Perhaps he was singing quietly. The other gentleman sitting closer to us had a bright and polished look about him. His greying hair suggested he might be in his mid-forties, but apart from that he seemed pretty well-preserved. He was reading the *Statesman* with great concentration. Feluda might have been able to guess a lot of things about the man, but I couldn't think of anything at all although I tried very hard.

'What are you gaping at?' Feluda asked under his breath, thereby startling me considerably. Then he cast a sidelong glance at the man and said, 'He's not as flabby as he might have been. After all, he does eat a lot, doesn't he?'

Yes, indeed. Now I remembered having seen him ask the air hostess for two cups of tea in the past hour, with which he had eaten half-a-dozen biscuits.

'What else can you tell me about him?' I asked curiously.

'He's used to travelling by air.'

'How do you know that?'

'Our plane had slipped into an air pocket a few minutes ago, remember?'

'Oh yes. I felt so strange! My stomach began to churn.'

'Yes, and it wasn't just you. Many other people around us had grown restless, but that gentleman didn't even lift his eyes from his paper.'

'Anything else?'

'His hair at the back is tousled.'

'So?'

'He has not once leant back in his seat in the plane. He's sat up straight throughout, either reading or having tea. So obviously at Dum Dum—'

'Oh, I get it! He must have had some time to spare at Dum Dum airport, at least time enough to sit back against a sofa and relax for a while. That's how his hair got tousled.'

'Very good. Now you tell me which part of India he comes from.'

'That's very difficult, Feluda. He's wearing a suit and he's reading an English newspaper. He could be a Bengali, a Punjabi, a Gujarati or a Maharashtrian, anything!'

Feluda clicked his tongue disapprovingly. 'You'll never learn to observe properly, will you? What's he got on his right hand?'

'A news—no, no, I see what you mean. He's wearing a ring.'

'And what does the ring say?'

I had to screw up my eyes to peer closely. Then I saw that in the middle of the golden ring was inscribed a single word: 'Ma'. The man had to be a Bengali.

I wanted to ask Feluda about other passengers, but at this moment there was an announcement to say that we were about to reach Bagdogra. 'Please fasten your seat-belts and observe the no-smoking sign.'

We were on our way to Gangtok, the capital of Sikkim. We might have gone to Darjeeling again, where we had been twice already to spend our summer holidays. But at the last minute Feluda suggested a visit to Gangtok, which sounded quite interesting. Baba had to go away to Bangalore on tour, so he couldn't come with us. 'You and Felu could go on your own,' Baba told me. 'I'm sure Felu could take a couple of weeks off. Don't waste your holiday in the sweltering heat of Calcutta.'

Feluda had suggested Gangtok possibly because he had recently read a lot about Tibet (I, too, had read a travelogue by Sven Hedin). Sikkim had a strong Tibetan influence. The King of Sikkim was a Tibetan, Tibetan monks were often seen in the gumphas in Sikkim, many Tibetan refugees lived in Sikkimese villages. Besides, many aspects of Tibetan culture—their music, dances, costumes and food—were all in evidence in Sikkim. I jumped at the chance to go to Gangtok. But then, I would have gone anywhere on earth, quite happily, if I could be with Feluda.

Our plane landed at Bagdogra at 7.30 a.m. Baba had arranged a jeep to meet us here. But before climbing into it, we went to the restaurant at the airport to have breakfast. It would take us at least six hours to reach Gangtok. If the roads were bad, it might take even longer. However, since it was only mid-April, hopefully heavy rains hadn't yet started. So the roads ought to be in good shape.

I had finished an omelette and just started on a fish-fry, when I saw the same gentleman from the plane rise from the next table and walk over to ours, grinning broadly. 'Are you Kang, or Dang, or Gang?' he asked, wiping his mouth with a handkerchief.

I stared, holding a piece of fish-fry a few inches from my mouth. What on earth did this man mean? What language was he speaking in? Or was it some sort of a code?

But Feluda smiled in return and replied immediately, 'We're Gang.'

'Oh good. Do you have a jeep? I mean, if you do, can I come with you? I'll pay my share, naturally.'

'You're welcome,' said Feluda, and it finally dawned on me that Kang meant Kalimpong, Dang was Darjeeling, and Gang was Gangtok. I found myself laughing, too.

'Thank you,' said the man. 'My name is Sasadhar Bose.'

'Pleased to meet you, Mr Bose. I am Pradosh Mitter and this is my cousin, Tapesh.'

'Hello, Tapesh. Are you both here on holiday?'

'Yes.'

'I love Gangtok. Have you been there before?'

'No.'

'Where will you be staying?'

'We're booked somewhere, I think the hotel is called Snow View,' Feluda replied, signalling at the waiter for our bill, and offering a Charminar to Mr Bose. Then he lit one himself.

'I know Gangtok very well,' Mr Bose told us. 'In fact, I've travelled all over Sikkim—Lachen, Lachung, Namche, Nathula, just name it! It's really beautiful. The scenery is just out of this world, and it's all so peaceful. There are mountains and rivers and flowers—you get orchids here, you know—and bright sunshine and rain and mist . . . nature in all her glory. The only thing that stops this place from being a complete paradise is its roads. You see, some of the mountains here are still growing. I mean, they are still relatively young, and therefore restless. You know what youngsters are like, don't you . . . ha ha ha!'

'You mean these mountains cause landslides?'

'Yes, and it can really be a nuisance. Halfway through your journey you may suddenly find the road completely blocked. That then means blasting your way through rocks, rebuilding the road, clearing up the mess . . . endless problems. But the army here is always on the alert and it's very efficient. Besides, it hasn't yet started to rain, so I don't think we'll have any problem today. Anyway, I'll be very glad of your company. I hate travelling alone.'

'Are you here on holiday as well?'

'Oh no,' Mr Bose laughed, 'I am here on business. But my job is rather a peculiar one. I have to look for aromatic plants.'

'Do you run a perfumery?'

'Yes, that's right. Mine's a chemical firm. Among other things, we extract essences from plants. Some of the plants we need grow in Sikkim. I've come to collect them. My business partner is already here. He arrived a week ago. He's got a degree in Botany and knows about plants. I was supposed to travel with him, but a nephew's wedding came up. So I had to go to Ghatshila to attend it. I returned to Calcutta only last night.'

Feluda paid the bill. We picked up our luggage and began walking towards our jeep with Mr Bose.

'Where are you based?' Feluda asked.

'Bombay. This company is now twenty years old. I joined it seven years ago. S. S. Chemicals. Shivkumar Shelvankar. The company is in his name.'

We set off in a few minutes. From Bagdogra we had to go to Siliguri, to find Sewak Road. This road wound its way through the hills, going up and down. It would finally take us to a place called Rongpo, where West Bengal ended, and the border of Sikkim began.

On our way to Rongpo, we had to cross a huge bridge over the river Tista. On the other side was a market called Tista Bazaar. We stopped here for a rest. By this time the sun had come up, and we were all feeling a little hot.

'Would you like a Coca-Cola?' asked Mr Bose. Feluda and I both said yes, and got out of the jeep. Two years ago, said Mr Bose, this whole area had been wiped out in a devastating flood. All the buildings and other structures, including the bridge, were new.

By the time I finished my own bottle of Coca-Cola, Mr Bose had emptied two. When we went to return the bottles, we noticed a jeep parked near the stall selling cold drinks. A few men were standing near it, talking excitedly. The jeep had come from the other side, and was probably going to Siliguri. Suddenly, all of us caught the word 'accident', and went across to ask them what had happened. What they told us was this: it had rained heavily in Gangtok a week ago. Although there had been 'no major landslide, somehow a heavy boulder had rolled off a mountain and fallen on a passing jeep, killing its passenger. The jeep had fallen into a ravine, five hundred feet below. It was totally destroyed. None of these men knew who the dead man was.

'Fate,' said Feluda. 'What else can you call this? The man was destined to die, or else why should just a single boulder slip off a mountain and land on his jeep? Such accidents are extremely rare.'

'One chance in a million,' said Mr Bose. As we got back into the jeep, he added, 'Keep an eye on the mountains, sir. One can't be too careful.' However, the scenery became so incredibly beautiful soon after we crossed Tista that I forgot all about the accident. There was a brief shower as we were passing through Rongpo. As we climbed up to three thousand feet, a mist rose from the valley just below, making us shiver in the cold. We stopped shortly to pull out our woollens from our suitcase. I saw Mr Bose dig out a blue pullover from an Air India bag and slip it on.

Slowly, through the mist, I began to notice vague outlines of houses among the hills. Most houses appeared to be Chinese in style. 'Here we are,' said Mr Bose. 'It took us less than five hours. We're very lucky.'

The city of Gangtok lay before us. Our jeep made its way carefully through its streets, past a military camp, sweet little houses with wooden balconies and flower-pots, groups of men and women in colourful clothes, and finally drew up before Snow View Hotel. The people in the streets, I knew, were not from Sikkim alone. Many of them were from Nepal, Bhutan or Tibet.

Mr Bose said he was staying at the dak bungalow. 'I'll make my own way there, don't worry,' he said. 'Thank you so much. No doubt we shall meet again. In a small place like this, it is virtually impossible to avoid bumping into one another every day.'

'Well, since we don't know anyone in Gangtok except you, I don't think we'd find that a problem. If you don't mind, I'll visit your dak bungalow this evening,' said Feluda.

'Very well. I'll look forward to it. Goodbye.'

With a wave of his hand, Mr Bose disappeared into the mist.

TWO

Although our hotel was called Snow View and the rooms at the rear were supposed to afford a view of Kanchenjunga, we didn't manage to see any snow the day we arrived, for the mist didn't clear at all. There appeared to be only one other Bengali gentleman among the other guests in the hotel. I saw him in the dining hall at lunch time, but didn't get to meet him until later.

We went out after lunch and found a paan shop. Feluda always had a paan after lunch, though he admitted he hadn't expected to find a shop here in Gangtok. The main street outside our hotel was quite large. A number of buses, lorries and station wagons stood in the middle of the road. On both sides were shops of various kinds. It was obvious that business people from almost every corner of India had come to Sikkim. In many ways it was like Darjeeling, except that the number of people out on the streets was less, which helped keep the place both quiet and clean.

Stepping out of the paan shop, we were wondering where to go next, when the figure of Mr Bose suddenly emerged from the mist. He appeared to be walking hurriedly in the direction of our hotel. Feluda waved at him as he came closer. He quickened his pace and joined us in a few seconds.

'Disaster!' he exclaimed, panting.

'What happened?'

'That accident . . . do you know who it was?'

I felt myself go rigid with apprehension. The next words Mr Bose spoke confirmed my fears. 'It was SS,' he said, 'my partner.'

'What! Where was he going?'

'Who knows? What a terrible disaster, Mr Mitter!'

'Did he die instantly?'

'No. He was alive for a few hours after being taken to a hospital. There were multiple fractures. Apparently, he asked for me. He said, "Bose, Bose" a couple of times. But that was all.'

'How did you find out?' Feluda asked, walking back to the hotel. We went into the dining hall. Mr Bose sat down quickly, wiping his face with a handkerchief. 'It's a long story, actually,' he replied. 'You see, the driver survived. What happened was that when the boulder hit the jeep, the driver lost control. I believe the boulder itself wasn't such a large one, but because the driver didn't know where he was going, the jeep tilted to one side, went over the edge and fell into a gorge. The driver, however, managed to jump out in the nick of time. All he got was a minor cut over one eye. But by the time he could scramble to his feet, the jeep had disappeared with Shelvankar in it. This happened on the North Sikkim Highway. The driver began walking back to Gangtok. On his way he found a group of Nepali labourers who helped him to go back to the spot and rescue Shelvankar. Luckily, an army truck happened to be passing by, so they could take him to a hospital almost immediately. But . . . well . . .'

There was no sign of the jovial and talkative man who had accompanied us from Bagdogra. Mr Bose seemed shaken and deeply upset.

'What happened to his body?' Feluda asked gently.

'It was sent to Bombay. The authorities here got through to his brother there. SS had married twice, but both his wives are dead. There was a son from his first marriage, who fought with him and left home fourteen years ago. Oh, that's another story. SS loved his son; he tried very hard to contact him, but he had vanished without a trace. So his brother was his next of kin. He didn't allow a post mortem. The body was sent to Bombay the next day.

'When did this happen?'

'On the morning of the eleventh. He had arrived in Gangtok on the seventh. Honestly, Mr Mitter, I can hardly believe any of this. If only I was with him . . . we might have avoided such a tragedy.'

'What are your plans now?'

'Well, there's no point in staying here any longer. I've spoken to a travel agent. I should be able to fly back to Bombay tomorrow.' He rose. 'Don't worry about this, please,' he added. 'You are here to have a good time, so I hope you do. I'll see you before I go.'

Mr Bose left. Feluda sat quietly, staring into space and frowning. Then he repeated softly the words Mr Bose had uttered this morning: 'One chance in a million . . . but then, a man can get struck by lightning. That's no less amazing.'

The Bengali gentleman I had noticed earlier had been sitting at an adjacent table, reading a newspaper. He folded it neatly the minute Mr Bose left, and came over to join us. 'Namaskar,' he said to Feluda, taking the chair next to him. 'Anything can happen in the streets of Sikkim. You arrived only this morning, didn't you?'

'Hm,' said Feluda. I looked carefully at the man. He seemed to be in his mid-thirties. His eyes were partially hidden behind tinted glasses. Just below his nose was a small, square moustache, the kind that was once known as a butterfly moustache. Not many people wore it nowadays.

'Mr Shelvankar was a most amiable man.'

'Did you know him?' Feluda asked.

'Not intimately, no. But from what little I saw of him, he seemed very friendly. He was interested in art. He bought a Tibetan statue from me only two days before he died.'

'Was he a collector of such things?'

'I don't know. I found him in the Art Emporium one day, looking at various objects. So I told him I had this statue. He asked me to bring it to the dak bungalow. When I showed it to him there, he bought it on the spot. But then, it was a piece worth having. It had nine heads and thirty-four arms. My grandfather had brought it from Tibet.'

'I see.' Feluda sounded a little stiff and formal. But I found this man quite interesting, especially the smile that always seemed to hover on his lips. Even the death of Mr Shelvankar appeared to have given him cause for amusement.

'My name is Nishikanto Sarkar,' he said.

Feluda raised his hands in a namaskar but did not introduce himself.

'I live in Darjeeling,' Mr Sarkar continued. 'We've lived there for three generations. But you'd find that difficult to believe, wouldn't you? I mean, just look at me, I am so dark!'

Feluda smiled politely without saying anything. Mr Sarkar refused to be daunted. 'I know Darjeeling and Kalimpong pretty thoroughly. But this is my first visit to Sikkim. There are quite a few interesting places near Gangtok, I believe. Have you already seen them?'

'No. We're totally new to Sikkim, like yourself.'

'Good,' Mr Sarkar grinned. 'You're going to be here for some time, aren't you? We could go around together. Let's visit

Pemiangchi one day. I've heard it's a beautiful area.'

'Pemiangchi? You mean where there are ruins of the old capital of Sikkim?'

'Not just ruins, dear sir. According to my guide book, there's a forest, old dak bungalows built during British times, gumphas, a first class view of Kanchenjunga—what more do you want?'

'We'd certainly like to go, if we get the chance,' said Feluda and stood up.

'Are you going out?'

'Yes, just for a walk. Is it necessary to lock up each time we go out?'

'Well, yes, that's always advisable in a hotel. But cases of theft are very rare in these parts. There is only one prison in Sikkim, and that's here in Gangtok. The total number of criminals held in there would be less than half-a-dozen!'

We came out of the hotel once more, only to find that the mist hadn't yet cleared. Feluda glanced idly at the shops and said, 'We should have remembered to buy sturdy boots for ourselves. These shoes would be no good if it rained and the roads became all slushy and slippery.'

'Couldn't we buy us some boots here?'

'Yes, we probably could. I'm sure Bata has a branch in Gangtok. We could look for it in the evening. Right now I think we should explore this place.'

The road that led from the market to the main town went uphill. The number of people and houses grew considerably less as we walked up this road. Most of the passers-by were schoolchildren in uniform. Unlike Darjeeling, no one was on horseback. Jeeps ran frequently, possibly because of the army camp. Sixteen miles from Gangtok, at a height of 14,000 feet, was Nathula. It was here that the Indian border ended. On the other side of Nathula, within fifty yards, stood the Chinese army.

A few minutes later, we came to a crossing, and were taken aback by a sudden flash of colour. A closer look revealed a man—possibly a European—standing in the mist, clad from head to foot in very colourful clothes: yellow shoes, blue jeans, a bright red sweater, through which peeped green shirt cuffs. A black and white scarf was wound around his neck. His white skin had started to acquire a tan.

He had a beard which covered most of his face, but he appeared to be about the same age as Feluda—just under thirty. Who was he? Could he be a hippie?

He gave us a friendly glance and said, 'Hello.'

'Hello,' Feluda replied.

Now I noticed that a leather bag was hanging from his shoulder, together with two cameras, one of which was a Canon. Feluda, too, had a Japanese camera with him. Perhaps the hippie saw it, for he said, 'Nice day for colour.'

Feluda laughed. 'When I saw you from a distance, that's exactly what I thought. But you see, colour film in India is so expensive that one has to think twice before using it freely.'

'Yes, I know. But I have some in my own stock. Let me know if you need any.' I tried to work out which country he might be from. He didn't sound American; nor did he have a British or French accent.

'Are you here on holiday?' Feluda asked him.

'No, not really. I'm here to take photographs. I'm working on a book on Sikkim. I am a professional photographer.'

'How long are you going to be here for?'

'I came five days ago, on the ninth. My original visa was only for three days. I managed to have it extended. I'd like to stay for another week.'

'Where are you staying?'

'Dak bungalow. See this road on the right? The dak bungalow is on this road, only a few minutes from here.'

I pricked up my ears. Mr Shelvankar had also stayed at the same place.

'You must have met the gentleman who died in that accident recently—' Feluda began.

'Yes, that was most unfortunate,' the hippie shook his head sadly. 'I got to know him quite well. He was a fine man, and—' he broke off. Then he said, more or less to himself, 'Very strange!' He looked faintly worried.

'What's wrong?' Feluda enquired.

'Mr Shelvankar acquired a Tibetan statue from a Bengali gentleman here. He paid a thousand rupees for it.'

'One thousand!'

'Yes. He took it to the local Tibetan Institute the next day. They said it was a rare and precious piece of art. But—' The man stopped again and remained silent for a few moments. Finally, he sighed and said, 'What is puzzling me is its disappearance. Where did it go?'

'What do you mean? Surely his belongings were all sent back to Bombay?'

'Yes, everything else he possessed was sent to Bombay. But not that statue. He used to keep it in the front pocket of his jacket. "This is my mascot," he used to say, "it will bring me luck!" He took it with him that morning. I know this for a fact. When they brought him to the hospital, I was there. They took out everything from his pockets. There was a notebook, a wallet and his broken glasses in a case. But there was no sign of the statue. Of course, it could be that it slipped out of his pocket as he fell and is probably still lying where he was found. Or maybe one of those men who helped lift him out saw it and removed it from the spot.'

'But I've been told people here are very honest.'

'That is true. And that is why I have my doubts—' the man seemed lost in thought.

'Do you know where Mr Shelvankar was going that day?'

'Yes. On the way to Singik there's a gumpha. That is where he was going. In fact, I was supposed to go with him. But I changed my mind and left a lot earlier, because it was a beautiful day and I wanted to take some photographs here. He told me he'd pick me up on the way if he saw me.'

'Why was he so interested in this gumpha?'

'I'm not sure. Perhaps Dr Vaidya was partly responsible for it.'

'Dr Vaidya?'

This was the first time anyone had mentioned Dr Vaidya. Who was he?

The hippie laughed. 'It's a bit awkward, isn't it, to chat in the middle of the road? Why don't you come and have coffee with me in the dak bungalow?'

Feluda agreed readily. He was obviously keen to get as much information as possible about Shelvankar.

We began walking up the road on our right. 'Besides,' added the hippie, 'I need to rest my foot. I slipped in the hills the other day and sprained my ankle slightly. It starts aching if I stand anywhere for more than five minutes.'

The mist had started to clear. Now it was easy to see how green the surroundings were. I could see rows of tall pine trees through the thinning mist. The dak bungalow wasn't far. It was rather an attractive building, not very old. Our new friend took us to his room, and quickly removed piles of papers and journals from two chairs for us to sit. 'Sorry, I haven't yet introduced myself,' he said. 'My name is Helmut Ungar.'

'Is that a German name?' Feluda asked.

'Yes, that's right,' Helmut replied and sat down on his bed. Clearly, he didn't believe in keeping a tidy room. His clothes (all of them as colourful as the ones he was wearing) were strewn about, his suitcases were open, displaying more books and magazines than clothes, and spread on a table were loads of photographs, most of which seemed to have been taken abroad. Although my own knowledge of photography was extremely limited, I could tell these photos were really good.

'I am Pradosh Mitter and this is my cousin, Tapesh,' said Feluda, not revealing that he was an amateur detective.

'Pleased to meet you both. Excuse me,' Helmut went out of the room, possibly to order three coffees. Then he came back and said, 'Dr Vaidya is a very interesting person, though he talks rather a lot. He stayed here in this dak bungalow for a few days. He can read palms, make predictions about the future, and even contact the dead.'

'What! You mean he can act as a medium?'

'Yes, something like that. Mr Shelvankar was startled by some of the things he said.'

'Where is he now?'

'He left for Kalimpong. He was supposed to meet some Tibetan monks there. But he said he'd return to Gangtok.'

'What did he tell Mr Shelvankar? Do you happen to know anything about it?'

'Oh yes. They spoke to each other in my presence. Dr Vaidya told Mr Shelvankar about his business, the death of his wives, and about his son. He even said Mr Shelvankar had been under a lot of stress lately.'

'What could have caused it?'

'I don't know.'

'Didn't Shelvankar say anything to you?'

'No. But I could sense something was wrong. He used to grow preoccupied, and sometimes I heard him sigh. One day he received a telegram while we were having tea on the front veranda. I don't know what it said, but it upset him a good deal.'

'Did Dr Vaidya say that Mr Shelvankar would die in an accident?'

'No, not in so many words; but he did say Mr Shelvankar must be careful over the next few days. Apparently, there was some indication of trouble and bad times.'

The coffee arrived. We drank it in silence. Even if Mr Shelvankar's death had been caused truly by a freak accident, I thought, there was something wrong somewhere. It was evident that Feluda was thinking the same thing, for he kept cracking his knuckles. He never did this unless there was a nasty suspicion in his mind.

We finished our coffee and rose to take our leave. Helmut walked with us up to the main gate.

'Thank you for the coffee,' Feluda told him. 'If you're going to be here for another week, I'm sure we shall meet again. We're staying at the Snow View. Please let me know if Dr Vaidya returns.'

In reply, Helmut said just one thing: 'If only I could find out what happened to that statue, I'd feel a lot happier.'

THREE

Although the mist had lifted, the sky was still overcast, and it was raining. I didn't mind the rain. It was only a faint drizzle, the tiny raindrops breaking up into a thin, powdery haze. One didn't need an umbrella in rain like this; it was very refreshing.

We found a branch of Bata near our hotel. Luckily, they did have the kind of boots we were looking for. When we came out clutching our parcels, Feluda said, 'Since we don't yet know our way about this town, we'd better take a taxi.'

'Where to?'

'The Tibetan Institute. I've heard they have a most impressive collection of tankhas, ancient manuscripts and pieces of Tantrik art.'

'Are you beginning to get suspicious?' I asked, though I wasn't at all sure that Feluda would give me a straight answer.

'Why? What should I be getting suspicious about?'

'That Mr Shelvankar's death wasn't really caused by an accident?'

'I haven't found a reason yet to jump to that conclusion.'

'But that statue is missing, isn't it?'

'So what? It slipped out of his pocket, and was stolen by someone. That's all there is to it. Killing is not so simple. Besides, I cannot believe that anyone would commit murder simply for a statue that had been bought for a thousand rupees.'

I said nothing more, but I couldn't help thinking that if a mystery did grow out of all this, it would be rather fun.

A row of jeeps stood by the roadside. Feluda approached one of the Nepali drivers and said, 'The Tibetan Institute. Do you know the way?'

'Yes sir, I do.'

We got into the jeep, both choosing to sit in the front with the driver. He took out a woollen scarf from his pocket, wrapped it round his neck and turned the jeep around. Then we set off on the same road which had brought us into town. Only this time, we were going in the opposite direction.

Feluda began talking to the driver.

'Have you heard about the accident that happened recently?'

'Yes, everyone in Gangtok has.'

'The driver of that jeep survived, didn't he?'

'Yes, he's very lucky. Last year there had been a similar accident: The driver got killed, not the passenger.'

'Do you happen to know this driver?'

'Of course. Everyone knows everyone in Gangtok.'

'What is he doing now?'

'Driving another taxi. SKM 463. It's a new taxi.'

'Have you seen the accident spot?'

'Yes, it's on the North Sikkim Highway. Three kilometres from here.'

'Could you take us there tomorrow.'

'Yes, sure. Why not?'

'Well then, come to the Snow View Hotel at 8 a.m. We'll be waiting for you.'

'Very well, sir.'

A road rose straight through a forest to stop before the Tibetan Institute. The driver told us that orchids grew in this forest, but we didn't have the time to stop and look for them. Our jeep stopped outside the front door of the Institute. It was a large two-storey building with strange Tibetan patterns on its walls. It was so quiet that I thought perhaps the place was closed, but then we discovered that the front door was open. We stepped into a big hall. *Tankhas* hung on the walls. The floor was lined with huge glass cases filled with objects of art.

As we stood debating where to go next, a Tibetan gentleman, clad in a loose Sikkimese dress, came forward to meet us.

'Could we see the curator, please?' Feluda asked politely.

'No, I'm afraid he is away on sick leave today. I am his assistant. How may I help you?'

'Well, actually, I need some information on a certain Tibetan statue. I do not know what it's called, but it has nine heads and thirty-four arms. Could it be a Tibetan god?'

The gentleman smiled. 'Yes, yes, you mean Yamantak. Tibet is full of strange gods. We have a statue of Yamantak here. Come with me, I'll show it to you. Someone brought a beautiful specimen a few days ago—it's the best I've ever seen—but unfortunately, that gentleman died.'

'Oh, did he?' Feluda feigned total surprise.

We followed the assistant curator and stopped before a tall showcase. He brought out a small statue from it. I gasped in horror. Good heavens, was this a god or a monster? Each of its nine faces wore a most vicious expression. The assistant curator then turned it in his hand and showed us a small hole at the base of the statue. It was customary, he said, to roll a piece of paper with a prayer written on it and insert it through that little hole. It was called the 'sacred intestine'!

He put the statue back in the case and turned to us once more. 'That other statue of Yamantak I was talking about was only three inches long. But its workmanship was absolutely exquisite. It was made of gold, and the eyes were two tiny rubies. None of us had ever seen anything like it before, not even our curator. And he's been all over Tibet, met the Dalai Lama—why, he's even drunk tea with the Dalai Lama, out of a human skull!'

'Would a statue like that be valuable? I mean, if it was made of gold—?'

The assistant curator smiled again. 'I know what you mean. This man bought it for a thousand rupees. Its real value may well be in excess of ten thousand.'

We were then taken on a little tour down the hall, and the assistant curator told us in great detail about some of the other exhibits. Feluda listened politely, but all I could think of was Mr Shelvankar's death. Surely ten thousand rupees was enough to tempt someone to kill? But then, I told myself firmly, Mr Shelvankar had not been stabbed or strangled or poisoned. He had died simply because a falling rock had hit his jeep. It had to be an accident.

As we were leaving, our guide suddenly laughed and said, 'I wonder why Yamantak has created such a stir. Someone else was asking me about this statue.'

'Who? The man who died?'

'No, no, someone else. I'm afraid I cannot recall his name, or his face. All I remember are the questions he asked. You see, I was very busy that day with a group of American visitors. They were our Chogyal's guests, so . . .'

When we got back into the jeep, it was only five to five by my watch; but it was already dark. This surprised me since I knew daylight could not fade so quickly. The reason became clear as we passed the forest and came out into the open again. Thick black clouds had gathered in the western sky. 'It generally rains at night,' informed our driver. 'The days here are usually dry.' We decided to go back to the hotel as there was no point now in trying to see other places.

Feluda did not utter a single word on our way back. He simply stared out of the jeep, taking in everything he saw. If we went up this road again on a different day, I was sure he'd be able to remember the names of all the shops we saw. Would I ever be able to acquire such tremendous powers of observation, and an equally remarkable memory? I didn't think so.

We saw Mr Bose again as we got out of our jeep in front of our hotel. He appeared to be returning from the market, still looking thoughtful. He gave a little start when he heard Feluda call out to him. Then he looked up, saw us and came forward with a smile. 'Everything's arranged. I am leaving by the morning flight tomorrow.'

'Could you please make a few enquiries for me when you get to Bombay?' asked Feluda. 'You see, Mr Shelvankar had bought a valuable Tibetan statue. We must find out if it was sent to Bombay with his other personal effects.'

'All right, I can do that for you. But where did you learn this?'

Feluda told him briefly about his conversation with Mr Sarkar and the German photographer. 'Yes, it would have been perfectly natural for him to have kept the statue with him. He had a passion for art objects,' Mr Bose said. Then he suddenly seemed to remember something, and the expression on his face changed. He looked at Feluda again with a mixture of wonder and amusement.

'By the way,' he said, 'you didn't tell me you were a detective.'

Feluda and I both gave a start. How had he guessed? Mr Bose began laughing. Then he pulled out his wallet and, from it, took out a small visiting card. To my surprise, I saw that it was one of Feluda's. It said: Pradosh C. Mitter, Private Investigator.

'It fell out of your pocket this morning when you were paying the driver of your jeep,' Mr Bose told us. 'He picked it up and gave it to me, thinking it was mine. I didn't even glance at it then, but saw it much later. Anyway, I'm going to keep it, if I may. And here's my own card. If there is any development here . . . I mean, if you think I ought to be here, please send me a telegram in Bombay. I'll take the first available flight . . . Well, I don't suppose I'll meet you tomorrow. Goodbye, Mr Mitter. Have a good time.' Mr Bose raised his hand in farewell and began walking briskly in the direction of the dak bungalow. It had started to rain.

Feluda took his shoes off the minute we got back into our room and threw himself down on his bed. 'Aaaah!' he said. I was feeling tired, too. Who knew we'd see and hear so many different things on our very first day?

'Just imagine,' Feluda said, staring at the ceiling, 'what do you suppose we'd have done if a criminal had nine heads? No one could possibly sneak up to him and catch him from behind!'

'And thirty-four arms? What about those?'

'Yes, we'd have had to use seventeen pairs of handcuffs to arrest him!'

It was raining quite hard outside. I got up and switched on the lights. Feluda stretched out an arm and slipped his hand into his handbag. A second later, he had his famous blue notebook open in front of him and a pen in his hand. Feluda had clearly made up his mind that there was indeed a mystery somewhere, and had started his investigation.

'Can you tell me quickly the name of each new person we have met today?'

I wasn't prepared for such a question at all, so all I could do for a few seconds was stare dumbly at Feluda. Then I swallowed and said, 'Today? Every new person? Do I have to start from Bagdogra?'

'No, you idiot. Just give me a list of people we met here in Gangtok.'

'Well . . . Sasadhar Datta.'

'Wrong. Try again.'

'Sorry, sorry. I mean Sasadhar Bose. We met him at the airport in Bagdogra.'

'Right. Why is he in Gangtok?'

'Something to do with aromatic plants, didn't he say?'

'No, a vague answer like that won't do. Try to be more specific.'

'Wait. He came here to meet his partner, Shivkumar Shelvankar. They have a chemical firm. Among other things, they . . .'

'OK, OK, that'll do. Next?'

'The hippie.'

'His name?'

'Helmet—'

'No, not Helmet. It's Helmut. And his surname?'

'Ungar.'

'What brought him here?'

'He's a professional photographer, working on a book on Sikkim. He had his visa extended.'

'Next?'

'Nishikanto Sarkar. Lives in Darjeeling. No idea what he does for a living. He had a Tibetan statue which he—'

I was interrupted by a knock on the door. 'Come in!' Feluda shouted.

The man I was just talking about walked into the room. 'I hope I'm not disturbing you?' asked Nishikanto Sarkar. 'I just thought I'd tell you about the Lama dance.'

'Lama dance? Where?' Feluda offered him a chair. Mr Sarkar took it, that same strange smile still hovering on his lips.

'In Rumtek,' he said, 'just ten miles from here. It's going to be a grand affair. People are coming from Bhutan and Kalimpong. The chief Lama of Rumtek—he is number three after the Dalai Lama—was in Tibet all this while. He has just returned to Rumtek. And the monastery is supposed to be new and worth seeing. Would you like to go tomorrow?'

'Not in the morning. Maybe after lunch?'

'OK. Or if you wish to have a darshan of His Holiness, we could go the day after tomorrow. I could get hold of three white scarves.'

'Why scarves?' I asked.

Mr Sarkar's smile broadened. 'That is a local custom. If you wish to meet a high class Tibetan, you have to present him with a scarf. He'll take it from you, and return it immediately. That's all, that takes care of all the formalities.'

'No, I don't think we need bother about a darshan,' said Feluda. 'Let's just go and see the dance.'

'Yes, I would actually prefer that myself. The sooner we can go the better. You never know what might happen to the roads.'

'Oh, by the way, did you tell anyone else apart from Shelvankar about that statue?'

Mr Sarkar's reply came instantly, 'No. Not a soul. Why do you ask?'

'I was curious, that's all.'

'I did think of taking it somewhere to have it properly valued, but I met Mr Shelvankar before I could do that, and he bought it. Mind you, he didn't pay me at once. I had to wait until the next day.'

'Did he pay you in cash?'

'No, he didn't have that much cash on him. He gave me a cheque. Look!' Mr Sarkar took out a folded cheque from his wallet and showed it to Feluda. I leant over and saw it, too. It was a National and Grindlays Bank cheque. Feluda returned it to Mr Sarkar.

'Did you notice anything sus-suspicious?' Mr Sarkar asked, still smiling. I realized later that he had a tendency to stammer if he was upset or excited. 'No, no.' Feluda yawned. Mr Sarkar rose to go. At this precise moment, there was a bright flash of lightning, followed almost immediately by the ear-splitting noise of thunder. Mr Sarkar went white. 'I can't stand thunder and lightning, heh heh. Good night!' He went out quickly.

It continued to rain throughout the evening. Even when I went to bed after dinner, I could hear the steady rhythm of the rain, broken occasionally by distant thunder. Despite that, it didn't take me long to fall asleep.

I woke briefly in the middle of the night and saw a figure walk past our window. But who would be mad enough to go out on a night like this? Perhaps I wasn't really awake. Perhaps the figure wearing a red garment that I saw only for a few seconds in the flash of lightning was no more than a dream . . . a figment of my imagination.

FOUR

I woke at 6.30 a.m. the next morning, to find that the rain had stopped and there was not a single cloud in the sky. The sun shone brightly on the world, and behind the range of mountains, now easily visible from our room, stood Kanchenjunga. The view from here was different from that in Darjeeling, but it was still unmistakably the same Kanchenjunga, standing apart from all the other mountains—proud, majestic and beautiful.

Feluda had risen before me and already had a bath. 'Be quick, Topshe. We have lots to do,' he said. It took me less than half an hour to get ready. By the time we went down for breakfast, it was only a little after 7 a.m. To our surprise, we found Mr Sarkar already seated in the dining hall.

'Good morning. So you're an early riser, too,' Feluda greeted him.

Mr Sarkar smiled, but seemed oddly preoccupied, even somewhat nervous. 'Er . . . did you sleep well?' we asked.

'Not too badly. Why, what's the matter?'

Mr Sarkar glanced around briefly before taking out a crumpled yellow piece of paper from his pocket. Then he handed it over to Feluda and said, 'What do you make of this?'

Feluda spread it out. There were some strange letters written with black ink. 'It looks like a Tibetan word. Where did you get it?'

'Last night . . . in the . . . I mean, d-dead of night . . . someone threw it into my room.'

'What!' My heart gave a sudden lurch. Mr Sarkar's room was next to ours. The same stretch of the veranda that ran in front of our room went past his. If the man I saw last night was real, and not something out of a dream, why, he might have—! But I chose not to say anything.

'I wish I knew what it said,' added Mr Sarkar.

'That shouldn't be a problem, surely? Dozens of people here can read Tibetan. You could go to the Tibetan Institute, if no one else will help you. But why are you assuming this is some sort of a threat? It could simply mean "May you live long", or "God be with you", or something like that. Is there a specific reason to think this is a warning or a threat?'

Mr Sarkar gave a little start, then smiled and said, 'No, no, certainly not. I do nothing but mind my own business. Why should anyone threaten me? But then again, why should anyone send me their good wishes? I mean, purely out of the blue like this?'

Feluda called a waiter and ordered breakfast. 'Stop worrying. We're right next to you, aren't we? We'll both look after you. Now, have a good breakfast, relax and think of the Lama dance this afternoon.'

Our jeep arrived on time. Just as we were about to get into it, I saw another jeep coming from the direction of the dak bungalow. As it came closer, I could read its number plate. SKM 463, it said. Why did it seem familiar? Oh, of course, this was the new jeep that Mr Shelvankar's driver was now driving. I caught a glimpse of the blue jacket the driver was wearing, and then, to my utter surprise, I saw Mr Bose sitting in the passenger's seat. He stopped his jeep at the sight of ours. 'I was waiting for information from the army,' he told us, leaning out. 'All that rain last night made me wonder if the roads were all right.'

'And are they?'

'Yes, thank God. If they weren't, I'd have had to go via Kalimpong.'

'Didn't Mr Shelvankar use the same driver?'

Mr Bose laughed. 'I can see you've started making enquiries already. But yes, you're right. I chose him deliberately, partly because his jeep is new, and partly because . . . lightning doesn't strike the same place twice, does it? Anyway, goodbye again!'

He drove off and soon disappeared. We climbed into our own jeep. The driver knew where he was supposed to take us, so we were off without wasting another minute. I glanced up as we approached the dak bungalow to see if I could see Helmut, but there was no one in sight. There was a slope to our left, leading to another street lined by buildings. One of them looked like a school for there was an open square ground in front of it with two tiny goal posts. A little later, we reached a crossing where four roads met. We drove straight ahead and soon came across a large sign that said, 'North Sikkim Highway'.

Feluda had been humming under his breath. Now he broke off and asked the driver, 'How far has this road gone?'

'Up to Chungtham, sir. Then it splits into two—one goes to Lachen, and the other to Lachung.'

I had heard of both these places. They were both at a height of nearly 9,000 feet and reported to be very beautiful.

'Is it a good road?'

'Yes, sir. But it gets damaged sometimes after heavy rain.'

The few buildings that could be seen by the road soon disappeared altogether. We were now well out of the town, making our way through hills. Looking down at the valley below, I could only see maize fields. It seemed as though someone had cut steps in the hillside to plant the maize. It looked most attractive.

After driving in silence for another ten kilometres, our driver slowed down suddenly and said, 'Here's the spot. This is where the accident took place.' He parked the jeep on one side and we got out. The place was remarkably quiet. I could hear nothing but the faint chirping of a bird, and the gurgling of a small river in the far distance.

On our left was a slope. The hill rose almost in a straight line on our right. It was from the top of this hill that the boulder had fallen. Pieces of it were still strewn about. The thought of the accident suddenly made me feel a little sick.

Feluda, in the meantime, had finished taking a few quick photos. Then he passed his camera to me and walked over to the edge of the road on the left. 'It may be possible to climb down this slope, if I go very carefully. Wait for me. I shouldn't take more than fifteen minutes,' he said. Before I could say or do anything to stop him, he had stepped off the road and was climbing down the slope, clutching at plants, bushes and rocks, whistling nonchalantly. But the sound of his whistling faded gradually, and in just a few minutes there was silence once more. Unable to contain myself, I moved towards the edge of the road and took a quick look. What I saw made me give an involuntary gasp. I could see Feluda, but he had climbed such a distance already that his figure looked like that of a tiny doll.

'Yes, he's found the right spot,' said the driver, joining me. 'That's where the jeep had fallen.'

Exactly fifteen minutes later, I heard Feluda climbing up, once again clutching and grasping whatever he could lay his hands on. When he came closer, I stretched an arm and helped him heave himself up on the road.

'What did you find, Feluda?'

'Just some nuts and bolts and broken parts of a vehicle. No Yamantak.'

This did not surprise me. 'Did you find nothing else?' I asked. In reply, Feluda took out a small object from his pocket. It was a white shirt button, possibly made of plastic. Feluda put it away, and made his way to the hill that rose high on the other side of the road. I heard him mutter 'rocks and boulders, rocks and boulders' a couple of times. Then he raised his voice and said, 'Felu Mitter must now turn into Tenzing.'

'What do you mean? Why Tenzing? Hey Feluda, wait for me!'

This time, I was determined not to be left behind. The hill that had looked pretty daunting at first turned out to have little clefts and hollows one could use as footholds. 'All right, you go before me,' Feluda said. I knew he wanted to be right behind me so that he could reach out and catch me if I slipped and fell. Luckily, that did not happen. A few minutes later, I heard Feluda say, 'Stop!' We had reached a place that was almost flat. I decided to sit on a small rock and rest for a while. Feluda began pacing, examining the ground carefully. I paid no attention until he stopped and said, 'Hm. This is where that boulder must have slipped from. Look at those bushes over there—and that small fern—see how they've been crushed?'

'How big do you think it was?'

'You saw the pieces, didn't you? It need not have been very big. A rock the size of a dhobi's bundle would be enough to kill, if it fell from such a height.'

'Really?'

'Yes. It's a matter of momentum, you see. Mass into velocity. If you stood at the bottom of Qutab Minar and someone threw a pebble aimed at your head from its top, you might end up with a fractured skull. Haven't you noticed when you play cricket that the higher the cricket ball is thrown in the air, the more difficult and painful it is for a fielder to catch it?'

'Yes, I see what you mean.'

Feluda turned and started to stare at a certain spot that looked more barren than its surroundings. There were grassy patches everywhere else.

'Topshe, do you want to find out how that stone slipped out? Come and have a look.' Feluda pointed at something in that barren portion of the hill. I got up and peered. There was a small hole. What could it mean?

'As far as I can see,' Feluda said slowly, 'yes, I am almost a hundred per cent sure about this—someone forced the rock out of the ground, using either a strong iron rod, or something like that. Otherwise there wouldn't be an empty space here. Which means—'

I knew what his next words were going to be. But I held my breath and let him finish.

'—Which means the accident that took Mr Shelvankar's life was caused by man, not nature. Someone killed him . . . someone incredibly cruel, and clever.'

FIVE

When we returned to the hotel from the place of the murder (I am not going to call it an accident any more), Feluda told me to wait in the hotel. He had to go out on some work. I didn't ask him for details for I knew he wouldn't tell me.

On our way back, we had met Helmut near the big crossing. When he heard we were going to Rumtek later in the afternoon, he said he'd like to join us. Nobody had told him about the Lama dance. I wondered where Mr Sarkar was. Had he managed to find out what that Tibetan word meant?

I found him in the dining hall, looking morose and depressed. However, my arrival seemed to cheer him up. 'Where's your cousin?' he asked with his usual smile.

'He's gone out for a while. He should be back soon.'

'Er . . . he's very strong, isn't he?'

I looked up in surprise at this question, but Mr Sarkar continued, 'You see, I am staying on in Gangtok only because he said he'd help me, if need be. Or else I'd have gone back to Darjeeling today.'

'Why?'

Mr Sarkar began looking nervous again. Then he slowly took out the same yellow paper from his pocket. 'I've ne-never done anyone any harm. Why should anyone try to threaten me?'

'Did you find out what that word means?'

'Ye-es. I took it to the Tibetan Institute. And they said . . . they said it means "death". Giangphung, or something like that. The Tibetan word for death. It's got me really worried. I am thirty-seven now, you see, and once an astrologer had told me my stars were all going to fall into unfavourable positions after I turned thirty-seven . . .'

This irritated me somewhat. 'I think you are jumping to conclusions,' I said a little sternly. 'All it says is "death". Does it say *you* have to die?'

'Yes, yes, you're right. It could be anybody's death, couldn't it? Even so . . . I don't know . . .' I thought of the figure in red I had seen last night. But obviously it was better not to mention it to Mr Sarkar. He was upset enough as it was. After a few moments of silence, he seemed to pull himself together with an effort. 'I mustn't brood,' he said. 'Your cousin's there to help me. The very sight of him inspires confidence. Is he a sportsman?'

'He used to play cricket. Now he does yoga.'

'I knew it! One doesn't often get to see a man looking so fit. Anyway, would you like a cup of tea?'

I was feeling quite tired after all that climbing. So I said yes, and Mr Sarkar ordered tea for both of us. Feluda arrived just as the waiter placed two steaming cups before us. Mr Sarkar told him of his problem at once. Feluda looked at the Tibetan word again and asked, 'Can you figure out why anyone should want to do this to you?'

'No, sir. I've thought a great deal, but I can't think of a reason at all.'

'Very well. If you're sure there's no one to bear you a grudge, then there's nothing to be worried about. I am sure that was dropped into your room by mistake. What is the point in threatening someone in a language he doesn't know? That warning must have been meant for someone who can read Tibetan. You were not the real target.'

'Yes, that makes a lot of sense. Besides, I can rely on you, can't I, if there's any trouble?'

'Yes, but perhaps there's something I should tell you here and now. Trouble follows me around wherever I go.'

'R-really?'

Feluda went up to our room without another word. I knew he couldn't stand people who were given to frequent attacks of nerves. If Mr Sarkar wanted his support, he'd have to stop whining all the time.

When I returned to our room after finishing my tea, Feluda was writing something in his blue notebook. 'I knew most people in telegraph offices were illiterate, but this is too much!' he exclaimed upon seeing me.

'Why, what happened?'

'I sent a telegram to Mr Bose. He will get it as soon as he reaches Bombay.'

'What did you tell him?'

'Have reason to suspect Shelvankar's death not accidental. Am investigating.'

'But why are you so cross with the telegraph office?'

'That's another matter. You see, I went to find out if Shelvankar had received any telegrams while he was here. It wasn't easy to get this information, of course, but in the end they told me there had been two. One was from Mr Bose, saying, "Am arriving fourteenth."'

'And the other?'

'Here, read this,' Feluda offered me his notebook. I saw what was written in it: YOUR SON MAY BE IS A SICK MONSTER. PRITEX.

I stared. What on earth did it mean? Were we now going to deal with demons and monsters?

'Some words have clearly been misspelt. But what could they be?' Feluda muttered.

'What is Pritex?'

'That probably refers to a private detective agency.'

'You mean Shelvankar had appointed a detective to trace his son?'

'Quite possibly. But "sick monster"? Dear God!'

'This is getting increasingly complicated, Feluda. How many mysteries will you solve all at once?'

'I was thinking the same thing. There is no end to the questions. In fact, it might not be a bad idea to write them down.' He bent over his notebook, pen in hand.

'Go ahead,' he invited.

'Number one—sick monster.'

'Yes. Next?'

'Who threw that boulder?'

'Good.'

'Number three—where did that statue disappear?'

'Carry on. You're doing quite well.'

'Number four—who threw that piece of paper into Mr Sarkar's room?'

'And why? All right, next?'

'Number five—whose shirt button did you find at the site of the murder?'

'Yes, although that might well have dropped from the shirt of the murder victim.'

'Number six—who, apart from ourselves, went to the Tibetan Institute to ask about Yamantak?'

'Splendid. If you keep going like this, in about ten years you'll become a full-fledged detective yourself!'

I knew Feluda was joking, but I felt quite pleased to think I had passed the test.

'There is only one person we haven't yet met and I feel we ought to.'

'Who is that?'

'Dr Vaidya. If he can make predictions for the future, speak to departed souls, and perform other tricks, he's got to be an interesting man.'

SIX

We left for Rumtek as planned, taking the road to Siliguri. The same road turned right to join a new road that went straight up to Rumtek. Both roads passed through picturesque villages and green and gold maize fields. I found the ride thoroughly enjoyable, despite the fact that the sun had disappeared and the sky had started to turn grey.

Our driver was driving very cautiously. Feluda and I sat with him in the front. Helmut and Mr Sarkar sat at the back, facing each other. Helmut's foot, he said, was now a lot better. The pain had gone, thanks to a German pain balm he had used. Mr Sarkar seemed much more cheerful. I Could hear him humming a Hindi song. Only Feluda was totally silent and withdrawn. I knew he was trying very hard to find answers to those six questions. If we hadn't already planned this trip, he would have spent the afternoon scribbling in his notebook.

Our jeep turned right, bringing into view new houses and buildings, and rows of what looked like bunting. I learnt later that Tibetans hung square pieces of cloth from ropes outside their houses in the belief that they ward off evil spirits.

A few minutes later, a faint noise that had already reached my ears grew louder. It was a mixture of the deep and sombre sound of a horn, clanking of cymbals and a shrill note from a flute. This must be the music for the Lama dance, I thought, as our jeep pulled up outside the huge gate of the monastery. 'The Lamas are dan-dancing,' informed Mr Sarkar, possibly for Helmut's benefit. All of us climbed out.

Passing through the gate, we found ourselves in a large open courtyard. A beautiful blue and white embroidered shamiana stood over it. The audience sat under the shamiana. About ten men, wearing bright costumes and rather grotesque masks, were dancing before this audience, jumping and swaying to the music. The musicians were all dressed in red. Small boys—barely ten years old—were blowing the horns, each one of which was several feet long. I had never seen anything like it.

Helmut started taking photos. He was carrying three cameras today.

'Would you like to sit down?' asked Mr Sarkar.

'What do you want to do?' Feluda said.

'I have seen this kind of thing before, in Kalimpong. I'm going to have a look at the temple behind this courtyard. Its inside walls are supposed to be beautifully carved.'

Mr Sarkar left. Feluda and I sat down on the floor. 'Tradition is a strange thing,' remarked Feluda. 'A traditional dance like this can make you forget you're living in the twentieth century. I don't think this form of dance has changed at all in the last thousand years.'

'Why is this place called a gumpha?'

'No, this isn't a gumpha. A gumpha is a cave. This is a monastery. See those little rooms on the other side? That's where the monks stay. All these little boys with shaved heads, wearing long Tibetan robes are being trained to become monks. In a monas—' Feluda broke off. I looked at him quickly to find him frowning, his mouth hanging open. Now what was the matter? What had he suddenly thought of? 'It's this mountain air,' he said finally, shaking his head. 'It's affecting my brain. I've stopped thinking. Why did it take me so long to work out what that telegram meant? It's so simple!'

'How is it simple? I still can't—'

'Look, it said "sick". That means Sikkim. And "monster" is monastery.'

'Hey, that makes sense! What does the whole thing say?'

'YOUR SON MAY BE IS A SICK MONSTER. If you read "IN" for "IS", it says YOUR SON MAY BE IN A SIKKIM MONASTERY.'

'Does that mean Mr Shelvankar's son, who left home fifteen years ago, is here right now?'

'That's what Pritex said. If Shelvankar had managed to figure out the meaning of this telegram, he might well have started to feel hopeful. From what I've heard, he loved his son and wanted him back.'

'Perhaps he was going to that gumpha the day he died only to look for his son.'

'That's entirely possible. And if his son was really somewhere in Sikkim, the chances of . . .' Feluda broke off again. Then I heard him mutter under his breath, 'Will . . . will . . . if Shelvankar made a will leaving everything to his son, he stood to gain a lot.' Feluda rose and made his way out of the crowd. I followed quickly. He was obviously feeling restless, having just discovered what the telegram had really meant. I saw him look around. Was he looking for an Indian among the Tibetans?

We began walking in the direction of the temple, where Mr Sarkar had disappeared a few minutes ago. There were fewer people on the other side of the courtyard. As we passed the rooms in which the monks lived, we saw a couple of very old monks sitting outside in the corridor, turning a prayer wheel silently, their eyes closed. If their heavily wrinkled faces were anything to go by, they must have been a hundred years old.

Behind the rooms was a long veranda. Its walls were covered with pictures depicting scenes from the Buddha's life. The veranda led to a dark hall. Inside it, flickering oil lamps stood in rows. A huge wooden door, painted red, had been thrown open, but there was no one at the door. Feluda and I stepped in quietly.

The dark, damp hall was filled with a strange scent of incense. Incredibly long lengths of bright silk, heavily embroidered, hung from the high ceiling. Benches, draped in colourful fabrics, stood in corners, as did what looked like very large drums. These were supported by bamboo rods. Behind these, in the darkest corner of the hall, were a number of tall statues, chiefly of the Buddha. Flowers had been arranged in a number of vases, and the oil lamps I had seen from outside were placed under the statues.

I was totally engrossed in looking at these things when suddenly Feluda placed a hand on my shoulder. I looked up swiftly and found him staring at a side entrance to the hall. A much smaller door on one side was open.

'Let's get out of here,' he said, speaking through clenched teeth, and started to move towards the door.

We emerged from the hall to find a flight of stairs going up. 'I can't tell where he went, but let's go upstairs, anyway,' Feluda said.

'Where who went?' I whispered, running up the stairs.

'A man in red. He was peeping into the hall. Ran away the moment he realized I had seen him.'

'Did you see his face?'

'No, it was too dark.'

We found a room on the first floor, but its door was closed. Perhaps this was the senior Lama's room, who had recently returned from Tibet. On the left was an open terrace. Here again, pieces of cloth hung from ropes. Strains of the music from the courtyard down below reached my ears. A dance like this could go on for seven or eight hours.

We walked across the terrace and stood by a railing, overlooking a green valley. A mist had started to rise, slowly engulfing everything that was visible. 'If Shelvankar's son was here—' Feluda began, but was interrupted by a loud scream.

'Help me! Oh God . . . save! . . . help . . . help!'

It was Mr Sarkar's voice.

We ran back to the stairs. It took us less than a minute to get down and find the rear exit from the monastery. We rushed out to find that the shrieks for help were coming from the bottom of a hill. The area was uneven, dotted with bushes and shrubs, one end leading to a steep drop of about a hundred feet. It was here that Mr Sarkar was hanging from a bush, right at the edge of the hill. Our appearance made him shout even louder. 'I am d-d-dying . . . save me, please save me!'

It wasn't too difficult to pull him up to safety. But the instant his feet touched solid ground, he rolled his eyes and fainted. Then we had to carry him back to the jeep and splash cold water on his face. He came round in a few moments and sat up slowly.

'What happened?' asked Feluda.

'D-don't remind me!' Mr Sarkar whimpered. 'After that long journey, I n-n-needed to . . . I mean . . . relieve myself, you see . . . so I thought I'd better go out of the monastery, and I found this place that seemed quite suitable, but . . . but who knew I had been followed?'

'Did someone give you a push from the back?'

'Absolutely. It was h-horrible! If I hadn't found that bush to hang on to, that Tibetan warning would have come t-true, in no t-time!'

'Did you see the man?'

'No, of course not! He stole up behind me, didn't he?'

There was no point in staying on in Rumtek after an incident like this. We decided to go back to Gangtok immediately. Helmut, who had seen us coming back to the jeep, agreed to return with us, although I suspect he was disappointed at not being able to take more photos.

Feluda had sunk into silence once more. But he spoke suddenly as our driver started the jeep. 'Mr Sarkar,' he said, 'surely you realize you have a certain responsibility in this whole business?'

'Res-responsibility?' croaked Mr Sarkar.

'There's no way we can figure out who's trying to frighten you unless you tell us what—or who—you are after.'

Mr Sarkar sat up, looking profoundly distressed. 'I swear, sir—I promise—I've never caused anyone any harm. Not knowingly, anyway.'

'You don't happen to have an identical twin, do you?'

'No, no. I am the only child of my parents.'

'Hm. I assume you're telling the truth. Mind you, if you tell me a lie, it is you who is going to be in trouble.'

The rest of the journey was made in total silence. Feluda spoke again only when our jeep stopped at the dak bungalow and Helmut tried to pay his share.

'No, no,' Feluda said, 'we invited you, didn't we? Besides, you are a guest in our country. We cannot allow you to pay a single paisa.'

'All right.' Helmut smiled. 'Will you at least allow me to offer you a cup of tea?'

This seemed like a very good idea, so all of us got out. Feluda and Mr Sarkar paid the driver. Helmut then took us to his room.

We had just found three chairs for ourselves, and Helmut had placed his cameras on the table, when a strange man walked into the room and greeted Helmut with a smile. A thick beard—flecked with grey—covered most of his face. Long hair came down to his shoulders. He was clad in loose flannel trousers and a shapeless orange jacket with a high neck. In his hand was a stout walking-stick.

Helmut smiled back, and turned to us. 'Allow me to introduce you,' he said. 'This is Dr Vaidya.'

SEVEN

'Are you from Bengal?' Dr Vaidya asked. He spoke with a funny accent.

'Yes,' Feluda replied. 'Helmut has told us about you.'

'Helmut is a nice boy,' Dr Vaidya nodded, 'but I've had to warn him about one thing. People here don't normally like being photographed. You see, it is their belief that if a part of a person is represented somewhere else in a different form, it reduces the vital force—the ability to live—of that person.'

'Do you believe this yourself?'

'What I believe is of no consequence, at least not to Helmut. He hasn't stopped taking pictures, has he? Why, I have been captured in his camera, too! What I say is this: one cannot disregard anything in life without studying it, or examining it thoroughly. I still have a lot to learn.'

'But there's such a lot you know already! I've heard you can see the future and even speak to the dead.'

'No, not always.' Dr Vaidya gave a slight smile. 'A lot depends on the immediate surroundings. But there are certain things that are fairly easy to tell. For instance, I can tell that this gentleman here is under a lot of stress,' he pointed at Mr Sarkar, who licked his lips nervously.

'Yes, you're right,' Feluda said. 'Somebody is trying to threaten him. He thinks his life is in danger. Can you tell us who is doing this?'

Dr Vaidya closed his eyes. He opened them a few seconds later and stared out of the window absently. 'Agent,' he said.

'Agent?'

'Yes. A man must be punished for his sins. Sometimes he is punished by the Almighty. At other times, God sends His agents out to do this job.'

'Enough!' shouted Mr Sarkar. His voice shook. 'I don't want to hear any more.'

Dr Vaidya smiled again. 'I am saying all this only because your friend asked me. If you can learn something yourself, there's no need to go looking for a teacher. But one thing I must tell you. If you wish to live, you will have to tread most carefully.'

'What does that mean?' asked Mr Sarkar.

'I can't say anything more than that.'

The tea arrived. Helmut poured it out and passed the cups around.

'I believe you met Mr Shelvankar,' said Feluda, sipping his tea.

'Yes. It's all very sad. I did warn him about a rough patch he might have to go through. But death? No, that's a different matter altogether, and no one has any control over it.'

No one spoke after this. We drank our tea in silence. Helmut sorted a few papers out on his table. Mr Sarkar stared absently into space, apparently unaware that his tea was getting cold. Only Feluda seemed totally at ease, happily finishing the biscuits that had arrived with the tea. After a while, Helmut rose to switch on a light. Daylight had almost gone by this time. But it turned out that there was a power cut. 'I'll get some candles,' said Helmut and went out to look for the bearer.

Feluda turned to Dr Vaidya again. 'Do you really believe Mr Shelvankar's death was accidental?'

Dr Vaidya took a moment to reply. Then he said, 'Only one person knows the answer to that question.'

'Who?'

'The person who died. Only he knows the truth. We who are living look upon this world and this life through eyes that take in every irrelevant and unnecessary detail. Just look out of that window. All those mountains and trees and rivers are irrelevant. They stand as a screen between ourselves and the truth. But death opens an inner eye that sees nothing but what is real and of true significance.'

Most of this speech went over my head, but I was sure Feluda had understood every word. 'You mean it is only Mr Shelvankar who could tell how he died?' Feluda asked.

'Yes. He couldn't have known the truth when he died. But now . . . yes, now he knows exactly what happened.'

I shivered suddenly. There was something eerie in the atmosphere, in so much talk about death, and the way Dr Vaidya smiled in the dark. It gave me goose-pimples.

The bearer came in at this moment. He cleared the table and placed a candle on it. Feluda took out a packet of Charminar, offered it to everyone else in the room, then lit one himself. 'It may be a good idea to consult Mr Shelvankar and see what he thinks,' he remarked, blowing out a smoke ring. I knew he had read a lot on seances and most things supernatural. He kept an open mind on every subject, never hesitating to read or hear about other people's views, even if he didn't believe in something himself.

Dr Vaidya closed his eyes. A few moments later, he opened them and said, 'Shut the door and windows.' There was something authoritative in his tone. Mr Sarkar got up like a man hypnotized and obeyed silently. We were left sitting around the table in the faint flickering light of the candle. On my right was Dr Vaidya. On my left sat Feluda. Mr Sarkar sat next to him. Helmut finished the circle.

'Place your hands, palms down, on this table. Your fingers must touch your neighbour's,' commanded Dr Vaidya. We did as we were told. Dr Vaidya placed his own hands between mine and Helmut's, and said, 'Look straight at that candle and think of the death of Shelvankar.'

The candle was burning steadily. A few drops of wax had fallen on the table. A small insect, trapped in the room, began buzzing around the flame. God knows how long we sat in silence. I did cast a few sidelong glances at Dr Vaidya, but he couldn't have seen me for his own eyes were closed.

After a long time, he spoke. His voice sounded very faint as though he was speaking from a great distance. 'What do you want to know?' he asked. Feluda answered him. 'Did Mr Shelvankar die in an accident?'

'No,' said that faint, strange voice.

'How did he die?'

Silence. All of us were now gazing at Dr Vaidya. He was leaning back in his chair. His eyes were shut tight. Lightning flashed outside, lighting up our room for a second. Feluda's question was answered the same instant.

'Murder,' said Dr Vaidya.

'Mu-h-h-u-rder?' Mr Sarkar gasped.

'Who killed him?' Feluda wanted to know. He was staring at Dr Vaidya's hands. Dr Vaidya sighed. Then he began breathing hard, as though the act of breathing was causing him a great deal of pain. 'Virendra!' he finally whispered. Virendra? Who was he? Feluda started to speak, but Dr Vaidya opened his eyes unexpectedly and said, 'A glass of water, please.'

Helmut rose and poured him water from his flask. Feluda waited until Dr Vaidya had finished drinking it. Then he asked, 'I don't suppose there's any chance of finding out who this Virendra is?'

Helmut answered him this time. 'Virendra is Mr Shelvankar's son. He told me about him.'

It was now time for us to leave. All of us stood up. Helmut opened the door and windows. The power came back a second later.

'You get nervous rather easily, don't you?' said Dr Vaidya, placing a hand on Mr Sarkar's shoulder. Mr Sarkar tried to smile. 'Anyway, I don't think you are in any danger now,' Dr Vaidya told him reassuringly. This time, Mr Sarkar smiled more naturally, looking visibly relieved.

'How long are you here for?' Feluda asked Dr Vaidya.

'I'd like to go to Pemiangchi tomorrow, if it doesn't rain. I've heard they've got some ancient valuable manuscripts in the monastery there.'

'Are you making a study of Tibet and the Tibetan culture?'

'Yes, you might call it that. It's the only ancient civilization that's left in the world. Egypt, Iraq, Mesopotamia . . . each one of those got destroyed. But for that matter, what is left in India, tell me? It's all a great hotch-potch. It's only Tibet that's managed to retain most of what it had. Luckily, some of the old monasteries in Sikkim have got pieces of their art and culture, so one doesn't have to go all the way to Tibet to find them.'

We came out, to find that the sky was covered by thick, dark clouds, being frequently ripped by lightning. It was certain that it would start raining again.

'Why don't you go to Pemiangchi as well?' Dr Vaidya asked.

'Yes, we might do that. I've heard a lot about the place.'

'If you do, don't forget to take a bag of salt with you.'

'Salt? Whatever for?'

'Leeches. There's nothing like salt to get rid of them.'

EIGHT

Feluda, Mr Sarkar and I were back in our hotel, sitting down to our dinner. Although the hotel was pretty average in many ways, it had an excellent cook.

'A most decent fellow, I must say,' remarked Mr Sarkar, trying to get the marrow out of a bone. A delicious lamb curry was on the menu tonight.

'Who? You mean Dr Vaidya?'

'Yes. What a remarkably gifted man, too. He seemed to know everything.'

'Yes, you should be pleased,' Feluda said, laughing. 'Didn't he tell you you were no longer in danger?'

'Why, didn't you believe what he said?'

'If what he said turns out to be true, then of course I shall believe him. But, right now, I think we should be careful in what or whom we believe. There are so many cheats in this line.' Feluda was frowning again. Something was obviously bothering him a great deal. I wish I knew what it was.

'Do you believe what he said about the murder?' Mr Sarkar persisted.

'Yes, I do.'

'Really? Why?'

'There is a reason.' Feluda refused to say anything more.

The two of us went out after dinner again to buy paan. It hadn't yet started to rain, but there was virtually no breeze. Feluda put a paan in his mouth and began pacing. After only a few minutes, however, he stopped and said, 'I'm only wasting my time like this. Tell you what, Topshe, why don't you go for a walk for half an hour? I'd like to work alone in our room, undisturbed.'

I agreed, and Feluda walked away. I ambled across to the opposite pavement and made my way slowly down the road that led to the main town. All the shops were closed. A few men were sitting in a circle in front of a shop and gambling. I heard someone rattle the dice, which was followed by a great shout and loud laughter.

The street lights were dim, but even so I didn't fail to notice the figure of a man coming from the opposite direction, walking very fast. As he came closer, I realized it was Helmut. Something stopped me from calling out to him. But he was so preoccupied that even when he passed me by, he didn't seem to notice me at all. I stared foolishly at his receding back, until it vanished from sight. Then I looked at my watch and returned to the hotel.

Feluda was lying flat on his back, resting his notebook on his chest.

'I brought the list of suspects up to date,' he told me as I came in.

'Well, Virendra Shelvankar was already a suspect, wasn't he? It's just that we didn't know his name. Have you added Dr Vaidya's name to your list?'

Feluda grinned. 'The man put up a jolly good show, I must admit. Yet, the whole thing could be genuine, who knows? But we mustn't forget that he and Shelvankar had talked to each other. There's no way of making sure whether Dr Vaidya is a fraud or not unless we can find out what exactly the two had discussed.'

'But he was right about Mr Sarkar, wasn't he?'

'That was easy enough. Mr Sarkar was biting his nails constantly. Anyone could have guessed he was tense.'

'And what about the murder?'

'He may have said that only to create an effect. A natural death, or death by a real accident, is too tame. Call it a murder, and it sounds so much more dramatic.'

'So who's on your list of suspects?'

'Everyone, as always.'

'Everyone including Dr Vaidya?'

'Yes. He may have known about the statue of Yamantak.'

'And Helmut? He walked past me just now, but didn't seem to see me.'

This did not appear to surprise Feluda. 'Helmut struck me as a mysterious character right from the start. He's supposed to be taking photographs for a book on Sikkim, and yet he didn't know about the Lama dance in Rumtek. That's reason enough to feel suspicious about him.'

'Why? What can it mean?'

'It can mean that he hasn't told us the real reason why he is here in Sikkim.' I began to feel quite confused, so I stopped asking questions. Feluda went back to scribbling in his notebook.

At a quarter to eleven, Mr Sarkar knocked on our door to say good-night. I tried to read a book after that, but couldn't concentrate. Feluda spent his time either sitting silently or studying the entries in his notebook. I do not know when I fell asleep. When I woke, the mountains outside were bright with sunshine.

Feluda was not in the room. Perhaps he was having a shower. I noticed a piece of paper on his bed, placed under an ashtray. Had he left a message for me? I picked it up and found a Tibetan word staring at me. I knew what it meant.

Death.

NINE

Feluda was not in the bathroom. I learnt later that he had risen early that morning to make a trunk call to Bombay. When I came down for breakfast, I found him speaking to someone on the telephone.

'I couldn't get Mr Bose,' he told me, putting the receiver down. 'He left very early this morning. Perhaps he got my telegram.'

We ordered breakfast. 'I'll have to conduct an experiment today,' Feluda revealed a few minutes later. 'I think I made a mistake somewhere. I have to make sure.'

'Where will you carry out this experiment?'

'I need a quiet spot.'

'You mean an empty room?'

'No, no, you idiot. I could use our hotel room if that's what I needed. I have to be out on the road, but I must not be seen. If anyone saw me, they'd definitely think I was mad. Let's go towards Nathula Road after breakfast.' We hadn't yet seen any of the other large streets of Gangtok. The prospect of doing a little more exploration on foot was quite exciting.

We ran into Dr Vaidya as we came out of the hotel. He was wearing sunglasses today. 'Where are you off to?' he asked.

'Just for a walk. We haven't really seen much of the city. We were thinking of going towards the palace.'

'I see. I am going to look for a jeep. It's a good day to make that trip to Pemiangchi. If you don't go there, you really will miss a lot.'

'We do intend going there one day.'

'Try to make it while I'm there. Gangtok isn't a very safe place, particularly for you.'

Dr Vaidya left with a smile and a friendly wave.

'Why did he say that?' he asked.

'He's a very clever man. He wanted to startle us, that's all. Clearly he's seen I am involved in a complex matter, so he decided to say something odd for more effect.'

'But you really have been threatened, haven't you? I saw that piece of paper.'

'That's nothing new, is it?'

'No, but—'

'But nothing. If you think I'll give up now simply because someone wrote a Tibetan word on a piece of paper, you don't know me at all.'

I didn't say anything, but thought to myself how well I did know him. Hadn't I seen him work wonders in the case of the Emperor's ring in Lucknow, despite being showered with threats and warnings?

We had been walking uphill and had now reached a point where the road spread out, almost like the Mall in Darjeeling. There was a small roundabout with yellow roadsigns. The one pointing right said 'Palace'. There was a large, heavily decorated gate at the end of this road, which was obviously the gate of the palace. The sign on the left said 'Nathula Road'. It seemed a quiet enough road. The few people we could see all appeared to be tourists, heading for the palace. 'Let's take this left turn. Quick!' Feluda said.

We turned left and took the road that led to the Chinese border.

There was no one in sight. Feluda kept looking up at the hills through which the road had been built. We had now come to the eastern side of Gangtok. Kanchenjunga was on the west. I couldn't see any of the snow-capped peaks from here, but what I could see was a ropeway.

It seemed so interesting that I stopped and stared at it, losing all track of time. I had to look up with a start a few minutes later, when I heard Feluda calling out to me. While I had been gazing at the busy ropeway, Feluda had climbed up the side of a hill, and was shouting from several feet above the road. 'Hey, Topshe, come here!'

I left the road and joined him. Feluda was standing near a rock, nearly as large as a football. 'I'm going down,' he said. 'I'll come walking past the hill. Push this stone down when I tell you to. Just a little push will make it roll off the hill. Is that clear?'

'Yes, sir. No problem!'

Feluda climbed down and disappeared in the direction from which I had come.

Then I heard him call, 'Ready?'

'Ready!' I replied.

Feluda started walking. I couldn't see him, but I heard his footsteps. A few moments later, he came vaguely within my line of vision, but before I could see him properly, I heard him shout, 'Go!' I pushed the rock, and it began to roll down. Feluda did not stop walking. By the time the rock landed on the road, he had crossed that area and gone ahead by at least ten steps.

'Wait right there!' he shouted again.

He then came back with the rock in his hand. It was still intact. 'Now you go down, and walk past this hill exactly as you saw me do. I will throw this stone at you, but you must continue walking. If you can see it rolling down at enormous speed and feel that it might hit you, you'll have to jump aside: Can you do that?'

'Sure.'

I scrambled down, and started walking, keeping an eye on Feluda. I saw him standing still, waiting for the right moment. Then he kicked the stone. I kept on walking. The stone hit the ground a few seconds before I could reach the spot. Then it rolled down the slope on the left and disappeared.

Feluda sat down, slapping his forehead. I didn't want to stand around like a fool, so I climbed up again.

'What an ass I've been, Topshe! What a perfect idiot. This simple—'

'Feluda!' I screamed, quickly pulling him to one side. In the same instant, a huge boulder came crashing from the top of the hill and went down, missing us by inches and crushing a large flowering bush on the way. By the time it struck the road and vanished from sight, my breathing was starting to return to normal. Thank God I had looked up when Feluda was speaking. Thank God I had seen the boulder. If I hadn't . . . I shuddered to think of the consequences.

'Thanks, Topshe,' Feluda said. 'This place really appears unsafe. Let's go back.'

We got down to the road and walked as fast as we could to the next crossing. There were benches on one side, placed under a canopy. We threw ourselves down on one of these. 'Did you see anyone?' asked Feluda, wiping his face.

'No. That boulder came from quite a height. I couldn't have seen who threw it even if I had had the time to look.'

'I've got to move faster now. I've got to find a final solution!'

'But there are so many questions that need to be answered.'

'And who told you I haven't found some of the answers already? Do you know what time I went to bed last night? At 2 a.m. I did a lot of thinking. And now this experiment merely confirmed every suspicion I had. Mr Shelvankar's jeep had not been hit by a falling rock. One cannot commit a murder banking on a chance that's one in a million. What really happened, I'm sure, was this: Mr Shelvankar was knocked unconscious. Then he was dropped into that ravine, along with the jeep. Someone pushed that boulder afterwards, just to make it look an accident.'

'But the driver? What about him?'

'He had been bribed. I'm sure of it.'

'Or the driver himself might have killed him?'

'No, that's unlikely. He wouldn't have had a sufficiently strong motive.'

Feluda rose. 'Let's get back, Topshe. We must find SKM 463.'

But SKM 463 was not in Gangtok, as it turned out. It had left for Siliguri the day before. 'I think people want to hire it because it's a new jeep,' Feluda remarked.

'What do we do now?'

'Wait, let me think. I'm getting muddled.'

We returned to the hotel from the jeep stand. Feluda ordered cold drinks in the dining hall. His hair was dishevelled and he seemed greatly perturbed.

'When did we arrive here?' he asked suddenly.

'Fourteenth April.'

'And when was Shelvankar killed?'

'On the eleventh.'

'Apart from Shelvankar, Mr Sarkar was here in Gangtok, and Helmut and Dr Vaidya.'

'And Virendra.'

'All right, let us make that assumption. When did Mr Sarkar get that Tibetan warning?'

'On the night of the fourteenth.'

'Right. Who was in town that day?'

'Helmut, Mr Bose, Virendra, and . . . and . . .'

'Mr Sarkar.'

'Yes, of course.'

'He may well have committed a crime. Maybe he is trying to remove suspicion from himself by showing us a piece of paper with a Tibetan word written on it. He may have written it himself. His shrieks for help in Rumtek could have been a clever piece of acting.'

'But what can he have done?'

'I don't know that yet, though I don't think he killed Shelvankar.'

'Well then, who is left?'

'Dr Vaidya. Don't forget him. We don't know for sure whether he did go to Kalimpong or not.'

Feluda finished a glass of Sikkim orange in one gulp. Then he continued, 'The only person whose movements cannot be questioned is Mr Bose, because he came with us and went to Bombay the next day. Someone in his house confirmed that he had indeed returned to Bombay. But he's not there now. Maybe he's on his way here. Perhaps our trip to Pemiangchi—' Feluda stopped speaking. Someone had walked into the dining hall and was talking to the manager. It was our German friend, Helmut Ungar. The manager pointed at us. Helmut wheeled around. 'Oh sorry, I didn't realize you were here,' he said, adding rather hesitantly, 'There's something I'd like to discuss with you. Do you think we could go up to your room?'

TEN

'May I close the door?' asked Helmut as we walked into our room.

Then he shut the door without waiting for an answer. I looked at him and began to feel vaguely uneasy. He was tall and strong, taller than Feluda by at least an inch. What did he want to do that required such secrecy? I had heard that some hippies took drugs. Was Helmut one of them? Would he—?

By this time, Helmut had placed his camera on my bed, and was opening a large red envelope with Agfa written on it.

'Would you like a cup of tea?' Feluda offered.

'No, thanks. I came here only to show you these photos. I couldn't get them printed here. So I had sent them to Darjeeling. I got the enlargements only this morning.'

Helmut took out the first photograph. 'This was taken from the North Sikkim Highway. The road where the accident took place goes right across to the opposite hill. You can get a wonderful view of Gangtok from there. That is where I was that morning, taking photos of this view. Mr Shelvankar had offered to pick me up on his way. But his jeep never got to the spot where I was standing. I heard a noise as I was clicking, which made me turn around. What I saw from where I was standing has been captured in these photos that I took with my telephoto lens.'

It was a strange photo. Most of the details were clear, although it had been taken from a distance. A jeep was sliding down a hill. A few feet above it, a man was standing on the road, looking at the falling jeep. This was probably the driver. He was wearing a blue jacket. His face couldn't be seen

Helmut took out the second photo. This was even stranger. Taken a few seconds after the first one, it showed the jeep lying wrecked by the side of the hill. Next to it, behind a bush, there was a partially hidden figure of a man in a dark suit, lying on the ground. The driver was still standing on the road, this time with his back to the camera, looking up at the hill. Right on top of the hill was another man, bending over a rock. His face was just as unclear, but he was wearing red clothes.

In the third photograph, this man in red could not be seen at all. The driver was running—in fact, he had nearly shot out of the frame. The jeep and the man in the dark suit were still lying on the ground. And the rock that was on top of the hill was now lying on the road, broken to pieces.

'Remarkable!' Feluda exclaimed. 'I have never seen photographs like these!'

'Well, it isn't often that one gets such an opportunity,' Helmut replied dryly.

'What did you do after taking these pictures?'

'I returned to Gangtok on foot. By the time I could walk across to the spot where the jeep had fallen, Mr Shelvankar had been taken away. All I could see was the broken jeep and the shattered rock. I heard about the accident the minute I reached Gangtok. I then went straight to the hospital where Mr Shelvankar had been taken. He remained alive for a couple of hours after I got there.'

'Didn't you tell anyone, about the photographs?'

'No. There was no point, at least not until I could have the film developed, and use it as evidence. Yet, I knew it was not an accident, but murder. Had I been a little closer, the face of the murderer might have been clearer in the picture.'

Feluda took out a magnifying glass and began examining the large prints again. 'I wonder if that man in red is Virendra?' he said.

'That's impossible!' Helmut declared. There was something in his voice that made us both look at him in surprise.

'Why? How can you be so sure?'

'Because I am Virendra Shelvankar.'

'What!' For the first time, I saw Feluda go round-eyed.

'What do you mean? How can you be Virendra? You are white, you have blue eyes, you speak English with a German accent, your name . . .'

'Please let me explain. You see, my father married twice. My mother was his first wife. She was a German. She met my father in Heidelburg when he was a student. That was where they got married. Her maiden name was Ungar. When I left India and settled in Germany, I started using this name, and changed my first name from Virendra to Helmut.'

My head started reeling. Helmut was Shelvankar's son? Of course, if he had a German mother, that would explain his looks.

'Why did you leave home?' Feluda asked after a brief pause.

'Five years after my mother died, my father married again. I couldn't bring myself to accept this. I loved my mother very much. It's not that I did not care for my father, but somehow when he remarried, I began to hate him. In the end, I thought leaving home was the only thing I could do to solve my problems. It wasn't easy to travel to Europe on my own, and make a new beginning. For about eight years, I moved from place to place, and job to job. Then I studied photography, and finally started to make money. A few years ago, I happened to be in Florence working on an assignment. A friend of my father's saw me there and recognized me. He came back and told my father about it, after which he approached a detective agency to track me down. When I came to know about this, I grew a beard and changed the colour of my eyes.'

'Contact lenses?'

Helmut smiled and took the lenses out of his eyes. His real eyes were brown, just like my own. He then put the lenses back and continued, 'A year ago, I came to India with a group of hippies. I hadn't stopped loving this country. But then I realized that the detective agency was still trying to trace me. I went to a monastery in Kathmandu. When someone found me even there, I came over to Sikkim.'

'Wasn't your father pleased to see you?'

'He did not recognize me at all. I have lost a lot of weight since he last saw me. Besides, my long hair, my beard and blue eyes must have all worked together to stop him from recognizing his own son. He told me about Virendra, and how much he missed him. By this time, I, too, had forgotten my earlier dislike of my father. After all, whatever happened between us was now in the past. But when he failed to recognize me, I did not tell him who I was. I probably would have told him eventually, but. . . well, I never got the chance.'

'Do you have any idea who the murderer might be?'

'May I speak frankly?'

'Of course.'

'I don't think we should let Dr Vaidya escape.'

'I agree with you,' said Feluda, lowering his voice.

'I began to suspect him the minute he mentioned the name of Virendra that evening in my room. Obviously, he didn't know I was the same person. I think he is a first class cheat, and I bet it was he who took that statue.'

'When Mr Shelvankar set out that morning, was he alone?'

'I don't know. I left quite early, you see. Dr Vaidya may well have stopped the jeep on the way and asked for a lift. Naturally, at that stage, my father had no reason to suspect him. In any case, he was a simple man. He trusted everyone.'

Feluda stood up and began pacing. Then he stopped abruptly and said, 'Would you like to go to Pemiangchi with us?

'Yes. I am prepared to go anywhere to catch my father's killer.'

'Do you know how far it is?'

'About a hundred miles from here. If the roads are good, we can get there in less than six hours. I think we should leave today, as soon as possible.'

'Yes, you're right. I'll try to find a jeep.'

'OK, and I'll get rooms booked at the dak bungalow in Pemiangchi. By the way—' Helmut turned back from the doorway, 'a dangerous man like him may well be armed. I have nothing except a flashgun. Do you—?'

Without a word, Feluda slipped a hand inside his suitcase and brought out his revolver. 'And here's my card,' he said, handing one of his cards of Helmut. 'Pradosh C. Mitter, Private Investigator', it said.

Unfortunately, we couldn't get a jeep that day. The few there were had all been hired by American tourists for a day trip to Rumtek. We booked one for the next morning and spent the day walking around in the streets of Gangtok.

We ran into Mr Sarkar near the main market. 'We're going to Pemiangchi tomorrow,' Feluda told him. 'Would you like to join us?'

'Oh sure. Thanks!'

In the evening, he came to our room carrying a strange object. A small white bundle was tied at the end of a stick. 'I bet you can't guess what this is,' he said, beaming. 'This is actually used to get rid of leeches. This small bundle contains salt and tobacco. If a leech attaches itself to your foot, just rub it once with this stick and it's bound to drop off.'

'But how can a leech attack anyone through heavy leather boots and nylon socks?'

'I don't know, but I've seen leeches slip through even very thick layers of clothes. The funny thing about leeches is that they can't see. Suppose a number of people were walking in single file, no leech would attack the person at the head of the file. It would simply pick up the vibrations created by his movements. Then it would get ready to strike as the second person passed it by; and for the third, there would be no escape at all. He would definitely get bitten.'

We decided to take four similar sticks with us the next day.

'It's Buddha Purnima the day after tomorrow,' Feluda remarked as we were getting ready for bed. 'There will be a big celebration here.'

'Shall we get to see it?'

'I don't know. But if we can catch the man who killed Mr Shelvankar, that will make up for everything we miss seeing.'

The sky remained clear that night. I spent a long time looking at a moon that was nearly full. Kanchenjunga gleamed in its light.

The next day, the four of us left for Pemiangchi at five in the morning, with just a few essentials. Mr Sarkar did not forget the 'leech-proof' sticks.

ELEVEN

There were two routes to Pemiangchi. Unfortunately, we couldn't take the shorter one as the main road had been damaged. Taking the longer route meant spending at least eight hours on the journey. Pemiangchi was a hundred and twenty-seven miles away. But it couldn't be helped. Our hotel had given us packed lunches, and we had two flasks. One was full of hot coffee, the other had water. So there was no need for us to stop anywhere for lunch, which would have taken up a lot of time.

Helmut was carrying only one camera today. Mr Sarkar, I noticed, had packed a pair of galoshes. 'No point in taking risks,' he told me. 'This is cent per cent safe.'

'Cent per cent? What if a leech fell on your head from a tree?'

'No, that's not likely. That happens in July and August. Leeches are normally to be found on the ground at this time of the year.'

Mr Sarkar didn't know we were going in search of a criminal. He was therefore perfectly happy and relaxed.

We reached Singtham at a quarter past six. We had passed through this town on our way to Gangtok. A left turn brought us to the river Tista again. We crossed it and found ourselves on a road none of us knew. This led straight to Pemiangchi. The jeep we were in wasn't new, but was in reasonably good condition. Its driver looked like a bandit from a Western film. He was dressed purely in black—the trousers, shirt and the leather jerkin he wore were all black. Even the cap on his head was dark enough to qualify as black. He was too tall to be a Nepali, but I couldn't figure out where he was from. Feluda asked him his name. 'Thondup,' he replied.

'That's a Tibetan name,' said Mr Sarkar, looking knowledgeable.

We drove in silence for about twenty kilometres. The next town on the way to Pemiangchi was Namchi. Just as we got close to it, a jeep behind us started blowing its horn loudly. Thondup made no attempt to let it pass.

'Why is he in such a hurry?' Feluda asked.

'No idea, sir. But if we let it go ahead, it'll only blow up clouds of dust.'

Thondup increased his speed. But the sound of the horn from the other jeep got more insistent. Mr Sarkar turned around irritably to see who it was. Then he exclaimed, 'Why, look, it's that same gentleman!'

'Who?' Feluda and I turned and saw, to our amazement, that Mr Bose was in the other jeep, still honking and waving madly.

'You'll have to stop for a minute, Thondupji,' Feluda said. 'That's a friend of ours.'

Thondup pulled up by the side of the road. Mr Bose came bounding out of the other jeep. 'Are you deaf or what?' he demanded. 'I yelled myself hoarse in Singtham, but none of you heard me!'

'Sorry, very sorry, Mr Bose. If we knew you were back, we wouldn't have left without you,' Feluda apologized.

'I could hardly stay on in Bombay after receiving your telegram. I've been following your jeep for miles.'

Thondup was absolutely right about the dust. Mr Bose was covered with it from head to foot, like an ash-smeared sadhubaba, thanks—no doubt—to the wheels of our own jeep.

'In your telegram you said you were suspicious about something. So where are you off to now? Why did you leave Gangtok?'

Instead of giving him a straight answer, Feluda asked, 'Do you have a lot of luggage?'

'No, just a suitcase.'

'In that case, why don't we move our own luggage into your jeep, and you can climb in with us? I'll fill you in.'

It took only a couple of minutes to transfer all the luggage. Mr Bose climbed in at the back with Mr Sarkar and Helmut, and we set off again. Feluda told Mr Bose briefly what had happened over the last two days. He even revealed that Helmut was Mr Shelvankar's son. Mr Bose frowned when Feluda finished. 'But who is this Dr Vaidya? He's bound to be a fraud. You should not have allowed him to get away, Mr Mitter. You could have—'

Feluda interrupted him. 'My suspicions fell on him when I learnt about Helmut's true identity. You are partly to blame, Mr Bose. You should have told us your partner's first wife was a German.'

'How was I to know that would matter? Besides, all I knew was that she was a foreigner. I had no idea about her nationality. Shelvankar married her about twenty-five years ago. Anyway, I just hope that Vaidya hasn't left Pemiangchi. Or our entire journey will come to nothing!'

We reached Namchi a little after ten. Here we stopped for a few minutes, to pour cold water into the engine, and hot coffee into ourselves. I could see clouds gathering in the sky, but wasn't unduly worried since I'd heard Namchi was considered by many to be the driest and cleanest place in Sikkim. Helmut was taking photographs, more out of habit than any real interest. He had hardly spoken since we left.

Now that Mr Sarkar had learnt the real reason for going to Pemiangchi, he seemed faintly uneasy; but the prospect of having an adventure was obviously just as appealing. 'With your cousin on one side, and the German Virendra on the other, I see no reason to worry,' he declared to me.

We left Namchi after ten minutes. The road went down from here, towards another river called Rangeet. This river was very different from the Tista. Its water was clear, with a greenish tinge, and it flowed with considerable force. Pools of foam formed where it struck against stones and rocks. I had never seen such a beautiful river in the hills. We had to cross another bridge and climb up the hill again to get to Pemiangchi, which was at a height of 9,000 feet.

As we wound our way up, I could see evidence of landslides almost everywhere. The thick green foliage on the hills had large gaps here and there. Great chunks of the hill had clearly slid down towards the river. Heaven knew how long it would take nature to repair the damage caused by these 'young mountains'!

We passed a gumpha on the way. Outside its entrance were a lot of flags strung from a thin rope, to ward off evil spirits. Each of them looked clean and fresh. 'Preparations for Buddha Purnima,' explained Mr Bose.

'When is it?' asked Feluda absent-mindedly.

'Buddha Purnima? Tomorrow, I think. On seventeenth April.'

'Seventeenth April . . . on the Indian calendar that would be the fourth of Baisakh . . . hmm . . . Baisakh . . . '

I looked at Feluda in surprise. Why was he suddenly so concerned about dates? And why was he looking so grim? Why was he cracking his knuckles?

There was no opportunity to ask him. Our jeep had entered a forest. The road here had been badly damaged by the recent rains. Thondup crawled along with extreme care, despite which there were a few nasty bumps. One of these resulted in Mr Sarkar banging his head against the roof of the jeep. 'Bloody hell!' I heard him mutter.

The forest grew thicker and darker. Helmut pointed at a tall tree with dark green leaves and a light bark, and said, 'That's a birch. If you ever went to England, you'd get to see a lot of them.' There were trees on both sides. The road coiled upwards like a snake. It wasn't just dark inside the forest, but also much more damp. From somewhere came the sharp cry of a strange bird.

'Th-thrilling, isn't it?' said Mr Sarkar. Suddenly, without any warning, the trees cleared. We found ourselves in front of a hillock, under an overcast sky. A few moments later, the tiled roof of a bungalow came into view, followed by the whole building.

This was the famous dak bungalow of Pemiangchi. Built during British times, it stood at a spot that was truly out of this world. Rows and rows of peaks rose behind the bungalow, their colours ranging from lush green to a hazy blue.

Our jeep stopped outside the front door. The chowkidar came out. On being told who we were, he nodded and confirmed that rooms had been booked for us.

'Is there anyone else staying here?' asked Mr Bose.

'No, sir. The bungalow's empty.'

'Empty? Why, did no one come here before us?' Feluda asked anxiously.

'Yes, but he left last night. A man with a beard, and he wore dark glasses.'

TWELVE

The chowkidar's words appeared to disappoint Helmut the most. He sat down on the grass outside, placing his camera beside him.

Mr Bose said, 'Well, there's nothing we can do immediately, can we? Let's have lunch. I'm starving.'

We went into the bungalow carrying our luggage. It was obvious that the bungalow had been built several decades ago. The wooden floor and ceiling, the wide verandas with wooden railings and old-fashioned furniture all bore evidence of an era gone by. The view from the veranda was breathtaking. If the sky wasn't cloudy, we would have been able to see Kanchenjunga, which was twenty-two miles away. There was no noise anywhere except the chirping of birds.

We crossed the veranda and went into the dining hall. Mr Bose found an easy chair and took it. He said to Feluda, 'I wasn't too sure about Vaidya before, although you did tell me you had your suspicions. But now I'm convinced he's our man. SS should never have shown him such a valuable object as that statue.'

Helmut had risen to his feet, but hadn't joined us. I could see him pacing in the veranda outside. Mr Sarkar went inside, possibly to look for a bathroom. Feluda began to inspect the other rooms in the bungalow. I sat quietly in the dining hall, feeling most depressed. Was our journey really going to turn out to be a complete waste of time?

There were two doors on one side, leading to two bedrooms. Feluda came out of one of these with a walking-stick in his hand. 'Dr Vaidya most certainly visited this place,' Feluda said, 'and he left this stick to prove it. How very strange!' Feluda's voice sounded different. I looked up quickly, but said nothing. Mr Sarkar returned, wiping his face with a handkerchief. 'What a weird place!' he exclaimed, taking the chair next to mine, yawning noisily. Feluda did not sit down. He stood before the fireplace, tapping the stick softly on the ground. His mouth was set in a grim line.

'Mr Sarkar!' called Mr Bose. 'Where are those packed lunches your hotel gave you? Let's eat.'

'No!' said Feluda, his voice sounding cold and remote. 'This is not the time to eat.'

Mr Sarkar had started to rise. He flopped back in his chair at Feluda's words. Mr Bose and I both looked at him in surprise. But Feluda's face remained without expression.

Then he sat down, lit a Charminar and inhaled deeply. 'Mr Bose,' he said conversationally, 'you know someone in Ghatshila, you said. Isn't that where you were before you caught a flight from Calcutta?'

'Yes. A nephew of mine got married.'

'You are a Hindu, aren't you, Mr Bose?'

'Why? What do you mean?'

'You heard me. What are you? A Hindu, or a Muslim, or a Christian, or what?'

'How does that—?'

'Just tell me.'

'I'm a Hindu, of course.'

'Hm.' Feluda blew out two smoke rings. One of them wafted towards Mr Bose, getting larger and larger, until it disappeared in front of his face.

'But,' Feluda frowned, 'you and I travelled together in the same plane. You had just got back from Ghatshila, hadn't you?'

'Yes, but why is that causing you such concern? I can't understand this at all, Mr Mitter. What has my nephew's wedding in Ghatshila got to do with anything?'

'It has plenty to do with things, Mr Bose. Traditionally, no Hindu would get married in the month of Chaitra. We left Calcutta on fourteenth April, which was the first of Baisakh. Your nephew's wedding took place before that, so it must have been in the preceding month, which was Chaitra. How did you allow this to happen?'

Mr Bose was in the middle of lighting a cigarette. He stopped, his hands shaking a little. 'What are you implying, Mr Mitter? Just what are you trying to say?'

Feluda looked steadily at Mr Bose, without giving him an immediate answer. Then he said, slowly and deliberately, 'I am implying a lot of things, Mr Bose. To start with, you are a liar. You never went to Ghatshila. Secondly, you betrayed someone's trust—'

'What the hell is that supposed to mean?' Mr Bose shouted.

'We have all heard how depressed Mr Shelvankar had been before he died. He had even mentioned it to Helmut, though he did not specify the reason. It is easy enough to get totally broken in spirit if one is betrayed by a person one has trusted implicitly. I believe you were that person. You were his partner, weren't you? Mr Shelvankar was a simple, straightforward man. You took full advantage of this and cheated him endlessly. But one day, he came to know of what you had done. When you realized this, you decided to get him out of the way forever. That wasn't possible in Bombay, so you had to wait until he came to Sikkim. You were not supposed to be here. But you came—possibly the next day—disguised as Dr Vaidya. Yes, *you* were Dr Vaidya! You met Shelvankar and impressed him a great deal by telling him a few things about his life that you knew already. Then you told him about the possibility of finding Virendra in a gumpha, and left with him that morning in the same jeep. On the way, you hit his head with this heavy stick. This made him unconscious, but he did not die. You went ahead with your plan, and had the jeep pushed into the gorge. The driver had, no doubt, been bribed; that must have been easy enough to do. Then you threw that stone from the hill, using the same heavy stick to dislodge it from the ground. In spite of all this, Mr Shelvankar remained alive for a few hours, long enough to mention your name. Perhaps he had recognized you at the last minute.'

'Nonsense! What utter rubbish are you talking, Mr Mitter?' shouted Mr Bose. 'Where is the proof that I am Dr Vaidya?'

In reply, Feluda asked him a strange question. 'Where is your ring, Mr Bose?'

'My ring?'

'Yes, the one with "Ma" engraved on it. There's a white mark on your finger, but you're not wearing your ring. Where did it go?'

'Oh, that . . .' Mr Bose swallowed. 'I took it off because . . . because it felt too tight.' He took the ring out of his pocket to show us he still had it with him.

'When you changed your make-up and your costume, you forgot to put it back on. I had noticed that mark that evening when you were supposed to be talking to the departed soul of Shelvankar. I found it odd then, but did not pay enough attention at the time.'

Mr Bose began to rise, but Feluda's voice rang out again, cold as steel, 'Don't try to move, Mr Bose. I haven't finished.' Mr Bose quickly sat down again, and began wiping his face. Feluda continued, 'The day after Mr Shelvankar died, Dr Vaidya said he was going to Kalimpong. He didn't. He shed his disguise, became Sasadhar Bose and returned to Calcutta. He had already sent a telegram to Shelvankar saying "Arriving Fourteenth". This upset him very much since Mr Bose wasn't supposed to be in Sikkim at all. Anyway, he came here on the fourteenth just to create an alibi for himself. Then he pretended to be greatly distressed by his partner's death and said he would go back to Bombay the next day. Again, he didn't. He remained in hiding somewhere near Gangtok. He returned as Dr Vaidya just to add to the confusion, and pretend he could speak to the dead. But by then he had come to know that I was a detective. So he tried to remove me from the scene, too, by throwing another boulder at me. He must have seen me walking towards Nathula Road, and had probably guessed what I was going to do. And it was he who had followed us to Rumtek—' Feluda was interrupted suddenly by a high-pitched wail. To my surprise, I discovered it was coming from Mr Sarkar.

'All right, Mr Sarkar,' said Feluda. 'Out with it! And I want the truth. Why did you go to the spot where the murder had taken place?'

Mr Sarkar raised his hands as though someone had shouted, 'Hands up!' Then he croaked, 'I d-didn't know, you see, how val-valuable that statue was. When they t-told me—'

'Was it you who went to the Tibetan Institute?'

'Yes. They s-said it was totally unique. So I th-thought—'

'So you thought there was no harm in stealing from a dead man if the statue was still lying at the accident site? Especially when it had once belonged to you?'

'Y-yes, something like th-that.'

'But didn't you see anyone at that particular spot?'

'No, sir.'

'All right. But it appears that someone did see you and was afraid that you had seen him. Hence the threats you received.'

'Yes, that explains it.'

'Where's the statue?'

'Statue? But I didn't find it!'

'What? You—?' Feluda was interrupted again, this time by Mr Bose. He jumped to his feet, overturning his chair, and rushed out of the room. Helmut, who was standing at the door, was knocked down by him. Since there was only one door that led to the veranda outside, and this exit was blocked for a few moments by Helmut, who had fallen to the ground, we were delayed by about ten seconds.

By the time all of us could get out, Mr Bose had climbed back into his jeep, and its engine had already roared into life. No doubt his driver had been warned and prepared for such an eventuality. His jeep made a quick about turn and began moving towards the forest. Without a word, Thondup, who was standing by our own jeep, threw himself back in it and started the engine, assuming we would want to follow Mr Bose. As it turned out, however, there was no need to do that. Feluda took out his revolver from his pocket and fired at the rear wheels of Mr Bose's jeep. The tyres burst instantly, making the jeep tilt to one side, run into a tree, and finally come to a halt. Mr Bose jumped out, and vanished among the trees. His driver came out, too, clutching the starting handle of his jeep. Feluda ignored him completely. He ran after Mr Bose, with Helmut, Mr Sarkar and me right behind him. Out of the corner of my eye, I saw Thondup pick up his own starting handle and move forward steadily, to deal with the other driver.

The four of us shot off in different directions to look for Mr Bose. I heard Helmut call out to us about ten minutes later. By the time I found him, Feluda and Mr Sarkar had joined him already. Mr Bose was standing under a large tree a few feet away. No, he wasn't just standing. He was actually hopping around, stamping his feet and wriggling in what appeared to be absolute agony.

The reason became clear as we got closer to him. He had been attacked by leeches. At least two hundred of them were clinging to his body, some on his legs, others on his neck, shoulders and elbows. Helmut pointed at a thick root that ran across the ground near the tree. Obviously, Mr Bose had stumbled against it and fallen flat on the ground.

Feluda caught him by his collar and pulled him out in the open. 'Get those sticks with the bundles of salt and tobacoo,' he said to me. 'Quick!'

We had finished eating, and were sitting on the veranda of the dak bungalow. Helmut was taking photographs of orchids. Thondup had gone and informed the police in the nearest town. Mr Bose had been handed over to them. The statue of Yamantak had been found amongst his belongings. He had forgotten to take it from Mr Shelvankar on the day of the murder. He went back later to look for it where the jeep had fallen, and found it behind a bush. As he was climbing up the hill, he saw Mr Sarkar going down, with the same purpose in mind. Fearing that he might have been seen, he started threatening and frightening Mr Sarkar.

It also turned out that Mr Bose had an accomplice in Bombay, with whom he had stayed in touch. It was this man who had answered Feluda's call, received his telegram and informed Mr Bose in Gangtok.

Having explained these details, Feluda turned to Mr Sarkar. 'You are a small-time crook yourself, aren't you? You're lucky you couldn't retrieve that statue. If you had, we'd have had to find a suitable punishment for you.'

'I've been punished adequately, believe me!' Mr Sarkar said, looking profusely apologetic. 'I found as many as three leeches in one of my socks. They must have drunk gallons of my blood. I feel quite weak, as a matter of fact.'

'I see. Anyway, I hope you'll have the sense not sell anything else that belonged to your grandfather. And look, here's your button.'

I noticed for the first time that the last button on Mr Sarkar's shirt was missing. Mr Sarkar took the button from Feluda and, after a long time, smiled his old smile.

'Th-thanks,' he said.

The Golden Fortress

ONE

Feluda stopped reading and shut his book with a bang. Then he snapped his fingers twice, yawned heavily and said, 'Geometry.'

I asked, 'Were you reading a book on geometry all this while?'

The book was covered with newspaper, so I could not see its title. All I knew was that Feluda had borrowed it from Uncle Sidhu, who was passionate about books. He bought quite a few, and took great care of them. In fact, he did not like lending his books to anyone, but Feluda was an exception. Feluda knew it, so he always put a protective cover on any book that he brought from Uncle Sidhu's house.

Feluda lit a Charminar and blew out two smoke rings, one after the other. 'There is no such thing as a book on geometry,' he told me. 'Any book may be seen as one because everything around us is related to geometry. Did you see those smoke rings? When they left my mouth, they were perfect circles. Now just think. There are circles everywhere. Look at your own body. The iris in your eye is a circle. With the help of the iris, you can look at the sun and the moon. If you think of them as flat objects, they are circles, but of course they are actually spheres—each a solid bubble. That's geometry. The planets in the solar system are orbiting the sun in elliptic curves. There's geometry again. When you spat out of the window a little while ago—you shouldn't have done that, it's most unhygienic and if you do it again, you'll get a sharp rap on the head, but anyway—that spit went out in a parabolic curve. Geometry, see? Have you ever looked at a spider's web in any detail? It starts with a simple square. Then two diagonal lines run through it and the square is divided into four triangles. After that, the spider starts weaving a spiral web from the intersecting point of those diagonal lines. That keeps growing in size, until it covers the entire square. If you think about it, your head will start reeling . . . it's something so amazing!'

It was a Sunday morning. The two of us were sitting in our living room on the ground floor. Baba had gone to visit his childhood friend, Subimal, as he did every Sunday. Feluda was seated on a sofa, his feet resting on a low table.

I was on a divan, leaning on a cushion placed against the wall. In my hand was a game. It was a maze, made of plastic. Inside the maze were tiny metal balls. Over the last half hour, I had been trying to make those metal balls slip through the various lanes in the maze and go straight to its centre. Now I realized that the game was a matter of complex geometry, too.

A Durga Puja was being held in Nihar and Pintu's house, which was near ours. Someone was playing a song over a loudspeaker— *Yeh jo muhabbat hai from the film Kati Patang*. Fine spiral grooves on a circular record. More geometry!

'Geometry applies not just to objects you can see,' Feluda continued. 'The human mind often follows geometric patterns. A simple man's mind will run along a straight line. Others who are not so simple may have minds that twist and wriggle like a snake. And the mind of a lunatic? No one can tell how that's going to run. It's a matter of the most convoluted geometry!'

Thanks to Feluda, I had come across plenty of people from every category. What kind of geometric pattern did he fall into? When I asked him, Feluda said, 'You might call me a many-pointed star.'

'And I? Am I a satellite of that star?'

'You are merely a point, something that indicates a position, but has no significance of its own.'

I like to think of myself as a satellite. The only problem is that I cannot play that role all the time. I managed to be with Feluda when we had trouble in Gangtok because that was during school holidays. Two cases had followed—one was a murder in Dhalbhoomgarh, and the other was to do with a forged will in Patna—which I missed altogether. Now my school was closed once again for Puja. I was wondering if a new case would come along. Who knew whether it really would? But then, Feluda did tell me that if one badly wants something to happen, and if one's will is strong enough, then a particular wish may well come true, more or less automatically. I quite like to think what happened that Sunday morning was simply a result of my willing it.

A song from the film Johnny Mera Naam had just started on the loudspeaker; Feluda had flicked a quantity of ash into an ashtray and picked up the Hindustan Standard; I was toying with the idea of going out, when someone rattled the knocker on our door very loudly. Baba, I knew, would not be back before twelve o'clock. This had to be someone else. I opened the door and found a simple, mild looking man, wearing a dhoti and a blue shirt.

'Does a Pradosh Mitter live in this house?' he asked, raising his voice to make himself heard. The loudspeaker was making quite a racket.

Feluda rose from the sofa and came to the door on hearing his name. 'Where have you come from?' he asked.

'All the way from Shyambazar,' the man replied.

'Please come in.'

The man stepped into the living room.

'Please sit down. I am Pradosh Mitter.'

'Oh. Oh, I see. I didn't know . . . I mean, I didn't realize you were so young!' The man sat down on a chair next to the sofa, looking visibly impressed. But the smile on his face disappeared almost at once.

'What can I do for you?' Feluda asked.

The man cleared his throat. 'I have heard a lot about you from Kailash Chowdhury. He seems to think very highly of you. He . . . he is one of my customers, you see. My name is Sudhir Dhar. I have a book shop in College Street—Dhar & Co. You may have seen it.'

Feluda nodded briefly, before saying to me, 'Topshe, please shut that window.'

I shut the window that overlooked the street. That reduced the noise, and Mr Dhar could then speak normally.

'About a week ago, there was a press report about my son. Did you . . .?'

'Press report? What did it say?'

'About his being a jatismar . . . I mean . . .'

'About a boy called Mukul?'

'Yes.'

'So the report's true?'

'You see, from the way he speaks, the kind of things he says, it does seem as if . . .' Mr Dhar broke off.

I knew what the word jatismar meant. A person who can recall events from a previous life is called a jatismar. Apparently, there are people who get periodic flashes of memory related to a life that they had lived long before they were born in their present incarnation. Mind you, even Feluda does not know whether or not there is any truth behind this whole business.

Feluda picked up the packet of Charminar and offered it to Mr Dhar, who smiled and shook his head. Then he said, 'Perhaps you remember what my son told the reporter? He's only eight, but he described a place which he is supposed to have seen. Yet I am sure nobody from ray family—not even my forefathers—has been there, let alone my son. We are very ordinary people, you see. I only have that shop, and the book trade these days is . . .'

'Doesn't your son talk of a fortress?' Feluda interrupted him.

'Yes, that's right. A golden fortress. There was a cannon on its roof, a lot of fighting, and several people were killed . . . my son says he has seen it all. He used to wear a turban and ride a camel on the sand. He mentions sand quite frequently. And animals—camels, elephants and horses. Oh, and peacocks. There is a mark near his elbow. We always thought it was a birthmark, but he says he was once attacked by a peacock, and the mark shows where the bird pecked him.'

'Has he ever mentioned exactly where he used to live?'

'No, but he does say that he could see this golden fortress from his house. Sometimes he draws funny squiggles with a pencil and says, "Look, that's my house!" If you look at it, well yes, it does appear to be a house.'

'Could he not have seen all that in a book? I mean, you have a book shop, don't you? So maybe he saw pictures of this place in a book?'

'Yes, that's a possibility. But other children also look at pictures in books; they don't talk incessantly about what they've seen, do they? If you'd seen my son, you'd know what I mean. To tell you the truth, his mind seems to be elsewhere. His own family—his parents, brothers and sisters, other relatives—no one seems to matter to him. In fact, he doesn't even look at us when he talks.'

'When did this whole thing start?'

'About two months ago. It started with those pictures, you see. One day, when I got back home from the shop—it had rained a lot that day—my son began showing me the pictures he had drawn. At first, I paid him no attention. Every child likes talking about imaginary lands, and he was chattering away. So I ignored him. It was my wife who first noticed that there was something odd. Then we listened more carefully to his words, and watched his behaviour over the next few weeks . . . then, one of my other customers, Dr Hemanga Hajra . . . have you heard of him?'

'Yes, yes. He's a parapsychologist, isn't he? I've certainly heard of him. But didn't that press report say he was going to travel somewhere with your son?'

'Not going to. Has gone. They've already left. Dr Hajra came to my house three times. He thought Mukul was talking of Rajasthan. So I said, yes, that could be true. Then, in the end, Dr Hajra told me he was doing research on this whole business of recalling a previous life. He wanted to take Mukul to Rajputana. He thought that if Mukul could actually go back to the same place, he might remember several other things, and that would help his research. So he said he'd pay for everything, and take great care of my son, I wouldn't have to worry.'

'And then?' Feluda leant forward. His voice had changed. Clearly, he was finding all this quite interesting.

'Then they left, that's all.'

'Didn't Mukul mind leaving home?'

Mr Dhar smiled a little wanly. 'Mind? Oh no. He was ready to go with Dr Hajra the minute he offered to show him the golden fortress. My son, you see, is not like other children. He's very different. We find him awake at three in the morning sometimes. He'd be humming a song. Not any film song, mind you. Something like a folk song, like the kind of music you hear in villages—but certainly it doesn't come from any village in Bengal. That much I can tell you. I know a little about music . . . I play the harmonium, you see.'

Mr Dhar had told us a lot about his son. But he had said nothing about why he had come to see Feluda, or why he needed to consult a detective. Feluda's next question made the whole conversation take a different turn.

'Didn't your son say something about hidden treasure?'

Mr Dhar began to look even more depressed. 'That is the biggest problem!' he sighed. 'He told me about it some time ago, but when he mentioned it to the reporter . . . well, that proved disastrous!'

'Why do you say that?' Feluda asked. Then he called out to our cook Srinath, and told him to bring tea.

'Let me explain,' Mr Dhar continued. 'Dr Hajra left for Rajasthan with Mukul yesterday morning by the Toofan Express. And . . .'

'Do you know where in Rajasthan he'll go?' Feluda interrupted.

'Jodhpur, so he said. Since Mukul had mentioned sand, he said he'd start with the northwest. Anyway, what happened was that yesterday evening, someone kidnapped a boy from our area. He was about Mukul's age.'

'And you think that boy was kidnapped by mistake? Because they thought he was Mukul?'

'Yes, there is no question about that. My son and this other boy happen to look similar. The other boy is Shivratan Mukherjee's grandson. Mr Mukherjee is one of our neighbours, he's a solicitor. The boy is called Neelu. They were naturally most upset, had to call the police, and there was an enormous fuss, as you can imagine. But now that they've got him back, things have calmed down.'

'Got him back? Already?'

'Early this morning. But how does that make any difference, tell me? I am going mad with anxiety, I tell you. Those kidnappers obviously realized they got the wrong boy. And Neelu has told them that Mukul has gone to Jodhpur. Suppose they chase Mukul all the way to Jodhpur just to lay their hands on that treasure?'

Feluda did not reply. He was lost in thought; four deep lines had appeared on his forehead. My heart was beating faster. Could it mean that we'd go to Rajasthan during these Puja holidays? Jodhpur, Chittor, Udaipur . . . I had only heard these names and read about these places in history books—and, of course, in Raj Kahini by Abanindranath Tagore. Uncle Naresh had given me a copy on my birthday.

Srinath came in with the tea. He placed the tray on a table. Feluda offered a cup to Mr Dhar.

'From what I heard about you from Kailash Chowdhury,' Mr Dhar began hesitantly, 'it appears that you were most . . . er . . . I mean . . . anyway, I was just wondering if you might be able to go to Rajasthan. If you found that Dr Hajra and Mukul were safe, that's well and good. But suppose they were in danger? Suppose you saw something odd? I mean, I've heard that you're brave, you'd tackle criminals. I am only an ordinary man, Mr Mitter. Perhaps it is impertinent of me to have come to you. But . . . if you did decide to go, I would certainly pay for your travel.'

Feluda continued to frown. After a minute's silence, he said, 'I shall let you know tomorrow what I decide. I assume you have got a photo of your son in your house? The one printed in the newspaper was not very clear.'

Mr Dhar took a long sip of his tea. 'My cousin is fond of photography. He took some photos of Mukul. My wife will have them.'

'Very well.'

Mr Dhar finished his tea, put the cup down on a table and rose. 'I have a telephone in my shop, 345116. I am usually in the shop from ten o'clock.'

'Where do you live?'

'Mechhobazar. 7 Mechhobazar Street. My house is on the main road.'

I went with Mr Dhar to see him out. When he'd gone, I shut the front door and returned to the living room. 'There's one word that I didn't quite understand,' I said to Feluda.

'You mean parapsychologist?'

'Yes.'

'Those who study certain hazy aspects of the human mind are called parapsychologists. Take telepathy, for instance. You can actually get into the mind of another person and read their thoughts. Or, if your own mind is strong enough, you can influence other people's thoughts, even change them totally. Strange things happen sometimes. Suppose you were sitting here, thinking of an old friend. Suddenly, out of the blue, the same friend rang you. A parapsychologist would tell you that there was nothing sudden or unexpected about it. If your friend rang you, it was because of strong telepathy. But there is more—like extra-sensory perception, or ESP for short. It can warn you about future events. Or, for that matter, take this business of recalling a previous life. All these could be subjects a parapsychologist might wish to study.'

'Is this Hemanga Hajra a famous parapsychologist?'

'Yes, one of the best known. He's been abroad, given lectures, and I think even formed a society.'

'Do you believe in such things?'

'What I believe is simply that it is foolish to accept or reject anything without sufficient evidence. If you don't keep an open mind, you're a fool. One look at history would show you plenty of examples of such stupidity. There was a time when some people thought that the earth was flat. Did you know that? They also thought that the earth came to an end at one particular point, and you couldn't travel beyond that. But when the navigator Magellan began his journey round the world from one place and returned to the same spot, all those who thought the earth was flat began scratching their heads. Then there have been people who thought the earth was fixed, and other planets, even the sun, moved around it. Some thought the sky was like a huge bowl turned upside down. All the stars were fixed on it like jewels, they thought. It was Copernicus who proved that the sun remained stationary, and the earth and other planets in the solar system orbited the sun. But Copernicus thought this movement followed a circular motion. Then Kepler came along and proved that everything moved in elliptic curves. After that, Galileo . . . but anyway, there's no point in talking about all that. Your mind is too young, and too immature to grasp such things!'

Clever detective though he was, Feluda did not seem to realize one simple thing. None of his jibes and jeers was going to spoil my excitement because my heart was already telling me that the holidays were going to be spent in Rajasthan. We would see a new place, and unravel a new mystery. What remained to be tested was the strength of my own telepathy.

TWO

Feluda had told Mr Dhar that he would take a day to make up his mind. But within an hour of Mr Dhar's departure, he decided that he would go to Rajasthan. When he told me about it, I asked, 'I am going with you, aren't I?'

'If you can name five places in Rajasthan that have forts—all within a minute—then you might stand a chance.'

'Jodhpur, Jaipur, Chittor, Bikaner and . . . and . . . Bundi!'

Feluda glanced at his watch and sprang to his feet. It took him exactly three and a half minutes to change from a kurta pyjama into a shirt and trousers. 'It's Sunday, so Fairlie Place will stay open till twelve o'clock. Let me go quickly and make our reservations,' he said.

It was one o'clock by the time Feluda returned. The first thing he did upon his return was to look up Hemanga Hajra's phone number in the directory and ring him. When I asked him why he was calling someone who was out of town, Feluda said, 'I needed proof that what Mr Dhar told us was true.'

'And did you get it?'

'Yes.'

After lunch, Feluda spent the whole afternoon stretched on his bed, a pillow tucked under his chest, going through five different books. Two of them were Pelican books on parapsychology. Feluda said he had borrowed them from a friend. Of the others, one was Todd's book on Rajasthan, the second was called A Guide to India, Pakistan, Burma and Ceylon, and the third was a book on Indian history, but I can't remember who wrote it.

In the evening, when we'd had our tea, Feluda said, 'Get ready, we're going out. We need to visit Mr Dhar.'

By this time, I had told Baba about our plans. He was very pleased to hear that we were going to Rajasthan. He had been there twice in his childhood with my grandfather. 'Don't miss Chittor,' he told me. 'The fort in Chittor is quite awe-inspiring. It's easy enough to guess what made the Rajputs such brave warriors.'

We arrived at Mr Dhar's house at around half past six. When he heard that Feluda was prepared to go to Rajasthan, Mr Dhar looked both relieved and grateful. 'I do not know how to thank you!' he exclaimed.

'It isn't yet time to start thanking me, Mr Dhar. You must assume that we are going purely as tourists, not because you asked us to. Anyway, we have very little time. There are two things we need. One is a photo of your son. The other is a chat with Neelu, that boy who was kidnapped.'

'Let me see what I can do. Usually, Neelu is never at home in the evenings, especially now that Puja is round the corner. But I don't think that today he'll be allowed to go out on his own. Wait, I'll get that photo.'

Shivratan Mukherjee, the solicitor, lived only three houses away, on the same side of the road. We found him at home, having a cup of tea in his living room with another gentleman. Mr Mukherjee's visitor seemed to have a skin disease—there were white patches on his face. When Mr Dhar explained why we were there, Mr Mukherjee remarked, 'My grandson seems to have become quite famous, thanks to your son! Please sit down. Manohar!'

Manohar turned out to be his servant. 'Bring more tea,' Mr Mukherjee told him, 'and see if you can find Neelu. Tell him I've sent for him.'

We found ourselves three chairs placed by the side of a large table. The walls on both sides were covered by very tall bookcases, almost reaching the ceiling. They were crammed with fat tomes. Feluda had once told me that no one needed to consult books as much as a lawyer.

While we were waiting for Neelu, I had a look at Mukul's photo. It had been taken on their roof. The little boy was standing in the sun, frowning straight at the camera. There was no smile on his face.

Mr Mukherjee said, 'We asked Neelu a lot of questions, too. At first, he was in such a state of shock that he wasn't talking at all. Now he appears more normal.'

'Have the police been told?' Feluda asked.

'Yes, we told the police when he went missing. But he came back before the police could do anything.'

The servant returned with Neelu. Mr Dhar was right. Neelu did bear a strong resemblance to the boy in the photo. He looked at us suspiciously. Clearly, he had not yet got over his ordeal.

Suddenly, Feluda asked him, 'Did you hurt your hand, Neelu?'

Mr Mukherjee opened his mouth to say something, but Feluda made a gesture and stopped him. Neelu answered the question himself. 'When they pulled my hand, it burned a lot.'

There was a cut over his wrist, clearly visible.

'They? You mean there was more than one person?'

'One man covered my eyes and my mouth. Then he picked me up and put me in a car. Another man drove the car. I felt very scared.'

'So would I,' Feluda told him. 'In fact, I would have felt much more scared than you. You are very brave. When they caught you, what were you doing?'

'I was going to Moti's house. They have a Durga Puja in their house. I wanted to see the idol. Moti is in my class.'

'Was it very quiet in the streets? Not many people about?'

'The day before yesterday,' Mr Mukherjee informed us, 'we had some trouble here. A bomb went off. So, since last evening, there have been fewer people out in the streets.'

Feluda nodded and said, 'Hmm.' Then he turned to Neelu once more. 'Where did they take you?'

'I don't know. They tied a cloth over my eyes. The car drove on and on.'

'And then?'

'Then they made me sit in a chair. One of them said, "Which school do you go to?" I told him. Then he said, "We're going to ask you a few questions. Tell us exactly what you know. If you do, we'll drop you in front of your school. Can you go home from there?" So I said, "Yes." Then I said, "You must hurry, my mother will scold me if I get late!" Then he said, "Where is the golden fortress?" I said, "I don't know, and nor does Mukul. He only knows there's a fort, that's all." Then the two men began talking with each other in English. I heard them say, "Mistake!" One man said to me, "What's

your name?" I said, "Mukul's my friend, but he's gone to Rajasthan."
He said, "Do you know where in Rajasthan he's gone?" I told him,
"Jaipur!"'

'You said Jaipur?' Feluda asked him.

'N-no, no. Jodhpur. Yes, that's what I said. Jodhpur.'

Neelu stopped. All of us remained silent. The servant had placed
tea and sweets before us, but no one seemed interested in them.

'Can you think of anything else?' Feluda prompted Neelu.

Neelu thought for a minute. Then he said, 'One of them was
smoking a cigarette. No, no, it was a cigar.'

'Do you know how a cigar smells?'

'Yes, my uncle smokes them.'

'All right. Where did you sleep at night?'

'I don't know.'

'You don't know? What do you mean?'

'Well, they said, "Here's some milk. Drink it." Then someone
handed me a very heavy glass. I drank the milk, then fell asleep. I
was still sitting in the chair!'

'And then? When you woke up?'

Neelu looked uncertainly at his grandfather. Mr Mukherjee smiled.
'He woke up only after he was brought home,' he explained. 'They
left him outside his school, possibly very early this morning. He was
still asleep. The man who delivers our newspaper every day happened
to be passing by a little later, and saw him. It was he who came and
told us. Then I went with my son and brought him back. Our doctor
has seen him. He said Neelu was given a sleeping draught—probably
a heavier dose than what might normally be given to a child.'

Feluda looked grave. He picked up his cup of tea and muttered
under his breath, 'Scoundrels!' Then, he patted Neelu's back and
said, 'Thank you, Neelu Babu. You may go now.'

When we had said goodbye to Mr Mukherjee and were out in the
street once more, Mr Dhar asked, 'Do you think there's reason for
concern?'

'What I can see is that some greedy and reckless people have
become unduly curious about your son. What's difficult to say is
whether they'll really go all the way to Rajasthan. By the way, I
think you should write to Dr Hajra, just to introduce me. After all,
he doesn't know me. So if I can show him your letter, it will help.'

Mr Dhar wrote the letter, handed it to Feluda and offered to pay
for our travel once more. Feluda paid no attention. As we approached

our bus stop, Mr Dhar said, 'Please let me know, sir, when you get there and find them. I'll be ever so worried. Dr Hajra has promised to write as well. But even if he doesn't, you must . . . at least one letter . . .!'

On reaching home, Feluda took out his famous blue notebook (volume six) before either of us began packing. Then he sat down on his bed and said, 'Let's get some dates sorted out. When did Dr Hajra leave with Mukul to go to Rajasthan?'

'Yesterday, 9 October.'

'When was Neelu kidnapped?'

'Yesterday, in the evening.'

'And he returned this morning, that's 10 October. We are leaving tomorrow morning, the 11th. We'll reach Agra on the 12th. Then we'll have to change trains there, and catch one in the evening that goes to Bandikui. Leave Bandikui at midnight, and reach Marwar the same day . . . that'll be the 13th evening . . . 13th . . . 13th . . .'.

Feluda continued to mutter and did some funny calculations. Then he said, 'Geometry. Even here you'll find geometry. A single point . . . and there are various lines converging to meet that point. Geometry!'

THREE

Half an hour ago, we boarded a train at the Agra Fort station to go to Bandikui. We had about three hours to kill in Agra. So we went to see the Taj Mahal again—after ten years—and Feluda gave me a short lecture on the geometry of the building.

Yesterday, before leaving Calcutta, we had to attend to some important business. Perhaps I should mention it here. Since the Toofan Express left at 9.30 in the morning, we were both up quite early. At around six o'clock, after we'd had tea, Feluda said, 'We ought to visit Uncle Sidhu before we go. If he can give us some information, it will really help.'

Uncle Sidhu lives in Sardar Shankar Road, which is only five minutes from our Tara Road. Uncle Sidhu is a strange character. He spent most of his life doing various kinds of businesses, earning a lot of money, and then losing much of it. Now he has retired. His main passion is books. He buys them in large numbers, and spends some of his time on reading, and the rest on playing chess all by himself. Sometimes, he consults a book on chess in between making moves.

His other passion is food—or rather, experimenting with food. He likes mixing one item with another. According to him, yoghurt mixed with an omelette tastes like ambrosia. To tell the truth, he is not related to us. He used to live next door to us back in our ancestral village (which I have never seen). So he's like an elder brother to my father, and we call him 'uncle'.

When we reached his house, he was seated on a low stool, blocking the entrance through his front door, and having his hair cut by his barber, although he has no hair except for some around the back of his head. Upon seeing us, he moved his stool a little and allowed us to go through. 'Make yourselves comfortable,' he said. 'Yell for Narayan, he'll give you some tea.'

Uncle Sidhu's room was very simply furnished. There was only a divan, two chairs and three very large bookcases. Books covered half the divan. We knew that the little empty space on it was where Uncle Sidhu liked to sit, so we took the two chairs. Feluda had remembered to bring the book he'd borrowed, which was still covered with newspaper. He slipped it back into an empty slot on a shelf.

The barber continued to work on Uncle Sidhu's hair. 'Felu,' said Uncle Sidhu, 'you are a detective. I hope you've read up on the history of criminal investigation? It doesn't matter what you specialize in. If you know something about the history of your profession, you'll gain more confidence and find your work much more interesting.'

'Yes, of course,' Feluda replied politely.

'Who was the first to discover the technique of identifying a criminal through his fingerprints? Can you tell me?'

Feluda winked at me and said, 'I can't remember. I did read about it somewhere, but now . . .'.

I could tell that Feluda knew the answer all right, but was pretending that he didn't, just to please Uncle Sidhu.

'Hmm. Most people would immediately tell you that it was Alphonse Bertillon. But that's wrong. The correct name is Juan Vucatich. Remember that. He was from Argentina. He was the first to emphasize the importance of thumbprints. Then he divided those prints into four categories. A few years later, Henry from England strengthened the system.'

Feluda glanced at his watch and decided to come straight to the point. 'You may have heard of Dr Hemanga Hajra, the parapsychologist—?'

'Certainly,' said Uncle Sidhu, 'Why, I saw his name in the papers only the other day! What's he done? Something fishy? But he's not the kind of man to get mixed up in funny business. On the contrary, he has exposed others . . . cheats and frauds.'

'Really?' Feluda looked up. We were about to hear an interesting story.

'Yes, don't you know about it? It happened about four years ago, and was reported in the press. A Bengali gentleman—no, I should not call him a gentleman, he was actually a scoundrel—started a centre for spiritual healing in Chicago. Bang in the city centre. Clients poured in every day. The Americans have plenty of money, and are easily impressed by new ideas. This Bengali claimed that he could use hypnotism and cure even the most complex diseases. The same sort of thing that Anton Mesmer did in Europe in the eighteenth century. Perhaps the Bengali managed to cure a couple of patients— that's not unusual; a few stray cases would be successful. But, around the same time, Hajra arrived in Chicago on a lecture tour. He went to see things for himself, and caught the man out. Oh God, it was a scandal! In the end, the American government forced him to leave the country. Yes, yes . . . I can remember his name now . . . he called himself Bhavananda. That man, Hajra, though, is a solid character. At least, that's the impression one gets from his articles. I've got two of them. See in the right hand corner of that bookcase on your left. You'll find three journals of the Parapsychological Society.'

Feluda borrowed all three journals. Now, sitting on the train, he was leafing through them. I was looking out of the window and watching the scenery. A little while ago, we had left Uttar Pradesh and entered Rajasthan.

'The sun here has a different brilliance. No wonder the men are so powerful!'

These words in Bengali came from the bench opposite us. It was a four-berth compartment, and there were four passengers. The man who had spoken those words looked perfectly meek and mild, was very thin and probably shorter than me by at least two inches. And I was only fifteen, so it was likely that I'd grow taller with time. This man was at least thirty-five; there was no chance that his height would ever change. As he was dressed in a bush shirt and trousers, I had been unable to guess from his clothes that he was another Bengali.

He glanced at Feluda, smiled and said, 'I've been listening to your conversation for a long time. I'm lucky to have found fellow Bengalis so far away from home. In fact, I'd assumed that for a whole month I'd be forced to boycott my mother tongue!'

Feluda asked, possibly purely out of politeness, 'Are you going far?

'Up to Jodhpur. Then I'll decide where else I might go. What about yourselves?'

'We are going to Jodhpur, too.'

'Oh, wonderful. Are you also a writer?'

'Oh no,' Feluda smiled, 'I am only a reader. Do you write?'

'Are you familiar with the name of Jatayu?'

'Jatayu?' I asked. 'The writer of all those thrillers?' I had read one or two of his books—Shivers in the Sahara and The Ferocious Foe. I had borrowed them from our school library.

'You are Jatayu?' Feluda asked.

'Yes, sir,' the man flashed his teeth, his head bent in a bow. 'I am Jatayu. At your service. I write under that pseudonym. Namaskar.'

'Namaskar. My name is Pradosh Mitter. And this is Sreeman Tapeshranjan.'

How could Feluda keep a straight face? I could feel laughter bubbling up inside me, threatening to burst forth. This was Jatayu? And I used to think a writer who could write such tales would have looks to match—perhaps even James Bond would be put in the shade!

'My real name is Lalmohan Ganguli. But please don't tell anyone. A pseudonym—like a disguise—must never be revealed. I mean, if it is, then it loses its impact, don't you think?'

We had bought a packet of sweet gulabi rewri in Agra. Feluda offered the packet to Jatayu and said, 'You seem to have been on the move for some time!'

'Yes, that's . . .' Jatayu picked up a rewri and suddenly broke off, looking a bit confused. Then he threw a startled glance at Feluda and asked, 'How can you tell?'

Feluda smiled. 'The strap on your wristwatch slips at times. When it does, it exposes the only part of your arm that isn't sunburnt.'

Jatayu's eyes grew round. 'Oh my God, what terrific powers of observation you have got! Yes, you're right. I left home about ten days ago, and travelled to Delhi, Agra and Fatehpur Sikri. So far, I've only written about adventures in foreign lands.

'I live in Bhadreshwar. So I thought I should travel a bit, see new places, it would help me in my writing. Besides, these areas are much better suited to adventure stories, aren't they? Look at those barren hills, rising high like biceps and triceps. Our Bengal has no muscles— except, of course, for the Himalayas. You can't have a successful adventure on the plains!'

The three of us continued to eat the rewri. Then I caught Jatayu casting sidelong glances at Feluda. Finally, he asked, 'What is your height? Please don't mind my asking.'

'Nearly six feet,' Feluda replied.

'Oh, that's a very good height, the same as my hero's. Prakhar Rudra—you do know his name, don't you? Prakhar is a Russian name, but it suits a Bengali, too, don't you think? The thing is, you see, I've got my hero to be everything I could never be myself. God knows I tried hard enough. When I was in college, I saw advertisements of Charles Atlas in British magazines. There he was, standing proudly, his chest and all his muscles expanded, his hands on his waist. He looked like a lion! There was not even an ounce of fat on his body. His muscles rippled like waves, from head to toe. And the advertisement said, "If you follow my system, you will look like me within a month!" Well, that may be true of Europeans. In Bengal, that kind of thing is impossible. My father was well off, so I wasted some of his money, sent for their lessons and followed them religiously.

'Nothing happened. I remained just the same. Then an uncle said, "Try swinging from a curtain rod. You'll grow taller in a month." A month? For several months, I swung from a rod until, one day, it came off and I fell down. That dislocated my knee, but my height remained stuck at five feet and three-and-half inches. That told me plainly that even if I were pulled in different directions by two teams— as they do in a tug-of-war—I would never grow any taller. So, eventually, I thought enough was enough. There was no point in thinking about the muscles in my body. I decided to pay more attention to the muscles in my brain. And increase my mental height. I began writing thrillers. But I knew Lalmohan Ganguli was not a name that would help sell books. So I took a pseudonym. Jatayu. A fighter. Just think of the fight he put up with Ravan!'

Although our train was called a 'fast passenger', it was stopping at so many stations that it was not able to run for more than twenty minutes at a stretch. Feluda left the journals on parapsychology and began reading a book on Rajasthan. It had pictures of all the forts.

Feluda was looking at those very carefully and reading the descriptions.

On the upper berth opposite us was a man whose moustache and clothes proclaimed clearly that he was not a Bengali. He was eating oranges—one after another—and collecting the peel and other debris on a sheet of a Urdu newspaper spread in front of him.

Feluda was marking a few places in his book with a blue pencil, when Lalmohan Babu said, 'May I ask you something? Are you a detective?'

'Why do you ask?'

'No, I mean . . . you could tell so easily about my travelling!'

'Well, I am interested in that kind of thing.'

'Good. You're also going to Jodhpur, didn't you say?'

'Yes.'

'In connection with a mystery? If so, I am going to join you . . . I mean, if you don't mind, that is. I'll never get such a chance again.'

'I hope you wouldn't object to riding a camel?'

'A camel? Oh my God!' Lalmohan Babu's eyes began to glint. 'Ship of the desert! It's always been my dream. I have written about Bedouins in one of my novels—Bloodbath in Arabia. And I've mentioned camels in Shivers in the Sahara. It's a fascinating creature. Just picture the scene. An entire row of camels, travelling through an ocean of sand, mile after mile, carrying their own water supply in their intestines. How romantic—oh!'

'Er . . . when you wrote your novel, did you mention that bit about the intestines?'

Lalmohan Babu began looking uncertain. 'Why, is that incorrect?'

Feluda nodded. 'Yes. You see, the source of the water is actually in a camel's hump. The hump is really an accumulation of fat. A camel can oxidize that fat and turn it into water. So it can survive without drinking any water for ten to fifteen days. But, once they do find water, camels have been known to drink as much as twenty-five gallons at one go.'

'Thank goodness you told me all this,' said Lalmohan Babu. 'I must correct that mistake in the next edition.'

FOUR

The train was slow, but at least it wasn't running significantly late.

When one has to take connecting trains, it can cause great problems if the first train is delayed.

We saw the first peacocks on reaching Bharatpur. Opposite our platform, there were three of them roaming freely on the tracks. Feluda said to me, 'You will find that peacocks and parrots are as common here as crows and sparrows in Calcutta.'

All the men we saw had turbans on their heads and sideburns on their cheeks—the size of which seemed to be getting larger as we travelled. They were all Rajasthanis, wearing short dhotis which reached their knees, and shirts with buttons on one side. On their feet were heavy naagras. Most men were carrying stout sticks in their hands.

We went to the refreshment room in the station in Bandikui to have dinner. Tucking into his roti and meat curry, Lalmohan Babu remarked, 'See all these men? There's a high probability that some of them are bandits. The Aravalli Hills act as a den for bandits—you know that, don't you? And I'm sure I don't have to tell you how powerful they are. When they are thrown into prison, they can push apart the iron bars on their windows with their bare hands, and escape through the gap!'

'Yes, I know,' Feluda replied. 'And do you know how they punish those who cross them?'

'They're killed, surely?'

'No. That's the beauty of it. If a bandit is annoyed with someone, he will hunt him down—no matter where that person is hiding—and then chop his nose off with a sword. That's all.'

Lalmohan Babu had just picked up a piece of meat. He forgot to put it in his mouth. 'Chop off his nose?' he asked.

'Yes, so I've heard.'

'It sounds most barbaric! Like something straight out of the dark ages. How terrible!'

We caught a train to Marwar in the middle of the night. It did involve scrambling in the dark, but we found enough room for ourselves and slept well.

In the morning, when I woke up, I glanced out of the window and saw an old fort in the distance, on top of a hill. Only a minute later, the train pulled into a station called Kisangarh.

'If you see the word "garh" attached to the name of a place, you may assume that somewhere in that area there is a fort on a hilltop,' Feluda said.

We got down on the platform and had tea. The earthen pots in which the tea was served were much larger and stronger than the pots used in Bengal. Even the tea tasted different. Feluda thought camel's milk had been used. Perhaps that was why Lalmohan Babu ordered a second pot when he finished the first.

When I'd finished mine, I found a tap on the platform and quickly brushed my teeth. Then I splashed cold water on my face and returned to our compartment.

There was a Rajasthani man sitting at one end of Lalmohan Babu's bench. On his head was a huge turban. One leg was folded up on the bench, and he was resting his chin on his raised knee. He had wrapped a shawl around himself, hiding most of his face. But I could see the colour of his shirt through the shawl. It was bright red.

Lalmohan Babu saw the man and promptly abandoned his bench and moved to ours. He tried to huddle in one corner. Feluda said, 'Why don't you two sit more comfortably?' He moved across to the other bench and sat down beside the Rajasthani.

I began to peer more closely at the man's turban. Heaven knew how many twists and turns the fabric had made before it was finally wound so tightly round his head. Lalmohan Babu addressed Feluda and said softly, 'Powerfully suspicious. He is dressed as an ordinary villager, but how come he is in a first-class compartment? Look at that bundle. God knows if it's packed with diamonds and other precious stones.'

The bundle was placed next to the man. Lalmohan Babu's comment made Feluda smile, but he said nothing.

The train started. Feluda took out the book on Rajasthan from his shoulder bag. I took out Newman's Bradshaw timetable and began looking up the stations we would stop at. Each place had a strange name: Galota, Tilonia, Makrera, Vesana, Sendra. Where had these names come from? Feluda had told me once that a lot of local history was always hidden in the name given to a place. But who was going to look for the history behind these names?

The train continued to chug on its way. Suddenly, I could feel someone tugging at my shirt. I turned to find that Lalmohan Babu had gone visibly pale. When he caught my eye, he swallowed and whispered, 'Blood!'

Blood? What was the man talking about?

Lalmohan Babu's eyes turned to the Rajasthani. The latter was fast asleep. His head was flung back, his mouth slightly open. My eyes fell on the foot on the bench. The skin around the big toe was badly grazed. It had obviously been bleeding, but now the blood had dried. Then I realized something else. The dark stains on his clothes, which appeared to be mud stains, were, in fact, patches of dried blood.

I looked quickly at Feluda. He was reading his book, quite unconcerned. Lalmohan Babu found his nonchalance too much to bear. He spoke again, in the same choked voice, 'Mr Mitter, suspicious blood marks on our new co-passenger!'

Feluda looked up, glanced once at the Rajasthani and said, 'Probably caused by bugs.'

The thought that the blood was simply the result of bites from bed bugs made Lalmohan Babu look like a pricked balloon. Even so, he could not relax. He continued to sit stiffly and frown and cast the Rajasthani sidelong glances from time to time.

The train reached Marwar Junction at half past two. We had lunch in the refreshment room, and spent almost an hour walking about on the platform. When we climbed into another train at half past three to go to Jodhpur, there was no sign of that Rajasthani wearing a red shirt.

Our journey to Jodhpur lasted for two-and-a-half hours. On the way, we saw several groups of camels. Each time that happened, Lalmohan Babu grew most excited. By the time we reached Jodhpur, it was ten past six. Our train was delayed by twenty minutes. If we were still in Calcutta, the sun would have set by now, but as we were in the western part of the country, it was still shining brightly.

We had booked rooms at the Circuit House. Lalmohan Babu said he would stay at the New Bombay Lodge. 'I'll join you early tomorrow morning, we can all go together to see the fort,' he said and went off towards the tongas that were standing in a row.

We found ourselves a taxi and left the station. The Circuit House wasn't far, we were told. As we drove through the streets, I noticed a huge wall—visible through the gaps between houses—that seemed as high as a two-storeyed house. There was a time, Feluda told me, when the whole of Jodhpur was surrounded by that wall. There were gates in seven different places. If they heard of anyone coming to attack Jodhpur, all seven gates were closed.

Our car went round a bend. Feluda said at once, 'Look, on your left!'

In the far distance, high above all the buildings in the city, stood a sprawling, sombre-looking fort—the famous fort of Jodhpur. Its rulers had once fought for the Mughals.

I was still wondering how soon I'd get to see the fort at close quarters, when we reached the Circuit House. Our taxi passed through the gate, drove up the driveway, past a garden, and stopped under a portico. We got out, collected our luggage and paid the driver.

A gentleman emerged from the building and asked us if we were from Calcutta, and whether Feluda was called Pradosh Mitter.

'Yes, that's right,' Feluda acknowledged.

'There is a double room booked in your name on the ground floor,' the man replied.

We were handed the Visitors' Book to sign. Only a few lines above our own names, we saw two entries: Dr H.B. Hajra and Master M. Dhar.

The Circuit House was built on a simple plan. There was a large open space as one entered. To its left were the reception and the manager's room. In front of it was a staircase going up to the first floor, and on both sides, there were wide corridors along which stood rows of rooms. There were wicker chairs in the corridors.

A bearer came and picked up our luggage, and we followed him down the right-hand corridor to find room number 3. A middle-aged man, sporting an impressive moustache, was seated on one of the wicker chairs, chatting with a man in a Rajasthani cap. As we walked past them, the first man said, 'Are you Bengalis?' Feluda smiled and said, 'Yes.' We were then shown into our room.

It was quite spacious. There were twin beds, each with a mosquito net. Set apart, at one end, was a two-seater sofa, a pair of easy chairs, and a round table with an ashtray on it. There was also a dressing table, wardrobes and bedside tables. Lamps, glasses and flasks of water were placed upon the tables. The door to the attached bathroom was to the left.

Feluda asked the bearer to bring us some tea and switched the fan on. 'Did you see those two names?' he asked, sitting down on the sofa.

'Yes, but I hope that man with the thick moustache isn't Dr Hajra!' I replied.

'Why? What if he is? Why should it matter?'

I couldn't immediately think of a good reason. Feluda saw me hesitate and said, 'You didn't like the man, did you? You want Dr

Hajra to be a pleasant, cheerful and friendly man. Right?'

Yes, Feluda was absolutely right. The man we just met appeared kind of crafty. Besides, he was probably quite tall and hefty. That was not how I would picture a doctor.

The tea arrived just as Feluda finished a cigarette. The bearer placed the tray on the table and left. Someone knocked on our door almost at once. 'Come in!' said Feluda in a grand manner, sounding like an Englishman. The man with the moustache moved aside the curtain and came in.

'I am not disturbing you, am I?' he said.

'No, not at all. Please sit down. Would you like a cup of tea?'

'No, thanks. I've just had some. Frankly speaking, the tea here isn't all that good. But then, that's true of most places. India is the land of tea, yet how many hotels, or dak bungalows, or circuit houses serve good quality tea, tell me? But if you go abroad, it's a different story. Even in a place like Albania, I have had very good tea—would you believe it? First-class Darjeeling tea, it was. And if you went to Europe? Every major city would give you good tea. The only thing I don't like is the business of tea bags. Your cup is filled with hot water, and you're handed a little bag packed with tea leaves. A piece of string is tied to this bag. You have to hold it by this string and dip it in the water to make your own tea. Then you might add milk to it, or squeeze a lemon, as you wish. Personally, I prefer lemon tea. But you need really good tea for that. The kind of tea they have here is very ordinary.'

'You have travelled a lot, have you?' Feluda asked.

'Yes, that's all I've done in life,' our visitor replied 'I am what you might call a globetrotter. And I'm fond of hunting. I got interested when I was in Africa. My name is Mandar Bose.'

I had heard of the globetrotter Umesh Bhattacharya, but not of Mandar Bose.

He probably guessed what I was thinking. 'I don't suppose my name will mean anything to you,' he said. 'When I first left home, my name appeared in the press. But that was thirty-six years ago. I've been back in India for only three months.'

'Really? I must say your Bengali has remained pretty good, considering you've been out of the country for so long.'

'Well, that's something entirely up to the person who's travelling abroad. If you want to forget your own language, you can do so in just three months. And if you don't, you'll not forget it even in thirty years. But I was lucky in that I came across other Bengalis frequently. When I was in Kenya, I ran a business trading in ivory. My partner there was a Bengali. We worked together for almost seven years.'

'Is there any other Bengali here in the Circuit House?' asked Feluda. I had noticed earlier that he seldom wasted time on idle chit-chat.

'Yes! That's what I find so surprising. But one thing's become clear to me. People in Calcutta are fed up. So they get out whenever they can. This man here, though, has come with a purpose. He's a psychologist. It's all a bit complicated. There's a little boy with him, about eight years old. He's supposed to be able to recall his previous life. Says he was born in some fort in Rajasthan, once upon a time. This man is roaming around everywhere with the boy, looking for that fort. What I can't tell is whether this psychologist is a fraud, or the boy is simply telling a pack of lies. His behaviour is certainly odd. He doesn't talk properly with anyone, doesn't answer questions. Very fishy. I've seen a lot of cheats and frauds all over the world—never thought I'd come across something like this back in my own country!'

'Was it your globetrotting that brought you here?'

Mr Bose smiled and stood up. 'To tell you the truth, I haven't yet seen much of this country . . . . By the way, I didn't catch your names!'

Feluda made the introductions. 'And I have never stepped out of this country,' he added.

'I see. Well, if you come to the dining hall at around half past eight, we'll meet again. I believe in early-to-bed and early-to-rise, you see.'

We left our room with Mr Bose and emerged into the corridor outside. A taxi was coming in through the gate. It stopped under the portico, and a man of about forty got out of it, accompanied by a thin little boy. I did not have to be told that they were Dr Hemanga Hajra and Mukul Dhar.

FIVE

Mr Bose said 'good evening' to Dr Hajra as he passed him, and went towards his own room. Dr Hajra began walking down the corridor, holding the boy by the hand. Then he saw us and stopped, looking a little confused. Perhaps the sight of two strangers had startled him.

Feluda smiled and greeted him. 'Namaskar. Dr Hajra, I presume?' he asked.

'Yes. But I don't think I. . .?'

Feluda took out one of his cards from his pocket and handed it to Dr Hajra. 'I need to talk to you. To tell you the truth, we are here at Mr Dhar's request. He has written you a letter.'

'Oh, I see. Mukul, why don't you go to your room? I'll have a chat with these people, then I'll join you. All right?'

'I'll go to the garden,' said Mukul.

His voice sounded as sweet as a flute, but his tone was flat and lifeless, almost as if the words had been spoken by a robot. Dr Hajra said, 'Very well, you may go to the garden, but be a good boy and don't go out of the gate, okay?'

Mukul jumped from the corridor straight on to the gravel path, without saying another word. Then he stepped over a row of flowers and stood quietly on the lawn. Dr Hajra turned back to us, gave a somewhat embarrassed smile and asked, 'Where should we sit?'

'Let's go to our room.'

The hair around Dr Hajra's ears had started to grey, I noticed. His eyes held a sharp, intelligent look. Now that I could see him more closely, he appeared older—probably in his late forties.

When we were seated, Feluda handed him Mr Dhar's letter and offered him a Charminar. Dr Hajra smiled, said, 'No, thanks', and began reading the letter. When he'd finished, he folded it and put it back in its envelope.

Feluda explained quickly about Neelu being kidnapped. 'Mr Dhar was afraid,' he said, 'that those men might have followed Mukul and arrived here. That is why he came to see me. In fact, I am here really because he wanted me to join you. But, even if nothing untoward happens and you do not require my protection, I can see that my visit will not go to waste as I've always wanted to see Rajasthan.'

Dr Hajra remained thoughtful for a few moments. Then he said, 'Fortunately, nothing has happened as yet that might be seen as untoward. But honestly, there was no need to talk to a press reporter and say so much. I told Mr Dhar to wait until I finished my investigation, and then he could get Mukul to speak to as many reporters as he liked, especially about the hidden treasure. I might think the story is possibly quite baseless, but there might well be people who'd be easily tempted to go and look for it!'

'What do you think of this whole business of recalling previous lives? Do you really believe in jatismars?'

'What I think amounts to shooting arrows in the dark or simply making guesses. Yet I cannot dismiss the idea as pure nonsense. After all, there have been similar cases in the past. What those people could recall turned out to be accurate, to the last detail. That is why, when I heard about Mukul, I decided to do a thorough investigation. If it turned out that everything Mukul could recall was true, then I would treat his case as a starting point and base my future research on it.'

'Have you made any progress?'

'One thing has become clear. I was right to think about Rajasthan and bring him here. Mukul's entire demeanour has changed from the moment we set foot in Rajasthan. Just think. For the first time in his life, he is away from his parents and others in his family and travelling with a virtual stranger. Yet he hasn't mentioned his own people even once in the last few days.'

'How is his relationship with you?'

'We've had no problems. He sees me as someone who's taking him to his dreamland. All he can think of is his golden fortress. So he jumps with joy each time he sees a fort.'

'Any sign of the golden fortress?'

Dr Hajra shook his head. 'No, I am afraid not. On our way here, I took him to the fort in Kisangarh. Yesterday evening, he saw the Jodhpur fort from outside. Today, we went to Barmer. Every time, he says, "No, not this one. Let's find another." One really needs patience in a case like this. I know there's no point in taking him to Chittor or Udaipur because there's no sand near those places. Mukul keeps talking of sand, and that's to be found only in these parts. So I'm thinking of going to Bikaner tomorrow.'

'Would you mind if we came along?'

'No, of course not. In fact, I'd feel quite reassured if you were with us because . . . something happened . . .'

Dr Hajra stopped. Feluda had taken out his packet of cigarettes, but did not open it.

'Yesterday evening,' Dr Hajra spoke slowly, 'there was a phone call.'

'Where?'

'Here in the Circuit House. I wasn't here; Mukul and I were out looking at the fort. In our absence, someone rang to ask if a man had arrived from Calcutta with a small boy. Naturally, the manager said yes.'

'But,' Feluda suggested, 'it could be that some of the locals know about the press report that appeared in Calcutta and simply wanted to verify it? After all, there are plenty of Bengalis in Jodhpur, aren't there? Surely a little curiosity in a matter like this is natural?'

'Yes, I can see that. But the question is, why didn't that man come here and meet me, or get in touch, even when he heard that I was here?'

'Hmm. Perhaps it's best that you and I stay together. And don't let Mukul go out on his own.'

'Are you mad? Of course I won't.' Dr Hajra rose. 'I have booked a taxi for tomorrow. As there are just two of you, we'll manage quite easily in one taxi.'

He began moving towards the door. Suddenly, Feluda asked a question rather unexpectedly: 'By the way, weren't you involved in a case in Chicago, about four years ago?'

Dr Hajra frowned. 'A case? Yes, I've been to Chicago, but. . .'

'Something to do with a spiritual healing centre?'

Dr Hajra burst out laughing. 'Ah, are you talking about Swami Bhavananda? The Americans used to call him Byavanyanda. Yes, there was a case, but what was reported in the press was grossly exaggerated. The man was certainly a cheat, but you'll find similar cheats among quacks of all kinds. It was small-time stuff, no more. In fact, his patients caught him out, and the news spread. Reporters from the press came to me for my opinion. I said very little, and tried to play things down. But those reporters blew everything out of proportion. Afterwards, I happened to meet Bhavananda. I explained the whole matter to him myself and we parted as friends.'

'Thank you. What I read in the papers told me something quite different.'

We went out of the room together with Dr Hajra. It was dark outside. Although the western sky was still glowing red, the streetlights had come on. But where was Mukul? He was last seen in the garden, but now he wasn't there. Dr Hajra had a quick look in his room, and came out, looking concerned.

'Where's that boy gone?' he said and climbed down from the corridor on to the gravel path. We followed him. Mukul was certainly not in the garden.

'Mukul!' Dr Hajra called. 'Mukul!'

'Yes, he's heard you. He's coming!' said Feluda.

In the twilight, I could see Mukul coming back from the road outside and turn into the gate. At the same time, I saw a man on the opposite pavement, walking briskly towards the new palace on the eastern side. I did not see his face, but could see—even in the dark—that the colour of his shirt was bright red. Had Feluda seen him?

Mukul came towards us. Dr Hajra went to him, his arms outstretched, a smile on his lips. Then he said gently, 'You shouldn't go out like that!'

'Why not?' asked Mukul coldly.

'You don't know this place. There are so many bad people about.'

'I know him.'

'Who?'

Mukul pointed at the road. 'That man . . . who was here.'

Dr Hajra placed a hand on his shoulder and turned to Feluda. 'That's the trouble, you see,' he said. 'It's difficult to say whether he's talking of someone he really knows in this life, or whether he's still talking about his previous life.'

I noticed a shiny piece of paper in Mukul's hand. Feluda had seen it, too. He said, 'May I see that piece of paper you're holding?'

Mukul handed it to Feluda. It was a piece of golden foil, about two inches long and half an inch wide.

'Where did you find it?'

'Over there,' Mukul pointed at the grass.

'May I keep it?' asked Feluda.

'No. I found it.' Mukul's voice hadn't changed. His tone was just as cold and as flat. Feluda was obliged to return the piece of foil to him.

Dr Hajra said, 'Come on, Mukul, let's go to our room. We'll have a wash, and then we'll both go and have dinner. Goodnight, Mr Mitter. Early breakfast at half past seven tomorrow morning, and then we'll leave.'

Feluda wrote a postcard to Mr Dhar with news of Mukul's welfare before we went to the dining hall. By the time we got there after a shower, Dr Hajra and Mukul had returned to their room.

Mandar Bose was sitting in the opposite corner, having his pudding with the Marwari gentleman he had been talking to earlier. They finished their meal and rose as we were served our soup. Mr Bose raised his hand and said, 'Good night!' as he went out through the door.

After two nights on the train, I was feeling quite tired. All I wanted to do after dinner was go to sleep, but Feluda made me stay awake for a while. He took out his blue notebook and sat on the sofa. I was lying in my bed. We had a cream to ward off mosquitoes, so there was no need to use the mosquito net.

Feluda pushed the little button on his ballpoint pen, got it ready to write and said, 'Who have we met so far? Give me the whole list.'

'Starting from . . . ?'

'Mr Dhar's arrival.'

'Okay, Sudhir Dhar. That's number one. Then Shivratan. Then Neelu. Oh, Shivratan's servant—'

'What was his name?'

Can't remember.'

'Manohar. Next?'

'Jatayu.'

'What's his real name?'

'Lalmohan.'

'Surname?'

'Surname . . . his surname is . . . Ganguli!'

'Good.'

Feluda continued to write as I proceeded with my list. 'Then we saw that man in the red shirt.'

'Did we actually meet him? Get to know him?'

'No.'

'All right. Go on.'

'Mandar Bose, and that other gentleman.'

'And then we met Mukul Dhar. Doctor—'

'Feluda!'

My sudden scream made Feluda stop in mid-sentence. My eyes had fallen on Feluda's bed. An ugly, creepy creature was trying to slip out from under his pillow. I pointed at it.

Feluda sprang to his feet, moved quickly and removed the pillow. A scorpion lay on the bed. Feluda pulled the bedsheet off in one swift motion and the scorpion fell on the ground. Then he grabbed his chappal and smacked it three times with all his might. After that, he tore off a piece from a newspaper, picked up the crushed creature with it and went into the bathroom. I saw him crumple the whole thing into a ball and throw it out of the back door.

He came back to the room and said', 'The door which the cleaners use was left open. That's how Mr Scorpion got into our room. Anyway, go to sleep now. We have an early start tomorrow.'

But I could not dismiss the matter so easily. Something told me . . . but I put the thought out of my mind. If I kept thinking of possible danger, and if my telepathy was strong enough, it might just drag that danger closer—who knew?

It would be far better to try to sleep.

SIX

The following morning, as soon as I emerged from our room, I heard a familiar voice say, 'Good morning!' It was Jatayu. Feluda was already seated on a chair on the corridor outside, waiting for his tea. Jatayu glanced round excitedly and said, 'Oh! This is such a thrilling place, Mr Mitter! Full of powerfully suspicious characters.'

'You are unharmed, I hope?' Feluda asked.

'Oh yes. I feel fitter than ever. This morning, you know what I did? I challenged the manager of our lodge to an arm-wrestle. But the fellow didn't accept.' Then he came a little closer and whispered, 'I have a weapon in my suitcase!'

'A catapult?'

'No, sir. A Nepali dagger, straight from Kathmandu. If I'm attacked, I'm going to stab my attacker with it—push it straight into his stomach, I tell you. Then let's see what happens. I've always wanted to build up a collection of weapons, you know.'

I wanted to laugh again, but my self-control was getting better, so I managed to stop myself. Lalmohan Babu sat down on the chair next to Feluda and asked, 'What's your plan today? Aren't you going to see the fort?'

'Yes, but not the fort in Jodhpur. We're going to Bikaner.'

'Bikaner? Why Bikaner?'

'We've got company. Somebody's arranged a car.'

Another voice said 'Good morning!' from a different part of the corridor. Mr Globetrotter was walking towards us. 'Did you sleep well?' he asked.

I caught Lalmohan Babu casting admiring glances at Mandar Bose's handsome moustache and muscular physique. Feluda introduced him to Mr Bose.

'Good heavens, a globetrotter!' Lalmohan Babu's eyes widened. 'I must cultivate you, dear sir. You must have had a lot of hair-raising experiences!'

'Plenty, I can assure you. The only thing that I have missed is being boiled in a cannibal's cooking pot. Apart from that, I have had virtually every experience a man can possibly have.'

Suddenly, I noticed Mukul. I hadn't seen him come out on the corridor. He was standing quietly in a corner, staring at the garden. Then Dr Hajra appeared, dressed and ready to go out. A flask was slung from one shoulder; from the other hung binoculars, and around his neck was the strap of his camera. He said, 'It will take us almost four and a half hours to get there. If you have a flask, take it with you. God knows if we'll get anything to drink on the way. But I've told the dining hall to give us four packed lunches.'

'Where are you off to?' asked Mandar Bose.

On being told where we were going, he became all excited. 'Why don't we all go together?' he asked.

'What a good idea!' exclaimed Lalmohan Babu.

Dr Hajra looked a little uncomfortable. 'Well then, how many are actually going?' he enquired.

'Look, there's no question of all of us going in one car,' Mr Bose reassured him. 'I will arrange another taxi. I think Mr Maheshwari would also like to go with me.'

'Are you going, too?' Dr Hajra asked Lalmohan Babu.

'If I go, I'll pay my share. I don't want anyone else to pay for me. Tell you what, why don't you four go in one taxi? I'll go with Mr Globetrotter.'

Obviously, Jatayu wanted to hear a few stories from Mr Bose and perhaps get ideas for a new plot. He had already written at least twenty-five adventure stories. To be honest, his remark made me feel quite relieved. Five in one car would have been cramped and uncomfortable.

Mr Bose spoke to the manager and booked a second taxi. Lalmohan Babu returned to New Bombay Lodge. 'Please pick me up on your way,' he said before he departed. 'I'll be ready in half an hour.'

Before I describe anything else about our visit to Bikaner, perhaps I ought to mention that Mukul rejected the fort there as soon as he saw it. But that was not the highlight of our visit. Something far more important happened in Devikund, which proved that we were truly up against a ferocious foe.

Nothing much happened on the way to Bikaner, except that we saw a group of gypsies. They were camping by the roadside. Mukul asked us to stop, got out of the car and roamed amongst the gypsies for a while. Then he returned and declared that he knew those people.

After that, Feluda and Dr Hajra spoke about Mukul for a few minutes. I cannot tell whether he heard the conversation from the front seat. If he did, his demeanour gave nothing away.

'Dr Hajra,' Feluda began, 'when Mukul talks of his previous life, what exactly does he say?'

'He mentions one thing repeatedly—a golden fortress. His house was apparently near that fortress. Gold and jewels were buried under the ground in that house. From the way he talks, it seems as if he was present when the treasure was buried. Apart from that, he talks of a battle. He says he saw a large number of elephants, horses, soldiers, guns, cannons—there was a lot of noise, and people were screaming. And he talks of camels. Says he's ridden camels. Then he talks of peacocks. Once a peacock had attacked him, pecked his hand so hard that it began bleeding. There's something else he mentions frequently. Sand. Haven't you noticed how animated he becomes when he sees sand?'

We reached Bikaner at a quarter to twelve. The road began going uphill a little before we reached the city, which was surrounded by a wall, on top of the hill. The most striking building there was a huge fort, made of red sandstone.

Our car drove straight to the fort. As it got closer, the fort appeared to grow bigger. Baba was right. The appearance of the forts in Rajasthan was a good indicator of the might of the Rajputs.

As soon as our taxi drew up at the entrance, Mukul said, 'Why have we stopped here?'

Dr Hajra asked him, 'Does this fort seem familiar, Mukul?'

Mukul replied solemnly, 'No. This is a stupid fort, not the golden one.'

By this time, we had all climbed out of the car. Just as Mukul finished speaking, a harsh raucous sound reached our ears. At once, Mukul ran to Dr Hajra and flung his arms around him. The sound had come from a park opposite the fort.

'That was a peacock. Has this happened before?' asked Feluda.

Dr Hajra stroked Mukul's head gently. 'Yes. It happened yesterday in Jodhpur. He can't stand peacocks.'

Mukul had turned quite pale. 'I don't want to stay here,' he said, in the same lifeless yet sweet voice.

Dr Hajra turned to Feluda. 'I'm going to take the car and go to the local Circuit House. Then I'll send it back here. Why don't you two see whatever you want to? You can join me at the Circuit House when the car comes back to pick you up. But please make sure we leave here by two o'clock, or it will be late by the time we get back to Jodhpur.'

There was reason to feel disappointed, particularly for Dr Hajra, but I didn't mind all that much. I was about to step into a Rajasthani fort for the first time in my life. The thought was giving me goose pimples.

We proceeded towards the main gate of the fort. Suddenly, Feluda stopped and laid a hand on my shoulder. 'Did you see?'

'What?'

'That man.'

Was he referring to the man in the red shirt? I followed his gaze, but could not spot a single red shirt anywhere. There were lots of people milling about, for there was a small market just outside the fort. 'Where is he?' I asked.

'Idiot! Are you looking for a red shirt?'

'Yes. Shouldn't I? Who are you talking about?'

'You're the biggest fool on earth. All you remember is the shirt, nothing else. It was the same man, he was wearing a shawl and most of his face was covered, all except his eyes. But today he had a blue shirt on. When we stopped to look at those gypsies, I saw a taxi going towards Bikaner. That's when I spotted that blue shirt.'

'But what is he doing here?'

'If we knew that, there would be no mystery!'

The man had vanished. I passed through the gate and entered the fort, feeling rather agitated. A large courtyard greeted me. The fort stood proudly to the right. There were pigeons everywhere, in every niche in the wall. A thousand years ago, Bikaner was a thriving city, but it had disappeared under the sand. Feluda told me that four hundred years ago, Raja Rai Singh began building the fort. He was a famous leader in Akbar's army.

Something had been bothering me for a while. Why hadn't Lalmohan Babu and the others arrived yet? Did they get late in setting

out? Or had their car broken down on the way? Then I told myself
not to worry. There was no point in spoiling the joy of seeing an
amazing historical sight.

What struck me as most amazing was the armoury. Not only did
it contain weapons, but also a very beautiful silver throne, called
Alam Ambali. It was said to be a gift from a Mughal badshah. Apart
from that, there were swords, spears, daggers, shields, armour,
helmets—there was no end to the weapons. The swords were so
large and so strong that it seemed incredible that they were meant to
be used by human beings. The sight of those weapons reminded me
of Jatayu again. Funnily enough, as soon as I thought of him, he
arrived, possibly dragged by the force of my telepathy. In that huge
room in the massive fort, standing near a very large door, Jatayu
looked smaller and more comical than ever.

When he saw us, he grinned, looked around and simply said, 'Was
every Rajput a giant? Surely these things weren't made to be used by
ordinary men?'

It turned out that my hunch was right. They had travelled for
about seventy kilometres, when their taxi got a flat tyre. 'Where are
the other two?' Feluda asked.

'They stopped to buy things in the market. I couldn't wait any
longer, so I came in.'

We left the armoury and went off to see Phool Mahal, Gaj Mandir,
Sheesh Mahal and Ganga Nivas. When we got to Chini Burj, we
saw Mandar Bose and Mr Maheshwari. They were both clutching
parcels wrapped with newspaper, so clearly they had done some
shopping. Mr Bose said, 'The weapons I saw in the forts and castles
in Europe—all built in medieval times—and the weapons I've seen
here today, all prove one thing. The human race is becoming weaker
every day, and smaller in size!'

'Like me, you mean?' Lalmohan Babu remarked with a smile.

'Right. Exactly like you,' Mr Bose replied. 'I don't think a single
Rajput would have matched your dimensions in the sixteenth century.
Oh, by the way,' he turned to Feluda, 'this was waiting for you at
the reception desk in the Circuit House.'

He took out a sealed envelope from his pocket and passed it to
Feluda. It had no stamp on it. Someone must have delivered it by
hand. 'Who gave it to you?' Feluda asked, opening the envelope.

'Bagri, the fellow who sits at the reception desk. He handed it to
me just as we were leaving. Said he had no idea who had dropped it

off.'

'Excuse me,' said Feluda. Then he read the note, replaced it in the envelope and put it in his pocket. I could not tell what it said, nor could I ask.

We spent another half an hour in the fort. Then Feluda looked at his watch and said, 'Time to go to the Circuit House!' I didn't want to leave the fort, but knew I had to.

Both taxis were waiting outside. This time, we decided to leave together. As we were getting into ours, the driver told us that Dr Hajra and Mukul had not gone to the Circuit House. Apparently, Mukul had declared that he had no wish to go there. So where did they go? 'Devikund,' said the driver. Where was that? Not far from Bikaner, it turned out. Feluda said there were cenotaphs there (locally known as 'chhatris'), built as memorials to Rajput warriors.

We had to travel five miles, and it took us ten minutes. Devikund really was beautiful, as were the cenotaphs. Each cenotaph had stone columns that rose from stone platforms, supporting a small canopy, also made of stone. The whole structure, from top to bottom, was exquisitely carved. There were at least fifty such cenotaphs spread over the whole area. There were plenty of trees, all of them full of parrots. The birds were flocking together on some, or flitting from one tree to another, crying raucously. I had never seen so many parrots in one place.

But where was Dr Hajra? And Mukul?

Lalmohan Babu was getting restless. 'Very suspicious and mysterious!' he exclaimed.

'Dr Hajra!' shouted Mandar Bose. His deep, booming voice made a number of parrots take flight, but no one answered.

We began a search. There were so many cenotaphs that the place was like a maze. As we roamed amongst them, I saw Feluda pick up a matchbox from the grass and put it in his pocket.

In the end, it was Lalmohan Babu who found Dr Hajra. We heard him shout and ran to join him. Under a mango tree, in front of a mossy platform, Dr Hajra was lying crumpled on the ground. His mouth was gagged, and his hands were tied behind his back. He was groaning helplessly.

Feluda bent over him quickly, removed the gag and untied his hands. A torn piece of a turban had been used to cover his mouth.

'How on earth did this happen?' asked Mr Bose.

Fortunately, Dr Hajra was not injured. He sat up on the grass and panted for a while. Then he told us what had happened. 'Mukul said he didn't want to go to the Circuit House,' he said, 'so we just drove on. Then we happened to come here. Mukul liked the place. "Those things are chhatris," he said. He had seen them before, and he wanted a closer look. So we got out of the car. Mukul began exploring, and I stood in the shade, under a tree. Suddenly someone attacked me from behind. He placed a hand over my mouth and knocked me down. I fell flat on my face. Then he pressed me down firmly—I think he kept his knee on the back of my head—and tied my hands, and then gagged my mouth.'

'Where's Mukul?' Feluda asked anxiously.

'I don't know. I did hear a car start soon after I was tied up.'

'You didn't see this man's face?'

Dr Hajra shook his head. 'No, but when we struggled, I got an idea of his clothes. He was wearing Rajasthani clothes, not a shirt and trousers.'

'There he is!' shouted Mandar Bose.

To my surprise, Mukul emerged from behind a chhatri, chewing a stalk of grass. Dr Hajra let out an audible sigh of relief. 'Thank God!' he cried.

'Where did you go, Mukul?'

No answer.

'Where were you all this while?'

'Behind that,' Mukul replied this time, pointing at a chhatri. 'I have seen such things before.'

Feluda spoke next. 'Did you see the man who was here?'

'Which man?'

Dr Hajra intervened, 'Mukul could not have seen him. He ran off to explore the area the minute he got out of the car. I never imagined such a thing would happen in Bikaner, so I wasn't unduly worried about him.'

Even so, Feluda tried again, 'Didn't you see the man who tied the doctor's hands?'

'I want to see the golden fortress,' said Mukul. It was clearly pointless to ask him anything else.

'Let's not waste our time any more,' Feluda spoke abruptly. 'In a way, I am glad that Mukul was nowhere near you. Or that man might have made off with Mukul. If he has returned to Jodhpur, we might be able to catch up with him, if we drive fast enough.'

In two minutes, we were all back in our cars and speeding back to

Jodhpur. This time, Lalmohan Babu decided to join us. 'Those men drink a lot. I can't stand the smell of alcohol!' he confided.

Our Punjabi driver, Harmeet Singh, managed to drive at sixty mph. At one point, a small bird flew into our windscreen and died. Mukul and I were sitting in the front with the driver. I turned around once to look at the three men in the back seat. Lalmohan Babu was sitting crushed between Feluda and Dr Hajra. His face looked pale and his eyes were closed; nevertheless, a smile hovered on his lips, which told me that he could smell an adventure. Perhaps he had even thought of a plot for his next novel.

We drove at that speed for a hundred miles, but by that time it had become clear that the criminal had got away, and we wouldn't be able to catch up with him. After all, there was no reason to think that he wasn't travelling in a fast new car.

When we reached Jodhpur, it was dark and all the lights in the city had been switched on. Feluda said to Lalmohan Babu, 'You'd like to be dropped at the New Bombay Lodge, wouldn't you?'

'Yes,' Lalmohan Babu squeaked, 'I mean, all my things are there, so naturally . . . but I was wondering if . . . after dinner, I might go over to your place . . .?'

'Very well,' Feluda said reassuringly, 'I will ask at the Circuit House if they have a vacant room. You can ring me at around nine. I should be able to tell you then.'

I was still mulling over all that had happened during the day. We were up against someone extremely clever and crafty—of that there was no doubt. Was it the man in the red shirt, who went to Bikaner today wearing a blue one? I didn't know. Nothing was making any sense to me. Perhaps Feluda was just as puzzled. If he had worked things out, his whole demeanour would have changed. Having spent so many years with him and watched his reactions, that was something I had learnt to read quite well.

Upon reaching the Circuit House, we dispersed and went to our individual rooms. Before going to our room, Feluda said to Dr Hajra, 'If you don't mind, may I keep this with me?' In his hand was the torn piece of cloth with which Dr Hajra had been tied.

'Certainly,' Dr Hajra replied. Then he moved a little closer and lowered his voice. 'As you can see, Mr Mitter, the situation is now quite serious. This is exactly what you were afraid of, isn't it? I must say I hadn't anticipated such trouble.'

'Don't worry,' Feluda told him. 'You carry on with your work I am going to be with you. If you had gone straight to the Circuit House in Bikaner today, I don't think there would have been any problem. Fortunately, whoever attacked you could not kidnap Mukul. That's the main thing. From now on, stay close to us. That should minimize the chances of something similar happening again.'

Dr Hajra continued to look troubled. He said, 'I am not worried about myself, you see. If a scientist has to do research, he has to take certain risks just to complete his work. I am worried about you two. You are outsiders, not involved in this case at all.'

Feluda smiled. 'You must assume that I, too, am a scientist involved in some research, and so I'm taking risks as well!'

Mukul was pacing up and down the corridor. Dr Hajra called him, said 'Good night' to us and went to his room with Mukul. He was still looking preoccupied.

We went to ours. Feluda called a bearer and ordered two Coca-Colas. Then he took out his cigarettes and lighter from his pocket and placed them on the table. He was looking worried. From a different pocket, he took out the matchbox he had found in Devikund. It had an ace printed on one side, and it was empty. Feluda stared at it for a few moments, before saying, 'We stopped at so many stations on the way to Jodhpur, and you saw so many paan stalls selling matches and cigarettes. Did you notice any of them selling this particular brand of matches?'

I had to admit the truth. 'No, Feluda, I didn't notice anything.'

'In western India, this brand with the ace on it is not sold anywhere—certainly not in Rajasthan. This matchbox has come from a different state.'

'Does that mean it doesn't belong to the man in the red shirt?'

'That is a foolish question. To start with, if a man is dressed as a Rajasthani, that doesn't automatically mean that he is one. Anyone can wear Rajasthani clothes. Secondly, plenty of other people could have gone to Devikund and attacked Dr Hajra.'

'Yes, of course. But we don't know who they are, do we? So what's the use of wondering about that?'

'See, you are speaking without thinking again. Lalmohan, Mandar Bose and Maheshwari—all three men reached the Bikaner fort quite late. Just think about that. Besides . . .'

'Oh. Yes, yes, now I can see what you mean!'

It just hadn't occurred to me before. Lalmohan Babu told us that their car had a flat tyre, which delayed them by forty-five minutes.

What if he had lied? Even if he had told the truth and was quite innocent, Mandar Bose and Maheshwari could well have gone to Devikund instead of going to the local market.

Feluda let out a deep sigh and took out another object from his pocket. My heart gave a sudden lurch. I had totally forgotten about it. It was the letter Mandar Bose had handed him that morning.

'Who wrote that letter, Feluda?' I asked, my voice trembling.

'No idea,' Feluda replied, passing it to me. Only one line was written in large letters with a ballpoint pen:

If you value your life, go back to Calcutta immediately.

The note shook in my hand. I put it quickly on the table and placed my hands on my lap, trying to steady them.

'What are you going to do, Feluda?'

Feluda was staring at the ceiling fan. His eyes remained fixed on it as he muttered, almost to himself, 'A spider's web . . . geometry. It is dark now . . . so you can't see it . . . but when the sun rises, the web will catch its light . . . it will glitter . . . and then you can see its pattern. Now, all we have to do is wait for sunrise. . .!'

SEVEN

I woke for a few moments in the middle of the night—God knows what time it was—and saw Feluda scribbling something in his blue notebook, by the light of the bedside lamp. I don't know how long he stayed awake, but when I woke at half past six, he had showered, had a shave and was dressed to go out. According to him, when your brain works at high speed, you tend to sleep a lot less, but that does not affect your health. At least, that's what he believes. In the last ten years, I have not known him to be ill, even for a single day. Even here in Jodhpur, he was doing yoga every day. By the time I left my bed, he had finished his exercises.

When we went to the dining room for breakfast, we met everyone else. Lalmohan Babu had moved to the Circuit House the previous night. He had been given a room only two doors away Mandar Bose. We found him eating an omelette. He had thought of a wonderful plot, he told us. Dr Hajra still seemed upset. He had not slept well. Only Mukul seemed totally unperturbed.

Mandar Bose decided to be direct with Dr Hajra. 'Please don't mind my saying this,' he began, 'but you're dealing with such a weird subject that you're bound to invite trouble. In a country where superstition runs rife, isn't it better not to meddle with such things? One day, you'll find little boys in every household claiming to be jatismars! If you look closely, you'll find that their parents want a little publicity—that's all there is to it. But what are you going to do if that happens? How many kids will you take with you and travel all over the country?'

Dr Hajra made no comment. Lalmohan Babu simply cast puzzled glances from one to the other, for no one had told him about Mukul being able to recall his past life.

Feluda had already told me that after breakfast, he wanted to go to the main market. I knew he had some other motive; it could not be just to see more of the city, or to shop. We left at a quarter to eight, accompanied by Lalmohan Babu. I tried a couple of times to imagine him as a ferocious foe, but the mere idea was so laughable that I had to wipe it from my mind.

The area round the Circuit House was quiet, but the main city turned out to be noisy and congested. The old wall was visible from virtually every corner. Along that wall stood rows of shops, tongas, houses and much else. Remnants of a five-hundred-year-old city were now inextricably tangled with the modern Jodhpur.

We walked through the bazaar, looking at various shops. I could tell Feluda was looking for something specific, but had no idea what it was. Suddenly, Lalmohan Babu asked, 'What is Dr Hajra's subject? I mean, what is he a doctor of? This morning, Mr Trotter was saying something . . .?'

'Hajra is a parapsychologist,' Feluda replied.

'Parapsychologist?' Lalmohan Babu frowned, 'I didn't know you could add "para" before "psychologist"! I know you can do that to "typhoid". So does it mean it's half-psychology, just as paratyphoid is half-typhoid?'

'No, in this case "para" means "abnormal", not "half". Psychology is a complex subject, in any case. Parapsychology deals with its more obscure aspects.'

'I see. And what was all that about a jatismar?'

'Mukul is a jatismar. At least, that's what he's been called.'

Lalmohan Babu's jaw fell open.

'You'll get plenty of material for a plot,' Feluda continued. 'That young boy talks of a golden fortress he saw in a previous life. And the house where he lived had hidden treasure, buried under the ground.'

'Are we . . . are we going to look for those things?' Lalmohan Babu's voice grew hoarse.

'I don't know about you. We certainly are.'

Lalmohan Babu stopped, bang in the middle of the road, and grasped Feluda's hand with both his own. 'Mr Mitter! This is the chance of a lifetime! Please don't disappear anywhere without taking me with you. That's my only request.'

'But I don't know where we're going next. Nothing's decided.'

Lalmohan Babu paused for a while, deep in thought. Then he said, 'Will Mr Trotter go with you?'

'Why? Would you mind if he did?'

'That man is powerfully suspicious!'

There was a stall by the roadside, selling naagras. Most people in Rajasthan wear these shoes. Feluda stopped at the stall.

'Powerful he might be. Why suspicious?' he asked.

'When we were travelling to Bikaner yesterday, he was bragging a lot in the car. Said he had shot a wolf in Tanganyika. Yet I know that there are no wolves anywhere in Africa. I have read books by Martin Johnson. No one can fool me that easily!'

'So what did you say?'

'What could I say? I could hardly call him a liar to his face. I was sitting sandwiched between those two men. You've seen how broad his chest is, haven't you? At least forty-five inches. Both sides of the road were lined with huge cactus bushes and prickly pear. If I dared to contradict him, he'd have picked me up and thrown me behind one of those bushes—and then, in no time, I'd have turned into fodder for vultures. Great squadrons of vultures would have landed on me and had a feast!'

'You think so? How many vultures could possibly feed on your corpse?'

'Ha ha ha ha!'

Feluda had, in the mean time, taken off his sandals and put on a pair of naagras. He was walking back and forth in front of the stall.

'Very powerful shoes. Are you going to buy those?' Lalmohan Babu asked.

'Why don't you try on a pair yourself?' Feluda suggested.

None of the shoes were small enough to fit Lalmohan Babu, but he did slip his feet into the smallest pair that could be found, and gave a shudder. 'Oh my God! This was made from the hide of a rhino. You'd have to be a rhino yourself to wear such shoes.'

'In that case, you must assume that ninety per cent of Rajasthanis are rhinos.'

Both men took the naagras off and wore their own shoes again. Even the shopkeeper began laughing, having realized that the Babus from the city were having a little joke.

We left the stall and walked on. From a paan shop, a film song was being played very loudly on a radio. That reminded me of Durga Puja in Calcutta. Over here, people celebrated not Durga Puja, but Dussehra. But that was a long way away.

A few minutes later, Feluda suddenly stopped at a shop selling stoneware. It was a prosperous looking shop called Solanki Stores. Displayed in the showcase were beautiful pots, bowls, plates and glasses, all made of stone. Feluda was staring at those fixedly. The shopkeeper saw us, came to the door and invited us into his shop.

Feluda pointed at a bowl in the glass case, and said, 'May I see it, please?'

The shopkeeper did not pick up the bowl that was displayed. Instead, he took out an identical one from a cupboard. It was beautiful, made of yellow stone. I couldn't remember having seen anything like it before.

'Was this made here?' Feluda asked.

'It was made in Rajasthan, but not in Jodhpur.'

'No? Where was it made then?'

'Jaisalmer. This yellow stone can be found only in Jaisalmer.'

'I see.'

I had heard of Jaisalmer, but only vaguely. I didn't know where exactly in Rajasthan it was. Feluda bought the bowl. Then we took a tonga back to the Circuit House. It was half past nine by the time we returned, after a most bumpy ride. But it did mean that, after such a journey, our breakfast was certainly digested.

Mandar Bose was sitting outside in the corridor, reading a newspaper. 'What did you buy?' he asked, looking at the packet in Feluda's hand.

'A bowl. After all, I must have a Rajasthani memento.'

'I saw your friend go out.'

'Who, Dr Hajra?'

'Yes. I saw him leave in a taxi, at around nine o'clock.'

'And Mukul?'

'He went with him. Perhaps they've gone to talk to the police. After what happened yesterday, Hajra must still be quite shaken.'

Lalmohan Babu returned to his room, on the grounds that he had to work on his new plot and change it a little. We went to ours.

'Why did you suddenly buy that bowl, Feluda?' I asked.

Feluda sat down on the sofa, unwrapped the bowl and placed it on the table, 'There is something special about it,' he said.

'What's so special?'

'Here is a bowl made of stone. Yet if I were to say it was a golden bowl, I wouldn't be far wrong! I have never seen anything like this in my life.'

After this, he lapsed into silence and began turning the pages of a railway timetable. There was little that I could do. I knew Feluda wouldn't open his mouth, at least for an hour. Even if I asked him questions, he wouldn't answer. So I left the room.

The corridor was now empty. Mandar Bose had gone. So had the European lady, who had been sitting at the far end earlier on. The sound of a drum reached my ears. Then someone started singing. I looked at the gate and found a boy and a girl, who looked like beggars. The boy was beating the drum and the girl was singing. They were walking towards the corridor. I went forward.

When I reached the open space, suddenly I felt like going upstairs. I had been walking past the staircase every day. I knew there was a terrace upstairs, but hadn't yet seen it. So I climbed up the steps.

There were four rooms upstairs. To the east and west of these was an open terrace. The rooms appeared to be unoccupied. Or it could be that the occupants had all gone out.

I went to the western side. The fort was clearly visible from here, looking quite majestic.

The two beggars downstairs were still singing. The tune of their song sounded familiar. Where had I heard it before? Suddenly I realized it was very similar to the tune I had heard Mukul hum at times. The same tune was being repeated every now and then, but it did not sound monotonous.

I went closer to the low wall that surrounded the terrace. It overlooked the rear portion of the Circuit House.

There was a garden at the back as well. I was considerably surprised to see it. All I had seen from one of the windows in our room was a single juniper tree standing at the back, but that gave no indication that there were so many trees spread over such a large area.

What was that bright blue object glittering behind a tree? Oh, it was a peacock. Most of its body was hidden behind the tree, so at first I couldn't see it properly. Now it emerged, and was pecking the ground. Was it looking for worms? As far as I knew, peacocks ate insects. Suddenly something I'd once read about peacocks came back to me. It is always difficult to find a peacock's nest. Apparently, they manage to choose the most inaccessible spots to lay their eggs and raise their young.

The peacock was moving forward, taking slow, measured steps, craning its neck and occasionally looking around. Its long tail followed the movement of its body.

Suddenly, the peacock stopped. It craned its neck to the right. What had it seen? Or had it heard something?

The peacock moved away. Something had disturbed it.

It was a man, standing right below the spot where I was. I could see him through the gaps in the trees. The man had a turban on his head. It wasn't very large. He had wrapped a white shawl around himself. As I was standing above him, I could not see his face. All I could see were his turban and his shoulders. His arms were hidden under the shawl.

He began walking stealthily, moving from the western side of the building. I was on the terrace facing the west. Our room was on the ground floor, in the opposite direction.

I wanted to see where the man was going. So I ran past the rooms in the middle of the terrace, and leant over the wall on the eastern side.

The man was standing below me once again. If he looked up, he would see me. But he didn't. He was creeping closer to our room, to one of its windows. Then one of his hands slipped out from under the shawl. What was that, close to his wrist, glinting in the sun?

The man stopped. My throat felt dry. Then he took another step forward.

Suddenly, a loud, harsh sound broke the silence. The peacock had cried from somewhere. The man gave a violent start and, at the same moment, I screamed, 'Feluda!'

The man in the turban turned and ran in the same direction from which he had come. He disappeared in a matter of seconds. I sprinted down the stairs, taking two steps at a time, ran along the corridor without stopping, crashed straight into Feluda at the door to our room, and stood there, stunned.

Feluda pulled me inside and asked, 'What's the matter? What happened?'

'I saw from the roof . . . a man . . . wearing a turban . . . walking towards your window!'

'What did he look like? Tall?'

'Don't know. Saw him from a height, you see. On his hand . . . was a . . .a . . .'.

'A what?'

'Watch . . .!'

I thought Feluda would either laugh the whole thing off, or tease me by calling me an idiot and a coward. He did neither. Looking a little grim, he simply peered out of the window and looked around.

Someone knocked on our door.

'Come in!'

A bearer came in with coffee.

'Salaam, saab!' He placed the tray on the table and took out a folded piece of paper from his pocket. He handed it to Feluda, saying, 'Manager saab asked me to give it to you.'

He left. Feluda read the note quickly, then flopped down on the sofa, with an air of resignation.

'Whose letter is that, Feluda?'

'Read it.'

It was a short note from Dr Hajra, written on a sheet of paper that had his name printed in a corner. It said:

I believe it is no longer safe for me to remain in Jodhpur. I am going somewhere else, where I hope to have better success. I see no reason to drag you and your cousin into further danger. So I am leaving without saying goodbye. I wish you both all the very best.
Yours, H.M. Hazra

'He has acted most hastily,' Feluda spoke through clenched teeth. Then he made for the reception desk without even drinking his coffee. Today, we found a different man at the desk. 'Did Dr Hajra say when he was going to be back?' Feluda asked.

'No, sir. He paid all his bills. Said nothing about coming back.'

'Do you know where he has gone?'

'To the railway station. That's all I know.'

Feluda thought for a moment. Then he said, 'It's possible to go to Jaisalmer by train from here, isn't it?'

'Yes, sir. We've had a direct line for two years.'

'When is the train?'

'It leaves at ten o'clock at night.'

'Is there a train in the morning?'

'Yes, but it goes only up to Pokhran. It should have left half an hour ago. One can go to Jaisalmer by this train, if one can arrange a car from Pokhran.'

'How far is it from Pokhran?'

'Seventy miles.'

'What other trains go from Jodhpur in the morning? I mean, to other destinations?'

The man consulted a book, leafing through a few pages. 'A train leaves for Barmer at eight o'clock. And at nine, there's the Rewari Passenger. That's all.'

Feluda's fingers beat an impatient tattoo on the counter. 'Jaisalmer is about 200 miles from here, isn't it?'

'Yes, sir.'

'Could you please arrange a taxi for us? We would like to leave for Jaisalmer at half past eleven.'

'Certainly, sir.' The receptionist picked up a telephone.

'Where are you off to?' asked a voice. It was Mandar Bose, coming out of his room with a suitcase in his hand. He had just had a shower and was smartly dressed.

'I'd like to see the Thar desert,' Feluda replied.

'Oh. So you're going to the northwest? I'm off to the east.'

'You are leaving Jodhpur, too?'

'My taxi should be here any minute. I don't like spending a very long time in any one place. Besides, if you leave as well, the Circuit House will become empty, in any case.'

The receptionist finished talking into the phone and turned to us. 'It's arranged,' he said.

'Topshe,' Feluda said to me, 'go and see if you can find Lalmohan Babu. Tell him we are going to Jaisalmer. If he wants to come with us, he should get ready immediately.'

I ran towards room number 10. It was not clear to me why we were suddenly going to Jaisalmer. Why did Feluda choose Jaisalmer, of all places? Was it because it was close to the desert? Had Dr

Hajra and Mukul also gone there? Did this mean that we were no longer in any danger? Or were we going to walk straight into it?

EIGHT

Pokhran was 120 miles from Jodhpur. Jaisalmer was another seventy. It should not take more than six or seven hours to cover 190 miles. Or, at least, that was what our driver, Gurbachan Singh, told us. He was a plump and cheerful Sikh. I saw him taking his hands off the steering wheel at times, and clasping them behind his head. Then he would lean back in his seat and take a little rest. But the car stayed on course because Gurbachan rested the steering wheel on his fat paunch, even moving it when necessary, without putting his hands back on it. This action was actually not as difficult as it may sound, for there was virtually no traffic on the road. Besides, the road ran straight, without curves or bends, for as much as five or six miles in many places. Unless something went wrong, we would reach Jaisalmer by six o'clock in the evening.

The scenery started to change when we were only ten miles out of Jodhpur. I had never seen anything like it. Jodhpur had a number of hills around it. The fort there was made of red sandstone that came from those hills. But now, those hills disappeared, and were replaced by an undulating terrain that stretched right up to the horizon. It was a mixture of grass, red earth, sand and loose stones. Ordinary trees and plants had disappeared, too. Now all I could see were acacia, cacti and similar plants whose names I didn't know.

The other thing I noticed was wild camels. They were roaming freely, like cattle and sheep. Some were light brown, like milky tea; others had darker coats, closer to black coffee. I saw one of them munching on a thorny plant. Feluda said that the thorns frequently injured a camel's mouth; but since those bushes were its only source of food, the camel put up with the discomfort.

Feluda also told me a little about Jaisalmer. It was built in the twelfth century, and became the capital of the Bhati Rajputs. Only sixty-four miles from there was the border between India and Pakistan. Even ten years ago, going to Jaisalmer was quite difficult. There were no trains, and what roads there were often disappeared under the sand. The place was so dry that if it rained just for a day in a whole year, people thought they were lucky. When I asked him about battles, Feluda said Alauddin Khilji had once attacked Jaisalmer.

We had travelled for nearly ninety kilometres (fifty-six miles), when purely out of the blue, we got a puncture, which made the car give an unpleasant shriek, lurch and come to a halt by the side of the road. I felt quite cross with Gurbachan Singh. He had assured us that he had checked the pressure in each tyre and all was well. As a matter of fact, the car appeared to be new and in good condition.

We got out with Gurbachan. It would take at least fifteen minutes to change the tyre.

As soon as our eyes fell on the flat tyre, we realized what had caused the puncture. Strewn over a large area on the road were hundreds of nails. It was obvious that they were new and had been bought recently.

We exchanged glances. Gurbachan let out an expletive through clenched teeth that I shall not repeat here. Feluda said nothing. He simply stood there, arms akimbo, and stared at the road, deep in thought. His brows were drawn together in a frown. Lalmohan Babu took out a green notebook—it looked like a diary—from an old Japan Airlines bag, and scribbled something in it with a pencil.

By the time we finished changing the tyre, removed all the nails from the road and were ready to leave, it was a quarter to two. Feluda said to Gurbachan, 'Sardarji, please keep an eye on the road. You can see that our enemies are trying to make things difficult for us!'

However, it wouldn't do to go too slowly, if we were to reach Jaisalmer before nightfall. So Gurbachan Singh reduced his speed from sixty to forty. If he were to keep his eye on the road all the time, he could hardly move faster than ten or fifteen miles an hour.

About forty miles later, when we had covered almost a hundred miles, the second disaster hit us. It simply could not be avoided.

This time, instead of nails, thousands of drawing pins had been strewn over at least twenty feet of the road. Obviously, whoever wanted us to have a flat tyre was not taking any chances.

What was also obvious was that Gurbachan Singh did not have another spare tyre.

We all climbed out again. If Gurbachan had not been wearing a turban, he would probably have scratched his head. Feluda asked him, 'Is Pokhran a town or a village?'

'It is a town, Babu.'

'How far is it?'

'About twenty-five miles.'

'Oh God. What are we going to do?'

Gurbachan tried to be reassuring. Every taxi that plied on that route, he said, was known to him. If we waited until another taxi came along, he would borrow a spare from its driver. Then we could go to Pokhran and have our own punctured tyres mended. The question was, would a taxi come along? If so, when? How long were we supposed to wait in the middle of nowhere?

A group of three men passed us by, leading five camels. They were going in the direction of Jodhpur. Each man had such dark skin that it looked almost black. One of them sported a snowy white beard and sideburns. I saw Lalmohan Babu move closer to Feluda, possibly because he had caught the men casting curious glances at us.

'Which is the nearest railway station from here?' Feluda asked, removing the pins from the road. We had all joined him in this good deed, to save other cars from a similar fate.

'Ramdeora. It is seven or eight miles from here.'

'Ramdeora . . .!'

When all the pins had been removed, Feluda took out a Bradshaw timetable from his shoulder bag. One particular page was folded. Feluda opened the timetable at that page, ran his eye over it and said, 'It's no use. The morning train that leaves Jodhpur reaches Ramdeora at 3.45. It must have left Ramdeora by now.'

'But isn't there another train to Jaisalmer at night?' I asked.

'Yes, but that will reach Ramdeora very early in the morning, at 3.53. If we began walking now, we'd take at least two hours to get to Ramdeora. There might have been a point in walking all that way, if there was any chance of catching the morning train. We could then have travelled to Pokhran, if nothing else. Now in this godforsaken . . .' Feluda broke off.

Even under such difficult circumstances, Lalmohan Babu smiled and said in a somewhat unsteady voice, 'Well, you must admit such a situation would be easier to find in a novel. Who knew even in real life . . .?'

Rather unexpectedly, Feluda raised a hand and stopped him. Our surroundings were completely silent, as if the entire world here had turned mute. In that silence, a faint noise reached our ears. There could be no mistake: chug-chug, chug-chug, chug-chug!

It was a train, the train to Pokhran. But where was the track?

I stared in the direction from which the noise was coming, and suddenly noticed a column of smoke. Almost immediately, I spotted a telegraph pole. I hadn't seen it before because the ground sloped down and the red pole practically merged with the reddish brown earth. Had it been standing on higher ground, outlined against the sky, it would have been far more easily visible.

'Run!' shouted Feluda and began running towards the smoke. I followed suit. Lalmohan Babu followed me. To my amazement, he ran so fast—despite his thin and scraggy appearance—that he nearly caught up with Feluda, leaving me behind.

I could see grass under my feet, but instead of being green, it was as white as cotton wool. We scrambled down the slope, still moving as fast as we could, and reached the railway track. The train was now within a hundred yards.

Without a second's hesitation, Feluda jumped into the middle of the track and began waving madly, both his arms raised high. The train began whistling loudly, but drowning the sound of the whistle rose Lalmohan Babu's voice: 'Stop! Stop! Halt, I say!'

Nothing worked. It was a small train, but not like the ones that Martin & Co. once used to run. If one stood by the tracks and raised a hand, those trains would stop, just like buses. This train, however, did nothing to reduce its speed. Whistling mightily, it came dangerously close, at which point Feluda was obliged to spring to safety. We simply stood and watched as the train coolly passed us by, clanging on its way, hiding the bright sun momentarily behind thick, black smoke. Even at a time like that, I couldn't help thinking that I might have seen such a scene only in a Hollywood western. Not once did I ever imagine I'd get to witness a scene like that in my own country!

'Such arrogance!' remarked Lalmohan Babu when the train had gone. 'It didn't look bigger than a caterpillar, did it?'

'Bad luck!' muttered Feluda, 'That train was running late, yet we couldn't take advantage of that. If we could have somehow got to Pokhran, we might have found another taxi.'

Gurbachan Singh, with great thoughtfulness, had collected our luggage and was carrying it over, but now there was no need for it. I glanced briefly at the track. All that could be seen was smoke.

Suddenly, Lalmohan Babu spoke excitedly. 'What about camels?' he said.

'Camels?'

'Over there—look!'

Yes. Another group with camels was coming our way, this time from the direction of Jodhpur.

'Good idea, let's go!'

At Feluda's words, we began running again. 'When a camel really gets going, I've heard that it can cover twenty miles in an hour!' Lalmohan Babu told me as he ran.

We managed to stop the group. This time, there were two men and seven camels. 'We need three camels, and we want to go to Ramdeora. How much would that be?' asked Feluda in Hindi. Then it turned out that the men spoke some local dialect. However, they could understand a little Hindi, and speak it, too, albeit haltingly. Gurbachan spoke on our behalf. In the end, they agreed to lend us their camels for ten rupees.

'Can your camels run fast?' Lalmohan Babu wanted to know, 'We have a train to catch!'

Feluda laughed. 'Don't worry about running. Get on the camel first.'

'Get on . . . on its back?'

Perhaps for the first time, face to face with a camel, Lalmohan Babu realized the complexities involved in climbing on to its back. I was looking carefully at the animals. They looked perfectly weird, but had been saddled with care. On their backs were the kind of sheets with fringes and tassels that I'd seen earlier on elephants. On top of this sheet was a wooden seat. The sheet was covered with red, blue, yellow and green geometric patterns. Each camel had its long neck wrapped with a length of red fabric decorated with cowrie shells. It was clear that, in spite of their strange appearance, their owners loved and cared for them.

Three camels were now kneeling on the ground. Gurbachan Singh, by this time, had fetched every piece of our luggage, which consisted of two suitcases, two holdalls and a few smaller items. Gurbachan told us to wait for him in Pokhran, if we could catch the train in Ramdeora. He would definitely get to Pokhran that night. Our luggage was tied securely on to two of the other camels.

The first three camels were still waiting for us.

'You saw how they sat down, didn't you?' Feluda asked Lalmohan Babu. 'A camel folds its forelegs first, and the front part of its body comes down before its rear. When it gets up, expect just the opposite. It will raise its hind legs first. If you can remember that and lean backwards and forwards accordingly, you can avoid a great deal of embarrassment.'

'Emb-embarrassment?' Lalmohan Babu croaked.

'Here, watch me!'

Feluda jumped on to the back of the first camel. One of the men made a funny noise through his teeth. At once, the camel raised itself—quickly but awkwardly—in exactly the same manner that Feluda had just described. But he managed very well, there was no awkwardness.

'Come on, Topshe! You two are smaller and lighter than me, it should be easier for you,' Feluda called.

Both the Rajasthani men were grinning at our antics. I gathered all my courage and got on the second camel, which stood up immediately. Now I could tell where the real problem lay. When the hind legs were raised, the rider on the camel's back was likely to slide forward in one swift motion. If one could lean back and remain in that position as the camel rose to its feet, it would be easier to maintain one's balance. If I ever had to ride a camel again, I must remember that, I told myself.

'Dear G-ya-aa-d!' said Lalmohan Babu.

'God' became 'Gyad' for the simple reason that, even as he was uttering those words, the rear portion of the camel's body jerked into motion and Lalmohan Babu slid forward on its back. In the next instant, he was thrown back in the opposite direction. I heard him gulp noisily, as he lay horizontal on the camel's back, cast into an undignified heap.

Having said goodbye to Gurbachan Singh, we three Bedouins began our journey to Ramdeora.

'We must get to Ramdeora in half an hour. It's eight miles from here, isn't it? We have a train to catch!' Feluda yelled to the two men. At these words, one of them jumped up on his camel and marched forward briskly to take the lead. The second man shouted, 'Hei! Hei!' and every camel broke into a run.

As it was, the animals were ungainly and not exactly easy to sit on. When they lurched forward, my whole body swung and shook from side to side; but I didn't mind. We were running across a sandy terrain, covered with dry, scorched grass, and the place was

Rajasthan—so, all in all, it was a thrilling experience.

Feluda was ahead of me, and Lalmohan Babu's camel was behind me. Feluda turned his head and called out, 'How do you find the ship of the desert, Mr Ganguli?'

I, too, looked back to see what Lalmohan Babu was doing. I found him making an awful grimace, as if he was in a freezing cold climate. His lips had parted, his teeth were clenched, and the veins on his neck were all standing out.

'What's the matter?' Feluda went on. 'Why don't you say something?'

Six words emerged from Lalmohan Babu, in five instalments: 'Ship . . . all right. . . but. . . talking . . . impossible!'

Laughter began bubbling up inside me once again, but I quelled it and focussed on the journey. We were now running alongside the railway track. In the distance, a column of smoke seemed to rise for a minute; then it disappeared. The sun was going down in the western horizon, and the landscape was changing. A hazy range of hills was visible in the far distance. On our right was a huge sand dune, unmarked by human feet. It was covered with wavy lines from top to bottom.

Perhaps the camels were not used to running fast for any length of time, so their speed faltered every now and then. When that happened, one of the men barked, 'Hei! Hei!' again, and the animals ran faster.

Around a quarter past four, a square structure came into view. It appeared to be a building, right next to the railway track. What could it be, if it wasn't a railway station?

As we got closer, it became clear that we were right. There was a signal, too. So it had to be a station, and the place had to be Ramdeora.

The camels had slowed down again. But now there was no need to shout at them. The train we were hoping to catch had come and gone. We couldn't tell when it had left, but there could be no doubt that we had missed it.

It meant only one thing. Until three o'clock in the morning, we would have to wait in this unknown place, in the middle of nowhere, by the side of the tiny structure that was trying to pass itself off as a station. And there was not a soul in sight.

NINE

It turned out that the station was in the process of being built. All it had at the moment was a platform and that structure, which was really a ticket window. Heaven knew when the building work would be completed. We selected a spot close to the ticket window and sat on our holdalls, preparing ourselves for a long wait. A kerosene lamp hung from a wooden post nearby, so when it got dark, we would at least be able to see one another.

There appeared to be signs of habitation not all that far from the station. Feluda went to have a look, then returned and said that although he had seen houses, there were no shops and nowhere to eat. All we had with us was a little water in our flasks, and Lalmohan Babu had a tin of goja (deep-fried pastry dipped in syrup). Perhaps we would have to spend the whole night on the strength of those.

The sun had set about ten minutes ago. It would soon be dark. Gurbachan Singh's arrival did not seem likely, as in the last three hours, we had not seen a single car go past, either towards Jodhpur or Jaisalmer. There was nothing to do but wait on the platform until the next train came at three o'clock.

Feluda was sitting on his suitcase and gazing steadily at the track. I watched him cracking the fingers of his right hand with his left. Obviously, he was anxious or agitated about something, which was why he wasn't saying much.

Lalmohan Babu opened his tin, bit into a goja and said, 'Who knew this would happen? If I didn't travel with you in the same compartment on the way from Agra, the entire nature of my holiday would not have changed like this, would it?'

'Why, do you mind?' Feluda asked.

'No, of course not!' Lalmohan Babu laughed. 'But it would certainly help if a few things were a bit clearer.'

'Which things in particular?'

'I don't really know what's going on, do I? I feel a bit like a shuttlecock—slapped from one side to the other, and back again. I mean, I don't even know who you are. Are you the hero, or the villain? Ha ha!'

'Why do you want to know? What would you do, anyway, if you knew?' Feluda asked with a smile. 'When you write a novel, do you reveal everything at the outset? Why don't you treat this entire

Rajasthani experience as a novel? When it comes to an end, every mystery will be cleared up.'

'And I? Will I still be alive, and in one piece?'

'Well, you've already proved that you can run faster than a rabbit, if you have to. Isn't that reassuring enough?'

I hadn't realized it before, but someone had come and lit the kerosene lamp while we were talking. In its light, I suddenly saw two men, clad in local Rajasthani garb with turbans on their heads, making their way towards us. In their hands were stout sticks, which they were tapping on the ground. They stopped a few feet away, squatted and began a conversation in a completely incomprehensible language.

One thing about those men made my jaw fall open. Both were sporting huge moustaches. They didn't just turn upward, but had, in fact, coiled at least four times on either side of the men's faces. The final effect was like the spring fitted inside a clock. If they were pulled straight, each side would probably measure eighteen inches. Lalmohan Babu, too, seemed totally dumbstruck by the sight.

'Bandits!' muttered Feluda under his breath.

'Really?' Lalmohan Babu quickly poured himself some water from the flask and gulped it down.

'Undoubtedly.'

Lalmohan Babu tried to replace the lid on his tin, but dropped it on the platform with a loud clang. The noise made him jump, and he became more nervous.

I looked at the two men closely. Their skin was as dark and shiny as a freshly polished shoe. One of them took out a cigarette, placed it between his lips, and slapped all his pockets until he found a matchbox in one of them. But it turned out to be empty, so he threw it away on the track.

A sudden noise made me glance at Feluda. He had flicked his lighter on and was offering it to the man. The man looked taken aback at first, then leant forward to light his cigarette. After that, he took the lighter from Feluda and examined it closely, pressing it here and there before finding the right spot and lighting it once more. Lalmohan Babu tried to speak, but his voice sounded choked.

The man switched the lighter on and off a few times, before returning it to Feluda. Lalmohan Babu began stuffing his tin back into his suitcase, but it slipped from his hand and, this time, the whole tin fell on the ground, making a racket that was ten times worse than the previous one. Feluda paid him no attention. He simply took out his blue notebook from his shoulder bag and began leafing through its pages in the dim light from the kerosene lamp.

Suddenly, my eyes fell on a thorny bush a little way beyond the ticket window. A light was falling on it. Where was it coming from?

It was growing brighter. Then I heard a car. It was coming from the direction of Jaisalmer. Oh good. Perhaps Gurbachan Singh would now be able to borrow a spare tyre.

The car came into view, then whooshed past the little station and vanished towards Jodhpur. My watch showed half past seven.

Feluda raised his eyes from his notebook and looked at Lalmohan Babu. 'Lalmohan Babu,' he said, 'you write novels, don't you? You must know a lot of things. Can you tell me what a blister is, and what causes it?'

'Blister? . . . Blister?' Lalmohan Babu sounded completely taken aback. 'Why does one get blisters, you mean? But one could, quite easily. I mean, suppose you burnt your finger while lighting your cigarette . . .'

'Yes. But why should that cause a blister?'

'Oh. I see. Why? You want to know the reason?'

'All right, never mind. Tell me something else. If you look at a man from a height, why does he appear short?'

Lalmohan Babu simply stared without a word. Even in that dim light, I could see him rubbing his hands uncertainly. The two Rajasthani men were still talking in that same language, using the same tone. Feluda's eyes were fixed on Lalmohan Babu's face.

Lalmohan Babu licked his lips and found his voice. 'Why are you . . . I mean, all these questions . . .?'

'I have one more. And I'm sure you know the answer to this one.'

Lalmohan Babu said nothing. It was as if Feluda had hypnotized him.

'This morning, what were you doing among the trees behind the Circuit House, creeping up to my window?'

Just for a moment, Lalmohan Babu remained motionless. Then life returned to his limbs, and he burst into speech. 'But I was going to see you!' he declared, gesticulating wildly. 'Believe me, Mr Mitter, it was you I wanted to see. But that peacock made such a racket, and then I heard someone scream . . . so I got all startled and nervous and so . . . .!'

'Was that the only way to get to my room? And was it necessary to wear a turban and a shawl to come and see me?'

'Look, that shawl was only a bed sheet. I took it from my room.
And the turban? That was a towel from the Circuit House. I had to
have some sort of a disguise, don't you see? Or how could I spy on
that man?'

'Which man?'

'Mr Trotter. Very suspicious, that man. But thank goodness I did
go there. See what I found, lying on the grass outside his window.
It's a secret code. I was going to pass it on to you, when that peacock
cried out and spoilt everything!'

I was looking carefully at Lalmohan Babu's watch. Yes, it was
the same watch I had seen from the terrace in the Circuit House.

Lalmohan Babu opened his suitcase and groped in it. He fished
out a crumpled piece of paper and handed it to Feluda. I could see
that it had been screwed into a ball, but straightened later.

I peered over Feluda's shoulder to see what was written on it with
a pencil. It said:

IP 1625+U

U – M

Feluda frowned darkly at the piece of paper. Was it algebra? I
couldn't make head or tail of it. Lalmohan Babu whispered a couple
of times, 'Highly suspicious!'

Feluda was muttering to himself, 1625 . . .1625 . . . where have
I seen that number recently?'

'Could it be the number of a taxi?' I asked.

'No. 1625 . . . sixteen twenty-fi—!' Feluda left his sentence
incomplete and pounced upon his shoulder bag. Then he took out
the railway timetable and opened it at the page that was folded. He
ran a finger quickly down the page, and stopped abruptly.

'Yes, here it is. 1625 is the arrival.'

'Where?'

'Pokhran.'

'In that case,' I remarked, 'the "P" might mean "Pokhran". 1625
in Pokhran. What about the rest?'

'The rest is . . . "IP" and then "+U" . . . what could it. . .?'

'I don't like that "M" in the second line,' Lalmohan Babu told us.
'The letter M always reminds me of the word "murder".'

'Wait, dear sir, let me first deal with the top line!'

Lalmohan Babu continued to mutter under his breath, 'Murder. . .
mystery . . . massacre . . . monster . . .!'

Feluda sat with the piece of paper on his lap, lost in thought.

Lalmohan Babu took out his tin of goja and offered it to me again. When I'd taken one, he turned to Feluda and said, 'By the way, how did you know I'd crept up to your window? Did you see me?'

Feluda helped himself to a goja. 'You took your turban off, but did not brush your hair. When I met you shortly after the incident. the state of your hair made me quite suspicious.'

Lalmohan Babu smiled. 'I hope you won't mind my saying it, sir, but you strike me as a detective. A hundred per cent, full-fledged detective!'

Without saying anything, Feluda handed him one of his cards. Lalmohan Babu's eyes began glinting.

'Oh. Pradosh C. Mitter! Is that your real name?'

'Yes. Why, is there something wrong with it?'

'No, no. But isn't it strange?'

'What is?'

'Your name. Look, it matches your profession. P-r-a-d-o-s-h, pronounced pro-dosh. "Pro" stands for "professional"; and "dosh" is the Bengali word for "crime". The "C" is "to see", that is "to investigate". So the whole thing works out as Pradosh C = Professional Crime Investigator!'

'Great. Well done. But what about "Mitter"?'

'Mitter? Oh, that . . . I'll have to think about it,' said Lalmohan Babu, scratching his head.

'There's no need. I can solve it for you. You have seen meters on taxis, haven't you? It's the same thing—that is to say, it's an indicator. So it doesn't just investigate, it also indicates. It picks out the criminal after an investigation and points a finger at him. Would you go along with that?'

'Bravo!' said Lalmohan Babu, clapping. But Feluda grew serious again. He glanced at the code, transferred it to his shirt pocket and took out a cigarette.

'The "I" and the "U" can be easily explained,' he said, 'that "I" is probably the fellow who wrote the code. And "U" is "you". But that plus sign doesn't make sense. And the second line is totally obscure . . . Look, Topshe, why don't you spread your holdall on the platform here and try to get some sleep? You, too, Lalmohan Babu. The train won't be here for another seven and a half hours. I will wake you up at the right time.'

It was not a bad idea. I unstrapped our holdall and spread it out.

As soon as I lay flat on my back, my eyes went to the sky and I realized I had never seen so many stars in my life. Was the sky so clear because we were close to a desert? Perhaps.

Soon, my eyes grew heavy with sleep. Once, I heard Lalmohan Babu say, 'I say, riding a camel has made my joints ache!' Then I thought I heard him mutter, 'M is murder.' After that I fell asleep.

The next thing I knew, Feluda was trying to shake me awake. 'Topshe! Get up, here comes the train!'

I scrambled to my feet and began rolling my holdall. By the time the straps had been fastened, the headlight on the train had come into view.

TEN

It was a passenger train running on meter gauge. Its compartments were therefore quite small. There were not many passengers, either; hence when we found an empty first-class compartment, it did not surprise me.

Inside the coach, it was dark. We groped for a switch, found it and pressed it—to no avail. Lalmohan Babu said, 'Bulbs in railway compartments tend to vanish even in civilized areas. In this land of bandits, one shouldn't even expect to find any!'

'The two of you can take the benches. I will spread a durrie on the floor and manage. We have six whole hours in hand—time enough for a nice, long nap!' said Feluda.

Lalmohan Babu raised a mild objection to this plan, 'Why should you be on the floor? Let me . . .!' But Feluda said, 'Certainly not!' so sternly that he said nothing more. I saw him spread his holdall on one of the benches, not merely because of Feluda's words, but perhaps also out of concern for his aching joints.

The train began pulling out of the platform. Within a minute of leaving the station, suddenly a figure jumped on to the footboard of our carriage. Lalmohan Babu said with a laugh, 'Hey, this is a reserved compartment. Ladies only!'

Then the door swung open quickly, and a bright light from a torch dazzled our eyes for a few seconds. We saw a hand coming towards us. The point of a gun shone in that light. All of us raised our arms high above our heads.

'Get up, dear hearts! The door's open, get out of the train. All of you!' It was the voice of Mandar Bose.

'But . . . but the train's still running!' said Lalmohan Babu in a trembling voice.

'Shut up!' roared Mandar Bose and inched a little closer. The torchlight was playing on our faces constantly, never standing still for more than a few moments.

'You trying to be funny?' Mr Bose went on. 'What do you do in Calcutta? Don't you climb in and out running buses? Get up, I tell you!'

Just as he finished speaking, something happened so totally unexpectedly that it took my breath away. I shall never forget it as long as I live. Feluda's right arm came down in a flash. He grasped a corner of the durrie and yanked it off the floor. As a result, Mandar Bose lost his balance. His feet slipped, then rose in the air for a second, before he fell, the top half of his body hitting the wall of the carriage with a bang. At the same time, the revolver was knocked out of his hand. It fell on Lalmohan Babu's bench, and the torch dropped from his left hand on to the floor.

All that happened in a split second. Even before Mandar Bose crashed down on the floor, Feluda had sprung up, clutching his own revolver, which had come out of his jacket pocket.

'Get up!' This time it was Feluda who ordered Mandar Bose.

The meter gauge train was swinging and swaying across the desert, making a lot of noise. Lalmohan Babu had, in the meantime, grabbed Mr Bose's revolver and stuffed it into his own Japan Airlines bag.

'Get up!' Feluda shouted again.

The torch was rolling on the floor. I could see that it should really be focussed on Mr Bose, or the fellow might take advantage of the darkness and try to trick us. Some such thought made me bend down to pick it up—which led to disaster. Even now, my blood runs cold when I think about it.

Mandar Bose was facing my bench. Just as I bent down, he suddenly lunged forward, grabbed me and got to his feet, holding me firmly in front of himself. As a result, I became a protective shield for him. Even at such a critical moment, I couldn't help admiring his cunning. It was clear that although round one had gone to Feluda most unexpectedly, he was certainly in a difficult position in the second round. And I was wholly to blame.

Mandar Bose kept a tight hold on me as he began moving towards the open door. I could feel something sharp hurting my shoulder.

Then I realized it was one of his nails. Suddenly, I remembered little Neelu complaining that his hand hurt.

We were now standing very close to the door. I could feel the biting cold night air. It was brushing against my left shoulder.

Mandar Bose took another step. Feluda's gun was pointed at him, but now Feluda couldn't really do anything. The torch was still rolling on the floor as the train swayed from side to side.

Suddenly, I was flung forward, with considerable force. It made me collide with Feluda. The sound that came a second later told me that Mandar Bose had jumped out of the moving train. What I could not tell was whether he had survived or not.

Feluda went to the door and peered out. He came back a couple of minutes later, replaced his revolver and said, 'I hope he breaks a few bones, or it will be a matter of great regret.'

Lalmohan Babu laughed—a trifle loudly—and said, 'Didn't I tell you the man was suspicious?'

I gulped some water from the flask. My heartbeat was gradually returning to normal, as was my breathing. I was still finding it difficult to grasp the enormity of what had just happened, in a matter of minutes.

'He got away this time only because of dear Topesh,' said Feluda, 'or I'd have used my gun to drag a full confession out of him. However . . .' he stopped. After a brief pause, he said, 'When I come face to face with danger, my brain starts working much more efficiently. I've noticed it before. Now I can see what that code meant.'

'Really?' Lalmohan Babu sounded amazed.

'It's actually quite simple. "I" is the man writing the note, "P" is Pokhran, "U" is "you", and "M" is "Mitter". Pradosh Mitter.'

'And the plus and minus signs?'

'IP 1625 + U. That means "I am arriving at Pokhran at 4.25. You must join me."'

'And U – M? What does that mean?'

'That's even simpler. It means "you get rid of Mitter".'

'Get rid . . .?' Lalmohan Babu could barely speak. 'You mean the minus sign stands for murder?'

'No, not necessarily. If you were forced to jump out of a moving train, chances are you'd be injured. And, in any case, you'd have to wait another twenty-four hours for the next train. The crooks would have finished their business in that time. What they really needed to do was stop us from going to Jaisalmer. That's why they littered the road with nails and pins. But when they realized that hadn't worked, Bose tried to get us off the train.'

Suddenly, I became aware of a smell. 'I can smell a cigar, Feluda!' I exclaimed.

'Yes, I got that smell as soon as the fellow jumped into the compartment. It was obvious even in the Circuit House that someone was smoking cigars. Remember that golden foil Mukul found? Cigars are wrapped in that kind of foil.'

'And there's something else. One of his nails is much longer than others. My shoulder must be as badly scratched as Neelu's hand.'

'All right, but who is the "I" who is giving all the instructions?' Lalmohan Babu wanted to know.

Feluda's voice sounded solemn when he spoke. 'That warning someone had left for me in the Circuit House, and this handwritten code both point to one person.'

'Who?' Lalmohan Babu and I cried together.

'Dr Hemanga Mohan Hajra.'

The rest of the night passed without further excitement. I slept for about three hours. When I woke, it was bright and sunny outside. Feluda was no longer lying on the floor. He was seated in one corner of my bench and staring out of the window. On his lap was his blue notebook, and in his hands were two notes. One was the warning, and the other was the letter Dr Hajra had left for us before leaving Jodhpur. I glanced at my watch. It was a quarter to seven. Lalmohan Babu was still fast asleep. I felt very hungry, but had no wish to eat another goja. We would reach Jaisalmer at nine. Somehow, I must put up with the pangs of hunger until then.

The scenery outside was really strange. For mile after mile stretched an undulating landscape—there was not a single house in sight, not a single human being, not even a tree. Yet I could not call it a desert because, although there was a little sand, most of it consisted of dry, pale grass, reddish earth and blackish-red chips of stone. It seemed incredible that, after such a landscape, we would find a whole town again.

The train stopped at a station called Jetha-chandan. I opened the railway timetable and discovered that the next station was called

Thaiyat Hamira, and the one after that was Jaisalmer. At Jetha-
chandan, there were no shops or stalls on the platform, no hawkers,
no porters, no passengers. It was as if our train had somehow arrived
at a place that had not yet been discovered by man. It was no different
from a rocket landing on moon.

Lalmohan Babu woke soon after the train started moving again.
He yawned and said, 'I had the most fantastic dream, you know.
There was this gang of bandits, each with a moustache that looked
like the horns of a ram. I had hypnotized them, and was leading
them through a castle. There was a tunnel. We went through the
tunnel and reached an underground chamber. I knew there was some
treasure buried in that chamber, but all I could see was a camel
sitting on the floor, chewing gojas!'

'How do you know that?' Feluda asked. 'Did the camel open its
mouth and show you what it was chewing?'

'No, no. But I saw my tin—there it was, lying in front of the
camel!'

Soon after we left Thaiyat Hamira, in the distance, the hazy outline
of a hill came into view. It was a Rajasthani table mountain with a
flat top. Our train appeared to be going in that direction.

Around eight o'clock, we could dimly see some sort of structure
on top of that hill. Slowly, it became clear that it was a fortress. It
stood like a crown atop the hill, spread all around its flattened top.
It was bathed in the bright light of the early morning sun, which was
falling directly upon it from a dazzling sky. Quite involuntarily, three
words slipped out of my mouth: 'The golden fortress!'

'That's right,' Feluda told me. 'This is the only golden fortress in
Rajasthan. That bowl in that shop in Jodhpur raised my suspicions.
Then I looked it up in the guide book, and my suspicions were
confirmed. The fort and the bowl were both made with the same
stone—yellow sandstone. If Mukul is truly a jatismar, and if there is
truly something like a previous life, then I think he was born
somewhere in this region.'

'But does Dr Hajra know that?' I asked.

Feluda did not reply. He was still staring at the fort. 'You know
something Topshe?' he said finally. 'There is something special about
that golden light. It has helped me see the whole pattern of the spider's
web, very clearly!'

ELEVEN

The first thing we did on getting off the train in Jaisalmer was to stop at a tea stall and have a cup of tea and some sweets. It was a new kind of sweet, one that we hadn't had before. Feluda said it would do us good as it had glucose in it. A lot of activity lay ahead, the glucose would provide extra energy.

We emerged from the station to find that there was not a single vehicle we could hire—no tongas, ekkas, cycle-rickshaws, or taxis. There was a jeep waiting, but it was obviously not meant for hire. When we got off the train, I had noticed a black Ambassador standing outside. But now even that had gone.

'It's a small town,' Feluda said. 'I don't think a place is all that far from another. My guide book says there's a dak bungalow. Let's go and find it.'

We set off, carrying our luggage. Soon enough, we found a petrol station, where a man gave us directions. In order to get to the dak bungalow, we would not have to climb the hill, he said. The bungalow was located on the plains, to the south of the hill. As we began walking again, Feluda looked at the tyre marks on the sand and said, 'That Ambassador must have come this way!'

About fifteen minutes later, we came upon a bungalow. A wooden board fixed to its gate told us that we had come to the right place. The black Ambassador was parked in front of it.

An old man wearing a khaki shirt and a short dhoti came out of an outhouse. On his head was a turban. Perhaps he had seen us arrive. Feluda asked him in Hindi if he was the chowkidar. The man nodded. It appeared from the way he was looking at us that our arrival was unexpected, and he didn't altogether approve of our sudden appearance, as no one was allowed to stay in the bungalow without prior permission.

Feluda said nothing about staying there. All we wanted to do, he told the man, was leave our luggage in the bungalow. Then we'd try to get the necessary permission. 'You'll have to see the Raja's secretary for that,' said the chowkidar and pointed us in the right direction. The palace, also made of yellow sandstone, was at some distance; but certain portions of it were visible, rising above the trees.

The chowkidar raised no objection to our luggage being left there,

He showed us into a small room, where we dumped our suitcases and holdalls. Then we filled our flasks with fresh water, slung them on our shoulders and asked him the way to the fort.

'You want to go to the fort?'

The question came from the far end of a passage. A gentleman had just come out of a room. He appeared no more than forty, had a clear complexion, and a sharp nose, under which was a thin moustache, very carefully trimmed. A second later, he was joined by an older man, who was clutching a stick—the kind that we had seen in the market in Jodhpur—and was wearing an odd, somewhat ill-fitting black suit. I could not tell which part of the country they might be from. The second man was limping slightly, which explained the need for the stick.

'Yes, a look at the fort might be interesting,' said Feluda.

'Come along with us, we are going that way.'

Feluda thought for a few moments, then agreed. 'Thank you very much, it is very kind of you,' he said

As we made our way to the car, Lalmohan Babu whispered into my ear: 'I hope these men won't try to throw us out of a moving car!'

The car began its journey to the fort. The man with the stick asked us, 'Are you from Calcutta ?'

'Yes,' Feluda replied.

To our left, in the distance, rising from the sand, were stone pillars. We had seen something similar in Devikund. Feluda said such structures were quite common in Rajasthan.

Our car started going uphill. About a minute later, we heard another car. It was tooting urgently. That was a bit surprising, since we were not driving all that slowly and getting in its way. Feluda was sitting at the back with the two gentlemen. He turned round, peered through the glass and suddenly said to our driver, 'Stop! Please stop!'

Our car pulled up by the side of the road. At once, a taxi came along and stopped on our right. Holding its steering wheel was Gurbachan Singh, greeting us with a smile.

The three of us climbed out. Feluda said to the two men, 'Thank you so much for your help. But this is our own taxi. It had broken down on the way to Jaisalmer, but now it's caught up with us.'

When we were back in his car, Gurbachan told us how, at half past six that morning, he had spotted another taxi going back from

Jaisalmer. He knew its driver, and managed to get a spare tyre from him. Then he covered ninety miles in two hours. When he reached Jaisalmer, he simply waited at the petrol station, until he spotted us inside the black Ambassador.

A little later, we found ourselves going through a market. There were shops everywhere, a loudspeaker was playing a Hindi song and, outside a small cinema, was a poster advertising a Hindi film.

'You want to see the fort?' Gurbachan asked.

'Yes,' Feluda told him. Gurbachan stopped the taxi and said, 'This is its gate.'

To our right was a massive gate, beyond which rose a road, paved with stone, which led to a second gate. That, I realized, was the real entrance to the fort, the first one acted as the front gate. Behind the entrance, rising steeply, was the golden fortress of Jaisalmer.

A guard was standing outside the front gate. Feluda went and asked him if he had seen a man with a small boy that morning. He indicated Mukul's height.

'Yes, sir, they were here. But they've now left,' replied the guard.

'When did they leave?'

'About half an hour ago.'

'Did they come by car?'

'Yes, sir. In a taxi.'

'Which way did they go? Can you remember?'

The guard nodded and pointed at the road that went further west. We got back to the car and followed it, passing through little alleys and more shops. Lalmohan Babu was sitting next to Gurbachan. Feluda and I were in the back seat. After a few minutes, Feluda suddenly asked, 'You didn't bring your weapon with you, did you?'

Startled by such a question, Lalmohan Babu said, 'The dodger? No, sorry, I mean that Nepali dagger?'

'Yes, sir. Your dagger.'

'That's in my suitcase.'

'In that case, take out Mandar Bose's revolver from your Japan Airlines bag and tuck it into your belt. Make sure it isn't visible.'

From Lalmohan Babu's movements, it became clear that he was following Feluda's instruction. I was dying to see his face, but couldn't.

'Don't worry,' Feluda said reassuringly, 'If things get sticky, all you have to do is take that gun out and point it in front of you.'

'What if b-b-behind me, there's . . .?'

'If you hear a noise behind you, then just turn around. Then your "behind" will become your "front", see?'

'And you? Are you . . . . I mean, today, are you going to be non-violent?'

'That depends.'

Our taxi left the market behind and came to an open space. We had already asked a couple of men on the way, and learnt that the other taxi had been seen coming this way. Besides, we had also seen tyre-marks in the sand from time to time, which told us that we were following the same route that Dr Hemanga Hajra had taken.

Gurbachan Singh came up with more information. 'This is the way to Mohangarh,' he said. 'I could drive for another mile, but after that the road gets really rough. Only jeeps can travel on that road, nothing else.'

But we didn't have to go another mile. Only a little later, we saw a taxi standing on one side of the road. To our right, at some distance, were a number of old, abandoned stone houses. All the roofs had caved in. Clearly, it had once been a village. We had seen similar villages elsewhere. People had moved out of them a long time ago. The walls of these houses were still standing only because they were made of stone.

We told Gurbachan to wait, and made our way to the houses. I saw Gurbachan get out of his car and go towards the other one, perhaps to chat with its driver.

Everything was eerily silent. If I turned my head, I could see the fort behind me, on top of the hill. Opposite the road, another hill rose steeply. At its foot, spread over a wide, open area were rows of yellow stones, embedded in the ground. They looked like giant spice-grinders. 'Graves of warriors,' whispered Feluda.

Lalmohan Babu spoke, in a hoarse yet squeaky voice, 'I . . . I . . . have low blood pressure!'

'Don't you worry,' Feluda replied. 'It will soon rise higher, I promise you, and stop exactly where it should.'

We were now quite close to the houses. A path ran straight through them. I realized this village was different from the ones I had seen in Bengal. It had a simple, geometric plan.

But where were the people who had travelled in the other taxi? Where was Mukul? And Dr Hajra?

Had something happened to Mukul?

Suddenly, I became aware of a noise. It was faint, but audible if I strained my ears: thud, thud, thud, thud!

We walked on, very carefully and very silently. Then we reached a crossroad where two lanes intersected. The noise was coming from the right. Ten or twelve houses stood by the road. There were yawning gaps between their walls and where once there must have been doors.

We turned right and resumed walking stealthily.

Feluda uttered one word through his teeth, almost inaudibly, 'Revolver!' I saw that his hand had disappeared under his jacket. Out of the corner of my eye, I saw a revolver in Lalmohan Babu's hand, which was trembling violently.

A sudden crunching noise made us come to a halt. In the next instant, through the door of a house at the far end on our left, appeared Mukul, running fast. Then he saw us, ran even faster, and flung himself on Feluda's chest. He was gasping, his face was deathly pale.

I opened my mouth to ask him what had happened, but Feluda placed a finger on his lips and stopped me from speaking aloud.

'Please look after him until I return!' he whispered to Lalmohan Babu, and left Mukul in his charge. Then he proceeded towards the house from which we had just seen Mukul emerge. I followed Feluda.

The strange noise was getting louder. It sounded as if someone was lifting stones. Thud! Bang! Clang! It went on.

Feluda flattened himself against the wall as we got close to the house. A couple of steps later, we were able to peer through the gap left by the missing door. With his back to us, crouching over a huge pile of rubble, was Dr Hajra. Like a madman, he was removing stone after stone from that heap, and casting each one aside. He had no idea that we were standing so close.

Feluda took another step, pointing his revolver at Dr Hajra.

Suddenly, we heard a flutter above our heads.

A peacock swooped down from the compound wall. It sped towards Dr Hajra the instant it landed, and attacked him, pecking hard just under his left ear. Dr Hajra, who was still crouching over the stones, could only scream in agony and press his hand over that spot. At once, the white cuff of his shirt turned red.

But the peacock hadn't finished. It continued to attack him, pecking wherever it could. Dr Hajra turned, took a step towards the door in an attempt to escape, and saw us. He started as if he'd seen a pair of ghosts. We stepped aside. The peacock chased him out through the door.

'You did not imagine, did you, that a peacock would have built its nest—and that nest would contain its eggs—in the same spot where the treasure was buried?'

Feluda's voice sounded as cold as steel. His revolver was pointed at Dr Hajra. It was clear to me now that the real culprit in this whole affair was Dr Hajra—and he had been suitably punished already—but there were so many other things that still seemed hazy that my head started reeling.

Then we heard a car.

Dr Hajra fell to the ground. He was lying on his stomach. He lifted his head and turned it slowly towards Feluda. His left hand, clutching a bloodstained handkerchief, was still pressed against his wound.

'There is absolutely no hope left for you. I hope you realize that? Every route of escape is closed, and . . .'

Before Feluda could finish speaking, Dr Hajra sprang to his feet and began running blindly in the opposite direction, away from the derelict house. Feluda lowered his gun because there really was no way that Dr Hajra could now escape. Two men, whom I recognized, were walking towards us. The one who was not hampered by a stick caught Dr Hajra neatly in his arms, as if he were a cricket ball.

The other man clutching the stick approached Feluda. I saw Feluda transfer his revolver to his left hand and offer the man his right hand. 'Hello, Dr Hajra!' he said.

What! That man was Dr Hajra?

He shook hands with Feluda. 'And you are Pradosh Mitter?'

'Yes. Those new naagras caused blisters on your feet, didn't they? Are they still bothering you?'

The real Dr Hajra smiled. 'I rang Mr Dhar the day before yesterday. He told me you were here. I had no problem in recognizing you from his description. Allow me to introduce you—this is Inspector Rathor.'

'And what about him?' Feluda pointed at the other man, whom until now we had known as Dr Hajra. He was now handcuffed and hanging his head, 'Is that Bhavananda?'

'Yes,' Dr Hajra replied, 'alias Amiyanath Burmun, alias the Great Bar-man—Wizard of the East!'

TWELVE

Bhavananda was handed over to the local police. The charges against him were many. They included an attempt to murder Hemanga Hajra, disappearing with his belongings, and trying to pass himself off as Dr Hajra.

We were back in the dak bungalow, having coffee (made with camel's milk) on the veranda. Mukul was romping happily on the lawn in front of us. He knew he would leave for Calcutta the same night. Having seen the golden fortress, he had no wish to remain in Rajasthan any longer.

Feluda turned to the real Dr Hajra and said, 'Bhavananda was truly a fraud, wasn't he? I mean, what he did in Chicago, and all that I read in the press reports . . . was all of it true?'

'Yes. One hundred per cent. Bhavananda and his accomplice cheated and swindled others in various countries, not just one. Besides, back in Chicago, they were doing something else. Not only were they out to deceive everyone, but they were also spreading evil tales and rumours about me, which was affecting my work. So, in the end, I was forced to take certain steps. But all that happened four years ago. I do not know when they returned to India. I came back only three months ago. One day, I happened to be in Mr Dhar's shop, when I heard about his son. So I went to meet him. You know the rest. When I decided to travel to Rajasthan with Mukul, I had no idea I'd be followed!'

'Who wouldn't want to kill two birds with one stone?' Feluda asked. 'There was the chance to grab that hidden treasure, plus settle scores with you . . . But didn't you see them anywhere in Calcutta?'

'No, not once. The first time I met them was in the refreshment room in the station at Bandikui. The two men came up to me and began chatting.'

'You didn't recognize them?'

'No, bow could I? I had only seen them in Chicago, where they had long hair, flowing beards and fat moustaches!'

'What happened next?'

'They sat at the same table and had a meal with us. They told Mukul they knew magic and even pulled some tricks. Then they got into the same compartment with us. I got off at Kisangarh to show Mukul the fort there, but didn't realize that those two characters had followed me. They reached the fort soon after us, and hid somewhere until the coast was clear. It was a deserted place, in any case. There was no one in sight. When they found an opportunity, they pushed me down a slope. I rolled down, perhaps a hundred feet. Luckily, my fall was broken by a clump of bushes. If I take my shirt off, you'll see that my body is still covered with bruises. Anyway, I remained by the side of that bush for a whole hour. I wanted them to think that they had managed to get rid of me, and leave with Mukul. At least, Mukul would then be safe. By the time I got up and walked to the station, the eight o'clock train to Marwar had gone. Those two criminals had left by the same train, with Mukul and my luggage. All my papers were in my suitcase, so there was no way I could prove to anyone who I really was.'

'Didn't Mukul mind going with them?'

Dr Hajra smiled. 'Mukul was in a totally distracted state of mind. Didn't you realize that? He had no problem leaving his own parents and setting off with me. So why should he make a distinction between one strange man and another? Bhavananda told him he would take him to the golden fortress. That was enough to entice Mukul. Anyway, I didn't give up. If anything, I was more determined now to get to the bottom of this business. Fortunately, I still had my wallet with me. So I could buy new clothes—local Rajasthani ones. I packed my old torn ones into a bundle. I wasn't used to wearing naagras, you see, so I got blisters on my feet.

'The next day, I boarded the train at Kisangarh and got into your compartment. Then I took the same train as you from Marwar to Jodhpur. I went to stay in a place called Raghunath Sarai. I knew someone in Jodhpur—one Professor Trivedi. But, at first, I told him nothing. If the matter came to be known, the two men might have tried to run away, or Mukul himself might have felt scared and refused to cooperate. By then I had guessed that the fort in Jaisalmer was where Mukul should be taken. All I had to do was wait until Bhavananda had the same idea and left with Mukul. Until then, my job was to keep an eye on the pair.'

'We saw someone hanging around the Circuit House on the very first day. It was you, wasn't it?'

'Yes, and that caused another problem. Mukul saw me, and seemed to recognize me! At least, that's how it appeared from the way he came out of the gate and began walking straight towards me.'

'So, later, you followed Bhavananda and got into the same train that was going to Pokhran?'

'Yes. The strangest thing was that I saw you from the train, trying to stop it!'

'Bhavananda must have seen me, too. He would then have realized we would try to catch the early morning train from Ramdeora.'

Dr Hajra continued with his story. 'Before I caught that train, I told Trivedi to inform the police in Jaisalmer. Before that, I had spoken to Mr Dhar from Trivedi's house; and then I borrowed one of his suits to dress normally.'

'And when you got to Pokhran, you saw that Bhavananda's assistant was already there with a taxi, is that right?' Feluda wanted to know.

'That's where things went wrong. I lost them. Then I had to wait another ten hours and catch that early morning train. I had no idea that you were on the same train. I saw you here in the dak bungalow. Now, what I would like to know is, when did you first start suspecting Bhavananda?'

Feluda smiled. 'It would be wrong to say that I suspected Bhavananda. It was the character of Dr Hajra that made me suspicious. Not in Jodhpur, but in Bikaner. When we went to Devikund, we found him with his hands tied, his mouth gagged. Just before that, I'd found a matchbox with an ace printed on it. I knew that particular brand isn't sold in Rajasthan. Then, when we saw Dr Hajra lying on the ground so helplessly, at first I thought that matchbox was dropped by whoever had attacked him. But then I noticed that there was something wrong with the way he was tied up. I mean, if a man's hands and legs are tied, that may make him perfectly immobile; but if only his hands are tied behind his back, any intelligent man will fold his legs, slip his hands below them and loosen his ties. Then he can set himself free. It became clear to me that Dr Hajra had tied himself up. But even so, it did not occur to me at the time that that man was not the real Dr Hajra. The scales fell from my eyes this morning, in the train to Jaisalmer, when I happened to be staring at a note Bhavananda had written to me. He had used a sheet of your letterhead.'

'So? How was that significant?'

'The printed name showed "Hajra" with a "j". But Bhavananda, pretending to be you, had signed his name "Hazra", with a "z". That told me that the man I had met in Jodhpur and who had written that note was not the real Dr Hajra. But in that case, who was he? He had to be one of those men who had kidnapped Neelu. And the other man was Mandar Bose, who had one long nail on his right hand, who smoked cigars—Neelu had recognized the smell, and so had we. The question now was, who was the real Dr Hajra, and where was he? There could be only one answer to that—Hajra had to be that same man who had got into our compartment at Kisangarh, who had new naagras and blisters on his feet, who was seen loitering outside the Circuit House and the Bikaner fort, and who we saw this morning in the dak bungalow in Jaisalmer, limping with a stick in his hand!'

Dr Hajra nodded. 'Mr Dhar did a most intelligent thing by asking you to come here. I don't think I could have managed entirely on my own. It was you who tackled Bhavananda's assistant. If he is arrested as well, we can then say that it all ended happily.'

Feluda pointed at Lalmohan Babu and said, 'He made a significant contribution towards raising the alarm against Mandar Bose.'

Lalmohan Babu was struggling all this while to get in a word. Now he blurted out, 'I say, what's going to happen to that hidden treasure?'

'Why don't you leave it to the peacock?' said Dr Hajra. 'It's guarding it quite admirably, isn't it? You saw what happens when you meddle with a peacock!'

'For the moment,' suggested Feluda, 'kindly return the treasure you have got hidden. Mind you, from the way your jacket is bulging near your waist, one can hardly call it "hidden"!'

Lalmohan Babu looked positively sad as he pulled out Mandar Bose's revolver and returned it to Feluda.

'Thank you,' said Feluda as he took it. Then his face suddenly grew grave. I saw him examine the revolver closely.

'I must hand it to you, Mr Trotter!' he muttered. 'Who knew you'd hoodwink Pradosh Mitter like this?'

'Why, what's happened?' we cried.

'This revolver's a fake! Made in Japan. Magicians use such guns on the stage!'

Just before everyone burst into laughter, Lalmohan Babu took the revolver back from Feluda, grinned and said, 'For my collection—and as a souvenir of our powerful adventure in Rajasthan. Thank you, sir!'

Incident on the Kalka Mail

ONE

I had only just finished reading a hair-raising account of an expedition by Captain Scott. Who knew I would have to travel to the land of mist and snow so soon after this? Well no, I don't mean the North or the South Pole. I don't think Feluda would ever be required to help solve mysteries in such remote corners. The place I am talking about is in our own country. Here I saw snowflakes floating down from the sky like cotton fluff. It spread on the ground like a carpet, dazzling my eyes as the sun fell on it; yet it stayed soft enough to be scooped and gathered into a ball.

This particular adventure started last March, on a Thursday morning. By this time, Feluda had become fairly well known as a detective, so his number of clients had grown. But he didn't accept a case unless it was one that gave him the chance to sharpen his remarkable brain. When I first heard about this case, it did not strike me as anything extraordinary. But Feluda must have sensed a great challenge, which was why he agreed so readily. The only other factor that might have influenced his decision was that the client seemed to be pretty well off, so perhaps he was expecting a fat fee. However, when I mentioned this to Feluda, he gave me such a glare that I had to shut up immediately.

The client was called Dinanath Lahiri. He rang us in the evening on Wednesday and made an appointment for eight o' clock the following morning. On the dot of eight on Thursday, we heard a car stop and blow its horn outside our house in Tara Road. The horn sounded strangely different from other cars. I sprang to my feet and moved towards the door, but Feluda stopped me with a gesture.

'You must learn,' he said, 'to play it cool. At least wait till the bell rings.'

It rang in a few seconds. When I opened the door, the first thing I saw was a huge car. Never before had I seen such a big car, except for a Rolls-Royce. The gentleman who emerged from it was equally impressive, though that had nothing to do with his size. A man in his mid-fifties, he had a remarkably fair complexion and was wearing a fine dhoti and kurta. On his feet were white nagras with an upturned front. In his left hand was a walking-stick with an ivory handle; and in his right hand he held a blue square attaché case, of a type which I had seen many times before. There were two in our own house—one was Baba's, the other belonged to Feluda. They were handed out by

Air-India as free gifts to their passengers.

Feluda offered the gentleman the most comfortable armchair in the living-room and took an ordinary chair himself to sit opposite him.

'I rang last night,' said our visitor. 'My name is Dinanath Lahiri.'

Feluda cleared his throat and said, 'Before you say anything further, may I ask you a couple of questions?'

'Of course.'

'First of all, would you mind having a cup of tea?'

Mr Lahiri folded his hands, bent his head politely and replied, 'You must forgive me, Mr Mitter, I am not used to having anything except at certain hours. But please don't let me stop you from having a cup of tea, if you so wish.'

'All right. My second question is—is your car a Hispano Suiza?'

'Yes, that's right. There aren't too many of those in this country. My father bought it in 1934. Are you interested in cars?'

Feluda smiled, 'Yes, among other things. But my interests are chiefly related to my profession.'

'I see. Allow me now to tell you why I'm here. You may find the whole thing totally insignificant. I am aware of your reputation, so there's no way I can insist that you take the case. I can only make a request.'

There was a certain polish and sophistication in his voice and the way he spoke, but not even the slightest trace of arrogance. On the contrary, Mr Lahiri spoke gently and quietly.

'Let's hear the details of your case,' said Feluda.

'You may call it my case,' said Mr Lahiri with a smile, pointing at the blue object in his hand, 'or the tale of my attaché case . . . ha ha. You see, my story revolves round this attaché case.'

Feluda glanced at the case and said, 'It seems to have gone abroad few times. The tags are torn but I can see the elastic bands on the handle—one, two, three, four . . .'

'Yes, the handle of my own case also has elastic bands hanging from it.'

'Your own case? You mean this one isn't yours?'

'No. This belongs to someone else. It got exchanged with mine.'

'I see. Where did this happen? In a plane, or was it a train?'

'It was a train. Kalka Mail. I was coming back from Delhi. There were four passengers in a first class compartment, including myself. My attaché case must have got mixed up with one of the other three.'

'I assume you do not know whose it was . . . ?'

'No. If I did, I don't suppose I'd need your help.'

'And you don't know the names of the others?'

'There was another Bengali. His name was Pakrashi. He travelled from Delhi, like me.'

'How did you get to know his name?'

'One of the other passengers happened to recognize him. I heard this other man say, "Hello, Mr Pakrashi!" and then they got talking. I think both were businessmen. I kept hearing words like contract and tender.'

'You didn't learn the name of this other man?'

'No. He was not a Bengali, though he was speaking the language quite well. I gathered he came from Simla.'

'And the fourth passenger?'

'He stayed on one of the upper berths most of the time. I saw him climb down only during lunch and dinner. He was not a Bengali, either. He offered me an apple soon after we left Delhi and said it was from his own orchard. So perhaps he was from Simla, too.'

'Did you eat that apple?'

'Yes, certainly. It was a good, tasty apple.'

'So you don't mind eating things outside your regular hours when you're in a train?'

Mr Lahiri burst out laughing.

'My God! I'd never have thought you'd pick that up! But you're right. In a moving train I am tempted to break my own rules.'

'OK,' said Feluda, 'I now need to know exactly where who was sitting.'

'I was on a lower berth. Mr Pakrashi was on the berth above mine. On the Other side, the man who gave me the apple sat on the upper berth and below him was the businessman who knew Mr Pakrashi.'

Feluda was silent for a few moments. Then he rubbed his hands together and said, 'If you don't mind. I am going to ask for some tea. Do have a cup if you want. Topshe, would you please go in?'

I ran in to tell our cook, Srinath, to bring the tea. When I returned, Feluda had opened the attaché case.

'Wasn't it locked?' he asked.

'No. Nor was mine. So whoever took it could easily have seen what was in it. This one is full of routine, ordinary stuff.'

True. It contained little besides two English dailies, a cake of soap, a comb, a hairbrush, a toothbrush, toothpaste, a shaving kit, a handkerchief and a paperback.

'Did your case contain anything valuable?' Feluda wanted to know.

'No, nothing. In fact, what my case had was probably of less value than what you see here. The only interesting thing in it was a manuscript. It was a travelogue, about Tibet. I had taken it with me to read on the train. It made very good reading.'

'A travelogue about Tibet?' Feluda was now clearly curious.

'Yes. It was written in 1917 by a Shambhucharan Bose. As far as I can make out, my uncle must have brought it, since it was dedicated to him. His name was Satinath Lahiri. He had lived in Kathmandu for many years, working as a private tutor in the household of the Ranas. He returned home about forty-five years ago, a sick old man. In fact, he died shortly after his return. Among his belongings was a Nepali box. It lay in a corner of our box room. We had all forgotten its existence until recently, when I called the Pest Control. The room had to be emptied for the men to work in. It was then that I found the box and, in it, the manuscript.'

'When did this happen?'

'The day before I left for Delhi.'

Feluda grew a little thoughtful. 'Shambhucharan?' he muttered to himself. 'Shambhucharan . . . Shambhucharan . . .'

'Anyway,' continued Mr Lahiri, 'that manuscript does not mean very much to me. To tell you the truth, I wasn't really interested in getting my attaché case back. Besides, there was no guarantee that I would find the owner of the one that got exchanged with mine. So I gave this case to my nephew. But since last night, I have been thinking. These articles that you see before you may not be expensive, but for their owner they might have a great deal of sentimental value. Look at this handkerchief, for instance. It's initialled "G". Someone had embroidered the letter with great care. Who could it be? His wife? Perhaps she is no more. Who knows? Shouldn't I try to return this attaché case to its rightful owner? I was getting worried, so I took it back from my nephew and came to you. Frankly, I don't care if my own case does not come back to me. I would simply feel a lot more comfortable if this one could be restored to whoever owns it.'

Srinath came in with the tea. Feluda, of late, had become rather fussy about his tea. What he was now going to drink had come from the Makaibari tea estate of Kurseong. Its fragrance filled the room the instant Srinath placed the cups before us. Feluda took a sip quietly and said, 'Did you have to open your case quite a few times in the train?'

'No, not at all. I opened it only twice. I took the manuscript out soon after the train left Delhi, and then I put it back before going to sleep.'

Feluda lit a Charminar and blew out a couple of smoke rings.

'So you'd like me to return this case to its owner and get yours back for you—right?'

'Yes. But does that disappoint you? Do you think it's all a bit too tame?'

Feluda ran his fingers through his hair. 'No,' he said, 'I understand your sentiments. And I must admit that your case is different from the ones I usually handle.'

Dinanath Babu looked visibly relieved. 'Your acceptance means a lot to me,' he said, letting out a deep breath.

'I shall, of course, do my best,' Feluda replied, 'but I cannot guarantee success. You must understand that. However, I should now like some information.'

'Yes?'

Feluda rose quickly and went into the next room. He returned with his famous blue notebook. Then, pencil in hand, he began asking questions.

'When did you leave Delhi?'

'On 5 March at 6.30 p.m. I reached Calcutta the next morning at nine-thirty.'

'Today is the 9th. So you arrived here three days ago, and you rang me yesterday.'

Feluda opened the attaché case and took out a yellow Kodak film container. As he unscrewed its lid, a few pieces of betel-nut fell out of it on the table. Feluda put one of these in his mouth and resumed speaking.

'Was there anything in your case that might give one an idea of your name and address?'

'No, not as far as I can recall.'

'Hm. Could you now please describe your fellow passengers?'

Dinanath Babu tilted his head and stared at the ceiling, frowning a little.

'Pakrashi would have been about the same age as me. Between sixty and sixty-five. He had salt-and-pepper hair, brushed back. He wore glasses and his voice was rather harsh.'

'Good.'

'The man who offered me the apple had a fair complexion. He was tall and slim, had a sharp nose, wore gold-framed glasses and was quite bald except for a few strands of black hair around his ears. He spoke to me only in English, with a flawless accent. And he had a cold. He kept blowing his nose into a tissue.'

'A pukka sahib, I see! And the third gentleman?'

'His appearance was really quite ordinary—there was nothing that one might have noticed in particular. But he was the only one who ordered a vegetarian thali.'

Feluda jotted all this down in his notebook. Then he looked up and asked, 'Anything else?'

'No, I can't recall anything else worth reporting. You see, I spent most of the day reading. And I fell asleep soon after dinner. I don't usually sleep very well in a train. But this time I slept like a baby until we arrived at Howrah. In fact, it was Mr Pakrashi who woke me.'

'In that case, presumably you were the last person to leave the coach?'

'Yes.'

'By which time one of the other three had walked out with your attaché case?'

'Yes.'

'Hm,' Feluda said, shutting his notebook, 'I'll see what I can do.' Dinanath Babu rose.

'I will, of course, pay your fee. But you will naturally need something to begin your investigation. I brought some cash today for this purpose.' He took out a white envelope from his pocket and offered it to Feluda, who took it coolly with a casual 'Oh, thanks' and stuffed it into his own pocket, together with his pencil.

Dinanath Babu came out and began walking towards his car. 'You will get my telephone number from the directory,' he said, 'please let me know if you hear anything. As a matter of fact, you can come straight to my house if need be. I am usually home in the evening.'

The yellow Hispano Suiza disappeared in the direction of Rashbehari Avenue, blowing its horn like a conch shell, startling all passers-by. We returned to the living-room. Feluda took the chair Dinanath Babu had occupied. Then he crossed his legs, stretched lazily and said, 'Another twenty-five years . . . and people with such an aristocratic style will have vanished.'

The blue case was still lying on the table. Feluda took its contents out one by one. Each object was really quite ordinary. Whoever bought them could not have spent more than fifty rupees.

'Let's make a list,' said Feluda. This was soon ready, and it contained the following:

Two English dailies from Delhi, neatly folded. One was the Sunday *Statesman*, the other the Sunday *Hindustan Times*.
A half-used tube of Binaca toothpaste. The empty portion had been rolled up.
A green Binaca toothbrush.
A Gillette safety razor.
Three thin Gillette blades in a packet.
An old and used Old Spice shaving cream. It was nearly finished.
A shaving brush.
A nail cutter—pretty old.
Three tablets of Aspro wrapped in a cellophane sheet.
A folded map of Calcutta. It measured 4' x5' when opened.
A Kodak film container with chopped betel-nuts in it.
A matchbox, brand new.
A Venus red-and-blue pencil.
A white handkerchief, with the letter 'G' embroidered in one corner.
A pen-knife, possibly from Moradabad.
A small face-towel.
A rusted old safety-pin.
Three equally rusted paper clips.
A shirt button.
A detective novel—Ellery Queen's *The Door Between*.

Feluda picked up the book and turned a few pages.

'No, there's no mention of the owner's name,' he said, 'but he clearly had the habit of marking a page by folding its corner. There are 236 pages in this book. The last sign of folding is at page 212. I assume he finished reading it.'

Feluda now turned his attention to the handkerchief.

'The first letter of his name or surname must be "G". No, it must be his first name, that's far more natural.'

Then he opened the map of Calcutta and spread it on the table.

'Red marks,' he said, looking closely at it, 'someone marked it with a red pencil . . . hmm . . . one, two, three, four, five . . . hm . . . Chowringhee . . . Park Street . . . I see. Topshe, get the telephone directory.'

Feluda put the map back into the case. Then he began turning the pages of the telephone directory. 'P . . . here we are,' he said. 'There are only sixteen Pakrashis listed here. Two of them are doctors , so we can easily leave them out.'

'Why?'

'The man who recognized him in the train called him Mr Pakrashi, not Doctor, remember?'

'Oh yes, that's right.'

Feluda picked up the telephone and began dialling. Each time he got through, I heard him say, 'Has Mr Pakrashi returned from Delhi? . . . Oh, sorry!'

This happened five times in a row. But the sixth number he dialled apparently got him the right man for, this time, he spoke for much longer. Then he said 'Thanks' and put the phone down.

'I think I've got him,' he said to me. 'N.C. Pakrashi. He answered the phone himself. He returned from Delhi by Kalka Mail the day before yesterday. Everything tallies, except that his luggage didn't get exchanged.'

'Then why did you make an appointment with him this evening?'

'Why, he can give us some information about the other passengers, can't he? He appears to be an ill-tempered fellow, but it would take more than ill-temper to put Felu Mitter off. Come, Topshe, let's go out.'

'Now? I thought we were meeting Mr Pakrashi in the evening?'

'Yes, but before calling on Pakrashi I think we need to visit your Uncle Sidhu. Now.'

TWO

Uncle Sidhu was no relation. He used to be Baba's next door neighbour when he lived in our old ancestral home, long before I was born. Baba treated him like a brother, and we all called him Uncle. Uncle Sidhu's knowledge about most things was extraordinary and his memory remarkably powerful. Feluda and I both admired and respected him enormously.

But why did Feluda want to see him at this time? The first question Feluda asked made that clear. 'Have you heard of a travel writer called Shambhucharan Bose? He used to write in English, about sixty years ago.'

Uncle Sidhu's eyes widened.

'Good heavens, Felu, haven't you read his book on the Terai?'

'Oh yes,' said Feluda, 'now I do remember. The man's name sounded familiar, but no, I haven't read the book.'

'It was called *The Terrors of Terai*. A British publisher in London published it in 1915. Shambhucharan was both a traveller and a shikari. But by profession he was a doctor. He used to practise in Kathmandu. This was long before the present royal family came into power. The powerful people in Nepal then were the Ranas. Shambhucharan treated and cured a lot of ailments among the Ranas. He mentioned one of them in his book. Vijayendra Shamsher Jung Bahadur. The man was keen on hunting, but he drank very heavily. Apparently, he used to climb a machan with a bottle in one hand and a rifle in the other. But both his hands stayed steady when it came to pressing the trigger. Except once. Only once did he miss, and the tiger jumped up on the machan. It was Shambhucharan who shot the tiger from the next machan and saved the Rana's life. The Rana expressed his gratitude by giving him a priceless jewel. A most thrilling story. Try and get a copy from the National Library. I don't think you'll get it easily anywhere else.'

'Did he ever go to Tibet?'

'Yes, certainly. He died in 1921, soon after I finished college. I saw an obituary on him, I remember. It said he had gone to Tibet after his retirement, although he died in Kathmandu.'

'I see.'

Feluda remained silent for a few moments. Then he said, in a clear, distinct tone, 'Supposing an unpublished manuscript was discovered today, written after his visit to Tibet, would that be a valuable document?'

'My goodness!' Uncle Sidhu's bald dome glistened with excitement. 'You don't know what you're saying, Felu! Valuable? I still remember the very high praise *Terai* had received from the *London Times*. It wasn't just the stories he told, Shambhucharan's language was easy, lucid and clear as crystal. Why, have you found such a manuscript?'

'No, but there might be one in existence.'

'If you can lay your hands on it, please don't forget to show it to me, Felu. And in case it gets auctioned, let me know. I'd be prepared to bid up to five thousand rupees . . .'

We left soon after this, but not before two cups of cocoa had been pressed upon us.

'Mr Lahiri doesn't even know his attache case contains such hot stuff,' I said as we came out. 'Aren't you going to tell him?'

'Wait. There's no need to rush things. Let's see where all this leads to. In any case, I have taken the job, haven't I? It's just that now I feel a lot more enthusiastic.'

Naresh Chandra Pakrashi lived in Lansdowne Road. It was obvious that his house had been built at least forty years ago. Feluda had taught me how to assess the age of a house. For instance, houses built fifty years ago had a certain type of window, which was different from those built ten years later. The railings on verandas and terraces, patterns on gates, pillars at porticos—all bore evidence of the period a building was made. This particular house must have been built in the 1920s.

The first thing I noticed as we climbed out of our taxi was a notice outside the main gate: 'Beware of the Dog'.

'It would have made better sense,' remarked Feluda, 'if it had said, "Beware of the Owner of the Dog".'

We passed through the gate and found a chowkidar standing near the porch. Feluda gave him his visiting card, which bore the legend: 'Pradosh C. Mitter, Private Investigator'. The chowkidar disappeared with the card and reappeared a few minutes later.

'Please go in,' he said.

We had to cross a wide marble landing before we got to the door of the living-room. It must have been about ten feet high. We lifted the curtain and walked in, to be greeted by rows and rows of books, all stashed in huge almirahs. There was quite a lot of other furniture, a wall-to-wall carpet, pictures on the walls, and even a chandelier. But the whole place had an unkempt air. Apparently, no one cared to clean it regularly.

We found Mr Pakrashi in his study, hidden behind the living-room. The sound of typing had already reached our ears. Now we saw a man sitting behind an ancient typewriter, which rested on a massive table, covered with green rexine. The table was placed on the right. On our left, as we stepped in, we saw three couches and a small round table. On this one stood a chess board with all the chessmen in place, and a book on the game. The last thing my eyes fell on was a large dog, curled up and asleep in one corner of the room.

The man fitted Dinanath Babu's description. A pipe hung from his mouth. He stopped typing upon our entry, and his eyes swept over us both. 'Which one of you is Mr Mitter?' he finally asked.

Perhaps it was his idea of a joke, but Feluda did not laugh. He answered civilly enough, 'I am Pradosh Mitter. This is my cousin.'

'How was I to know?' said Mr Pakrashi. 'Little boys have gone into so many different things . . . music, acting, painting; why, some have even become religious gurus! So your cousin here might well have been the great sleuth himself. But anyway, tell me why you're here. What do you want from a man who's never done anything other than mind his own business?'

Feluda was right. If ever a competition was held in irascibility, this man would have been a world champion.

'Who did you say sent you here?' he wanted to know.

'Mr Lahiri mentioned your name. He arrived from Delhi three days ago. You and he travelled in the same compartment.'

'I see. And is he the one whose attaché case got lost?'

'Not lost. Merely mistaken for someone else's.'

'Careless fool. But why did he have to employ you to retrieve it? What precious object did it contain?'

'There was nothing much, really, except an old manuscript. There is no other copy.'

I could tell why Feluda mentioned the manuscript. If he told Mr Pakrashi the real reason why he had been employed, no doubt Mr Pakrashi would have laughed in derision.

'Manuscript?' he asked somewhat suspiciously.

'Yes. A travelogue written by Shambhucharan Bose. Mr Lahiri had read it on the train, then put it back in the case.'

'Well, the man is not just a fool, he seems to be a liar, too. You see, although I had an upper berth, I spent most of the day sitting right next to him. He never read anything other than a newspaper and a Bengali magazine.'

Feluda did not say anything. Mr Pakrashi paused for breath, then continued, 'I don't know what you'd make of it as a sleuth. I find the whole thing distinctly suspicious. Anyway, if you wish to go on a wild-goose chase, suit yourself. I cannot offer any help. I told you on the phone I have about three of those Air-India bags, but on this trip I didn't take any with me.'

'One of the other passengers knew you, didn't he?'

'Who, Brijmohan? Yes. He is a moneylender. I've had a few dealings with him.'

'Could he have had a blue case?'

'How on earth should I know?' Mr Pakrashi frowned darkly.

'Could you give me Brijmohan's telephone number?'

'Look it up in the directory. S. M. Kedia & Co. SM was Brijmohan's father. Their office is in Lenin Sarani. And one more thing—you're wrong in thinking I knew only one of the other passengers. As a matter of fact, I knew two of them.'

'Who's the second one?' Feluda sounded surprised.

'Dinanath Lahiri. I had seen him before at the races. He used to be quite a lad. Now I believe he's changed his lifestyle and even found himself a guru in Delhi. Heaven knows if any of this is true.'

'What about the fourth man in your coach?' asked Feluda. He was obviously trying to gain as much information as he could.

'What's going on?' shouted Mr Pakrashi, pulling a face, in spite of the pipe still hanging from his mouth. 'Are you here simply to ask questions? Am I an accused standing trial or what?'

'No, sir,' said Feluda calmly. 'I am asking these questions only because you play chess all by yourself, you clearly have a sharp brain, a good memory, and . . .'

Mr Pakrashi thawed a little. He cleared his throat and said, 'Chess has become an addiction. The partner I used to play with is no more. So now I play alone.'

'Every day?'

'Yes. Another reason for that is my insomnia. I play until about three in the morning.'

'Do you never take a pill to help you sleep?'

'I do sometimes. But it doesn't always help. Not that it matters. I go to bed at three, and rise at eight. Five hours is good enough at my age.'

'Is typing also . . . one of your addictions?' Feluda asked with his lopsided smile.

'No, but there are times when I do like to do my own typing. I have a secretary, who's pretty useless. Anyway, you were talking about the fourth passenger, weren't you? He had sharp features, was quite bald, a non-Bengali, spoke very good English and offered me an apple. I didn't eat it. What else would you like to know? I am fifty-three and my dog is three-and-a-half. He's a boxer and doesn't like visitors to stay for more than half an hour. So . . .'

'An interesting man,' Feluda remarked. We were out in the street, but not walking in the direction of home. Why Feluda chose to go in the opposite direction, I could not tell; nor did he make any attempt at hailing either of the two empty taxis that sailed by.

One little thing was bothering me. I had to mention it to Feluda.

'Didn't Dinanath Babu say he thought Pakrashi was about sixty? But Mr Pakrashi himself said he was fifty-three and, quite frankly, he didn't seem older than that. Isn't that funny?'

'All it proves is that Dinanath Babu's power of observation is not what it should be,' said Feluda.

A couple of minutes later, we reached Lower Circular Road. Feluda turned left. 'Are you going to look at that case of robbery?' I asked. Only three days ago, the papers had reported a case of a daylight robbery. Apparently, three masked men had walked into a jeweller's shop on Lower Circular Road and got away with a lot of valuable jewellery and precious stones, firing recklessly in the air as they made their escape in a black Ambassador car. 'It might be fun tracing those daredevils,' Feluda had said. But sadly, no one had come forward to ask him to investigate. So I thought perhaps he was going to ask a few questions on his own. But Feluda paid no attention to me. It seemed as though his sole purpose in life, certainly at that moment, was to get some exercise and so he would do nothing but continue to walk.

A little later, he turned left again rather abruptly, and walked briskly into the Hindustan International Hotel. I followed him quickly.

'Did anyone from Simla check in at your hotel on 6 March?' Feluda asked the receptionist, 'His first name starts with a "G" . . . I'm afraid I can't recall his full name.'

Neither Brijmohan nor Naresh Pakrashi had names that started with a 'G'. So this had to the applewalla.

The receptionist looked at his book.

'There are two foreigners listed here on 6 March,' he said, 'Gerald

Pratley and G. R. Holmes. Both came from abroad.'

'Thank you,' said Feluda and left.

We took a taxi as we came out. 'Park Hotel,' Feluda said to the driver and lit a Charminar.

'If you had looked carefully at those red marks on the map,' he said to me, 'you'd have seen they were markers for hotels. It's natural that the man would want to stay at a good hotel. At present, there are five well-known hotels in Calcutta—Grand, Hindustan International, Park, Great Eastern and Ritz Continental. And those red marks had been placed on, these. The Park Hotel would be our next port of call.'

As it turned out, no one with a name starting with 'G' had checked in at the Park on 6 March. But the Grand offered some good news. Feluda happened to know one of its Bengali receptionists called Dasgupta. He showed us their visitors' book. Only one Indian had checked in on the 6th. He did arrive from Simla and his name was G. C. Dhameeja.

'Is he still here?'

'No, sir. He checked out yesterday.'

The little flicker of hope in my mind was snuffed out immediately. Feluda, too, was frowning. But he didn't stop asking questions.

'Which room was he in?'

'Room 216.'

'Is it empty now?'

'Yes. We're expecting a guest this evening, but right now it's vacant.'

'Can I speak to the room boy?'

'Certainly. I'll get someone to show you the way.'

We took the lift up to the second floor. A walk down a long corridor finally brought us to room 216. The room boy appeared at this point. We went into the room with him. Feluda began pacing.

'Can you remember the man who left yesterday? He was staying in this room.'

'Yes, sir.'

'Now try to remember carefully. What luggage did he have?'

'A large suitcase, and a smaller one.'

'Was it blue?'

'Yes. When I came back to the room after filling his flask, I found him taking things out of the blue case. He seemed to be looking for something.'

'Very good. Can you remember if this man had a few apples—perhaps in a paper bag?'

'Yes. There were three apples. He took them out and kept them on a plate.'

'What did this man look like?'

But the description the room boy gave did not help. At least a hundred thousand men in Calcutta would have fitted that description.

However, there was reason to feel pleased. We now had the name and address of the man whose attaché case had got exchanged with Mr Lahiri's. Mr Dasgupta gave us a piece of paper as we went out. I glanced over Feluda's shoulder and saw what was written on it:

G. C. Dhameeja
'The Nook'
Wild Flower Hall
Simla.

THREE

'Kaka has gone out. He'll return around seven,' we were told.

So this was Dinanath Babu's nephew. We had come straight from the Grand Hotel to Dinanath Babu's house to report our progress, stopping on our way only to buy some meetha paan from a shop outside the New Empire.

Lined on one side of the gate of Mr Lahiri's house were four garages. Three of these were empty. The fourth contained an old, strange looking car. 'Italian,' said Feluda. 'It's a Lagonda.'

The chowkidar took our card in, but, instead of Dinanath Babu, a younger man emerged from the house. He couldn't have been more than thirty. Of medium height, he had fair skin like his uncle; his hair was long and tousled; and running down from his ears were broad sideburns, the kind that seemed to be all the rage among fashionable men. The man was staring hard at Feluda.

'Could we please wait until he returns?' asked Feluda. 'We have something rather important to discuss, you see.'

'Please come this way.'

We were taken into the living-room. The walls and the floor were littered with tiger and bear skins; a huge head of a buffalo graced the wall over the main door. Perhaps Dinanath Babu's uncle had been a shikari, too. May be that was why he and Shambhucharan had been so close?

'My uncle goes out for a walk every evening. He'll be back soon.'

Dinanath Babu's nephew had an exceptionally thin voice. I wondered if it was he who had been given Mr Dhameeja's attaché case.

'Are you,' he asked, 'the same Felu Mitter who solved the mystery of the Golden Fortress?'

'Yes,' said Feluda briefly, and leant back in his chair, crossing his legs, perfectly relaxed.

I kept looking at the other man. His face seemed familiar. Where had I seen him before? Then something seemed to jog my memory.

'Have you ever acted in a film?' I asked.

The man cleared his throat.

'Yes, in *The Ghost*. It's a thriller. I play the villain. But it hasn't yet been released.'

'Your name . . . ?'

'My real name is Prabeer Lahiri. But my screen name is Amar Kumar.'

'Oh yes, now I remember. I have seen your photograph in a film magazine.'

Heavens, what kind of a villain would he make with a voice like that?

'Are you a professional actor?' asked Feluda. For some strange reason, Prabeer Babu was still standing.

'I have to help my uncle in his business,' he replied, 'which means going to his plastic factory. But my real interest is in acting.'

'What does your uncle think?'

'Uncle isn't . . . very enthusiastic about it.'

'Why not?'

'That's the way he is.'

Amar Kumar's face grew grave. Clearly, he had had arguments with his uncle over his career in films.

'I have to ask you something,' Feluda said politely, possibly because Amar Kumar was beginning to look belligerent.

'I don't mind answering your questions,' he said. 'What I can't stand is my uncle's constant digs at my—'

'Did your uncle recently give you an Air-India attaché case?'

'Yes, but someone pinched it. We've got a new servant, you

see . . .'

Feluda raised a reassuring hand and smiled.

'No, no one stole that case, I assure you. It's with me.'

'With you?' Prabeer Babu seemed perfectly taken aback.

'Yes. Your uncle decided to return the case to its owner. He hired me for this purpose. What I want to know is whether you removed anything from it.'

'I did, naturally. Here it is.'

Prabeer Babu took out a ballpoint pen from his pocket. 'I wanted to use the blades and the shaving cream,' he added, 'but of course I never got the chance.'

'You do realize, don't you, that the case must go back to the owner with every item intact?'

'Yes, yes, naturally.'

He handed the pen over to Feluda. But he was obviously still greatly annoyed with his uncle. 'At least,' he muttered, 'I should have been told the case was going back. After all, he did give . . .'

He couldn't finish his sentence. Dinanath Babu's car sounded its horn at this moment, thereby causing the film villain to beat a quick retreat.

'Oh no, have you been waiting long?' Dinanath Babu walked into the room, looking slightly rueful, his hands folded in a namaskar. We stood up to greet him. 'No, no, please sit down,' he said hurriedly. 'You wouldn't mind a cup of tea, would you?'

His servant appeared almost immediately and left with an order to bring us tea. Dinanath Babu sat down on the settee next to ours. 'So . . . tell me . . . ?' he invited.

'Your case got exchanged with the man who gave you the apple. His name is G. C. Dhameeja.'

Dinanath Babu grew round-eyed. 'You found that out in just a day? What is this—magic?'

Feluda gave his famous lopsided smile and continued, 'He lives in Simla and I've got his address. He was supposed to spend three days at the Grand, but he left a day early.'

'Has he left already?' Dinanath Babu asked, a little regretfully.

'Yes. He left the hotel, but we don't know whether he returned to Simla. One telegram to his house in Simla, and you shall get an answer to that.'

Dinanath Babu seemed to ponder for a few moments. Then he said, 'All right. I will send a cable today. But if I discover he has indeed gone back to Simla, I still have to return his case to him, don't I?'

'Yes, of course. And yours has to come back to you. I am quite curious about that travelogue.'

'Very good. Allow me to make a proposal, Mr Mitter. Why don't you go to Simla with your cousin? I shall, of course, pay all your expenses. It's snowing in Simla, I hear. Have you ever seen it snow, Khoka?'

At any other time, I would have been affronted at being called a child. But now it did not seem to matter at all. Go to Simla? Oh, how exciting! My heart started to race faster.

But Feluda's next words were most annoying. 'You must think this one through, Mr Lahiri,' he said. 'It's just a matter of taking an attaché case to Simla, and bringing one back, isn't it? So anyone can do the job. It doesn't necessarily have to be me.'

'No, no, no,' Dinanath Babu protested rather vehemently, 'where will I find anyone as reliable as you? And since you began the investigation, I think you should end it.'

'Why, you have a nephew, don't you?'

A shadow passed over Dinanath Babu's face.

'He is no good, really. I'm afraid my nephew's sense of responsibility is virtually nonexistent. Do you know what he has done? He's gone into films! No, I cannot rely on him at all. I'd rather the two of you went. I'll tell my travel agents to make all arrangements. You can fly up to Delhi and then catch a train. When you've done your job, you can even have a holiday in Simla for a few days. It would give me a lot of pleasure to be of service to a man like you. What you've done in just a few hours is truly remarkable!'

The tea arrived, together with cakes and sandwiches. Feluda picked up a piece of chocolate cake and said, 'Thank you. There is one little thing I am still feeling curious about. The Nepali box in which you found the manuscript. Is it possible to see it?'

'Of course. That's not a problem at all. I'll get my bearer to bring it.'

The box appeared in a few moments. About two feet in length and ten inches in height, its wooden surface was covered by a sheet of copper. Red, blue and yellow stones were set on the lid. The smell that greeted my nostrils as soon as the lid was lifted was the same as that in Naresh Pakrashi's study. Dust-covered old furniture and threadbare curtains gave out the same musty smell.

Dinanath Babu said, 'As you can see, there are two compartments in the box. The manuscript was in the first one, wrapped in a Nepali newspaper.'

'Good heavens, it's stuffed with so many different things!' exclaimed Feluda.

'Yes,' Dinanath Babu smiled. 'You might call it a mini curio shop. But it's so filthy I haven't felt tempted to handle anything.'

It turned out that the compartments could be removed. Feluda brought out the second one and inspected the objects it contained. There were stone necklaces, little engraved discs made of copper and brass, two candles, a small bell, a couple of little bowls, a bone of some unknown animal, a few dried herbs and flowers, reduced to dust—truly a little junk shop.

'Did this box belong to your uncle?'

'It came with him, so I assume it did.'

'When did he return from Kathmandu?'

'In 1923. He died the same year. I was seven.'

'Very interesting,' said Feluda. Then he took a last sip from his cup and stood up. 'I accept your proposal, Mr Lahiri,' he said, 'but we cannot leave tomorrow. We'll have to collect our warm clothes from the dry-cleaner's. The day after tomorrow might be a better idea. And please don't forget to cable Dhameeja.'

We returned home at around half-past-eight to find Jatayu waiting for us in the living-room, a brown parcel on his lap.

'Have you been to the pictures?' he asked with a smile.

FOUR

Jatayu was the pseudonym of Lalmohan Ganguli, the famous writer of best-selling crime thrillers. We had first met him on our way to the golden fortress in Rajasthan. There are some men who appear strangely comical without any apparent reason. Lalmohan Babu was one of them. He was short—the top of his head barely reached Feluda's shoulder; he wore size five shoes, was painfully thin, and yet would occasionally fold one of his arms absentmindedly and feel his biceps with the other. The next instant, he would give a violent start if anyone so much as sneezed loudly in the next room.

'I brought my latest book for you and Tapesh,' he said, offering the brown parcel to Feluda. He had started coming to our house fairly regularly ever since our adventure in Rajasthan.

'Which country did you choose this time?' Feluda asked, unwrapping the parcel. The spine-chilling escapades of Lalmohan Babu's hero involved moving through different countries.

'Oh, I have covered practically the whole world this time,' Lalmohan Babu replied proudly, 'from the Nilgiris to the North Pole.'

'I hope there are no factual errors this time?' Feluda said quizzically, passing the book to me. Feluda had had to correct a mistake in his last book, *The Sahara Shivers*, regarding a camel's water supply.

'No, sir,' Lalmohan Babu grinned. 'One of my neighbours has a full set of the "Encyclopaedia Britannia". I checked every detail.'

'I'd have felt more reassured, Lalmohan Babu, if you had consulted the Britannica rather than the Britannia.'

But Jatayu ignored this remark and went on, 'The climax comes— you've got to read it—with my hero, Prakhar Rudra, having a fight with a hippopotamus.'

'A hippo?'

'Yes, it's really a thrilling affair.'

'Where does this fight take place?'

'Why, in the North Pole, of course. A hippo, didn't I say?'

'A hippopotamus in the North Pole?'

'Yes, yes. Haven't you seen pictures of this animal? It has whiskers like the bristles of a garden broom, fangs that stick out like a pair of white radishes, it pads softly on the snow . . .'

'That's a walrus, surely? A hippopotamus lives in Africa!'

Jatayu turned a deep shade of pink and bit his lip in profound embarrassment. 'Eh heh heh heh!' he said. 'Bad mistake, that! Tell you what, from now on I'll show you my manuscript before giving it to the publisher.'

Feluda made no reply to this. 'Excuse me,' he said and disappeared into his room.

'Your cousin appears a little quiet,' Lalmohan Babu said to me. 'Has he got a new case?'

'No, it's nothing important,' I told him. 'But we have to go to Simla in the next couple of days.'

'A long tour?'

'No, just about four days.'

'Hmm . . . I've never been to that part of the country . . .'

Lalmohan Babu grew preoccupied. But he began to show signs of animation the minute Feluda returned.

'Tapesh tells me you're going to Simla. Is it something to do with an investigation?'

'No, not exactly. It's just that Tom's case has got exchanged with Dick's. So we have to return Dick's case to him and collect Tom's.'

'Good lord, the mystery of the missing case? Or, simply, a mysterious case?'

'Look, I have no idea if there is any real mystery involved. But one or two things make me wonder . . . just a little . . .'

'Felu Babu,' Jatayu interrupted, 'I have come to know you pretty well in these few months. I'm convinced you wouldn't have taken the case unless you felt there was . . . well, something in it. Do tell me what it is.'

I could sense Feluda was reluctant to reveal too much at this stage. 'It's difficult to say anything,' he said guardedly, 'without knowing for sure who is telling lies, and who is telling the truth, or who is simply trying to conceal the truth. All I know is that there is something wrong somewhere.'

'All right, that's enough!' Jatayu's eyes began to shine. 'Just say the word, and I'll tag along with you.'

'Can you bear the cold?'

'Cold? I went to Darjeeling last year.'

'When?'

'In May.'

'It's snowing in Simla now.'

'What!' Lalmohan Babu rose from his chair in excitement. 'Snow? You don't say! It was the desert the last time and now it's going to be snow? From the frying pan into the frigidaire? Oh, I can't imagine it!'

'It's going to be an expensive business.'

I knew Feluda was trying gently to discourage him, but Jatayu paid no attention to his words.

'I am not afraid of expenses,' he retorted, laughing like a film villain. 'I have published twenty-one thrillers, each one of which has seen at least five editions. I have bought three houses in Calcutta, by the grace of God. It's in my own interest that I travel as much as possible. The more places I see, the easier it is to think up new plots. And not everyone is clever like you, so most people can't see the difference between a walrus and a hippo, anyway. They'll happily swallow what I dish out, and that simply means that the cash keeps rolling in. Oh no, I am not bothered about the expenses. But if you give me a straight "no",' then obviously it's a different matter.'

Feluda gave in. Before taking his leave, Jatayu took the details of when and how we'd be leaving and for how long, jotted these down in his notebook and said, 'Woollen vests, a couple of pullovers, a woollen jacket and an overcoat . . . surely that should be enough even for Simla?'

'Yes,' said Feluda gravely, 'but only if you add to it a pair of gloves, a Balaclava helmet, a pair of galoshes, woollen socks and something to fight frostbite. Then you may relax.'

I hate exams and tests in school, but I love the kind of tests Feluda sets for me. These are fun and they help clear my mind.

Feluda told me to come to his room after dinner. There he lay on his bed, flat on his stomach, and began throwing questions at me. The first was, 'Name all the people we've got to know who are related to this case.'

'Dinanath Lahiri.'

'OK. What sort of a man do you think he is?'

'All right, I guess. But he doesn't know much about books and writers. And I'm slightly doubtful about the way he is spending such a lot of money to send us to Simla.'

'A man who can maintain a couple of cars like that doesn't have to worry about money. Besides, you mustn't forget that employing Felu Mitter is a matter of prestige.'

'Well, in that case there is nothing to be doubtful about. The second person we met was Naresh Chandra Pakrashi. Very ill-tempered.'

'But plain spoken. That's good. Not many have that quality.'

'But does he always tell the truth? I mean, how do we know that Dinanath Lahiri really used to go to the races?'

'Perhaps he still does. But that doesn't necessarily mean that he's a crook.'

'Then we met Prabeer Lahiri, alias Amar Kumar. Didn't seem to like his uncle.'

'That's perfectly natural. His uncle is a stumbling block in his way forward in films, he gives him an attaché case full of things one day, and then takes it back without telling him . . . so obviously he's annoyed with his uncle.'

'Prabeer Babu seemed pretty well built.'

'Yes, he has strong and broad wrists. Perhaps that's why his voice sounds so odd. It doesn't match his manly figure at all. Now tell me the names of the other passengers who travelled with Dinanath Lahiri.'

'One of them was Brijmohan. And his surname was . . . let me see . . .'

'Kedia. Marwari.'

'Yes. He's a moneylender. Nothing remarkable in his appearance, apparently. Knew Mr Pakrashi.'

'He really does have an office in Lenin Sarani. I looked it up in the telephone directory.'

'I see. Well, the other was G. C. Dhameeja. He lives in Simla. Has an orchard.'

'So he said. We don't know that for sure.'

'But it is his attaché case that got exchanged with Mr Lahiri's. Surely there is no doubt about that?'

The case in question was lying open next to Feluda's bed. He stared absentmindedly at its contents and muttered, 'Hm . . . yes, that is perhaps the only thing one can be . . .' He broke off and picked up the two English newspapers that were in the case and glanced at them. 'These,' he continued to mutter, 'are the only things that . . . you know . . . make me feel doubtful. They don't fit in somehow.'

At this point, he had to stop muttering for the phone rang. Feluda had had an extension put in his own room.

'Hello.'

'Is that you, Mr Mitter?'

I could hear the words spoken from the other side, possibly because it was quiet outside.

'Yes, Mr Lahiri.'

'Listen, I have just received a message from Dhameeja.'

'You mean he's replied to your telegram? Already?'

'No, no. I don't think I'll get a reply before tomorrow. I am talking about a phone call. Apparently, Dhameeja had gone to the railway reservation office and got my name and address from them. But because he had to leave very suddenly, he could not contact me himself. He left my attaché case with a friend here in Calcutta. It was this friend who rang me. He'll return my case to me if I bring

Dhameeja's. So, you see . . .'

'Did you ask him if the manuscript was still there?'

'Oh yes. Everything's fine.'

'That's good news then. Your problem's solved.'

'Yes, most unexpectedly. I'm leaving in five minutes. I'll collect Dhameeja's case from you and then go to Pretoria Street.'

'May I make a request?'

'Certainly.'

'Why should you take the trouble of going out? We were going to go all the way to Simla, weren't we? So we'd quite happily go to Pretoria Street and collect your case for you. If you let me keep it tonight, I can skim through Shambhucharan's tale of Tibet. You may treat that as my fee. Tomorrow morning I shall return both the case and the manuscript to you.'

'Very well. I have no objection to that at all. The man who rang me is a Mr Puri and his address is 4/2 Pretoria Street.'

'Thank you. All's well that ends well.'

Feluda replaced the receiver and sat frowning. I, too, sat silently, fighting a wave of disappointment. I did so want to go to Simla and see it snow. Now I had missed the chance and would have to rot in Calcutta where it was already uncomfortably hot, even in March. Well, I suppose I ought to be with Feluda in this last chapter of the story.

'Let me go and get changed, Feluda,' I said. 'I won't be a minute.'

'All right. Hurry up.'

Twenty minutes later, we were in a taxi, cruising up and down Pretoria Street. It was a quiet street and, it being nearly half past eleven at night, not a soul was to be seen. We drove from one end of the street to the other, but it was impossible to see the numbers on the houses from the car. 'Please wait here, Sardarji,' Feluda said to the driver. 'We'll find the house and come back. We simply have to drop this case. It won't take long.'

An amiable man, the driver agreed to wait. We got out of the taxi at one end of the road and began walking. Beyond the wall on our left stood the tall and silent Birla building, dwarfing every other building in its vicinity with all its twenty-two floors. I had often heard Feluda remark that the creepiest things in a city after nightfall were its skyscrapers. 'Have you ever seen a corpse standing up?' he had asked me once. 'These buildings are just that in the dark—just a body without life or soul!'

A few minutes later, we found a house with '4' written on its gate. The next house, which was at some distance, turned out to be number 5. So 4/2 was probably in the little lane that ran between numbers 4 and 5. It was very difficult to see anything clearly. The few dim streetlights did nothing to help. We stepped into the lane, walking cautiously. How quiet it was!

Here was another gate. This must be 4/1. Where was 4/2? Somewhere further down, hidden in the dark? There didn't seem to be another house in the lane and, even if there was, it certainly did not have a light on. There were walls on both sides of the lane. Overgrown branches of trees on the other side hung over these. A very faint noise of traffic came from the main road. A clock struck in the distance. It must be the clock in St Paul's Church. It was now exactly half past eleven. But these noises did nothing to improve the eerie silence in Pretoria Street. A dog barked nearby. And, in that instant—

'Taxi! Sardarji, Sardarji!' I screamed, quite involuntarily.

A man had jumped over the wall on our right and fallen over Feluda. He was followed by another. The attaché case Feluda was carrying was no longer in his hand. He had dropped it on the ground and was trying to tackle the first man. I could feel the two men struggling with each other, but could see nothing. The blue case was lying on the road, right in front of me. I stretched my hand to pick it up, but the second man turned around at this moment and knocked me aside. Then he snatched the case and rushed to the entrance of the lane, through which we had just stepped. On my left, Feluda and the other man were still grappling with each other, but I could not figure out what the problem was. Feluda, by this time, should have been able to overpower his opponent.

'God!'

This exclamation came from our driver. He had heard me scream and rushed out to help. But the man who was making off with the case knocked him down and vanished. I could see the poor driver lying flat on the ground under a streetlight. In the meantime, the first man managed to wriggle free from Feluda's grasp and climbed over the wall.

Feluda took out his handkerchief and began wiping his hands.

'That man,' he observed, 'had oiled himself rather well. Must have rubbed at least a kilo of mustard oil on his body, making him slippery as an eel. I believe it's an old trick with thieves.'

True. I had smelt the oil as soon as the two men arrived, but had not been able to guess where it was coming from.

'Thank God!'

For the life of me, I could not understand why Feluda said this. How could he, even after such a disaster? 'What do you mean?' I asked, puzzled. Feluda did not reply at once. He helped the driver, who appeared unhurt, to his feet. Then he said, as the three of us began walking towards the taxi, 'You don't think what those scoundrels got away with was Dhameeja's property, do you?'

'Wasn't it?' I was even more mystified.

'What they took was the property of Pradosh C. Mitter. And what it contained were three torn vests, five threadbare handkerchiefs, several pieces of rag and a few old newspapers, torn to shreds. I rang telephone enquiries when you went to change. They told me there was no telephone at 4/2 Pretoria Street. But, of course, I didn't know that even the address was a fake one.'

My heart started pounding once more. Something told me the visit to Simla was now imperative.

FIVE

We rang Dinanath Babu as soon as we got home. He was completely nonplussed. 'Goodness me!' he exclaimed, 'I had no idea a thing like this could happen! One possible explanation is, of course, that those two men were just ordinary thieves without any particular motive to steal Dhameeja's attaché case. But even so, the fact remains that both this man called Puri and the address he gave, were totally fictitious. That means Mr Dhameeja never really went to the railway reservation office. Who, then, made the phone call?'

'If we knew that, there would be no need for further investigations, Mr Lahiri.'

'But tell me, what made you suspicious in the first place?'

The fact that the man rang you so late in the night. Mr Dhameeja went back yesterday. So why didn't Mr Puri give you a call yesterday or during the day today?'

'I see. Well, it looks as though we have to go back to our original plan of sending you to Simla. But considering the turn this whole business is taking, frankly I am now scared to send you anywhere.'

Feluda laughed, 'Don't worry, Mr Lahiri. I can't call your case tame and insipid any more. It's definitely got a taste of excitement. And I am glad, for I would have felt ashamed to take your money otherwise. Anyway, I would now like you to do something for me, please.'

'Yes?'

'Let me have a list of the contents of your case. It would make it easier for me to check when Dhameeja returns it.'

'That's easy since there wasn't anything much, anyway. But I'll let you have the list when I send you your tickets.'

Feluda left home early the next morning. His whole demeanour had changed in just a few hours. I could tell by the way he kept cracking his knuckles that he was feeling restless and disturbed. Like me, he had not been able to work out why anyone should try to steal a case that contained nothing of value. He had examined each item carefully once more, going so far as to squeeze some of the toothpaste out and feeling the shaving cream by pressing the tube gently. He even took out the blades from their container and unfolded the newspapers. Still, he found nothing suspicious. Feluda left at about 8 a.m. 'I will return at eleven,' he said before leaving. 'If anyone rings the calling bell in the next three hours, don't open the door yourself. Get Srinath to do it.'

I resigned myself to wait patiently for his return. Baba had gone out of town. So I wrote a letter for him, explaining why Feluda and I had to go to Simla before he got back. Having done this, I settled down on the settee in the living-room with a book. But I could not read. The more I thought about Feluda's new case, the more confused I felt. Dinanath Babu, his nephew who acted in films, the irascible Mr Pakrashi, Mr Dhameeja of Simla, the moneylender called Brijmohan . . . everyone seemed unreal, as though each was wearing a mask. Even the contents of the Air-India case seemed false. And, on top of everything else, was last night's frightening experience . . .

No, I must stop thinking. I picked up a magazine. It was a film magazine called *Sparkling Stars*. Ah yes, here was the photograph of Amar Kumar I had seen before. 'The newcomer, Amar Kumar, in the latest film being made by Sri Guru Pictures', said the caption. Amar Kumar was staring straight into the camera, wearing a cap very much in the style of Dev Anand in *Jewel Thief*, a scarf around his throat, a cruel smile under a pencil-thin moustache. There was a pistol in his hand, very obviously a fake, possibly made of wood.

Something made me suddenly jump up and turn to the telephone directory. Here it was—Sri Guru Pictures, 53 Bentinck Street. 24554.

I dialled the number quickly. It rang several times before someone answered at the other end.

'Hello.'

'Is that Sri Guru Pictures?'

My voice had recently started to break. So I was sure whoever I was speaking to would never guess I was really no more than fifteen-and-a-half.

'Yes, this is Sri Guru Pictures.'

'This is about Amar Kumar, you know . . . the newcomer in your latest film—'

'Please speak to Mr Mallik.' The telephone was passed to another man.

'Yes?'

'Mr Mallik?'

'Speaking.'

'Is there someone called Amar Kumar working in your latest film? *The Ghost*, I think it's called?'

'Amar Kumar has been dropped.'

'Dropped?'

'Who am I speaking to, please?'

'I . . . well, I . . .'

Like a fool, I could think of nothing to say and put the receiver down hurriedly.

So Amar Kumar was no longer in the cast! It must have been because of his voice. How unfair, though, to reject him after his picture had been published in a magazine. But didn't the man know, or did he simply pretend to us that he was still acting in the film?

I was lost in thought when the telephone rang, startling me considerably.

'Hello!' I gasped.

There was no response for a few seconds. Then I heard a faint click. Oh, I knew. Someone was calling from a public pay phone.

'Hello?' I said again. This time, I heard a voice, soft but distinct.

'Going to Simla, are you?'

This was the last thing I'd have expected to hear from a strange voice. Rendered speechless, I could only swallow in silence.

The voice spoke again. It sounded harsh and the words it uttered chilled my blood. 'Danger. Do you hear? You are both going to be in great danger if you go to Simla.' This was followed by another click. The line was disconnected. But I didn't need to hear any more. Those few words were enough. Like the Nepali Rana in Uncle Sidhu's story, whose hand shook while shooting at a tiger, I replaced the receiver with a trembling hand.

Then I flopped down on a chair and sat very still. About half an hour later, I heard another ring. This nearly made me fall off the chair, but this time I realized it was the door bell, not the telephone. It was past eleven, so I opened the door myself and Feluda walked in. The huge packets in his hands meant that he had been to the laundry to collect our warm clothes.

Feluda gave me a sidelong glance and said, 'Why are you licking your lips? Has there been a strange phone call?'

'How did you guess?' I asked, astonished.

'From the way you've kept the receiver. Besides, the whole thing's become so complicated that I'd have been surprised if we didn't get a few weird calls. Who was it? What did he say?'

'Don't know who it was. He said going to Simla meant danger for both of us.'

Feluda pushed the regulator of the fan to its maximum speed and sat casually down on the divan.

'What did you say to him?'

'Nothing.'

'Idiot! You should have said going to Simla cannot possibly be more dangerous than going out in the street in Calcutta. A regular battlefield is probably the only place that can claim to be more full of danger than the streets in this city.'

Feluda's nonchalance calmed my nerves. I decided to change the subject.

'Where did you go?' I asked. 'Apart from the laundry, I mean.'

'To the office of S. M. Kedia.'

'Did you learn anything new?'

'Brijmohan seemed a friendly enough fellow. His family has lived in Calcutta for three generations. And yes, he knows Mr Pakrashi. I got the impression that Pakrashi still owes him some money. Brijmohan, too, had eaten the apple Dhameeja had offered him. But no, he doesn't have a blue Air-India attaché case; and he had spent most of his time on the train either sleeping or just lying with his eyes closed.'

I told Feluda about Amar Kumar.

'If he knows he has been dropped but is pretending he isn't,' remarked Feluda, 'then the man is truly a fine actor.'

We finished our packing in the late afternoon. Since we were going for less than a week, I didn't take too many clothes. At six-thirty in the evening, Jatayu rang us.

'I am taking a new weapon,' he informed us. 'I'll show it to you when we get to Delhi.'

We knew he was interested in collecting weapons of various kind. He had taken a Nepali dagger on our journey through Rajasthan, although he did not get the chance to use it.

'I have bought my ticket,' he added. 'I'll see you tomorrow at the airport.'

Our tickets arrived a couple of hours later, together with a note from Dinanath Babu. It said:

Dear Mr Mitter,
I am enclosing your air tickets to Delhi and train tickets to Simla. I have made reservations for you for a day in Delhi at the Janpath Hotel; and you are booked at the Clarkes in Simla for four days. I have just received a reply from Mr Dhameeja. He says he has my attaché case safe. He expects you to call on him the day after tomorrow at 4 p.m. You have got his address, so I will not repeat it here. I have not made a list of the items in my case because, thinking things over, it struck me that there is only one thing in it that is of any value to me. It is a bottle of enterovioform tablets. These are made in England and definitely more effective than those produced here. I should be happy simply to get these back. I hope you have a safe and successful visit.
Yours sincerely,
Dinanath Lahiri

We were planning to have an early night and go to bed by ten o' clock, but at a quarter to ten, the door bell rang. Who could it be at this hour? I opened the door and was immediately struck dumb to find a man who I never dreamt would ever pay us a visit. If Feluda was similarly surprised, he did not show it.

'Good evening, Mr Pakrashi,' he said coolly, 'please come in.'

Mr Pakrashi came in, a slightly embarrassed look on his face, a smile hovering on his lips. His ill-tempered air was gone. What had happened in a day to bring about this miraculous change? And what had he come to tell us so late in the evening?

He sat down on a chair and said, 'Sorry to trouble you. I know it's late. I did try to ring you, but couldn't get through. So I thought it was best to call personally. Please don't mind.'

'We don't. Do tell us what brings you here.'

'I have come to make a request. It is a very special request. In fact, it may strike you as positively strange.'

'Really?'

'You said something about a manuscript in Dinanath Lahiri's attaché case. Was it . . . something written by Shambhucharan Bose? You know, the same man who wrote about the Terai?'

'Yes, indeed. An account of his visit to Tibet.'

'My God!'

Feluda did not say anything. Naresh Pakrashi, too, was quiet for a few moments. Then he said, 'Are you aware that my collection of travelogues is the largest and the best in Calcutta?'

'I am fully prepared to believe that. I did happen to glance at those almirahs in your room; and I caught the names of quite a few very well-known travel writers.'

'Your powers of observation must be very good.'

'That is what I live by, Mr Pakrashi.'

Mr Pakrashi now took the pipe out of his mouth, looked straight at Feluda and said, 'You are going to Simla, aren't you.'

It was Feluda's turn to be surprised. He did not actually ask, 'How do you know.' But his eyes held a quizzical look.

Mr Pakrashi smiled. 'A clever man like you,' he said, 'would naturally not find it too difficult to discover that Dinu Lahiri's attaché case had got exchanged with Dhameeja's. I had seen Dhameeja's name written on his suitcase. He did, in fact, take out his shaving things from the blue Air-India case, so I knew it was his.'

'Why didn't you say so yesterday?'

'Isn't it a greater joy to have worked things out for yourself? It is your case, after all. You will work on it and get paid for your pains. Why should I voluntarily offer any help?'

Feluda appeared to be in agreement. All he said was, 'But you haven't yet told me what your strange request is.'

'I am coming to that. You will—no doubt—manage to retrieve Dinanath's case. And the manuscript with it. I would request you not to give it back to him.'

'What!' This time Feluda could not conceal his surprise. Nor could I.

'I suggest you pass the manuscript to me.'

'To you?' Feluda raised his voice.

'I told you it would sound odd. But you must listen to me,' Mr Pakrashi continued, leaning forward a little, his elbows resting on his knees. 'Dinanath Lahiri cannot appreciate the value of that book. Did you see a single good book in his house? No, I know you did not. Besides, don't think I'm not going to compensate you for this. I have got—'

Here he stopped and took out a long blue envelope from the inside pocket of his jacket. Then he opened it and offered it to Feluda. It was stuffed with new, crisp, sweet-smelling hundred-rupee notes. 'I have two thousand here,' he said, 'and this is only an advance payment. I will give you another two thousand when you hand over the manuscript to me.'

Feluda did not even glance at the envelope. He took out a cigarette from his pocket, lit it casually and said, 'I don't think it's of any relevance whether Dinanath Lahiri appreciates the value of the manuscript or not. I have promised to collect his case from Dhameeja in Simla and return it to him, with all its contents intact. And that is what I am going to do.'

Mr Pakrashi appeared to be at a loss to find a suitable answer to this. After a few moments, he simply said, 'All right. Let's forget about your payment. All I am asking you to do is give me the manuscript. Tell Lahiri it was missing. Say Dhameeja said he didn't see it.'

'How,' asked Feluda, 'can I put Mr Dhameeja in a position like that? Can you think of the consequences? You can't seriously expect me to tell lies about a totally innocent man? No, Mr Pakrashi, I cannot do as you ask.'

Feluda rose and added, perfectly civilly, 'Good-night, Mr Pakrashi. I hope you will not misunderstand me.'

Mr Pakrashi continued to sit, staring into space. Then he replaced the envelope into his pocket, stood up, gave Feluda a dry smile and went out without a word. It was impossible to tell from his face whether he felt angry, disappointed or humiliated.

Would any other sleuth have been able to resist such temptation and behave the way Feluda had done? Perhaps not.

SIX

Feluda, Jatayu and I were sitting in Indian Airlines flight number 263, on our way to Delhi. The plane left at 7.30 a.m. Feluda had explained to Jatayu, while we were waiting in the departure lounge, about our visit to Pretoria Street and the ensuing events. Jatayu listened, round-eyed, occasionally breaking into exclamations like 'thrilling!' and 'highly suspicious!' Then he jotted down in his notebook the little matter of the thief and the mustard oil.

'Have you flown before?' I asked him.

'If,' he replied sagely, 'a man's imagination is lively enough, he can savour an experience without actually doing anything. No, I've never travelled by air. But if you asked me whether I'm feeling nervous, my answer would be "not a bit" because in my imagination, I have travelled not just in an aeroplane but also in a rocket. Yes, I have been to the moon!'

Despite these brave words, when the plane began to speed across the runway just before take-off, I saw Lalmohan Babu clutching the armrests of his seat so tightly that his knuckles turned white. When the plane actually shot up in the air, his colour turned a rather unhealthy shade of yellow and his face broke into a terrible grimace.

'What happened to you?' I asked him afterwards.

'But that was natural!' he said. 'When a rocket leaves for outer space, even the faces of astronauts get distorted. The thing is, you see, as you're leaving the ground, the laws of gravity pull you back. In that conflict, the facial muscles contract, and hence the distortion of the whole face.'

I wanted to ask if that was indeed the case, why should Lalmohan Babu be the only person to be singled out by the laws of gravity, why didn't everyone else get similarly affected; but seeing that he had recovered his composure and was, in fact, looking quite cheerful, I said nothing more.

Breakfast arrived soon, with the cutlery wrapped in a cellophane sheet. Lalmohan Babu attacked his omelette with the coffee spoon, used the knife like a spoon to scoop out the marmalade from its little pot, putting it straight into his mouth without bothering to spread it on a piece of bread; then he tried to peel the orange with his fork, but gave up soon and used his fingers instead.

Finally, he leant forward and said to Feluda, 'I saw you chewing betel-nut a while ago. Do you have any left?'

Feluda took out the Kodak container from the blue attaché case and passed it to Lalmohan Babu. I couldn't help glancing again at Mr Dhameeja's case. Did it know that we were going to travel twelve hundred miles to a snow-laden place situated at a height of seven thousand feet, simply to return it to its owner and pick up an identical one? The thought suddenly made me shiver.

Feluda had said virtually nothing after we took off. He had taken out his famous blue notebook (volume seven) and was scribbling in it, occasionally looking up to stare out of the window at the fluffy white clouds, biting the end of his pen. It was impossible to tell what he was thinking. I, for my part, had given up trying to think at all. It was all too complex.

We soon landed in Delhi and came out of the airport. There was a noticeable nip in the air. 'This probably means there has been a fresh snowfall in Simla,' Feluda observed. He was still clutching the blue case. Not for a second had he allowed himself to be separated from it.

'I think I can get a room at the Agra Hotel,' said Lalmohan Babu. 'I will join you at the Janpath by noon. Then we can have lunch together and have a little roam around. The train to Simla doesn't leave until eight this evening, does it?'

The Janpath was a fairly large hotel. We were given room 532 on the fifth floor. Feluda put our luggage on the luggage-rack and threw himself on the bed. I decided to take this opportunity to ask him something that I had been feeling curious about.

'Feluda,' I said, 'in this whole business of blue cases and jumping hooligans, what strikes you as most suspicious?'

'The newspapers.'

'Er . . . would you care to elaborate?' I asked hesitantly.

'I cannot figure out why Mr Dhameeja folded the two newspapers so neatly and put them in his case with such care. A newspaper, once read, especially on a train, is useless. Most people would leave it behind without a second thought. Then why . . . ?'

This was Feluda's technique. He would begin to worry about a seemingly completely irrelevant point that would escape everyone else. Certainly I couldn't make head or tail of it.

In the remaining hours that we spent in Delhi, two things happened. The first was nothing remarkable, but the other was horrifying.

Lalmohan Babu turned up at about half past twelve. We decided to go to the Jantar Mantar, which was not far from our hotel. Jatayu and I were both keen to see this observatory built two hundred and fifty years ago by Sawai Jai Singh. Feluda said he'd much rather stay in the hotel, both to keep an eye on Dhameeja's attaché case and to think more about the mystery.

The first incident took place within ten minutes of our arrival at the Jantar Mantar. We were strolling along peacefully, when suddenly Lalmohan Babu clutched at my sleeve and whispered, 'I think . . . I think a rather suspicious character is trying to follow us!'

I looked at the man he indicated. It was an old man, a Nepali cap on his head, cotton wool plugged in his ears, his eyes hidden behind a pair of dark glasses. It did appear as though he was interested in our movements. How very strange!

'I know that man!' said Jatayu.

'What!'

'He sat next to me on the plane. Helped me fasten my seat belt.'

'Did he speak to you?'

'No. I thanked him, but he said nothing. Most suspicious, I tell you!'

Perhaps the man could guess we were talking about him. He disappeared only a few minutes later.

By the time we returned to the hotel, it was almost half past three. I asked for our key at the reception, but the receptionist said he didn't have it. This alarmed me somewhat, but then I remembered I had not handed it in at all. It was still in my pocket. Besides, it was rather foolish to worry about the key when Feluda was in the room to let us in. 'Just goes to show you're not used to staying in hotels,' I told myself.

Our room was on the right, about thirty yards down the corridor. I knocked on the door. There was no response.

'Perhaps your cousin is having a nap,' remarked Lalmohan Babu.

I knocked again. Nothing happened.

Then I turned the handle and discovered that the door was open. But I knew Feluda had locked it from inside when we left.

I pushed the door, but it refused to open more than a little. Something pretty heavy must be lying behind it. What could it be?

I peered in through the little gap, and my blood froze.

Feluda was lying on the floor, face down. His right elbow was what the door was knocking against.

I could hardly breathe, but knew that I must not panic. Together with Lalmohan Babu, I pushed the door harder and eventually we both managed to slide in.

Feluda was unconscious. But, possibly as a result of our pushing and heaving, he was beginning to stir and groan. Lalmohan Babu, it turned out, could keep a calm head in a crisis. It was he who splashed cold water on Feluda's face and fanned him furiously until he opened his eyes.

Then he raised a hand gingerly and felt the centre of his head, making a face. 'It's gone, I assume?' he asked. I had already checked.

'Yes, Feluda,' I had to tell him, 'that attaché case has vanished.'

Feluda staggered to his feet, declining our offer of assistance.

'It's all right,' he insisted, 'I can manage. I've got a bump on my head, but I think that's all. It might have been worse.'

It might indeed. Feluda took a few minutes to rest and to make sure nothing was broken. Then he rang room service, ordered tea for us all and told us what had happened.

'I studied the entries in my notebook for about half an hour after you had gone. Then I began to feel tired. I hadn't slept for more than a couple of hours last night, you see. So I thought I'd have a little rest, but just at that moment the telephone rang.'

'The telephone? Who was it?'

'Wait, let me finish. It was the receptionist. He said, Mr Mitter, there's a gentleman here who has recognized you. He says he'd like to take the autograph of such a brilliant sleuth as yourself. Shall I send him up?'

Feluda paused here, turned to me and continued, 'I realized one thing today, Topshe, and I don't mind admitting it—to give an autograph is as tempting as taking it. I shall, of course, be more careful in future. But I needed this lesson.'

'What does that mean?'

'I felt so pleased that I told the receptionist to send the man up. He came, knocked on the door, I opened it, felt a sharp knock on my own head, and . . . everything went black. The man had covered his face with a large handkerchief, so I don't even know what he looked like.'

'Since we are in Delhi,' suggested Jatayu, 'wouldn't it be a good idea to inform the Prime Minister?'

Feluda smiled wryly at this. 'God knows what that man gained by stealing that blue case,' he remarked, 'but he has certainly put us in an impossible situation. What a reckless devil!'

For the next few minutes, no one spoke. All that could be heard in the room was the sound of sighs. At last, Feluda uttered a few significant words. 'There is a way,' he said slowly. 'Not, I admit, a simple way. But it's the only one I can think of, and we've got to take it because we cannot go to Simla empty-handed.'

He reached for his blue notebook, and ran his eyes through the list of contents in Dhameeja's case.

'There is nothing in this list,' he said, 'that we can't get here in Delhi. We've got to get every item. I remember what each one looked like and what condition it was in. So that's one thing we needn't worry about. I could make the toothpaste and the shaving cream look old and used. And it should be possible to get hold of a white handkerchief and have it embroidered. I remember the pattern. The newspapers will, of course, have a different date, but I don't think Mr Dhameeja will notice it. The only expensive thing would be a roll of Kodak film . . .'

'Hey!' Lalmohan Babu interrupted. 'Hey, look, I completely forgot to give this back to you. You passed it to me on the plane, remember?' He returned the Kodak container to Feluda.

'Good, that's one problem solved . . . but what is that sticking out of your pocket?'

A piece of paper had slipped out with the little box of betel-nuts. We could all see what was written on it:

'Do not go to Simla if you value your life.'

SEVEN

It was now 9.30 p.m. Our train was rushing through the darkness in the direction of Kalka. We would have to change at Kalka to go on to Simla. There were only the three of us in our compartment. The fourth berth was empty. I couldn't guess how the other two were feeling, but in my own mind there was a mixture of so many different emotions that it was impossible to tell which was the uppermost: excitement, pleasure, an eager anticipation or fear.

Lalmohan Babu broke the silence by saying, somewhat hesitantly,

'Tel! me, Mr Mitter, the dividing line between a brilliant detective and a criminal with real cunning is really quite thin, isn't it?'

Feluda was so preoccupied that he did not reply. But I knew very well what had prompted the question. It was related to a certain incident that took place during the evening. I should describe it in some detail, for it revealed a rather unexpected streak in Feluda's character.

It had taken us barely half an hour to collect most of the things we needed to deceive Mr Dhameeja. The only major problem was the attaché case itself.

Where could we find a blue Air-India case? We didn't know anyone in Delhi we could ask. It might be possible to get a similar blue case in a shop—but that wouldn't have Air India written on it. And that would, naturally, give the whole show away.

In the end, however, in sheer desperation, we did buy a plain blue case and, clutching it in one hand, Feluda led us into the main office of Air-India.

The first person our eyes fell on was an old man, a Parsee cap on his head, sitting right next to the 'Enquiries' counter. On his left, resting against his chair, was a brand new blue Air India attaché case, exactly the kind we were looking for.

Feluda walked straight up to the counter and placed his own case beside the old man's. 'Is there an Air-India flight to Frankfurt from Delhi?' he asked the man behind the counter. In a matter of seconds, he got the necessary information, said, 'Thank you,' picked up the old man's case and pushed his own to the spot where it had been resting and coolly walked out. Lalmohan Babu and I followed, quite speechless. Then we returned to the hotel and Feluda began to work on the attaché case. By the time he finished, no one—not even Mr Dhameeja—could have said that it was not the one we had been given by Dinanath Lahiri. The same applied to its contents.

Feluda had been staring at his notebook. Now he shut it, rose and began pacing. 'It was just like this,' he muttered. 'Those four men were in a coach exactly like this . . .'

I have always found it difficult to tell what would attract Feluda's attention. Right now, he was staring at the glasses that stood inside metal rings attached to the wall. Why should these be of any interest to him?

'Can you sleep in a moving train, or can't you?' he asked Lalmohan Babu, rather abruptly.

'Well, I . . .' Lalmohan Babu replied, trying to suppress a giant yawn, 'I quite like being rocked.'

'Yes. I know the rocking generally helps one sleep. But not everyone, mind you. I have an uncle who cannot sleep a wink in a train,' said Feluda and jumped up on the empty berth. Then he switched on the reading lamp, opened the book that was in Dhameeja's attaché case, and turned a few pages. We had bought a second copy at a book stall in the New Delhi railway station.

Laying the book aside, Feluda stretched on the upper berth and stared up at the ceiling. It was completely dark outside. Nothing could be seen except a few flickering lights in the distance.

I was about to ask Lalmohan Babu if he had remembered to bring his weapon and, if so, when would he show it to us, when he spoke unexpectedly.

'We forgot one thing,' he said, 'betel-nuts. We must check with the fellow from the dining car if they have any. If not, we shall have to buy some at the next station. There's just one left in this little box.'

Lalmohan Babu took out the Kodak container, the only original object left from Dhameeja's attaché case, and tilted it on his palm. The betel-nut did not slip out.

'How annoying!' he exclaimed. 'I can see it, but it won't come out!' He began to shake the container vigorously, showering strong words on the obstinate piece of betel-nut, but it refused to budge.

'Give it to me!' said Feluda and leapt down from the upper berth, snatching the container from Lalmohan Babu's hand. Lalmohan Babu could only stare at him, completely taken aback.

Feluda slipped his little finger into the box and pushed at the small object, using a little force. It now came out like an obedient child. Feluda sniffed a couple of times and said, 'Araldite. Someone used Araldite on this piece of betel-nut. I wonder why—? Topshe, shut the door.' There were footsteps outside in the corridor. I did shut the door, but not before I had caught a glimpse of the man who went past our compartment. It was the same old man we had seen at the Jantar Mantar. He was still wearing the dark glasses and his ears were still plugged with cotton wool.

'Sh-h-h-h,' Feluda whistled.

He was gazing steadily at the little betel-nut that lay on his palm. I went forward for a closer look. It was clear that it was not a betel-nut at all. Some other object had been painted brown to camouflage it.

'I should have guessed,' said Feluda softly. 'I should have known a long time ago. Oh, what a fool I have been, Topshe!'

Feluda now lifted one of the glasses from its ring, poured a little water from our flask and dipped the betel-nut in it. The water began to turn a light brown as he gently rubbed the object. Then he wiped it with a handkerchief and put it back on his palm.

The betel-nut had disappeared. In its place was a beautifully cut, brilliant stone. From the way it glittered even in our semi-dark compartment, I could tell it was a diamond. And it was pretty obvious that none of us had seen such a large one ever before. At least, Lalmohan Babu made no bones about it.

'Is that . . .' he gasped, 'a d. . .di. . .di. . .?'

Feluda closed his fist around the stone, went over to the door to lock it, then came back and said, 'We've already had warnings threatening our lives. Why are you talking of dying?'

'No, no, not d-dying. I mean, is that a diam-m-m-?'

'Very probably, or it wouldn't be chased so persistently. But mind you, I am no expert.'

'Well then, is it val-val-val-?'

'I'm afraid the value of diamonds is something I don't know much about. I can only make a rough guess. This one, I think, is in the region of twenty carats. So its value would certainly exceed half a million rupees.'

Lalmohan Babu gulped in silence. Feluda was still turning the stone between his fingers.

'How did Dhameeja get hold of something so precious?' I asked under my breath.

'I don't know, dear boy. All I know about Dhameeja is that he said he had an orchard and that he likes reading thrillers on trains.'

Lalmohan Babu, in the meantime, had recovered somewhat. 'Will this stone now go back to Dhameeja?' he asked.

'If we can be sure that it is indeed his, then certainly it will go back to him.'

'Does that mean you suspect it might actually belong to someone else?'

'Yes, but there are other questions that need to be answered. For instance, I don't know if people outside Bengal are in the habit of chewing chopped betel-nuts.'

'But if that is so—' I began.

'No. No more questions tonight, Topshe. This whole affair has taken another new turn. We have to take every step with extreme caution. I can't waste any more time chatting.'

Feluda took out his wallet, put the sparkling stone away safely, pulled the zip and climbed on to his berth. I knew he didn't want to be disturbed. Lalmohan Babu opened his mouth to speak, but I laid a finger against my lips to stop him. He glanced once at Feluda and then turned to me. 'I think I'll give up writing suspense thrillers,' he confided.

'Why?'

'The few things that have happened in the last couple of days . . . they're beyond one's imagination, aren't they? Haven't you heard the saying, truth is stronger than fiction?'

'Not stronger. I think the word is stranger.'

'Stranger?'

'Yes, meaning more . . . amazing. More curious.'

'Oh really? I thought a stranger was someone one hadn't met before. Oh no, no, I see what you mean. Strange, stranger, strangest . . .'

I decided to cheer him up. 'We found the diamond only because of you,' I told him. 'If you hadn't finished all the real betel-nuts, that diamond would have remained hidden forever.'

Lalmohan Babu grinned from ear to ear.

'You mean to say even I have made a little contribution to this great mystery? Heh, heh, heh, heh . . .' Then he thought for a minute and added, 'You know what I really think? I am sure your cousin knew about the diamond right from the start. Or how could we have survived two attempts to steal it from us?'

This made me think. The thief had not yet managed to lay his hands on the real stuff. Not even by breaking into our hotel room. That precious stone was still with us. This meant we were probably still being followed, and therefore, in constant danger.

And we wouldn't be safe even in Simla . . .

Heaven knows when I fell asleep. I woke suddenly in the middle of the night. It was totally dark in the compartment, which meant even Feluda had switched off the reading lamp and gone to sleep. Lalmohan Babu was sleeping on the lower berth opposite mine. I was about to switch on my own lamp to look at the time, when my eyes fell on the door. The curtain from our side was drawn partially over the frosted glass. But there was a gap, and on this gap fell the shadow of a man.

What was he doing there? It took me a few seconds to realize he was actually trying to turn the handle of the door. I knew the door was locked and would not yield to pressure from outside; but even so, I began to feel breathless with fear.

How long the man would have persisted, it is difficult to say. But, only a few seconds later, Lalmohan Babu shouted 'Boomerang!' in his sleep, and the shadow disappeared.

I realized that even in the cool night air, I had broken into a cold sweat.

EIGHT

I had seen snow-capped mountains before—Kanchenjunga in Darjeeling and the top of Annapurna from a plane; and certainly I had seen snow in films. But nothing had startled me as much as what I saw in Simla. If it wasn't for other Indians strolling on the streets, I could have sworn we were in a foreign country.

'This town was built by the British, like Darjeeling,' Feluda told me, 'so it does have the appearance of a foreign city. One Lt. Ross built a wooden cottage here in 1819 for himself. That was the beginning. Soon, the British turned this into their summer capital, since in the summer months life on the plains became pretty uncomfortable.'

We had taken a metre gauge train at Kalka to reach Simla. Nothing remarkable happened on the way, although I noticed that the old man with the earplugs travelled on the same train and checked in at the Clarkes just like us. Since the main season had not yet started, there were plenty of rooms available and Lalmohan Babu, too, found one at the Clarkes without any problem.

Feluda went looking for a post office soon after checking in. I offered to go with him, but he said someone should stay behind to guard the new attaché case; so Lalmohan Babu and I remained at the hotel. Feluda hadn't made a single remark on the snow or the beautiful town. Lalmohan Babu, on the other hand, appeared to be totally overwhelmed. Everything he saw struck him as 'fanastatic'. When I pointed out that the word was 'fantastic', he said airily that the speed with which he read English was so remarkable that not often did he find the time to look at the words carefully. Besides, there were a number of other questions he wanted answered—was it possible to find polar bears in Simla, did the Aurora Borealis appear here, did the Eskimos use the same snow to build their ilgoos (at which point I had to correct him again and say that it was igloos the Eskimos built, not ilgoos). The man was unstoppable.

The Clarkes Hotel stood on a slope. A veranda ran by the side of its second floor, which led to the street. The manager's room, the lounge, as well as our own rooms, were all on the second floor. Wooden stairs ran down to the first floor where there were more rooms and the dining-hall.

Feluda got delayed on his way back, so it was past 2 p.m. by the time we finished our lunch. A band was playing in one corner of the dining-hall. Lalmohan Babu called it a concert. The old man with the earplugs was also having lunch in the same room, as were three foreigners—two men and a woman. I had seen a man with dark glasses and a pointed beard leave the room when we came in. It did not appear as though there was anyone else in the hotel apart from these people and ourselves.

'We are going to see Mr Dhameeja today, aren't we?' I asked, slowly sipping the hot soup.

'Yes, at four o'clock. We needn't leave before three,' Feluda replied.

'Where exactly does he live?'

'The Wildflower Hall is on the way to Kufri. Eight miles from here.'

'Why should it take an hour to get there?'

'Most of the way is snowed under. The car might skid if we try to do anything other than crawl.' Then Feluda said to Lalmohan Babu, 'Wear all your warm clothes. This place we're going to is a thousand feet higher than Simla. The snow there is a lot worse.'

Lalmohan Babu put a spoonful of soup into his mouth, slurping noisily, and asked, 'Is a sherpa going to accompany us?'

I nearly burst out laughing, but Feluda kept a straight face. 'No,' he said seriously, 'there is actually a road that leads up there. We'll be going in a car.'

We finished our soup and were waiting for the next course, when Feluda spoke again. 'What happened to your weapon?' he asked Lalmohan Babu.

'I have it with me,' Lalmohan Babu replied, chewing a bread stick, 'haven't had the chance to show it to you, have I?'

'What is it?'

'A boomerang.'

Ah, that made sense. I had been wondering why he had shouted 'boomerang!' in his sleep.

'Where did you get a thing like that?'

'An Australian was selling some of his stuff. He had put an advertisement in the paper. There were many other interesting things, but I couldn't resist this one. I have heard that if you can throw it correctly, it would hit your target and return to you.'

'No, that's not quite true. It would come back to you only if it misses the target, not if it hits it.'

'Well yes, you may be right. But let me tell you one thing. It's damn difficult to throw it. I tried from my terrace, and it went and broke a flower pot on the balcony of the house opposite. Thank goodness, those people knew me and were kind enough to return my weapon without making a fuss about their flower pot.'

'Please don't forget to take it with you today.'

Lalmohan Babu's eyes began to shine with excitement.

'Are you expecting trouble?'

'Well, I can't guarantee anything, can I? After all, whoever has been trying to steal that diamond hasn't yet got it, has he?' Feluda spoke lightly, but I could see he was not totally easy in his mind.

At five to three, a blue Ambassador drove up and stopped before the main entrance. 'Here's our taxi,' said Feluda and stood up. Lalmohan Babu and I followed suit. The driver was a local man, young and well built. Feluda joined him on the front seat, clutching Mr Dhameeja's (fake) attaché case. Jatayu and I sat at the back. The boomerang was hidden inside Jatayu's voluminous overcoat. I had taken a good look at it. It was made of wood and looked a bit like the bottom half of a hockey stick, although it was a lot thinner and smoother.

The sky had started to turn grey and the temperature dropped appreciably. But the clouds were not very heavy, so it did not seem as though it might rain. We left for the Wildflower Hall on the dot of 3 p.m.

Our hotel was in the main town. We hadn't had the chance to go out of the hotel since our arrival. The true spirit of the cold, sombre, snow-covered mountains struck me only when our car left the town and began its journey along a quiet, narrow path.

The mountains rose on one side, on the other was a deep ravine. The road was wide enough to allow another car to squeeze past, but that was just about all it could do. A thick pine forest grew on the mountains.

The first four miles were covered at a reasonable speed since the snow on the road was almost negligible. Through the pine trees, I could catch glimpses of heavier snow on the mountains at a distance; but, soon, the snow on the road we were on grew very much thicker. Feluda was right.

We had to reduce our speed and crawl carefully, following the tyre marks of cars that had preceded us. The ground was so slippery that, at times, the car failed to move forward, its wheels spinning furiously.

The tip of my nose and my ears began to feel icy. Lalmohan Babu told me at one point that his ears were ringing. Five minutes later he said he had a blocked nose. I paid little attention. The last thing I was worried about was how my body would cope with the cold. All I could do was look around me and wonder at this remarkable place. Did man indeed live here? Wasn't this a corner nature had created only for animals and birds and insects that lived in snowy mountains? Shouldn't this stay unspoilt and untouched by the human hand? But no, the road we were travelling on had been built by man, other cars had driven on the same road and, no doubt, others would follow. In fact, if this wonderful place had not already been discovered by man, I would not be here today.

The unmarred strange whiteness ended abruptly about twenty minutes later, with a black wooden board by the side of the road that proclaimed in white letters: Wildflower Hall. I had not expected our journey to end so peacefully.

A little later we came upon a gate with The Nook written on it. Our car turned right and drove through this gate. A long driveway led to a large, old-fashioned bungalow, very obviously built during British times. Its roof and parapets were covered with a thick layer of snow. Its occupant had to be a pukka sahib, or he wouldn't live in a place like this.

Our taxi drew up under the portico. A man in a uniform came out and took Feluda's card. A minute later, the owner of the house came out himself with an outstretched arm.

'Good afternoon, Mr Mitter. I must say I am most impressed by your punctuality. Do come in, please.'

Mr Dhameeja might have been an Englishman. His diction was flawless. His appearance fitted Mr Lahiri's description. Feluda introduced me and Lalmohan Babu, and then we all went in. The floor was wooden, as were the walls of the huge drawing-room. A fire crackled in the fireplace.

Feluda handed over the blue attaché case before he sat down. The smile on Mr Dhameeja's face did not falter. Our attempt at deception was thus rewarded with complete success.

'Thank you so much. I've got Mr Lahiri's case and kept it handy.'

'Please check the contents in your case,' said Feluda with a slight smile.

'If you say so,' replied Mr Dhameeja, laughing, and opened the case. Then he ran his eyes over the items we had so carefully placed in it and said, 'Yes, everything's fine, except that these newspapers are not mine.'

'Not yours?' asked Feluda, retrieving the two English dailies.

'No, and neither is this.'

Mr Dhameeja returned the box of betel-nuts, which had been filled at the Kalka railway station. 'Oh, I see,' said Feluda. 'Those must have got there by mistake.'

Well, at least it proved that Mr Dhameeja knew nothing about the diamond. But, in that case, how did the box get inside the attaché case?

'And here is Mr Lahiri's case,' said Mr Dhameeja, picking up an identical attaché case from a side table and handing it over to Feluda. 'May I,' he added, 'make the same request? Please check its contents.'

'There's really only one thing Mr Lahiri is interested in. A bottle of enterovioform tablets.'

'Yes, it's there.'

'. . . And, a manuscript?'

'Manuscript?'

Feluda had opened the case. A brief glance even from a distance told me that there was not even a scrap of paper in it, let alone a whole manuscript.

Feluda was frowning deeply, staring into the open attaché. 'What manuscript are you talking about?' asked Mr Dhameeja.

Feluda said nothing. I could see what a difficult position he was in; either Mr Dhameeja had to be accused of stealing, or we had to take our leave politely, without Shambhucharan's tale of Tibet.

Mercifully, Mr Dhameeja continued to speak. 'I am very sorry, Mr Mitter, but that attaché case now contains exactly what I found in it when I opened it in my room in the Grand Hotel. I searched it thoroughly in the hope of finding its owner's address. But there was nothing, and certainly not a manuscript. On my return to Simla, I kept it locked in my own cupboard. Not for a second did anyone else touch it. I can guarantee that.'

After a speech like that, there was very little that Feluda could do. He rose to his feet and said with a slightly embarrassed air, 'It must be my mistake, then. Please don't mind, Mr Dhameeja. Thank you very much for your help. We should perhaps now be making a move.'

'Why? Allow me at least to offer you a cup of tea. Or would you prefer coffee?'

'No, no, nothing, thank you. It's getting late. We really ought to go. Good-bye.'

We came out of the bungalow and got into our taxi. I was feeling even more confused. Where could the manuscript have disappeared? Naresh Pakrashi had told us that he didn't see Mr Lahiri read on the train. Was that the truth?

Had Dinanath Lahiri simply told us a pack of lies?

NINE

It grew darker soon after we left. But it was only 4.25 p.m. Surely the sun wasn't setting already? I looked at the sky, and found the reason. The light grey clouds had turned into heavy, black ones. Please God, don't let it rain. The road was already slippery. Since we were now going to go downhill, the chances of skidding were greater. The only good thing was that traffic was virtually nonexistent, so there was no fear of crashing into another car.

Feluda was sitting next to the driver. I couldn't see his face, but could tell that he was still frowning. And I also knew what he was thinking. Either Dinanath Babu or Mr Dhameeja had lied to us. Mr Dhameeja's living-room had been full of books. Perhaps he knew the name of Shambhucharan. An account of a visit to Tibet fifty years ago—and that, too, written in English—might well have been a temptation. It was not totally impossible, was it? But if the manuscript was with Mr Dhameeja, how on earth would Feluda ever retrieve it?

Clearly, there were two mysteries now. One involved the diamond, and the other the missing manuscript. What if such a terrible tangle proved too much to unravel, even for Feluda?

The temperature had dropped further. I could see my breath condensing all the time. Lalmohan Babu undid the top button of his overcoat, slipped his hand in and said, 'Even the boomerang feels stone cold. It comes from a warm country, doesn't it? I hope it'll work here in this climate.' I opened my mouth to tell him there were places in Australia where it snowed, but had to shut it. Our car had come to a complete halt. And the reason was simple. A black Ambassador blocked our way. About a hundred yards away, diagonally across the road, stood this other car, making it impossible for us to proceed.

When the loud blowing of our horn did not help, it became obvious that something was wrong. The driver of the other car was nowhere in sight.

Feluda placed a hand on the steering wheel and quietly told the driver to move his car to one side, closer to the hill. The driver did this without a word. Then all four of us got out and stepped on to the slushy path.

Everything was very quiet. Not even the twitter of a bird broke the eerie silence. What was most puzzling was that there was neither a driver nor a passenger in the black car. Who would place a car across the road like that and then abandon it totally?

We were making our way very cautiously along the tyre marks on the snow, when a sudden splashing noise made Lalmohan Babu give a violent start, stumble and go sprawling on the snow. He landed flat on his face. I knew the noise had been caused by a chunk of thawing ice that had dislodged itself from a branch. In the total silence of the surroundings, it did sound as loud as a pistol shot. Feluda and I pulled Lalmohan Babu up to his feet and we resumed walking.

A few yards later, I realized I had been wrong. There was indeed a figure sitting in the car, in the driver's seat. 'I know this man,' said our driver, Harbilas, peering carefully, 'he is a taxi driver like me. And this taxi is his own. He's called Arvind. But . . . but . . . I think he's unconscious, or perhaps . . . dead?'

Feluda's right hand automatically made its way to his pocket. I knew he was clutching his revolver.

Splash!

Another chunk of ice fell, a lot closer this time. Lalmohan Babu started again, but managed to stop himself from stumbling. In the next instant, however, a completely unexpected ear-splitting noise made him lose control and he went rolling on the snow once more. This time, it was a pistol shot.

The bullet hit the ground less than ten yards ahead of us, making the snow spray up in the air. Feluda had pulled me aside the moment the shot was fired, and we had both thrown ourselves on the ground. Lalmohan Babu came rolling half a second later. The driver, too, had jumped behind the car. Although young and strong, clearly he had never had to cope with such a situation before.

The sound of the shot echoed among the hills. Someone hiding in the pine forest had fired at us. Presumably, he couldn't see us any more for we were shielded by the black Ambassador.

Lying prostrate on the ground, I tried to come to terms with this new development. Something cold and wet was tickling the back of my neck. I turned my head a few degrees and realized what it was. A fine white curtain of snow had been thrown down from the sky. Even in such a moment of danger, I couldn't help staring— fascinated—at the little flakes that fell like cotton fluff. For the first time in my life, I discovered falling snow made no noise at all. Lalmohan Babu looked as though he was about to make a remark, but one gesture from Feluda made him change his mind.

At this precise moment, the silence was shattered once more, but not by a pistol shot, or a chunk of ice, or the sound of wheels turning in the slippery snow. This time, we heard the voice of a man.

'Mr Mitter!'

Who was this? Why did the voice sound vaguely familiar?

'Listen carefully, Mr Mitter,' it went on. 'You must have realized by now that I have got you where I want you. So don't try any clever tricks. It's not going to work and, in fact, your lives may be in danger.'

It was some time before the final echo of the words died down. Then the man spoke again.

'I want only one thing from you, Mr Mitter.'

'What is it?' Feluda shouted back.

'Come out from where you're hiding. I would like to see you, although you couldn't see me even if you tried. I will answer your question when you come out.'

For a few minutes, I had been aware of a strange noise in my immediate vicinity. At first I thought it was coming from inside the car. Now I turned my head and realized it was simply the sound of Lalmohan Babu's chattering teeth.

Feluda rose to his feet and slowly walked over to the other side of the car, without uttering a word. Perhaps he knew under the circumstances, it was best to do as he was told. Never before had I seen him grapple with such a difficult situation.

'I hope,' said the voice, 'that your three companions realize that a single move from them would simply spell disaster.'

'Kindly tell me what you want,' said Feluda.

I could see him standing from behind one of the wheels. He was looking up at the mountain. In front of him lay a wide expanse of snow. The pine forest started at some distance.

'Take out your revolver,' commanded the voice. Feluda obeyed.

'Throw it across on the slope.' Feluda did.

'Do you have the Kodak container?'

'Yes.'

'Show it to me.'

Feluda took out the yellow container from his pocket and raised it.

'Now show me the stone you found in it.'

Feluda slipped his hand into the pocket of his jacket. Then he brought it out and held it high once more, holding a small object between his thumb and forefinger.

No one spoke for a few seconds. No doubt the man was trying to take a good look at the diamond. Did he have binoculars, I wondered.

'All right,' the voice came back. 'Now put that stone back into its container and place it on that large grey boulder by the side of the road. Then you must return straight to Simla. If you think . . .'

Feluda cut him short.

'You really want this stone, don't you?' he asked.

'For God's sake, do I have to spell it out?' the voice retorted sharply.

'Well then, here it is!'

Feluda swung his arm and threw the stone in the direction of the forest. This was followed by a breath-taking sequence of events.

Our invisible adversary threw himself out of his hiding place in an attempt to catch the diamond, but fell on a slab of half-frozen snow. In the next instant, he lost his foothold and was rolling down the hill like a giant snowball. He finally came to rest near the snow-covered nullah that ran alongside the road. By this time, the pistol and binoculars had dropped from his hands. A pair of dark glasses and a pointed beard lay not far from these.

There was no point in our hiding any more. The three of us leapt to our feet and ran forward to join Feluda. I had expected the other man to be at least unconscious, if not dead. He had slipped from a considerable height at enormous speed. But, to my surprise, I found him lying flat on his back, glaring malevolently at Feluda and breathing deeply.

It was easy enough now to understand why his voice had sounded familiar. The figure stretched out on the snow was none other than the unsuccessful film star, Amar Kumar, alias Prabeer Lahiri, Dinanath Babu's nephew.

Feluda spoke with ice in his voice. 'You do realize, don't you, that the tables have turned? So stop playing this game and let's hear what you have to say.'

Prabeer Lahiri did not reply. He continued to lie on his back, snow drifting down on his upturned face, gazing steadily at Feluda.

Nothing was as yet clear to me, but I hoped Prabeer Babu would throw some light on the mystery. But still he said nothing.

'Very well,' said Feluda, 'if you will not open your mouth, allow me to do the talking. Pray tell me if I get anything wrong. You had got the diamond from that Nepali box, hadn't you? It was possibly the same jewel that the Rana of Nepal had given to Shambhucharan as a token of his gratitude. That box, in fact, must have been Shambhucharan's property; and he must have left it before his death with his friend, Satinath Lahiri. Satinath brought it back to India with him, but was unable to tell anyone about the diamond, presumably because by the time he returned, he was seriously ill. You found it only a few days ago purely by chance. Then you painted it brown and kept it together with chopped betel-nuts in that empty film container. When your uncle gave you the Air India attaché case, you thought it would be perfectly safe to hide your diamond in it. But what you didn't foresee was that only a day later, the case would make its way from your room to mine. You eavesdropped, didn't you, when your uncle was talking to us that evening in your house? So you decided to steal it from me. When the telephone call from a fictitious Mr Puri and the efforts of your hired hooligans failed, you chased us to Delhi. But even that didn't work, did it? You took a very great risk by breaking into our room in the hotel, but the diamond still eluded your grasp. There was really only one thing you could do after that. You followed us to Simla and planned this magnificent fiasco.'

Feluda stopped. We were all standing round, staring at him, totally fascinated.

'Tell me, Mr Lahiri, is any of this untrue?'

The look in Prabeer Lahiri's eyes underwent a swift change. His eyes glittered and his lips spread in a cunning smile. 'What are you talking about, Mr Mitter?' he asked almost gleefully. 'What diamond? I know nothing about this!'

My heart missed a beat. The diamond was lost in the snow. Perhaps forever. How could Feluda prove—?

'Why, Mr Lahiri,' Feluda said softly, 'are you not acquainted with this little gem?'

We started again. Feluda had slipped his hand into a different pocket and brought out another stone. Even in the fading light from the overcast sky, it winked merrily.

'That little stone that's buried in the snow was something I bought this morning at the Miller Gem Company in Simla. Do you know how much I spent on it? Five rupees. This one is the real . . .'

He couldn't finish. Prabeer Lahiri sprang up like a tiger and jumped on Feluda, snatching the diamond from his hand.

Clang!

This time, Feluda, too, gave a start. This unexpected noise was simply the result of Lalmohan Babu's boomerang hitting Prabeer Lahiri's head. He sank down on the snow again, unconscious. The diamond returned to Feluda.

'Thank you, Lalmohan Babu.'

But it was doubtful whether Lalmohan Babu heard the words for he was staring, dumbfounded, at the boomerang that had shot out in the air from his own right hand and found its mark so accurately.

TEN

The budding film star, Amar Kumar, was now a sorry sight. He had made a full confession in the car on the way back to Simla. This was made easier by the revolver in Feluda's hand, which he had recovered soon after the drama ended. It had not taken Prabeer Babu long to come round. Lalmohan Babu, having thrown the boomerang at him, had made an attempt at nursing him by scooping up a handful of snow and plastering his head with it. I cannot tell if it helped in any way, but he opened his eyes soon enough.

The driver called Arvind had also regained consciousness and was, reportedly, feeling better. He had, at first, been offered money to join Prabeer Lahiri. But when he refused to be tempted, Prabeer Babu lost his patience and simply knocked him out.

Things had started to go wrong for Prabeer Lahiri ever since he was dropped from the film. It had been a long-cherished dream that he would be a famous film star one day, living in luxury, chased by thousands of admirers. When his voice let him down and this dream was shattered, Prabeer Lahiri, in a manner of speaking, lost his head.

He had to get what he wanted. If it was not possible to fulfil his dream by fair means, he was prepared to adopt unfair ones. By a strange twist of fate, the Nepali box fell into his hands, like manna from heaven. In it he found a stone beautifully cut and sparkling bright. When he had it valued, it took his breath away; and his plans took a different shape. He would produce his own film, he decided, and take the lead role. No one—but no one—could have him dropped. What followed this decision was now history.

We handed him over to the Himachal Pradesh state police. It turned out that Feluda's suspicions had fallen on Prabeer Babu as soon as we had found the diamond. So he had called Dinanath Lahiri immediately on arrival in Simla, and asked him to join us. Mr Lahiri was expected to reach Simla the next day. It would then be up to him to decide what should be done with his nephew. The diamond would probably return to Dinanath Babu, since it had been found amongst his uncle's belongings.

'That's all very well,' I said, after Feluda explained the whole story, 'but what about Shambhucharan's travelogue?'

'That,' said Feluda, 'is mystery number two. You've heard of double-barrelled guns, haven't you? This one's a double-barrelled mystery.'

'But are we anywhere near finding its solution?'

'Yes, my dear boy, yes. Thanks to the newspapers and that glass of water.'

Feluda's words sounded no less mysterious, so I decided not to probe any further. He, too, said nothing more.

We returned to the hotel without any other excitement on the way. A few minutes later, we were seated on the open terrace of the hotel under a colourful canopy, sipping hot chocolate. Seven other tables stood on the terrace. Two Japanese men sat at the next one and, at some distance, sat the old man who had travelled with us from Delhi. He had removed the cotton wool from his ears.

The sky was now clear, but the evening light was fading rather quickly. The main city of Simla lay among the eastern hills. I could see its streets and houses being lit up one by one.

Lalmohan Babu had been very quiet, lost in his thoughts. Now he took a long sip of his chocolate and said, 'Perhaps it is true that there is an underlying current of viciousness in the mind of every human being. Don't you agree, Felu Babu? When one blow from my boomerang made that man spin and fall, I felt so . . . excited. Even pleased. It's strange!'

'Man descended from monkeys,' Feluda remarked. 'You knew that, didn't you? Well, a modern theory now says that it was really a special breed in Africa that was man's ancestor. It's well known for its killer instinct. So, if you are feeling pleased about having hit Prabeer Lahiri, your ancestors are to blame.'

An interesting theory, no doubt. But I was in no mood to discuss monkeys. My mind kept going back to Shambhucharan. Where was his manuscript? Who had got it? Or could it be that no one did, and the whole thing was a lie? But why should anyone tell such a lie?

I had to speak.

'Feluda,' I blurted out, 'who is the liar? Dhameeja or Dinanath Babu?'

'Neither.'

'You mean the manuscript does exist?'

'Yes, but whether we'll ever get it back is extremely doubtful.' Feluda sounded grave.

'Do you happen to know,' I asked tentatively, 'who has got it?'

'Yes, I do. It's all quite clear to me now. But the man who has it is so remarkably clever that it would be very difficult indeed to prove anything against him. To tell you the truth, he almost managed to hoodwink me.'

'Almost?' The word pleased me for I would have hated to think Feluda had been totally fooled by anyone.

'Mitter sahib!'

This came from a bearer who was standing near the door,

glancing around uncertainly.

'Here!' Feluda shouted, waving. The bearer made his way to our table, clutching a brown parcel.

'Someone left this for you in the manager's room,' he said.

Feluda's name was written on it in large bold letters: MR P. C. MITTER, CLARKES HOTEL.

Feluda's expression had changed the minute the parcel was handed to him. Now he opened it swiftly and exclaimed, 'What! Where did this come from?'

A familiar smell came from the parcel. Feluda held up its content. I stared at an ancient notebook, the kind that was impossible to find nowadays. The front page had these words written on it in a very neat hand:

A Bengalee in Lamaland
Shambhucharan Bose
June 1917

'Good heavens! It's that famous manusprint!' said Lalmohan Babu.

I did not bother to correct him. I could only look dumbly at Feluda, who was staring straight at something specific. I turned my gaze in the same direction. The two Japanese had gone. There was only one other person left on the terrace, apart from ourselves. It was the same old man we had seen so many times before. He was still wearing a cap and dark glasses. Feluda was looking straight at him.

The man rose to his feet and walked over to our table. Then he took off his glasses and his cap. Yes, he certainly seemed familiar. But there was something odd . . . something missing . . . what had I seen before . . . ?

'Aren't you going to wear your false teeth?' Feluda asked.

'Certainly.'

The man took out a set of false teeth from his pocket and slipped it into his mouth. Instantly, his hollowed cheeks filled out, his jaw became firm and he began to look ten years younger. And it was easy to recognize him.

This was none other than that supremely irritable man we had visited in Lansdowne Road, Mr Naresh Chandra Pakrashi.

'When did you get the dentures made?' asked Feluda.

'I had ordered them a while ago. But they were delivered the day after I returned to Calcutta from Delhi.'

That explained why Dinanath Babu had thought him old. He had not worn his dentures on the train. But he had started using them by the time we met him in his house.

'I had guessed from the start that the attaché cases had been exchanged deliberately,' Feluda told him. 'I knew it was no accident. But what I did not know—and it took me a long time to figure that one out—was that you were responsible.'

'That is natural enough,' Mr Pakrashi replied calmly. 'You must have realized that I am no fool.'

'No, most certainly you are not. But do you know where you went wrong? You shouldn't have put those newspapers in Mr Dhameeja's attaché case. I know why you did it, though. Dinanath Lahiri's case was heavier than Dhameeja's because it had this notebook in it. So you stuffed the newspapers in Dhameeja's case, so that its weight became more or less the same as Dinanath's. When Dinanath Babu picked it up, naturally he noticed nothing unusual. But people don't normally bother to pack their cases with papers they've read on the train, do they?'

'You're right. But then, you are more intelligent than most. Not many would have picked that up.'

'I have a question to ask,' Feluda continued. 'Everyone, with the sole exception of yourself, slept well that night, didn't they?'

'Hmmm . . . yes, you might say that.'

'And yet, Dinanath Lahiri says he cannot sleep in a moving train. Did you drug him?'

'Right.'

'By crushing a pill and pouring it into a glass of water?'

'Yes. I always carry my sleeping pills with me. Everyone had been given a glass of water when dinner was served, and two of the passengers went to wash their hands. Only Dhameeja didn't.'

'Does that mean you couldn't tamper with Mr Dhameeja's drinking water?'

'No, and as a result of that I couldn't do a thing during the night. At six in the morning, Dhameeja got up to have a shave and then went to the bathroom. I did what I had to do before he came back Lahiri and the other one were still fast asleep.'

'I see. You took one hell of a risk, didn't you, with Dhameeja actually in the compartment, when you poured the pill into Dinanath's water?'

'I was lucky. He didn't even glance at me.'

'Yes, lucky you certainly were. But, later, you did something that gave you away. It was a clever move, no doubt, but what made you offer me money even after you had got hold of Shambhucharan's manuscript?'

Mr Pakrashi burst out laughing, but said nothing.

'That phone call in Calcutta and that piece of paper in Delhi . . . you were behind both, weren't you?'

'Yes, of course. I did not want you to go to Simla—at least, not at first. I knew a man like you would tear apart my perfect crime. So I rang your house and even slipped a written threat into your friend's pocket when I found him sitting next to me in the plane. But then . . . slowly, I began to change my mind. By the time I reached Simla, I was convinced I should return the stolen property to you.'

'Why?'

'Because if you went back without the manuscript, you yourself might have been under suspicion. I did not want that to happen. I have come to appreciate you and your methods in these few days, you see.'

'Thank you, Mr Pakrashi. One more question.'

'Yes?'

'You made a duplicate copy of the whole manuscript before returning it to me, didn't you?'

All the colour from Mr Pakrashi's face receded instantly. Feluda had played his trump card.

'When we went to your house, you were typing something. It was the stuff in this notebook, wasn't it? You were typing every word in it.'

'But . . . you . . .'

'There was a funny smell in your room, the same as the smell in Shambhucharan's old Nepali box. And now I can see that this notebook has it, too.'

'But the copy—'

'Let me finish. Shambhucharan died in 1921. Fifty-one years ago. That means the fifty-year copyright period was over a year ago. So anyone can now have it printed, right?'

'Of course!' Mr Pakrashi shouted, displaying signs of agitation. 'Are you trying to tell me I did wrong? Never! It's an extraordinary tale, I tell you. Dinanath wouldn't have known its value, nor would he have had it published. I am going to print it now, and no one can stop me.'

'Oh, sure. No one can stop you, Mr Pakrashi, but what's wrong with a bit of healthy competition?'

'Competition? What do you mean?'

Feluda's famous lopsided smile peeped out. He stretched his right hand towards Mr Pakrashi.

'Meet your rival, Naresh Babu,' he said. 'When Dinanath Lahiri arrives tomorrow, I shall not ask for my fees with regard to this mysterious case. All I do want from him is this old notebook. And I happen to know a few publishers who might be interested. Now do you begin to see what I mean?'

Naresh Pakrashi glared in silence.

Lalmohan Babu, however, suddenly found his voice, and uttered one word, without any apparent rhyme or reason.

'Boomerang!' he yelled.

A Killer in Kailash

ONE

It was the middle of June. I had finished my school final exams and was waiting for the results to come out. Feluda and I were supposed to have gone to a film today, but ten minutes before we were to leave, it began raining so heavily that we had to drop the idea. I was now sitting in our living room, immersed in a Tintin comic (*Tintin in Tibet*). Feluda and I were both very fond of these comics which had mystery, adventure and humour, all in full measure. I already had three of these. This one was new. I had promised to pass it on to Feluda when I finished with it. Feluda was stretched out on the divan, reading a book called *Chariots of the Gods?* He had nearly finished it.

After a while, he shut the book, placed it on his chest and lay still, staring at the whirring ceiling fan. Then he said, 'Do you know how many stone blocks there are in the pyramid of Giza? Two hundred thousand.'

Why was he suddenly interested in pyramids? He went on, 'Each block weighs nearly fifteen tonnes. From what is known of ancient engineering, the Egyptians could not have polished to perfection and placed together more than ten blocks every day. Besides, the stone it's made of had to be brought from the other side of the Nile. A rough calculation shows that it must have taken them at least six hundred years to build that one single pyramid.'

'Is that what your book says?'

'Yes, but that isn't all. This book mentions many other wonders that cannot be explained by archaeologists and historians. Take our own country, for instance. There is an iron pillar at the Qutab Minar in Delhi. It is two thousand years old, but it hasn't rusted. No one knows why. Have you heard of Easter Island? It's a small island in the South Pacific Ocean. There are huge rocks facing the sea, on which human faces were carved thousands of years ago. These rocks were dragged from the middle of the island, taken to its edge and arranged in such a way that they were visible from the sea. Each weighs almost fifty tonnes. Who did this? How did the ancient tribal people get hold of adequate technology to do this? They didn't have things like lorries, tractors, cranes or bulldozers.'

Feluda stopped, then sat up and lit a Charminar. The book had clearly stirred him in a big way. 'In Peru,' he went on, 'there is an area which has geometric patterns drawn on the ground. Everyone knows about these patterns, they are visible from the air, but no one can tell when and how they came to be there. It is such a big mystery that scientists do not often talk about it.'

'Has the author of your book talked about it?'

'Oh yes, and he's come up with a very interesting theory. According to him, creatures from a different planet came to earth more than twenty-five thousand years ago. Their technological expertise was much higher than man's. They shared their knowledge with humans, and built structures like the pyramids—which, one must admit, modern man has not been able to match despite all his technical know-how. It is only a theory, mind you, and of course it need not necessarily be true. But it makes you think, doesn't it? The weapons described in our *Mahabharata* bear resemblances to atomic weapons. So maybe . . .'

' . . . The battle of Kurukshetra was fought by creatures from another planet?'

Feluda opened his mouth to reply, but was interrupted. Someone had braved the rain and arrived at our door, pressing the bell three times in a row. I ran and opened it. Uncle Sidhu rushed in, together with sprays of water. Then he shook his umbrella and shut it, sending more droplets flying everywhere.

Uncle Sidhu was not really a relation. He and my father used to be neighbours many years ago. Since my father treated him like an elder brother, we called him Uncle.

'What a miserable day get me a cup of tea quick the best you've got,' he said in one breath. I ran back inside, woke Srinath and told him to make three cups of tea. When I returned to the living room, Uncle Sidhu was seated on a sofa, frowning darkly and staring at a porcelain ashtray.

'Why didn't you take a rickshaw? In this weather, really, you shouldn't have—' Feluda began.

'People get murdered every day. Do you know there's a different type of murder that's much worse?' Uncle Sidhu asked, as if Feluda hadn't spoken at all. We remained silent, knowing that he was going to answer his own question.

'I think most people would agree that our present downfall notwithstanding, we have a past of which every Indian can be justly proud,' Uncle Sidhu went on. 'And, today, what do we see of this glorious past? Isn't it our art, chiefly paintings and sculptures? Tell me, Felu, isn't that right?'

'Of course,' Feluda nodded.

'The best examples of these—particularly sculptures— are to be found on the walls of old temples, right?'

'Right.'

Uncle Sidhu appeared to know about most things in life, but his knowledge of art was probably the deepest, for two out of his three bookcases were full of books on Indian art. But what was all this about a murder?

He stopped for a minute to light a cheroot. Then he coughed twice, filling the whole room with smoke, and continued, 'Several rulers in the past destroyed many of our temples. Kalapahar alone was responsible for the destruction of dozens of temples in Bengal. You knew that, didn't you? But did you know that a new Kalapahar has emerged today? I mean, now, in 1973?'

'Are you talking of people stealing statues from temples to sell them abroad?' Feluda asked.

'Exactly!' Uncle Sidhu almost shouted in excitement. 'Can you imagine what a huge crime it is? And it's not even done in the name of religion, it's just plain commerce. Our own art, our own heritage is making its way to wealthy Americans, but it's being done so cleverly that it's impossible to catch anyone. Do you know what I saw today? The head of a yakshi from the Raja-Rani temple in Bhubaneshwar. It was with an American tourist in the Grand Hotel.'

'You don't say!'

I had been to Bhubaneshwar when I was a child. My father had shown me the Raja-Rani temple. It was made of terracotta and its walls were covered by beautiful statues and carvings.

Uncle Sidhu continued with his story. 'I had a few old Rajput paintings which I had bought in Varanasi in 1934. I took those to Nagarmal to sell. I have known him for years. He has a shop in the Grand Hotel arcade. Just as I was placing my paintings on the counter, this American arrived. It seemed he had bought a few things from Nagarmal before. In his hand was something wrapped in a newspaper. It seemed heavy. Then he unwrapped it, and—oh God!—my heart jumped into my mouth. It was the head of a yakshi, made of red stone. I had seen it before, more than once. But I had seen the whole body. Now the head had been severed.

'Nagarmal didn't know where it had come from, but could tell that it was genuine, not a fake. The American said he had paid two thousand dollars for it. If you added two more zeros after it, I said to myself, even then you couldn't say it was the right value. Anyway, that man went up to his room. I was so amazed that I didn't even ask him who had sold it to him. I rushed back home and consulted a few of my books just to make sure. Now I am absolutely positive it was from a statue on the wall of Raja-Rani. I don't know how it was done—possibly by bribing the chowkidar at night. Anything is possible these days. I have written to the Bhubaneshwar Archaeological Department and sent it by express delivery, but what good is that going to do? The damage is already done!'

Srinath came in with the tea. Uncle Sidhu picked up a cup, took a sip, and said, 'This has to be stopped, Felu. I am now too old to do anything myself, but you are an investigator, it is your job to find criminals. What could be worse than destroying and disfiguring our ancient art, tell me? Shouldn't these criminals be caught? I could, of course, write to newspapers and try to attract the attention of the police, but do you know what the problem is? Not everyone understands the true value of art. I mean, an old statue on a temple wall isn't the same as gold or diamonds, is it? You cannot put a market price on it.'

Feluda was quiet all this while. Now he said, 'Did you manage to learn the name of that American?'

'Yes. I did speak to him very briefly. He gave me his card. Here it is.' Uncle Sidhu took out a small white card from his pocket and gave it to Feluda. Saul Silverstein, it said. His address was printed below his name.

'A Jew,' Uncle Sidhu remarked. 'Most undoubtedly very wealthy. The watch he was wearing was probably worth a thousand dollars. I had never seen such an expensive watch before.'

'Did he tell you how long he's going to stay here?'

'He's going to Kathmandu tomorrow morning. But if you ring him now, you might get him.' Feluda got up and began dialling. The telephone number of the Grand Hotel was one of the many important numbers he had memorized.

The receptionist said Mr Silverstein was not in his room. No one knew when he might be back. Feluda replaced the receiver, looking disappointed. 'If we could get even a description of the man who sold that statue to him, we might do something about it.'

'I know. That's what I should have asked him,' Uncle Sidhu sighed, 'but I simply couldn't think straight. He was looking at my paintings. He said he was interested in Tantric art, so if I had anything to sell I should contact him. Then he gave me that card. But I honestly don't see how you'll proceed in this matter.'

'Well, let's just wait and see. The press may report the theft. After all, Raja-Rani is a very famous temple in Bhubaneshwar.'

Uncle Sidhu finished his tea and rose. 'This has been going on for years,' he said, collecting his umbrella. 'So far, the target seems to have been smaller and lesser known temples. But now, whoever's involved has become much bolder. Perhaps a group of reckless and very powerful people are behind this. Felu, if you can do something about it, the entire nation is going to appreciate it. I am positive about that.'

Uncle Sidhu left. Feluda then spent all day trying to get hold of Saul Silverstein, but he did not return to his room. At 11 p.m., Feluda gave up. 'If what Uncle Sidhu said is true,' he said, frowning, 'whoever is responsible is a criminal of the first order. What is most frustrating is that there's no way I can track him down. No way at all.'

A way opened the very next day, in such a totally unexpected manner that, even now, my head reels when I think about it.

TWO

What happened was a terrible accident. But, before I speak about it, there's something else I must mention. There was a small report in the newspaper the next day, which confirmed Uncle Sidhu's suspicions:

The Headless Yakshi

The head from the statue of a yakshi has been stolen from the wall of the Raja-Rani temple in Bhubaneshwar. This temple serves as one of the best examples of old Indian architecture. The chowkidar of the temple is said to be missing. The Archaeological Department of Orissa has asked for a police investigation.

I read this report aloud, and asked, 'Would that mean the chowkidar is the thief?'

Feluda finished squeezing out toothpaste from a tube of Forhans and placed it carefully on his toothbrush. Then he said, 'No, I don't think stealing the head was just the chowkidar's idea. A poor man like him would not have the nerve. Someone else is responsible, someone big enough and strong enough to think he is never going to be caught. Presumably, he—or they—simply paid the chowkidar to get him out of the way for a few days.'

Uncle Sidhu must have seen the report too. He would probably turn up at our house again to tell us proudly that he was right.

He did arrive, but not before half past ten. Today being Thursday, our area had been hit by its regular power cut since nine o'clock. Feluda and I were sitting in our living room, staring occasionally at the overcast sky, when someone knocked loudly at the door. Uncle Sidhu rushed in a minute later, demanding a cup of tea once more. Feluda began talking of the headless yakshi, but was told to shut up.

'That's stale news, young man,' Uncle Sidhu barked. 'Did you hear the last news bulletin?'

'No, I'm afraid not. Our radio is not working. Today is . . .'

'I know, it's Thursday, and you've got a long power cut. That is why, Felu, I keep asking you to buy a transistor. Anyway, I came as soon as I heard. You'll never believe this. That flight to Kathmandu crashed, not far from Calcutta. It took off at seven-thirty, but crashed only fifteen minutes later. There was a storm, so perhaps it was trying to come back. There were fifty-eight passengers. All of them died, including Saul Silverstein. Yes, his name was mentioned on the radio.'

For a few moments, neither of us could speak. Then Feluda said, 'Where did it crash? Did they mention the place?'

'Yes, near a village called Sidikpur, on the way to Hasnabad. Felu, I had been praying very hard for that statue not to leave the country. Who knew my prayer would be answered through such a terrible tragedy?'

Feluda glanced at his watch. Was he thinking of going to Sidikpur?

Uncle Sidhu looked at him sharply. 'I know what you're thinking. There must have been an explosion and everything the plane contained must have been scattered over miles. Suppose, among the belongings of the passengers, there is—?'

Feluda decided in two minutes that he'd take a taxi and go to Sidikpur to look for the head of the yakshi. The crash had occurred three hours ago. It would take us an hour and a half to get there. By this time, the police and the fire brigade would have got there and started their investigation. No one could tell whether we'd succeed in our mission, but we could not miss this chance to retrieve what was lost.

'Those paintings I sold to Nagarmal fetched me a tidy little sum,' Uncle Sidhu told Feluda. 'I would like to give you some of it. After all, you are going to get involved only because of me, aren't you?'

'No,' Feluda replied firmly. 'It is true that you gave me all the details. But, believe me, I wouldn't have taken any action if I didn't feel strongly about it myself. I have thought a great deal about this, and—like you—I have come to the conclusion that those who think they can sell our ancient heritage to fill their own pockets should be caught and punished severely.'

'Bravo!' Uncle Sidhu beamed. 'Please remember one thing, Felu. Even if you don't need any money, you may need information on art and sculpture. I can always help you with that.'

'Yes, I know. Thank you.'

We decided that if we could find what we were looking for, we would take it straight to the office of the Archaeological Survey of India. The thief might still be at large, but at least the stolen object would go back to the authorities.

We quickly got ready, and got into a yellow taxi. It was 10.55 when we set off. 'I've no idea how long this is going to take,' Feluda said. 'We can stop for lunch at a dhaba on Jessore Road on our way back.'

This pleased me no end. The food in dhabas—which were usually frequented by lorry drivers—was always delicious. Roti, daal, meat curry . . . my mouth began to water. Feluda could eat anything anywhere. I tried to follow his example.

There was a shower as soon as we left the main city and reached VIP Road. But the sun came out as we got close to Barasat. Hasnabad was forty miles from Calcutta. 'If the road wasn't wet and slippery, I could have got there in an hour,' said our driver. 'There's been a plane crash there, sir, did you know? I heard about it on the radio.'

On being told that that was where we were going, he became very excited. 'Why, sir, was any of your relatives in that plane?' he asked.

'No, no.'

Feluda could hardly tell him the whole story, but his curiosity was aroused and he went on asking questions.

'I believe everything's been reduced to ashes. What will you get to see, anyway?'

'I don't know.'

'Are you a reporter?'

'I . . . well, I write stories.'

'Oh, I see. You'll get all the details and then use it in a story? Very good, very good.'

We had left Barasat behind us. Now we had to stop every now and then to ask people if they knew where Sidikpur was. Finally, a group of young men standing near a cycle repair shop gave us the right directions. 'Two miles from here, you'll see an unpaved road on your left,' said one of them. 'This road will take you to Sidikpur. It's only a mile from there.' From the way he spoke, it seemed obvious that he and his friends had already given the same directions to many others.

The unpaved road turned out to be little more than a dirt track. It was muddy after the recent rain and bore several sets of tyre marks. Thank goodness it was only June. A month later, this road would become impossible to drive through. Three other Ambassadors passed us. Several people were going on foot, and some others were returning from the site of the crash.

A number of people were gathered under a banyan tree. Three cars and a jeep were parked near it. Our taxi pulled up behind these. There was no sign of the crash anywhere, but it became clear that we couldn't drive any further. To our right was an open area, full of large trees. Beyond these, in the distance, a few small houses could be seen.

'Yes, that's Sidikpur,' one of the men told us. 'There's a little wood where the village ends. That's where the plane crashed.'

By this time, our driver had introduced himself to us. His name was Balaram Ghosh. He locked his car and came with us. As it turned out, the wood wasn't large. There were more banana trees than anything else. Only half a dozen mango and jackfruit trees stood amongst them. Each of them was badly charred. There were virtually no leaves left on their branches, and some of the branches looked as if they had been deliberately chopped off. The whole area was now teeming with men in uniform, and some others who were probably from the airline. There was a very strong pungent smell, which made me cover my face with a handkerchief. The ground was littered with endless pieces of broken, burnt and half-burnt objects, some damaged beyond recognition, others more or less usable.

Feluda clicked his tongue in annoyance and said, 'If only we could have got here an hour ago!'

The main site had been cordoned off. There was no way we could get any closer. So we started walking around the cordon. Some of the policemen were picking up objects from the ground and inspecting them: a portion of a stethoscope, a briefcase, a flask, a small mirror that glinted brightly in the sun. The site was on our right. We were slowly moving in that direction, when suddenly Feluda saw something on a mango tree on our left and stopped.

A little boy was sitting on a low branch, clutching a half-burnt leather shoe. He must have found it among the debris. Feluda glanced up and asked, 'You found a lot of things, didn't you?' The boy did not reply, but stared solemnly at Feluda. 'What's the matter? Can't you speak?' Feluda asked again. Still he got no reply. 'Hopeless!' he exclaimed and walked on, away from the debris and towards the village. Balaram Ghosh became curious once more.

'Are you looking for something special, sir?' he asked.

'Yes. The head of a statue, made of red stone.'

'I see. Just the head? OK.' He started searching in the grass.

There was a peepul tree about a hundred yards away, under which a group of old men were sitting, smoking hookahs. The oldest among them asked Feluda, 'Where are you from?'

'Calcutta. Your village hasn't come to any harm, has it?'

'No, babu. Allah saved us. There was a fire as soon as the plane came down—it made such a big noise that we all thought a bomb had gone off—and then the whole village was filled with smoke. We could see the fire in the wood, but none of us knew what to do . . . but soon it started to rain, and then the fire brigade arrived.'

'Did any of you go near the plane when the fire went out?'

'No, babu. We're old men, we were simply glad to have been spared.'

'What about the young boys? Didn't they go and collect things before the police got here?'

The old men fell silent. By this time, several other people had gathered to listen to this exchange. Feluda spotted a boy and beckoned him. 'What's your name?' he asked as the boy came closer. His tone was gentle and friendly.

'Ali.'

Feluda placed a hand on his shoulder and lowered his voice. 'A lot of things scattered everywhere when the plane crashed. You've seen that for yourself, haven't you? Now, there should have been the head of a statue among those things. Just the head of a statue of a woman. Do you know if anyone saw it?'

'Ask him!' Ali replied, pointing at another boy. Feluda had to repeat the whole process once more.

'What's your name?'

'Panu.'

'Did you see the head of a statue? Did you take it?'

Silence. 'Look, Panu,' Feluda said even more gently, 'it's all right. No one's going to get angry with you. But if you can give me that head, I'll pay you for it. Have you got it with you?'

More silence. This time, one of the old men shouted at him, 'Go on, Panu, answer the gentleman. He hasn't got all day.'

Panu finally opened his mouth. 'I haven't got it with me now.'

'What do you mean?'

'I found it, babu. I swear I did. But I gave it to someone else, only a few minutes ago.'

What! Could this really be true? My heart started hammering in my chest.

'Who was it?' Feluda asked sharply.

'I don't know. He was a man from the city, like you. He came in a car, a blue car.'

'What did he look like? Was he tall? Short? Thin? Fat? Did he wear glasses?'

This prompted many of Panu's friends to join the conversation. From the description they gave, it seemed that a man of medium height, who was neither thin nor fat, neither fair nor dark, and whose age was between thirty and fifty, had arrived half an hour before us and had made similar enquiries. Panu had shown him the yakshi's head, and he had bought it from him for a nominal sum. Then he had driven off in a blue car.

When we were driving to Sidikpur, a blue Ambassador had come from the opposite direction, passed us and gone towards the main road. All of us remembered having seen it.

'OK. Come on, Topshe. Let's go, Mr Ghosh.'

If Feluda was disappointed by what we had just learnt, he did not show it. On the contrary, he seemed to have found new energy. He ran all the way back to the taxi, with the driver and me in tow.

God knew what lay in store.

THREE

We were now going back the same way we had come. It was past one-thirty, but neither of us was thinking of lunch. Balaram Ghosh did suggest stopping for a cup of tea when we reached Jessore Road, but Feluda paid no attention. Perhaps our driver smelt an adventure in all this, so he, too, did not raise the subject of food again.

Our car was now going at 75 kmph. I was aware of only one thought that kept going over and over in my mind: how close we had got to retrieving the yakshi's head! If we hadn't had a power cut this morning, we would have heard the news on the radio, and then we would have reached Sidikpur much sooner and most certainly we would have got hold of Panu. If that had happened, by now we would have been making our way to the office of the Archaeological Survey of India. Who knows, Feluda might have been given a Padma Shree for recovering the country's lost heritage!

The sun had already dried the road. I was beginning to wonder why we couldn't go a little faster, when my eyes caught sight of something by the roadside that caused a sharp rise in my pulse rate.

A blue Ambassador was standing outside a small garage.

'Should I stop here, sir?' Balaram Ghosh asked, reducing his speed. He had obviously paid great attention to what those boys had told us.

'Yes, at that tea stall over there,' Feluda replied. Mr Ghosh swept up to the stall and pulled up by its side with a screech. We got out and Feluda ordered three cups of tea. I noticed that tea was being served in small glasses, there were no cups.

'What else have you got?' Feluda asked.

'Biscuits. Would you like some? They're fresh, sir, and very tasty.'

Two glass jars stood on a counter, filled with large, round biscuits. Feluda asked for half-a-dozen of those.

My eyes kept darting back to the blue car. A mechanic was in the process of replacing a punctured tyre. A man—medium height, age around forty, thick bushy eyebrows, hair brushed back—was pacing up and down, inhaling every now and then from a half-finished cigarette.

Our tea was almost ready. Feluda took out a Charminar, then pretended he had lost his lighter. He patted his pocket twice, then shrugged and moved over to join the other man. The driver and I stayed near our taxi, but we could hear what was said.

'Excuse me.' Feluda began, 'do you . . . ?'

The man took out a lighter and lit Feluda's cigarette for him.

'Thanks,' Feluda inhaled. 'A terrible business, wasn't it?'

The man glanced at Feluda, then looked away without replying. Feluda tried once more.

'Weren't you at the site where that plane crashed? I thought I saw your car there!'

This time, the man spoke. 'What plane crash?'

'Good heavens, haven't you heard? A plane bound for Kathmandu crashed near Sidikpur.'

'I am coming from Taki. No, I hadn't heard of the crash.'

Taki was a town near Hasnabad. Could the man be telling the truth? If only we had noted the number of his car when he passed us!

'How much longer will it take?' he asked the mechanic impatiently.

'A couple of minutes, sir, no more.'

Our tea had been served by this time. Feluda came back to pick up a glass. The three of us sat down on a bench in front of the stall. 'He denied everything . . . the man's a liar,' Feluda muttered.

'How can you be so sure, Feluda? There are millions of blue Ambassadors.'

'His shoes are covered by ash. Have you looked at your own sandals?'

I glanced down quickly and realized the colour of my sandals had changed completely. The other man's brown shoes were similarly covered with dark patches.

Feluda took his time to finish his tea. We waited until the blue car got a new tyre—this took another fifteen minutes instead of two—and went towards Jessore Road. Our own taxi left a minute later. There was quite a big gap between the two cars which, Feluda said, was no bad thing. 'He mustn't see that we're following him,' he told Mr Ghosh.

It began raining again as we reached Dum Dum. Everything went hazy for a few minutes and it became difficult to keep the blue car in view. Balaram Ghosh was therefore obliged to get a bit closer, which helped us in getting the number of the car. It was WMA 5349.

'This is like a Hindi film, sir!' Mr Ghosh enthused. 'I saw a film only the other day—it had Shatrughan Sinha in it—which had a chase scene, exactly like this. But the second car went and crashed into a hill.'

'We've already had a crash today, thank you.'

'Oh, don't worry, sir. I've been driving for thirteen years. I haven't had a single accident. I mean, not yet.'

'Good. Keep it that way.'

Balaram Ghosh was a good driver, I had to admit. We were now back in Calcutta, but he was weaving his way through the busy roads without once losing sight of the blue car. I wondered where it was going.

'What do you think the man's going to do with the statue?' I asked Feluda after a while.

'Well, he's certainly not going to take it back to Bhubaneshwar,' Feluda replied. 'What he might do is find another buyer. After all, it isn't often that one gets the chance to sell the same thing twice!'

The blue car finally brought us to Park Street. We drove past the old cemetery, Lowdon Street, Camac Street, and then suddenly, it turned left and drove into a building called Queen's Mansion.

'Should I go in, sir?'

'Of course.'

Our taxi passed through the front gates. A huge open square faced us, surrounded by tall blocks of flats. A number of cars and a couple of scooters were parked before these. The blue car went to the far end and stopped. We waited in our taxi to see what happened next.

The man got out with a black bag, wound up the windows of his car, locked it and slipped into Queen's Mansion through a large door. Feluda waited for another minute, then followed him.

By the time we reached the door, the old-fashioned lift in the lobby had already gone up, making a great deal of noise. It came back a few seconds later. An old liftman emerged from behind its collapsible gate. Feluda went up to him.

'Did I just miss Mr Sengupta?' he asked anxiously.

'Mr Sengupta?'

'The man who just went up?'

'That man was Mr Mallik of number five. There's no Sengupta in this building.'

'Oh. I must have made a mistake. Sorry.'

We came away. Mr Mallik, flat number five. I must remember these details.

Feluda paid Balaram Ghosh and said he was no longer needed. Before driving off, he gave us a piece of paper with a phone number scribbled on it. 'That's my neighbour's number,' he said. 'If you ever need me, ring that number. My neighbour will call me. I'd love to be able to help, sir. You see, life's usually so boring that something like this comes as a tremendous . . . I mean, it makes a change, doesn't it?'

We made our way to the Park Street police station. Feluda knew its OC, Mr Haren Mutsuddi. Two years ago, they had worked together to trace the culprit who had poisoned a race horse called Happy-Go-Lucky. It turned out that Mr Mutsuddi was aware of the theft in Bhubaneshwar. Feluda told him briefly about our encounter with Mr Mallik and said, 'Even if Mallik is not the real thief, he has clearly taken it upon himself to recover the stolen object and pass it on to someone else. I have come to make two requests, Mr Mutsuddi. Someone must keep an eye on his movements, and I need to know who he really is and where he works. He lives in flat number five, Queen's Mansion, drives a blue Ambassador, WMA 5349.'

Mr Mutsuddi heard Feluda in silence. Then he removed a pencil that was tucked behind his ear and said, 'Very well, Mr Mitter. If you want these things done, they will be done. A special constable will follow your man everywhere, and I'll see if we have anything in our files on him. There's no guarantee, mind you, that I'll get anything, particularly if he hasn't actually broken the law.'

'Thank you. But please treat this matter as urgent. If that statue gets passed on to someone else, we'll be in big trouble.'

'Why?' Mr Mutsuddi smiled, 'Why should you be in big trouble, Mr Mitter? You'll have me and the entire police force to help you. Doesn't that count for anything? We're not totally useless, you know. But there's just one thing I'd like to tell you. The people who are behind such rackets are usually quite powerful. I'm not talking of physical strength. I mean they often manage to do things far worse and much more vile than ordinary petty criminals. I am telling you all this, Mr Mitter, because you are young and talented, and I look upon you as a friend.'

'Thank you, Mr Mutsuddi. I appreciate your concern.'

We left the police station and went to the Chinese restaurant, Waldorf, to have lunch. Feluda went to the manager's room to make a call after we had placed our order.

'I rang Mallik,' he said when he came back. 'He was still in his room and he answered the phone himself. I rang off without saying anything.' He sounded a little relieved.

We returned home at three o'clock. Mr Mutsuddi called us a little after four. Feluda spoke for nearly five minutes, noting things down in his notebook. Then he put the phone down and told me everything even before I could ask.

'The man's called Jayant Mallik. He moved into that flat about two weeks ago. It actually belongs to a Mr Adhikari, who is away in Darjeeling at the moment. Perhaps he's a friend, and he's allowed Mallik to use his flat in his absence. That blue Ambassador is Adhikari's. Mallik took it to the Grand Hotel at three o'clock today. He went in for five minutes, then came out and was seen waiting in his car for twenty minutes. After that, he went in once more and emerged in ten minutes. Then he went to Dalhousie Square. Mutsuddi's man lost him for a while after this, but then found him in the railway booking office in Fairlie Place. He bought a ticket to Aurangabad, second class reserved. Mutsuddi's man will ring him again if there's more news.'

'Aurangabad?'

'Yes, that's where Mallik is going. And we are going immediately to Sardar Shankar Road, to visit Uncle Sidhu. I need to consult him urgently.'

FOUR

'Aurangabad!' Uncle Sidhu's eyes nearly popped out. 'Do you realize what this means? Aurangabad is only twenty miles from Ellora, which is a sort of depot for the best specimens of Indian art. There is the Kailash temple, carved out of a mountain. Then there are thirty-three caves—Hindu, Buddhist, Jain—that stretch for a mile and a half. Each is packed with beautiful statues, wonderful carvings . . . oh God, I can hardly think! But why is this man going by train when he can fly to Aurangabad?'

'I think he wants to keep the yakshi's head with him at all times. If he went by air, his baggage might be searched by security men. No one would bother to do that on a train, would they?'

Feluda stood up suddenly.

'What did you decide?' Uncle Sidhu asked anxiously.

'We must go by air,' Feluda replied.

The look Uncle Sidhu gave him at this was filled with pride and joy. But he said nothing. All he did was get up and select a slim book from one of his bookcases. 'This may help you,' he said. I glanced at its title. *A Guide to the Caves of Ellora*, it said.

Feluda rang his travel agent, Mr Bakshi, as soon as we got back home.

'I need three tickets on the flight to Bombay tomorrow,' I heard him say. This surprised me very much. Why did he need three tickets? Was Uncle Sidhu going to join us? When I asked him, however, Feluda only said, 'The more the merrier. We may need an extra pair of hands.'

Mr Bakshi came back on the line. 'I'll have to put you on the waiting list,' he said, 'but it doesn't look too bad, I think it'll be OK.'

He also agreed to make our hotel bookings in Aurangabad and Ellora. The flight to Bombay would get us there by nine o'clock. Then we'd have to catch the flight to Aurangabad at half past twelve, reaching there an hour later. This meant we would arrive in Aurangabad on Saturday, and Mr Mallik would get there on Sunday.

Feluda rang off and began dialling another number. The doorbell rang before he could finish dialling. I opened it to find Lalmohan Babu. Feluda stared, as though he had seen a ghost, and exclaimed, 'My word, what a coincidence! I was just dialling your number.'

'Really? Now, that must mean I have got a telepathetic link with you, after all,' Lalmohan Babu laughed, looking pleased. Neither of us had the heart to tell him the correct word was 'telepathic'.

'It's so hot and stuffy . . . could you please ask your servant to make a lemon drink, with some ice from the fridge, if you don't mind?'

Feluda passed on his request to Srinath, then came straight to the point.

'Are you very busy these days? Have you started writing anything new?'

'No, no. I couldn't have come here for a chat if I had already started writing. All I've got is a plot. I think it would make a good Hindi film. There are five fights. My hero, Prakhar Rudra, goes to Baluchistan this time. Tell me, how do you think Arjun Mehrotra would handle the role of Prakhar Rudra? I think he'd fit the part very well—unless, of course, you agreed to do it, Felu Babu?'

'I cannot speak Hindi. Anyway, I suggest you come with us to Kailash for a few days. You can start thinking of Baluchistan when you get back.'

'Kailash? All the way to Tibet? Isn't that under the Chinese?'

'No. This Kailash has nothing to do with Tibet. Have you heard of

Ellora?'

'Oh, I see, I see. You mean the temple? But isn't that full of statues and rocks and mountains? What have you to do with those, Felu Babu? Your business is human beings, isn't it?'

'Correct. A group of human beings has started a hideous racket involving those rocks and statues. I intend to put a stop to it.'

Lalmohan Babu stared. Feluda filled him in quickly, which made him grow even more round-eyed.

'What are you saying, Felu Babu? I had no idea stone statues could be so valuable. The only valuable stones I can think of are precious stones like rubies and emeralds and diamonds. But this—!'

'This is far more precious. You can get diamonds and rubies elsewhere in the world. But there is only one Kailash, one Sanchi and one Elephanta. If these are destroyed, there would be no evidence left of the amazing heights our ancient art had risen to. Modern artists do not—they cannot—get anywhere near the skill and perfection these specimens show. Anyone who tries to disfigure any of them is a dangerous criminal. In my view, the man who took that head from the statue of the yakshi is no less than a murderer. He has got to be punished.'

This was enough to convince Lalmohan Babu. He was fond of travelling, in any case. He agreed to accompany us at once, and began asking a lot of questions, including whether or not he should carry a mosquito net, and was there any danger of being bitten by snakes? Then he left, with a promise to meet us at the airport.

Neither of us knew how long we might have to stay in Aurangabad, but decided to pack enough clothes for a week. Since Feluda was often required to travel, he always had a suitcase packed with essentials such as a fifty-foot steel tape, an all-purpose knife, rail and air timetables, road maps, a long nylon rope, a pair of hunting boots, and several pieces of wire which came in handy to unlock doors and table-drawers if he didn't have a key. None of this took up a lot of space, so he could pack his clothes in the same suitcase.

He also had guide books and tourist pamphlets on various parts of the country. I leafed through the ones I thought might be relevant for this visit. Feluda set the alarm clock at 4 a.m. before going to bed at ten o'clock, then rang 173 and asked for a wake-up call, in case the alarm did not go off for some reason.

Ten minutes later, Mr Mutsuddi rang again. 'Mallik received a trunk call from Bombay,' he said. 'The words Mallik spoke were these: "The daughter has returned to her father from her in-laws. The father is taking her with him twenty-seventy-five." The caller from Bombay said: "Carry on, best of luck." That was all.'

Feluda thanked him and rang off. Mallik's words made no sense to me. When I mentioned this to Feluda, he simply said, 'Even the few grey cells you had seem to be disappearing, my boy. Stop worrying and go to sleep.'

The flight to Bombay was delayed by an hour. It finally left at half past seven. There were quite a few cancellations, so we got three seats pretty easily.

Lalmohan Babu had flown with us for the first time when we had gone to Delhi and Simla in connection with Mr Dhameeja's case. This was possibly the second time he was travelling by air. I noticed that this time he did not pull faces and grip the arms of his chair when we took off; but, a little later, when we ran into some rough weather, he leant across and said, 'Felu Babu, this is no different from travelling in a rickety old bus down Chitpur Road. How can I be sure the whole plane isn't coming apart?'

'It isn't, rest assured.'

After breakfast, he seemed to have recovered a little, for I saw him press a button and call the air hostess. 'Excuse please Miss, a toothpick,' he said smartly. Then he began reading a guide book on Bombay. None of us had been to Bombay before. Feluda had decided to spend a few days there with a friend on our way back—provided, of course, that our business in Ellora could be concluded satisfactorily.

When the 'fasten seat belts' sign came on just before landing, there was something I felt I had to ask Feluda. 'Will you please explain what Mr Mallik's words meant?'

Feluda looked amazed. 'What, you mean you really didn't understand it?'

'No.'

'The daughter has returned to her father from her in-laws. "The daughter" is the yakshi's head, the "in-laws" refers to Silverstein who had bought it, and the "father" is Mallik himself.'

'I see . . . What about "twenty-seventy-five"?'

'That refers to the latitude. If you look at a map, you'll see that's where Aurangabad is shown.'

We landed at Santa Cruz airport at ten. Since our flight to Aurangabad was at half past twelve, we saw no point in going into the town, although an aerial view of the city had impressed me very much. We remained in the airport, had chicken curry and rice for lunch at the airport restaurant, and boarded the plane to Aurangabad at quarter to one. There were only eleven passengers, since it was not the tourist season.

This time, Lalmohan Babu and I sat together. Feluda sat on the other side of the aisle, next to a middle-aged man with a parrot-like nose, thick wavy salt-and-pepper hair brushed back and wearing glasses with a heavy black frame. We got to know him after landing at the small airport at Aurangabad. He was expecting to be met, he said, but no one had turned up. So he decided to join us to go to town in the bus provided by the airline.

'Where will you be staying?' he asked Feluda.

'Hotel Aurangabad.'

'Oh, that's where I shall be staying as well. What brings you here? Holiday?'

'Yes, you might call it that. And you?'

'I am writing a book on Ellora. This is my second visit. I teach the history of Indian art in Michigan.'

'I see. Are your students enthusiastic about this subject?'

'Yes, much more now than they used to be. India seems to inspire young people more than anything else.'

'I believe the Vaishnavas have got a strong hold over there?' Feluda asked lightly. The other gentleman laughed. 'Are you talking of the Hare Krishna people?' he asked. 'Yes, their presence cannot be ignored. They are, in fact, very serious about what they do and how they dress. Have you heard their keertan? Sometimes it is impossible to tell they are foreigners.'

It took us only fifteen minutes to reach our hotel. It was small, but neat and tidy. We checked in and were shown into room number 11. Lalmohan Babu went to room 14. Feluda had bought a newspaper at Bombay airport. I had seen him read it in the plane. Now he sat down on a chair in the middle of our room, spread it once more and said, 'Do you know what "vandalism" means?'

I did, but only vaguely. Feluda explained, 'The barbarian invaders who sacked Rome in the fifth century were called Vandals. Any act related to disfiguring, damaging or destroying a beautiful object has come to be known as vandalism.' Then he passed the newspaper to me and said, 'Read it.'

I saw a short report with the heading, 'More Vandalism'. According to it, a statue of a woman had been broken and its head lifted from one of the walls of the temple of Kandaria Mahadev in Khajuraho. A group of art students from Baroda who were visiting the complex were the first to notice what had happened. This was the third case reported in the last four weeks. There could be no doubt that these statues and other pieces of sculpture were being sold abroad.

As I sat trying to grasp the full implications of the report, Feluda spoke. His tone was grim.

'As far as I can make out,' he said, 'there is only one octopus. It has spread its tentacles to various temples in different parts of the country. If even one tentacle can be caught and chopped off, it will make the whole body of the animal squirm and wriggle. It should be our aim here to spot that one tentacle and seize it.'

FIVE

Aurangabad was a historical city. An Abyssinian slave called Malik Ambar had been brought to India. In time, he became the Prime Minister of the King of Ahmednagar and built a city called Khadke. During the time of Aurangzeb, Khadke changed its name and came to be known as Aurangabad. In addition to Mughal buildings and structures, there were about ten Buddhist caves—thirteen hundred years old—that contained statues worth seeing.

The gentleman we had met at the airport—whose name was Shubhankar Bose—came to our room later in the evening for a chat. 'You must see the caves here before going to Ellora,' he told us. 'If you do, you'll be able to see that the two are similar in some ways.'

Since it was drizzling outside, we decided not to go out immediately. Tomorrow, if the day was fine, we would see the caves and the mausoleum built in the memory of Aurangzeb's wife, called Bibi ka Makbara. We would have to remain in Aurangabad until the next afternoon, anyway, since Jayant Mallik was supposed to get here at eleven o'clock. He would probably go to Ellora the same day, and we would then follow him.

After dinner, Feluda sat down with his guide book on Ellora. I was wondering what to do, when Lalmohan Babu turned up.

'Have you looked out of the window, Tapesh?' he asked. 'The moon has come out now. Would you like to go for a walk?'

'Sure.'

We came out of the hotel to find everything bathed in moonlight. In the distance was a range of hills. Perhaps that was where the Buddhist caves were located. A paan shop close by had a transistor on, playing a Hindi song. Two men were sitting on a bench, having a loud argument. They were probably speaking in Marathi, for I couldn't understand a word. The road outside had been full of people and traffic during the day, but was now very quiet. A train blew its whistle somewhere far away, and a man wearing a turban went past, riding a cycle. I felt a little strange in this new place—there seemed to be a hint of mystery in whatever I saw, some excitement and even a little fear. At this moment, Lalmohan Babu suddenly brought his face close to my ear and whispered, 'Doesn't Shubhankar Bose strike you as a bit suspicious?'

'Why?' I asked, considerably startled.

'What do you think his suitcase contains? Why does it weigh 35 kgs?'

'Thirty-five?' I was very surprised.

'Yes. He was before me in the queue in Bombay, when we were told to check in. I saw how much his suitcase weighed. His was thirty-five, your cousin's was twenty-two, yours was fourteen and mine was sixteen kilograms. Bose had to pay for excess baggage.'

This was news to me. I had seen Mr Bose's suitcase. It wasn't very large. What could have made it so heavy?

Lalmohan Babu provided the answer.

'Rocks,' he said, still whispering, 'or tools to break something made of stone. Didn't your cousin tell us there was a large gang working behind this whole business? I believe Bose is one of them. Did you see his nose? It's exactly like Ghanashyam Karkat's.'

'Who is Ghanashyam Karkat?'

'Oh ho, didn't I tell you? He is the villain in my next book. Do you know how I'm going to describe his nose? "It was like a shark's fin, rising above the water."'

I paid no attention to this last bit, but couldn't ignore his remarks about Mr Bose. I would not have suspected him at all. How could a man who knew so much about art be a criminal? But then, those who go about stealing art must know something about the subject. Besides, there really was something sharp about his appearance.

'I only wanted to warn you,' Lalmohan Babu went on speaking, 'just keep an eye on him. He offered me a toffee, but I didn't take it. What if it was poisoned? Tell your cousin not to let on that he is a detective. If he does, his life may be at risk.'

The next day, we left in a taxi at half past six in the morning and went to see Bibi ka Makbara (also known as the 'second Taj Mahal'). Then we went to the Buddhist caves. The taxi dropped us at the bottom of a hill. A series of steps led to the caves. Mr Bose had accompanied us, and was talking constantly about ancient art, most of which went over my head. I still couldn't think of him as a criminal, but caught Lalmohan Babu giving him sidelong glances. This often made him stumble, but he did not stop.

Two other men had already gone into the caves. I had seen them climbing the steps before us. One of them was a bald American tourist, dressed in a colourful bush shirt and shorts; the other was a guide from the tourist department.

Feluda took out his Pentax camera from his shoulder bag and began taking photos of the hills, the view and, occasionally, of us. Each time he peered at us through the camera, Lalmohan Babu stopped and smiled, looking somewhat self-conscious. After a while, I was obliged to tell him that he didn't necessarily have to stop walking and, in fact, photos often came out quite well even if one didn't smile.

When we reached the caves, Feluda suddenly said, 'You two carry on, I'll join you in a minute. I must take a few photos from the other side.'

'Don't miss the second and the seventh cave,' Mr Bose called out to us. 'The first five are all in this area, but numbers six to nine are half a mile away, on the eastern side. A road runs round the edge of the hill.'

The bright sun outside was making me feel uncomfortably hot, but once I stepped into the first cave, I realized it was refreshingly cool inside. But there wasn't much to see. It was obvious that it had been left incomplete, and what little work had been done had started to crumble. Even so, Mr Bose began inspecting the ceiling and the pillars with great interest, jotting things down in his notebook.

Lalmohan Babu and I went into the second cave. Feluda had given us a torch. We now had to switch it on. We were in a large hall, at the end of which was a huge statue of the Buddha. I shone the torch on the walls, to find that beautiful figures had been carved on these. Lalmohan Babu was silent for a few moments, taking it all in. Then he remarked, 'Did you realize, Tapesh, how physically strong these ancient artists must have been? I mean, a knowledge of art and a creative imagination alone wasn't enough, was it? They had to pick up hammers and chisels and knock through such hard rock . . . makes the mind boggle, doesn't it?'

The third cave was even larger, but the guide was speaking so loudly and rapidly that we couldn't stay in it for more than a few seconds. 'Where did your cousin go?' Lalmohan Babu asked as we emerged. 'I can't see him anywhere.'

This was true. I had assumed Feluda would catch up with us, but he was nowhere to be seen. Nor was Mr Bose. 'Let's check the other caves,' Lalmohan Babu suggested.

The fourth and the fifth caves were not far, but something told me Feluda had not gone there. I began to feel faintly uneasy. We started walking towards cave number six, which was half a mile away. This side of the hill was barren and rocky, there were few plants apart from the occasional small bush. I glanced at my watch. It was only a quarter past eight, but we could not afford to stay here beyond ten o'clock, for Mr Mallik was going to arrive at eleven.

Fifteen minutes later, we looked up and saw another cave. It was probably cave number six. There was no way of telling whether Feluda had come this way. Lalmohan Babu kept peering at the ground in the hope of finding footprints. It was a futile exercise, really, since the ground was absolutely dry.

Was there any point in going any further? Might it help if we called his name?

'Feluda! Feluda!' I started shouting.

'Pradosh Babu! Felu Babu! Mr Mit-te-er!' Lalmohan Babu joined me.

There was no answer. I began to get a sinking feeling in the pit of my stomach.

Had he climbed up the hill and gone to the other side? Had he seen or heard something that made him forget all about us?

After a while, Lalmohan Babu gave up. 'He's obviously nowhere here,' he said, shaking his head, 'or he'd have heard us. Let's go back. I'm sure we'll find him this time. He couldn't have left us without a word. He would not do an irresponsible thing like that, would he?'

We turned back and retraced our steps. In a few minutes, we saw the foreigner and his guide making their way to the sixth cave. I could see that the American was finding it difficult to cope with the guide and his endless patter. 'Look, here's Mr Bose!' Lalmohan Babu cried. Mr Bose was walking towards us with a preoccupied air. He raised his eyes as he heard his name. I went to him quickly and asked, 'Have you seen my cousin?'

'No. Didn't he say he was going off to take pictures?'

'Yes, but that was a long time ago. Maybe he's in one of these caves?'

'No. I have been to each one of them. If he was there, I would certainly have seen him.'

Perhaps my face registered my anxiety, for his tone softened. 'He may have climbed a little higher. There is, in fact, a fantastic view of the whole city of Aurangabad if you can get to the top of the hill. Why don't you walk on and keep calling his name? He's bound to hear you sooner or later,' Mr Bose said reassuringly, and went off in the direction of cave number six.

Lalmohan Babu lowered his voice. 'I don't like this, Tapesh,' he said. 'I never thought there would be cause for anxiety even before we got to Ellora.'

I pulled myself together and kept walking. My speed had automatically become faster. All I could think of was that we were running out of time, we had to get back to the hotel by eleven to find out if Mr Mallik had arrived, but what were we to do if we couldn't find Feluda?

Without him . . .

'Charminar!' Lalmohan Babu cried suddenly, making me jump.

We were standing near the pillars of the fifth cave. A yellow packet of Charminar was lying under a bush a few feet away from the pillars. It had either not been there when we were here earlier, or we had somehow missed it. Had it dropped out of Feluda's pocket? I picked it up quickly and opened its top. It was empty. Just as I was about to throw it away, Lalmohan Babu said, 'Let me see, let me see!' and took it from me. Then he opened it fully, and a small piece of paper slipped out. There was a brief message scribbled on it in

Feluda's handwriting.

'Go back to the hotel', it said.

Considerably relieved, we debated on what to do next. I couldn't think very clearly as Feluda's message said nothing about where he was or why he was asking us to go back. The empty feeling in my stomach continued to linger.

'How can we go back?' Lalmohan Babu said. 'Mr Bose is with us, and he has four more caves to see.'

'Why don't we return to the hotel,' I said slowly, forcing myself to think, 'and send the taxi back to fetch him?'

'Ye-es, we could do that, but shouldn't we stay here to watch his movements?'

'No. I don't think so, Lalmohan Babu. Feluda said nothing about Mr Bose. He just wanted us to go back, and that's what we ought to do.'

'Very well. So be it,' Lalmohan Babu replied, sounding a little disappointed.

Since he wrote mystery stories, Lalmohan Babu occasionally took it into his head to act like a professional sleuth. I could see that he wanted to follow Mr Bose, but I felt obliged to stop him. Our taxi dropped us at the hotel, then went back to the caves. It was nine o'clock. God knew how long we'd have to wait for Feluda.

Neither of us could remain in our room, so we came out of the hotel and began strolling on the road outside. The sky had started to cloud over. If it rained, it might cool down a bit, I thought.

Mr Bose returned at nine forty-five and looked rather puzzled when we told him Feluda had not returned. Naturally, we could not tell him the real reason why we were worried. After all, we did not know him well and Lalmohan Babu was still convinced he was one of the criminals involved. In order to stop him from asking further questions, I said quickly, 'I'm afraid my cousin often does things without telling others. He's done this before—I mean, he's gone off like this, but has returned later. I'm sure he'll be back soon.'

We stayed out for nearly an hour, then I went back to my room and began reading *Tintin in Tibet*. Just after eleven, I thought I heard a train whistle, and at quarter to twelve, a car drew up outside in the porch. Unable to contain myself, I went out to have a look.

Two men got out of the taxi. One of them was of medium height and pretty stout. His broad shoulders seemed to start just below his jaws; his neck was almost non-existent. For some reason, he seemed as if he might easily fly into a temper. The other man was just the opposite: tall, lanky, wearing bell-bottoms and a loose, cotton embroidered shirt. His face was covered by an unkempt beard and his hair rippled down to his shoulders. He looked like a hippie. The stout man had an old leather suitcase; the hippie had a new canvas bag. Both walked into the hotel. Another taxi arrived as soon as these men had gone in.

Jayant Mallik got out of it.

A sudden surge of relief swept over me. At least, this meant that we were on the right track. Our journey from Calcutta had not simply been a wild-goose chase.

But where on earth was Feluda?

SIX

I waited for another ten minutes to see if Feluda turned up. When he didn't, I went in and knocked on Lalmohan Babu's door. He opened it at once and said with large, round eyes, 'I've seen it all from the lobby! Don't both those characters look highly suspicious? I wonder if they'll go to Ellora? One of them—you know, the bearded one—might well be into ganja and other drugs.'

I nodded. 'Jayant Mallik has also arrived and checked in,' I told him.

'Really? I didn't see him. I came back to my room as soon as that hippie walked in. What does Mallik look like?'

When I described him, Lalmohan Babu grew even more excited. 'Oh, I think he's been given the room next to mine. I saw him arrive and something struck me as very odd. A bearer was carrying his suitcase, but it was obviously extremely heavy. The poor man could hardly move. And no wonder. Isn't the yakshi's head supposed to be in it?'

I could think of nothing except Feluda's disappearance, so I said, 'What is much more important now is finding Feluda. Never mind about Mallik's suitcase. We've made no arrangements to go to Ellora. Mallik, I am sure, hasn't come here simply to see the sights of Aurangabad. If he reaches Ellora before us, he might damage more—'

'What's that?' Lalmohan Babu interrupted me, staring at the door. I had shut it after coming into the room. Someone had slipped a piece of paper under it. I leapt and grabbed it quickly. It was another note, written by Feluda:

'Collect all our luggage and wait outside the hotel at one-thirty. Look out for a black Ambassador taxi, number 530. Have your lunch before you leave. All hotel bills have been paid in advance.'

I ran my eyes over these few lines and opened the door. There was no one in sight. A second later, however, Jayant Mallik came out of his room and went busily towards the reception desk. He caught my eye briefly, but did not seem to recognize me.

'He didn't lock his room,' Lalmohan Babu whispered. 'There's no one about. Shall I go in and have a look? Think of the stolen statue—!'

'No! We mustn't do anything like that without telling Feluda. It's nearly one o'clock now. I think we should both be getting ready to leave.'

Sometimes, Lalmohan Babu's enthusiasm caused serious problems. Luckily, he agreed to restrain himself.

We had a quick lunch and came out with our luggage—including Feluda's—at one twenty-five. An empty taxi arrived in a few minutes, but it was green and had a different number. Its driver stopped it a few feet away from us. I saw him raise his arms and stretch lazily.

Three minutes later, another taxi drove up to us. A black Ambassador, number 530. Its driver peered out of the window and said, 'Mr Mitter's party?'

'Yes, yes,' Lalmohan Babu replied with an important air. The driver got out and opened the boot for us. I put the three suitcases in it.

Two men came out of the hotel: Shubhankar Bose and Jayant Mallik. I had seen them having lunch together. They got into the green taxi. It roared to life and shot off down Adalat Road, which headed west. Ellora lay in the same direction.

All this suspense is going to kill me, I thought. Where were we going to go? Why wasn't Feluda with us? I couldn't help feeling annoyed with him for having vanished, although I knew very well he never did anything without a good reason.

Another man emerged from the hotel. It was the tall hippie, carrying his canvas bag. He came straight to us, stopped and said, 'Get in, Topshe. Quick, Lalmohan Babu!'

Before I knew it, I was sitting in the back of the taxi. The hippie opened the front door, pushed the bemused Lalmohan Babu in, then got in beside me. 'Chaliye, Deendayalji,' he said to the driver.

I knew Feluda was good at putting on make-up and disguises, but had no idea he could change his voice, his walk, even the look in his eyes so completely. Lalmohan Babu appeared to be speechless, but he did turn around and shake Feluda's hand. My heart was still speeding like a race horse, and I was dying to know why Feluda was in disguise.

Feluda opened his mouth only when we had left the main town and reached the open country. 'The disguise was necessary,' he explained, 'because Mallik might have recognized me, although we had exchanged only a few words in that garage in Barasat. Naturally, his suspicions would have been aroused if he saw that the same man who had asked him awkward questions was also going to Ellora. I didn't tell you about my plan, for I wanted to see if my make-up was good enough. When neither of you recognized me, I knew I didn't have to worry about Mallik . . . I had these clothes and everything else in my shoulder bag this morning. When I said I was going off to take photos, I actually walked ahead and disappeared into cave number six. Not many people go in there, since it's far from the others and one has to climb higher to get there. When I finished, I climbed down and walked back to town. First I arranged this taxi, then went to the station to see if Mallik got off the train. When he did, I followed his taxi, having collected another passenger who also wanted to go to our hotel. This helped me as I could then share the taxi fare with him. Now, if Shubhankar Bose asks you anything about me, tell him I've sent you a message saying I had to go to Bombay on some urgent business. I cannot remove my disguise until I go to bed. In fact, we shouldn't even let Mallik see that you and I know each other. You and Lalmohan Babu will share a room. I will be in a separate room wherever we stay.'

'But who are you?'

'You don't have to bother with a name. I am a photographer. I'm here to take photos for the *Asia* magazine of Hong Kong.'

'OK. What about Lalmohan Babu and myself?'

'You are his nephew. He teaches history in the City College. You are a student in the City School. You are interested in painting, but you want to join your uncle's college next year to study history. Your name is Tapesh Mukherjee. Lalmohan Babu need not change his name, but please read up on Ellora. Basically, all you need to remember is that the Kailash temple was built during the reign of Raja Krishna of the Rashtrakut dynasty, in the eighth century.'

Lalmohan Babu repeated these words to himself, then took out his little red notebook and noted them down, although writing wasn't easy in the moving car. Now I could see why Feluda had asked him to come with us. He must have known he'd have to be in disguise and pretend he didn't know me. Lalmohan Babu's presence ensured that there was an extra pair of eyes to check on Mallik's movements, and I had an adult to accompany me. I didn't mind having to call Lalmohan Babu 'Uncle', but pretending Feluda was a total stranger was going to be most difficult. Well—I had no choice.

I looked out of the window. There were hills in the distance, and the land on either side of the road was dry and barren. Cactus grew here and there, but it was a different kind of cactus, not the familiar prickly pear I had seen elsewhere. These bushes were larger and taller by several feet.

Another car behind us had been honking for some time. Our driver slowed down slightly to let it pass. It had the bald American we had seen this morning, and the stout man who had travelled with Feluda in the same taxi.

Half an hour later, we found ourselves getting closer to the distant hills. To our left stretched a small town, called Khuldabad. We were going to stay in the dak bungalow here. At any other time, it would have been impossible to find rooms at such short notice. Thank goodness it was not the regular tourist season. However, the absence of tourists also meant that the thieves and vandals could have a field day.

A little later, to our right, the first of the many caves of Ellora came into view.

'To the dak bungalow?' our driver asked. 'Or would you like to see the caves first?'

'No, let's go straight to the dak bungalow,' Feluda replied.

Our car made a left turn where the road curved towards Khuldabad. I was still staring at the rows of caves in the hills. Which one of them was Kailash?

There were two major places to stay in Khuldabad. One was the dak bungalow where we were booked, and the other was the more expensive and posh Tourist Guest House. The two stood side by side, separated by a strong fence. I spotted the green taxi standing outside the guest house, which meant that was where Jayant Mallik had checked in. Our bungalow was smaller, but neat and compact. Feluda paid the driver, then asked him to wait for fifteen minutes. We would leave our things in our rooms, and go to Kailash. The driver could drop us there, and return to Aurangabad.

There were four rooms in the bungalow. Each had three beds. Feluda could have remained with us, but decided to take a separate room. 'Remember,' he whispered before he left us, 'your surname is Mukherjee. Lalmohan Babu is your uncle . . . Rashtrakut dynasty . . . eighth century . . . Raja Krishna . . . I'll join you in ten minutes.' Then he went into his own room and shouted, 'Chowkidar!' in a voice that was entirely different from his own.

Lalmohan Babu and I had a quick wash and went into the dining hall, where we were supposed to wait for Feluda. We found another gentleman in it, the same man we had just seen travelling with the American. Clearly, he was going to stay in the bungalow with us. At first, he had struck me as a boxer or a wrestler. Now I noticed his eyes: they were bright and intelligent, which suggested he was educated and, in fact, might well be a writer or an artist, for all I knew. His eyes twinkled as they caught mine.

'Off to Kailash, are you?' he asked with a smile.

'Yes, yes,' Lalmohan Babu replied eagerly, 'we are from Calcutta. I am a . . . what d'you call it . . . professor of history in the City College; and this is my nephew, you see.'

There was no need to tell him anything else. But, possibly because he was nervous about playing a new role, Lalmohan Babu went on speaking, 'I thought . . . you know . . . that we must see this amazing creation of the Rashtraput—I mean kut—dynasty. My nephew is . . . you know . . . very interested in art. He wants to get into an art college. He paints quite well, you know. Bhuto, don't forget to take your drawing book.'

I said nothing in reply, for I had not brought my drawing book.

Thankfully, Feluda came out at this moment and glanced casually at us.

'If any of you want to go to the caves, you may come with me. I've still got my taxi,' he said in his new voice.

'Oh, thank you, that's very kind,' Lalmohan Babu turned to him, looking relieved. Then courtesy made him turn back to the other gentleman. 'Would you like to come with us?' he asked.

'No, thank you. I'll go later. I must have a bath first.'

We went out of the bungalow.

'Tell me a bit more about the history of this place, Felu Babu,' Lalmohan Babu pleaded in a low voice. 'I can't manage unless I have a few more details.'

'Do you know the names of different periods in Indian history?'

'Such as?'

'Such as Maurya, Sunga, Gupta, Kushan, Chola . . . things like that?'

Lalmohan Babu turned pale. Then, getting into the taxi, he said, 'Tell you what, why don't I pretend to be deaf? Then, if anyone asks me anything about the history of the caves, or anything else I might find difficult to answer, I can simply ignore them. Isn't that a good idea?'

'All right. I have no objection to that, but remember your acting must be consistent at all times.'

'No problem with that. Anything would be better than trying to remember historical facts. Didn't you see how I messed things up just now? I mean, saying "put" instead of "kut" was hardly the right thing to do, was it?'

We were passing the guest house. Jayant Mallik was standing outside, his hands in his pockets, staring at our bungalow. The green Ambassador was still parked by the road. On seeing Mr Mallik, Feluda took out a small comb from his bag and passed it to me. 'Change your parting,' he said, 'make a right parting.' I looked at myself in the rearview mirror and quickly changed the parting in my hair as Feluda suggested. Who knew a little thing like that would make such a lot of difference? Even to my own eyes, my face looked different.

We reached the main road. Another road rose up the hill from here, curved around and finally brought us to the famous Kailash temple. We got out here, and the taxi returned to Aurangabad.

At first, I didn't realize what the temple was like. However, as soon as I had passed through its huge entrance, my head began reeling. For a few moments, I forgot all about the yakshi's head, the gang of crooks, Mr Mallik, Shubhankar Bose, everything. All I was aware of was a feeling of complete bewilderment. I closed my eyes and tried to imagine a group of men, carving the whole temple out of the hill twelve hundred years ago, using no other tools but hammers and chisels. But I could not. It seemed as if the temple had always been there. It couldn't be manmade at all. Or maybe it had been created by magic; or perhaps—as Feluda's book had suggested—creatures from a different planet had come and built it.

The temple had hills rising on three sides. A narrow passage went around it. On both sides of the temple were a number of caves—that looked like cells—which had more statues in them. We started walking down the passage to go around the temple. Feluda kept up a running commentary: 'This place is three hundred feet in length, one hundred and fifty feet in width and the height of the temple is a hundred feet. Two hundred thousand tonnes of rock must have been excavated to build it . . . they built the top first, then worked their way down to the base . . . the statues include gods and goddesses, men and women, animals, events from the *Ramayana* and the *Mahabharata*, the lot. Just think of their skill, the precision of their calculations, their knowledge of engineering, quite apart from the aesthetics . . .' he stopped. There were footsteps coming towards us. Feluda fell behind deliberately and began inspecting the statue of Ravana shaking Kailash.

Shubhankar Bose emerged from behind the temple. In his hand was a notebook, and a bag hung from his shoulder. He seemed engrossed in looking at the carvings. Then his eyes fell on us. He smiled, then seemed to remember something and asked anxiously, 'Any news of your cousin?'

'Yes,' I replied, trying to sound casual, 'he sent a message. He had to go to Bombay on some urgent work. He'll be back soon.'

'Oh, good.' Mr Bose went back to gazing at the statues. A faint click behind us told me Feluda had taken a picture. His camera was hanging from his neck. If he was to pass himself off as a photographer, the camera naturally had to stay with him whenever he went out.

I turned my head slightly and saw that Feluda was following us. We finished walking around the temple, and had almost reached the main entrance again when we saw someone else. Blue shirt, white trousers. Mr Jayant Mallik. He had probably just arrived. He was standing quietly, but moved towards the statue of an elephant as soon as he saw us. In his hand was the same bag I had seen him carrying before. He had travelled from Barasat to Calcutta with it. I had seen him walk into Queen's Mansion, clutching it. Feluda had now almost caught up with us. I was dying to know what that bag contained. Why didn't Feluda go up to the man, grab him by his collar and challenge him straightaway? Why didn't he say, 'Where's that broken head? Take it out at once!'

But no, I knew Feluda would not do that. He could not, without sufficient evidence. It was true that Mallik had gone to Sidikpur where that plane had crashed; it was true that he had travelled all the way to Ellora, and had been heard speaking to someone in Bombay, talking about a daughter having returned to her father. But that was not really enough. Feluda would have to wait a bit longer before speaking to him.

There was, however, one way of finding out if Mallik's bag contained anything heavy. I saw Feluda walk past us, go up to Mallik and give him a push. 'Oh, sorry!' he said quickly, and began focusing his camera on a statue. I saw the bag swing from side to side with the push. Its contents did not appear to be very heavy.

We left the temple. On our way out, we saw two other men. One of them was the stout gentleman Lalmohan Babu had recently tried to impress, and the other was the bald American.

The former was explaining something with elaborate gestures; the latter was nodding in agreement.

For some strange reason, I suddenly began to think everyone around us was a suspicious character. Each one of them should be watched closely.

Was Feluda thinking the same thing?

SEVEN

Feluda wanted to stop at the guest house on our way back. 'I want to see what newspapers they get,' he said by way of an explanation.

Lalmohan Babu and I returned to the bungalow. We were both feeling hungry, so Lalmohan Babu called out to the chowkidar and asked him to bring us tea and biscuits. The dining room faced the small lobby. The room to its right—number one—was ours. Number two was empty. Opposite these two were rooms three and four. The stout gentleman was in one of them, and Feluda had the other.

Lalmohan Babu was still in a mood to snoop. 'Listen, Tapesh,' he said, sipping his tea, 'I think we can leave the American out of this, at least for the moment. That leaves us with three other people: Bose, Mallik and that man who's staying here. We know something about Bose and Mallik—true or false, God only knows—but we know absolutely nothing about the third man, not even his name. We could peep into his room now, it doesn't appear to be locked.'

I did not like the idea, so I said, 'What if the chowkidar sees us?'

'He cannot see us if I go in, and you stay here to look out for him. If you see the chowkidar coming this way, start coughing. I will get out of that room at once. I think your cousin will appreciate a helping hand. This man's suitcase also struck me as quite heavy.'

The whole world was suddenly full of heavy suitcases. But I could not stop him. To be honest, although I had never done anything like this before for anyone except Feluda, there was a scent of adventure in the suggestion, so I found myself agreeing.

I went to the back veranda. There was a small courtyard facing the veranda, across which was the kitchen and, next to it, the chowkidar's room. A cycle stood outside this room. A boy of about twelve—presumably his son—was cleaning it with great concentration. I turned my head as I heard a faint creaking noise and saw Lalmohan Babu sneak into room number three. A couple of minutes later, it was he who coughed loudly to indicate that he had finished his job. I returned to our room.

'There was nothing much in there,' Lalmohan Babu said. 'His suitcase seemed pretty old, but it was locked and it did not open even when I pulled the handle. On the table was an empty spectacle-case with "Stephens Company, Calcutta" stamped on it, a bottle of indigestion pills and a tube of Odomos. Apart from these things, there was nothing that I . . .'

'Whose possessions are you talking about?' asked Feluda. We looked up with a start. He had walked into our room silently, almost like a ghost.

This called for an honest confession. Much to my surprise, he did not get cross with either of us. All he said was, 'Was there any particular reason for doing this?'

'No, it's just that we don't know anything about the man, do we?' Lalmohan Babu tried to explain. 'I mean, he hasn't even told us his name. And he looks kind of hefty, doesn't he? Didn't you say there was a whole gang involved in this? So I thought . . .'

'So you thought he must be one of them? There was no need to search his room just to get his name. He's called R.N. Raxit. His name's written on one side of his suitcase. I don't think we need to know any more about him at this moment. Please don't go into his room again. It simply means taking unnecessary risks. After all, we haven't got any concrete reason to suspect him.'

'Very well. That just leaves the American.'

'He's called Lewison, Sam Lewison. Another Jew, and also very wealthy. He owns an art gallery in New York.'

'How do you know all this?' I asked, surprised.

'The manager of the guest house told me. We got talking. He's a very nice man, passionately fond of detective novels. In fact, he's been waiting for thieves and crooks to arrive here ever since he read about the thefts in other temples.'

'Did you tell him why you were here?'

'Yes. He can help us a great deal. Don't forget Mallik is staying in his guest house. Apparently, Mallik has already tried to ring someone in Bombay, but the call didn't come through.'

That night, all four guests in the bungalow sat down to dinner together. Feluda did not speak a word. Mr Raxit turned to Lalmohan Babu and tried to make conversation by asking him if he specialized in any particular period of history. In answer to that, Lalmohan Babu said he didn't know very much about pyramids, except that they were in Egypt. Then he went back to dunking pieces of chapati into his bowl of daal. Mr Raxit cast me a puzzled glance. I placed a hand on my ear and shook my head to indicate that my 'uncle' was hard of hearing. Mr Raxit nodded vigorously and refrained from asking further questions.

After dinner, Feluda went straight to his room and Lalmohan Babu and I went out for a walk. It was quite windy outside. A pale moon shone between patches of dark clouds. From somewhere came the fragrance of hasnahana. Lalmohan Babu, inspired by all this, decided to start singing a classical raga. I suddenly felt quite lighthearted. Just at that moment, we saw a man walking towards us from the guest house. Lalmohan Babu stopped singing (which was a relief since he was singing perfectly out of tune) and stood still. As the man got closer, I recognized him. It was Shubhankar Bose. 'I wish your cousin was here!' Lalmohan Babu whispered.

'Out for a walk, eh?' Mr Bose asked. Then he cleared his throat, looked around a couple of times, lowered his voice and said, 'Er . . . do you happen to know that man in the blue shirt?'

This time, Lalmohan Babu couldn't pretend to be deaf. Mr Bose had spoken with him before.

'Why, did he say he knew us?' Lalmohan Babu asked.

Mr Bose looked over his shoulder again. 'That man is most peculiar,' he told us. 'He says he is interested in Indian art and this is his first visit to Ellora. Yet, when I met him at the temple, he didn't seem moved by any of it. I mean, not at all. I felt just as thrilled by everything, even though this is my second visit. Now, if the man does not care for art and sculpture, why is he here? Why is he pretending to be something he clearly isn't?'

We remained silent. What could we say?

'Have you read the papers recently?' Mr Bose went on.

'Why do you ask?'

'Pieces of our ancient art are being sold off. Statues from temples are disappearing overnight.'

'Really? No, I didn't know that. What a shame! It's a regular crime, isn't it?' Lalmohan Babu declared. His acting was not very convincing, but luckily Mr Bose did not seem to notice. He came closer and added, 'The man left the guest house a while ago.'

'Which man?'

'Mr Mallik.'

'What!' We both spoke together. Lalmohan Babu was right. Feluda ought to have been here.

'Why don't we go, too?' Mr Bose asked, his voice trembling with excitement.

'N-now? Wh-where to?' Lalmohan Babu stammered.

'To the caves.'

'But they must be closed now. Surely there are chowkidars?'

'Yes, but there are only two guards for thirty-four caves. So that shouldn't be a problem. I saw Mallik leave with a bag. He and that hippie in your bungalow keep going about with bags. In fact, that hippie also strikes me as suspicious. Do you know who he is?'

Lalmohan Babu nearly choked. 'He . . . he is a photographer. A very good one. He showed us some of his photos. He's here on an assignment.'

Someone came out of the bungalow. It was Mr Raxit, carrying a stout walking stick in one hand, and a torch in the other. He was wearing a dark, heavy raincoat. He stopped for a minute to shout into Lalmohan Babu's ear: 'After dinner, walk a mile!' Then he smiled and disappeared in the direction of the guest house. Mr Bose said, 'Good night!' and followed him. Lalmohan Babu frowned and said, 'Why did that man tell me to walk a mile?'

'That should help your digestion. Come on now, let's go and find Feluda. He must be told what we just heard. Everyone seems to have gone off to the caves. I don't like it. Let's see what Feluda thinks.'

It was dark inside the bungalow, except for a lantern in the chowkidar's room. This surprised us. Mr Raxit had naturally switched off his light before going out, and so had we. But why was Feluda's door closed? Why couldn't I see any light under it? Had he already gone to sleep? It was only ten-thirty.

His room had a window that opened out on the veranda. At this moment, however, it was firmly shut and the curtains drawn. I walked up to it and softly called out Feluda's name. There was no reply. He must have gone out. But if he had used the main exit, we would certainly have seen him. Perhaps he had gone out of the little back door behind the chowkidar's room?

Rather foolishly, we went back to our own room and switched the light on. At once, our eyes fell on a piece of paper that was lying on the floor. 'Stay in your room,' it said in Feluda's handwriting.

'Tapesh, my boy,' Lalmohan Babu said with a sigh, 'do you know what is worrying me the most? It's your cousin's behaviour. That is what is most mystifying. Otherwise, frankly, I cannot see too many mysteries in this case.'

Feluda had told us to stay in, but had said nothing about when he might return. There was no question of going to bed. So I spent the next thirty minutes playing noughts-and-crosses with Lalmohan Babu. Then he said he'd tell me the plot of his next novel. 'This time,' he announced, 'I've introduced a new type of fight. My hero's hands and feet are going to be tied, but he'll still manage to defeat the villain, simply by using his head.'

I was about to ask whether by this he meant Prakhar Rudra's brain power, or was his hero simply going to butt his way to victory, when Feluda returned. We looked up expectantly, but he said nothing. By this time, we had both learnt that if Feluda did not wish to part with information, even a thousand questions couldn't make him open his mouth. On the other hand, he'd tell us everything, if he so wished.

What he finally said took us by surprise. 'Lalmohan Babu,' he asked solemnly, 'did you bring a weapon this time?'

Lalmohan Babu had a passion for collecting weapons. When we had gone to Rajasthan, he had taken a Nepali dagger with him. Then, when he went to Simla, he had a boomerang. At Feluda's question, his eyes started glinting. 'Yes, sir,' he said. 'This time, I've got a bomb.'

'A bomb?'

I could hardly believe him. Lalmohan Babu opened his suitcase and took out a heavy brown object, shaped a little like a torch. He passed it to Feluda, saying, 'My neighbour Mr Samaddar's son, Utpal, is in the army. He came to my house last March and gave it to me. "Look, Uncle, see what I brought for you!" he said, "This is a bomb. It is used in serious warfare." Utpal loves reading my novels.'

Feluda inspected it briefly before saying, 'Let me keep this. It's too dangerous to remain anywhere else.'

'Very well. How many metaguns do you think it weighs?'

What he meant obviously was 'megaton', but Feluda ignored this last remark completely. He put the 'bomb' in his shoulder bag and said, 'Let's go out. Everyone else has gone, so why should we stay in?'

When we left the dak bungalow, it was half past eleven. The moon was now almost totally obliterated by clouds. It was still windy. One of the rooms in the guest house had a light on. It was the American's room, Feluda said. It was impossible to tell whether Bose and Mallik had returned.

By the time we reached the main road, the eastern sky was heavily overcast. A loud rumble in the sky made Lalmohan Babu exclaim, 'Good heavens, what if we get caught in the rain?'

'If we can get to the caves before it starts raining, we'll have plenty of places to seek shelter,' Feluda reassured us.

Fortunately, it remained dry for quite some time after this. We reached Kailash, but Feluda did not go in through the main entrance. He turned left instead. A little later, he left the path and began climbing up the hill. I was familiar enough with his techniques to realize that he was trying to see if there was another way to get into the temple, without using the main passage. There were bushes and loose stones everywhere, but the moonlight—fleeting though it was—helped us find our way.

Feluda turned right. We were now going back the way we came, but were walking several feet above the path that visitors normally used. A few minutes later, Feluda suddenly stopped. He was looking at something on his right. I followed his gaze.

In the distance, it seemed as if a long silk ribbon was spread on the ground. It was the road that led to the main town. A man was quickly walking down this road, either to the guest house or to the bungalow.

'Not Raxit,' Lalmohan Babu whispered.

'How do you know?'

'Raxit was wearing a raincoat.' He was right.

The man turned a corner and vanished from sight. We resumed walking. Only a few moments later, however, we had to stop again. There was a strange noise—something like a cross between a scrape and a rustle. Where was it coming from?

Feluda sat down. So did we. A large cactus bush hid us from view. The noise continued for sometime, then stopped abruptly.

We emerged cautiously. Huge, dark clouds had now spread all over the sky. We could hardly see our way. Nevertheless, Feluda kept going. Soon, we could vaguely see the temple again. Its spire was before us. Several feet below the spire, on the roof, stood four lions, facing the east, west, north and the south. Far below them were the two elephants that stood at the entrance.

We kept walking. The noise had come from this direction, but I couldn't see anything suspicious. Feluda had a torch, but I knew he wouldn't switch it on, in case it was seen by whoever happened to be in the vicinity.

We passed the temple and came to a cave. It was cave number fifteen. We moved on to the next. Feluda stopped again. I could see that his whole body was tense. 'Torch,' he whispered. 'Someone in number fifteen has switched on a torch. Look at the courtyard in front of it. Doesn't it seem brighter than the others?'

It was true. Neither Lalmohan Babu nor I had noticed it. Only Feluda's sharp eyes had picked it up. We stood holding our breath for a couple of minutes. Then Feluda did something entirely unexpected. He picked up a small pebble and threw it in the direction of the courtyard. I heard it fall with a soft thud. A second later, the faint light coming from the cave went out. The torch was switched off. Then a man came out and slipped away, moving stealthily like a thief. 'Could that be Raxit?' Lalmohan Babu said softly. I couldn't recognize the man, but could see that he was not wearing a raincoat.

What followed next took my breath away. Without a word of warning, Feluda began climbing down. He leapt, crawled, scraped himself on the ground, then swinging from a branch like a monkey, disappeared from sight. I stared speechlessly. Lalmohan Babu said, after a moment's silence, 'He'll do very well in a circus!'

Cave number fifteen was at a lower level. That was where Feluda had gone. Three minutes later (it felt like three hours), he climbed up

again, more or less in a similar fashion. How he could do it with a
torch in one hand, a bag hanging from his shoulder and a revolver
tucked into his waist, I do not know.

'That one's the Das Avatar cave,' he told us, panting. 'It has two
storeys, and some exquisite statues.'

'Did you . . . did you see who it was?' I asked breathlessly.

Feluda did not reply immediately. Then he said, 'It's not as simple
as I had thought. It'll take me a while to unravel this tangled mess.'

We found the main path again and climbed down to the bottom of
the temple. But Feluda had not finished. He found one of the
chowkidars and asked him if he had seen anyone going up.

'No, sir,' the chowkidar replied.

'Did you hear any noise? Anything suspicious at all?'

'No, sir. There's been a lot of thunder. I didn't hear anything else.'

'Can we go into the temple?'

I knew the man would refuse, and he did.

'No, sir. I have orders not to let anyone in at this time of night.'

We made our way back to the bungalow. As we got closer, we saw
something extremely strange. Two windows on the eastern side of
the building overlooked the street. We could see these from outside.
One of them was Feluda's, the other was Mr Raxit's. Feluda's room
was in darkness, but a light flashed in Mr Raxit's room. It was the
light from a torch, but it did not stay still. In fact, whoever was
holding it seemed to have gone mad. The light danced all over the
room, then came to the window, shone once in the direction of the
guest house, fell and moved on the bushes by the road before going
back to the room. We could not see who it was. 'Highly interesting!'
Feluda muttered.

We returned to the bungalow. By now, it had started to drizzle,
and was pitch dark outside.

EIGHT

I had noticed in the past that our adventures often took totally-
unexpected turns. When this happened, Feluda seldom lost his
equanimity. In fact, I had always marvelled at his ability to keep
calm while dealing with unforeseen complications. This time,
however, what happened made him very cross.

Before going to bed at night, we had decided to leave early in the morning to go back to the spot where we had heard that funny noise. It required investigation, Feluda said. So we rose at five o'clock and left the bungalow half an hour later after having a cup of tea. Feluda was up before us to replace his make-up. I remembered to maintain a right parting in my hair. Lalmohan Babu expressed the desire to make some change in his appearance as well, but Feluda said 'No!' so firmly that he had to desist.

The caves were going to open for visitors as soon as the sun rose. We wanted to be the first, so we got there at 6 a.m. To our complete astonishment, we found the place crawling with people. A large number of cars and vans were parked outside. It was the sight of a reflector that told me what was going on. This was a film unit. They had arrived from Bombay to shoot a Hindi film, we learnt. The actors hadn't yet arrived, but the rest of the crew were getting things ready. 'Oh no!' Feluda cried in dismay. 'Why couldn't they find some other place?'

A young man was bustling about, clutching a film magazine. Lalmohan Babu called him aside.

'What is the name of this film, do you know?' he asked.

'Oh yes. *Krorepati*.'

'Who's acting in it?'

'Three of the top stars. Today's shots will include Rupa, Arjun Mehrotra and Balwant Chopra. The heroine, hero and the villain.'

The mention of Arjun Mehrotra made Lalmohan Babu grow round-eyed. 'Will there be songs?' he asked.

'No, no. We've come to shoot fights. Stuntmen, doubles and the fight director are all here. The hero will chase the villain from a cave into the main temple.'

'And the heroine?'

'She'll stay in the cave. The villain has imprisoned her in there, you see. But now the hero's here, so the villain has to run for his life. The climax takes place on the spire.'

'The spire?'

'Yes.'

'Who's the director?'

'Mohan Sharma. But these shots today will be taken by the fight director, Appa Rao.'

'How long do you think the whole thing will take?'

'Well . . . that's difficult to say. We hope to start by ten o'clock. Then we should finish by one.'

That meant they would occupy the whole complex virtually the whole day.

'I don't believe this!' Feluda said through clenched teeth. 'How did they get permission to take the whole place over?'

Since we couldn't get into the temple, we decided to climb over it, just as we had done the previous night. But even the hills around the temple had men from the film unit setting up equipment. We learnt here that although the film crew were not letting ordinary visitors into the temple, they could not go in themselves, as the official letter giving them the necessary permission to shoot had not yet arrived. It was being brought in a different car. The chowkidar on duty had flatly refused to unlock the main door unless the letter was produced.

Feluda clicked his tongue in annoyance and said, 'Let's not waste any more time. Let's see if we can get into cave number fifteen. At least we can look at those beautiful statues, away from all this noise.'

We climbed down from the other side and were walking towards the cave when we saw a huge yellow American car making its way to the temple. The three major stars and the fight director had arrived.

Feluda had already told us the fifteenth cave was the Das Avatar cave. We ran into two modern avatars on our way. They were Lewison and Raxit. We had spotted them from a distance, standing near the entrance and speaking rather animatedly. As we got closer, we heard the American say angrily, 'I see no point in my staying here any longer.' Then he strode off in a huff. Mr Raxit walked up to us, shrugged and smiled somewhat bitterly. 'He was complaining about the arrangements here. I mean, in the guest house. He said to me, "How can you expect me to spend my dollars here, when you don't even know how to fry an egg?" Just because he's rich, he thinks he owns the whole world.'

'That's strange!' Feluda remarked. 'Isn't he supposed to be a connoisseur of art? How can he talk of fried eggs, standing in a place like this, surrounded by the best specimens of Indian art?'

'How,' Lalmohan Babu wanted to know, 'do they fry eggs in America, anyway?'

Mr Raxit opened his mouth to speak, but had to shut it immediately. A loud scream from the temple made us all start violently. Lalmohan Babu was the first to recover. 'That must be the villain!' he exclaimed. 'They've started shooting. The villain's shouting and making his escape.'

But no. A babble had broken out. There were many other voices, also screaming and yelling. There was something wrong, obviously. Feluda had already begun walking in that direction. We followed him quickly. As we returned to the temple's entrance, we saw a man in a purple bush shirt being carried out. He appeared to be unconscious. He was taken to the yellow car. Then came the three stars. Rupa was walking slowly, leaning heavily on Arjun Mehrotra. Balwant was holding her hand, and murmuring into her ear, as if she were a frightened child, in need of comforting.

A second later, we saw the same young man we had spoken to earlier.

'What happened? What's wrong?' Lalmohan Babu asked him.

'There's a . . . there's a dead body lying behind the temple. It's horrible!'

'Oh my God! Who was that man they carried out to the car?'

'Appa Rao. He was the first to discover the body. One look, and he fainted.'

Feluda and Mr Raxit had gone into the temple. The film crew were all coming out. There was now no question of shooting a film here today.

Lalmohan Babu and I walked along the passage to our left. To our right, below us, were several statues of elephants and lions. They looked as though they were carrying the whole temple on their shoulders. We stopped as the passage turned right. There was a group of men, peering down into a gorge. Perhaps that was where the body was lying. Mr Raxit emerged from the crowd and stopped us. 'Don't go any further,' he said. 'It's not a pretty sight.' Quite frankly, I had no wish to see the body, but I did feel curious about the dead man. Who was he? Feluda came out and answered this question even before I could ask it.

'Shubhankar Bose,' he said. 'I think he fell off the edge of the cliff straight onto the rocks below.'

'Strange, how strange!' Lalmohan Babu muttered under his breath. 'This is exactly how my own villain, Ghanashyam Karkat, is supposed to die!'

Feluda started walking away, so Lalmohan Babu and I had to move on. Mr Raxit was ahead of us, but he turned and stopped. 'I saw him last night,' he said, shaking his head, 'I told him not to try climbing in the dark. But he paid no attention to me. How was I to know that he was planning to commit suicide?'

Mr Raxit left, having given us something to ponder on. The idea of a suicide had not occurred to me. I looked at Feluda, but he had started to climb the hill on the left of the temple. Mr Bose must have climbed the same hill.

The people gathered near the cliff had gone. Mr Base's death had, in a way, made things easier for our investigation. Feluda went close to the edge of the cliff and examined the area carefully.

There was a small hole in the ground, only a few feet away from the edge. People had walked over it and around it, making it almost disappear. But when Feluda took out a steel tape from his bag and pushed it in, we realized it was a fairly deep hole. Now Feluda peered closely at the ground again. Lalmohan Babu and I both saw what had claimed his attention.

There was a deep crease on the ground, running from the edge of the cliff to the hole.

'Do you know what this is?' Feluda asked me. I couldn't answer. Feluda went on, 'This mark was left by a rope. Someone had tied a rope to a crowbar, dug the crowbar deep into the ground, and gone down—or tried to go down—the cliff, using that rope. Remember the noise we heard yesterday? It was the noise of the rope being pulled back. Since there was no way to get into the cave below from the front, someone found this way to reach it from the rear.'

'But. . . what sort of a rope could it have been?' Lalmohan Babu asked. 'I mean . . . if you had to climb down a hundred feet, you'd need a remarkably strong rope, wouldn't you?'

'Yes. A nylon rope would to the trick. It would be light, but very, very strong.'

'That means there was a second person here,' I said slowly. 'I mean, apart from Mr Bose.'

'Right. This second person removed the rope, and the crowbar. We don't yet know whether he was Bose's friend or foe, but there is something that indicates he might have been the latter.'

I looked quickly at Feluda. What did he mean? In reply, he took out a small object from his pocket and placed it on his palm. It was a piece of blue cloth, torn presumably from a shirt. Who was wearing a blue shirt yesterday?

Mr Jayant Mallik!

'Where did you find it?' I asked. My voice shook.

'Bose was lying on his stomach. His arms were spread wide. His right hand was closed around this piece of cloth, but a small bit was sticking out between two fingers. He and this other man must have struggled with each other by the cliff. Bose clutched at the shirt the other man was wearing. But then he fell, taking this little piece with him.'

'You mean he was deliberately pushed off the cliff?' Lalmohan Babu gasped, 'You m-mean it was m-m-murder?'

Feluda did not give a direct answer. After a few seconds of silence, he simply said, 'If the statues in the temple are still intact, we must thank Mr Bose for it. It was because of his presence here last night that the thief couldn't get away with it.'

NINE

When we climbed down eventually and went back to the main entrance to the temple, the members of the film unit had all disappeared. There were knots of local people, curious and excited. The big American car had been replaced by a jeep. An intelligent and smart looking man—possibly in his mid-thirties—saw Feluda and came forward to greet him. It turned out to be Mr Kulkarni, the manager of the Tourist Guest House.

'We realized only this morning that Mr Bose had not returned last night,' he said, shaking his head regretfully. 'I sent a bearer to look for him, but of course he couldn't find him anywhere.'

'What is going to happen now?' Feluda asked.

'The police in Aurangabad have been informed. They're sending a van to collect the body. Mr Bose had a brother in Delhi. He'll have to be informed, naturally. . . It is really very sad. The man was a true scholar. He came once before, in 1968. I believe he was writing a book on Ellora.'

'Isn't there a police station here?'

'Yes, but it's only a small outpost. An assistant sub-inspector is in charge, a man called Ghote. He's inspecting the body at the moment.'

'Could I meet him?'

'Certainly. Oh, by the way—' Mr Kulkarni stopped, looking doubtfully at Lalmohan Babu and me.

'They are friends, you may speak freely before them,' Feluda said quickly.

'Oh. Oh, I see,' Mr Kulkarni sounded relieved. 'Well, some

rang Bombay this morning.'

'Mallik?'

'Yes.'

'What did he say?'

Mr Kulkarni took out a piece of paper from his pocket and read from it: 'The daughter's fine. Leaving today.'

'Today? Did he tell you anything about leaving today?'

'He did. He wanted to leave this morning. But I thought of you, Mr Mitter, and had a word with his driver. Mallik has been told there's something wrong with his car, it'll take a while to repair it. So he cannot leave immediately.'

'Bravo! Thank you, Mr Kulkarni, you've been a great help.'

Mr Kulkarni looked pleased. Feluda lit a Charminar and asked, 'Tell me, what kind of a man is this Ghote?'

'A very good man, I should say. But he doesn't like it here. He longs for a promotion and a posting in Aurangabad. Come with me, I will introduce you to him.'

Mr Ghote had emerged from the cave. Mr Kulkarni brought him over and introduced Feluda as 'a very famous private detective'. Mr Ghote's height was about five feet five inches. His width matched his height and, to top it all, he had a moustache like Charlie Chaplin. But his movements were surprisingly brisk and agile.

'Why don't you go back to the bungalow?' Feluda said to me. 'I'll have a word with Mr Ghote, and then join you there.'

Neither of us had the slightest wish to return without Feluda, but there was no point in arguing. So we went back. On reaching the bungalow, we realized we were both quite hungry; so I stopped to tell the chowkidar to send us toast and eggs. Then I walked into our room, to find Lalmohan Babu sitting on his bed, looking a little foolish.

'Tell me, Tapesh,' he said on seeing me, 'did we lock our room before going out this morning?'

'Why, no! There was no need to. We have nothing worth stealing. Besides, the cleaners usually come in the morning, so I thought . . . why, has anything been taken?'

'No. But someone has been through my things. Whoever did it sat on my bed and opened my suitcase. In fact, when I came in, the bed was still warm. See if he touched your suitcase as well?'

He had; I realized this the minute I opened the case. Nothing was in place. Not only that, one of my pillows was lying on the floor.

Judging by the way my chappals had been thrown in two different directions, the intruder had even looked under the bed.

'I was most worried about my notebook,' Lalmohan Babu confided, 'but he didn't take it, thank God.'

'Did he take anything else?'

'No, I don't think so. What about you?'

'The same. Whoever came in was looking for something specific, I think. He didn't find it here.'

'Let's ask the chowkidar if he saw anything.'

But the chowkidar could not help. He had gone out shopping for a while, so if anyone stole in while he was out, he couldn't have seen him. Normally, theft was a rare occurrence in these parts. The chowkidar seemed most puzzled by the thought that anyone's room should be broken into and their belongings searched.

Had Feluda's room been similarly ransacked? I went to have a look, but saw that his room was locked. He had to be extra careful because of his disguise. 'Should we try asking Raxit?' Lalmohan Babu asked.

Having seen the flashing light in his room the night before, I was feeling rather curious about the man. So I agreed and we both went up to his room. I knocked softly. The door opened almost at once.

'What is it? Come in.'

Mr Raxit did not seem very pleased to see us; but we went into his room, anyway.

'Did anyone break into your room as well?' Lalmohan Babu asked as soon as he had stepped in.

From the way Mr Raxit looked at Lalmohan Babu, it was obvious that he was not in a good mood. He spoke in a low voice, but his tone was sharp. 'What's the use of speaking to you?' he said. 'You can't hear a word, can you? Let me speak to your nephew. Not only did someone get into my room, but he actually removed something valuable.'

'What. . . what was it?' I asked timidly.

'My raincoat. I had bought it in England, and had been using it for the last twenty-five years.' Lalmohan Babu looked at me silently. He wasn't supposed to have heard anything. I repeated the words to him, speaking loudly, trying not to laugh.

'Could it have been stolen last night?' Lalmohan Babu suggested. 'We saw you looking for something. I mean, we saw your torch . . .'

'No. A small bat had somehow got into my room last night. I

switched the main lights off and used my torch to get rid of it. Nothing was stolen yesterday. It happened this morning. I believe the culprit is that young boy of the chowkidar's.'

I had to shout once more and repeat the whole thing to Lalmohan Babu.

'I am very sorry to hear this,' Lalmohan Babu said gravely. 'We must keep an eye on the boy.'

There didn't seem to be anything else to say. We apologized for disturbing him and came away.

The chowkidar had served us breakfast in the dining hall. We began eating. I had no idea what American fried eggs tasted like, but what I had been given here was quite tasty. I kept wondering who might have broken into our room, but decided in the end that it must have been the chowkidar's son. I had seen him walking in the backyard and throwing curious glances in the direction of our rooms.

Feluda had told us to go back to the bungalow, but hadn't said that we had to stay in. So after breakfast, we locked our room, and went out in the street.

The guest house was not clearly visible from the main gate of our bungalow, the view being partially obstructed by a large tree. The sudden noise of a car starting made us go forward quickly. Now the guest house was fully visible. The taxi that had brought Mr Raxit and Lewison from Aurangabad was now ready to leave. The luggage-rack on its roof was loaded. Mr Sam Lewison, the American millionaire, was giving a tip to one of the bearers.

But who was that?

Another man had come out of the guest house and was speaking to Lewison. Lewison nodded twice, which clearly meant that he had agreed to do something for the other man. The latter went back to the guest house and reappeared with a suitcase. The driver opened the boot of the car, and placed the suitcase in it. My heart began beating faster. Lalmohan Babu clutched my sleeve. There could be no doubt about the implication of what we had just seen. Mr Jayant Mallik was not going to wait for his own car to be repaired. He was trying to escape with Sam Lewison.

The driver took his seat.

'The cycle!' I cried. 'The chowkidar's cycle!'

The car started. I ran back to the bungalow and managed to drag the cycle out. Luckily, no one saw me.

'Come on!' I said to Lalmohan Babu. He stood there looking as though he had never ridden on the crossbar of a cycle before. But there was no time to argue, our culprit was running away. He jumped up a second later, and I began pedalling as fast as I could. Feluda had taught me to cycle when I was seven. Now I could put it to good use.

If we had walked, it would have taken us twenty minutes to get back to the temple. I covered that distance in five. There was Feluda, and Ghote, and Kulkarni!

'Feluda!' I panted. 'Mr Mallik went off . . . in that American's car . . . five minutes ago!'

Just that one remark from me set so many things in motion that the whole thing now seems almost like a blur. Mr Ghote jumped into his jeep, with Feluda beside him, and Lalmohan Babu and myself at the back. I had no idea even a jeep could travel at 60 kmph. Very soon, we saw Lewison's taxi, overtook it and made it stop. Lewison got out, looking furious and giving vent to his anger by uttering a range of specially chosen American swear words. These had no effect on Mr Ghote. He ignored Lewison completely and approached Mallik, who turned visibly pale. Mr Ghote then opened his suitcase, quelling an abortive attempt by Mallik to stop him, and took out an object wrapped heavily in a large Turkish towel. With one swift movement, he removed the towel and revealed the yakshi's head. Sam Lewison shut up immediately, gaped in horror and stammered, 'B-b-but . . . b-but I . . . I . . . !' Lalmohan Babu heaved a sigh of relief and proclaimed, 'End's well that all's well!' Finally Lewison was allowed to travel back to Aurangabad. We returned to Khuldabad with the culprit, caught red-handed.

Mr Ghote took Mallik away, to keep him somewhere in the police outpost. He went quietly, too dazed to say anything.

We were dropped at the guest house, for Mr Kulkarni was waiting anxiously for our return. He appeared very pleased on being told that our mission had been entirely successful. However, Feluda seemed to pour cold water over his enthusiasm by saying, 'We haven't yet finished our job, Mr Kulkarni. There's plenty more to be done. Don't forget to make enquiries about that number in Bombay, and let me know as soon as you hear anything.'

I didn't understand what this last instruction meant, but thought no more about it.

Mr Kulkarni had ordered coffee for all of us. When it arrived, I suddenly remembered we had not told Feluda about our room being searched. He sipped his coffee quietly as I quickly explained what had happened. Then he frowned and asked Mr Kulkarni, 'What sort of a man is that chowkidar?'

'Who, Mohanlal? A very good man, most trustworthy. He's been doing this job for the last seventeen years. I have never heard anyone complain against him.'

Feluda thought for a second, then turned to me. 'Are you sure nothing was stolen?'

'Yes. We are both absolutely sure. Mr Raxit thinks it was the chowkidar's boy who did it.'

'Very well. Let's go and have a look, especially since Lalmohan Babu says the intruder actually sat on his bed and kept it warm for him. See you soon, Mr Kulkarni; perhaps you had better keep this with you.' He passed the yakshi's head—still wrapped in the towel—to Mr Kulkarni, who put it in a safe in his office and locked it.

We returned to the bungalow. Feluda came into our room with us, bolted the door and then went through our belongings with meticulous care. Apart from his clothes, Lalmohan Babu's suitcase contained a small box of homoeopathic pills, two books on criminology, one on Baluchistan and his own notebook. For some reason, Feluda spent a long time going through this notebook, but did not tell us what was so intriguing about it. Finally, he put everything away and said, 'If my guesses turn out to be correct, this whole business is going to be settled tonight, one way or the other. If that happens, you will both have to play an important role. Please remember, at all times, that I am with you, keeping an eye on you, even if you cannot see me. Don't tell anyone about Mallik's arrest. And don't leave your room. In any case, I don't think you can, for it looks like it's going to rain.'

Feluda peered out of the window as he spoke, then got up silently and went and stood by it. I followed him. We were looking out of the western side. There was a lawn, across which stood a number of tall trees. I could recognize eucalyptus amongst them. A man came out of the trees, crossed the lawn and went to the front of the bungalow. A minute later, he entered the dining hall. This was followed by the sound of a room being unlocked, and then locked again from inside.

Feluda nodded and muttered 'Yes, yes!' almost to himself.

The man who had come in was Mr Raxit.

'Wait until you hear from me,' Feluda said, 'and then simply do as you're told. Don't be afraid.'

He opened the door and went out.

We remained in our room. Thunder rumbled outside. The sky was overcast.

Staring at the walls, thinking things over, it suddenly occurred to me that the man who was probably the most mysterious was Mr Raxit. We did not know anything about him.

And Mallik? How much had we learnt about Jayant Mallik?

Not much. Not enough. Suddenly, it seemed to me that we had made no progress at all.

TEN

It began pouring soon after twelve o'clock. The rain was accompanied by frequent thunder. Lalmohan Babu and I sat in our room trying—in vain—to work out what possible role we might have to play later in the day. Mallik had been arrested, the yakshi's head was safely locked away. As far as we were concerned, that was the end of the story. What else could Feluda be thinking of?

The chowkidar told us at one o'clock that lunch was ready. We went into the dining hall without Feluda. He was probably having lunch with Mr Kulkarni in the guest house.

Mr Raxit joined us. He had seemed extremely cross this morning when we had spoken to him, but now he appeared cheerful once more. 'On a day like this,' he said, 'a Bengali ought to have kedgeree, *pakoras* and fried hilsa. I have lived out of Bengal for many years, but haven't forgotten Bengali habits.'

The meal we were served here was different, but no less tasty. I finished my bowl of daal, and had just helped myself to the meat curry, when a car drew up outside the front door and a thin, squeaky voice cried: 'Chowkidar!' The chowkidar rushed out, clutching an umbrella. Mr Raxit soaked a piece of his chapati in the curry, put it in his mouth and said, 'A tourist? In this weather?'

A tall man walked in, taking off his raincoat. Most of his hair was grey. He had a short moustache and goatee, and he wore glasses. 'I've already had my lunch,' he told the chowkidar, who was carrying his aged leather suitcase. Then he turned to us and asked, 'Who has been arrested?'

Feluda had told us not to say anything about Mallik's arrest, so we simply stared foolishly. Mr Raxit gave a start and said, 'Arrested?'

'Yes. Some vandal. He was apparently trying to steal a statue from one of the caves, and was caught. At least, that's what I've just heard. I only hope they won't decide to close the caves because of this. I've travelled quite far simply to see the statues here. Why, haven't you heard anything?'

'No.'

'Anyway, I'm glad the fellow was caught. I must say the police here are quite efficient.'

The man was given the third empty room. He disappeared into it, but we could hear him talking to himself. Perhaps he was slightly mad.

The rain stopped at around two-thirty. Half an hour later, I saw the new arrival walking towards the eucalyptus trees. He came back in five minutes.

The chowkidar brought us our tea at four-thirty. I noticed a small piece of paper on the floor as he left. It turned out to be another message from Feluda: 'Go to cave number fifteen at seven o'clock. Wait in the south-eastern corner on the first floor.'

He was still running a campaign, totally unseen. This had never happened before.

Fortunately, it did not rain again. When we left the bungalow at six-thirty, both Mr Raxit and the man with the goatee appeared to be in their rooms, for their lights were on. Lalmohan Babu muttered a short prayer as we set out. My own feelings were so confused that I am not even going to try to describe them. My hands felt cold. I thrust them into my pockets.

We reached Kailash ten minutes before seven. The western sky was still quite bright since the sun did not set here at this time of year until after six-thirty. The caves and hills seemed darker, but the sky had cleared.

We turned right after reaching Kailash. The next cave was number fifteen, the Das Avatar cave. It was at this one that Feluda had thrown a pebble last night.

There was no one around. We walked on. The courtyard before the cave was large. There was a small shrine in the middle of it. We crossed it quickly and climbed a few steps to go through the main entrance that took us into the cave. We had been told to find the first floor. I could dimly see a flight of steps going up. God knew if there was anyone already hiding in the dark. We went up the steps, trying not to make any noise at all.

The stairs led us to a huge hall. Rows of carved pillars stood supporting the roof, as though they were carrying it on their heads. There were scenes from Indian mythology, beautifully carved on the northern and the southern walls.

We found the south-eastern corner. It was too dark inside to see clearly. I had taken off my sandals before climbing the stairs, but now the rocky floor felt so cold that I had to put them on again. As neither of us knew how long we might have to wait, we sat down, leaning against the wall. Who knew what was going to happen next in this cave, built twelve hundred years ago, and filled with amazing specimens of ancient art?

Something happened almost immediately. As soon as we had sat down, my eyes fell on something that made me give an involuntary gasp. Only a few feet away from where we were sitting, barely visible in the dark, was a solid round object lying on the floor. Sticking out from under it was a white square object. Neither was a part of the temple decorations. Someone had placed them there deliberately. What could they be? Who had kept them there, and for whom?

'P-paper?' Lalmohan Babu whispered, pointing at the white object.

We rose and went closer. What we saw made us stare in utter disbelief. It was indeed a piece of paper, but what had been used as a paperweight was the yakshi's head! There could be no mistake. We had seen it only this morning—first in Mr Ghote's hand, and then in Mr Kulkarni's, who had locked it away in his safe.

I shone the torch on the piece of paper. It was another message from Feluda, this time addressed to Lalmohan Babu. 'Keep the head with you,' it said. 'If anyone demands it, hand it over to him.'

What could this mean? But there was no time to think. Lalmohan Babu said, 'Jai Guru!' and picked up the head. I put Feluda's message into my pocket, and we returned to our positions.

Our eyes were now getting used to the dark. There appeared to be a faint moonlight outside. We could see a portion of the western sky through the pillars. It had turned a deep purple. Gradually, it changed its hue. Perhaps the moon had risen higher. It didn't seem as dark inside the cave as before.

'Eight o'clock!' Lalmohan Babu muttered, letting go of a long sigh.

Suddenly, a faint noise reached my ears. Someone was coming up the stairs, placing each foot with extreme caution. Then the noise stopped. A second later, the footsteps continued. The man was now walking on flat ground, among the pillars. There, now he was visible through a couple of pillars. He stopped, and looked around. Then, with a click, he lit a lighter. The small flame went out almost as soon as it had appeared, but it was enough to illuminate his face. We recognized him instantly.

Jayant Mallik!

How could he be here? He was supposed to be in police custody. My head began reeling. After this, I thought, if the dead Shubhankar Bose turned up in person, I should not be surprised.

Mr Mallik resumed walking, but did not come toward us. He made his way to the north-eastern corner. That part of the hall was in total darkness. He disappeared from sight.

My throat felt dry. I could hardly think clearly. Only one thing kept going round and round in my head. Where was Feluda Where was Feluda? Where was Feluda? Lalmohan Babu had once declared he would give up writing crime stories because his real-life experiences were so much stranger. What would he say after today?

The moonlight grew stronger as we waited. A dog barked somewhere in the distance. Then it was quiet once more.

But not for long. A second man was climbing up the steps. Like Mr Mallik, he stopped for a moment on reaching the flat surface where the stairs ended. Then we could see him walking, but could not tell who he was. He did not stop to use a lighter.

He was coming towards us, getting closer and closer, walking with slow, measured steps. Then, without the slightest warning, our eyes were dazzled by a powerful light. The man was shining a torch directly into our eyes. The footsteps came even closer, and a voice spoke, softly, but with biting sarcasm.

'Dreaming of the moon, weren't you, you puny little dwarf? Who taught you to write threatening letters? "Come to the Das Avatar cave at 8 p.m. . . . then you'll get back what you've lost, or else . . ." where did you learn all this, Professor? A professor of history, didn't you say? Can you hear me now? Or are you still pretending to be deaf? How did you get involved in this, anyway? You had noted everything down in your notebook, hadn't you? I saw it myself—"a Fokker Friendship crashes", "a yakshi from Bhubaneshwar gets stolen", "the Kailash temple in Ellora", even plane timings . . . ! Why have you got a child with you? Is he your bodyguard? Can you see what I've got in my right hand?'

I had recognized the voice as soon as it had started to speak. It was Mr Raxit. In his left hand was a torch. In his right was a pistol.

'I . . . I . . .' Lalmohan Babu stammered.

'Stop whimpering!' Mr Raxit's voice boomed out. 'Where's the real thing?'

'Here it is. I kept it for you,' Lalmohan Babu offered him the yakshi's head.

Mr Raxit took it with his left hand, making sure his right hand did not waver. 'Not everyone can play this game, do you understand?' he went on, still sounding furious. 'It's not for the likes of you, you stupid little—' he broke off.

A strange thing had started to happen. Great clouds of smoke were coming into the cave, spiralling up and slowly enveloping everything—the pillars, the carvings, the statues. As we stood gaping in absolute amazement at this thick sheet of haze, another voice rang out, almost like a bullet. It was Feluda.

'Mr Raxit!' he called, his voice as cold and hard as the stony floor we were standing on. 'Not one, but two revolvers are pointing at you at this very moment. Put your gun down. Go on, throw it down.'

'What . . . what's the meaning of this?' Mr Raxit cried, his voice suddenly uncertain.

'Let me explain,' Feluda replied. 'We are here to punish you for your crime, and it isn't just one crime, either. First, you destroyed and damaged a part of India's history. Second, you sold bits of your—and our—own heritage to foreigners. Third, you killed Shubhankar Bose.'

'No! Lies, these are all lies!' Mr Raxit shrieked. 'Bose slipped and fell into the gorge. It was an accident.'

'If anyone is lying, it is you. The crowbar you had used has been found behind a cactus bush fifty yards from where Bose's body was found. It is heavily stained with blood. Had Mr Bose slipped and fallen by accident, he would certainly have screamed for help. None of the guards here heard a scream. Besides, you had hidden a blue shirt among the plants behind the bungalow where we were all staying. A portion of this shirt is torn. I found it. The piece of blue fabric Bose was found clutching is the same—'

Mr Raxit did not stop to hear any more. He leapt up and tried to dash out of the smoky curtain, only to find himself being embraced by three different men. To our right, Jayant Mallik lit his torch. Now I could see Feluda, who had taken off his make-up. Next to him was Mr Ghote and a constable. At a nod from him, the constable put handcuffs on Mr Raxit.

Feluda turned to Mr Mallik. 'I must ask you to do something for me,' he said. 'See that other cave over there? You'll find Mr Raxit's raincoat in it, tucked away in the left-hand corner. Could you get it for me, please? Well, we mustn't stay in this smoke any longer. Come along, Topshe. Are you all right, Lalmohan Babu? This way, please.'

Feluda explained everything to us over dinner that night. We had dinner at the guest house. With us were Mr Kulkarni, Mr Ghote and Mr Mallik.

'The first thing I should tell you,' Feluda began, 'is that Raxit isn't his real name. His real name is Chattoraj. He is a member of a gang of criminals, who operate from Delhi. Their main aim is to steal valuable statues, or even parts of statues, from old temples, and sell them to foreign buyers, thereby filling their own pockets with tidy little sums. There must be many other gangs like this one, but at least we have managed to get hold of one. Chattoraj was made to come clean, and he gave us all the details we needed. It was he who had stolen that head, brought it to Calcutta and sold it to Silverstein. Then, when he heard of the plane crash, he rushed to the spot, bought it back from that boy called Panu for just ten rupees, and then chased Lewison all the way to Ellora. He wanted to kill two birds with one stone. The yakshi's head could be sold to Lewison, and Chattoraj could steal another statue from Kailash. Sadly for him, he didn't manage to do either of these things. Lewison agreed to buy the stolen statue, but Chattoraj lost it before he could pass it on to Lewison. As a result, Lewison got very cross with him and left. He might have succeeded in removing a statue from Kailash, but two things stopped him. One was the sudden appearance of Shubhankar Bose. The other was a small pebble, thrown on the courtyard before cave number fifteen.'

Feluda stopped for breath. I started feeling most confused. 'What about Mr Mallik?' I blurted out.

Feluda smiled. 'The presence of Jayant Mallik can be very easily explained. In fact, it was so simple that even I could not figure it out at first. Mr Mallik was simply following Chattoraj.

'Why?'

'For the same reason that I was chasing him! He wanted to retrieve the statue, like me. But that isn't all. He and I do the same job. Yes, he's a private detective, just like me.'

I cast a startled glance at Mr Mallik. He said nothing, but I saw that he was grinning, looking at Feluda and waiting for him to explain further.

'When I made enquiries about him,' Feluda went on, 'I discovered that he worked for an agency in Bombay. They sent him to Calcutta recently, in connection with a case. He stayed in a friend's flat in Queen's Mansion, and used his car while the friend was away on holiday. Normally, the kind of cases these agencies handle are all ordinary and pretty insignificant. Mr Mallik was getting bored with his job. He wanted to do something exciting, much more worthwhile and become famous. Is that right?'

'Yes.' Mr Mallik admitted. 'I got the chance to work on such a case, most unexpectedly. My old job took me to the Grand Hotel last Thursday, and I happened to be in Nagarmal's shop when an American visitor showed that yakshi's head to him. At that time, I paid no attention. All that I grasped was that the man was immensely wealthy, and his name was Silverstein. But, when I heard about the plane crash the next morning and they said he had been on that flight, it suddenly struck me that it might be possible to retrieve that statue. I have a little knowledge of ancient art, and I knew that what I had seen Silverstein carrying was extremely valuable. So I thought if I could get it back, it might be reported in the press, which would be a good thing for the agency as well. So I rang my boss in Bombay and told him what I wanted to do. He agreed, and asked me to keep him posted. I left for Sidikpur immediately, but it was too late. I missed Chattoraj by just five minutes. He got there first and bought the head back. There didn't seem to be anything I could do, but—'

'Do you remember the colour of his car?' Feluda interrupted him.

'Oh yes. It was a blue Fiat. I decided to follow Chattoraj. But I ran into some more problems. A burst tyre meant an unnecessary delay . . . so I lost him for the moment. However, by then I was absolutely determined not to give up. I knew he'd want to sell the statue again. So I went back to the Grand Hotel. It meant waiting for a while, but eventually I found him and followed him to the Railway Booking Office. He bought a ticket to Aurangabad. So did I. He was still carrying a heavy bag, so it was clear that he had not been able to get rid of the statue. I came back to my flat, rang my office in Bombay and told them what had happened.'

'Yes, we know about that. You had said, "The daughter has returned to her father". What we did not know was that by "father" you meant Chattoraj, not yourself.'

Mr Mallik smiled, then continued, 'I kept waiting for a suitable opportunity to remove the stolen object. I knew if I could catch the thief at the same time, it would be even better. But that proved much too difficult. Anyway, last night I went and hid near Kailash. When I saw that everyone from the bungalow had gone out in the direction of the caves, I returned quickly, slipped into the bungalow through the side door that only the cleaners use, and removed the statue from Chattoraj's room.'

'I see. Did you have any idea you were being watched by a detective?'

'Oh no. That's why I couldn't speak a word when you arrested me! I must have looked very foolish.'

Mr Ghote burst out laughing. Feluda took up the tale, 'When I saw that you had travelled with Lewison in the same car for many miles, but had done nothing to sell him the statue, I realized you were innocent. Until then, although I'd come to know you were a detective, I could not drop you from my list of suspects.'

'But Chattoraj was also on this list, wasn't he?'

'Yes. Mind you, initially it was no more then a slight doubt. When I saw that this his name had been freshly painted on an old suitcase, I began to wonder if the name wasn't fake. Then, Lalmohan Babu told us yesterday that he had gone out wearing a raincoat. When we were passing cave number fifteen, I noticed someone was in it, and threw a pebble in the courtyard. That made the man run away. I then went into the cave and began searching the surrounding area. In a smaller cave behind the big one, I found the raincoat. It had a specially large pocket, in which was a hammer, a chisel and a nylon rope. I left everything there. It became obvious that Raxit—or Chattoraj—was the real culprit. As we returned to the bungalow, we saw him desperately searching for something in his room. In fact, he seemed to have gone mad, which is understandable since he had come back to his room to find that his precious statue had gone. This morning, Mr Kulkarni told me you had called Bombay and said, "The daughter is fine". That meant you had the stolen statue with you. So you had to be arrested.'

Feluda stopped. No one said anything. After a short pause, he went on, 'While we were worrying about statues and thieves, Shubhankar Bose got killed. On examining his dead body, we found a piece of blue cloth in one of his hands. You were wearing a blue-shirt yesterday. But I didn't think of you, since my suspicions had already fallen on Chattoraj. What really happened was that he reached Bose's body before me and, pretending that he was trying to feel his pulse, pushed in that torn piece into the dead man's hand. It had become essential for Chattoraj to throw suspicion on someone else for Bose's death. The torn piece had, of course, come from Chattoraj's own shirt. He had cut out a piece and hidden the shirt amongst the plants and bushes behind the bungalow. I found it myself.

'However, although I had gathered some evidence against Chattoraj, it was not enough to actually accuse him of murder and theft. As I was wondering what to do, Tapesh and Lalmohan Babu told me that someone had been through their belongings. This had to be Chattoraj, for he had lost something valuable and was naturally looking for it everywhere. In Lalmohan Babu's suitcase was his notebook, which mentioned the theft of the statue from Bhubaneshwar, Silverstein and the plane crash. I knew at once that Chattoraj had read every detail and was feeling threatened, thinking it was Lalmohan Babu who had stumbled on the truth. So I sent him a little note, pretending it had been written by Lalmohan Babu, asking Chattoraj to meet him in the Das Avatar cave at 8 p.m. Before that, however, I told Chattoraj that whoever had tried to steal a statue from Kailash the night before had been arrested. I knew this would set his mind at rest, and he would stop being on his guard.'

'That man with the goatee!' Lalmohan Babu and I cried together, 'Was that you?'

'Yes,' Feluda laughed. 'That was my disguise number two. I felt I had to stay close to you, since we were dealing with a dangerous man. Anyway, he swallowed my bait at once. He thought a few sharp words from him would really make Lalmohan Babu return the head to him, and he could get away with it once again. Well, we all know what happened next.

'There is only one thing left for me to say: Mr Mallik and his agency will get full credit for their share in catching this gang. And I will pray for a promotion for Mr Ghote. I must also thank Mr Kulkarni for the important role he played, but if a medal for courage and bravery could be given to anyone, it should go jointly to Tapeshranjan Mitter and Lalmohan Ganguli.'

'Hear, hear!' said Mr Mallik, and the others clapped enthusiastically.

When the applause died down, Lalmohan Babu turned to Feluda and said a little hesitantly, 'Does that mean . . . this time my weapon didn't come into any use at all?'

Feluda looked perfectly amazed. 'Not come into use? What are you talking about? Where do you think all that smoke came from? It was no ordinary bomb, sir. Do you know what it was? A three hundred and fifty-six megaton special military smoke bomb!'

The Key

ONE

The Key

ONE

'Do you know why the sight of trees and plants have such a refreshing effect on our eyes?' asked Feluda. 'The reason is that people, since primitive times, have lived with greenery all around them, so that their eyes have developed a healthy relationship with their environment. Of course, trees in big cities these days have become rather difficult to find. As a result, every time you get away from town, your eyes begin to relax, and so does your mind. It is mostly in cities that you'll notice people with eye disorders. Go to a village or a hill-station, and you'll hardly find anyone wearing glasses.'

Feluda himself had a pair of sharp eyes, didn't wear glasses, and could stare at any object for three minutes and fifteen seconds without blinking even once. I should know, for I had tested him often enough. But he had never lived in a village. I was tempted to point this out to him, but didn't dare. The chances of having my head bitten off if I did were very high.

We were travelling with a man called Monimohan Samaddar. He wore glasses (but then, he lived in a city), was about fifty years old and had sharp features. The hair around his ears had started to turn grey. It was in his Fiat that we were travelling, to a place called Bamungachhi, which was a suburb of Calcutta. We had met Moni Babu only yesterday.

He had turned up quite out of the blue in the afternoon, as Feluda and I sat in our living room, reading. I had been watching Feluda reading a book on numerology, raising his eyebrows occasionally in both amazement and appreciation. It was a book about Dr Matrix. Feluda caught me looking at him, and smiled. 'You'd be astonished to learn the power of numbers, and the role they play in the lives of men like Dr Matrix. Listen to this. It was a discovery Dr Matrix made. You know the names of the two American Presidents who were assassinated, don't you?'

'Yes. Lincoln and Kennedy, right?'

'Right. Now tell me how many letters each name has.'

'L-i-n-c-o-l-n—seven. K-e-n-n-e-d-y—also seven.'

'OK. Now listen, carefully. Lincoln was killed in 1865 and Kennedy died in 1963, a little less than a hundred years later. Both were killed on a Friday, and both had their wives by their side. Lincoln was killed in the Ford Theatre. Kennedy was killed in a car called Lincoln, manufactured by the Ford company. The next President after Lincoln was called Johnson, Andrew Johnson. Kennedy was succeeded by Lyndon Johnson. The first Johnson was born in 1808, the second in 1908, exactly a hundred years later. Do you know who killed Lincoln?'

'Yes, but I can't remember his name right now.'

'It was John Wilkes Booth. He was born in 1839. And Kennedy was killed by Lee Harvey Oswald. He was born in 1939! Now count the number of letters in both names.'

'Good heavens, both have fifteen letters!'

Feluda might have told me of a few more startling discoveries by Dr Matrix, but it was at this point that Mr Samaddar arrived, without a prior appointment. He introduced himself, adding, 'I live in Lake Place, which isn't far from here.'

'I see.'

'Er . . . you may have heard of my uncle, Radharaman Samaddar.'

'Oh yes. He died recently, didn't he? I believe he was greatly interested in music?'

'Yes, that's right.'

'I read an obituary in the local newspaper. I hadn't heard about him before that, I'm afraid. He was quite old, wasn't he?'

'Yes, he was eighty-two when he died. I'm not surprised that you hadn't heard of him. When he gave up singing, you must have been a young boy. He retired fifteen years ago, and built a house in Bamungachhi. That is where he lived, almost like a recluse, until his death. He had a heart attack on 18 September, and died the same night.'

'I see.'

Mr Samaddar cleared his throat. After a few seconds of silence, he said a little hesitantly, 'I'm sure you're wondering why I've come to disturb you like this. I just wanted to give you a little background, that's all.'

'Of course. Don't worry, Mr Samaddar, please take your time.'

Moni Babu resumed speaking. 'My uncle was different from other men. He was actually a lawyer, and he made a lot of money. But he stopped practising when he was about fifty, and turned wholly to music. He didn't just sing, he could play seven or eight different instruments, both Indian and Western. I myself have seen him play the sitar, the violin, piano, harmonium, flute and the tabla, besides others. He had a passion for collecting instruments. In fact, his house had become a mini-museum of musical instruments.'

'Which house do you mean?'

'He had started collecting before he left Calcutta. Then he transferred his collection to his house in Bamungachhi. He used to travel widely, looking for instruments. Once he bought a violin from an Italian in Bombay. Only a few months later, he sold it in Calcutta for thirty thousand rupees.'

Feluda had once told me that three hundred years ago, in Italy there had been a handful of people who had produced violins of such high quality that, today, their value was in excess of a hundred thousand rupees.

Mr Samaddar continued to speak. 'As you can see, my uncle was gifted. There were a lot of positive qualities in his character that made him different from most people. But, at the same time, there was an overriding negative factor which eventually turned him into a recluse. He was amazingly tight-fisted. The few relatives he had stopped seeing him because of this. He didn't seem to mind, for he wasn't particularly interested in staying in touch with them, anyway.'

'How many relatives did he have?'

'Not a lot. He had three brothers and two sisters. The sisters and two of his brothers are no more. The third brother left home thirty years ago. No one knows if he's alive. Radharaman's wife and only child, a son called Muralidhar, are both dead. Muralidhar's son, Dharanidhar, is his only grandchild. Radharaman was very fond of him once. But when he left his studies and joined a theatre under a different name, my uncle washed his hands off him. I don't think he ever saw him again.'

'How are you related to him?'

'Oh, my father was one of his elder brothers. He died many years ago.'

'I see; and is Dharanidhar still alive?'

'Yes, but I believe he's moved on to another group, and is now doing a jatra. I tried contacting him when my uncle passed away, but he wasn't in Calcutta. Someone told me he was off on a tour, travelling through small villages. He's quite well known now in the theatre world. He was interested in music, too, which was why his grandfather was so fond of him.'

Mr Samaddar stopped. Then he went on, speaking a little absently. 'It's not as if I saw my uncle regularly. I used to go and meet

him, maybe once every two months or so. Of late, even that had
become difficult as my work kept me very busy. I run a printing press
in Bhawanipore, called the Eureka Press. We've had such frequent
power cuts recently that it's been quite a job clearing all our backlog.
Anyway, my uncle's neighbour, Abani Babu, telephoned me when he
had a heart attack. I left immediately with Chintamoni Bose, the
heart specialist. My uncle was unconscious at first, but opened his
eyes just before he died, and seemed to recognize me. He even spoke
a few words, but then . . . it was all over.'

'What did he say?' Feluda leant forward.

'He said, "In . . . my . . . name." Then he tried to speak, but
couldn't. After struggling for sometime, he could get only one word
out. "Key . . . key," he said. That was all.'

Feluda stared at Mr Samaddar, a frown on his face. 'Have you any
idea what his words might have meant?'

'Well, at first I thought perhaps he was worried about his name,
and his reputation. Perhaps he'd realized people called him a miser.
But the word "key" seemed to matter to him. I mean, he sounded
really concerned about this key. I haven't the slightest idea which key
he was referring to. His bedroom has an almirah and a chest. The
keys to these were kept in the drawer of a table that stood by the side
of his bed. The house only has three rooms, barring a bathroom
attached to his bedroom. There is hardly any furniture, and almost
nothing that might require a key. The lock he used on the main door
to his bedroom was a German combination lock, which didn't work
with a key at all.'

'What did he have in the almirah and the chest?'

'Nothing apart from a few clothes and papers. These were in the
almirah. The chest was totally empty.'

'Did you find any money?'

'No. In the drawer of the table was some loose change and a few
two and five rupee notes, that's all. There was a wallet under his
pillow, but even this had very little money in it. Apparently, he kept
money for daily use in this wallet. At least, that's what his old
servant Anukul told me.'

'What did he do when he finished spending what he had in his
wallet or in his table drawer? Surely he had a bigger source to draw
on?'

'Yes, that's what one has to assume.'

'Why do you say that? Didn't he have a bank account?'

Mr Samaddar smiled. 'No, he didn't. If he had had one, there would've been nothing unusual about him, would there? To tell you the truth, there was a time when he did keep his money in a bank. But many years ago, that bank went out of business, and he lost all he had put in it. He refused to trust another bank after that. But—' Mr Samaddar lowered his voice, 'I know he had a lot of money. How else do you suppose he could afford to buy all those rare and expensive instruments? Besides, he didn't mind spending a great deal on himself. He ate well, wore specially tailored clothes, maintained a huge garden, and had even bought a second hand Austin. He used to drive to Calcutta occasionally. So . . .' His voice trailed away.

Feluda lit a Charminar, and offered one to Mr Samaddar. Mr Samaddar took it, and waited until Feluda had lit it for him. 'Now,' he said, inhaling deeply, 'do you understand why I had to come to you? What will the key unlock? Where has all my uncle's money gone? Which key was he talking about, anyway? Shall we find any money or something else? Had he made a will? Who knows? If he had, we must find it. In the absence of a will, his grandson will get everything, but someone has to find out what that consists of. I have heard such a lot about your intelligence and your skill. Will you please help me, Mr Mitter?'

Feluda agreed. It was then decided that Mr Samaddar would pick us up today at 7 a.m. and take us to his uncle's house in Bamungachhi. I could tell Feluda was interested because this was a new type of mystery. Or perhaps it was more a puzzle than a mystery.

That is what I thought at first. Later, I realized it was something far more complex than a mere puzzle.

TWO

We drove down Jessore Road, and took a right turn after Barasat. This road led straight to Bamungachhi. Mr Samaddar stopped here at a small tea shop and treated us to a cup of tea and jalebis. This took about fifteen minutes. By the time we reached Radharaman Samaddar's house, it was past eight o'clock.

A bungalow stood in the middle of a huge plot of land (it measured seven acres, we were told later), surrounded by a pink boundary wall and rows of eucalyptus trees. The man who opened the gate for us was probably the mali, for he had a basket in his hand. We drove up to the front door, passing a garage on the way. A black Austin stood in it.

As I was getting out of the car, a sudden noise from the garden made me look up quickly. I found a boy of about ten standing a few yards away, wearing blue shorts and clutching an air gun. He returned my stare gravely.

'Is your father at home?' asked Mr Samaddar. 'Go tell him Moni Babu from Calcutta has come back, and would like to see him, if he doesn't mind.'

The boy left, loading his gun.

'Is that the neighbour's son?' Feluda asked.

'Yes. His father, Abani Sen, is a florist. He has a shop in New Market in Calcutta. He lives right next door. He has his nursery here, you see. Occasionally, he comes and spends a few weeks with his family.'

An old man emerged from the house, looking at us enquiringly. 'This is Anukul,' Mr Samaddar said. 'He had worked for my uncle for over thirty years. He'll stay on until we know what should be done about the house.'

There was a small hall behind the front door. It couldn't really be called a room, all it had was a round table in the middle, and a torn calendar on the wall. There were no light switches on the wall as the whole area did not receive any electricity at all. Beyond this hall was a door. Mr Samaddar walked over to it, and said, 'Look, this is the German lock I told you about. One could buy a lock like this in Calcutta before the Second World War. The combination is eight-two-nine-one.'

It was round in shape, with no provision for a key. There were four grooves instead. Against each groove were written numbers, from one to nine. A tiny object like a hook stuck out of each groove. This hook could be pushed from one end of the groove to the other. It could also be placed next to any of the numbers. It was impossible to open the lock unless one knew exactly which numbers the hooks should be placed against.

Mr Samaddar pushed the four hooks, each to rest against a different number—eight, two, nine and one. With a faint click, the lock opened. It seemed almost as though I was in a magic show. 'Locking the door is even easier,' said Mr Samaddar. 'All you need to do is push any of those hooks away from the right number. Then it locks automatically.'

The door with the German lock opened into Radharaman Samaddar's bedroom. It was a large room, and it contained all the furniture Radharaman's nephew had described. What was amazing was the number of instruments the room was packed with. Some of these were kept on shelves, others on a long bench and small tables. Some more hung on the wall.

Feluda stopped in the middle of the room and looked around for a few seconds. Then he opened the almirah and the chest, and went through both. This was followed by a search of the table drawers, a small trunk he discovered under the bed (all it revealed was a pair of old shoes and a few rags) and all the instruments in the room. Feluda picked them up, felt their weight and turned them over to see if any of them was meant to be operated by a key. Then he stripped the bed, turned the mattress over, and began tapping on the floor to see if any part of it sounded hollow. It didn't. It took him another minute to inspect the attached bathroom. He still found nothing. Finally, he said, 'Could you please ask the mali to come here for a minute?' When the mali came, he got him to remove the contents of two flower-pots kept under the window. Both pots were empty. 'All right, you can put everything back into those pots, and thank you,' he told the mali.

In the meantime, Anukul had placed a table and four chairs in the room. He then put four glasses of lemonade on the table, and withdrew. Mr Samaddar handed two glasses to us, and asked, 'What do you make of all this, Mr Mitter?' Feluda shook his head. 'If it wasn't for those instruments, it would've been impossible to believe that a man of means had lived in this room.'

'Exactly. Why do you suppose I ran to you for help? I've never felt so puzzled in my life!' Mr Samaddar exclaimed, taking a sip from his glass.

I looked at the instruments. I could recognize only a few like the sitar, sarod, tanpura, tabla and a flute. I had never seen any of the others, and I wasn't sure that Feluda had, either. 'Do you know what each one of these is called?' he asked Mr Samaddar. 'That string instrument that's hanging from a hook on the wall over there. Can you tell me its name?'

'No, sir!' Mr Samaddar laughed. 'I know nothing of music. I haven't the slightest idea of what these might be called, or where they came from.'

There were footsteps outside the room. A moment later, the boy with the airgun arrived with a man of about forty. Mr Samaddar did the introductions. The man was Abani Sen, the florist who lived next door. The boy was his son, Sadhan. 'Mr Pradosh Mitter?' he said. 'Of course I've heard of you!' Feluda gave a slight smile, and cleared his throat. Mr Sen took the empty chair and was offered the fourth glass of lemonade. 'Before I forget, Mr Samaddar,' he said, picking it up, 'do you know if your uncle had wanted to sell any of his instruments?'

'Why, no!' Mr Samaddar sounded quite taken aback.

'A gentleman came yesterday. He went to my house since he couldn't find anyone here. He's called Surajit Dasgupta. He collects musical instruments, very much like your uncle. He showed me a letter written by Radharaman Babu, and said he'd already been to this house and spoken to Radharaman Babu once. Anukul told me later he had seen him before. The letter had been written shortly before your uncle died. Anyway, I told him to come back today. I had a feeling you might return.'

'I have seen him, too.'

This came from Sadhan. He was playing with a small instrument that looked a bit like a harmonium, making slight tinkling noises. His father laughed at his words. 'Sadhan used to spend most of his time in or around this house. In fact, he still does. He and his Dadu were great friends.'

'How did you like your Dadu?' Feluda asked him.

'I liked him a lot,' Sadhan answered, with his back to us, 'but sometimes he annoyed me.'

'How?'

'He kept asking me to sing the sargam.'

'And you didn't want to?'

'No. But I can sing.'

'Ah, only songs from Hindi films.' Mr Sen laughed again.

'Did your Dadu know you could sing?'

'Yes.'

'Had he ever heard you?'

'No.'

'Well then, how do you think he knew?'

'Dadu often used to tell me that those whose names carry a note of melody are bound to have melodious voices.'

This made very little sense to us, so we exchanged puzzled glances.

'What did he mean by that?' Feluda asked.

'I don't know.'

'Did you ever hear him sing?'

'No. But I've heard him play.'

'What!' Mr Samaddar sounded amazed. 'Are you sure, Sadhan? I thought he had given up playing altogether. Did he play in front of you?'

'No, no. I was outside in the garden, killing coconuts with my gun. That's when I heard him play.'

'Could it have been someone else?'

'No, there was no one in the house except Dadu.'

'Did he play for a long time?' Feluda wanted to know.

'No, only for a little while.'

Feluda turned to Mr Samaddar. 'Could you please ask Anukul to come here?'

Anukul arrived in a few moments. 'Did you ever hear your master play any of these instruments?' Feluda asked him.

'Well . . .' Anukul replied, speaking hesitantly. 'My master spent most of his time in this room. He didn't like being disturbed. So really, sir, I wouldn't know whether he played or not.'

'I see. He never played in your presence, did he?'

'No, sir.'

'Did you ever hear anything from outside, or any other part of the house?'

'Well. . . only a few times . . . I think . . . but I can't hear very well, sir.'

'Did a stranger come and see him before he died? The same man who came yesterday?'

'Yes, sir. He spoke to my master in this room.'

'When did he first come?'

'The day he died.'

'What! That same day?' Mr Samaddar couldn't hide his surprise.

'Yes, sir.' Anukul had tears in his eyes. He wiped them with one end of his chaddar and said in a choked voice, 'I came in here soon after that gentleman left, to tell my Babu that the hot water for his bath was ready, but found him asleep. At least, I thought he was sleeping until I found I just couldn't wake him up. Then I went to Sen Babu's house and told him.'

'Yes, that's right,' Mr Sen put in. 'I rang Mr Samaddar immediately, and told him to bring a doctor. But I knew there wasn't much that a doctor could do.'

A car stopped outside. Anukul left to see who it was. A minute later, a man entered the room, and introduced himself as Surajit Dasgupta. He had a long and drooping moustache, broad side-burns and thick, unruly hair. He wore glasses with a very heavy frame. Mr Sen pointed at Mr Samaddar and said, 'You should speak to him, Mr Dasgupta. He's Radharaman Babu's nephew.'

'Oh, I see. Your uncle had written to me. So I came to meet—'

'Can I see that letter?' Mr Samaddar interrupted him.

Surajit Dasgupta took out a postcard from the inside pocket of his jacket and passed it on to Mr Samaddar. Mr Samaddar ran his eyes over it, and gave it to Feluda. I leant across and read what was written on it: 'Please come and meet me between 9 and 10 a.m. on 18 September. All my musical instruments are with me in my house. You can have a look when you come.' Feluda turned it over to take a quick look at the address: Minerva Hotel, Central Avenue, Calcutta 13. Then he glanced at the bottle of blue-black ink kept on the small table next to the bed. The letter did seem to have been written with the same ink.

Mr Dasgupta sat down on the bed, with an impatient air. Mr Samaddar asked him another question. 'What did you and my uncle discuss that morning?'

'Well, I had come to know about Radharaman Samaddar only after I read an article by him that was published in a magazine for music lovers. So I wrote to him, and came here on the eighteenth as requested. There were two instruments in his collection that I wanted to buy. We discussed their prices, and I made an offer of two thousand rupees for them. He agreed, and I started to write out a cheque at once. But he stopped me and said he'd much rather have cash. I wasn't carrying so much cash with me, so he told me to come back the following Wednesday. On Tuesday, I read in the papers that he had died. Then I had to leave for Dehra Dun. I got back the day before yesterday.'

'How did he seem that morning when you talked to him?' Mr Samaddar asked.

'Why, he seemed all right! But perhaps he had started to think that he wasn't going to live for long. Some of the things he said seemed to suggest that.'

'You didn't, by any chance, have an argument, did you?'

Mr Dasgupta remained silent for a few seconds. Then he said

coldly, 'Are you, holding me responsible for your uncle's heart attack?'

'No, I am not suggesting that you did anything deliberately,' Mr Samaddar returned, just as coolly. 'But he was taken ill just after you left, so . . .'

'I see. I can assure you, Mr Samaddar, your uncle was fine when I left him. Anyway, it shouldn't be difficult for you to make a decision about my offer. I have got the money with me.' He took out his wallet. 'Here's two thousand in cash. It would help if I could take the two instruments away today. I have to return to Dehra Dun tomorrow. That's where I live, you see. I do research in music'

'Which two do you mean?'

Mr Dasgupta rose and walked over to one of the instruments hanging on the wall. 'This is one. It's called *khamanche*, it's from Iran. I knew about this one, but hadn't seen it. It's quite an old instrument. And the other was—'

Mr Dasgupta moved to the opposite end of the room and stopped before the same instrument Sadhan had been playing with. 'This is the other instrument I wanted,' he said. 'It's called melochord. It was made in England. It is my belief that the manufacturers released only a few pieces, then stopped production for some reason. I had never seen it before, and since it's not possible to get it any more, I offered a thousand for it. Your uncle agreed to sell it to me for that amount.'

'Sorry, Mr Dasgupta, but you cannot have them,' said Feluda firmly. Mr Dasgupta wheeled around, and cast a sharp look at us all. Then his eyes came to rest on Feluda. 'Who are you?' he asked dryly.

'He is my friend,' Mr Samaddar replied, 'and he is right. We cannot let you buy either of these. You must appreciate the reason. After all, there is no evidence, is there, that my uncle had indeed agreed to sell them at the price you mentioned?'

Mr Dasgupta stood still like a statue, without saying a word. Then he strode out of the room as quickly as he could.

Feluda, too, rose to his feet, and walked slowly over to the instrument Mr Dasgupta had described as a *khamanche*. He didn't seen perturbed at all by Mr Dasgupta's sudden departure. The instrument looked a little like the small violins that are often sold to children by roadside hawkers, although of course it was much larger in size, and the round portion was beautifully carved. Then he went across to the melochord, and pressed its black and white keyboard. The sweet notes that rang out sounded like an odd mixture of the piano and the sitar.

'Is this the instrument you had heard your Dadu play?'

'Maybe.'

Sadhan seemed a very quiet and serious little boy, which was rather unusual for a boy of his age.

Feluda said nothing more to him, and moved on to open the almirah once more. He took put a sheaf of papers from a drawer, and asked Mr Samaddar, 'May I take these home? I think I need to go through them at some length.'

'Oh yes, sure. Is there anything else . . . ?'

'No, there's nothing else, thank you.'

When we left the room, I saw Sadhan staring out of the window, humming a strange tune. It was certainly not from a Hindi film.

THREE

'What do you think, Mr Mitter?' asked Mr Samaddar on our way back from Bamungachhi. 'Is there any hope of unravelling this mystery?'

'I need to think, Mr Samaddar. And I need to read these papers I took from your uncle's room. Maybe that'll help me understand the man better. Besides, I need to do a bit of reading and research on music and musical instruments. Please give me two days to sort myself out.'

This conversation was taking place in the car when we finally set off on our return journey. Feluda had spent a lot of time in searching the whole house a second time, but even that had yielded nothing.

'Yes, of course,' Mr Samaddar replied politely.

'You will have to help me with some dates.'

'Yes?'

'When did Radharaman's son Muralidhar die?'

'In 1945, twenty-eight years ago.'

'How old was his son at that time?'

'Dharani? He must have been seven or eight.'

'Did they always live in Calcutta?'

'No, Muralidhar used to work in Bihar. His wife came to live with us in Calcutta after Muralidhar died. When she passed away, Dharani was a college student. He was quite bright, but he began to change after his mother died. Very soon, he left college and joined a theatre group. A year later, my uncle moved to Bamungachhi. His house was built in—'

'—Nineteen fifty-nine. Yes, I saw that written on the main gate.'

Radharaman Samaddar's papers proved to be a collection of old letters, a few cash memos, two old prescriptions, a catalogue of musical instruments produced by a German company called Spiegler, musical notation written on pages torn out of a notebook, and press reviews of five plays, in which mention of a Sanjay Lahiri had been underlined with a blue pencil.

'Hm,' said Feluda, looking at the notation. 'The handwriting on these is the same as that in Surajit Dasgupta's letter.' Then he went through the catalogue and said, 'There's no mention of a melochord.' After reading the reviews, he remarked, 'Dharanidhar and this Sanjay Lahiri appear to be the same man. As far as I can see, although Radharaman refused to have anything to do with his grandson, he did collect information on him, especially if it was praise of his acting.'

Feluda put all the papers away carefully in a plastic bag, and rang a theatre journal called *Manchalok*, to find out which theatre group Sanjay Lahiri worked for. It turned out that the group was called the Modern Opera. Apparently, Sanjay Lahiri did all the lead roles. Feluda then rang their office, and was told that the group was currently away in Jalpaiguri. They would be back only after a week.

We went out after lunch. I had never had to go to so many different places, all on the same day! Feluda took me first to the National Museum. He didn't tell me why we were going there, and I didn't ask because he had sunk into silence and was cracking his knuckles. This clearly meant he was thinking hard, and was not to be disturbed. We went straight to the section for musical instruments. To be honest, I didn't even know the museum had such a section. It was packed with all kinds of instruments, going back to the time of the *Mahabharata*. Modern instruments were also displayed, although there was nothing that might have come from the West.

Then we went to two music shops, one in Free School Street, and the other in Lal Bazaar. Neither had heard of anything called melochord. 'Mr Samaddar was an old and valued customer,' said Mr Mondol of Mondol & Co. which had its shop in Lal Bazaar (Feluda had found one of their cash memos among Radharaman's papers yesterday). 'But no, we never sold him the instrument you are talking about. What does it look like? Is it a wind instrument like a clarinet?'

'No. It's more like a harmonium, but much smaller in size. The sound it gives out is a cross between a piano and a sitar.'

'How many octaves does it have?'

I knew the eight notes—sa re ga ma pa dha ni sa—made one octave. The large harmoniums in Mondol's shop had provision for as many as three octaves. When Feluda told him a melochord had only one octave, Mr Mondol shook his head and said, 'No, sir, I don't think we can help you. This instrument might well be only a toy. You may wish to check in the big toy shops in New Market.'

We thanked Mr Mondol and made our way to College Street. Feluda bought three books on music, and then we went off to find the office of *Manchalok*. We found it relatively easily, but it took us a long time to find a photograph of Sanjay Lahiri. Finally, Feluda dug out a crumpled photo from somewhere, and offered to pay for it. 'Oh, I can't ask you to pay for that picture, sir!' laughed the editor of the magazine. 'You are Felu Mitter, aren't you? It's a privilege to be able to help you.'

By the time we returned home after stopping at a café for a glass of lassi, it was 7.30 p.m. The whole area was plunged in darkness because of load shedding. Undaunted, Feluda lit a couple of candles and began leafing through his books. When the power came back at nine, he said to me, 'Topshe, could you please pop across to your friend Poltu's house, and ask him if I might borrow his harmonium just for this evening?'

It took me only a few minutes to bring the harmonium. When I went to bed quite late at night, Feluda was still playing it.

I had a strange dream that night. I saw myself standing before a huge iron door, in the middle of which was a very large hole. It was big enough for me to slip through; but instead of doing that, Feluda, Monimohan Samaddar and I were all trying to fit a massive key into it. And Surajit Dasgupta was dancing around, wearing a long robe, and singing, 'Eight-two-o-nine-one! Eight-two-o-nine-one!'

FOUR

Mr Samaddar had told us he'd give us a call the following Wednesday. However, he rang us a day earlier, on Tuesday, at 7 a.m. I answered the phone. When I told him to hold on while I went to get Feluda, he said, 'No, there's no need to do that. Just tell your cousin I'm going over to your house straightaway. Something urgent's cropped up.'

He arrived in fifteen minutes. 'Abani Sen rang from Bamungachhi. Someone broke into my uncle's room last night,' he said.

'Does anyone else know how to operate that German lock?' Feluda asked at once.

'Dharani used to know. I'm not sure about Abani Babu—no, I don't think he knows. But whoever broke in didn't use that door at all. He went in through the small outer door to the bathroom. You know, the one meant for cleaners.'

'But that door was bolted from inside. I saw that myself.'

'Maybe someone opened it after we left. Anyway, the good news is that he couldn't take anything. Anukul came to know almost as soon as he got into the house, and raised an alarm. Look, are you free now? Do you think you could go back to the house with me?'

'Yes, certainly. But tell me something. If you now saw Radharaman's grandson, Dharani, do you think you could recognize him?'

Mr Samaddar frowned. 'Well, I haven't seen him for years, but . . . yes, I think I could.'

Feluda went off to fetch the photo of Sanjay Lahiri. When he handed it over to Mr Samaddar, I saw that he had drawn a long moustache on Sanjay's face, and added a pair of glasses with a heavy frame. Mr Samaddar gave a start. 'Why,' he exclaimed, 'this looks like—!'

'Surajit Dasgupta?'

'Yes! But perhaps the nose is not quite the same. Anyway, there is a resemblance.'

'The photo is of your cousin Muralidhar's son. I only added a couple of things just to make it more interesting.'

'It's amazing. Actually, I did find it strange, when Dasgupta walked in yesterday. In fact, I wanted to ring you last night and tell you, but I got delayed at the press. We were working overtime, you see. But then, I wasn't absolutely sure. I hadn't seen Dharani for fifteen years, not even on the stage. I'm not interested in the theatre at all. If what you're suggesting is true . . .'

Feluda interrupted him, 'If what I'm suggesting is true, we have to prove two things. One—that Surajit Dasgupta doesn't exist in real life at all; and two—that Sanjay Lahiri left his group and returned to Calcutta a few days before your uncle's death. Topshe, get the number of Minerva Hotel, please.' The hotel informed us that a Surajit Dasgupta had indeed been staying there, but had checked out the day before. There was no point in calling the Modern Opera, for they had already told us Sanjay Lahiri was out of town.

On reaching Bamungachhi, Feluda inspected the house from outside, following the compound wall. Whoever came must have had to come in a car, park it at some distance and walk the rest of the way. Then he must have jumped over the wall. This couldn't have been very difficult, for there were trees everywhere, their overgrown branches leaning over the compound wall. The ground being totally dry, there were no footprints anywhere.

We then went to find Anukul. He wasn't feeling well and was resting in his room. What he told us, with some difficulty, was this: mosquitoes and an aching head had kept him awake last night. He could see the window of Radharaman's bedroom from where he lay. When he suddenly saw a light flickering in the room, he rose quickly and shouted, 'Who's there?' But before he could actually get to the room, he saw a figure slip out of the small side door to the bathroom and disappear in the dark. Anukul spent what was left of the night lying on the floor of his master's bedroom.

'I don't suppose you could recognize the fellow?' Mr Samaddar asked.

'No, sir. I'm an old man, sir, and I can't see all that well. Besides, it was a moonless night.'

Radharaman's bedroom appeared quite unharmed. Nothing seemed to have been touched. Even so, Feluda's face looked grim. 'Moni Babu,' he said, 'you'll have to inform the police. This house must be guarded from tonight. The intruder may well come back. Even if Surajit Dasgupta is not Sanjay Lahiri, he is our prime suspect. Some collectors are strangely determined. They'll do anything to get what they want.'

'I'll ring the police from next door. I happen to know the OC,' said Mr Samaddar and went out of the room busily.

Feluda picked up the melochord and began inspecting it closely. It was a sturdy little instrument. There were two panels on it, both beautifully engraved. Feluda turned it over and discovered an old and faded label. 'Spiegler,' he said. 'Made in Germany, not England.' Then he began playing it. Although he was no expert, the sound that filled the room was sweet and soothing. 'I wish I could break it open and see what's inside,' he said, putting it back on the table, 'and obviously I can't do that. The chances are that I'd find nothing, and the instrument would be totally destroyed. Dasgupta was prepared to pay a thousand rupees for it, imagine!'

Despite his splitting headache, Anukul got up and brought us some lemonade again. Feluda thanked him and took a few sips from his glass. Mr Samaddar returned at this moment. 'The police have been informed,' he told us. 'Two constables will be posted here from tonight. Abani Babu wasn't home. He and Sadhan have gone to Calcutta for the day.' ,

'I see. Well, tell me, Moni Babu, who—apart from yourself—knew about Radharaman's habit of hiding all his money?'

'Frankly, Mr Mitter, I realized the money was hidden only after his death. Abani Babu next door is aware that we're looking for my uncle's money, but I'm sure he hasn't any idea about the amount involved. If it was Dharani who came here disguised as Dasgupta, he may have learnt something that morning before my uncle died. In fact, I'm convinced Dharani had come only to ask for money. Then they must have had a row, and—' Mr Samaddar broke off.

Feluda looked at him steadily and said, '—And as a result of this row, your uncle had a heart attack. But that didn't stop Dharani. He searched the room before he left. Isn't that what you're thinking?'

'Yes. But I know he didn't find any money.'

'If he had, he wouldn't have returned posing as Surajit Dasgupta, right?'

'Right. Perhaps something made him think the money was hidden in one of those two instruments.'

'The melochord.'

Mr Samaddar gave Feluda a sharp glance. 'Do you really think so?'

'That's what my instincts are telling me. But I don't like taking shots in the dark. Besides, I can't forget your uncle's last words. He did use the word "key", didn't he? You are certain about that?'

Mr Samaddar began to look unsure. 'I don't know . . . that's what it sounded like,' he faltered, rubbing his hands in embarrassment. 'Or it could be that my uncle was talking pure nonsense. It could have been delirium, couldn't it? Maybe the word "key" has no significance at all.'

I felt a sudden stab of disappointment at these words. But Feluda remained unruffled. 'Delirium or not, there is money in this room,' he said. 'I can smell it. Finding a key is not really important. We've got to find the money.'

'How? What do you propose to do?'

'Just at this moment, I'd like to go back home. Please tell Anukul not to worry, I don't think anyone will try to break in during the day. All he needs to do is not let any stranger into the house. There will be those police constables at night. I must go back and think very hard. I can see a glimmer of light, but unless that grows brighter, there's nothing much I can do. May I please spend the night here?'

Mr Samaddar looked faintly surprised at this question. But he said immediately, 'Yes, of course, if that's what you want. Shall I come and collect you at 8 p.m.?'

'All right. Thank you, Moni Babu.'

'First of all, my boy, write down the name of the dead man.'

Feluda was back in his room, sitting on his bed. I was sitting in a chair next to him, a notebook on my lap and a pen in my hand.

'Radharaman Samaddar,' I wrote.

'What's his grandson called?'

'Dharanidhar Samaddar.'

'And the name he uses on the stage?'

'Sanjay Lahiri.'

'What's the name of the collector of musical instruments who lives in Dehra Dun?'

'Surajit Dasgupta.'

'Who's Radharaman's neighbour?'

'Abani Sen.'

'And his son?'

'Sadhan.'

'What were Radharaman's last words?'

'In my name . . . key . . . key.'

'What are the eight notes in the sargam?'

'Sa re ga ma pa dha ni sa.'

'Very well. Now go away and don't disturb me. Shut the door as you go. I am going to work now.'

I went to the living room and picked up one of my favourite books to read. An hour later, I heard Feluda dialling a number on the telephone extension in his room. Unable to contain myself, I tiptoed to the door of his room and eavesdropped shamelessly.

'Hello? Can I speak to Dr Chintamoni Bose, please?'

Feluda was calling the heart specialist who had accompanied Mr Samaddar the day Radharaman died. I returned to the living room, my curiosity satisfied. Ten minutes later, there was the sound of dialling again. I rose once more and listened at the door.

'Eureka Press? Who's speaking?'

This time, Feluda was calling Mr Samaddar's press. I didn't need to hear any more, so I went back to my book.

When our cook Srinath came in with the tea at four, Feluda was still in his room. By the time I had finished my tea and read a few more pages of my book, it was 4.35. I was now feeling more mystified than ever. What on earth could Feluda be doing, puzzling over those few words I had scribbled in a notebook? After all, there wasn't anything in them he didn't know already. Before I could think any further, Feluda opened his door and came out with a half-finished Charminar in his hand. 'My head's reeling, Topshe!' he exclaimed, a note of suppressed excitement in his voice. 'Who knew it would take me so long to work out the meaning of a few words spoken by a very old man at his deathbed?'

In reply, I could only stare dumbly at Feluda. What he had just said made no sense to me, but I could see that his face looked different, which could simply mean that the light he had seen earlier was now much stronger than a glimmer.

'Sa dha ni sa ni . . . notes from the sargam. Does that tell you anything?'

'No, Feluda. I've no idea what you're talking about.'

'Good. If you could catch my drift, one would have had to assume your level of intelligence was as high as Felu Mitter's.'

I was glad of the difference. I was perfectly happy being Feluda's satellite, and no more.

Feluda threw his cigarette away, and picked up the telephone once again.

'Hello? Mr Samaddar? Can you come over at once? Yes, yes, we have to go to Bamungachhi as soon as we can . . . I think I've finally got the answer . . . yes, melochord . . . that's the important thing to remember.'

Then he replaced the receiver and said seriously, 'There is a risk involved, Topshe. But I've got to take it, there is no other choice.'

FIVE

Mr Samaddar's driver was old, but that didn't stop him from driving at eighty-five kilometres per hour when we reached VIP Road. Feluda sat fidgeting, as though he would have liked to have driven faster. Soon, we had to reduce our speed as the road got narrower and more congested. However, only a little while later, it shot up to sixty, despite the fact that the road wasn't particularly good and it had started to get dark.

There was no one at the main gate of Radharaman's house. 'Perhaps it's not yet time for those police constables to have arrived,' Feluda remarked.

We found Sadhan in the garden with his airgun.

'Why, Sadhan Babu, what are you killing in the dark?' Feluda asked him, getting out of the car.

'Bats,' Sadhan replied promptly. There were a number of bats hanging from the branches of a peepul tree just outside the compound.

The sound of our car had brought Anukul to the front door. Mr Samaddar told him to light a lantern and began unlocking the German lock. 'I'm dying to learn how you solved the mystery,' he said. I could understand his feelings, for Feluda hadn't uttered a single word in the car. I, too, was bursting with curiosity.

Feluda refused to break his silence. Without a word, he stepped into the room and switched on a powerful torch, It shone first on the wall, then fell on the melochord, still resting peacefully on the small table. My heart began to beat faster. The white keys of the instrument gleamed in the light, making it seem as though it was grinning from ear to ear. Feluda did not move his arm. ,'Keys . . .' he said softly. 'Look at those keys. Radharaman didn't mean a lock and a key at all. He meant the keys of an instrument, like a piano, or—'

He couldn't finish speaking. What followed a split second later took my breath away. Even now, as I write about it, my hand trembles.

At Feluda's words, Mr Samaddar suddenly sprang in the air and pounced upon the melochord like a hungry tiger on its prey. Then he picked it up, struck at Feluda's head with it, knocked me over and ran out of the door.

Feluda had managed to raise his arms in the nick of time to protect his head. As a result, his arms took the blow, making him drop the torch and fall on the bed in pain. As I scrambled to my feet, I heard Mr Samaddar locking the door behind him. Even so, I rushed forward, to try and push it with my shoulder. Then I heard Feluda whisper, 'Bathroom.' I picked up the torch quickly, and we both sped out of the small bathroom door.

There was the sound of a car starting, followed by a bang. A confused babble greeted us as we emerged. I could hear Anukul shouting in dismay, and Abani Sen speaking to his son very crossly. By the time we reached the front door, the car had gone, but there was someone sitting on the driveway.

'What have you done, Sadhan?' Mr Sen was still scolding his son furiously. 'Why did do you that? It was wrong, utterly wrong—!'

Sadhan made a spirited reply in his thin childish voice, 'What could I do? He was trying to run away with Dadu's instrument!'

'He's quite right, Mr Sen,' Feluda said, panting a little. 'He's done us a big favour by injuring the culprit, though in the future he must learn to use his airgun more carefully. Please go back home and inform the police. The driver of that car must not be allowed to get away. Tell them its number is WMA 6164.'

Then he walked over to the figure sitting on the driveway and, together with Anukul, helped him to his feet. Mr Samaddar allowed himself to be half pushed and half dragged back into the house, without making any protest. A pellet from Sadhan's airgun had hit one corner of his forehead. The wound was still bleeding.

The melochord was still lying where it had fallen on the cobbled path. I picked it up carefully and took it back to the house.

Feluda, Mr Sen, Inspector Dinesh Guin from the Barasat police station and I were sitting in Radharaman's bedroom, drinking tea. A man—possibly a constable—stood at the door. Another sat huddled in a chair. This was our culprit, Monimohan Samaddar. The wound on his forehead was now dressed. Sadhan was also in the room, standing at the window and staring out. On a table in front of us was the melochord.

Feluda cleared his throat. He was now going to tell us how he had learnt the truth. His watch was broken, and one of his arms was badly scraped. He had found a bottle of Dettol in the bathroom, and dabbed his arm with it. Then he had tied a handkerchief around his arm. If he was still in pain, he did not show it.

He put his cup down and began speaking. 'I started to suspect Monimohan Samaddar only from this afternoon. But I had nothing to prove that my suspicions weren't baseless. So, unless he made a false move, I could not catch him. Fortunately, he lost his head in the end and played right into my hands. He could never have got away, but Sadhan helped me in catching him immediately . . . Something he told me about working late on Monday first made me suspicious, not at the time, but later. He said he got very late on Monday evening because he had to work overtime. This was odd since a friend of mine lives in the same area where his press is, and I have often heard him complain that they have long power cuts, always starting in the evening and lasting until quite late at night. So I rang the Eureka Press, and was told that no work had been done on Monday evening because of prolonged load shedding. Moni Babu himself had left the press in the afternoon, and no one had seen him return. This made me wonder if a man who had told me one lie hadn't also told me another. What if Radharaman's last words were different from what I had been led to believe? I remembered he wasn't the only one present at the time of his death. I rang Dr Chintamoni Bose, and learnt that what Radharaman had really said was, "Dharani . . . in my name . . . key . . . key." It was Dharani's name that Moni Babu had failed to mention. Dharani was, after all, Radharaman's only grandchild. He was still fond of him. If there were good reviews of his performance, Radharaman kept those press cuttings. So it was only natural that he should try to tell his grandson—and not his nephew—the secret about his money. I don't think he had even recognized his nephew. Nevertheless, it was his nephew who heard his last words. He could make out that Radharaman was talking about his hidden money. But he couldn't find a key anywhere, so he decided to come to me, the idea being that I would find out where the key was, and Moni Babu would grab all the money. Nobody knew if there was a will. If a will could not be found, everything Radharaman possessed would have gone directly to Dharani. In any case, I doubt very much if Radharaman would have considered leaving anything to his nephew. It is my belief that he wasn't particularly fond of Moni Babu.'

Feluda stopped. No one spoke. After a brief pause, he continued, 'Now, the question was, why did Moni Babu lie to me about working late on Monday? Was it because he spent Monday evening indulging in some criminal activity, which meant that he needed an alibi? Radharaman's room was broken into that same evening. Could the intruder have been Moni Babu himself? The more I thought about it, the more likely did it seem. He was the only one who could use the combination lock, go into the room, unbolt the bathroom door, then come out again and lock the main door to the bedroom. That small bathroom door was most definitely bolted from inside when I saw it during the day. No cleaner could have come in after we left since it's not being used at all. I suspect Moni Babu had worked out what his uncle had meant by the word "key", so he'd come back in the middle of the night to steal the melochord. Am I right?'

All of us turned to look at Mr Samaddar. He nodded without lifting his head. Feluda went on, 'Even if Moni Babu could get away with stealing the melochord, I am positive he could never have decoded the rest of Radharaman's message. I stumbled on the answer only this evening, and for that, too, I have to thank little Sadhan.'

We looked at Sadhan in surprise. He turned his head and stared at Feluda solemnly. 'Sadhan,' Feluda said, 'tell us once again what your Dadu said about music and people's names.'

'Those who have melody in their names,' Sadhan whispered, 'are bound to have melody in their voices.'

'Thank you. This is merely an example of Radharaman's extraordinary intelligence. "Those who have melody in their names," he said. All right, let's take a name. Take Sadhan, for instance. Sadhan Sen. If you take away some of the vowels, you get notes from the sargam—sa dha ni sa ni. When I realized this, a new idea struck me. His last words were "in my name . . . key". Could he have meant the keys on the melochord that corresponded with his own name? Radharaman—re dha re ma ni. Samaddar—sa ma dha dha re. Dharanidhar was a singer, too; and he had melody in his name as well—dha re ni dha re. What a very clever idea it was, simple yet ingenious. Radharaman was obviously interested in mechanical gadgets. That German combination lock is an example. The melochord was also made in Germany, by a company called Spiegler. It was made to order, possibly based on specifications supplied by Radharaman himself. It acted as his bank. Thank goodness Surajit Dasgupta hadn't walked away with it, although I'm sure Radharaman would have emptied its contents before handing it over. Maybe he didn't feel the need for a bank any more. Maybe he knew he didn't have long to live . . . I learnt two other things. Surajit Dasgupta is a genuine musician, absolutely passionate about music and instruments. The few books on music I have read in the last two days mentioned his name. I was quite mistaken in thinking it was Dharani in disguise. Dharani is truly away in Jalpaiguri, he hasn't the slightest idea of what's going on. What we have to do now is see if there is anything left for him to inherit. He wants to form his own group, according to an interview published in Manchalok. So I'm sure a windfall would be most welcome. Topshe, bring that lantern here.'

I picked up the lantern and brought it closer to the melochord. Feluda placed it on his lap. 'It's had to put up with some rough handling today,' he said, 'but it was designed so well that I don't think it was damaged in any way. Now let's see what Radharaman's brain and German craftsmanship has produced.' Feluda began pressing the keys that made up Radharaman's full name—re dha re ma ni sa ma dha dha re. A sweet note rang out with the pressing of every key. As Feluda pressed the last one, the right panel slid open silently. We leant over the instrument eagerly, to find that there was a deep compartment behind this panel, lined with red velvet, and packed with bundles of hundred rupee notes.

Sheer amazement turned us into statues for a few moments. Then Feluda began pulling out the bundles gently. 'I think we have at least fifty thousand here,' he said. 'Come on, Mr Sen, help me count it.'

A bemused Abani Sen rose to his feet and stepped forward. The light from the lantern fell on Feluda's face and caught the glint in his eye. I knew it wasn't greed, but the pure joy of being able to use his razor-sharp brain once more, and solve another mystery.

The Royal Bengal Mystery

Old Man hollow,
pace to follow,
people's tree.
Half ten, half again
century.
Rising sun,
whence it's done,
can't you see?
Between hands,
below them stands,
yours, it be.

Feluda said to me, 'When you write about our adventure in the
forest, you must start with this puzzle.'

'Why? We didn't get to know of the puzzle until we actually got
there!'

'I know. But this is just a technique, to tickle the fancy of the
reader.'

I wasn't happy with this answer. Feluda realized it, so a couple of
minutes later, he added, 'Anyone who reads that puzzle at the outset
will get the chance to use his own intelligence, you see.'

So I agreed to start my story with it. I should, however, point out
at once that it's no use trying to work out what it means. It's not easy
at all. In fact, it took even Feluda quite a long time to discover its
meaning, although when he eventually explained it to me, it seemed
simple enough.

In talking about our past experiences, I have so far used real
names and real places. This time, I have been specifically asked not
to do so. I had to turn to Feluda for advice on fictitious names I
might use. 'You can mention the place was near the border of
Bhutan, there's no harm in that,' Feluda said, 'but you can change its
name to Laxmanbari. The chief character might be called Mr
Sinha-Roy. Many old zamindar families used to have that name. In
fact, some of them originally came from Rajputana. They came to
Bengal and joined the army of Todar Mal to fight the Pathans. Then
they simply stayed on, and their descendants became Bengalis.'

I am doing what Feluda told me to do. The names of places and
people are fictitious, but not the events. I shall try to relate

everything exactly as I saw or heard it.

The story began in Calcutta. It was Sunday, 27 May. The time was 9.30 a.m. My summer holidays had started. Of late, the maximum temperature had hit 100°F, so I was keeping myself indoors, pasting stamps from Bhutan into my stamp album. Feluda had recently finished solving a murder case (catching the culprit by using a common pin as a clue), which had made him quite famous. He had also been paid a fat fee. At this moment he was resting at home, stretched out on a divan, reading Thor Heyerdahl's *Aku-Aku*. A minute later, Jatayu turned up.

Lalmohan Ganguli—alias Jatayu—the writer of immensely popular crime thrillers, had started visiting us at least twice a month. The popularity of his novels meant that he was pretty well off. As a matter of fact, he was once rather proud of his writing prowess. But when Feluda pointed out dozens of factual errors in his books, Lalmohan Babu began to look upon him with a mixture of respect and admiration. Now, he got his manuscripts corrected by Feluda before passing them on to his publisher.

Today, however, he was not carrying a sheaf of papers under his arm, which clearly meant that there was a different reason for his visit. He sat down on a sofa, took out a green face towel from his pocket, wiped his face with it, and said without looking at Feluda, 'Would you like to see a forest, Felu Babu?'

Feluda raised himself a little, leaning on his elbow. 'What is your definition of a forest?'

'The same as yours, Felu Babu. Cluster of trees. Dense foliage. That sort of thing.'

'In West Bengal?'

'Yes, sir.'

'Where? I can't think of any place other than the Sunderbans, or Terai. Everything else has been wiped clean.'

'Have you heard of Mahitosh Sinha-Roy?'

The question was accompanied by a rather smug smile. I had heard of him, too. He was a well-known shikari and a writer. Feluda had one of his books. I hadn't read it, but Feluda had told me it was most interesting.

'Doesn't he live in Orissa, or is it Assam?' Feluda asked.

'No, sir,' Lalmohan Babu replied, taking out an envelope from his pocket with a flourish, 'he lives in the Dooars Forest, near the border of Bhutan. I dedicated my latest book to him. We have exchanged letters.'

'Oh? You mean you dedicate your books even to the living?'

Perhaps I should explain here the business of Lalmohan Babu's dedications. Nearly all of them are made to famous people who are now dead. *The Antarctic Anthropophagi* was dedicated to the memory of Robert Scott; *The Gorilla's Grasp* said, 'In the memory of David Livingstone', and *The Atomic Demon* (which Feluda said was the most nonsensical stuff he had ever read) had been dedicated to Einstein. Then, when he wrote *The Himalayan Hemlock*, he dedicated it to the memory of Sir Edmund Hillary. Feluda was furious at this.

'Why, Lalmohan Babu, why did you have to kill a man who is very much alive?'

'What! Hillary is alive?' Lalmohan Babu asked, looking both apologetic and embarrassed, 'I didn't know. I mean . . . he hasn't been in the news for a long time, and he does go about climbing mountains, doesn't he? So I thought perhaps he had slipped and . . . well, you know . . .' His voice trailed away.

The mistake was rectified when the second edition of the book came out.

Mahitosh Sinha-Roy might be a well-known shikari, but was he really as famous as all these other people? Why was the last book dedicated to him?

'Well, you see,' Lalmohan Babu explained, 'I had to consult his book *The Tiger and the Gun* quite a few times when I was writing my own. In fact,' he added with a smile, 'I used a whole episode. So I felt I had to please him in some way.'

'Did you succeed?'

Lalmohan Babu took out the letter from its envelope. 'Yes. He wouldn't send an invitation otherwise, would he?'

'Well, he may have invited you, but surely he didn't include me?'

Lalmohan Babu looked faintly annoyed. 'Look, Felu Babu,' he said, frowning, 'I know you would never go anywhere unless you were invited. You are well known yourself, and you have your prestige. I am well aware of that. What happened was that I told him that the book had seen four editions in four months. And I also told him—only a hint, that is—that I knew you. So he sent me this letter. Read it yourself. We've both been invited.'

The last few lines of Mahitosh Sinha-Roy's letter said, 'I believe your friend Pradosh Mitter is a very clever detective. If you can bring him with you, he might be able to help me out in a certain matter. Please let me know if he agrees to come.'

Feluda stared at the letter for a few moments. Then he said, 'Is he an old man?'

'What do you mean by old?' Lalmohan Babu asked, his eyes half-closed.

'Say, around seventy?'

'No, sir. Mr Sinha-Roy is much younger than that.'

'His writing is like an old man's.'

'How can you say that? This writing is absolutely beautiful.'

'I agree. But look at the signature. I think the letter was written by his secretary.'

It was decided that we would leave for Laxmanbari the following Wednesday. We could go up to New Jalpaiguri by train. After that we'd have to go by car to Laxmanbari, which was forty-six miles away. Mahitosh Babu had already offered to send his own car to collect us at the New Jalpaiguri station.

It came as no surprise to me that Feluda agreed to visit a forest so readily. My own heart was jumping with joy. The fact was that one of our uncles was a shikari as well. Our ancestral home was in the village of Shonadeeghi, near Dhaka. My father was the youngest of three brothers. The oldest worked as the manager of an estate in Mymansinh. He was renowned in the area for having killed wild deer, boars and even tigers in the Madhupur forest to the north of Mymansinh. The second brother—Feluda's father—used to teach mathematics and Sanskrit in a school. However, that did not stop him from being terrific at sports, including swimming, wrestling and shooting. Unfortunately, he died very young after only a brief spell of illness. Feluda was nine years old at the time. Naturally, his father's death came as an enormous shock to everyone. Feluda was brought to our house and raised by my parents. My own father has never shown any interest in anything that calls for great physical strength, but I do know that his will power and mental strength is much stronger than most people's.

Feluda himself has always been fascinated by tales of shikar. He has read every book written by Corbett and Kenneth Anderson. Although he's never been on a shikar, he did learn to shoot and is now a crack shot. There is no doubt in my mind that he could easily kill a tiger, should he be required to do so. He has often told me that the mind of an animal is a lot less complex than that of humans. Even the simplest of men would have a more complex mind than a ferocious tiger. Catching a criminal was, therefore, no less difficult than killing a tiger.

Feluda was trying to explain this to Lalmohan Babu in the train. Lalmohan Babu was carrying the first book Mahitosh Sinha-Roy had written. The front page had a photograph of the writer, which showed him standing with one foot on a dead Royal Bengal tiger, a rifle in his hand. His face wasn't clear, but it was easy to spot the set of his jaws, his broad shoulders and an impressive moustache under a sharp, long nose.

Lalmohan Babu stared at the photo for a few seconds and said, 'Thank goodness you are going with me, Felu Babu. In front of such a personality, I'd have looked like a . . . a worm!' Jatayu's height was five foot four inches, and at first glance his appearance suggested that he might be a comedian on the stage or in films. Anyone even slightly taller and better built than him made him look like a worm. Certainly, when he stood next to Feluda, the description seemed apt enough.

'What is strange,' he continued, 'is that although this is his first book—and he began writing at the age of fifty—it reads as though it's been written by an experienced writer. He has a wonderful style.'

'He probably turned to writing when hunting as a sport was banned by the Indian government,' Feluda remarked. 'Many other shikaris have proved to be skilful writers. Corbett's language is wonderful. Perhaps it's something to do with being close to nature. Think of the sages who wrote the scriptures. Didn't they live in jungles?'

I had noticed lightning ripping the sky soon after we left Calcutta. By the time we reached the New Farakka station, it was past midnight. I woke when the train stopped to find that it was pouring outside, and there was frequent thunder. However, when we alighted at New Jalpaiguri in the morning, there was no evidence of rain, although the sky was overcast.

The man who had been sent to meet us turned out to be Mahitosh Babu's secretary, Torit Sengupta. He was under thirty, thin, fair, wore glasses with thick black frames, and his hair was dishevelled. He greeted us politely, but without any excessive show of warmth. I told myself hurriedly that it might not necessarily mean he was displeased to see us. Feluda had warned me often enough not to jump to conclusions or judge people simply by their outward behaviour. But Mr Sengupta was clearly an intelligent man, for he didn't have to be told who amongst us was Lalmohan Ganguli, and who was Pradosh Mitter.

We stopped for ten minutes to have toast and omelettes. Then we climbed into the jeep waiting outside. Our luggage consisted only of two suitcases and a shoulder-bag. There was plenty of room in the jeep to sit comfortably. 'Mr Sinha-Roy sent his apologies for not being able to receive you himself,' Mr Sengupta said before we started. 'His brother has not been keeping well. So he had to stay home because the doctor was expected.'

This was news to us. None of us knew Mahitosh Babu had a brother.

'I hope it's nothing serious?' Feluda asked. I could tell he wasn't happy about staying in a house where someone was ill. Our visit might well turn into an imposition on our host.

'No, no,' Mr Sengupta replied, 'Devtosh Babu—that's his brother—doesn't have a physical problem. His problems are mental, and he's been . . . well, not quite normal . . . for many years. But don't get me wrong. He isn't mad. In fact, he seems fine most of the time. But occasionally he gets very restless. So the doctor has to put him on sedatives.'

'How old is he?'

'Sixty-four. He's older by five years. He was once a very learned man. He had . . . has . . . an extensive knowledge of history.'

I looked out of the jeep. To the north were the Himalayas. Somewhere in that direction lay Darjeeling. I had been there three times, but never to Laxmanbari. It wasn't very warm as there was no sun. The scenery changed as soon as we left the town. We passed a few tea estates. Now I could see mountains even to the east.

'Bhutan,' Mr Sengupta said briefly, pointing at these. The tea estates gave way to forests soon after we crossed the river Teesta. At one point, we saw a herd of goats emerging from a wood. Lalmohan Babu got very excited, and shouted, 'Look, deer, deer!'

'At least he didn't say tigers. Thank heaven for that!' Feluda muttered under his breath.

'There is a forest called Kalbuni within a mile of where we live,' Mr Sengupta informed us. 'It was once full of tigers, many of which were killed by the Sinha-Roys. Now, I'm not sure if any Royal

Bengals are left, but about three months ago there were rumours of a man-eater in Kalbuni.'

'Rumours? How do you mean?'

'Well, the body of an adivasi boy was found in the jungle. There were scratches on it that suggested it had been attacked by a tiger.'

'Just scratches? Didn't the tiger eat the flesh?'

'Yes, the flesh was partially eaten. But a hyena or a jackal may have been responsible for that.'

'What did Mahitosh Babu have to say?'

'He wasn't here at the time. He had gone to visit his tea estate near Hasimara. The officers of the Forest Department thought it might be a tiger, but when Mr Sinha-Roy got back, he said that couldn't be. A lot has been done in these few months to find that tiger, without success whatsoever.'

'I see. No one else was attacked after that one incident?'

'No.'

The very mention of a man-eater gave me goose pimples. But Mahitosh Babu must have been right. Lalmohan Babu said, 'Highly interesting!' and began staring at the trees, a frown across his brows.

We crossed a small river, went past a village and another forest, and turned left. The road was unpaved here, so our ride became noticeably bumpy. It did not last for very long, however. Only five minutes later, I saw the top of a building, towering over the trees. The rest of it came into view in a few moments. The trees thinned out to reveal a large mansion that stood behind tall iron gates. Once it must have been white, but now there were black marks all over its walls, making the whole house look as if it had been attacked and left badly bruised. Only the window panes glowed with colour. Not a single one from the colours of a rainbow was missing.

The gates were open. Our jeep passed through them and stopped at the portico. I noticed a marble slab on the gate that said: 'The Sinha-Roy Palace'.

TWO

Mahitosh Sinha-Roy turned out to be a little different from his photograph. The photo had not done justice to his complexion. He was remarkably fair. His height seemed nearly the same as Feluda's, and he had put on a little weight since the photo had been taken. His voice was deep and strong. Enough to frighten a tiger if he simply spoke to it, I thought.

He met us at the front door and ushered us into a huge drawing room.

'Please sit down,' he invited warmly. Feluda mentioned his writing as soon as we had all been introduced. 'The events you describe are amazing enough. But even apart from those, your language and style are so good that from the literary point of view as well, I think you have made a remarkable contribution.'

A bearer had come in and placed glasses of mango sherbet on a low table. Mahitosh Babu gestured at these and said, 'Please help yourselves.' Then he smiled and added, 'You are very kind, Mr Mitter. It may be that writing was in my blood, but I didn't know it until four years ago when I first started to write. My grandfather and father were both writers. Mind you, I don't think their forefathers had anything to do with literature. We were originally Kshatriyas from Rajputana. Oh, you knew that, did you? So, once we were in the business of fighting with other men. Then we left the men and turned to animals. Now I've been more or less forced to abandon my gun and pick up a pen.'

'Is that your grandfather?' Feluda asked, looking at an oil painting on the wall.

'Yes. That is Adityanarayan Sinha-Roy.'

It was an impressive figure. His eyes glinted, in his left hand was a rifle, and the right one was placed lightly on a table. He looked directly at us, holding himself erect, his head tilted proudly. His beard and moustache reminded me of King George V.

'My grandfather exchanged letters with Bankim Chandra Chatterjee. He was in college at the time *Devi Chowdhurani* was published. He wrote to Bankim after reading the book.'

'The novel was set in these parts, wasn't it?'

'Yes,' Mahitosh Babu replied with enthusiasm, 'The Teesta you crossed today was the Trisrota river described in the book. Devi's barge used to float on this river. But the jungles Bankim described have now become tea estates.'

'When did your grandfather become a shikari?' Lalmohan Babu asked suddenly.

Mahitosh Babu smiled. 'Oh, that's quite a story,' he replied, 'My grandfather was very fond of dogs. He used to go and buy pups from all over this region. There was a time when there must have been at least fifty dogs in this house, of all possible lineages, shapes, sizes and temperament. Among these, his favourite was a Bhutanese dog. There is a Shiva temple near here called the temple of Jalpeshwar. The local people hold a big fair every year during Shivaratri. A lot of people from Bhutan come down for that fair, bringing dogs and pups for sale. My grandfather bought one of these—a large, hairy animal, very cuddly—and brought it home. When the dog was three and a half years old, he was attacked and killed by a cheetah. Grandfather was then a young man. He decided he would settle scores by killing all the cheetahs and any other big cats he could find. He got himself rifles and guns, learnt to shoot and then . . . that was it. He must have killed around one hundred and fifty tigers in twenty-two years. I couldn't tell you how many other animals he killed—they were endless.'

'And you?'

'I?' Mahitosh Babu grinned, then turned to his right. 'Go on, Shashanka, tell them.'

I noticed with a start that while we were all listening to Mahitosh Babu's story, another gentleman had quietly entered the room and taken the chair to our left.

'Tigers? Why, you have written so many books, you tell them!' Shashanka Babu replied with a smile.

Mahitosh Babu turned back to us. 'I haven't been able to reach three figures, I must admit. I killed seventy-one tigers and over fifty leopards. Meet my friend, Shashanka Sanyal. We've known each other since we were small children. He looks after my timber business.'

There seemed to be a world of difference between Mahitosh Babu and his friend. The latter was barely five feet eight inches tall, his complexion was dark, his voice quiet, and he spoke very gently. Yet, there had to be some common interest to hold them together as friends.

'Mr Sengupta mentioned something about a man-eater. Has there been any further news?' Feluda asked.

Mahitosh Babu moved in his chair. 'A tiger doesn't become a man-eater just because a few people choose to call it so. I would have known, if I had been here and could have seen the body. However, the good news is that whatever animal attacked that poor boy has not yet shown further interest in human flesh.'

Feluda smiled. 'If indeed it was a man-eater, I am sure you would have dropped your pen and picked up your gun, at least temporarily,' he remarked.

'Oh yes. If a tiger went about eating men in my own area, most certainly I would consider it my duty to destroy it.'

We had finished our drinks. Mahitosh Babu said, 'You must be tired after your journey. Why don't you go to your room and have a little rest? I'll get someone in the evening to take you around in my jeep. A road goes through the forest. You may see deer, or even elephants, if you are lucky. Torit, please show them the trophy room and then take them to their own.'

The trophy room turned out to be a hall stashed with the heads of tigers, bears, wild buffalo and deer. Crocodile skins hung on a wall. There was hardly enough room for us all. I felt somewhat uncomfortable to find dozens of dead animals staring at me through their glassy eyes. But that wasn't all. The weapons that had been used to kill these animals were also displayed on a huge rack. None of us had ever seen so many guns: single-barrelled, double-barrelled, guns to kill birds with, guns for tigers, and even some for elephants. There seemed to be no end to them.

'Have you ever been on a shikar?' Feluda asked Torit Sengupta, looking at the various weapons. Mr Sengupta laughed and shook his head. 'No, no, not me. You are a detective. Can't you tell by looking at me I have nothing to do with killing animals?'

'One doesn't have to be physically very large and hefty to be a shikari. It's all to do with a steady nerve, isn't it? You do not strike me as someone who might lack it.'

'No, my nerve is steady enough. But I come from an ordinary middle-class family in Calcutta. Shikar is something I've never even thought of.'

We left the trophy room and began climbing a staircase. 'What is a man from a city doing in a place like this?' Feluda asked.

'He is simply doing a job, Mr Mitter. I couldn't find one in the city, when I finished college. Then I saw the advertisement Mr Sinha-Roy had put in for a secretary. I applied, came here for an interview and got it.'

'How long have you been here?'

'Five years.'

'You like walking in the forest, don't you? I mean, even if you're not a shikari?'

Mr Sengupta looked at Feluda in surprise. 'Why, what do you

mean?'

'There are scratch marks on your right hand. Bramble?'

Mr Sengupta smiled again. 'Yes, you're right. You are remarkably observant, I must say. I got these marks only yesterday. Walking in the forest has become something like an addiction for me.'

'Even if you're unarmed?'

'Yes. Normally, there's nothing to be afraid of,' Mr Sengupta replied quietly. 'The only things I have to watch out for are snakes and mad elephants.'

'And man-eaters?' Lalmohan Babu whispered.

'If a man-eater's existence is proved one day, I suppose I shall have to give up my walks.'

There was a door at the top of the stairs, beyond which lay a long veranda. There were several rooms running down one side. The first of these was Mahitosh Babu's study. Mr Sengupta worked in it during the day. The veranda curved to the left a little later, taking us to the west wing of the building. Our rooms were among the ones that lined this section of the veranda.

'Are all these in use? Who stays in these rooms?' asked Feluda.

'No one. Most of these stay locked. Mr Sinha-Roy and his brother live in the eastern side. Shashanka Sanyal and I are in the southern wing. Two rooms in our side of the house are always kept ready for Mr Sinha-Roy's sons. He has two sons. Both work in Calcutta. They come here occasionally.'

Now I noticed another figure standing on the opposite veranda: a man wearing a purple dressing gown, leaning against the railing and staring straight at us. 'Is that Mahitosh Babu's brother?' Feluda asked. Before Mr Sengupta could reply, the man spoke. His voice was as deep as his brother's.

'Have you seen Raju? Where is he?'

The question was clearly meant for us. He moved closer quickly. There were visible resemblances between the two brothers, specially around the jaw. Mr Sengupta answered on our behalf, 'No, they haven't seen him.'

'No? What about Hussain? Have they seen Hussain?'

His eyes were odd, unfocussed. His hair was much thinner than his brother's, and almost totally white. He might have been just as tall, but he stooped and so appeared shorter.

'No, they haven't seen Hussain, either,' said Mr Sengupta and motioned us to go inside our room. 'They know nothing,' he added firmly, 'They are only visiting for a few days.' Devtosh Babu looked openly disappointed. We slipped into our room quickly.

'Who are Raju and Hussain?' Feluda wanted to know. Mr Sengupta laughed.

'Raju is another name for Kalapahar. And Hussain is Hussain Khan, who used to be the Sultan of Gaur. Both of them destroyed several Hindu temples in Bengal. The head of the statue in the temple of Jalpeshwar here was broken by Hussain Khan.'

'Were you a student of history?'

'No, literature. But Mr Sinha-Roy is writing the history of his family. So, as his secretary, I am having to pick up a few details here and there about past events in this area.'

Mr Sengupta left. For the first time since our arrival, we were left by ourselves. I could now relax completely. The room was large and comfortable. There were two deer heads fixed over the door. Spread on the floor was a leopard skin, including the head. Perhaps it had not been possible to accommodate it anywhere else. There were two proper beds, and a smaller wooden cot, which had clearly been added because there were three of us. All three beds had been carefully made, with thick mattresses, embroidered bedsheets and pillowcases. Mosquito nets hung around each bed. Feluda looked at the cot and said, 'This one was probably once used as a machaan. Look, there are marks where it must have been tied with ropes. Topshe, you can sleep on it.'

Lalmohan Babu seemed quite satisfied with what he saw. He sat down on his bed and said, 'I think we are going to enjoy the next three days. But I hope Devtosh Babu won't come back to ask about his friend Raju. Frankly speaking, I feel very uncomfortable in the presence of anyone mentally disturbed.'

The same thought had occurred to me. But Feluda did not appear concerned at all. He began unpacking, stopping only for a moment to frown and say, 'We still don't know what kind of help Mahitosh Babu is expecting from me.'

THREE

Mr Sengupta could not go with us in the evening as he had some important work to see to. Mahitosh Babu's friend, Shashanka Sanyal, came with us instead. Having lived in these parts for many years, he, too, seemed to have learnt a lot of about the local flora and fauna. He kept pointing out trees and plants to us, although it was quickly getting dark and not very easy to see from the back of the jeep. He had lived here for thirty years, he said. Before that, he was in Calcutta. Mahitosh Babu and he had attended the same school and college.

Our jeep stopped by the side of a small river. The sun was just about to set.

'Let's get down for a while,' Mr Sanyal said. 'You'll never get the feel, the real atmosphere in a forest from a moving jeep.'

I realized the minute we stepped out how dense and quiet the forest was. There was no noise except the gently rippling river and the birds going back to roost. Had there not been a man carrying a rifle, I would certainly have felt uneasy. This man was called Madhavlal. He was a professional shikari. When shikaris from abroad used to come here, it was always Madhavlal who used to act as their guide. Apparently, he knew everything about where a machaan should be set up, where a tiger was likely to be spotted, what might it mean if an animal cried out. He was about fifty, tall and well built without even a trace of fat on his body. I was very glad he had been sent with us.

We walked slowly over to the sandy bank and stood on the pebbles that were spread on the ground like a carpet. After chatting with Mr Sanyal for a few minutes, Feluda suddenly asked, 'What is the matter with Devtosh Babu? How did he happen to . . .?'

'Heredity. There is a history of madness in their family. Mahitosh's grandfather went mad in his old age.'

'Really? Did he have to stop hunting?'

'Oh yes. Every firearm was removed out of sight. But, one day, he found an old sword hanging on the wall in the drawing room. He grabbed it and went into the jungle to kill yet another tiger. Rumour has it that he wanted to do what Sher Shah had done. You must have been told in your history lessons in school how Sher Shah got his title: "In his later years, he is said to have beheaded a tiger with one stroke of his sword, which earned him the title of Sher Shah". In a fit of madness, Adityanarayan wanted to do the same.'

'And then?' Lalmohan Babu asked, his eyes round and his voice hushed.

'He never returned. This time, the tiger won. There was virtually nothing left, except his sword.'

An animal called loudly from behind a bush. Lalmohan Babu nearly jumped out of his skin. Mr Sanyal laughed. 'Mr Ganguli, you are a writer of adventure stories. You shouldn't get frightened so easily. That was only a fox.'

Lalmohan Babu pulled himself together. 'Er . . . you see, it is because I am a writer that my imagination is livelier than others. We were talking about tigers, weren't we, and then I heard that animal. So I thought I could actually see a flash of yellow behind that bush.'

'Well . . . something yellow and striped may well start moving behind bushes if we hang around,' Mr Sanyal remarked, suddenly lowering his voice.

'What!'

'Was that a barking deer?' Feluda whispered.

A different animal had started to call. It sounded like the barking of a dog. Feluda had told me once that if a tiger was spotted close by, barking deer often called out to warn other animals. Mr Sanyal nodded in silence and motioned us to get back into the jeep. We crept back and took our places in absolute silence. It was now appreciably darker. My heart started thumping loudly. Madhavlal, too, had moved closer to the jeep, clutching his rifle tightly. Lalmohan Babu touched my hand briefly. His palm felt icy.

We waited in breathless anticipation until six o'clock; but no animal came into view. We had to return disappointed.

It was totally dark by the time we reached our room. To our surprise, we realized that in this short time, large thick clouds had gathered in the western sky. Thunder rumbled in the distance, and lightning spread its roots everywhere in the sky, dazzling our eyes. We were all staring out of the window, watching this spectacle, when someone knocked at the door. It had been left open. We turned around to find Mahitosh Sinha-Roy standing there.

'How was your trip to the forest?' he asked in his deep voice.

'We almost saw a tiger!' Lalmohan Babu shouted, excited like a child.

'If you had come here even ten years ago, you would certainly have seen one,' said our host. 'If you failed to see one today, I must admit I—and other shikaris like me—are to blame, for shikar was considered to be a sport. Even in ancient times, kings used to go on hunting expeditions which they called *mrigaya*. So did Mughal badshahs, and in modern times, our British masters. It became a tradition, which we followed blindly. Can you imagine how many animals have been killed in these two thousand years? But that isn't all, is it? Just think of the number of animals that are caught every year for zoos and circuses!'

None of us knew what to say. Was a famous shikari now sorry for what he had done? Feluda offered him a chair, but he declined. 'No, thank you,' he said, 'I didn't come here to stay. I came only to show you something. Let's go to my grandfather's room. I think you'll find it interesting.'

Adityanarayan's room was in the northern wing. 'We heard how he had lost his mind in his old age,' Feluda said as we began moving in that direction.

Mahitosh Babu smiled. 'Yes, but until that happened, till he was about sixty, there were few men with his intelligence and sharpness.'

'Do you still have the sword he had taken to kill a tiger?'

'Yes, it's kept in his room. Come, I'll show you.'

Bookshelves occupied three sides of Adityanarayan's room. Each of them was packed with books, papers, manuscripts and stacks of old newspapers. The fourth side had two chests and a glass case. It is impossible to make a list of its contents that ranged from tigers' nails and a rhino's horn to metal statues and jewellery from Bhutan. The collar that his favourite dog had worn was also there. It was studded with stones, like all the Bhutanese jewellery. Apart from these, there was a silver pen and ink-well, binoculars from Mughal times and two human skulls. All these things occupied the top two shelves. The bottom two contained only weapons: a three hundred year old carved pistol, eight daggers and kukris, and the famous sword. Only a madman could think it would be enough to kill a tiger, for it was neither very big nor heavy. The swords I had seen in Bikaner fort that had once belonged to Rajput rulers were much more impressive.

While we were examining these objects, Mahitosh Babu had opened one of the chests and brought out a small ivory box. Now he took out a folded piece of paper from it and said, 'Detectives, I believe, have a special gift to unravel puzzles and riddles. See what you make of this one, Mr Mitter.'

'A riddle? I was once interested in things of that sort, but. . .'

Mahitosh Babu passed the piece of paper to Feluda. 'You said you wanted to spend three days here. If you cannot figure it out in that time, I am prepared to give you another three days; but no more than that.'

His tone changed as he spoke the last few words, as did the look in his eyes. I realized with a shock that our genial host had a streak of cold sternness—perhaps even ruthlessness—in him. Obviously, there were times when this side to his character was exposed. Feluda asked quickly, even before Mahitosh Babu's eyes could lose their cold, remote look: 'And what if I succeed?' His own tone was light, and there was a hint of a smile around his lips. But it was clear that Feluda didn't lack the ability to deal with Mahitosh Babu, no matter how stern he might be.

Mahitosh Sinha-Roy laughed, his good humour restored. 'If you succeed, Mr Mitter, I will give you a whole tiger skin, taken from one of the biggest tigers I have killed.'

This was quite generous, I had to admit. The value of a whole tiger skin today was not to be laughed at.

Feluda now looked at the piece of paper and read aloud the riddle:

Old man hollow,
pace to follow,
people's tree.
Half ten, half again,
century.
Rising sun,
whence it's done,
can't you see?
Between hands,
below them stands,
yours, it be.

'Hidden treasure,' Feluda murmured.

'You think so?'

'Yes, that's what the last line seems to indicate. I mean, "yours, it be" could only mean finding something after solving that riddle and being rewarded for it. It has to be money. But what we must consider is whether your grandfather was the kind of man who'd hide his wealth and then leave a coded message for its recovery. Not many people would think of doing such a thing.'

'My grandfather would. He was very different from ordinary men, I have told you that. He loved practical jokes, and having a laugh at the expense of others. When he was a child, I believe one day, he was cross with all the grown-ups for some reason. So he stole their shoes in the middle of the night and hung them in bundles from the highest branches of a tree. Yes, I can well believe—what is it, Torit?'

None of us had noticed Torit Sengupta come into the room. He was standing near the door. 'I came to return a dictionary I had taken from that shelf,' he replied quietly.

'Very well, put it back. And . . . have you finished with those proofs?'

'Yes, sir.'

'Then you must take them with you tomorrow. And ask them why there were so many errors even in the second proof. Don't let them get away with it!'

Mr Sengupta slipped the book he was carrying into an empty space on a shelf, and left.

'Torit is going to Calcutta tomorrow for a week. His mother is ill,' Mahitosh Babu explained. Feluda was still staring at the rhyme.

'Who else knows about this riddle?' he asked.

Mahitosh Babu switched the light off and began moving towards the door. 'We found it only ten days ago. I was going through old papers and correspondence as I want to start writing the history of our family. Many of my grandfather's personal papers were found in an old steel trunk. That ivory box was hidden under a pile of letters. Only three people know about it: Shashanka, Torit and myself. But none of us have the required skill to decipher the message. One needs to know about words—one single word can have different meanings, can't it? Do you think you can crack it, Mr Mitter?'

Feluda returned the piece of paper of Mahitosh Babu.

'What! Are you giving up already?' he cried in dismay.

'No, no,' Feluda smiled, 'I can remember all the words. I'll go and write them down in my notebook. That paper belongs to you and your family. It should stay with you.'

FOUR

'You will get a tiger skin, Felu Babu, but what about me?' Lalmohan Babu asked, sounding disappointed.

We had finished dinner an hour ago. Our host had regaled us after dinner with exciting stories about his experiences in the wild. We had only just wished him a good night and returned from the drawing room.

'Why do you say that, Lalmohan Babu? Whoever solves this code will get that skin. At least, he should. So why don't you give it a go yourself, eh? You are a writer, you have a good command over your language, and you have imagination. So come on!'

'Pooh! My command over language would never get me through all that hollow-follow and hands-stands and what have you. You're the one who is going to get the reward. Do you think he might give you this one?' He looked at the skin that lay sprawling on the floor.

'No, I don't think so. Didn't he mention a big tiger? I have no interest in leopards.'

Feluda had already written down the few lines that made up the puzzle and was now staring at his notebook.

'Is it making any sense at all?' Lalmohan Babu persisted.

'No, not really, except that I am positive it involves hidden treasure,' Feluda replied without looking up.

'How can you tell? What's all that about following a hollow old man?'

'I don't know yet, but I think the word "follow" is important, and so is "pace". Perhaps it's simply telling you where you should go—take paces to something, or from something. Nothing else is clear. So we must—' Feluda couldn't finish speaking. Someone had walked in through the open door. It was Devtosh Babu.

He was still wearing the purple dressing gown. His eyes held the same wild look, as though he suspected everyone he met of having committed a crime. He looked straight at Lalmohan Babu and said, 'Did the Bhot Raja send you?'

'Bh-bhot?' Lalmohan Babu gulped. 'Do you mean vote? El-elections?'

'No, I think he is talking of the Raja of Bhutan,' Feluda said softly. Devtosh Babu turned his eyes immediately on Feluda, thereby releasing Lalmohan Babu from an extremely awkward situation.

'Are the Bhots coming back?' he wanted to know.

'No, I don't think so,' Feluda replied, his voice absolutely normal, 'but it is possible now to travel to Bhutan quite easily.'

'Really?' Devtosh Babu sounded as though this was the first time he'd heard the news. 'Good,' he said, 'That's good. They had once been very helpful. It was only because of them that the soldiers of the Nawab couldn't do anything. They know how to fight. But not everyone knows that, do they?' He sighed deeply, then added, 'Not everyone can handle weapons. No, not everyone can be like

Adityanarayan.'

He turned abruptly and began walking to the door. Then he stopped, turned back, looked at the leopard skin on the floor and said something perfectly weird.

'Do you know about the wheels of Yudhisthir's chariot? They never touched the ground. Yet . . . in the end, they did. They had to.' Then he quickly left the room.

We sat in silence after he had gone. After a few minutes, I heard Feluda mutter: 'He was wearing clogs. The soles were lined with rubber to muffle the noise.'

Our first night turned out to be quite eventful. I shall try to describe what happened in the right order. A grandfather clock on the top of the stairs helped me to keep track of time.

The first thing we realized within ten minutes of going to bed was that although we had been given thick mattresses and beautiful linen, no one had thought of checking the mosquito nets. There were holes in all three, which simply meant an open invitation to all the mosquitoes in the region. Thank goodness Feluda always carried a tube of Odomos with him. Each of us had to use it before going back to bed. When I did, suitably embalmed, I could hear the clock outside strike eleven. The clouds had dispersed to make way for the moon. I could see a patch of moonlight on the floor and was looking at it when, suddenly, someone spoke on the veranda.

'I am warning you for the last time. This is not going to do you any good!'

It was Mahitosh Sinha-Roy. He sounded furious. There was no reply from the other person. On my right, Lalmohan Babu had started to snore. I turned to my left and whispered, 'Feluda, did you hear that?'

'Yes,' Feluda whispered back, 'go to sleep.'

I said nothing more. I must have fallen asleep almost immediately, but woke again a little later. The moon was still there, but the thunder was back, rolling in the distance. I lay quietly listening to it, but as the last rumble died away, it was replaced by another noise: khut-khut, khut-khut, khut-khut! It did not continue at a regular pace, but stopped abruptly. Then it started again. Now it became clear that it was coming from inside our room. It got drowned occasionally by the thunder outside, but it did not stay silent for long. I could hear Feluda breathing deeply and regularly. He was obviously fast asleep.

But why had Lalmohan Babu stopped snoring? I glanced at his bed, but could see nothing through the nets. Then I became aware of another noise, a faint, chattering noise which I recognized instantly. A few years ago, during a visit to Simla, Lalmohan Babu had slipped and fallen on the snow as a bullet came and hit the ground near his feet. He had made the same noise then. It was simply the sound of his teeth chattering uncontrollably.

Khut-khut, khut-khut, khut!

There it was again. I raised my head to look at the floor. The mosquito net rustled with this slight movement, which told Lalmohan Babu that I was awake.

'T-t-t-tapesh!' he cried in a strange, hoarse voice. 'The l-l-l-eopard!'

I sat up to look properly at the leopard skin. What I saw froze my blood. Moonlight was still streaming in through a window to shine directly on the head of the leopard. It was rising and turning every now and then, first to the left and then to the right, making that strange noise. 'Feluda!' I called, unable to stop myself. I knew Feluda would wake instantly and be totally alert, no matter how deeply he had been sleeping.

'What is it? Why are you shouting?' he asked. I tried to tell him, but discovered that, like Lalmohan Babu, my throat had gone completely dry. All I could manage was, 'Look . . . floor!'

Feluda climbed out of his bed and stood staring at the moving head of the leopard. Then he stepped forward coolly and placed a finger under its chin, tilting it up. A large beetle crawled out. With unruffled calm, he picked it up and threw it out of the window. 'Didn't you know about the demonic strength of a beetle? If you place a heavy brass bowl over it, it will drag it about all over the house!' Feluda said.

I could feel myself go limp with relief. From the way Lalmohan Babu sighed, I could tell he was feeling the same. But why was Feluda still standing at the window? What was there to see in the dead of night?

'Topshe, come and have a look,' he invited. Lalmohan Babu and I joined him. Our room, which was in the rear portion of the house, overlooked the Kalbuni forest. In the last couple of minutes, thick clouds had once again obliterated the moon. There was lightning and the sound of thunder appeared closer. But what surprised me was that, in addition to the lightning, another light flashed in the distance. It kept moving about among the trees in the forest. Someone with a torch was out there. There was no doubt about that.

'Highly suspicious!' Lalmohan Babu muttered.

Then the torch was switched off. In the same instant, there was a blinding flash, followed by an ear-splitting noise. Almost immediately, it began to pour in great torrents. We had to pull the shutters down quickly.

'It's past one o'clock,' Feluda said. 'Let's try and get some sleep. We're supposed to go to the temple of Jalpeshwar in the morning, remember?'

The three of us got back into bed, behind the mosquito nets. I stared at the windows. Although they were shut, their multicoloured panes shone brightly each time there was a flash of lightning, flooding the room with all the hues of a rainbow.

I couldn't tell when this colourful display stopped, and when I fell asleep.

FIVE

The next morning, I woke at seven o'clock. Feluda was already up, and had finished doing his yoga, bathing and shaving. Mr Sengupta was supposed to collect us at eight, and take us to the temple. One of the three bearers, called Kanai, brought us our morning tea at half past seven. Feluda picked up his cup, then went back to staring at the notebook lying open in his lap. 'Bravo, Adityanarayan!' I heard him murmur. 'What a brain you had!'

Lalmohan Babu slurped his tea noisily, and said, 'Very good tea, I must say. Why, Felu Babu, have you made any progress?'

Feluda continued to mutter, '"Half ten". That's five. "Half again, century". Century would mean a hundred, so half of that is fifty. Five and fifty, that's fifty-five. OK, he probably means fifty-five paces. But what does it relate to? The tree? What is a people's tree? I must think . . .'

My heart lifted suddenly. He had started to solve the riddle. I felt sure he'd be able to get the entire meaning before we left—with the tiger skin, of course.

The clock outside struck eight. Mr Sengupta should be here soon,

I thought. A few minutes passed, but there was no sign of him. Feluda didn't seem to be aware of the delay. He was still engrossed in the puzzle.

'Rising sun?' I heard him say. 'Could it mean the east? Yes. Fifty-five paces to the east of something. What can it mean? The tree . . . the tree . . .'

Someone knocked on the door. It was Shashanka Sanyal, not Mr Sengupta.

'Er . . . haven't you finished your tea? Oh, I'm sorry,' he said. Feluda put his notebook away and got to his feet. Mr Sanyal was looking visibly upset.

'What is it? What is the matter?' Feluda asked quickly. Mr Sanyal cleared his throat, then spoke somewhat absently, 'There's some bad news, Mr Mitter. Torit Sengupta . . . Mahitosh's secretary . . . died last night.'

'Wha-at! How?' Feluda asked. Lalmohan Babu and I simply stared speechlessly.

'It seems he went into the forest last night. No one knows why. His body was found only a little while ago, by a woodcutter.'

'But how did he die? What happened?'

'Apparently, his body has been partially eaten by some animal. Quite possibly, a tiger.'

The man-eater! My hands suddenly felt cold and clammy. Lalmohan Babu had been standing in the middle of the room. He now took three steps backwards to grab the corner of a table and lean against it. Feluda stood still, looking extremely grim.

'I am sorry,' Mr Sanyal said again. 'You only came yesterday for a holiday and now this has happened. I'm afraid we are going to be rather busy . . . I mean, we have to go and see the body for ourselves, naturally.'

'Can we go with you?'

At this question, Mr Sanyal glanced swiftly at us and said, 'You may be used to gory deaths, Mr Mitter, but the others . . . ?'

'They will stay in the jeep. I will not let them see anything unpleasant.'

Mr Sanyal agreed. 'Very well. We have two jeeps. You three can travel in one.'

'Are we going to carry a gun?'

This question came from Lalmohan Babu. At any other time, Mr Sanyal would have laughed at the idea. But now he said seriously,

'Yes. There's nothing to be afraid of during the day, but we are going to be armed.'

None of us spoke in the jeep. I hadn't yet got over the shock. Only last evening, he was alive. He had spoken with us. And now he was dead . . . killed by a man-eater. What was he doing in the forest in the middle of the night? The light we saw moving among the trees . . . was it coming from Mr Sengupta's torch?

There was another jeep in front of ours. In it were Mahitosh Babu, Mr Sanyal, a man called Mr Datta from the Forest Department, the shikari Madhavlal, and the woodcutter who had found the body and come running to the house. Mahitosh Babu, who had told us so many exciting stories only the previous night, seemed to have aged considerably in the last couple of hours. What I couldn't figure out was whether it was because of the tragic death of his secretary, or because of the implications of having a man-eater running loose in the area.

We did not have to go very far into the forest. Only five minutes after taking the road that ran through the forest, the jeep in front of us slowed down, and then stopped. The road was lined with large trees. I recognized teak, silk-cotton and neem. There was a huge jackfruit tree and a number of bamboo groves. Evidence of last night's rain lay everywhere. Every little hole and hollow in the ground was full of water.

'Look!' Feluda said as our jeep stopped. I looked in the direction he pointed and noticed, after a few seconds, a light green object on a bush. It was a torn piece of the shirt Mr Sengupta had worn the night before, I had no problem in recognizing it.

Our jeep stood at least fifty yards away from where Mr Sengupta's body lay—hidden out of sight, thankfully. Everyone from the other jeep climbed out. The woodcutter began walking. Feluda, too, got out and said, 'You two wait here. It must be a horrible sight.'

The others disappeared behind a bamboo grove. Although we were at some distance from them, I could hear what they said, possibly because the forest was totally silent. The first person to speak was Mahitosh Babu. 'My God!' he exclaimed, slapping his forehead with his palm.

'It's useless now to look for pug marks—the rain would have washed them away—but it does look like an attack by a tiger, doesn't it?' asked Mr Datta.

'Yes, undoubtedly,' Mahitosh Babu replied.

'It stopped raining after two o'clock last night. From the way the blood's been washed away, it seems he was killed before it started to rain.'

Feluda spoke next: 'But does a man-eater always start eating its prey on the same spot where it kills it? Doesn't it often carry its dead prey from one place to another?'

'Yes, that's true,' Mahitosh Babu replied, 'but don't think we can find traces of the body being dragged on the ground. No mark would have stayed for very long in all that rain. In any case, a tiger is quite capable of carrying the body of a man in such a way that it wouldn't touch the ground at all. So I don't think we'll ever find out where exactly Torit was attacked.'

'If we could find his glasses, maybe that would . . .' Feluda's voice trailed away.

This was followed by a few minutes' silence. Through the leaves, I saw Mr Sanyal move. Perhaps he was trying to look for pug marks.

'Madhavlal!' called Mahitosh Babu, but could get no further, for Feluda interrupted him.

'Can a tiger use just one single nail to leave a deep wound?' he asked.

'Why? What makes you say that?'

'Perhaps you didn't notice—there's a wound on his chest. Something narrow and very sharp pierced through his clothes and went into his body. If you come this way, sir, I'll show you what I mean.'

Everyone gathered round the body once more. Then I heard Mahitosh Babu cry, 'Oh God! Dear God in heaven, this is murder! That kind of injury couldn't possibly have been caused by an animal. Someone killed him before the tiger found him. Oh, what a terrible disaster!'

'Murder . . . or it may be attempted murder,' Feluda spoke slowly 'He was stabbed, that much is clear. But maybe his assassin left him injured and ran away. When the tiger came along, an injured prey must have made his job that much easier. If only we could find the weapon!'

'Shashanka, please inform the police at once,' Mahitosh Babu said.

Everyone then returned to the jeep, leaving only Madhavlal with his gun to guard the body. When Feluda joined us, I was shocked to see how grim he looked. He didn't speak another word on the way back; neither were we in the mood to talk. We passed a herd of deer a few moments later, but even that did not bring me any joy. We had faced danger many times in the past, and had had to deal with unforeseen complexities, but this seemed utterly bizarre. Not only was there a mysterious death, a possible murderer to be found and arrested, but—to top it all—a man-eater!

I stole a glance at Lalmohan Babu. Never before had I seen him look so ashen.

SIX

We were back in our room. It was now 5 p.m. Shashanka Sanyal had informed the police, who had started their investigation. At this moment, there was really nothing for us to do. We had just had tea. Despite all my mental turmoil, I couldn't help noticing just how good the tea was. It was from Mahitosh Babu's own estate, we were told. Feluda was pacing, frowning and cracking his knuckles, stopping occasionally to light a Charminar, then stubbing it into a brass ashtray after just a couple of puffs. I sat staring out of the window. The sky today was quite clear. Lalmohan Babu kept lifting up the head of the leopard on our floor and inspecting its teeth. I saw him do this at least three times.

'If only I had had the chance to get to know him better!' Feluda muttered. This was truly unfortunate. Mr Sengupta had died before we could learn anything about him. How could Feluda get anywhere unless he knew what kind of a man he had been, who would want to kill him, whether he had had any enemies?

A few minutes after the clock on the veranda struck five, a servant came up to inform us that Mahitosh Babu wanted to see us. We rose at once and went to the drawing room. Besides our host and Mr Sanyal, there was a third man in the room, wearing a police uniform.

'This is Inspector Biswas,' Mahitosh Babu said. 'When I told him you were the first one to suspect murder, he said he'd like to meet you.'

'Namaskar,' said Feluda and took a chair opposite the inspector. We found a settee for ourselves.

Mr Biswas was very dark and quite bald, although he could not have been more than forty. He sported a thin moustache, one side of which was longer than the other. Perhaps he hadn't been paying attention while trimming it. He cast a sharp glance at Feluda and said, 'I believe you are an amateur detective?'

Feluda smiled and nodded.

'Do you know the difference between your lot and mine? There's usually a murder when you visit a place; we visit a place after there's been a murder.' Mr Biswas laughed loudly at his own joke.

Feluda went straight to the point. 'Has the murder weapon been found?'

Mr Biswas stopped laughing and shook his head. 'No, but we're still looking for it. You can imagine how difficult it is to find something in a forest, especially when there's a man-eater lurking in it. Even the police are men, aren't they? I mean, which man wants to get eaten? Ha ha ha ha!'

Feluda forced a smile since the inspector was laughing so much, but grew serious immediately.

'Is it true that he died because he was stabbed?' he asked.

'That's impossible to tell, from what's left of the body. The tiger finished nearly half of it. There will be a post-mortem, naturally, but I don't think that's going to be of any use. There is no doubt that he was stabbed. We have to catch whoever did it. Now, whether he died as a result of stabbing, or whether it was because of the tiger's attack, we do not know. In any case, what the tiger did is not our concern. That's for Mr Sinha-Roy to sort out.'

Mahitosh Babu was staring at the carpet. 'Already,' he said grimly, 'there is pretty widespread panic among the villagers. Some of my own men who work as woodcutters come from local villages. They have to work for another couple of months, after which the monsoon will start, so their work will have to stop. But they're not willing to risk their lives right now. I . . . I simply do not know what to do. Before I do anything at all, I must learn who killed Torit, why did he have to die? If I cannot hunt the tiger down, the Forest Department must find someone. After all, I am not the only shikari in this area.'

Mr Biswas cleared this throat. 'There is only one question in my mind,' he said. 'Why did your secretary go to the forest in the middle of the night? The motive for killing, I think, is relatively simple. We didn't find a wallet or any money or any other valuables on his person. So whoever killed him simply wanted those, I think. Plain robbery, there's your motive.'

'If that was the case,' Feluda said quietly, lighting a cigarette, 'he could simply have been knocked unconscious with a rod, or even a heavy walking stick. He did not have to be killed.' Mr Biswas laughed again, a little dryly this time. 'No,' he said, 'but if you rule out robbery, can you think of a suitable motive, Mr Mitter? Torit Sengupta worked for Mr Sinha-Roy, his world consisted of books and papers, he arrived here five years ago, didn't go out much and didn't know anyone except those in this house. Who would wish to kill a man like that, unless he—or they—came upon him by chance and decided to rob him of what possessions he had?'

Feluda frowned in silence.

'Yes, I know an amateur detective wouldn't appreciate the idea of a simple robbery,' Mr Biswas mocked. 'You like complications, don't you? You like mysteries? Well then, here's a first class mystery for you, Mr Mitter: why did Mr Sengupta go into the forest in the first place? What was he doing there? Try and solve that one!'

No one made a reply. Mr Sanyal was sitting next to his friend in absolute silence. Mahitosh Babu was still looking pale and exhausted. He kept shaking his head and muttering under his breath, 'I don't understand . . . nothing makes sense . . .!'

There didn't seem to be anything else to say. We rose a minute later. To my surprise, Mr Biswas spoke quite kindly before we left. 'You may carry on with your own investigation, Mr Mitter,' he said, 'we don't mind that in the least. After all, you were the first person to notice the stab wound.'

We left the drawing room, but did not return to our own. Feluda went out of the front door, through the portico and turned right to go behind the house, past the old stables, and possibly where elephants used to be kept.

I glanced up once we were at the back of the house, and saw a row of windows on the first floor. Some were shut, others open. Through one of the open windows, I could see Lalmohan Babu's towel hanging on his bedpost. Had it not been there, it would have been impossible to identify our own room. There was a door on the ground floor, directly below our window. Perhaps this acted as the back door. Mr Sengupta might have slipped out of it to go to the forest last night.

About fifty yards away, there was a tiny hut with a thatched roof. A group of men were huddled before it. I recognized one of them. It was Mahitosh Babu's chowkidar. Perhaps the hut belonged to him. Feluda strode forward in that direction, closely followed by Lalmohan Babu and me. The forest Kalbuni stretched in the background, behind which lay a range of bluish-grey mountains.

The chowkidar gave us a salute as we got closer.

'What is your name?' Feluda asked him.

'Chandan Mishir, huzoor.' He was an old man, with close-cropped hair and wrinkles around his eyes. From the way he spoke, it was obvious that he chewed tobacco. Feluda started chatting with him. From what he told us, it appeared that the local people were far more worried about the man-eater than about Mr Sengupta's death. Chandan—who had spent fifty years working for the Sinha-Roys—had seen or heard of mad elephants in the jungle which came out at times, but there hadn't been a man-eater for at least thirty years.

It was Chandan's belief that the tiger had been injured by a poacher, which now hampered its ability to find prey in the forest. This could well be true. Or maybe the tiger was old. Sometimes tigers became man-eaters when their teeth became worn and weak. I had even read that trying to eat a porcupine might injure a tiger to such an extent that it would then be forced to kill humans, which is easier than hunting other animals in the wild.

'Do the locals want Mahitosh Babu to kill this tiger?' Feluda asked.

Chandan scratched his head. 'Yes, of course. But our babu has never been on a shikar in these parts. He's been to the jungles in Assam and Orissa, but not here,' he said.

This came as a big surprise to us all.

'Why? Why hasn't he ever hunted here?'

'Babu's grandfather and father were both killed by tigers, you see. So Mahitosh Babu went away from here.'

We had no idea his father had also been killed by a tiger. Chandan told us what had happened. Apparently, Mahitosh Babu's father had shot a tiger from a machaan. The tiger fell and lay so still that everyone thought it had died. Ten minutes later, when he climbed down from the machaan and went closer to the tiger, it sprang up and attacked him viciously. Although he was taken to a hospital, his wounds turned septic and he died in a few days.

Feluda stood frowning when Chandan finished his tale. Then he pointed at the hut and said, 'Is that where you live?'

'Ji, huzoor.'

'When do you go to sleep?'

Chandan looked profoundly startled by this question. Feluda stopped beating about the bush.

'The man who was killed last night—'

'Torit Babu?'

'Yes. He left the house quite late at night and went into the forest. Did you see him go?'

'No, not last night. But I saw him go in there the day before yesterday, and a few days before that. He went there more than once, often in the evening. Last night . . .'

'Yes?'

'I saw not Torit Babu, but someone else.'

The expression on Feluda's face changed instantly. 'Who did you see?' he asked urgently.

'I don't know, huzoor. The torch Torit Babu used to carry was a large one—an old one with three cells. This man had a smaller torch, but its light was just as strong.'

'Is that all you saw? Just the light from a torch? Nothing else?'

'No, huzoor. I didn't see who it was.'

Feluda started to ask something else, but had to stop. One of the servants from the house was running towards us.

'Please come back to the house, sir!' he called. 'Babu wants to see you at once.'

We quickly went back to the front of the house. Mahitosh Babu was waiting for us near the portico.

'You were right,' he said as soon as he saw Feluda, 'Torit was not killed by a passing hooligan in the forest.'

'How can you be so sure?'

'The murder weapon was taken from our house. Remember the sword I showed you yesterday? It is missing from my grandfather's room!'

SEVEN

It was the servant called Kanai who had first noticed that the sword was missing when he went in to dust the room. He informed his master immediately. The room was not locked, since it contained several books and papers which Mahitosh Babu frequently needed to refer to. All the servants were old and trusted. Nothing had been stolen from the house for so many years that people had stopped worrying about theft altogether. What it meant was that anyone in the house could have taken the sword.

Feluda examined the glass case carefully, but did not find a clue. It was just the sword that was missing. Everything else was in place. 'I'd like to see Mr Sengupta's bedroom, and the study where he worked,' Feluda said when he had finished. 'But before I do that, I need to know if you suspect anyone.'

Mahitosh Babu shook his head. 'No, I simply cannot imagine why anyone should want to kill him. He hardly ever saw anyone outside this house. All he did was go on long walks. If that sword was used to kill him, then it has to be someone from this house who did it. No, Mr Mitter, I cannot help you at all.'

We made our way to Mr Sengupta's bedroom. It was as large as ours. Among his personal effects were his clothes, a blue suitcase, a shoulder bag and a shaving kit. On a table were a few magazines and books, a writing pad and a couple of pencils. A smaller bedside table held a flask, a glass, a transistor radio and a packet of cigarettes. The suitcase wasn't locked. Feluda opened it, to find that it was very neatly packed. 'He was obviously all set to leave for Calcutta,' he remarked, closing it again.

Five minutes later, we came out of the bedroom and went into his study.

'What exactly did his duties involve?' Feluda asked Mahitosh Babu.

'Well, he handled all my correspondence. Then he made copies of my manuscripts, since my own handwriting is really quite bad. He used to go to Calcutta and speak to my publishers on my behalf, and correct the proofs. Of late, he had been helping me gather information about my ancestors to write a history of my family. This meant having to go through heaps of old letters and documents, and making a note of relevant details.'

'Did he use these notebooks to record all the information?' Feluda asked, pointing at the thick, bound notebooks neatly arranged on a desk. Mahitosh Babu nodded.

'And are these the proofs for your new book he was correcting?'

Stacks of printed sheets were kept on the desk, next to the notebooks. Feluda picked up a few sheets and began leafing through them.

'Tell me, was Mr Sengupta a very reliable proof-reader?'

Mahitosh Babu looked quite taken aback by the question. 'Yes, I think so. Why do you ask?'

'Look, there's a mistake in the first paragraph of the first page, which he overlooked. The "a" in the word "roar" is missing; and . . . again, look, the second "e" in "deer" hasn't been printed. But he didn't spot it.'

'How strange!' Mahitosh Babu glanced absently at the mistakes Feluda pointed out.

'Had he seemed worried about something recently? Did he have anything on his mind?'

'Why, no, I hadn't noticed anything!'

Feluda bent over the desk, and peered at a writing pad on which Mr Sengupta had doodled and drawn little pictures.

'Did you know he could draw?'

'No. No, he had never told me.'

There was nothing else to see. We stepped out of the room and reached the veranda outside. A deep, familiar voice reached our ears, speaking in a somewhat theatrical fashion: 'Doomed . . . doomed! Destruction and calamity! The very foundation of truth is being rocked . . . the end is nigh!'

We only heard his voice. Devtosh Babu remained out of sight. His brother sighed and said, 'Every summer, he gets a little worse. He'll be all right once the rains start, and it cools down.'

We had reached our room. Feluda said, 'I was thinking of going back to the forest tomorrow. I need to search . . . find things for myself. What do you say?'

Mahitosh Babu thought for a moment. Then he said, 'Well, I don't think the tiger will return to the spot where Torit's body was found, at least not during the day. That's what my experience with tigers tells me, anyway. So if you stay relatively close to that area, you're going to be safe. To tell you the truth, what I find most surprising is that a large tiger is still left in Kalbuni!'

'May we take Madhavlal with us, and a jeep?'

'Certainly.'

Mahitosh Babu left. The police had to be informed about the missing sword.

It was now quite dark outside, although the sky was absolutely clear. Lalmohan Babu switched the fan on and sat down on his bed.

'Did you think you'd get a murder mystery on a short holiday? It's a bonus, isn't it, Felu Babu? You have to thank me for it,' he laughed.

'Sure, Lalmohan Babu, I am most thankful,' Feluda replied, sounding a little preoccupied. He had picked up two things from Torit Sengupta's room and brought them back with him. One was a book on the history of Coochbehar, and the other was the writing pad. I saw him staring at the little pictures, frowning deeply.

'These are not just funny doodles,' he said, almost to himself. 'I am sure it has a meaning. What could it be? Why do I feel there's something familiar about these pictures?'

Lalmohan Babu and I went and stood next to him. Mr Sengupta had drawn a tree on the pad. A tree with a solid trunk and several leafy branches. A few leaves were lying loose at the bottom of the tree. Their base was broad, but they tapered off to end on a thin narrow point. I had no problem in recognizing them. They were peepul leaves.

But that was not all. He had drawn footprints, going away from the tree, towards what looked like a couple of hands I peered more closely. Yes, they were two hands—or, rather, two open palms. He had even drawn tiny lines on them, just as they appear on human hands. Behind these was a sun. Not a full round one, but one that had only half-risen. Between the two hands was a tiny cross. Something began stirring in my own mind. This picture was meant to convey a message. Was it a message that perhaps I had heard before? Where? I began to feel quite confused.

Feluda cleared all confusion in less than a minute. 'Yes, yes, yes!' he exclaimed softly. 'Of course! Well done, Mr Sengupta, well done!' Then he caught me looking expectantly at him. 'Do you see what this is, Topshe? It's a picture of the puzzle. Torit Sengupta had cracked it, possibly quite soon after they found it among Adityanarayan's papers. Let's have a look.' He opened his notebook. "Old man hollow". Now, that's the only bit that's not clear. But "pace to follow" means fifty-five paces—those are the footprints—going from the "people's tree", which is simply a peepul tree. Adityanarayan called it a people's tree either because it sounded similar to "peepul", or because it was for some reason important to people. That rising sun, as! had guessed myself, means the east. So, fifty-five paces to the east of a peepul tree are . . .'

' . . . Two hands?' Lalmohan Babu asked hopefully.

'Yes and no. Look at the picture. They are palms. So there must be two palms—palm trees—near the peepul. And if you dig the ground between these palms, you'll probably find the treasure.'

'It makes no sense to me,' Lalmohan Babu complained. 'Tell me what the whole message is.'

'But I just did! In the forest somewhere, there is a peepul tree. Fifty-five paces—that would be about fifty-five yards—to the east of this tree are two palms. And . . .'

'OK, between those palms—"below them stands"—so you mean below the ground is the buried treasure, whatever that might be. I get it now. But, Felu Babu, there may be dozens of peepul trees in that forest and scores of palms, all within fifty yards of one another. How many will you look for?'

Feluda was silent, still frowning. 'Yes,' he said at last, 'the first line—"old man hollow"—is probably an indicator. I mean, that's what actually identifies the tree, and tells you which particular peepul tree to look for. But what can it mean? Even this picture doesn't tell us anything, does it? The old man—' he had to stop.

'Who is talking of old men?' asked Devtosh Babu, lifting the curtain and walking into the room. He was still wearing the same purple dressing gown. Didn't he have anything else to wear?

'Oh, please do come in, sir, have a seat,' Feluda invited.

Devtosh Babu paid no attention to him. 'Do you know why Yudhisthir's chariot got stuck to the ground?' he asked. He had said this before. Why was he obsessed with Yudhisthir's chariot?

'No. Why?' Feluda answered calmly.

'Because he had told a lie. He had to be punished. One single lie . . . and it can finish you.'

'Devtosh Babu,' Feluda said conversationally, 'may I ask you something?'

He looked perfectly amazed. 'Ask me something? Why? No one ever asks me anything.'

'I'd like to, because I know about your knowledge of local history. Can you tell me if there's a tree associated with an old man? I mean, here in the forest? Did an old man sit under a tree?'

It was a shot in the dark. But it made Devtosh Babu's sad and intense face suddenly break into a smile. It transformed his whole appearance.

'No, no. No old man actually sat under the tree. It was in the tree itself.'

What! Was he talking nonsense again? But his eyes and his voice seemed perfectly normal.

'There was a hollow in the tree trunk,' he explained quickly, 'that looked like the face of an old man. You think I'm mad, don't you? But I swear, that hollow looked exactly as though an old man was gaping with his mouth open. We loved that tree. Grandfather used to call it the tree of the toothless fakir. He used to take us there for picnics.'

'What kind of a tree was it?'

'A peepul. Have you seen the temple of the Chopped Goddess? That was Raju's doing. This tree was behind the temple. In fact, it was from this same tree that Mahi—'

'Dada! Come back here at once!' shouted a voice outside the door.

Devtosh Babu broke off, for his brother had appeared at the door, looking and sounding extremely cross. Mahitosh Babu stepped into the room. His face was set, his eyes cold.

'Did you take your pills?' he asked sternly.

'What pills? I am fine, there's nothing wrong with me. Why should I have to take pills?'

Without another word, Mahitosh Babu dragged his brother out of our room. We could hear him scolding him as they moved away, 'Let the doctor decide how you are. You will kindly continue to take the pills you have been prescribed. Is that understood?'

Their footsteps died away.

'Pity!' Lalmohan Babu remarked. 'He seemed quite normal today, didn't he?'

Feluda did not appear to have heard him. He was looking preoccupied again.

'The tree of the toothless fakir,' he said under his breath. 'Well, that takes care of both the old man and the hollow. All we need to do now, friends, is find the temple of the Chopped Goddess!'

EIGHT

Feluda did not go to bed until late that night. Lalmohan Babu and I stayed up with him until eleven, talking about Torit Sengupta's death. None of us could figure out why a young and obviously intelligent man like him had to die such an awful and mysterious death. Even Feluda could not find answers to a lot of questions. He made a list of these:

1. Who, apart from Mr Sengupta, had gone to the forest that night? Was it the murderer? Was it the person who had stolen the sword? Or was it a third person? Who could have a small but powerful torch?
2. We had all heard Mahitosh Sinha-Roy having an argument with someone the same night. Who was he speaking to?
3. Devtosh Babu was about to tell us something concerning the peepul tree and his brother, when the latter interrupted him. What was he going to say?
4. Why did Devtosh Babu mention Yudhisthir's chariot, more than once? Was it simply the raving of a madman, or did it have any significance?
5. Why does Shashanka Sanyal speak so little? Was he quiet and reserved by nature, or was there a specific reason behind his silence?

Lalmohan Babu heard him read out this list, then said, 'Look, Felu Babu, there's one man who continues to make me feel uneasy. Yes, I am talking of Devtosh Babu. He spoke quite normally a few hours ago, but at other times he isn't normal, is he? What if he came upon someone accidentally in the forest, and decided it was Kalapahar, or Raju as he calls him? He might attack this person, mightn't he?'

Feluda stared at Lalmohan Babu for a few seconds before speaking. 'Working with me has clearly improved both your imagination and powers of observation,' he remarked. 'Yes, I agree Devtosh Babu is certainly physically capable of striking someone with a sword. But consider this: whoever took that sword knew Mr Sengupta had gone to the forest. So he deliberately took the weapon, followed him—don't forget it was a stormy night—found him, and then killed him. Could a madman have thought all this out and acted upon it, especially when it meant finding his way in the dark in inclement weather, then holding the torch in one hand and using the sword with the other? No, I don't think so. What is essential now is a return visit to the forest, and seeing if we can pick up a clue. There's no point in speculating here. The only thing I am sure of is that Mr Sengupta had gone into the forest to look for the hidden treasure. Perhaps he wanted to collect it and take it back to Calcutta. But what still doesn't make sense is why he was so sorely tempted in the first place. He was living here very comfortably, and was clearly very well paid. Did you see his clothes and toiletries? Everything was expensive and of good quality. Even the cigarettes he smoked were imported.'

Lalmohan Babu shook his head, and declared he was now ready for bed. I fell asleep soon after this, but Feluda stayed awake for a long time.

I woke to find the sky overcast once again, and Feluda dressed and ready. Then we heard the sound of a jeep arriving, and a servant came up to say we were wanted in the drawing room.

Inspector Biswas was waiting for us.

'Are you happy now?' he asked Feluda.

'Why should I be happy?'

'You found a mystery, didn't you? The murderer took the weapon from this house and finished his victim with it. Isn't that great news?'

'It is true that a sword is missing. But surely you are not assuming that the same sword was used to kill Mr Sengupta, just because it is no longer here?'

'No, I am not assuming anything at all. But what about you? Didn't the thought cross your mind?'

Both men were speaking politely, but it was obvious that a silent undercurrent of rivalry was flowing between them. This was quite unnecessary. I felt cross with the inspector. It was he who had started it. Feluda lit a cigarette and spoke quietly, 'I haven't yet reached any conclusion. And if you think I am happy about any aspect of this case, you are quite wrong. Murder never makes me happy, particularly when it is the murder of a young and clever man.'

'A clever man?' Mr Biswas jeered openly. 'Why should a clever man leave the comforts of his room and go walking in a dark forest in the middle of the night? What's so clever about that? Can you find a satisfactory answer to this question. Mr Mitter?'

'Yes, I can.'

All the three men present in the room, apart from ourselves, seemed to stiffen at Feluda's words. 'There was a very good reason for Mr Sengupta's visit to the forest that night,' Feluda said clearly, looking at Mahitosh Babu. 'I have worked out the meaning of the puzzle you showed me. But Torit Sengupta had done the same, long before me. That tiger skin should really have gone to him. It is my belief that he was in the forest looking for the treasure.'

Mahitosh Babu opened his mouth to speak, but could not find any words. His eyes nearly popped out. Feluda hurriedly explained about the puzzle and how he had discovered its meaning. But

Mahitosh Babu continued to look perplexed.

'The tree of the toothless fakir?' he said, surprised. 'Why, I have never heard of it!'

'Really? But your brother told us you used to go for picnics with your grandfather when you were both small. He said you sat under that tree? . . .'

'My brother?' Mahitosh Babu said a little scornfully, 'Do you realize how much fact there is in what my brother says, and how much of it is fiction? Don't forget he isn't normal.'

Feluda could not say anything in reply. How could he possibly comment on Mahitosh Babu's brother's illness? After all, he was only an outsider.

Mahitosh Babu, however, had now started to look openly distressed. 'This means . . . this means Torit was planning to run away to Calcutta with the treasure! And I had no idea.' Mr Biswas stood up, curling his right hand into a fist. Then he struck his left palm with it and said, 'Well, at least we know why he was in the forest. That's one problem solved. Now we must find his assassin.'

'It has to be someone from this house. I hope you realize that, Mr Biswas?' Feluda blew out a smoke ring.

Mr Biswas gave a twisted smile. 'Sure,' he replied, narrowing his eyes, 'but that would have to include you. You had seen the sword, you knew where it was kept. You had every opportunity to remove it, just like the others in this house. We don't know whether you knew Torit Sengupta before you came here, or whether there was any enmity between the two of you, do we?'

Feluda sent another smoke ring floating in the air. 'You're right,' he said, 'no one knows anything about that. However, everyone is aware of two things. One, I was invited here. I did not come on my own. Two, I was the one who pointed out that Mr Sengupta had been attacked by a sharp instrument. If I didn't, people would have assumed a wild animal had killed him, and no further questions would have been asked.'

Mr Biswas laughed unexpectedly. 'Relax, Mr Mitter,' he said, 'why are you taking me so seriously? Don't worry, we are not interested in you. Someone else concerns us far more.' I noticed that when he said this, he exchanged a glance with Mahitosh Babu, just for a fleeting second.

'You told me something yesterday, Mr Biswas. Does that still stand?' Feluda asked.

'What did I tell you?'

'Can I continue with my own investigation?'

'Of course. But we must not clash with each other, you know.'

'We won't. I wish to confine myself to working in the forest. You're not interested in that, are you?'

The inspector shrugged. 'As you wish,' he said carelessly.

Feluda turned to Mahitosh Babu. 'You mean to say there is absolutely no point in talking to your brother?'

Mahitosh Sinha-Roy seemed to clench his jaw at this question. Was he perhaps beginning to lose his patience? However, when he spoke, he sounded perfectly friendly. 'My brother seems to have taken a turn for the worse,' he explained quietly. 'I really don't think he should be disturbed.'

Feluda stubbed his cigarette out in an ashtray and stood up. 'Well, I can hardly remain here indefinitely as your guest. Tomorrow will be the last day of our visit. May we go to the forest today? If you could please tell Madhavlal, and get us a jeep—'

Mahitosh Babu nodded. It was now eight-thirty. We decided to leave by ten o'clock. Feluda and I had brought hunting boots to walk in the forest. We put these on, although I had a feeling I wouldn't be allowed to climb out of the jeep at all. I had expected Lalmohan Babu to say he had no wish to leave the jeep but, to my surprise, he disappeared into the bathroom and changed into khaki trousers. Then he took out a pair of rather impressive sturdy boots from his suitcase and began to slip them on. Feluda gave him a sidelong glance, but made no comment.

'Felu Babu,' Lalmohan Babu began, marching up and down in his new boots in military style, 'is it true what they say about a tiger's eyes? I mean, the look in its eyes is supposed to be absolutely terrifying, or so I've heard. Could it be true?'

Feluda was staring out of the window, waiting to be told that Madhavlal and the jeep had arrived. We were all ready to leave.

'Yes, I've heard the same,' he replied. 'But do you know what some famous shikaris have said? Tigers are just as afraid of men. If a man can manage to return a tiger's stare and just stand with a steady eye contact, the tiger would make an about turn and go away. And if simply a stare doesn't help, then screaming and shouting and waving may produce the same result.'

'But . . . what about a man-eater?'

'That's different.'

'I see. So why are you? . . .'

'Why am I going? I am going because the chances of the tiger coming out during the day are virtually nil. Even if it does appear, we will have a rifle to deal with it. Besides, we'll have the jeep; so we can always make a quick escape, if need be.'

Lalmohan Babu did not say another word until the jeep arrived. When it did, he simply said, 'I can't understand anything about this murder. Nothing makes sense, I am in total darkness.'

'Efforts are being made to make sure we do not see the light, Lalmohan Babu. It should be our job to foil every attempt.'

NINE

We reached the spot where Mr Sengupta's body had been found. The clouds having dispersed, it was much brighter today. Sunlight streamed through the leaves to form little patterns on the ground here and there. There also appeared to be many more birds chirping in the trees. Lalmohan Babu gave a start each time he heard a bird call, thinking it was an alarm call for an approaching tiger.

The body had been removed the same day. Torit Babu's family in Calcutta had been informed, and his brother had arrived to take care of the funeral. There was no sign left of that hideous incident near the bamboo grove. Even so, Feluda began inspecting the ground closely, assisted by Madhavlal. The more I saw Madhavlal, the more I liked him. He seemed a cheerful fellow. He smiled often, which made deep creases appear on both sides of his mouth. Even when he didn't smile, his eyes twinkled. He told us on the way that the news of the man-eater had spread through people in the Forest Department. Apparently, a number of shikaris had offered to kill it. Among them was a Mr Sapru, who had killed many tigers and other animals in the Terai. He was expected to arrive the next day.

Now he stopped to chat with us and began telling us stories of the many expeditions he had been on. At this moment, Feluda called him from the bamboo grove. Madhavlal stopped his tale and went forward quickly, closely followed by Lalmohan Babu and myself. Feluda had raised no objection today to our getting out of the jeep.

We found him kneeling on the ground, bending over a bamboo stem.

'Take a look at this!' he said to Madhavlal.

Madhavlal glanced at it briefly and declared, 'It was hit by a bullet, sir.'

There was a mark on the stem which I now saw. All of us—including Feluda—felt astounded.

'Can you tell me how old that mark might be?' Feluda asked, a little impatiently.

'Not older than a couple of days,' Madhavlal replied.

'What can it mean?' Feluda muttered, half to himself. 'A sword . . . a gun . . . I'm getting all confused. Torit Sengupta was struck by the sword, then someone shot at the tiger but missed, by the looks of things. Or else . . .' he broke off. Madhavlal had found something under the bamboo. I saw what it was only when I got closer. He was clutching what looked like fluff, about two inches in length.

'Hair from the tiger's body?' Feluda asked.

'Yes, sir. The bullet must have scraped one side.'

'Is that why the tiger ran away without finishing its meal?'

'Looks like it.'

Feluda began moving forward without another word. Madhavlal followed him, rifle in hand, his eyes alert. Lalmohan Babu and I placed ourselves between these two men, which struck us as the safest thing to do. Feluda was carrying a loaded revolver, but that wasn't enough to deal with a man-eater. The sound of an engine starting told me the driver of our jeep was following us. It meant that he would get closer, although he couldn't actually be by our side for we had left the road and were now amidst the trees and bushes.

Three minutes later, Feluda appeared to notice something on a thorny bush, and quickly made his way to it, walking diagonally to the right. There was a piece of green cloth stuck to it, which had undoubtedly come from Mr Sengupta's shirt. The tiger had obviously come this way carrying his body, and the shirt had got stuck on that bush.

When we started walking again, Madhavlal took the lead. He could probably guess which way the man-eater had come from. He moved with extreme caution, partly because we were behind him and partly because the area abounded with briar and other prickly plants. He stopped abruptly under a large tamarind tree, looking closely at the ground. We gathered around him and saw what had caught his attention. I had never seen such a thing before, but knew instantly I was looking at a pug mark. There were several others that seemed to have come from the same direction we were now going in.

Lalmohan Babu whispered, 'Is th-this a t-two legged tiger?'

Madhavlal laughed. 'No,' Feluda explained, 'that is how a tiger walks. It puts its hind legs exactly where it puts its forelegs. So it seems as if it's a two-legged animal.'

Madhavlal continued walking. I could no longer hear the jeep. A faint gurgling noise told me there was a nullah somewhere in the vicinity. Lalmohan Babu's new boots, which had been squeaking rather loudly at first ('ideal for arousing the man-eater's curiosity,' Feluda had remarked) were now silent, being heavily streaked with mud.

We passed a silk-cotton tree, and then Madhavlal stopped again.

'You have a revolver, sir, don't you?' he asked Feluda. His voice was low.

A few yards ahead of us, something was emerging from the long grass, parting it to make its way. 'Krait,' Madhavlal said softly. I had read about kraits. They were extremely poisonous snakes. A second later, it came into view and stopped. It was black, striped with yellow. It had no hood.

I did not see Feluda take out his revolver, but heard the earsplitting noise as he fired it. The head of the snake disappeared, and it was all over. A number of birds cried out, and a group of monkeys grew rather agitated, but the body of the snake lay still. 'Shabaash!' said Madhavlal. Lalmohan Babu made a noise that appeared to be a mixture of laughter, a sneeze and a cough.

We resumed walking. The forest was not thick everywhere. The trees thinned to our left. 'That's where the nullah is,' Madhavlal said, 'and the area is rocky. Tigers often rest there during the day behind rocks and boulders. I suggest we walk straight on.'

We took his advice. Feluda was still looking around everywhere, hoping for more clues. This time, Lalmohan Babu helped him find one, purely by accident. He stumbled against something and kicked it, making it spring up in the air and land a few feet away.

It was a dark brown leather wallet. Feluda picked it up and opened it. There were two hundred-rupee notes, and a few smaller ones. Besides these, in the smaller compartments, were two folded old stamps, cash memos and a prescription. The wallet was wet and dirty, but the money inside it could be used quite easily. Feluda put everything back in the wallet, then put it in his pocket.

We began walking again. The trees had suddenly grown very thick. Almost unconsciously, I began to look for a peepul tree. I knew Feluda was doing the same. I did see a couple of peepuls, but there were no palms near them. Madhavlal had stopped for a minute to cut two small branches from a tree, which he then passed on to Lalmohan Babu and me. We were now using these as walking sticks.

'A pug mark can tell you a lot about the size of the tiger, can't it?' Feluda asked.

'Yes, sir,' Madhavlal replied. 'Our man-eater appears to be a big fellow.'

Feluda asked another question: 'Mahitosh Babu has never killed anything in this forest, has he?'

'No, sir. Many shikaris have superstitions. Mahitosh Babu is no exception. My own father did. Once, he happened to brush against a stinging nettle just as he set off from home. He killed a ten-foot tiger that day. From then on, every time he went on shikar, he used to rub his hands on stinging nettle, no matter how much it hurt.'

'Jim Corbett was superstitious, too. If he could see a snake before going off to look for a tiger, that used to make him happy.'

If his grandfather and father had both been killed here, it was entirely understandable why Mahitosh Babu had taken himself off to Assam and Orissa.

Twenty minutes later, Feluda finally found what he was really looking for. Telling Madhavlal to stop, he began peering behind a thick bush, which was laden with small purple flowers. We joined him and saw it. The stone-studded handle of Adityanarayan's sword was visible just outside the bush. The blade was hidden behind it.

Feluda picked it up in one swooping movement. The blade was stained with blood, although the stains had faded to some degree. Feluda turned it over and inspected the handle closely. 'Madhavlalji,' he said, 'the actual spot where the murder took place cannot be far from here. Can we walk on?'

'Sure. But a hundred yards from here, you'll find a temple.'

'A temple?' Feluda asked sharply.

'Yes, sir. The locals call it the temple of the Chopped Goddess. There's nothing left in it. Only the basic structure is still standing somehow.'

None of us said anything. Behind this temple was the tree of the toothless fakir. And fifty-five yards to the east . . .! Without a word, Feluda strode ahead, the sword in his hand, as though he was Sher Shah, out to destroy a tiger.

Madhavlal was right about the temple. It was certainly an ancient building, its walls broken and cracked. Plants had grown out of the cracks. Roots from a banyan tree hung down from all sides, as if they wanted to crush what was left of the roof. What must have been the inner sanctum was still there, but it was so dark inside that I didn't think there was any question of going in.

Feluda, however, was not looking at the temple at all. He was staring behind it. About twenty yards away, just as Devtosh Babu had said, stood a large, old peepul tree. Its branches were dry, shrivelled and bare. There were virtually no leaves left. But what the tree did have, visible even from a distance, was a big hollow, at least five feet up from the ground.

We followed Feluda in breathless anticipation. As we got closer, we saw to our amazement that funny marks and patches on the tree trunk near the hollow, together with its uneven surface, had truly helped create the appearance of an old, toothless man with a gaping mouth. 'Is that the east?' Feluda asked, turning his eyes to the right.

'Yes, sir,' Madhavlal replied.

'Look, the two palms! And I don't think I need even bother with measuring the distance. It's got to be fifty-five paces.'

The two palms were clearly visible, fifty-five yards away. We moved towards them, and spotted it almost immediately: the ground between the palms had been dug quite recently. There was a fairly large hole, now filled with water. Any treasure that might have been there had gone.

'What! Hidden treasure vanished?' Lalmohan Babu was the first to find his tongue. He forgot to whisper.

Feluda was looking grim again, although what we had just seen could hardly be regarded as a new mystery. Whoever killed Mr Sengupta had obviously removed the treasure. Feluda stared at the hole in the ground for a few seconds, then said, 'Why don't you rest for a while? I'd like to make a quick survey.'

My legs were aching after walking stealthily for such a long time. I was quite thankful for this chance to rest, and so was Lalmohan Babu. We found a dry area under the peepul tree, and sat down. Madhavlal put his rifle down, placing it against the tree trunk and began to tell us a story of how he had been attacked by a bear when he was thirteen, and how he had managed to escape. But I couldn't give him my full attention, for my eyes kept following Feluda. He lit a cigarette, placed it between his lips and began examining the ground around the ancient temple. I saw him pick something up—possibly a cigarette stub—and then drop it again. Then he knelt, and bent low to look closely at the ground, his face almost touching it.

After ten minutes of close scrutiny outside, Feluda went into the dark hall. I could only marvel at his courage, the temple was probably crawling with snakes and other reptiles. When the temple was in use, it was supposed to have had a statue of Durga. Kalapahar chopped off its head and four of its ten arms. Hence its current name.

Feluda emerged a minute later, and made a rather cryptic remark. 'This is amazing!' he exclaimed. 'Who knew one would have to step into darkness in order to see the light?'

'What, Felu Babu, do you mean the darkness has gone?' Lalmohan Babu shouted.

'Partly, yes. You might call it the first night after a moonless one.'

'Oh. That would mean waiting for a whole fortnight to get a full moon!'

'No, Lalmohan Babu. You are only thinking of the moon. There is such a thing as the sun, remember? It comes out at the end of each dark night, doesn't it?'

'You mean to say tomorrow . . . tomorrow we might see the climax of this story? The end?'

'I am saying nothing of the kind, Lalmohan Babu. All I am prepared to tell you is that, after hours of darkness, I think I am beginning to see a glimmer of light. Come on, Topshe, let's go home.'

TEN

We had left the house at ten o'clock. By the time we got back, it was half past twelve. Feluda wanted to return the sword to Mahitosh Babu, but we discovered on our return that he had gone with Mr Sanyal to visit the Head of the Forest Department in the forest bungalow in Kalbuni. So we went to our room, taking the sword with us.

Before we did this, however, we spent some time on the ground floor. Feluda went to the trophy room. I could not tell what he was thinking, but he began to examine all the guns that were displayed there. He picked up each one, and inspected its barrel, its butt, trigger and safety catch. Lalmohan Babu began to ask him something, but Feluda told him to be quiet.

'This is a time to think, Lalmohan Babu,' he said, 'not to chat.' By this time, Lalmohan Babu had become quite familiar with Feluda's moods, so he promptly shut up.

Feluda finished inspecting the trophy room and turned to go upstairs. We followed silently. He spoke again on reaching the veranda on the first floor. 'What's this?' he asked, stopping suddenly and staring at Devtosh Babu's room. 'Why is the elder brother's room locked?'

There was a padlock on the door. Where could he have gone? Why had he left the room locked? Feluda said nothing more. We reached our room.

Feluda spent the next few minutes sitting quietly, frowning; then he got up and paced restlessly, stopped short and sat down again. Two minutes later, he was back on his feet. I knew this mood well. He always acted like this as he got closer to unravelling a complex mystery.

'Since there is no one about, and Devtosh Babu's room is locked,' he said suddenly, 'it might not be a bad idea to do a bit of snooping.'

He left the room. I stuck my head out of the door and saw him go into Mahitosh Babu's study. I came back into our room to find Lalmohan Babu stretched on the leopard skin on the floor. He was using its head as a pillow. Clearly, seeing a tiger's pug mark in the forest had gone a long way to boost his courage. After a few seconds of silence, he remarked, 'Thank goodness I thought of dedicating my book to Mahitosh Sinha-Roy! Could we ever have had such a thrilling experience if I hadn't? Just take this morning: a bullet in a bamboo grove, a snake in the grass, pug marks of a Royal Bengal, a ruined old temple, a famous peepul tree . . . what more could anyone want? All that's left to make the experience complete is an encounter with the man-eater.'

'Do you really want that?' I asked.

'I am not scared any more,' he replied, yawning noisily. 'If you have Madhavlal on one side, and Felu Mitter on the other, no man-eater can do anything to you!'

He closed his eyes, and seemed to go to sleep. I picked up Mahitosh Babu's book and had read a few pages, when Feluda returned. His footsteps made Lalmohan Babu open his eyes and sit up.

'Did you find anything?'

'No. I did not find what I was looking for, but that is what is significant.' After a brief pause, Feluda asked, 'Do you remember why Yudhisthir's chariot got stuck to the ground?'

'Because he told a lie?'

'Exactly. But these days, a liar doesn't always get punished by God. Other men have to catch and punish him.'

I could not ask him what he meant, for a jeep arrived as he finished speaking. Only a few minutes later, a servant turned up to say Mahitosh Babu had returned, and lunch had been served.

Despite all that had happened, we had all enjoyed our meals every day. Mahitosh Babu obviously had a very good cook. Today, the food looked inviting enough, but our host began a conversation on a rather sombre note. 'Mr Mitter,' he said solemnly, 'since you have discovered the meaning of Adityanarayan's message, I don't think I have the right to keep you here any longer. If you like, I can make arrangements for your return. One of my men is going to Jalpaiguri. He can book your tickets for you.'

Feluda did not reply immediately. Then he said slowly, 'I was thinking of going back myself. You have been an excellent host, but naturally we cannot stay here indefinitely. But, if you don't mind, I'd like to stay here tonight and leave tomorrow morning. You see, I am a detective, and there's been a murder. I'm sure you'll appreciate why I want to stay a bit longer to see if any light can be thrown on the case. It is immaterial whether I can discover the truth, or the police do their job. I only want to know what happened, and how it happened.'

Mahitosh Babu stopped eating and looked straight at Feluda. 'There is no one in this house who would plan a murder in cold blood, Mr Mitter,' he said firmly.

Feluda paid no attention. 'Where is your brother?' he asked casually. 'Has he been taken somewhere else? His room was locked.'

Mahitosh Babu replied in the same grave tone, 'My brother is in his room. But since last night, his . . . ailment has become worse. He has to be restrained, or he might cause serious damage to whoever came his way, yourself included. Sometimes, he starts imagining he's seen people who died hundreds of years ago—you know, characters out of a history book. Then he attacks them if he thinks they did anything wrong in the past. Once he mistook Torit for Kalapahar and nearly throttled him to death. One of the servants saw him, luckily, and managed to take him away.'

Feluda continued to eat. 'Did you know,' he said conversationally, 'the death of Mr Sengupta is not the only mystery we are dealing with? Someone ran off with your treasure, possibly the same night.'

'What!' Mahitosh Babu turned into a statue, holding his food a few inches from his mouth. 'You mean you went and checked?'

'Yes, the treasure's gone, but we found the sword, with bloodstains on it.'

Mahitosh Babu opened his mouth to speak, but could only gulp in silence. Feluda dropped the third bombshell. 'When the tiger attacked Mr Sengupta, someone shot at the tiger. The bullet hit a bamboo stem, but it is likely that it grazed the tiger's body, for we found a few strands of hair. So it seems Torit Sengupta was not the only one who had gone to the forest that night. Different people with different purposes in mind . . .'

'Poacher!' Mr Sanyal spoke unexpectedly. 'It must have been a poacher who entered the forest after Torit was killed. It was this poacher who shot at the tiger.'

Feluda nodded slowly. 'That possibility cannot be ruled out. So, for the moment, we need not worry about where the bullet came from. However, we still have the bloodstained sword and the missing treasure to explain.'

'Never mind the sword. The treasure is far more important,' Mahitosh Babu declared. 'Mr Mitter, we've got to find it. The history of the family of Sinha-Roys will remain incomplete unless it is found.'

'Very well,' Feluda suggested, 'if that is the case, why don't we all return to the spot later today? It is very close to the temple of the Chopped Goddess.'

Mahitosh Babu agreed to accompany us back to the forest. However, torrential rain—which began at half past three and continued well after six—forced us to abandon our plan. Feluda had been looking withdrawn; now he looked positively depressed. It was obvious that Mahitosh Babu wanted us to leave. If the weather did not improve the next day, we might well have to go back without solving the mystery surrounding Mr Sengupta's death. How another visit to the temple could make a difference, I could not tell, but I knew Feluda was definitely on to something. The occasional glint in his eyes told me that very clearly.

Unable to sit in our room doing nothing, we came out and stood on the veranda when the grandfather clock struck five. The door to Devtosh Babu's room was still locked.

'There's no one around,' Lalmohan Babu whispered. 'Why don't we try looking through the shutters? What can the man be doing?'

Like many of Lalmohan Babu's other suggestions, Feluda ignored this one.

The sky cleared after seven. When the stars came out, they looked as if someone had polished them before pasting them on an inky-black sky. Feluda sat on his bed, holding the sword. Lalmohan Babu and I were standing at the window, admiring the stars, when suddenly he clutched at my sleeve and said in a low voice, 'A small torch!'

The chowkidar's hut was visible from our window. There was a large tree near it. A man was standing under it. Another man—carrying a torch—was approaching him. His torch was of the kind that can be plugged into an electric socket and recharged. It had a small bulb, and an equally small point, but the light it gave out was very bright.

Feluda switched the light off in our room and joined us at the window.

'Madhavlal!' he murmured. I, too, had recognized the man who had been waiting under the tree as Madhavlal, for I could vaguely see his yellow shirt even in the dark. But it was impossible to see the other man. It could have been Mahitosh Babu, his brother, Mr Sanyal, or someone else.

The torch was switched off, but the two men were still standing close, talking. After a while, the yellow shirt moved away. The torch light came back on and returned to the house. Feluda waited for a few seconds before switching on our own light.

Lalmohan Babu was probably carrying out an investigation on his own. I saw him slip out to the veranda and return a moment later.

'What did you see? Is that door still locked?' Feluda asked.

Lalmohan Babu gave an embarrassed laugh. 'Yes,' he replied.

'Did you really think it was Devtosh Babu who was speaking with Madhavlal?'

'Yes. I told you I did not trust him. A madman must not be trusted. We used to have one where I live. He was often seen standing in the middle of the road, throwing stones at passing trams and buses. Just think how dangerous that was?'

'What did the locked door prove?'

'That he didn't go down just now.'

'How can you be so sure? Have you heard any noises from that room today? How do you know that room isn't empty?'

Lalmohan Babu began to look rather crestfallen.

'Felu Babu, I try so hard to follow your methods and work on the same lines as you, but somehow . . . I get it all wrong!'

'That is only because you work in reverse gear. You pick your criminal first, then try to dump the crime on him. I try to understand the nature of the crime before looking for the person who might have committed it.'

'Are you doing the same in this case?'

'Of course. There is no other way.'

'But where did you start from?'

'Kurukshetra.'

After this, Lalmohan Babu did not dare ask another question.

When I went to bed that night, I had no problem in falling asleep, for the mosquito nets had been changed. But, in the middle of the night, a sudden shout woke me. I sat up, startled, to find Feluda standing in the middle of the room, clutching Adityanarayan's sword. Moonlight poured in through an open window, making the weapon shine brightly. Feluda looked steadily at the metal blade, and repeated the word he had just spoken very loudly. Only, this time he lowered his voice.

'Eureka! Eureka!' he said.

Thousands of years ago, Archimedes had said the same thing when he had found what he was looking for. There was no way of telling what Feluda had discovered.

ELEVEN

Mr Sanyal arrived in our room the following morning, just as we finished our bed-tea. What did he want so early in the morning? I looked at him in surprise, but Feluda greeted him warmly. 'We haven't really had the chance to get to know each other, have we?' he said, offering our visitor a seat. 'As Mahitosh Babu's friend, you must have had a lot of interesting experiences yourself.'

Mr Sanyal took a chair opposite the table. 'Yes. I have known

Mahitosh for fifty years, since our school days.'

'May I ask you something?'

'About Mahitosh?'

'No, about Torit Sengupta.'

'Yes?'

'What sort of a man was he? I mean, what was your impression?'

'He was a very good man. I found him intelligent, diligent and very patient.'

'How was he at his work?'

'Brilliant. Absolutely brilliant.'

'Yes, I got that impression myself.'

Mr Sanyal gave Feluda a level look. 'I have come to make a request, Mr Mitter,' he said simply.

'A request?' Feluda asked, offering him a cigarette. Mr Sanyal accepted it and waited until it had been lit for him. I saw him smoking for the first time. He inhaled deeply before replying. 'Yes. You have seen a lot in the last three days,' he said. 'You are far more clever than ordinary men, so obviously you have drawn your own conclusions from what you've seen. Today is probably the last day of your stay. No one knows what the day has in store. No matter what happens today, Mr Mitter, I'd be very grateful if you could keep it to yourself. I am sure Mahitosh would want the same thing. If you look at the history of any old family in Bengal—particularly the zamindars—I'm sure you'll find a lot of skeletons in their cupboards. The Sinha-Roys are no exception. However, I see no reason why the facts that come to light should be made public. I am making the same appeal to your friend, and to your cousin.'

'Mr Sanyal,' Feluda replied, 'I have enjoyed Mahitosh Babu's hospitality for three days. I am very grateful to him for his generosity. I can never go back to Calcutta and start maligning him. None of us could do that. I give you my word.'

Mr Sanyal nodded silently. Then Feluda asked another question, possibly because he couldn't help himself. 'Devtosh Babu's room is still locked. Can you explain why?'

Mr Sanyal looked a little oddly at Feluda. 'By the end of this day, Mr Mitter, the reason will become clear to you.'

'I take it that the police are still working on this case?'

'No.'

'What! Why not?'

'Well, suspicion has fallen on someone . . . but Mahitosh does not want the police to harass this person at all.'

'You mean Devtosh Babu?'

'Yes, who else could I mean?'

'But even if that's true, even if he did kill, he's not going to be charged or punished in the usual way, is he? I mean, considering his medical condition?'

'Yes, you are probably right. Nevertheless, the news would spread, wouldn't it? Mahitosh doesn't want that to happen.'

'Simply to save the good name of his family?'

'Yes. Yes, that's the reason, Mr Mitter. Let's just leave it at that, shall we?'

Mr Sanyal rose, and left.

We left at half past eight. There were two jeeps once again, like the first day. Feluda, Lalmohan Babu and I were in one; in the other were Mahitosh Babu, Mr Sanyal, Madhavlal and a bearer called Parvat Singh. There were three rifles with us today. Madhavlal had his, Mahitosh Babu had another, and the third was with Feluda. He himself had asked for a rifle. Having heard from Madhavlal how he had killed the snake with his revolver, Mahitosh Babu had raised no objection. 'You can choose whatever you like,' he had said. 'The 375 would be suitable for a tiger.'

I did not understand what the number signified, but could see that the rifle was most impressive in size, and probably also in weight.

As a matter of fact, I was the only one who was not armed. Feluda had handed the sword to Lalmohan Babu this morning, saying, 'Hang on to it. This sword has an important role to play today. You'll soon get to see what I mean.' Lalmohan Babu was therefore clutching it tightly, wearing an air of suppressed excitement.

When we woke this morning, the sky was clear. But now it had started to cloud over again. The road being muddy and slippery, we took longer to reach the forest. Each driver took his jeep half a mile further into the forest than the last time, but then could go no further. 'Never mind,' Madhavlal said, 'I know the way. We have to cross a nullah and walk for fifteen minutes to get to the temple.'

We began our journey amidst the rustle of leaves, a cool breeze and the occasional rumble in the sky. Feluda loaded his gun before getting out of the jeep. Mahitosh Babu's gun was being carried by Parvat Singh. Apparently, he had always accompanied his master on hunting expeditions. A short but well-built man, he clearly did not lack physical strength.

I saw a herd of deer in a few minutes. A sudden surge of joy filled my heart, but then it leapt in fear. Somewhere in this forest—perhaps not very far away—was a man-eater. Normally, a tiger could easily walk more than twenty miles and travel from one forest to another to look for a prey. But if it was injured, it might not be able to walk very far. In any case, the forest here was not all that big. Large areas of woodland had been cleared to make tea estates, and farms. Besides, although tigers didn't usually come out of hiding during the day, they were likely to do so if the day was dark and cloudy. This was something I had learnt from Feluda only this morning.

Soon, we came to the nullah. It had probably been quite dry even a day ago, but was now gurgling merrily. A lot of animals had left their footprints on the wet sand by its sides. Madhavlal pointed out the marks left by deer, wild boars and a hyena; but there was no sign of a tiger. We crossed it and continued to walk. I could hear a hoopoe in the distance, a peacock cried out once, and there were crickets in the bushes we passed. The faint rustling noise in the grass told me lizards and other smaller reptiles were quickly moving out of our way to avoid being crushed to death under our feet.

The route we took today was a different one, but it did not take us very long to reach the spot we had visited yesterday. There was the bush with the purple flowers. That was where we had found the sword. Madhavlal moved silently, and each one of us tried to do the same. Actually, it was not all that difficult to muffle the noise our feet made, for the ground was wet and there were no dry leaves.

Piles of broken bricks came into view. We had reached the temple of the Chopped Goddess. No one spoke. Madhavlal stopped in front of the temple. We joined him noiselessly. Since my attention had been wholly taken up the day before by the peepul tree and the two palms, I hadn't noticed the other big trees in the area. A cool breeze now wafted through their leaves, and the nullah still rippled faintly in the background.

Feluda walked over to the palms. Mahitosh Babu followed him swiftly. The hole in the ground was even more full of water today. After a while, Feluda broke the silence.

'This is where Adityanarayan had hidden his treasure,' he said.

'But. . . where did it go?' Mahitosh Babu asked hoarsely.

'It has not gone far, unless someone removed it yesterday after we left.'

Mahitosh Babu's eyes began gleaming with hope.

'Do you really think so? Are you sure?' he asked eagerly.

Feluda turned to face him squarely. 'Mahitosh Babu, can you tell us what that treasure consists of? What exactly was buried under the ground?'

Mahitosh Babu's face had gone red with excitement. A couple of veins stood out on his forehead.

'I don't know, Mr Mitter, but I can guess,' he spoke with an effort. 'One of my ancestors—called Yashwant Sinha-Roy—was the chief of the army in the princely state of Coochbehar. The money he had been paid by the Maharaja was kept in our house. There were more than a thousand silver coins, four hundred years old. When Adityanarayan decided to hide these, he had crossed sixty and was beginning to lose his mind. He had started to indulge in childish pranks. No one could find those coins after he died. Now, after all these years, his coded message has told us where they were hidden. I can't afford to lose them again, Mr Mitter. I have got to find them!'

Feluda turned from Mahitosh Babu and began walking towards the temple. He stopped for a second as he passed me, and said, 'Here, Topshe, hold my rifle for me. I don't think I'll need it inside that hall. A revolver should be good enough.'

My hands started to tremble, but I pulled myself together and took the rifle from him. Then I realized just how heavy it was.

Feluda walked on and entered the dark hall once more. I saw him put his hand into his pocket before he disappeared through its broken door.

In less than five seconds, we heard him fire twice. No one said anything, but I could feel a shiver go down my spine. Then Feluda's voice spoke from inside the temple: 'Mahitosh Babu, could you please send your bearer here?'

Parvat Singh handed the rifle to his master, and went into the temple. A couple of seconds later, he emerged with a dirty, muddy brass pitcher in his hands. Feluda followed him. Mahitosh Babu rushed forward towards his bearer.

'Who knew a cobra would be attracted to silver coins? Feluda said with a smile. 'I had heard its hiss yesterday. Today, I found it wound around that pitcher, as if it was giving it a tight embrace!

Mahitosh Babu had thrown aside his rifle. I saw him pounce upon the pitcher and put his hand into it. Just as he brought it out, clutching a handful of coins, an animal cried out nearby. It was a barking deer. Monkeys joined it immediately, jumping from branch to branch, making an incessant noise.

A lot of things happened at once. Even now, as I write about it, I feel shaken and confused. To start with, a remarkable change came over Mahitosh Babu. Only a moment ago, he had seemed overjoyed at the sight of his treasure. Now, he dropped the coins, jumped up and took three steps backwards, as if he had received an electric shock. Each one of us turned into a statue. Feluda was the first to speak, but his voice was low. 'Topshe,' he whispered, 'climb that tree. You, too, Lalmohan Babu. Go on, be quick!'

We were standing near the famous peepul tree. I returned the rifle to Feluda, placed a foot in the big hollow and grasped a branch. In about ten seconds, I was a good ten feet from the ground. Lalmohan Babu followed suit, with surprising agility, having passed me the sword. Soon, he was sitting on a branch higher than mine. He told us afterwards that he had had a lot of practice in climbing trees as a child, but I had no idea he could do it even at the age of forty.

I saw what followed from the treetop. Lalmohan Babu saw some of it, then fainted quietly. But his arms and legs were so securely wrapped around a big branch that he did not fall down.

It was obvious to everyone that there was a tiger in the vicinity. That was why Feluda had told us to get out of the way. Mahitosh Babu's reaction was the most surprising. I could never have imagined he would behave like that. He turned to Feluda and spoke fiercely through clenched teeth, 'Mr Mitter, if you value your own life, go away at once!'

'Go away? Where could I go, Mahitosh Babu?'

Both men were holding their rifles. Mahitosh Babu raised his, pointing it at Feluda.

'Go!' he said again. 'The jeep is still waiting, over there. Get out of here. I command you—' He couldn't finish. His voice was drowned by the roar of a tiger. It sounded as if not one, but fifty wild animals had cried out together.

Then I saw a flash of yellow—like a moving flame—through the leaves of the trees that stood behind the temple. It moved swiftly through the tall grass and all the undergrowth, and slowly took the shape of a huge, striped animal: a Royal Bengal tiger. It began making its way to the open area where the others were still standing.

Mahitosh Babu lowered his gun. His hands were trembling uncontrollably.

Feluda raised his own rifle. There were three other men—Shashanka Sanyal, Madhavlal and Parvat Singh. Parvat Singh gave a sudden leap and vanished from sight. I could not see what the other two were doing, for my eyes kept moving between Feluda and the tiger. It was now standing beside the temple. It bared its fangs and growled. Never before had it had such a wide choice of prey.

Then I saw it stop, and crouch. It would spring up and attack perhaps in less than a second. I had read about this. Sometimes a tiger could—

Bang! Bang!

Shots rang out almost simultaneously from two different rifles. My ears started ringing. Just for a moment, even my vision seemed to blur. But I did not miss seeing what happened to the tiger. It shot up in the air, then seemed to strike against an invisible barrier, which made it take a somersault and drop to the ground. It crashed where the brass pitcher stood, its tail lashing at it, making it turn over noisily, spilling its contents. Then the tiger lay still, surrounded by four-hundred-year-old silver coins.

Feluda slowly put his rifle down.

'It's dead, sir,' Madhavlal announced, sounding pleased.

'Who killed it? Which of the two bullets did the trick, I wonder?' Feluda asked.

Mahitosh Babu was in no condition to reply. He was sitting on the ground, clutching his head between his hands. His rifle had been snatched away by his friend, Shashanka Sanyal. It was he who had fired the second shot.

Mr Sanyal walked over to the dead tiger.

'Come and have a look, Mr Mitter,' he invited. 'One of the bullets caught him under the jaw and went through the head; the other hit him near an ear. Either of those could have killed him.'

TWELVE

The sound of double shots had brought the local villagers running to the spot. Thrilled to see their enemy killed, they were now making arrangements to tie the tiger to bamboo poles and carry it to their village. There was no doubt that this was the man-eater, for two other bullet marks had been found on its body: one on a hind leg, the other near the jaw. These had clearly made the tiger lose its natural ability to hunt for prey in the wild. Besides, the heavy growth of hair on its jowls indicated it was an old tiger, anyway. Perhaps that was another reason why it had become a man-eater.

Parvat Singh had returned and helped his master to get up and sit on one of the broken steps of the temple. Mahitosh Babu was still looking shaken and was wiping his face frequently. Lalmohan Babu had regained consciousness and climbed down from the tree, with a little assistance from me. Then he had calmly taken the sword back, as though carrying a sword and climbing trees was something he did every day.

After a few minutes' silence, Feluda spoke. 'Mahitosh Babu,' he said, 'you are worrying unnecessarily. I had already promised Mr Sanyal I would not disclose any of your secrets. No one will ever find out that you are not a shikari, and that you cannot even hold a gun steadily. I had my suspicions right from the start. Your signature on Lalmohan Babu's letter made me think you were old. So I began to wonder how you could shoot, if you could not even write with a steady hand. Then I thought perhaps your hands had been affected only recently and all those tales in your books were indeed true. I started to believe this, but something your brother said raised fresh doubts in my mind. Yes, I know most of what he said was irrelevant, but I didn't think he would actually make up a story. On the contrary, what he said often made perfect sense, if one thought about it. He obviously knew you had written books on shikar, and that the whole thing was based on lies. This distressed him very much, which is why he kept talking about Yudhisthir's punishment for telling a lie. He also told me not everyone could be like your grandfather. Not everyone could handle weapons . . .'

'Yes, they could!' Mahitosh Babu interrupted, breathing hard and speaking very fast. 'I killed mynahs and sparrows with my airgun when I was seven, from a distance of fifty yards. But . . .' he glanced at the peepul tree. 'One day, we came here for a picnic, and I climbed that tree. In fact, I was sitting on the same branch where your cousin was sitting a while ago, when my brother suddenly said he could see a tiger coming. I jumped down to see the tiger, and—'

'—You broke your arm?'

'Compound fracture,' Mr Sanyal stepped forward. 'It never really healed properly.'

'I see. And yet you wanted to be known as a shikari, just because that was your family tradition? So you moved from here and went to

Assam and Orissa where no one knew you? It was Mr Sanyal who killed all those animals, but everyone was convinced you were a worthy successor of your forefathers. Is that right, Mahitosh Babu?'

'Yes,' Mahitosh Babu sighed deeply, 'that's right. What Shashanka did for his friend is unbelievable. He is a much better shikari than anyone in my family.'

'But recently . . . were you two drifting apart?'

Both men were silent. Feluda continued, 'I hadn't heard of Mahitosh Sinha-Roy before his books began to be published. Nor, I am sure, had thousands of others. But when these books came out, Sinha-Roy became a famous name, didn't it? He was praised, admired, even revered. And what was his fame based on? Nothing but lies. No one knew the name of Shashanka Sanyal. No one ever would. You had begun to resent this, Mr Sanyal, hadn't you? You had done a lot for your friend, but perhaps the time had come to draw a line? We heard Mahitosh Babu speak very sternly to someone on our first night. I assume he was speaking to you. You two had started to disagree on most things, hadn't you?'

Neither man made a reply. Feluda stared steadily at Mahitosh Babu for a few moments.

'Very well,' he said, 'I shall take silence for assent. But there is another thing. I suppose silence is the only answer to that, as well.'

Mahitosh Babu cast a nervous glance at Feluda.

'I am now talking of Torit Sengupta,' Feluda went on. 'You never wrote a single line yourself, just as you never killed a single animal. You said something about your manuscript, which made me go and look for it in your study. But I didn't find anything with your handwriting on it. All you ever did was just relate your stories to Mr Sengupta. It was he who wrote them out beautifully. They were his words, his language, his style; yet, everyone thought they were yours, and you earned more praise, also as a gifted writer. Yes, it is true that you paid him well and he lived here in great comfort. But how long could he go on seeing someone else take the credit for his talent, his own hard work? Anyone with creative abilities wants to see his efforts appreciated. If he continued to work for you, there was no way his own name could ever become well known. Disappointed and frustrated, he was probably thinking of leaving, but suddenly you chanced upon that puzzle left by Adityanarayan, and Mr Sengupta saw it. It could be that he had already found references to those coins among your grandfather's papers; so he knew what the treasure consisted of. He solved the puzzle, and decided to leave with the treasure. He even found it . . . but then things went horribly wrong.'

Mahitosh Babu struggled to his feet, not without difficulty. 'Yes, Mr Mitter, you are quite right in all that you've said,' he remarked. 'It is very painful for me to hear these things, but do tell me this: who killed Torit? He might have resented—even hated—me for what I was doing, but who could have disliked him so intensely? I certainly know of no one. Nor can I imagine who else might have come to the forest that night.'

'Perhaps I can help you there.'

Mahitosh Babu had started to pace. He stopped abruptly at Feluda's words and asked, 'Can you?'

Feluda turned to Mr Sanyal. 'Didn't you pick up a Winchester rifle from the trophy room that night and come here, Mr Sanyal? I noticed traces of mud on its butt.'

Perhaps being a shikari had given him nerves of steel. Mr Sanyal's face remained expressionless. 'What if I did, Mr Mitter?' he asked coolly. 'What exactly are you trying to say?'

Feluda remained just as calm. 'I am not suggesting for a moment that you came looking for the hidden treasure,' he said. 'You were and still are loyal to your friend. You would never have cheated him. But is it not true that you knew Mr Sengupta had solved the puzzle?'

'Yes,' Mr Sanyal replied levelly, 'I did. As a matter of fact, Torit had offered me half of the treasure since he felt we were both being deprived in the same way. But I refused. Moreover, I told him more than once not to go into the forest, because of the man-eater. But that night, when I saw the light from his torch, I had to follow him in here. Yes, I took that rifle from the trophy room. When I got here, I found that he had dug the ground and found that pitcher, but there was no sign of him. Then I looked around closely, and saw blood on the grass, and pug marks. So I quickly put the pitcher away inside the temple, and followed the marks up to the bamboo grove. Then . . . there was a flash of lightning, and I saw the tiger crouched over Torit's body. It was too dark to see clearly, but I shot at it, and made it run away. I knew I couldn't do anything to help Torit. It was too late. However . . .' He broke off.

'However, that isn't all, is it? Please allow me to finish your story. Correct me if what I say is wrong. I can only guess the details.'

'Very well.'

'You were talking to Madhavlal last night, weren't you?'

Mr Sanyal did not deny this. Feluda asked another question: 'Were you asking him to place a bait for the tiger? See those vultures over that tree? I think they are there because a dead animal is lying under it.'

'A calf,' Mr Sanyal muttered.

'That means you wanted the tiger to come out today, while we were here, so that you could show at least a few people you were the real shikari, not your friend. Is that right?'

Mr Sanyal nodded silently. Before Feluda could say anything else, Mahitosh Babu came forward and placed a hand on Feluda's shoulder.

'Mr Mitter,' he pleaded, 'I'd like to give you something. Please do not refuse.'

'What are you talking about?'

'These coins. This treasure. You are entitled to at least some of it. Please let me—'

Feluda smiled, looking at Mahitosh Babu. 'No, I don't want your silver coins,' he said, 'but there is something I'd like to take back with me.'

'What is it?'

'Adityanarayan's sword.'

Lalmohan Babu walked over to Feluda immediately and handed him the sword.

'What!' Mahitosh Babu sounded amazed. 'You would like that old sword instead of these priceless coins?'

'Yes. In a way, this sword is priceless, too. It is not an ordinary sword, Mahitosh Babu. No, I don't mean just the history attached to it. There is something else.'

'You mean something to do with Torit's murder?'

'No. Mr Sengupta was not murdered.'

'What! You mean he killed himself?'

'No, it was not suicide, either.'

'Then what was it, for heaven's sake? Why are you talking in riddles?' Mahitosh Babu said impatiently, sounding stern once more.

'No, no, I am not talking in riddles. Let me explain what happened. We were so busy looking for a murderer that the obvious answer did not occur to anyone. Mr Sengupta had removed the sword himself.'

'Really? Why?'

'Because he needed something to dig the ground with. He didn't have time to look for a spade. That sword was handy, so he took it.'

'And then?'

'I am coming to that. But before I do, I'd like to show you what's so special about it.'

Feluda stopped and began moving towards Mr Sanyal with the open sword in his hand. Brave though he was, Mr Sanyal moved restlessly as Feluda got closer. But Feluda did not hurt him. He merely stretched his arm, so that the iron blade could get closer to the point of the gun in Mr Sanyal's hand. A second later, the two pieces of metal clicked together with a faint noise.

'Good heavens, what is this? A magnet?' Mr Sanyal cried.

'Yes, it is now a magnet. I mean the sword, not your gun. Let me point out that when I saw this sword the first time, it was no different from other swords. There were various pieces of metal lying near it, but they were not sticking to the blade. It was magnetized the same night when Mr Sengupta died.'

'How did that happen?' Mahitosh Babu asked. We were all waiting with bated breath to hear Feluda's explanation.

'If a person happens to be carrying a piece of metal in his hand when lightning strikes, that piece of metal gets magnetized,' Feluda went on. 'Not only that, it may actually attract the lightning. What happened that night, I think, was this: it started raining as soon as Mr Sengupta finished digging the ground. He got the pitcher, but had to leave it there. I think he then ran towards that peepul tree to avoid getting wet. He was still carrying the sword, perhaps without even realizing it. Lightning struck the tree only a few seconds later. Mr Sengupta was lifted off the ground and flung aside under its impact . . . As he fell, the point of the sword pierced his clothes and left a deep wound in his body, purely by accident. No one killed him. It is my belief that he was already dead when he fell. Then the tiger found him.'

Mahitosh Babu was shaking violently. He looked up and stared at the peepul tree.

'That's why . . . that explains it!' he said, his voice sounding choked. 'I was wondering all this while why that tree had suddenly grown so old!'

We were going back to Calcutta today. The sun was shining brightly, but because of the recent rains, it felt pleasantly cool. We had finished packing, and were sitting in our room. Devtosh Babu's room was now unlocked. I could hear his voice from time to time. Lalmohan Babu had grazed a knee while climbing down from the tree. He was placing a strip of sticking plaster on it, when a servant arrived, carrying a steel trunk on his head. He put it down on the ground and said Mahitosh Babu had sent it. Feluda opened it, and revealed a beautiful tiger skin, very carefully packed. There was a letter, too. It said, 'Dear Mr Mitter, I am giving you this tiger skin as a token of my gratitude. I should be honoured if you accept it. The tiger was killed by my friend, Shashanka Sanyal, in a forest near Sambalpur, in 1957.'

Lalmohan Babu read the letter and said, 'Ah, so you get both the sword and this skin!'

'No, Lalmohan Babu. I am going to present the tiger skin to you.'

'To me? Why?'

'For your remarkable achievement. I have never known anyone who could lose consciousness on the top of a tree, and yet manage to stay put, without crashing to the ground. I would not have thought it possible at all. But you have proved it can be done!'

Lalmohan Babu waved a dismissive hand.

'Did I tell you why I fainted in the first place? It was only because of my very lively imagination, Felu Babu. When you mentioned a tiger, do you know what I saw? I saw a burning torch, its orange flame shooting up to the sky. An awful monster sat in the middle of it, pulling evil faces, and I could hear the roar of engines. An aircraft was about to take off . . . and I knew it was going to land on me! Hey, what else could I do after this, except close my eyes and pass into oblivion?'

The Locked Chest

Village: Ghurghutia
P.O. Plassey
Dist. Nadia
3 November 1974
To:
Mr Pradosh C. Mitter

Dear Mr Mitter,
I am writing to invite you to my house. I have heard a lot about
your work and wish to meet you in person. There is, of course,
a special reason for asking you to come at this particular time.
You will get to know the details on arrival. If you feel you are
able to accept this invitation from a seventy-three-year-old
man, please confirm your acceptance in writing immediately.
In order to reach Ghurghutia, you need to disembark at Plassey,
and travel further south for another five-and-a-half-miles.
There are several trains from Sealdah, out of which the Up
Lalgola Passenger leaves at 1.58 p.m. and reaches Plassey at
6.11. I will arrange for you to be met at the station and brought
here. You can spend the night at my house, and catch the same
train at 10.30 a.m. the following morning to Calcutta.
I look forward to hearing from you.

With good wishes,
Yours sincerely,
Kalikinkar Majumdar

I handed the letter back to Feluda, and asked, 'Is it the same
Plassey where that famous battle was fought?'

'Yes. There is no other Plassey in Bengal, dear boy. But if you
think the place has got any evidence left of that historic battle, you
are sadly mistaken. There is absolutely no sign left, not even the
palash trees in the woods that stood in Siraj-ud-daula's time. The
name "Plassey" came from these trees. Did you know that?'

I nodded. 'Will you go, Feluda?'

Feluda stared at the letter for a few seconds.

'I wonder why an old man wants to see me,' he said thoughtfully.
'It doesn't seem right to refuse. To be honest, I am quite curious.
Besides, have you ever been to a village in the winter? Have you seen
how the mist gathers in open fields at dawn and dusk? All that
remains visible are tree trunks and a little area over one's head.

Darkness falls suddenly, and it can get really cold . . . I haven't seen all this for years. Go on, get me a postcard, Topshe.'

Mr Majumdar was told to expect us on 12 November. Feluda chose this date, keeping in mind that a letter from Calcutta would take at least three days to reach him.

We took the 365 Up Lalgola Passenger and reached Plassey at 6.30 p.m. I saw from the train what Feluda had meant by darkness falling quickly. The last lingering rays of the setting sun disappeared from the rice fields almost before I knew it. By the time we left the station after handing over our tickets to the collector at the gate, all lights had been switched on, although the sky still held a faint reddish glow. The car that was parked outside had to be Mr Majumdar's. I had never seen a car like that. Feluda said he might have seen one or two when he was a child. All he knew was that it was an American car. Its colour must have been dark red once, but now the paint had peeled off in many places. The hood, too, bore patches here and there and showed signs of age. In spite of all this, there was something rather impressive about the car. I couldn't help feeling a certain amount of awe.

A car like that ought to have had a chauffeur in uniform. The man who was leaning against it, smoking a cigarette, was dressed in a dhoti and a shirt. He threw away his cigarette when he saw us and straightened himself. 'To see Mr Majumdar?' he asked.

'Yes, to Ghurghutia.'

'Very well, sir. This way, please.'

The driver opened a door for us, and we climbed into the forty-year-old car. He then walked over to the front of the car to crank the handle, which made the engine come to life. He got behind the wheel, and began driving. We settled ourselves comfortably, but the road being full of potholes and the springs in the seat being old, our comfort did not last for very long. However, once we had passed through the main town of Plassey and were actually out in the country, the scenery became so beautiful that I ceased to feel any discomfort. It wasn't yet totally dark, and I could see tiny villages across large rice fields, surrounded by trees. In their midst, the mist rose from the ground and spread like a smoky blanket a few feet above the ground. 'Pretty as a picture' was the phrase that came to mind.

An old, sprawling mansion in a place like this came as a total surprise. Ten minutes after we started, I realized that we were passing through private land, for the trees were now mango, jamun and jackfruit. The road then turned right. We passed a broken and abandoned temple, and suddenly found ourselves facing a huge white, moss-covered gate, on the top of which was a naubatkhana (a music room). The driver sounded his horn three times before passing through the gate. The mansion came into view immediately.

The last traces of red had disappeared from the sky, leaving a deep purple hue. The dark house stood against the sky, like a towering cliff. We got out and followed the driver. As we got closer, I realized the whole house could be kept in a museum. Its walls were all damp, plaster had peeled off in several places, and small plants had grown out of cracks in the exposed bricks. We stopped before the front door.

'No one in this area has electricity, I take it?' Feluda asked.

'No, sir. For nearly three years, all we've heard are promises. But nothing's happened yet,' the driver replied.

I glanced up. From where I was standing, a lot of windows on the first floor were visible. But each room was in darkness. On our right, through a couple of bushes, a light flickered in a tiny hut. Perhaps that was where a mali or chowkidar lived. I shivered silently. What sort of a place was this? Perhaps Feluda should have made more enquiries before agreeing to come.

Light from a lantern fell in the doorway. Then an old servant appeared at the door. The driver had gone, possibly to put the car away. The servant glanced at us with a slight frown, then said, 'Please come in.' We stepped in behind him.

There was no doubt that the house sprawled over a large area. But everything inside it seemed surprisingly small. The doors were not high, the windows were half the size of windows in any house in Calcutta, and it was almost possible to touch the ceiling if I raised my arm. 'This house clearly belonged to a zamindar.' Feluda remarked. 'All the houses built by zamindars in the villages in Bengal about two hundred years ago were built like this.'

We crossed a long passage, then turned right to go up a flight of stairs. A strange contraption met my eyes as we got to the first floor. 'This is called a "covered door". It's like a trapdoor, really,' Feluda told me. 'These were built to stop burglars and dacoits from getting in. If you shut it, it would cease standing upright. Then it would fold automatically and lie flat, stretching diagonally across, to from a kind of ceiling over out heads. So anyone trying to climb up would be shut out. See those holes in the door? Spears used to be slipped out of those holes to fight intruders.'

Luckily, the door was now standing wide open. We began crossing another long corridor. An oil lamp burnt in a niche in the wall where it ended. The servant opened a door next to this niche, and ushered us in.

The room we stepped into was quite large. It might have seemed even larger had it not been stuffed with so much furniture. Nearly half of it had been taken up by a massive bed. To the left of this bed was a table and a chest. Besides these, there were three chairs, a wardrobe, and bookshelves that went right up to the ceiling. Each shelf was crammed with books. An old man was lying on the bed, a blanket drawn upto his chin. In the flickering light of a candle I saw that through a salt-and-pepper beard and moustache, he was smiling at us.

'Please sit down,' he invited.

'Thank you. This is my cousin, Tapesh. I wrote to you about him,' Feluda said. Mr Majumdar smiled again and nodded. I noticed that he did not fold his hands in reply to my 'namaskar'.

We took the chairs nearest to the bed.

'My letter must have made you curious,' Mr Majumdar observed lightly.

'Yes, it certainly did. Or I'd never have travelled this distance.'

'Good.' Mr Majumdar looked genuinely pleased. 'If you hadn't come, I would have felt very disappointed, and thought you to be arrogant; and you would have missed out on something. But perhaps you have read these books already?' Mr Majumdar's eyes turned towards the table. Four bound volumes were arranged in a pile next to a candle. Feluda got up and picked them up. 'Good heavens!' he exclaimed. 'These are all extremely rare, and they are all to do with my profession. Did you ever . . .?'

'No, no,' Mr Majumdar laughed, 'I never tried to become a detective myself. It has always been a hobby. You see, fifty-two years ago, someone in our family was murdered. An English investigator called Malcolm caught the killer. After speaking to Malcolm and learning something about his work, I became interested in criminology. That was when I bought those books. I was also very fond of reading detective novels. Have you heard of Emile Gaboriau?'

'Yes, yes,' Feluda replied with enthusiasm, 'wasn't he a French writer? He wrote the first detective novel, I think.'

'That's right,' Mr Majumdar nodded. 'I've got all his books. And, of course, books by writers like Edgar Allan Poe and Conan Doyle. I bought all these forty years ago. Of late, I believe, there has been a lot of progress, and now there are many scientific and technical ways to catch a criminal. But from what little I know of your work, you strike me as one who depends more on old-fashioned methods, and uses his brain more than anything else, very successfully. Am I right?'

'I do not know how successful I've been, but you're certainly right about my methods.'

'That is why I asked you to visit me.'

Mr Majumdar paused. Feluda returned to his chair. After a while, Mr Majumdar resumed speaking, staring straight at the flame of the candle. 'I am not only old—I crossed seventy some years ago—but also ailing. God knows what's going to happen to my books when I die. So I thought if I could give you a few, they'd be appreciated and looked after.'

Feluda looked at the books in the shelves in surprise. 'Are all of those your own?' he asked.

'Yes. I was the only one in my family with an interest in books. Criminology wasn't the only subject that held my interest, as you can see.'

'Yes, of course. I can see books on archaeology, painting, gardening, history, biographies, travelogues . . . even drama and the theatre! Some of them appear to be new. Do you still buy books?'

'Oh yes. I have a manager called Rajen. He goes to Calcutta two or three times every month. I make him a list of books, and he goes and gets them from College Street.'

Feluda looked once more at the books kept on the table. 'I don't know how to thank you.'

'You don't have to. It would have given me a lot of pleasure if I could actually hand them over to you myself, but both my hands are useless.'

Startled, we stared at him. His hands were hidden under the blanket, but I would never have thought that that had a special significance.

'Arthritis,' Mr Majumdar explained, 'has affected all my fingers. My son happens to be visiting me at the moment, so he's looking after me now. Usually, it is my servant Gokul who feeds me every day.'

'Did you get your son to write the letter to me?'

'No, Rajen wrote it. He takes care of everything. If I need to see a doctor, he fetches one from Behrampore. Plassey doesn't have good doctors.'

I had noticed Feluda casting frequent glances at the chest kept near the bed while he was talking to Mr Majumdar. 'That chest appears to be different from most,' he now said. 'I can't see any provision for a key. Does it have a combination lock?'

'Correct,' Mr Majumdar smiled. 'All it has is a knob, with numbers written around it. The chest opens only if you move the knob to rest against some specific numbers. These areas were once notorious for armed burglars. You knew that, didn't you? In fact, my ancestors became wealthy enough to buy masses of land chiefly by looting others. Years later, we ourselves were attacked by dacoits, more than once. So I thought a chest with a combination lock might be safer than any other.'

Mr Majumdar stopped speaking, and frowned for a second. Then he called, 'Gokul!'

The old servant appeared almost instantly. 'Bring that bird over here,' his master commanded. 'I'd like these people to see it.'

Gokul disappeared and came back a minute later with a parrot in a cage. Mr Majumdar turned to it and said softly, 'Go on, sweetie. Say it. Shut the door . . . say it!'

For a few seconds, nothing happened. Then, suddenly, the parrot spoke in an amazingly clear voice. 'Shut the door!' it said. I gave a start. I had never heard a bird speak so distinctly. But that wasn't all. 'O big fat hen!' the bird added. This time, I saw Feluda turn his head sharply. Before anyone could say anything, the parrot said both things together, very rapidly: 'Shut the door, O big fat hen!'

'What does it mean?' Feluda asked after a moment's pause. Mr Majumdar burst out laughing. 'I am not going to tell you. All I can say is that what you just heard was a code, and it has to do with that locked chest over there. You have twelve hours to work it out.'

'I see. May I ask why the bird has been taught to say it?'

'You may indeed, and I am going to tell you why. Age does strange things to one's memory. About three years ago, one day, I suddenly discovered that I couldn't remember the combination that would open the chest. Can you believe that? After using the same numbers for years, almost every day, it had simply vanished from my mind, just like that. All day, I tried to remember the numbers. Then, finally, it came back in a flash, in the middle of the night. I could have written it down, but didn't want to, in case it fell into the wrong hands. It was far better to keep it in my head, but now I realized I could no longer depend ort my memory. So the next morning, I made up that code and taught my parrot to say it. Now it says it every now and then, just as other parrots say, "Radhey Shyam" or "how are you?"'

Feluda was still staring at the chest. I saw him frown suddenly and get up to peer at it closely. Then he picked up the candle and began examining its lid.

'What is it?' Mr Majumdar asked anxiously. 'What have you found? Do your trained eyes tell you anything?'

'I think, Mr Majumdar, someone tried to force this chest open.'

'Are you sure?' Mr Majumdar had stopped smiling.

Feluda put the candle back on the table. 'There are some marks on it,' he said. 'Ordinary dusting and cleaning couldn't have left marks like those. But is there anyone who'd want to open it?'

Mr Majumdar thought for a moment. Then he said slowly, 'Not many people live here, Mr Mitter. Apart from myself, there's Gokul, Rajen, my driver Monilal, a cook and a mali. Vishwanath—that's my son—arrived five days ago. He lives in Calcutta and visits me rarely. He's here now because of my illness. You see, last Monday I had been sitting in the garden. When I tried to get up, everything suddenly went dark and I fell down on the bench. Rajen rang Vishwanath from Plassey, and he came the next day with a doctor from Calcutta. It appears to have been a mild stroke. In any case, I know I haven't got long to live. But . . . don't tell me I have to spend my last few days in doubt and anxiety? Always afraid that a thief might get into my room and force open that chest?'

'No, no. There is no need to jump to conclusions. I may be quite wrong,' Feluda said reassuringly. 'Those marks may have appeared when the chest was first installed in that corner. I can't see very clearly in the light from one candle, so I cannot tell whether those marks are old or new. I'll have another look in the morning. Is your servant trustworthy?'

'Absolutely, He's been with me for thirty years.'

'And Rajen?'

'Rajen has also spent a good many years here. But then, where's the guarantee that someone who has honoured my trust until today won't betray it tomorrow?'

Feluda nodded in agreement. 'No, there's no guarantee at all, unfortunately. Anyway, tell Gokul to keep an eye on things. I don't really think there's any immediate danger.'

'Oh. Good.' Mr Majumdar appeared relieved. We rose.

'Gokul will show you your room,' he said. 'You'll find blankets and quilts and mosquito nets. Vishwanath has gone to Behrampore, he should be getting back soon. You must have your dinner as soon as he returns. Tomorrow morning, if you like, you can go for a ride in my car, though there isn't much to see in this area.'

Feluda picked up the books from the table and thanked him again. Before saying good night, Mr Majumdar reminded him about the code. 'If you can crack it, Mr Mitter, I will give you the whole set by Gaboriau.'

Gokul came back with a lantern and took us to our room. It was smaller than Mr Majumdar's but with less furniture, which made it easier to move about. Two beds had been made with considerable care. A lantern burnt in a corner. Feluda sat down on the spotless sheet that covered his bed, and said, 'Can you remember the code?'

'Yes.'

'Very well. Here's my notebook and a pen. Write it down. I would love to get those books by Gaboriau.'

I wrote the words down. None of it made any sense. How on earth was Feluda going to find its meaning?

'I simply cannot see how the numbers for a combination lock can be hidden in this strange message!' I complained. 'I mean, this is pure nonsense, isn't it? How can a hen shut a door?'

'That's where the challenge lies, don't you see? Nobody's actually asking a hen to shut a door. That much is obvious. Each word has a separate meaning. I have to figure it out somehow by tomorrow morning.'

Feluda got up and opened a window. The moon had risen by this time, and everything was bathed in moonlight. I went and stood by his side. Our room overlooked the rear portion of the house. 'There's probably a pond over there on the right,' Feluda remarked, pointing. Through a thick growth of plants and shrubs, I could see the shimmering surface of water. The only noise that could be heard was that of jackals calling in the distance, and crickets chirping in the bushes. Never before had I visited a place so totally isolated and remote.

Feluda shut the window again to keep out the cold night air. In the same instant, we heard a car arrive. It was obviously a different car, not the American one we had travelled in.

'That's probably Vishwanath Majumdar,' Feluda remarked.

Good, I thought. This might mean we'd soon be called in to dinner. To tell the truth, I was feeling quite hungry. We had left after an early lunch, since our train was at two o'clock. We did get ourselves a cup of tea and some sweets at Ranaghat, but even that was a long time ago. Ordinarily, I would probably not be thinking of food at eight in the evening, but since there was nothing else to do in a place like this, I quite liked the idea of dinner and an early night.

Looking around in the room, my eyes suddenly fell upon something I hadn't noticed before. It was the portrait of a man that took up most of the opposite wall. There could be no doubt that he was one of Mr Majumdar's ancestors. He was sitting in a chair, looking rather grim. His torso was bare, which showed to perfection his very broad shoulders. His eyes were large, and his moustache thick, its edges turning upwards. His hair rippled down to his shoulders.

'I bet he used to wrestle, and use heavy clubs regularly,' Feluda whispered. 'Perhaps he was the first bandit who became a zamindar.'

There were footsteps outside. Both of us looked at the door. Gokul had left a lantern on the veranda. A shadow blocked out its light for a second, then fell on the threshold. It was followed by the figure of a man. Could this be Vishwanath Majumdar? Surely not? This man was wearing a short dhoti and a grey kurta, had a bushy moustache and glasses with thick lenses. He was peering into the room, trying to find us.

'What is it, Rajen Babu?' Feluda asked.

Rajen Babu finally found what he was looking for. His eyes came to rest upon Feluda.

'Chhoto Babu has just returned,' he said in a gruff voice that suggested he might have a cold. 'I have asked Gokul to serve dinner. He'll come and call you in a few minutes.'

He left. 'What is that smell, Feluda?' I asked as soon as he had gone.

'Naphthalene. I think he just took that woollen kurta out of a suitcase and put it on.'

Silence fell once more as the sound of footsteps faded away. Had Feluda not been with me, I could never have spent even five minutes in such an eerie atmosphere. How did Mr Majumdar and the others manage to live here day after day? Suddenly, I remembered someone had been murdered in this house. God knew in which room it had taken place.

Feluda, in the meantime, had dragged the table with the lantern on it closer to his bed and opened his notebook to look at the code. I heard him mutter, 'Shut the door . . . shut the door . . .' a couple of times. Thoroughly bored, I decided to step out of the room and stand on the veranda outside.

Oh God, what was that? My heart nearly jumped into my mouth. Something was moving in the distance, where the faint light from the lantern gave way to complete darkness. I forced myself to stay silent and stared at the moving object. A couple of seconds later, I realized it was only a cat, not black or white, but one with stripes on its body like a tiger. It returned my stare sombrely, then gave a yawn before walking lazily back into the darkness. A few moments later, the parrot gave a raucous cry, and then all was silent once more. I wondered where Vishwanath Majumdar's room was. Was it on the ground floor? Where did Rajen Babu live? Why had we been given a room from which it was impossible to hear noises in other parts of the house?

I came back to the room. Feluda was sitting crosslegged on the bed, his notebook in his lap. 'Why are they taking so long?' I couldn't help sounding cross. Feluda looked at his watch. 'You're right, Topshe. Rajen Babu left at least fifteen minutes ago.' He then went back to staring at his notebook.

I began going through the books Feluda had been given. One was on analysing fingerprints, one was simply called *Criminology*, and the third was called *Crime and its Detection*. I picked up the fourth, but could not understand what its name meant. It was full of pictures, chiefly of firearms. Had Feluda brought his revolver?

No, why should he? After all, he hadn't come here to solve a crime. There was no reason for him to have brought his revolver. I put the books in our suitcase and was about to sit down, when the sound of an unfamiliar voice startled me again. Another man was standing at the door. This time, there was no problem in recognizing him. He wasn't Gokul, or Rajen Babu, or the driver Mondal. He had to be Kalikinkar's son, Vishwanath.

'Sorry to have kept you waiting,' he said, folding his hands and looking at Feluda. 'My name is Vishwanath Majumdar.'

Now I could see that he resembled his father to a great degree. He had the same eyes and the same nose. He was probably in his mid-forties. His hair was still black, he was clean-shaven and had very thin lips. I took an instant dislike to him, though I couldn't find a proper reason for it. It was perhaps simply because he had made us wait a long time, and I was tired. Or it could be that—but this could just be my imagination—when he smiled, his eyes remained cold and aloof. He seemed as though he wasn't really pleased to see us. Perhaps it was only our departure that would make him happy.

Feluda and I went with him down to the ground floor to the dining room. I had half expected to be asked to sit down on the floor for a traditional meal, but found to my surprise that there was a dining table. Silver plates and bowls and glasses were placed on it.

When we were all seated, Vishwanath Majumdar said, 'I like having a bath twice a day, be it summer or winter. That's what took so long, I'm afraid.'

He was still reeking of perfumed soap and, possibly, an expensive cologne. Clad in grey trousers, a white silk shirt and a dark green sleeveless pullover, he was clearly a man fond of the good things in life.

We began eating. Several little bowls were placed in a semicircle around our plates, each containing a different dish. There were three different vegetables, daal and fish curry.

'Have you spoken to my father?' Vishwanath Majumdar asked.

'Yes. I am rather embarrassed by what he did.'

'You mean the books he gave you?'

'Yes. Even if those books were still available, they would have cost at least a thousand rupees.'

Vishwanath Majumdar laughed. 'When he told me he had asked you to come here, I was at first quite annoyed with him,' he told us. 'I didn't think it was fair to invite people from the city to a place like this.'

'Why not?' Feluda protested. 'Why should you have objected to that? I have lost nothing by coming here. On the contrary, I have gained such a lot!'

Vishwanath Majumdar did not pay much attention to these words. 'Speaking for myself,' he declared, 'I'd be perfectly happy to go back tomorrow. The last four days have been quite enough for me, thank you. I have no idea how my father can live here permanently.'

'Doesn't he go out at all?'

'No. He spends most of his time in that dark room. He used to go out and sit in the garden a couple of times every day. But now the doctor has forbidden all movement.'

'Did you say you were returning tomorrow?'

'Yes. Father is not in any immediate danger. Will you be catching the train at half past ten?'

'Yes.'

'I see. That means I shall leave soon after you get to the station.'

Feluda poured daal over his rice. 'Your father is interested in so many different subjects. Are you interested in anything other than your business?'

'No, sir. I simply don't have the time for anything else once my day's work is done. I am entirely happy being a businessman, and no more.'

By the time we said good night to Vishwanath Majumdar and returned to our room, it was half past nine. It didn't really matter what time my watch showed, for time seemed to have very little significance here. Seven o'clock had seemed like midnight.

'Do you mind if I keep my pillow on the other side?' I asked Feluda.

'No, but why do you want to do that?'

'I have no wish to see that grim face on the wall the minute I open my eyes in the morning.'

Feluda laughed. 'All right. I think I'll do the same,' he said. 'I must say I don't like the look in his eyes, either.'

Just before going to bed, Feluda picked up the lantern and turned its light down. The room seemed to shrink in size. In just a few minutes, I could feel my eyes growing heavy with sleep. But, just as I was about to drop off, I heard Feluda muttering, which made me open them at once.

'Shut the door . . . and open the gate . . . no, that's wrong. Pick up sticks. Yes, that comes first.'

'Feluda!' I cried, slightly alarmed. 'Wake up, Feluda! You are talking in your sleep. What's the matter with you?'

'No, no,' I heard him chuckle in the darkness. 'I am fully awake, and no, I haven't gone mad, I assure you. What has just happened, Topshe, is that I think I've won that set by Gaboriau.'

'What! You've cracked the code?'

'Yes, I think so. It was actually ridiculously simple. I should have spotted it at once.'

'It still makes no sense to me.'

'That's only because you aren't thinking. How were you taught to count when you were a child?'

'Very simply. One, two, three, four . . . that was all.'

'Was it? Think, dear boy, think. Did no one try to make it easier for you? Weren't you taught a rhyme?'

'A rhyme to go with numbers? You mean something that began with one, two . . . no, I don't think . . . hey, wait a minute! Feluda, Feluda, I know what you mean! Yes, I've got it.' I sat up in excitement. I could dimly see Feluda turn his head to look at me. He was grinning.

'Very well. Let's have it, then.'

Softly, I began to chant a rhyme I had been taught in nursery school:

'One, two
Buckle my shoe.
Three, four
Shut the door.
Five, six
Pick up sticks.
Seven, eight
Open the gate.
Nine, ten
A big fat hen.
Eleven, twelve
Dig and delve . . .'

'That'll do. Now what do you think the full message means?'

'Shut the door . . . that would mean three and four. Big fat hen would mean nine and ten. Right?'

'Right. But there's an "O" before "big fat hen". That means the whole number is 340910. Simple, isn't it? Now, go to sleep.'

I lay down again, marvelling at Feluda's cleverness. But just as I began to close my eyes once more, footsteps sounded on the veranda. It was Rajen Babu again. What did he want at this time of night?

'Yes, Rajen Babu?' Feluda called.

'Chhoto Babu told me to find out if you needed anything.'

'No, no. We're fine, thank you.'

Rajen Babu disappeared silently. This time, sleep came very quickly. All I was aware of as I closed my eyes was that the moonlight that had seeped through closed shutters had suddenly gone pale. I thought I heard distant thunder, and the cat meeaowed a couple of times. Then I fell asleep.

When I woke in the morning, Feluda was opening the windows. 'It rained last night,' he said. 'Did you hear it?'

I hadn't. But now I could see through the window that the clouds had gone. The sun shone brightly on the leaves I could see from my bed.

Gokul appeared with two cups of tea half an hour later. Looking at him in daylight, I was considerably surprised. Not only did he seem old, but his face held an expression of deep distress.

'Has Kalikinkar Babu woken up?' Feluda asked. Perhaps Gokul was hard of hearing. He did not answer Feluda's question at first. All he did was stare at him vacantly. Feluda had to raise his voice and ask again before he nodded and left the room quickly.

We made our way to old Mr Majumdar's room at a round seven-thirty, and found him exactly as we'd left him the night before. He was still lying in his bed, a blanket covering most of his body including his arms. The window next to his bed was shut, possibly to avoid direct sunlight. The only light that came into the room was through the open door. I noticed a photograph on the wall over his bed. It must have been taken many years ago, for it showed a much younger Kalikinkar Majumdar. His hair and beard were both jet black.

He greeted us with a smile.

'I got Rajen to take out the books by Gaboriau. I knew you could do it,' he said.

'Well, it is for you to decide whether I've got the right number. 340910. Is that it?'

'Well done!' Mr Majumdar's voice held both pleasure and admiration. 'Go on, take those books and put them in your bag. And please take another look at those marks on the chest. I had a look myself. They didn't strike me as anything to worry about.'

'Well then, that settles it. If you're not worried about it, nothing else matters.'

Feluda thanked him once more before collecting the four books written by the first writer of detective fiction.

'Have you had tea?' Mr Majumdar asked.

'Yes, sir.'

'I told the driver to bring the car out. Vishwanath left very early this morning. He said he wanted to reach Calcutta by ten. Rajen has gone to the local market. Gokul will help you with your luggage. Would you like to go for a drive before you catch your train?'

'I was actually thinking of going by an earlier train. We don't really have to wait until ten-thirty. If we left immediately, perhaps we could catch the 372 Down.'

'Very well. I have no wish to keep anyone from the city in this small village any longer than is necessary. But I'm really pleased that you could come. I mean that.'

Soon, we were on our way to the railway station. The road went through rice fields, which glistened in the early morning sun after a rainy night. I was looking at these with admiration, when I heard Feluda ask a question. 'Is there any other way to get to the station?'

'No, sir, this is the only way,' Monilal replied.

Feluda was suddenly looking rather grave. I wanted to ask him if he had noticed anything suspicious, but didn't dare open my mouth.

The road being wet and muddy, it took us longer to reach the station. Feluda took the luggage out of the car and thanked the driver, who then drove off. But Feluda made no attempt to go to the ticket counter to buy tickets for our return journey. He found the stationmaster's room instead and left our luggage with him. Then he came out once more and approached one of the cycle-rickshaws that were waiting outside.

'Do you know where the local police station is?'

'Yes, sir.'

'Can you take us there? We're in a hurry.'

We climbed into the rickshaw quickly. The driver began pedalling fast, honking as loudly as he could, weaving his way through the milling crowds, narrowly avoiding collisions more than once. We reached the police station in five minutes. The officer left in charge was Sub-inspector Sarkar. It turned out that he knew Feluda's name. 'We have heard a lot about you, sir,' he said. 'What brings you here?'

'What can you tell me about Kalikinkar Majumdar of Ghurghutia?'

'Kalikinkar Majumdar? As far as I know, he is a perfect gentleman, who keeps himself to himself. Why, I've never heard anything nasty said about him!'

'What about his son, Vishwanath? Does he live here?'

'No. I think he lives in Calcutta. Whatever's the matter, Mr Mitter?'

'Can you take your jeep and come with me? There's something seriously wrong.'

Mr Sarkar did not waste another minute. We began bumping our way back to Ghurghutia in a police jeep, splashing mud everywhere. Feluda's face held a look of suppressed excitement, but he opened his mouth only once. I was the only one who could hear his words:

'Arthritis, those marks on the chest, the late dinner, the hoarseness in Rajen Babu's voice, the naphthalene . . . every little piece has fallen into place, Topshe. I tend to forget sometimes that there are other people just as clever as Felu Mitter.'

The first thing that I noticed with considerable surprise on reaching the old mansion was a black Ambassador standing outside the main gate. It obviously belonged to Vishwanath Majumdar. 'Look at its wheels,' Feluda said as we got out of the jeep. 'There is no trace of mud anywhere. This car has only just come out of a garage.'

A man—possibly its driver, whom I hadn't seen before—was standing near the car. He turned visibly pale and frightened at the sight of our jeep.

'Are you the driver of this car?' Feluda asked him.

'Y-yes, s-sir.'

'Is Vishwanath Majumdar at home?'

The man hesitated. Feluda ignored him and walked straight into the house, followed closely by the inspector, me and a constable.

Together, we ran up the stairs, and down the long passage that led to Kalikinkar's room. It was empty. The blanket lay on the bed, all the furniture was in place, but its occupant had vanished.

'Oh no!' Feluda exclaimed. I found him staring at the chest. It was open. Judging by its gaping emptiness, nearly all of its contents had been removed.

Gokul came and stood outside the door. He was trembling violently. There were tears in his eyes. He looked as though he might collapse any minute. Feluda caught him by his shoulders.

'Gokul, where is Vishwanath Majumdar?'

'He . . . he ran out of the back door!'

'Mr Sarkar!'

The inspector left with the constable without a word.

'Listen,' Feluda shook Gokul gently, 'if you tell me a single lie, you will go to prison. Do you understand? Where is your master?'

Gokul's eyes widened in fear, looking as though they would soon pop out of their sockets.

'He . . . he has been murdered!' he gasped.

'Who killed him?'

'Chhoto Babu.'

'When?'

'The day he arrived, that same night. He had an argument with his father, and asked for the numbers to open the chest. The master said, "I am not going to give it to you. Ask my parrot." Then . . . a while later . . . Chhoto Babu and his driver . . . they got together . . .' Gokul choked. He uttered the next few words with great difficulty: 'The two of them dropped the dead body into the lake behind the house. They . . . they tied a stone round its neck. And Chhoto Babu said if I breathed a word to anyone, he'd k-kill me, too!'

'I see,' Feluda helped him sit down. 'Now tell me, am I right in thinking there is no one called Rajen Babu at all?'

'Yes, sir. We did once have a manager by that name, but he died two years ago.'

Feluda and I leapt out of the room, and began running down the stairs. There was a door to the left where the stairs ended, which led to the rear of the house. We heard Mr Sarkar's voice as we emerged through this door.

'It's no use trying to escape, Mr Majumdar. I have a gun in my hand!' he shouted.

This was followed immediately by a loud splash and the sound of a revolver going off.

We continued running, jumping over small bushes and crashing through thick foliage. Eventually, we found Mr Sarkar standing under a large tamarind tree, with a revolver in his hand. Behind the tree was the lake we had glimpsed last night through our window. Its surface was covered almost totally with weed and algae.

'He jumped before I could fire,' Mr Sarkar said, 'but he cannot swim. Girish, see if you can drag him out.'

Vishwanath Majumdar was fished out in a few minutes by the constable, and transferred behind bars, very much like his father's parrot. The money and the jewellery he had stolen from the chest were recovered by the police. It appeared that although he ran a successful business, he used to gamble rather heavily, and was up to his neck in debt.

Feluda explained how he had arrived at the truth. 'Rajen Babu came to our room twenty minutes after we left Kalikinkar; and we saw Vishwanath Majumdar half an hour after Rajen Babu's departure. Then Rajen Babu came back briefly after dinner. Not once did we see father and son and their manager together. This made me wonder whether there were indeed three different people, or whether one single person was playing different roles. Then I remembered the books on drama and acting. Perhaps those books belonged to Vishwanath Majumdar? Maybe he was interested in acting and was good at putting on make-up? If so, it wouldn't have been difficult for him to wear a false beard and different wigs and change his voice, to fool a couple of visitors in a dark house. He had to hide his hands, though, for presumably his knowledge of make-up wasn't adequate to turn his own hands into those of a seventy-three- year-old man. But my suspicions were confirmed when I noticed this morning that although he was supposed to have left quite early, there were no tyre marks on the ground.'

'But who had actually written to you, asking you to come here?' I put in.

'Oh, that letter was written by Kalikinkar himself, I am sure. His son knew about it. So he did nothing to stop our arrival, for he knew he could use me to find out the combination numbers.'

In the end we got so delayed that we couldn't catch a train before half past ten. Before we left, Feluda took out the eight books he had been given and handed them to me. 'I have no wish to accept gifts from a murderer,' he said. 'Topshe, go and put these back.'

I replaced the books, filling each gap in the shelves and came out quietly. The parrot's cage was still hanging outside in the veranda.

'Shut the door!' it said to me. 'Shut the door . . . O big fat hen!'

The Mystery of the Elephant God

ONE

Lalmohan Babu—alias Jatayu—broke open a groundnut carefully, and promptly transferred its contents into his mouth. Then he dropped the shell into an ashtray, rubbed his hands and asked, 'Have you ever seen the Vijaya Dashami celebrations in Varanasi? You know, when Durga Puja ends and all the idols are immersed in the river at Dashashwamedh Ghat?'

Feluda was sitting with a chessboard in front of him, and a book called Great Games of Chess by his side. He had recently started playing chess by himself. Jatayu had arrived when he was almost halfway through the game. He told Srinath, our cook, to bring a fresh pot of tea and began answering Jatayu's questions between moves.

'No,' he replied briefly.

'Oh, it's . . . it's really a spectacular affair! You can't imagine what it's like!'

Feluda made the last move, stared for a second at the board and asked, 'Are you trying to . . . tempt me?'

'Well, yes, you've guessed it. Heh heh!'

'In that case, Lalmohan Babu, you'll have to describe the scene much better than that. What you just said won't do at all.'

'Why?' Lalmohan Babu raised his eyebrows.

Feluda began putting the chessmen away. 'Because,' he said, 'the word "spectacular" does not, by itself, evoke an image. It doesn't explain why Vijaya Dashami is special. You are a writer, Lalmohan Babu. You should be able to be a bit more graphic.'

'Yes, you're right, of course,' said Lalmohan Babu quickly. 'It was nearly twenty-five years ago, you see, when I saw the celebrations. So the details are a little hazy in my mind. But I still remember both my eyes and ears being dazzled by what I saw.'

'There you are! You said it. Eyes and ears. Your description should have something that appeals to one's senses.'

'What?'

'Yes. Try to think of exactly what you saw or heard or even smelt! Don't look so surprised. A particular place has a particular smell, haven't you noticed? The little alley that leads to the Vishwanath temple in Varanasi smells of incense, flowers, cow dung, dust and sweat. If you came out of the alley and began walking towards the river, you'd pass through a relatively smell-free zone, until you came

face to face with a herd of goats. The smell would then be most
unpleasant, I can tell you. But then you'd walk on and would soon be
greeted with another scent which would be a mixture of the scent of
the earth, water, oil, sandalwood, flowers and more incense.'

'Hey, that means you've been to Banaras!'

'Yes, when I was in college. I'd gone to play in a cricket match
with the Hindu University.'

Lalmohan Babu began fishing in his pocket.

'The paper cutting you're looking for,' said Feluda, 'slipped out of
your pocket and fell on the floor as soon as you walked in. There it
is, near that stool.'

'Eh heh . . . when I took my handkerchief out, it must have . . .'

I picked it up and handed it to Lalmohan Babu.

'Is it that story about the sadhubaba in Banaras?' asked Feluda.

'You knew!' Lalmohan Babu complained. 'Why didn't you say
something? Isn't it a strange story? All very mysterious.'

I took the cutting back from him and read it. It said:

Machchli Baba in Varanasi

The arrival of a certain holy man in Varanasi last Thursday has
created quite a stir. A senior resident of the city, Abhaycharan
Chakravarty, was the first to meet this sadhu at Kedar Ghat
and discover that he possessed very special supernatural
powers. The sadhu has since been staying in Abhaycharan's
house. His devotees call him 'Machchli Baba'. According to
them, he arrived in Varanasi from Prayag, floating on the river.

Yet another Wonder Man. The report did not strike me as
anything extraordinary, but Lalmohan Babu was clearly very
excited about it.

'Just imagine!' he said. 'Maybe he began his journey from Tibet,
right from the source of the Ganges. Oooh, the very thought gives
me goosepimples!'

'Who told you the source of the Ganges was in Tibet?'

'Oh, I'm sorry. Do I mean the Brahmaputra? But never mind. The
Ganges starts from the Himalayas, doesn't it? Isn't that good
enough?'

'Would you like to meet this man?'

'Wouldn't you? I mean, can't you smell a mystery in all this?
Machchli Baba—even the name is unique!'

'Yes, the name is somewhat unusual, I admit,' said Feluda, 'but that's about the only thing in that story that makes an impression. If one must go to Banaras, why should it be because of a certain sadhu? I would go back just to taste the *rabri* you can get in Kachauri Gali.'

'And suppose you found that the man who makes the rabri was murdered by a person or persons unknown . . . and his blood had splashed on the white *rabri* and turned it pink—well, that would make your day, wouldn't it? You'd have a case in Kashi, and earn some cash, ha ha! You haven't been very busy lately, have you?'

This was true. For about three months Feluda had not accepted a single case, because none had been challenging enough. He had spent the time reading, doing yoga, trying to cut down on smoking, playing chess and seeing films. He even tried growing a beard for a week. On the eighth day, he had taken one look at himself in the mirror and reached for his razor.

'Look,' Lalmohan Babu continued, 'you haven't got a case, and I haven't got a plot. For the first time, I couldn't think up a plot good enough for the Puja sales. For the first time, there won't be a new book by Jatayu for the pujas. I could have lifted ideas from foreign books and films and produced something anyhow, but I knew you would have caught me out. So I thought that if we could get out of Calcutta, maybe a few original ideas for a story would come floating along.'

'All right. I'll go with you. But there is a risk.'

'What is that?'

'Have you considered the possibility that a visit to Varanasi may well fail to provide you with a plot, and me with a case?'

Feluda was proved wrong. Lalmohan Babu did find a plot, although when his book eventually came out, the story sounded suspiciously like a certain Tintin comic.

And Feluda? He got a case that pitted him against the most cunning opponent he had ever had to deal with. He told me afterwards, 'All my life, Topshe, I had been waiting for a man like this. Fighting against such a man—and winning—worked like a tonic!'

The Calcutta Lodge stood by the side of a road that led to Dashashwamedh Ghat. It was a fifty-year-old hotel, run by Bengalis. Lalmohan Babu's cousin knew the manager and had made reservations for us. We arrived at about ten in the morning.

The manager, Niranjan Chakravarty, happened to be away. Another gentleman helped us check in, and a bearer took our luggage up to our room. The room turned out to be a mini-dormitory, with four beds in it. One of them had a suitcase under it, a bedroll carelessly rolled up, and a few clothes on a rack by the bed.

Feluda glanced at these objects and said, 'Lalmohan Babu, the sound of snoring doesn't disturb your sleep, I hope?'

'Why? You don't snore.'

'I'm not talking of myself. I mean our roommate.'

'You mean you have deduced that the man snores just by looking at his clothes and his suitcase?'

'No, I'm only making a guess. You see, usually it's large men who tend to snore. The size of this man's clothes suggests that his build isn't slight. And look, on that shelf over there is a bottle of nasal drops. So perhaps the man gets a blocked nose occasionally. That increases the chances of snoring.'

'My goodness! Is there anything else you've guessed about this man in these few seconds?'

'Well, you'll see that there isn't a shaving kit in sight. So unless he's hidden it somewhere, I'd say the fellow has a beard.'

A few minutes later, the bearer brought us tea. We took our cups and came out on the balcony. The road to Dashashwamedh Ghat stretched before us.

'If you were asked to leave Calcutta and come and settle here, do you think you could?' Feluda asked me.

I thought for a moment and said, 'No, I don't think so.'

'And yet, you're quite excited to be here, aren't you?'

Feluda was right. I wouldn't wish to spend my whole life in Banaras, but knowing that I would be spending only a little more than a week here, it seemed a very nice place to be in.

'Do you know why you feel like this? It's because you're thinking of the ancient traditions we associate with Banaras. Kashi, Banaras, Varanasi—each name evokes a special feeling, doesn't it? Not just because it's considered a holy place, but also because of the age of the city. Every old building could tell a story of its own. To a newcomer, that is what counts, no matter how dirty or filthy the place might be. That is the magic of Varanasi.'

Lalmohan Babu had slipped inside. Now he reappeared with a

gentleman, who turned out to be Niranjan Babu, the manager of the hotel. About fifty years old, salt-and-pepper hair parted in the middle, his mouth slightly stained with the juice of a paan, he smiled as he greeted us.

'Lalmohan Babu has just told me who you are. It's a privilege to have you stay in our hotel. Come to my room, sir. Allow me to offer you another cup of tea.'

We trooped downstairs. With the tea came a plate of sweets.

'You must sign my own visitors' book,' said Niranjan Babu to Feluda. 'A number of famous people have stayed in this hotel. I would like to see your name added to the list.'

'I hope you're aware,' Feluda replied with a slight smile, 'that my friend here is no less famous as a writer?'

Lalmohan Babu tried to look modest. The manager laughed, 'Of course! His cousin has already told me about him. Your coming was a total surprise, so . . .'

Lalmohan Babu intervened at this point. Clearly, there was. something on his mind, and he wanted to get it off his chest.

'We saw in the papers before we came . . . is it true about the sadhubaba?'

'Who? You mean Ebony Baba?'

'Ebony? Why ebony? I thought he was called Machchli—'

'Yes, yes. It's the same man. The locals are calling him Machchli Baba. I decided on Ebony. You'll know what I mean when you see him.'

'Did he really swim all the way?'

Lalmohan Babu was asking all the questions. Feluda was listening in silence. Niranjan Babu shook his head. 'I don't know,' he said. 'So they say. He's supposed to have started from Haridwar. From here he'll go to Munger and Patna. After that, who knows?'

'What about his supernatural powers?'

'I can only tell you what I've heard. Abhaycharan Chakravarty is seventy years old. For the last thirty-five years, he's been going to Kedar Ghat at four in the morning every day to bathe in the river. He doesn't see very well, but that doesn't stop him from going to the ghat, come rain or shine. On this particular day, as he went down the steps and reached the edge of the river, he stepped on something soft. When he looked closely he saw that it was a man, apparently unconscious. His skin was all wrinkled, as though he had been in the water for a long time. Before Abhaycharan could say or do anything, the man opened his eyes and said, "Look, there's water everywhere. Why are you still afraid of fire?" And that was that. Old Abhaycharan was won over instantly.'

We stared. Niranjan Babu explained further, 'You see, Abhaycharan once used to live near Calcutta. His wife and child got killed in a fire. After such a tragedy, he found it impossible to go on living in the same place; so he moved to Kashi. He's a very amiable, simple old man. So you can imagine what an impression Machchli Baba's words made on him!'

'And the Babaji has been staying in his house since then?'

'Oh yes. Apparently, Abhaycharan has been specially initiated by the Baba. Word spread like wildfire. People started pouring in. Abhaycharan's house is not far from the river. There is an open courtyard inside. This is where Babaji receives visitors. Each one is given a fish scale, blessed and purified by the holy man.'

'A fish scale? Oh, I see. In keeping with his name? But does one have to eat it?' Lalmohan Babu made a face.

'No, no. All you have to do is go to the river the next day before sunrise and drop it in the water.'

'Has it really made any difference to anyone?'

'I don't know about anyone else. I can only talk of myself. I had been getting a mild pain in my stomach. My doctor told me it might be a colic pain, and told me to take Mag Phos, which I did. Then I heard about Machchli Baba's arrival and went and got a fish scale. I dropped it in the river the next day, and now the pain has gone. Whether it's thanks to homoeopathy, or fishopathy, I don't know!'

'How long will he stay here?'

'He doesn't stay anywhere for very long. But it is always his followers who decide when he must leave.'

'How?'

'If you come with me this evening, you will find out.'

TWO

We chatted in Niranjan Babu's room for a while, then went for a walk. Niranjan Babu came with us.

We came out of the hotel and began walking towards the river. The road turned right and a slope began, to join the steps of the ghat. Beggars lined the steps and amidst them, a large number of goats roamed freely.

'What a nose you must have, Felu Babu!' exclaimed Jatayu. 'I recognize the smell now, but how could I have forgotten it?'

A strange noise rose above the general noise of the traffic. It was simply the din that came from Dashashwamedh Ghat. Hundreds of people milled around, doing hundreds of different things. 'Spectacular' was the word that automatically came to my mind, but I didn't dare mention it.

I could see the railway bridge from the steps of the ghat. Across the river lay Ram Nagar, where the Maharajah had his palace.

We walked over to Man Mandir Ghat, which was adjacent to Dashashwamedh. There was a building here that contained some astronomical instruments designed nearly three hundred years ago. It was a mini 'Jantar Mantar', like the one in Delhi. Feluda began walking towards this building, possibly with a view to looking at these instruments, when something happened.

It was much more quiet here. All that could be heard were strains of a Hindi song being played somewhere on a loudspeaker, and the noise of people washing clothes at the ghat, a few feet below. On our right was a banyan tree. Its top branches leant towards the roof of a yellow two-storey house. A shout from the roof made us all glance up quickly.

A boy was standing on the parapet on top of the roof, facing a red house just opposite. There was obviously someone on the roof of the red house as well, though he was hidden from sight. It was this unseen figure the boy was shouting at.

'Shaitan Singh!' he shouted again, like a film hero.

'That child's from the Ghoshal family,' whispered Niranjan Babu. 'A reckless devil!'

My stomach began to churn. If the boy lost his balance just once, he'd drop straight to the concrete pavement. No one could save him.

'There is no point in hiding any more!' he yelled. 'I know where you are!'

Lalmohan Babu spoke this time. His voice sounded hoarse. 'Shaitan Singh is a creation of my rival writer Akrur Nandi.'

'I am coming to get you!' said the boy. 'Get ready to surrender.'

The boy disappeared. An instant later, a long bamboo pole appeared from one corner of the roof of the yellow house, stretching to that of the red one, making a bridge between the two.

'What is he trying to do?' Feluda said softly.

'Shaitan Singh, I'll grab you before you can finish counting up to ten!' What followed made us break into a cold sweat.

The boy climbed over the railing, and began swinging from the bamboo pole.

'One . . . two . . . three . . . four. . .'

Shaitan Singh was counting from the red house. The boy started making his way to his adversary, still hanging from the pole.

'Do something!' urged Niranjan Babu. 'My colic pain's coming back!'

'Sh-h-h,' hissed Feluda. There was nothing we could do, except watch breathlessly what happened next.

' . . . six . . . seven . . . eight. . . nine . . .'

The boy had reached the opposite house. Now he swung himself over the wall and dropped on to the roof. This was followed by a piercing scream from Shaitan Singh and gleeful laughter from our hero.

'Did he actually kill him, do you think?' Lalmohan Babu asked anxiously. 'I thought I saw something like a dagger hanging from his waist.'

Feluda began striding towards the red house. 'God knows what the villain is like, but the hero is clearly remarkably brave,' he said.

'We must tell the child's father,' observed Niranjan Babu.

We didn't actually have to enter the red house. Just as we reached its front door, we heard footsteps coming down a flight of stairs, and the voice of the first boy.

'. . . Then he'll fall into the river with a loud splash, and the river will carry him straight to the sea. Then a shark will come and swallow him. But when this shark charges at Captain Spark, Captain Spark will strike it with a harpoon, and . . .'

He couldn't finish, for the two boys had come out of the door and seen us. They stopped abruptly, staring. The first one was a very good-looking child, about ten years old. The other seemed a bit older, and clearly not from a Bengali family. Both had chewing gum in their mouth.

Feluda said to the first boy, 'I can see that your friend is Shaitan Singh. Who are you?'

'Captain Spark,' said the boy sharply.

'Don't you have another name? What does your father call you?'

'My name is Captain Spark. Shaitan Singh killed my father in the jungles of Africa with a poisoned arrow. I was seven then. My eyes sparkle with the light of revenge. That's why I am called Captain Spark.'

'Good Lord!' exclaimed Lalmohan Babu. 'This boy seems to have memorized every word Akrur Nandi ever wrote!'

The boy glared at him, then walked away with his friend with infinite dignity. Soon they were both out of sight.

'A born actor,' remarked Lalmohan Babu.

'Do you happen to know the Ghoshals?' Feluda asked Niranjan Babu.

'Of course. Everyone in Kashi knows them. They have been living here for nearly a hundred years. That little boy's grandfather, Ambika Ghoshal, lives here permanently. He used to be a solicitor, but has retired now. The boy's father, Umanath Ghoshal, lives in Calcutta. He runs a business of his own. He comes here with his family every year before Durga Puja. They have the puja in their own house. Theirs is an old aristocratic family. I believe they once used to be zamindars in East Bengal.'

'Would it be possible to meet Umanath Babu, do you think?'

'Why, certainly. We might see him this evening where Ebony Baba is staying. I heard something about Umanath wanting to be initiated as well.'

One look at Ebony Baba told us why Niranjan Babu had chosen the name. I had never seen anyone quite so dark. But that was not all. His skin was so smooth that it seemed as though he was wearing a tight-fitting black costume. His wavy hair rippled down to his shoulders; his beard came down to his chest. Both were jet black. He was well-built, and he didn't appear to be older than thirty-five. Naturally, he could not swim so much if he wasn't young and strong. He wore a scarlet lungi, and around his shoulders was draped a red silk scarf. This made him a particularly impressive figure.

The four of us were standing behind a group of devotees. Babaji was sitting on a mat spread on the veranda that faced the courtyard. Behind him were two bolsters covered with yellow velvet. On his left sat an old man with folded hands, his eyes closed. This must be Abhaycharan Chakravarty, I thought. Another man was sitting in one corner of the veranda, singing a Hindi bhajan. Machchli Baba sat in padmasan, swaying his body gently to the rhythm of the song.

He was not going to give out fish scales today. We were to witness something quite different. Today, the Baba's followers would tell him how long he was to stay in Varanasi. No one appeared to know quite how this was going to be accomplished.

Lalmohan Babu seemed to have turned quite religious since his arrival here. This morning I had heard him shout 'Jai Baba Vishwanath!' more than once at the ghat. Now the very sight of the Baba had made him fold his hands. How did he hope to think up a plot for a thriller if he let his religious fervour carry him away? Or was he hoping the Baba would appear in his dream and reveal a suitable idea for a story?

At this point, a young man came in and joined us. He looked at the crowd, perhaps wondering how he could push his way forward. Niranjan Babu leant towards him and asked, 'Hasn't Mr Ghoshal come with you?'

'No,' replied the young man. 'Some guests arrived from Calcutta today, so he decided not to come.' The man had a polished, smart appearance.

'Allow me to introduce you,' Niranjan Babu said. 'This is Vikas Sinha, Umanath Ghoshal's secretary. And this is Pradosh Mitter, who's visiting with his cousin Tapesh here and friend, Lalmohan Ganguli.'

Vikas Sinha frowned. 'Pradosh Mitter? You mean the Pradosh Mitter, the investigator?'

'Yes, yes,' Niranjan Babu raised his voice in excitement, none other. Of course, Mr Ganguli here is also—'

He pointed at Lalmohan Babu, but Mr Sinha continued to stare at Feluda. It seemed as though he wanted to say something, but didn't know how to begin.

'Where are you staying?' he asked at last.

'In my hotel,' Niranjan Babu answered for Feluda.

'All right, I mean . . .' Vikas Sinha still hesitated. 'It might be wise . . . never mind, I'll contact you tomorrow.' He said 'namaskar' to all of us and disappeared into the crowd. At this precise moment, Machchli Baba spoke.

'One!' he shouted. The bhajan stopped. Everyone in the crowd fell silent. I noticed for the first time that opposite Abhaycharan was sitting another man with a brightly designed bag in front of him. Next to the bag, lying in a heap, were some strange black objects.

'There is only one sun, and one moon. One!' Babaji continued. 'Two ears and two eyes and two hands and two feet. Two!'

This sounded like pure nonsense to me. There was no way of telling whether anyone else could make head or tail of it. But the Baba was still speaking. 'The past, present and future—three! The east, west, north and south—four! Water, air, fire, earth and the sky—five! One, two, three, four, five!' He stopped. Every eye was fixed on him. 'Thrilling!' whispered Lalmohan Babu into my ear. The Baba went on counting in this rather cryptic manner until he reached ten, referring to the six seasons, the seven stars in the Great Bear, the eight metals considered pure and very special, the nine planets and, finally, the ten incarnations of Vishnu. Then he stopped and nodded at the man with the bag, who whispered something to him and turned to face the crowd.

'This bag contains blank pieces of paper,' said the man in a thin, squeaky voice. 'You are requested to take a piece of paper and a piece of charcoal from here and write any number from one to ten. Please return the paper to me with your chosen number on it.'

Feluda turned to Niranjan Babu.

'Will the number that's written by most people determine the length of his stay?' he asked.

'Maybe. He didn't say, did he?'

'If that is the case, I don't think he's going to be here for more than seven days.'

'Are you going to write a number?'

'No. I'm not interested in the Baba's stay. What I am curious about is something quite different. Tell me, are all these people just stooges, or are there a few well-known people present here?'

'What are you saying, sir?' Niranjan Babu raised his eyebrows. 'Many of these people might be called the cream of Kashi. Look, see that man over there in a white shirt? He's Srutidhar Mahesh Vachaspati, a Sanskrit scholar of renown. And there's a well-known doctor, and a bank manager. The man with the bag over there is Abhaycharan's nephew. He's a professor of English in Aligarh. You'll find somebody from every profession, I can tell you. Look at how many women are here. Some of them are well-known and highly qualified, too. And look, look—' he nodded towards a rather large man, clad in a white kurta, a white zari cap on his head. He was sitting with his back to us.

'Do you know who he is? That's Maganlal Meghraj. The richest and most powerful man in Banaras.'

'Maganlal Meghraj? That seems to ring a bell.'

Niranjan Babu lowered his voice. 'The police raided his house twice. His office in Calcutta was raided, too.'

'But nothing was found, I take it?'

'No, of course not. A man like him knows how to protect himself and keep the police happy.'

We started walking towards the exit. Just as we reached it, Mr Sinha emerged from the crowd. 'Are you leaving?' he asked Feluda anxiously. Then continued before Feluda could reply, 'Do you think you could come to our house right away? I think Mr Ghoshal would be pleased to meet you.'

Feluda glanced at his watch. 'There's no reason why we can't go with you. Only Niranjan Babu may have to return to the hotel.'

'That's right,' said Niranjan Babu. 'You three go along. But don't be late getting back if you want your dinner served hot. I've ordered a special chicken curry for you!'

THREE

'I have certainly heard of you,' said Umanath Ghoshal.

Feluda smiled as modestly as he could. Umanath Babu was a mart in his forties. His complexion was as fair as that of his son, and he had light hazel eyes. He now turned these on us and asked, 'Er . . . these are . . . ?'

'My cousin, Tapesh,' said Feluda quickly, 'and this is my friend, Lalmohan Ganguli. He writes stories of adventure under the pseudonym of Jatayu.'

'Jatayu?' Umanath Ghoshal raised an eyebrow. 'I seem to have heard the name. I think Ruku has a number of your books. Isn't that so, Vikas?'

'Yes, sir,' said Vikas Sinha. 'I think so.'

'You should know! You are the one who buys all those books for him.'

'I have to, sir. He doesn't read anything other than adventure and mystery stories.'

'That's natural,' Jatayu piped up, 'especially at his age.' I was glad to note that Lalmohan Babu had perked up a little. He had been looking decidedly morose ever since our encounter with Captain Spark. Akrur Nandi was clearly a popular writer and liable to cause Jatayu pangs of envy.

Feluda said, 'We were going to call on you anyway. You see, we met your son this morning. I don't know what his real name is, but I've learnt the name of the character he was playing.'

'He does that all the time. In fact, he even gets others to join him. Aren't you playing a special character for him, Vikas? He calls you by a different name, doesn't he?'

'It isn't just a single name or a single role, sir. I am quite versatile!' Vikas Sinha laughed.

'Anyway, where did you meet my son?'

Feluda told him as briefly as he could. Umanath Babu nearly fell off his chair. 'I don't believe this! My God, he might have been killed! Vikas, ask Ruku to come here at once!'

Mr Sinha left the room.

'What is Ruku's real name?' asked Feluda.

'Rukmini Kumar. He's my only child. So you can imagine how upset I'm feeling. I knew he was naughty, but this—!'

I looked around while we waited for Ruku to turn up. From one corner of the living room I could see a portion of the veranda where artists were working on an idol of Durga. Puja was only a few days away.

A bearer came in with a tray. We were handed cups of tea and plates of sweets.

'You went to see Machchli Baba, I believe,' said Mr Ghoshal. 'What did you think of him?'

'We didn't stay very long. You, too, were supposed to go, weren't you?'

'Well, I have been to see him once. I have no wish to go back. If only I hadn't gone out that evening, we might have been spared the disaster.'

'Disaster?'

'Yes,' Mr Ghoshal sighed. 'Last Wednesday, when I went to visit Machchli Baba, an extremely valuable object was stolen from my father's room. If you can get it back for me, Mr Mitter, I shall be eternally grateful. And, of course, I will pay you adequately.'

A familiar race began in my heart.

'May I ask what it was?' said Feluda.

'Ganesh. It was a small figure of Ganesh,' Mr Ghoshal spread his fingers slightly to indicate its size, 'made of gold and studded with precious stones. It was only about two-and-a-half inches high.'

'How did you get it?'

'I'll tell you. It might sound like a fairy tale, but I can assure you it's true.' He lit a cigarette and began. 'My great-grandfather, Someshwar Ghoshal, was a great traveller. He travelled all over the country, using whatever mode of transport he could get, ranging from bullock carts to trains. When he could get nothing, he simply walked. Once, when he was in south India, he happened to be going through a heavily wooded area near Madurai in a bullock cart. It was dark, and the path was a narrow one. Three robbers attacked him. But Someshwar was exceptionally strong. He used a heavy bamboo rod, and managed to knock one of his attackers unconscious. The other two ran away, leaving behind a bag that contained, among other things, this little figure of Ganapati. He returned home with the statuette, and things changed dramatically in our family. Don't think I am old-fashioned and superstitious, but I have heard it said that the Ganesh brought us good luck. Two years after its arrival, there was a devastating flood. Our house was quite close to the river, but was miraculously saved. There are other instances, too, which I needn't go into. My main concern is that we had had the Ganesh for a hundred years. Now it has been taken from us. Puja will start in a few days, the house is full of guests, but no one can relax and enjoy themselves. You do see my predicament, don't you?'

Mr Ghoshal leant back, sighing wearily.

'When did you visit Machchli Baba?' Peluda asked.

'Three days ago, on Wednesday. We arrived from Calcutta about ten days ago. My wife was very keen to see the Baba, so I took her and Ruku that evening.'

'Did your son really want to go?'

'Yes, I guess he was intrigued by the name. He told me he had read about a man who had swum seventy miles through a shark-infested sea. But when he actually saw the Baba, he didn't seem too impressed. He began to fidget and, only about ten minutes later, we left. We returned to find the Ganesh missing.'

'This little figure of Ganesh was kept in a chest, I presume? In your father's room, did you say?'

'Yes, but I have the key. Normally, it stays with my wife. That evening, since she was coming with me, I took it from her and put it in a drawer in my father's room. It was a foolish thing to do, of course, for my father is an opium addict and usually sleeps in the evening. Anyway, I pushed the drawer shut firmly, but when I got back, it was open by about an inch. This made me suspicious, so I looked into the drawer immediately. The key was where I had left it, but the Ganesh had gone.'

Feluda frowned. 'May I ask who was present in the house at the time?'

Feluda had not brought his notebook. But I had no doubt that he would be able to remember everything Mr Ghoshal was saying, and would write it down later in our hotel room.

'Well,' said Mr Ghoshal, 'you saw Trilochan, our chowkidar, at the gate. He's been with our family for thirty-five years. There are a couple of servants and maids—all have been with us for a long time. Shashi Babu, the artist, is working on the idol of Durga, together with his son. I've known him for thirty years. He's a most gifted artist. Apart from these people in the house, there was our mali, and Vikas, who brought you here.'

'How long have you had him as your secretary?'

'About five years. But he's spent virtually all his life in our house. His father used to work on our estate in Bengal. He died when Vikas was small. One of my uncles brought Vikas home to look after him, and he stayed on. He's no different from a family member. He's an intelligent man, did well in school and college.'

'Didn't you inform the police about the theft?'

'Of course. I rang them the same evening. But they haven't been able to do anything yet.'

'Did anyone outside your family know about the Ganesh?'

Before Mr Ghoshal could make a reply, Ruku arrived with Vikas Babu. I looked at Ruku's father, expecting him to explode. But Mr Ghoshal showed admirable control, going only so far as to give his son a sidelong glance and say in a steely voice, 'You are forbidden from stepping out of the house until puja is over. You can play in the garden and the terrace, but unless I personally take you out, you are to remain indoors at all times. Is that understood?'

'What about Shaitan Singh?' asked Ruku sharply.

'Who on earth is that?'

'He's broken out of the prison. He must be caught!'

'Never mind, I'll track him down for you,' said Vikas Babu lightly. Ruku gave him a grateful look, and went quietly out of the room with him, without saying another word about his punishment.

'As you've seen, Mr Mitter,' Mr Ghoshal said, 'this child is exceptionally imaginative. But anyway, let me answer your question. Yes, a lot of people knew about the Ganesh, especially when we were still living in our ancestral home. The story of Someshwar's fight with the robbers had spread like a legend. But that was long before I was born. When we moved to Calcutta, there weren't many people left to talk about it. While I was in college in Calcutta, I mentioned it casually to a few friends. One of them—but mind you, I don't consider him a friend any more—now lives here in Banaras. His name is Maganlal Meghraj.'

'Oh yes,' said Feluda, 'I know who you mean. We saw him this evening at Machchli Baba's meeting.'

'Yes, I know. He was there last Wednesday as well. There is a reason why he keeps going back for the Baba's help. He's going through a bad time, you see. His plywood factory got burnt down last year. Then there were rumours about certain shady dealings. So the police raided his house and office both here and in Calcutta. He came to see me two days after I arrived. He told me straightaway that he wanted to buy the Ganesh. He knew we kept it here in my father's room. He offered me thirty thousand rupees, but I refused. In the end, he left saying he'd get it by hook or by crook. Five days after his visit, the Ganesh vanished.'

Mr Ghoshal fell silent. Feluda was silent, too. He sat quietly, a deep crease between his brows. Something told me his three-month-long vacation had come to an end. Lalmohan Babu's prophecy was going to come true. Here in Kashi was a case, but the cash, of course, depended on . . .

'We're very fortunate to have you here at this time,' Mr Ghoshal broke the silence. 'Now, if only you'd accept. . .'

'Yes, of course. Certainly.' Feluda rose to his feet. 'I'd like to come back tomorrow, if I may, and talk to your father. Would that be possible?'

'Why not? My father isn't always very easy to talk to, but his aggressive air is just a pretence. Come at around eight. I'll make sure you find Father ready and waiting. Besides, if you wish to walk around in the garden or elsewhere in our compound, please feel free to do so. I'll tell Trilochan to let you in whenever you wish to visit. Vikas can help you, too.'

We took our leave soon after this. On our way back to the hotel, I noticed a man following us. He was wrapped up in a blanket. I could not see his face. But when I tried to warn Feluda we were being followed, he didn't pay any attention at all and continued to hum—quite tunelessly—a song from a Hindi film.

FOUR

The cook at the Calcutta Lodge produced an excellent chicken curry. He also served fish, which was equally tasty, but Lalmohan Babu did not touch it.

'After having seen Machchli Baba this evening,' he informed us, 'I couldn't eat fish, ever again.'

'Why?' Feluda laughed, 'would that make you feel you were chewing the Baba's flesh? Do you suppose Machchli Baba himself abstains from consuming what you are proposing to give up?'

'Doesn't he?'

'Well, you have heard he spends most of his time in water. So what could he possibly live on except fish? Certain species of fish eat other fish, didn't you know?'

Lalmohan Babu did not say anything. I felt quite sure he'd go back to being his fish-eating self from the next day.

After an eventful day, I was looking forward to a good night's sleep. But that was not to be. Our roommate, Jeevan Babu (short and fat and with a beard, just as Feluda had predicted), turned out to be a champion snorer. I spent most of the night tossing and turning in my bed, wondering why, just this once, Feluda could not have been proved wrong.

The next morning, as we were coming out of the hotel after breakfast, we met Niranjan Babu. Feluda exchanged pleasantries before asking, 'Do you happen to know where Maganlal Meghraj lives?'

'Meghraj? As far as I know, he has two houses, both in the heart of Banaras. One of them is not far from the Vishwanath temple. Anyone will show you the way.'

Niranjan Babu told us one more thing. Machchli Baba was going to be in Banaras for another six days. Feluda's famous lopsided smile peeped out at this, but he said nothing.

We arrived at the Ghoshal residence on the dot of eight. Trilochan opened the gate for us with a bright smile and a smart salute. He must be about seventy, I thought; but he certainly did not look it. His back was ramrod straight, and the size of his moustache most impressive.

Vikas Babu came out to greet us. 'I saw you arrive,' he said. He had probably just finished shaving, for there was a little soap stuck under his right ear.

'Would you like to come in? Old Mr Ghoshal is waiting for you. You wanted to see him in particular, didn't you?'

'Yes, but before we do that, do you mind telling me a few things?'

'No, not at all.'

Feluda asked a few rapid questions and noted the answers in his notebook. The following points emerged:

1. Maganlal came to meet Mr Ghoshal at his house on the 10th of October.

2. Mr Ghoshal took his wife and child to see Machchli Baba on the 15th, at 7.30 p.m. He returned a little more than an hour later. The figure of Ganesh was stolen during that time.

3. In the house between 7.30 and 8.30 p.m. were Umanath Ghoshal's father, Ambika Ghoshal, Vikas Sinha, Trilochan, two bearers, a maid, a cook, a mali and the two artists. Assuming that no one came in from outside, it had to be one of these people who had taken the Ganesh out of the chest in Ambika Ghoshal's room.

Feluda put his notebook away and said, 'You must forgive me for this, but I cannot possibly leave anyone out, not even you.'

'Yes, I understand that. I've already had to face the police. I suppose you want to know what I was doing in the house during that time?'

'Yes, but there's something else I'd like to ask first.'

'All right. But let's go to my room.'

We went into the house. A staircase went up from the front hall. Vikas Babu's room was on the left on the ground floor.

'You must have known about the Ganesh,' Feluda remarked, taking a chair.

'Yes, of course. I've known about it for ages.'

'Were you at home when Maganlal came to visit Umanath Babu?'

'Yes. In fact, I received Maganlal and took him to the living room. Then I got one of the bearers to go upstairs and inform Mr Ghoshal.'

'And then?'

'Then I returned to my room.'

'Did you know the two had an argument?'

'No. You cannot hear from my room anything that's said in the living room. Besides, I was playing the radio.'

'Were you in your room the evening the Ganesh got stolen?'

'Yes, for most of the time. When Mr Ghoshal left with his wife and Ruku, I walked with them up to the gate. From there I went to look at Shashi Babu and his son working in the veranda. Shashi Babu appeared a little unwell. So I came back to my room to fetch some medicine for him.'

'Homoeopathic medicine? I can see a couple of books on homoeopathy on that shelf.'

'Yes, you're right. I gave him a dose of Pulsetilla 30.'

'And then did you return to your room?'

'Yes.'

'What did you do?'

'I listened to the radio. The Lucknow station was playing records of Begum Akhtar.'

'How much time do you think you spent listening to the radio?'

'Well, the radio had been left on for some time. I was reading a magazine—the *Illustrated Weekly*—and was listening to the music at the same time.'

'Did you stay in your room until Mr Ghoshal returned?'

'Yes. You see, a few members of the Bengali Club were supposed to be calling to invite Mr Ghoshal to their play, *Kabuliwala*. I was waiting for them.'

'Did they come?'

'Yes, but much later; well after 9 p.m.'

Feluda pointed at the staircase. 'Can you remember seeing anyone going up or coming down those stairs?'

'No. But there is another staircase at the back of the house. If anyone came in or went out using this other staircase, I could not have seen them.'

'Thank you,' said Feluda and rose. Vikas Sinha then took us to meet Ambika Ghoshal.

We found him sitting by the window in an easy chair, reading the *Statesman*. The sound of our footsteps made him look up and peer at us over the golden frame of his glasses. His head was quite bald, except for a few strands of snowy white hair around his ears. Knitted in a frown were dark, bushy eyebrows, flecked with grey.

Vikas Babu made the introductions. Ambika Ghoshal looked straight at Lalmohan Babu and asked, 'Are you from the police?'

Taken aback, Lalmohan Babu began to stammer, 'No-no, I . . . I'm nothing!'

'Nothing? You're nothing? Is that just modesty, or . . . ?'

'No, what I mean is, I am not the d-d-d . . .'

Vikas Babu came to his rescue. 'This is Pradosh Mitter,' he said, pointing at Feluda, 'a well-known private investigator. Since the police couldn't catch the thief, Mr Ghoshal felt. . .'

Ambika Ghoshal turned his eyes on Feluda. 'What did my son tell you? Did he say our whole family is going to be destroyed because the Ganesh has gone? Nonsense! How old is he? Not even forty. And I am seventy-three. Does he think he knows more than me about the history of the Ghoshal family? Pooh! How have we survived all these years? How did we manage to do so well? Not because the Ganesh protected us, but because of our own intelligence and hard work. My son is a shrewd businessman all right, but I fear he should have been born a hundred years ago. I hear he's even thinking of adopting a guru!'

'Does that mean you have no regrets about the Ganesh's disappearance?'

Ambika Babu took off his glasses and trained his pale eyes on Feluda once more. 'Did Umanath tell you there was a diamond on the figure of that Ganesh?'

'Yes, he did.'

'Did he tell you what diamond it was?'

'No, I'm afraid not.'

'There you are, you see? He didn't tell you because he didn't know! Have you ever heard of the Vanaspati diamond?'

'You mean the one that has a greenish tinge?'

Ambika Babu sat up. When he spoke again, his tone had softened.

'Oh, I see. So you do know about these things, then. That kind of diamond is extremely rare. But that doesn't worry me so much; nor do I believe that the Ganesh brought us luck, or watched over us, or any such thing. What I am sorry about is that it was a work of art. And, as such, it is a pity—a great pity—to have lost it.'

'Was the key kept in the drawer of that table over there?' asked Feluda. A few yards away from where Ambika Babu was sitting, between two windows was a table. The chest was in the opposite corner. Between the two was a large, old-fashioned bed.

Instead of giving Feluda an answer, Ambika Babu asked another question.

'Did my son also tell you that I take opium?'

'Yes, sir.'

Very seldom had I heard Feluda speak to anyone so politely.

'I am generally dead to the world in the evening. So if anyone came into my room after seven, I wouldn't know.'

Feluda walked over to the table and pulled at the drawer carefully. It opened smoothly, without making a sound. Feluda pushed it back and made his way to the chest. Like the bed, it was a huge affair.

'The police searched it thoroughly, I presume?'

'Yes, of course,' Vikas Babu replied. 'They even looked for fingerprints, but found nothing.'

We took our leave and came out of Ambika Babu's room. We passed through a smaller room on the right, and found ourselves on a large veranda with a marble floor. From here, I could see the river in the distance through a number of neem and tamarind trees. The skyline was dotted with several temple-tops.

I had started to count these, and Feluda and Vikas Babu had both lit cigarettes, when something came floating down from the roof. Lalmohan Babu reached out and caught it. It proved to be a chewing gum wrapper.

'Mr Rukmini Kumar appears to be on the roof,' said Feluda.

'Where else could he play? He's now a prisoner in his own house.' Vikas Sinha smiled. 'He has a room of his own on the roof, you see.'

'Could we see it?'

'Of course. Come with me, please. I can show you the other staircase as well.'

It turned out to be a spiral staircase that went straight up to the roof. Ruku's room was on one side where the stairs ended. We found him kneeling on the floor, getting a kite ready for flying. He dropped the kite and sat back as he saw us arrive.

It was obvious that his room was really an old storeroom, filled with rusted trunks, packing cases, torn mattresses and piles of old newspapers and magazines.

'Are you a detective?' asked Ruku, looking at Feluda steadily. From the way his jaw moved, it was obvious that he had chewing gum in his mouth.

'How did Captain Spark get this information?' Feluda said with a smile.

'My assistant told me,' Ruku replied gravely, picking up his kite once more.

'Who is your assistant?'

'Captain Spark's assistant is Little Raxit, didn't you know? What kind of a sleuth are you?'

Lalmohan Babu cleared his throat. 'Khudiram Raxit,' he explained. 'Height: four-and-a-half feet. Captain Spark's right hand. He calls him Little Raxit.'

'Oh, I see,' Feluda said quickly. 'Yet another creation of Akrur Nandi?'

'Yes.'

Feluda turned to Ruku. 'Where is your assistant?'

Vikas Babu replied this time. 'Er . . . I am playing that role for the moment,' he said, looking somewhat embarrassed.

'Do you have a revolver?' Ruku asked suddenly.

'Yes,' Feluda answered.

'What kind?'

'Colt.'

'And a harpoon?'

'No, I haven't got a harpoon.'

'Don't you go looking for prey under water?'

'No, I haven't had to do that yet.'

'Do you have a dagger?'

'No, I haven't got a dagger, either. Not even one like this.'

Feluda pointed at a plastic dagger that hung on the wall. We had seen it dangling from Ruku's waist the day before.

'I will kill Shaitan Singh with that dagger.'

'Very well,' Feluda sat down on the floor beside Ruku. 'But what about your Ganesh? Did Shaitan Singh take it? Or was it someone else?'

'Shaitan Singh could never get into this house.'

'If Captain Spark hadn't gone to visit Machchli Baba that evening, the Ganesh would still be safe, wouldn't it?'

'Machchli Baba is as dark as Gongorilla of Congo.'

'Well done!' Lalmohan Babu spoke suddenly. 'Have you read *The Gorilla's Grasp*, Ruku Babu?'

Gongorilla was the name of a ninety-foot-high gorilla in Lalmohan Babu's book *The Gorilla's Grasp*. He freely admitted to having pinched the idea from King Kong. 'That book, you see,' he continued eagerly, 'was written by—' He broke off at a stern glance from Feluda.

But Ruku paid no attention. 'Our Ganesh is with a king,' he declared. 'Shaitan Singh couldn't find it, ever. No one could. Not even Daku Ganderia.'

'Oh no!' sighed Lalmohan Babu. 'Akrur Nandi again!'

Vikas Babu laughed. 'You'd need to read every book in the adventure series to follow his conversation,' he said.

Feluda was still sitting on the floor, gazing thoughtfully at Ruku, as though he was trying to make some sense out of his apparently meaningless chatter.

'Which king are you talking about, Ruku? Where does he live?' he asked softly. Ruku's reply came at once.

'Africa,' he said.

We spoke to one other person before leaving Mr Ghoshal's house. It was Shashi Bhushan Pal, the artist. He was painting the statue of Kartik when we found him. A man in his mid-sixties, he said he had spent nearly fifty years making idols of Durga and other gods and goddesses.

'We heard about your illness,' said Feluda. 'I hope you're feeling better now?'

'Yes, thank you. Sinha Babu's medicine helped a lot,' Shashi Babu replied, without stopping his work.

'When do you think you can finish the whole thing?'

'Puja begins the day after tomorrow. I hope to get everything ready by tomorrow evening. I'm getting old, you see, I can't work as fast as I used to.'

'Even so, your work is exquisite.'

'Thank you, babu. People only look at the goddess. Who thinks of the poor artist's hard work?'

'Something from this house got stolen the day Vikas Babu gave you the medicine. Are you aware of that?'

The brush in Shashi Babu's hand trembled a little. His voice had a slight catch in it as he made his reply. 'I have been working in this house for so many years. Never did I think one day I would be questioned by the police! When I do my work, babu, I forget everything else. Ask Sinha Babu, ask the little boy, ask anyone who's seen me at work. I don't leave this veranda for a minute!'

A young man of about twenty was working with Shashi Babu. He turned out to be his son, Kanai. He confirmed that neither of them had left the veranda between seven and eight-thirty the evening when the Ganesh went missing.

Vikas Babu came to the gate to see us off.

'I did not disturb Umanath Babu,' Feluda told him, 'because knew he was busy with his guests. Please tell him that I may drop it from time to time, and ask a few questions.'

'Since he has asked you to make an investigation, that is your right and privilege,' Vikas Babu remarked.

Just as we stepped out, a sudden noise from above made us all look up. Ruku was still on the roof, flying his kite. We could only see his little hands from where we stood, pulling at the thread.

Feluda stared at the kite, now flying freely in the sky.

'That child seems very lonely,' he said to Vikas Babu.

'Yes, he is. He's an only child, you see. At least he's found a friend here. You've seen Suraj, haven't you? He doesn't have a single friend in Calcutta.'

FIVE

On our way back from Mr Ghoshal's house, we decided to take a short cut through an alley, away from the traffic on the main road.

Here too, a few sheep and lambs were roaming about. Lalmohan Babu prodded a lamb gently with his umbrella to get it out of the way, and said, 'Shall I tell you something, Felu Babu, about myself? You see, when I visit a new place, I like to get into the spirit of things—you know, live like the locals, act like the natives. In fact, when we were in Rajasthan, I kept thinking of myself as a Rajput. A couple of times I even put up my hand to feel my *pugri*, and was most surprised to find my bald dome instead!'

'And here? Have you been startled to discover the absence of long, matted hair like a sadhu?'

'No, but I must confess the thought that the whole world is but an illusion did cross my mind yesterday when we were at the ghat. Today, walking through this alley, I would have been quite happy to have a dagger hanging from my waist. It's the atmosphere, isn't it . . .?'

He continued to expound on his theory, but I did not pay much attention. I had caught sight of the same figure that had followed us the day before. Among the various people who were either returning from the ghat or going to it, or crowding around shops, was this man, wearing tight pyjamas that peeped out from under a purple blanket which covered the rest of his body, including his face. He was following us doggedly at a distance of about ten yards. Since Feluda had appeared quite unconcerned the previous day, I didn't raise the matter again, but began to feel uncomfortable.

Lalmohan Babu hadn't stopped talking. 'This business of the Ganesh is going to be complicated, as far as I can see,' he was saying.

'It is difficult to say whether a case is going to be complex or simple before it reaches a certain stage. Are you telling me that we have come to such a stage already?'

'Haven't we?'

'No, not in the least.'

'But the real villain could not have taken it, could he?'

'Who are you referring to, may I ask?'

'Why, it's that man called Meghlal . . . or is it Meghram? . . . You know, the man we saw where Machchli Baba's staying? My God, I've never seen a man with such broad shoulders. Give him a pair of horns, and he could easily join those massive bulls Banaras is famous for!'

'You mean you think Maganlal Meghraj would have turned up personally to jump over the wall, steal into Ambika Babu's room and remove the Ganesh?'

'Oh, I see. He would have used an agent, right?'

'Isn't that far more natural? Besides, he might have threatened to get the Ganesh somehow, but that does not necessarily make him the real culprit.'

We had reached the hotel. Niranjan Babu's room was next to the reception. We found a well-built young man sitting opposite him, explaining something rather animatedly.

Niranjan Babu looked up as we arrived. 'Here they are. This visitor has been waiting for you for nearly twenty minutes. Allow me to introduce you. This is Inspector Tiwari, and these are . . .' He rattled off our names quickly.

Mr Tiwari was looking straight at Feluda. His eyes twinkled. Feluda frowned for a moment, then his face broke into a grin.

'You were in Allahabad, weren't you?' he asked.

'Yes, but I wasn't sure that you'd remember me,' Mr Tiwari replied, shaking his hand.

'It would've been difficult, I must admit. You have lost a lot of weight. If I may say so, it's done you some good!'

Mr Tiwari laughed. His height was about the same as Feluda's, and he looked just as trim. A couple of years ago, Feluda had had to go to Allahabad in connection with a case. He had obviously met Mr Tiwari then.

'I'd gone to meet Mr Ghoshal last night,' said Mr Tiwari, 'after you had left. He told me of your arrival and where you were staying.'

Niranjan Babu rang for tea. We all sat down.

'I must say this is a relief,' Feluda said to the inspector. 'I was beginning to worry about how the police might react to my presence. I know I won't have any problems with you. Two heads are better than one, aren't they? And it does appear to be a difficult case.'

Mr Tiwari's face fell. He forced a smile, and said slowly, 'Yes, Mr Mitter, it is so very difficult that I came to tell you to stay out of it.'

'Why?'

'Because Maganlal is involved in this. In fact, I'm concerned that you've already been to Mr Ghoshal's house. You must be very careful. Maganlal has a team of hired hooligans working for him.'

A bearer came in with the tea. Feluda picked up a cup, looking slightly worried, and asked, 'But how can you be sure that Maganlal is truly involved?'

'The line of investigation we're following points towards Maganlal. I have never seen anyone with such cunning.'

'But what is this line of investigation?'

'I'll tell you. Have you met everyone in the Ghoshal household?'

'Yes, all except the servants.'

'Did you see Shashi Babu?'

'Yes, we met him this morning.'

'And his son?'

'Yes, he was working with his father.'

'Did you know Shashi Babu has another son?'

'Does he? No, we didn't know that.'

'This other son is called Nitai. A bad type, very bad. He's only eighteen, but there's very little he hasn't tried his hand at. Supposing he has joined Maganlal's gang . . .'

Feluda raised a hand. 'I get it. Maganlal would get Nitai to work through either his father or brother to get the Ganesh.'

'Exactly. Nitai could easily be persuaded to use force, even on his own family. So I suggest you take it easy, at least for the time being. There is a lot to see in Banaras during the time of Durga Puja and Dussehra. So do enjoy yourselves, but don't go anywhere near the Ghoshal family.'

Feluda smiled and changed the subject. 'Aren't you thinking of investigating the case of Machchli Baba?' he asked.

Mr Tiwari put his cup down on the table and burst out laughing. 'You've already been to see him, have you? What did you think of it all?'

'Since I raised the question of an investigation, you must assume he didn't arouse any religious ardour in me.'

'Yes, Mr Mitter, but you're talking only of yourself. What about his devotees? Do you think they'd stand by and watch quietly if we openly tried to carry out an enquiry? They'd skin us alive!'

Mr Tiwari spoke the last sentence with a sidelong glance at Niranjan Babu, who threw up his hands in protest. 'Don't look at me, Tiwariji!' he exclaimed. 'What do I know of devotion? All I can say is that in our otherwise boring and eventless life, Machchli Baba is an event, an excitement—but that's all.'

'There is something you can do,' said Feluda. 'Try and find out if anyone called Machchli Baba had appeared recently in Haridwar or Allahabad.'

'Very well. That shouldn't be a problem. I'll get you this information in a couple of days.'

Mr Tiwari looked at his watch and rose. Just before stepping out of the room, he stopped for a minute and slapped Feluda on the back. 'Why don't you come to my office one day and see how we deal with crime in Varanasi? But do remember—and I mean this seriously—you must stay away from the case of the missing Ganesh.'

After lunch that afternoon, we went out for a walk again. I didn't know whether Feluda had anywhere specific in mind, but Lalmoham Babu and I followed him into an alley opposite the hotel.

'I think your cousin is looking for a sweet shop for a plate of rabri,' whispered Lalmohan Babu into my ear. I had to laugh, but I knew he was wrong.

The alley was both narrow and winding. Houses with two or three storeys stood on both sides. The sun hardly came in at all. Feluda told us most of these houses, like many others in Varanasi, were more than a hundred years old. Some had paintings of animals and birds on their front walls. A few had handwritten posters and advertisements in Hindi.

As we made our way carefully through this dim, dingy alley, several new noises began to reach my ears. The loudest among them was that of pealing bells. We were getting closer to the temple of Vishwanath.

Sheep and lambs had been replaced here by large cows and bulls. Each time we saw a particularly strong bull, Lalmohan Babu exclaimed, 'Look, there goes Meghraj!' In the end, Feluda was obliged to say, 'Look Lalmohan Babu, I do think those poor bulls are a lot less harmful than Meghraj, so please stop making a comparison. Anyway, I am trying to picture him as a man with thin, cruel lips and a malicious glint in his eyes. You are spoiling it for me by constantly harping on the bulls!'

It soon became impossible to walk freely. The crowd pushed us along in one direction. Pandas were scattered everywhere, each one pouncing on us eagerly. '*Darshan*? Would you like a *darshan* of Baba Vishwanath, babu?' they kept asking. We walked straight ahead, ignoring them as best we could. My attention was taken up totally in trying to protect my pocket and my wallet in it, and stop myself from stepping into the many puddles that dotted the way. When I finally looked up, I found Lalmohan Babu gazing at the golden dome of the temple, wonder and amazement in his eyes. I saw him ask Feluda something, but couldn't quite catch what he said. Only the word 'carat' reached my ears. All thoughts of God and religion had clearly been abandoned, at least for the moment.

Then I saw the kite. It was a red and white kite, identical to the one Ruku had been flying earlier. There it was, disappearing behind the temple.

Feluda, too, was staring at it. 'Most interesting,' he said briefly.

'It's not just interesting, my friend,' said Lalmohan Babu. 'I find it positively disturbing. No, I am not talking of that kite. But do you realize this place might be infested with Meghraj's spies? In fact, one of them can't take his eyes off you. I've been watching him for nearly three minutes.'

'Is it someone dressed as a sadhu, with a long flowing beard and a brand new robe?' Feluda asked, still staring at the sky.

'Full marks,' Jatayu replied.

Now I noticed the man. He was standing near a shop laden with flowers, incense and vermilion. As we passed him, Feluda stopped for a second and said, 'Jai Baba Vishwanath!' in a very loud voice. This nearly made me burst out laughing, but I controlled myself.

By now we had come out of the alley, having left the temple behind us. Close to where we were standing was the mosque built by Aurangzeb, and a huge open terrace. I looked up again as we reached the terrace, but couldn't see the kite any more. Steps ran down from the terrace to the road below. Feluda turned towards these. I did have a vague suspicion about where he wanted to go, but as it turned out, the same idea had occurred to Lalmohan Babu too.

'Are you, by any chance, heading for Meghraj's house?' he asked.

'Who else would I wish to call on? If there were no criminals, Lalmohan Babu, your friend here would starve. So don't you think we should pay a visit to the temple of the biggest criminal in Kashi?'

My heart began thudding faster. Since the crowd had thinned somewhat, Lalmohan Babu had to lower his voice to ask the next question, 'I hope you haven't come without your weapon?'

'If by a weapon you mean my revolver, no, I didn't bring it with me. But I've got all the other three, thank you.'

Lalmohan Babu looked up, startled, and nearly stumbled against a step. But he said nothing more. I knew that when Feluda mentioned three other weapons, he was simply referring to his powerful brain, steady nerves and strong muscles.

A tailor's shop stood where the steps ended. An old man was sitting just outside its entrance, working on a sewing machine. He told us where Maganlal lived. 'Go straight, past the Hanuman Mandir, and take the first right turn. You'll find Maganlal's house easily enough; it's the one with two large paintings of guards with swords,' he said.

'And aren't there real guards outside the main door?' Feluda asked.

'Oh yes, you'll find those as well.'

In less than two minutes, we were standing outside Maganlal's house. Two armed guards were painted on the wall, but there was no one in sight. The street, unlike the ones we had passed through, was remarkably quiet. Not even a goat or a lamb could be seen.

The front door was wide open. How very strange! Where had the guards gone? Were they perhaps having their lunch? Feluda sniffed a couple of times and said, 'I can smell tobacco.' Then he looked around and added, 'Come on, let's go in. If we're stopped, we can always say we're new and slipped in by mistake, thinking it was a temple.'

Lalmohan Babu and I followed him in. Goodness, was this where the great Maganlal lived, I thought in wonder, staring at the cows that stood in the dark, damp courtyard. Our appearance did not bother them at all. Each continued to chew the cud, gazing at us calmly.

'This is quite common here,' Feluda whispered. 'Very few people have any open space to keep their cows in. So they keep them in their courtyard inside the house, for they can't do without large quantities of milk and ghee.'

On our right and left were corridors, leading to nothing but darkness, as far as I could see. Presumably, there was a staircase somewhere, for I had noted outside that the house had three floors.

As we stood debating what to do next, my eyes suddenly fell on a figure that had emerged silently from the dark depths and was standing on our right.

It was a middle-aged man, of medium height, clad in a green kurta-pyjama, an embroidered white cotton cap on his head. A thick moustache drooped down, brushing against his chin. When he spoke, his voice sounded like an old, worn out gramophone record.

'Sethji would like to meet you,' he said.

'Which Sethji?'

'Seth Maganlalji.'

'All right. Let's go.'

SIX

'Jai Baba Vishwanath!'

I couldn't see the look on Lalmohan Babu's face, but I could tell from his voice how he felt.

'Do you really have a lot of faith in Vishwanath?' asked Feluda. I couldn't imagine how he could speak so lightly.

'Jai Baba Felunath!' whispered Lalmohan Babu.

'That's better!'

We were groping our way upstairs, climbing a series of stairs that were amazingly high. Everything was in total darkness. The man who had come to fetch us hadn't bothered to bring a light. Lalmohan Babu was still muttering under his breath. I caught the word 'black hole' a couple of times.

At last, we reached the top floor. Our emissary passed through a door. We followed him. He then took us through a room, a narrow passage, another chamber, and finally stopped before a small door, motioning us to go in.

We stepped into the room. At first I could see nothing except some coloured glass. Then I realized I was looking at a window. The light from outside was shining through its colourful panes.

'Namaskar, Mr Mitter,' said a deep, gruff voice.

A few things became visible. A thick mattress, covered with a white sheet, was spread on the floor. On it were four bolsters, also covered in white. The figure that sat leaning on one of these was that of the man we had seen from the rear at Abhay Chakravarty's house.

With a faint click, a light on the ceiling came on. We were finally face to face with Maganlal Meghraj. The eyes that regarded us solemnly were sunk in, set under thick, bushy eyebrows. A blunt nose, thick lips and a pointed chin completed the picture. He too was wearing a kurta-pyjama. The buttons on his kurta might well have been diamonds. Besides these, on eight of his ten fingers flashed other stones of every possible colour.

'Why are you standing? Do sit down,' he invited. 'Take a chair, if you like.'

There were low, Gujarati chairs placed by the side of the mattress. We took three of these.

'I wanted to meet you, Mr Mitter. I would have invited you properly, but luckily you came here yourself.' After a moment's pause he added, 'You may not know me, Mr Mitter, but I know all about you.'

'I have heard your name,' Feluda replied politely. 'You're pretty well known yourself.'

'Well known?' Maganlal laughed loudly, displaying paan-stained teeth. 'Not well known, Mr Mitter. What you mean is infamous. Notorious. Come on, admit it!'

Feluda remained silent. Maganlal's eyes turned towards me. 'Is this your brother?'

'My cousin.'

'And who is this? Your uncle?' Maganlal was smiling.

'This is my friend, Lalmohan Ganguli.'

'Very good! Lalmohan, Mohanlal, Maganlal . . . it's all just the same, isn't it? What d'you say, eh?'

Lalmohan Babu had been shaking his legs with an 'I-don't-feel-nervous-at-all' air. Maganlal's words made his knees knock against each other. At this point, Maganlal suddenly brought his hand down on a bell, making it ring sharply. This startled Lalmohan Babu so much that he choked and began to splutter.

'Does your throat feel a bit . . . dry?' queried Maganlal.

The man who had brought us upstairs reappeared silently. 'Bring some sherbet,' ordered Maganlal.

It was now possible to see everything quite clearly. There were two steel almirahs in one corner. Behind Maganlal, the wall was covered with pictures of Hindu gods and goddesses. On the mattress, on his right, were a few papers and files, a small metal cash-box and a red telephone. On his left was a silver box stuffed with paan, and a silver spittoon.

'Well, Mr Mitter,' he asked gravely, 'have you come to Banaras on holiday?'

'That was my original plan,' Feluda replied, looking straight at him.

'Then . . . why . . . are . . . you . . . wasting . . . your . . . time?' Maganlal spoke through clenched teeth, uttering each word distinctly.

'Have you been to Sarnath?' he went on. 'Ramnagar? Durga Bari, Man Mandir, Hindu University? No, I know you haven't seen any of these famous places. You walked past the Vishwanath temple today, but did not go in. Yet, you keep going back to Umanath Ghoshal's house. Why? Forget what he told you. I can make your stay in Kashi so much more enjoyable. I have my own barge, did you know that? Come any day to the river. I'll take you on a cruise from one side to the other. You'd love it!'

'You seem to be forgetting,' said Feluda, still speaking calmly, 'that I am a professional investigator. Mr Ghoshal has given me a specific task. I cannot think about having a holiday or going on a cruise on your boat until that task has been completed.'

'What is your fee?'

Feluda was quiet for a few seconds. Then he said, 'That depends—'

'Here, take this!'

I gave an involuntary gasp. Maganlal had opened the cash-box and taken out a large fistful of hundred rupee notes. He was now offering these to Feluda. Feluda's lips became set. 'I do not,' he said clearly, 'accept a fee without having done anything to earn it.'

'I see, I see!' Maganlal bared his paan-stained teeth again. 'But how will you earn it, Mr Mitter? How can you catch a thief when there has been no theft?'

'What do you mean?' This time even Feluda sounded surprised. 'If no one stole anything, where has it gone?'

'It,' said Maganlal, 'was sold to me. I paid Umanath thirty thousand for it.'

'What rubbish is this?'

How could Feluda talk like this? My hands began to feel clammy. Lalmohan Babu, too, was looking decidedly pale.

Maganlal had started to laugh, but Feluda's words instantly wiped the laughter from his face. A deep frown creased his brow, his eyes glinted under the light. 'Rubbish? Maganlal doesn't talk rubbish, Mr Mitter. Obviously, you don't know enough about Umanath and his affairs. Did you know his business isn't doing well? Are you aware how much he owes people? Did anyone tell you Umanath himself called me over to his house and took the Ganesh out of the chest? How do you propose to catch the culprit when it is none other than your client himself?'

'I still don't understand, Maganlalji,' Feluda answered. 'Why should Mr Ghoshal have to steal the Ganesh? Why couldn't he simply take it out openly if he had decided to sell it to you?'

'That Ganesh did not belong only to Umanath. It was the property of his family. His brother—who lives in England—and his father had an equal claim on it. It was his father who had had it all along, and he has certainly been lucky. Just look at how much money he's earned, and what comfort he lives in. Umanath would never have dared tell his father he was selling their most precious heirloom!'

Feluda appeared to be thinking. Was he beginning to believe Maganlal?

'I'll tell you.' Maganlal sat up. 'He called me over to his house on the tenth of October, and offered to sell the Ganesh. I agreed. I have recently had a run of bad luck, as you may have heard. So I thought the Ganesh would help change my luck. Umanath knows nothing of the value of that green diamond. It's actually worth far more than what I paid. Anyway, we had a chat on the tenth. He said he needed a little time to get things organized. So I said fine, take your time. On the fifteenth, he rang me again and said he had actually got the Ganesh. I told him to come to Machchli Baba's meeting. We both arrived with a little bag in our pockets. His had the Ganesh. Mine had thirty thousand in hundred rupee notes. It didn't take us long to exchange the bags. And that's all. End of story.'

If what Maganlal was saying was true, then one had to admit Mr Ghoshal had deceived not just us but also the police. Perhaps he had hired Feluda only as a cover-up. But why was Maganlal telling us all this? What did he stand to gain?

To my surprise, Feluda asked him the same question. Maganlal's small eyes narrowed further. 'I know you are an intelligent man, Mr

Mitter,' he proclaimed. 'In fact, your intelligence is reputed to be extraordinary. If you began an investigation, would you not have discovered the truth? And if you did, how do you suppose Umanath and I would have looked? The police would have driven us mad! After all, our dealing wasn't exactly legal and above board, was it? Surely you can see that?'

Feluda did not say anything immediately. While Maganlal was talking, a man had brought in three glasses of sherbet, which were placed before us on a low table. Feluda picked up a glass and said, 'That means you have got the Ganesh. May I see it? I am naturally curious to have a look at this object that's created such a furore.'

Maganlal shook his head regretfully. 'Very sorry, Mr Mitter, I do not have it here. You know this house was raided once. So I couldn't keep it here. I've had to send it to a safer place.'

'All right,' Feluda spoke casually. 'You did what you thought best, and I shan't argue with that. But don't you see that I have to carry on with my investigation simply to find out if you're telling the truth? If you are, we have nothing to worry about. But what if you're not?'

Maganlal's eyes virtually disappeared. His lips curled ominously.

'You mean you don't believe me?'

Feluda raised the glass to his lips and took a sip. Then he said, 'You told me yourself I didn't know you. So how can you expect me to believe all that you've just said? Would you believe everything a man told you the first time you met him? Especially if he clearly appeared to be tampering with the truth?'

Maganlal went on staring at him. In the silence, all I could hear was a clock ticking somewhere, but couldn't see it. Then Maganlal raised his right arm and extended it towards Feluda. He was still clutching the money. 'I have three thousand here,' he said. 'Take it, Mr Mitter, and enjoy yourself. Have a good holiday with your cousin and your uncle.'

'No, Maganlalji, I do not take money like this.'

'Does that mean you'll continue working on this case?'

'Yes. I have to.'

'Very well.'

Maganlal struck the bell again. The same man came back. Maganlal said, without even looking at him, 'Call Arjun. And get that box—number thirteen. And the wooden board.'

The man disappeared. God knew what he would come back with.

Maganlal now turned towards Lalmohan Babu, a smile hovering

on his lips. Lalmohan Babu's right hand was curled around a glass, but it looked as though he couldn't bring himself to drink from it.

'What is it, Mohanbhog Babu, don't you like my sherbet?'

'No, no, I mean . . .' Lalmohan Babu quickly brought the glass to his lips and swallowed some of its contents.

'Don't worry, Mohan Babu, that sherbet hasn't been poisoned.'

'No, no—'

'I don't like poison.'

'Yes, of course. P-poison is,' Lalmohan Babu gulped, 'very bad.'

'There are other things far more effective.'

'Other things?'

'I'll show you what I mean.'

Lalmohan Babu choked again. There were footsteps outside. A strange creature entered the room. It was a man, I had to admit, but I had never seen a man like him. About five feet in height, he was remarkably thin. Every vein in his body stood out. His eyes suggested he might have been a Nepali, but his nose was long and sharp. His hair was cut very short, and his ears stuck out. There was not a single hair on his body. I could see his arms and legs and chest, for he was wearing a dirty, torn sleeveless vest and an old pair of shorts. It was impossible to guess his age.

The man gave Maganlal a salute, then stood waiting for instructions.

Two men now came in carrying a long wooden box. This was probably the box number thirteen Maganlal had mentioned. The noise it made when set down on the floor suggested that its contents were made of either iron or brass.

A large wooden board was then brought in and placed against the closed door behind us. Maganlal opened his mouth once more.

'Do you know what knife-throwing is, Mr Mitter? Have you ever seen it in a circus?'

'Yes, I have.'

I hadn't, but I knew what it was. A man stood with his back to a board. Another threw knives at him which, instead of hitting him, hit the board, just a few inches away from his body. Even a slight mistake made by the thrower could result in serious—even fatal—injury. Was this creature called Arjun going to throw knives? At whom?

One of the men opened the box. It was filled with knives, each with an ivory handle, an identical pattern at one end.

'The king of Harbanspur had a private circus. Arjun used to perform in it. Now he performs for me, in my own circus . . . ha ha ha!'

Twelve knives had been selected from the box and spread out on a marble table like a Japanese fan. 'Come on, Uncle!' said Maganlal.

Lalmohan Babu gave a violent start, spilling most of the remaining liquid in his glass on the floor. Feluda spoke this time. 'Why are you calling him?' he asked, ice in his voice.

Maganlal's fat body rocked with laughter. 'Who else can stand before the board, tell me? If I asked you to stand there, you couldn't see the game, could you? No, don't say another word. You have insulted me today by calling me a liar. Let me warn you that I have other weapons, too. I don't use just knives. Look at those small windows. Two guns are, at this moment, pointed at you. If you behave and don't start an argument, you'll come to no harm. Nor will your friend. Arjun is a master in this game, believe me.'

I didn't dare look at the windows. A moment later, Lalmohan Babu rose shakily to his feet, saying, 'If I l-live, no wo-worries about a p-plot . . .' A couple of men grabbed him and took him to stand before the board. He closed his eyes. I couldn't bear to look any more.

Lalmohan Babu was standing behind me. Before me stood Arjun, picking up the knives one by one, slowly but steadily. Each one flew over the top of my head and hit the board with a faint swish. Feluda must have been facing Lalmohan Babu and actually watching the show, or no doubt one of the guns would have been fired.

At last, the last knife was thrown. Arjun stood mutely before the empty table, breathing heavily. Maganlal said, 'Well done!' The invisible clock ticked away.

No one else spoke. Nobody moved. Then, a few seconds later, just as my own breathing was beginning to get normal, Lalmohan Babu staggered forward, and grabbed Arjun's hand.

'Thank you, sir,' he said.

Then he swayed from side to side, and fell down on the mattress, unconscious.

SEVEN

It was nearly 2 p.m. The sky had turned grey. There were very few people left at Dashashwamedh Ghat. The three of us were sitting near the water.

It was almost an hour since our horrific experience in Maganlal's house. Two of his men had splashed cold water on Lalmohan Babu's face to help him regain consciousness. Then Maganlal himself had offered him a glass of milk and brandy, and said, 'Uncle, you are a brave man.'

We were allowed to leave shortly after this, but not before Maganlal had made it obvious that Feluda's life was in danger if he insisted on continuing with his investigation. Feluda did not argue, but managed to get a small concession. 'I must go back to Mr Ghoshal's house at least once more,' he said, 'if only to tell him I'm opting out. If I disappear without a word, it's not going to do much good to my image, is it?'

To my surprise, Maganlal agreed. 'Just one more visit,' he said. 'Remember, Mr Mitter, if you step out of line, you do so at your own risk. I don't need to tell you I've got the means to keep an eye on everything you do.'

I felt awful thinking Maganlal had had the last word. Feluda had, so far, never been defeated by an adversary. But then, none had been quite so cruel and powerful as Maganlal.

Lalmohan Babu had said very little after we came away. The only thing he asked was whether all his hair had turned grey, at which both Feluda and I assured him that not a single new grey hair could be seen on his head.

After a few minutes of silence, Feluda said with a sigh, 'The Ganesh hasn't left Mr Ghoshal's house. I am now certain of that. If Maganlal had already got it, he would not offer me money to get off the case. The big question is, where has it gone? Why hasn't Maganlal been able to lay his hands on it? Besides, who took it out, and who in that house is acting for Maganlal?'

By the time we left the ghat, the sky had turned a darker shade of grey. Was it going to rain? I looked up, and saw the red and white kite again. Feluda, too, had seen it.

I recognized the house over which the kite hovered. It was the same red house where Shaitan Singh had had to surrender to Captain Spark. Who was standing on the roof? Wasn't it Shaitan Singh in person? Yes, indeed. It was Ruku's friend, Suraj. Like us, he was staring at the kite.

Whoever was flying the kite now pulled at the thread. It started to come down rapidly. Suraj threw up his right hand into the air, aiming at the kite. We saw a stone fly past and disappear behind the kite. The stone was tied to the end of a long thread. Suraj had captured the red kite. As he pulled at the thread, the kite began to get closer and closer to him.

We decided to pay our last visit to Mr Ghoshal's house the same afternoon. It was about 4 p.m. when we arrived. Trilochan saluted us again and opened the gate.

Once again, we found Vikas Sinha coming out to greet us.

'Any news?' he asked.

'No, I'm afraid not. We just roamed all over the city.'

'Mr Ghoshal and the others have gone out.'

'Where?'

'Sarnath. A few more guests arrived today. Quite a large party went out, only a little while ago. They won't be back for some time.'

'Has Ruku gone with them?'

'No, one of his uncles took him to see a film, *Tarzan, the Ape Man*.'

'I see.'

'Would you like to sit in my room?'

'Yes, but before that I'd like to go up on the roof once more, if I may.'

'Of course.'

As we went into the house, we found Shashi Babu still engrossed in his work. 'He'll finish tomorrow, won't he?' Feluda asked.

'Yes, the poor man's still got a high temperature, but he hasn't stopped working for a moment.'

We climbed the steps to the roof. Here was Ruku's room. I had guessed that it was really this room that Feluda wanted to see. Would he search it thoroughly? Since Ruku was away, this appeared to be just the right time to look for . . . Then I remembered Maganlal's warning. Feluda must not spend too long in this house.

As it turned out, he found what he was looking for practically immediately. The red and white kite was lying on the floor. We had seen Suraj take it only a couple of hours ago. It was clear that it was damaged in many places. This kite would never fly again.

Feluda picked it up. Now we saw something none of us had noticed before. There was a message written on the kite. No, there were, in fact, two messages written in different places. One said, 'I have been imprisoned. But all is well, ha ha. Again in the evening.

Yours, Capt. Spark.'

The other was more brief: 'Going to see Tarzan. Tomorrow morning. Capt. Spark.'

'Good heavens!' exclaimed Lalmohan Babu. 'What are these boys up to?'

Feluda replaced the kite just as he had found it, and said, 'This is a clear example of what books from your adventure series can do to a young mind.'

We returned to Vikas Babu's room. Bharadwaj, the old bearer, came in with the tea. It was a fairly large room. The bed was on one side, and opposite it, a table and a chair. Besides these was a sofa for visitors. Feluda took the chair, Lalmohan Babu and I chose the sofa. Vikas Babu sat on the bed.

'How is Mr Ghoshal's business doing?' Feluda asked, sipping his tea.

'Reasonably well, I should imagine,' Vikas Babu replied. If he was surprised by the question, he did not show it. 'The workers do occasionally go on strike, but that happens everywhere, in every business, doesn't it?'

'Hm.' Feluda stood up suddenly and said, 'Can I see the living room?'

'Yes, certainly. This way, please.'

We put our cups down and followed Vikas Babu. The living room was across a veranda. 'Can you show me where Umanath Babu and Maganlal had sat the day Maganlal came visiting?' Feluda asked.

Vikas Babu pointed at two chairs facing each other.

'I see. And where do those doors lead to? More rooms? Or is there another veranda?'

'No, those are rooms'. One of them used to be old Mr Ghoshal's office. The other was a waiting room for his clients.'

We examined them briefly before going back to Vikas Babu's room.

'Where was the Ganesh normally kept?' Feluda now asked. 'Was it always here in Varanasi, or did anyone ever take it to Calcutta?'

'No, it always stayed with Ambika Babu, right here in this house. It is the old man who is much more upset by its loss than his son, though he may not show it. In fact, Umanath Babu hired you mainly to reassure his father, you see.'

Feluda nodded absently. He had picked up the transistor radio that stood on the table, and was turning a knob. Nothing happened until he turned it in the opposite direction. It gave a sudden click, which brought a frown to his face. 'That's funny,' he muttered, 'your radio had been left on!'

'Oh, r-r-r-eally?' Vikas Babu stammered, suddenly looking rather ill at ease. Feluda took out the batteries. 'These batteries have leaked,' he observed, 'which means that your radio stopped working some time ago.'

Vikas Babu remained silent.

'You are fond of listening to the radio, but you haven't done so in the last few days. Can you tell me why?'

Still Vikas Babu said nothing. 'Very well,' said Feluda, 'if you won't speak, I must do all the talking.' A familiar note of authority and confidence had crept into his voice. 'You were unable to resist the temptation to eavesdrop when Maganlal came to visit Umanath Babu, isn't that right? You turned down the volume of your radio and crept up to the door of the living room that opens on the veranda. You heard every word. You knew about Maganlal's offer of thirty thousand rupees. You heard him threaten Mr Ghoshal.'

Vikas Babu was looking down at the floor. He nodded in silence.

'Now please be good enough to answer this question, and I want the truth,' said Feluda, throwing the batteries away into a waste-paper basket. 'What were you doing between 7.30 and 8.30 p.m. the day the Ganesh was stolen? You could not have been listening to your radio, for it had stopped functioning five days—'

'Yes!' Vikas Sinha raised his head, and spoke quickly, almost desperately. 'I'll tell you everything. Please try and believe me.' He took a deep breath and continued, 'I did hear Maganlal's threat, and was deeply worried. Every day, I wanted to open the chest in Ambika Babu's room simply to make sure the Ganesh was still there. But I got the chance to do this only when Mr Ghoshal went with his family to see Machchli Baba. I waited for only ten minutes after they left. Then I went into Ambika Babu's room, took the key out of the drawer and opened the chest.'

'What happened next?' Vikas Sinha did not reply.

'Tell me, Mr Sinha, what did you see when you opened the chest?' This time, Vikas Babu raised a white face and spoke in a whisper.

'I saw . . . I saw that the Ganesh had gone!'

'Gone?' Feluda's frown deepened.

'Yes. I know you find it difficult to believe this, but I swear the Ganesh had been stolen before I opened the chest. You must realize why I did not mention this before, either to you or the police. To tell you the truth, I cannot begin to describe the state of mind I've been in ever since that day!'

Feluda picked up his cup of tea. 'How often was that chest opened?'

'Almost never. As far as I know, it was opened once the day after Umanath Babu arrived from Calcutta. He took out some old documents related to their property and had a chat with his father about those. That was all.'

Feluda sat silently. Vikas Babu looked at him, eyes pleading. After about two minutes, he couldn't contain himself any longer and blurted out, 'Do you find it impossible to believe me, Mr Mitter?'

When Feluda spoke his voice sounded rough.

'I am sorry, Mr Sinha, but if someone doesn't tell the truth in the first instance, it is rather difficult to eliminate him from the list of suspects.'

EIGHT

I woke the next morning to find the sky overcast. It was drizzling softly and, judging by the puddles on the road, it had rained fairly heavily during the night.

Feluda was already up, sitting on the balcony, his feet resting on the railing. His famous blue notebook lay open on his lap. He was turning its pages with great concentration, quite oblivious of the fact that his feet were getting wet. A number of people were making their way to the ghat, undaunted by the rain. But I knew that the noise from the street below would do nothing to disturb Feluda.

Lalmohan Babu rose a little later. 'I had such a strange dream, Tapesh,' he said. 'There I was, with knives and daggers sticking out from virtually every inch of my body. And I was standing before my publisher, asking for the proofs of my novel. Do you know what he said to me? He said, "Lalmohan Babu, why don't you change your pseudonym? Drop Jatayu. Porcupine would be more apt—and your books will sell much better." Ho!'

Feluda came back into the room a few minutes later, as Lalmohan Babu and I sat sipping our first cup of tea.

'Tell me, Mr Jatayu,' he said, 'do any of your books mention sending messages through a kite?'

'No, I'm afraid not,' Lalmohan Babu shook his head regretfully. 'I rather wish I had thought of that. As far as I can see, Ruku got the idea from a book by another writer.'

'Perhaps I should not have laughed at your adventure series. Considering the impact it's had on Ruku's mind, it deserves to be taken a bit more seriously. Oh, by the way, can you tell me a number between one and ten?'

'Seven.'

'Did you know that seventy per cent of people would say "seven" if asked the same question?'

'Really?'

'Yes. And they'd say "three" if you asked them to choose a number between one and five. Try asking them to name a flower, and they'd say "rose".'

We went down to breakfast at eight. About half-an-hour later, one of the waiters came looking for Feluda. 'There is a phone call for you,' he said, 'in the manager's room.'

Phone call for Feluda? Who would be ringing him so early in the morning? But there was nothing for me to do, except wait patiently until he came back and explained. He reappeared only a few minutes later.

'That was Tiwari,' he said. 'Neither Prayag nor Haridwar could confirm that anyone by the name of Machchli Baba had been seen or heard of in recent times.'

'How interesting! Does that mean the man here is a fraud?'

'He might be, but that does not bother me. I mean, there are scores of people who claim to have magical powers. What we have to establish is that there is no sinister motive behind Machchli Baba's little deception.'

'Didn't Mr Tiwari say anything else?' I asked.

'Yes,' Feluda replied. 'Three weeks ago, a man escaped from the Rai Bareli jail. He was serving a sentence for deception and fraud. His description fits Machchli Baba somewhat, although he is reported to be clean-shaven and not quite so dark.'

'He might have used make-up,' Lalmohan Babu remarked. 'Why don't we go and have a good look at him in broad daylight? We could wait for him at the ghat. Surely he'd go to Dashashwamedh, or perhaps Kedar?'

'Not a chance. He receives visitors only in the evening. His days are spent behind a closed door. I believe he doesn't step out of his

room at all. No one but Abhay Chakravarty is allowed to go in. His
meals are served in his room. He doesn't even bother with having a
bath.'

What! A supposedly great sadhu like him went without a bath
every day?

'Did Mr Tiwari tell you all this?'

Feluda turned his head to give me a cold look. Then he shook his
head sadly and said, 'Failed. You have just failed in an observation
test. Didn't you notice my wet clothes hanging on the line on the
balcony upstairs? If you did, didn't that tell you anything? Have you
ever heard of anyone getting drenched without stepping out?'

I couldn't say a word. Feluda was right, of course. I should have
been more observant. But why had he gone out anyway?

He explained. 'I got up at four this morning and went to Kedar
Ghat to wait for Abhay Chakravarty. He turned up at 4.30. It wasn't
difficult to start a conversation with him. He's a very good, kind,
simple man, just as Niranjan Babu had said. I learnt about the Baba's
habits from him. When he mentioned the Baba didn't have a bath, I
must have wrinkled my nose or something, for he said, "Does it
matter, son, when his mind is clean and pure? After all, it's just a
matter of ten days. He rose from the water, didn't he, and he will go
back to it." I didn't dare ask if he smelt! I believe a man comes in
every morning with a basket full of fish scales. These are distributed
in the evening. I stayed on at the ghat after Abhay Chakravarty left,
and spoke to a panda called Lokenath, who also comes to the ghat
every day. Lokenath said he had actually witnessed the first meeting
between Mr Chakravarty and Machchli Baba, though by the time he
arrived, the Baba was fully conscious. Apparently, he called
Lokenath by his name and told him a few startling things. Even if he
is a crook, he must have a very clever and efficient manager.'

'Could that perhaps be Abhay Chakravarty himself?' Lalmohan
Babu asked.

'No. Mr Chakravarty is undoubtedly sincere. I asked him if he
didn't find it difficult to believe that a man could swim all the way
from Prayag. To this he replied, "Nothing is impossible, my dear, if
your dedication and faith is strong enough." It is people like
Abhaycharan Chakravarty who have kept the spirit of Kashi alive.
Their belief in ancient values will never change. No, Lalmohan
Babu, he cannot be an accomplice.'

The rain stopped around half past four in the evening. We left at five. Feluda was a full-fledged tourist today. A camera hung from his shoulder. 'Let's go and have some *rabri*,' he said. Lalmohan Babu and I readily agreed.

Kachauri Gali wasn't far from the temple of Vishwanath. Feluda found the right shop easily enough. We sat on a bench, and were handed the most delicious *rabri* in small earthen pots. Lalmohan Babu had just stuffed a spoonful into his mouth, remarking, 'The discovery of this heavenly stuff is no less important than the discovery of the telephone, don't you think?' when I saw the same man who had been following us the day before. He was standing with his back to us, talking to someone.

I had been trying all day to forget about Maganlal and what he had said. But the sight of this man brought back all the horror of that meeting vividly. However, I forced myself to concentrate on eating and not dwell upon unpleasant thoughts.

'Let's go,' said Feluda. I gave my spoon one last lick and came out with him and Lalmohan Babu.

From Kachauri Gali, we made our way to Godhulia. In the last couple of days, these streets had become quite familiar to me. We walked slowly, with Feluda stopping occasionally to take a picture. I kept looking over my shoulder to see if the man was still following us, but he appeared to have vanished. Feluda saw what I was doing and said, 'Where did you get the idea that Maganlal appointed just that one man to cover our movements?'

I kept my eyes straight ahead after this.

There was the hardware shop I had seen before. Abhay Chakravarty's house was only a few steps from here.

'Mr Mitter! Pradosh Babu!' called a voice from behind us. All of us wheeled around.

Two Bengali gentlemen stood before us, smiling politely. We had not met them before.

'We went to your hotel to look for you,' said one of them.

'Is anything the matter?' asked Feluda.

'We are from the Bengali Club. My name is Sanjay Roy, and this is Gokul Chatterjee. We came to invite you to our play, the day after tomorrow.'

'*Kabuliwala?*'

'You knew?' Both men sounded pleased and surprised.

'Didn't you invite Mr Ghoshal a few days ago?'

'My God, you seem to know everything!' said Sanjay Roy.

'That's not surprising, is it?' Gokul Chatterjee laughed. Feluda's reputation as a sleuth was obviously not unknown to the members of the Bengali Club.

'We left the card with Niranjan Babu. You must all come. We'll expect you.'

'Thank you very much. We'll be there, if I don't get involved in anything important, that is.'

'Involved in something important? Why, are you . . . I mean, *here?*'

I looked at Feluda. His lips had parted in that mysterious smile which, I knew, he reserved for situations like this. It could mean 'yes', or it could mean 'no'; it could even mean 'maybe'. Neither Mr Roy nor Mr Chatterjee wanted to look foolish. So both nodded vigorously, indicating that they had fully grasped his meaning, and took their leave.

We resumed walking. It was getting dark. The streetlights had come on. They sky had started to change from royal blue to blue-black, and a transistor had been turned on at full blast in a shop. The voice of Lata Mangeshkar began to compete with the blare of rickshaw horns. At this point, Feluda announced that his heart was suddenly awash with a wave of *bhakti,* and he couldn't possibly go back without another look at Machchli Baba.

We arrived at Abhay Chakravarty's house to find a larger crowd, possibly because the Baba was going to leave in five days. 'Stand still,' said Feluda to me, placing his camera on my shoulder. Then he took a photograph of Machchli Baba using his telephoto lens. I couldn't see Maganlal anywhere. Maybe he didn't come every day. We left in five minutes.

A right turn took us into a new lane. A large cow stood blocking the way. Lalmohan Babu gave a small cough and stopped. 'What's the matter?' asked Feluda.

'Er. . . what do you suppose its height is?'

'Why?'

'I was once quite good at high jump. I even had a record in school. But, a few years ago, an attack of dengue . . . I mean, my knees are no longer . . .'

'Come with me.' Feluda went forward and patted the cow gently on its back. It moved to one side obligingly, allowing us to pass.

'Where are we going now?' Lalmohan Babu asked five minutes later.

'I don't know.'

Lalmohan Babu and I exchanged glances. The light from a street lamp shone directly on Lalmohan Babu's face. He was looking decidedly perplexed. 'Walking aimlessly often helps clear the mind,' Feluda explained. 'What we need now is a clear mind, clear thoughts.'

'And is your mind showing signs of clearing?'

Feluda started to reply, but something happened at this moment to distract all of us.

The winding lanes we had passed through in the last few minutes had brought us to an alley that was very quiet. No one spoke here, or played the radio. I couldn't even hear a child cry. All that could be heard was the faint sound of bells from a temple in the far distance. But, as we made our way down the lane, another rhythmic noise reached our ears: dhup, dhup, dhup, dhup, dhup . . .

Lalmohan Babu was walking between Feluda and me. The noise made him slow down and clutch at our sleeves. 'Highly suspicious!' he whispered.

Feluda disengaged himself. 'There's nothing suspicious about that. Someone's using a hand grinder, that's all. What I would call suspicious is over there. Look!'

A man had entered the lane from the other side. He stopped upon seeing us, standing with his back to a street light. The lamp cast a long shadow that almost touched our feet. The shadow was swaying strangely. Was the man drunk?

Feluda peered through the telephoto lens of his camera.

'Shashi Babu!' he exclaimed and rushed forward. Lalmohan Babu and I followed quickly.

Shashi Babu had fallen on the ground. His eyes were open wide, and between gasps, he was trying to speak.

'What is it?' Feluda bent over him.

'The . . . the . . .'

'Yes? What happened, Shashi Babu? What are you trying to say?'

'L-l-li . . . lie . . . lie . . .'

Shashi Babu's body gave a sudden jerk and was still. The street light fell on his back. It was soaked with blood.

NINE

'I may as well give up. I do not deserve to be called a sleuth,' said

Feluda. I had never heard him talk like this. But then, we had never been in a situation like this before.

A whole day had passed after Shashi Babu's death. Durga Puja had begun the day before. We had just finished breakfast and were sitting in our room. Mr Tiwari had rung a few minutes earlier to say that Shashi Babu's son, Nitai, had been arrested. He had never got on well with his father. In fact, Shashi Babu had threatened to hand him over to the police on many occasions. So Nitai might have had a motive for killing his father, although he had denied it. He had apparently been watching a film at the time of the murder. The police did find a torn ticket in his pocket. The knife with which Shashi Babu was stabbed had not been found.

According to what Vikas Sinha had told the police, Shashi Babu had finished painting the eyes of the goddess and put the last finishing touches by 6 p.m. that evening. Then he had gone straight to Vikas Babu to get some more medicine as his temperature had risen again. Vikas Babu gave him a fresh dose of homoeopathic medicine, and Shashi Babu left for his home soon afterwards. Someone stabbed him on the way.

'It is perhaps a good thing,' Feluda continued to speak, more to himself than the two of us, 'to fall flat on my face occasionally. At least it stops me from getting arrogant, and reminds me that I am no different from most men . . . Hey, Lalmohan Babu, you'll come with us to the play, won't you? I believe their standard of acting is pretty high.'

'Yes, of course, that is if you decide . . .'

'And what shall we do tomorrow? See a film? Why not? Let's go and see *Tarzan*. And a Hindi film after that. I'll also take you to Durga Bari. You'll find lots of monkeys there. Each one of them has more intelligence than your Felu Mitter.'

In the end, we did go and see *Kabuliwala* at the Bengali Club, and discovered that Feluda was right. It was a very good performance.

The next day was Mahashtami, the third day of Durga Puja. We went out to visit a few places where Puja was being held, including Mr Ghoshal's house. He invited us to lunch, but Feluda declined.

We ordered lunch in the hotel. Feluda normally had a light meal but, to my surprise, today he had a huge plate of rice and curry and went to sleep straight after. I realized later that this was only the lull before a storm. But, at this precise moment, it broke my heart to see

Feluda so depressed.

In the evening, we went to see *Tarzan, the Ape Man*. But Feluda, for some reason, left the hall virtually as soon as the film began. All he got to see was the name Metro-Goldwyn-Mayer, followed by the title of the film. He did not explain where he was going, but shot up from his chair and left immediately, with a brief: 'You stay here and watch the film. I've got some work to do.'

Lalmohan Babu and I did stay on till the end of the film, but neither of us could enjoy it properly. Where had Feluda gone? And why?

We returned to the hotel at a quarter past eight, to find Feluda deeply engrossed in making new entries in his notebook.

'You go ahead and have your dinner,' he said as we appeared. 'I've ordered a cup of coffee for myself.'

'Won't you eat anything at all?'

'No, I'm not hungry. Besides, I'm expecting an urgent call from Tiwari.'

The cook had produced a special meal today because of puja, but I had to rush through it. This time, I was determined to hear myself what Feluda said to Tiwari.

His call came half an hour after we had finished eating. This is what Feluda said to him:

'Yes, Mr Tiwari? Yes, very good . . . no, no, don't do anything yet, wait till the last moment . . . Yes, that's why there was such confusion at first . . . And did you find out about the house? Yes, all right. . . See you tomorrow. . . . Good night.'

Lalmohan Babu had gone to our room straight after dinner. 'I must get some writing done,' he had told me on our way back from the cinema. 'Your cousin's behaviour has got me all confused and mixed up. I must think carefully and chalk out my plot.'

When Feluda and I returned to the room, he was sitting with a writing pad and a pen in his hand, looking a bit put out. Feluda did not seem to notice him at all. He lit a Charminar and began pacing the floor.

Lalmohan Babu pushed the writing pad away. 'This,' he declared, 'is most unfair. I cannot concentrate on my own writing; nor can I make out what's going on. Why are you being so secretive? Why can't you tell us if you're on to something? After all, we're not entirely brainless, are we? Why don't you give us a chance?'

'All right,' said Feluda, blowing out a smoke ring, 'I'll give you five clues.'

'Go ahead.'

'The king of Africa, Shashi Babu's "lie", the mouth of a shark, one to ten, and Maganlal's barge.'

Lalmohan Babu stared at him for a few seconds, then let out a long sigh, shaking his head slowly.

'Promise me one thing,' Feluda said seriously. 'From tomorrow, you are not going to ask me any more questions.'

'I wouldn't dare. I've learnt my lesson, thank you.'

'I may have to go out from time to time,' Feluda went on, 'but not with you. You are free to go where you like, there's no risk in that. I will, of course, tell you if I think there's any danger anywhere. And—Lalmohan Babu, you can swim, can't you?'

'Swim? Why, yes, I mean—'

'That'll do. As long as you can stay afloat if thrown into the water. Can you manage that?'

'Yes, I think so.'

'Very well. It may not be necessary, but it's good to know, just in case.'

The next day was the last day of Durga Puja. Lalmohan Babu and I went sightseeing. When we returned at about 11 a.m., Feluda was stretched out on his bed, looking carefully at the enlargements of some of his photos. He had dropped in at a studio on our way to the Bengali Club two days ago to get the film developed.

Mr Tiwari rang again in the evening. Feluda went down to take the call and returned only a couple of minutes later. I did not bother to go with him this time. A little later, Lalmohan Babu and I left again for a long walk. We were both getting bored with having nothing to do in the hotel.

Feluda was still in the room when we came back.

'I don't think anyone followed us today,' said Lalmohan Babu for the third time. Feluda said nothing.

'Did you go out?' I asked.

'No. Mr Ghoshal rang. He asked me if I had given up.'

'What did you tell him?'

'Only that I hadn't.'

I rose at six the next morning, and found, to my surprise, that Feluda had already gone out. His bed was neatly made; on it was a small bowl that he had been using as an ashtray. Under this bowl was a piece of paper with 'I'll ring you' scrawled on it.

This meant that we could not leave the hotel. I didn't mind waiting, but I couldn't help worrying about Feluda's safety. Although he had said nothing to us, we suspected that Shashi Babu had been killed by one of Maganlal's men. If he could get rid of one man, why would he spare Feluda?

Lalmohan Babu said over breakfast, 'After what Maganlal said the other day, your cousin should simply have withdrawn from the case.'

'He did, didn't he? Then God knows what happened to him when we went to see that Tarzan film.'

'Who knew Tarzan would cause such trouble?'

We waited until lunch time, but Feluda did not call. After lunch, possibly for want of anything better to do, Lalmohan Babu told me his own theory about the theft of the Ganesh.

'You see, dear Tapesh,' he said, 'I don't think that the little Ganesh was stolen at all. Ambika Babu opened the chest that evening after he had had a dose of opium and took it out. The next morning, when the effect of the drug had worn off, he forgot all about it!'

'Oh? Well then, where is it now?'

'Did you notice the size of his slippers? I did. His slippers were much larger than his feet. If an old man sits in his room with his slippers on his feet, who is going to look inside them?'

I felt a little suspicious. 'Is your new story going to have a little detail like this?' I asked.

Lalmohan Babu smiled, 'Yes, you guessed it. But in my story, it's not a statuette, but a diamond. Two thousand carats.'

'What! Two thousand? The biggest known diamond in the world is called the Star of Africa. Do you know how much it weighs?'

'How much?'

'Five hundred carats. And the Koh-i-noor is only a hundred and ten.'

Lalmohan Babu shook his head gravely. 'My readers would not be impressed by anything less than two thousand,' he said.

At half past four, a waiter came up to say that there was a call for me. I sped downstairs as fast as I could and almost snatched the receiver from Niranjan Babu's hand.

'Is that you, Feluda?'

'Yes. Listen carefully,' Feluda's voice sounded solemn. 'On one side of Dashashwamedh Ghat is Munshi Ghat. Next to it is Raja

Ghat. Are you listening?'

'Yes, yes.'

'Between Munshi and Raja Ghat is a quiet spot, where one set of steps ends and another begins.'

'Yes, I've got that.'

'There is a big hand-painted poster on the wall, and just below it, quite a large shed.'

'OK.'

'You two should get there by 5.30 and wait for me by the shed. I'll meet you at six.'

'All right.'

'I'll be in disguise.'

My heart missed a beat. I couldn't say a thing. If Feluda was going to be in disguise, it could only mean that the drama was reaching its climax.

'Are you there?'

'Yes, yes.'

'I'll try and be there by six. Wait for me. Do you understand?'

'Yes. But are you all right?'

'Bye.'

With a click, the line was disconnected. Where was Feluda?

TEN

We knew Dashashwamedh would be crowded as it was Bijaya Dashami. So we decided to take a different route, past Abhay Chakravarty's house, to reach Kedar Ghat. Raja Ghat wasn't far from Kedar.

While we were waiting for Feluda's call, Lalmohan Babu had stepped out for a minute and bought a few ayurvedic pills. 'To calm my nerves,' he explained. I noticed now that the pills had had the desired effect. The first lane we turned into had a huge bull standing diagonally across, blocking our way completely. Lalmohan Babu, instead of getting nervous, walked boldly up to it and said, 'Get out of the way, you!' The bull stepped aside. Lalmohan Babu passed through. I lingered deliberately, simply to see what he would do next. To my amusement, he turned around, beckoned to me, and said, 'Come along, Tapesh. Don't be afraid.'

The number of people gathered both in and outside Abhay

Chakravarty's house seemed much larger than usual. Then I remembered that this was the day Machchli Baba was supposed to leave Varanasi. This meant that there was going to be another big event, in addition to the immersion of Durga.

I saw a man from our hotel standing outside. 'Do you know which ghat Machchli Baba will go from?' I asked him. 'Would it be Kedar?'

'No, I think it's going to be Dashashwamedh.'

'We'll have to witness the event from a distance,' I said to Lalmohan Babu.

'Good,' he replied cheerfully. 'At least we won't get trampled in the rush!'

It took us five minutes to reach Raja Ghat from Kedar. A number of tall buildings on one side blocked out the sunlight. The river had risen considerably after the rains. The buildings cast long shadows up to the edge of the water. It was only a matter of minutes before the sun would disappear altogether.

A row of boats stood by the side of the ghat. From Dashashwamedh came a constant cacophony. It included the sound of drums and bursting of crackers. The immersion of Durga had started.

We had crossed Raja Ghat and were walking towards Munshi. I saw the hand-painted poster on the wall a minute later. The spot Feluda had chosen was really very quiet. Besides, we could see Dashashwamedh fairly clearly, although we were not very close.

'*Durga Mai ki jai*!' shouted the crowd. A figure of Durga was raised on top of a barge and lowered into the water. The sun had gone. But the crowd at Dashashwamedh seemed to have swollen further. Lalmohan Babu looked at his watch. 'Twenty to six,' he said. 'If only your cousin was here with his telefocus—' he couldn't finish. A fresh shout had risen from the crowd.

'*Guruji ki jai*! *Machchli Baba ki jai*!'

At one end of Dashashwamedh, about twenty-five yards from where we were standing, facing us was a platform. A few people were standing on it. Now they suddenly grew a bit restless. Each one of them was craning his neck and staring at the steps of the ghat. The reason soon became clear.

A large group was coming down the steps, making its way to the platform. Its leader was none other than Machchli Baba. He was still clad in bright red, except for a yellow patch round his throat. Clearly, his followers had heaped garlands on him.

Most of the people got down from the platform. Only a couple of them remained, to help the baba climb up. He raised his arms and faced the crowd. We couldn't hear what he said. Then he turned around and began walking towards the edge of the platform, his arms raised high. He stood still for a moment, facing the river. 'Machchli Baba ki jai!' shouted his devotees. The baba dived into the water.

A strange noise rose from the crowd. Lalmohan Babu called it 'mass wailing'. Machchli Baba could be seen swimming for a few minutes. Then he disappeared.

'He'll swim all the way to Patna, not stopping anywhere, not seen by anyone . . . thrilling, isn't it?' said Lalmohan Babu. I turned my head to answer him, but froze at what I saw. While we were both taking in the events at Dashashwamedh Ghat, a figure had stolen up silently in the fading light, and was standing next to us. His face was hidden behind a thick beard and moustache. He wore a turban, a long shirt, a waistcoat, loose pyjamas and Afghani shoes.

An Afghan? Here? Then it dawned upon me. Kabuliwala!

The figure raised a reassuring hand.

Feluda! He had come dressed as a Kabuliwala. Why, wasn't this the costume an actor at the Bengali Club was wearing the other day?

'Wonder—' began Lalmohan Babu. Feluda put a finger against his lips and stopped him. Neither of us knew what was about to happen, or why Feluda had found it necessary to put on a disguise What we did know—very well—was that if Feluda asked us to keep our mouths shut, we would have to.

I glanced at him. He was looking straight at Dashashwamedh Ghat. My eyes automatically followed his gaze. There were two barges on the river. One was waiting near the steps. The other was at some distance, slowly making its way to the ghat. Five or six men were sitting on its roof. It was impossible to see them clearly.

'*Durga Mai ki jai*! *Jai Durga Mai ki*!' began the crowd once more.

Another figure of Durga was being brought down the steps. It glittered as it caught the light from the gas lamps. I could recognize it easily even from afar. It was the one from Mr Ghoshal's house. The three of us stood like statues, watching the process of immersion.

The idol was carried to the top of the barge, which began to move slowly towards the centre of the river, where the water was deeper. Then, with a sudden movement, the idol rose high into the air, tilted to one side, and disappeared behind the barge. The sound of a loud splash came a moment later.

What Shashi Babu had created with such devotion was now sunk under several feet of water. Perhaps all the paint had already been washed away.

A few of the garlands Machchli Baba had been wearing came floating past.

The second barge, which had been at a distance, had, by now, crossed Dashashwamedh and was coming towards the spot where we were standing. I could now see whose barge it was. Maganlal was sitting on its roof. Four other men sat with him.

Feluda's right hand was placed on his waist. His left was curled around a stout stick. I could see it, even in the dark.

The loud, thudding noise I had heard in that alley a few days ago began again. Only, it was not a grinder this time, but my own heart.

My throat began to feel dry. I couldn't take my eyes off Feluda's left hand. I knew the little finger of his left hand had a long nail.

The Kabuliwala's nails were all cut short.

Feluda had a mole on his left wrist.

There was no sign of a mole on this man's wrist.

This man was definitely not Feluda. Who was he? What was he doing here?

Did Lalmohan Babu realize this man was an impostor? Should I tell him?

The barge was getting closer to the platform from which Machchli Baba had taken his departure. Feluda—no, the stranger—motioned us to get into the shed. Before I could say anything, Lalmohan Babu stepped in, pulling me in with him. We could still see the barge, although no one from it could see us.

The barge had almost come to a halt.

What was that, moving in the water behind the platform? A head bobbed up from the water. Lalmohan Babu clutched at my sleeve.

One of the men from the barge detached himself silently from the group and jumped into the water. No, it was not a man. It was a boy.

Suraj! It was Ruku's friend, Suraj. He was swimming across to the platform.

The head bobbed up again; but this time I could see up to his shoulders. Good heavens, was I dreaming? It was Machchli Baba! There he was again, raising himself higher. He appeared to be holding something in his hands. What was it? A large ball?

Suraj was swimming quickly. Very soon, he would join the baba.

Everyone from the barge was watching these two figures.

Two things happened at this moment that took my breath away. Machchli Baba rose from the water and threw the strange object in his hand on the steps of our ghat. In a flash, the man dressed as Kabuliwala rushed out, picked it up with one hand and, with the other, took out a revolver from his pocket, aiming it at the barge.

Maganlal leapt to his feet. I saw that he, too, was holding a gun in his hand. His companions were probably armed as well. Suddenly, there was a flurry of activity around us. A number of policemen jumped over the wall that had the poster on it, and came and stood beside our shed. Each carried a rifle.

The noise began a second later. It was difficult to say who fired first, but for a few moments there was nothing but the ear-splitting noise of gunfire. A bullet came and hit the wall of our shed, making a small portion of it crumble. Lalmohan Babu sneezed.

A scream from the barge made me look at it again. Maganlal's gun had been knocked out of his hand. He was now running to the opposite end of the barge, moving remarkably quickly for a man of his size. Then he gave a loud yell, raised his arms over his head and threw himself into the water, making it spray high into the air.

But it was no use. Two boats were already by his side, filled with policemen.

And what was Machchli Baba doing?

Why, there he was, coming out of the water with Suraj in his arms.

'Thank you, Tiwariji,' he said as he reached the steps.

The Kabuliwala grinned and stretched out an arm to pull him out of the water.

'Thank you, Mr Mitter,' he replied.

Lalmohan Babu and I sat down quickly. If we hadn't we might have fainted.

Suraj was handed over to a constable. Now that Feluda was standing so close, I could see just how good his make-up was, although some of it had washed away. His real skin peeped through these gaps.

'I hope it doesn't look as though I've got a skin disease,' he remarked casually.

'Wonderful!' exclaimed Lalmohan Babu, suddenly finding his voice. 'Now I can tell why the real Machchli Baba never had a bath!'

Feluda turned to Mr Tiwari.

'My towel and clothes are in your jeep. Could you tell one of your men to get them for me, please?'

ELEVEN

It was now nearly 10 p.m. We were sitting in Mr Ghoshal's living room. Besides ourselves and Inspector Tiwari, in the room were Ambika Ghoshal, Umanath Ghoshal and his wife, Ruku, Vikas Sinha, and visiting guests. Occasionally peering through the curtain were Trilochan and Bharadwaj.

We had just finished demolishing a great mountain of sweets. Usually, people feel depressed after the immersion. Today, however, in the Ghoshal household, all sadness had been wiped out by the prospect of the return of the Ganesh.

Perhaps I should mention here that we didn't yet know where the Ganesh was. What had been revealed was the story of Machchli Baba.

An hour before his devotees arrived, at 4 p.m., the police got in through the back door of Abhay Chakravarty's house and arrested him. His real name, it turned out, was Purinder Raut, and he was indeed the same man who had escaped from prison.

Purinder Raut had started his career with little magic shows near the Monument in Calcutta. Over a period of time, he moved to serious fraud and deception. At some point, he came in contact with Maganlal Meghraj. To have him promoted as Machchli Baba was, apparently, Maganlal's idea. The police managed to get the whole story from Purinder, including every detail of the drama Maganlal had planned at the ghat this evening.

Feluda had just finished explaining all this. Every eye was fixed on him. Only Lalmohan Babu kept breaking into fits of laughter without any apparent reason. Perhaps someone had given him a glass of *bhang* to celebrate Bijaya Dashami. I had heard that *bhang* often made people laugh.

Feluda had paused to have a drink of water. Now he replaced the glass carefully on a Kashmiri table and continued, 'Maganlal, for reasons of his own, wanted to spread the story about Machchli Baba's so-called supernatural powers. It wasn't difficult for a man like him to get a few details about the lives of Abhay Chakravarty and Lokenath. The rest was easy, partly because of Abhay Babu's gullibility, and the faith of the people of Kashi.'

Feluda stopped. Lalmohan Babu threw his head back and opened his mouth to laugh once more. I had to prod him sharply with my elbow to make him stop.

'I spoke to Maganlal recently. He told me he had the Ganesh, and that Umanath Babu had sold it to him,' said Feluda.

'What!' Umanath Ghoshal jumped to his feet, outraged. 'Did you believe him?'

'At first it simply struck me as a new angle to the case. I did not reject the idea straightaway, I have to admit. But when Maganlal offered me money to stop the investigation, I began to have doubts. He did give me a reason, of course, but I couldn't quite believe it. If what he said was true, it would have made better sense for Mr Ghoshal to stop all enquiries. After all, if the truth came to be known, he would have been in a very embarrassing position. But it was he who had asked me to find the Ganesh. It just didn't make sense!'

'Nonsense!' said Lalmohan Babu, gurgling uncontrollably. 'No sense at all! Ha ha ha!'

Feluda ignored him. 'It was then that I began to suspect that the Ganesh had not left your house, and that Maganlal was still hopeful of getting it,' he continued. 'But if it was not in the chest, where was it? And who was Maganlal in touch with in this house? Surely he couldn't expect to get the Ganesh unless someone here was going to help him? While I was trying to think things through, I discovered that Vikas Babu had kept back a piece of evidence. When I questioned him closely, he confessed that he had overheard the conversation between Maganlal and Umanath Babu. Concerned about the safety of the Ganesh, he had opened the chest the day Umanath Babu went out with his wife and son. The Ganesh was missing.'

'Missing? You mean it had already been stolen?' asked Mr Ghoshal, frowning.

'No, not stolen.' Feluda stood up. 'It wasn't stolen. A highly intelligent person had hidden it, simply to keep it out of Maganlal's grasp.'

'Captain Spark!' said Ruku.

All eyes turned on him. He was standing in a corner, clutching at a curtain.

'Yes, you're right. It was Captain Spark, alias Rukmini Kumar. Tell me, Captain Spark, that day when your father was talking to that fat man—'

'Daku Ganderia! Captain Spark fools him each time!'

'All right. But did you hear their conversation from the next room?'

'Yes, sure I did. And that's why I took the Ganesh out immediately and hid it. Or Daku Ganderia would've found it, wouldn't he?'

'Yes, you did right,' Feluda turned to the others. 'I asked Ruku before if he knew where the Ganesh was. He told me it was with the king of Africa. I didn't realize then what he meant. It dawned upon me when we went to see the Tarzan film.'

'What! Tarzan? Why Tarzan?' asked a lot of voices, all at once.

Feluda did not reply. He turned to Ruku again. 'Captain Spark, can you tell me how that film begins?'

'Yes, of course. It says, "Metro-Goldwyn-Mayer presents", and then the lions roars.'

'Thank you. Mr Tiwari!'

Inspector Tiwari bent down and brought out an object wrapped with a newspaper. He then removed the newspaper, and several amazed eyes fell on the disfigured and damaged head of a lion. Even a few hours ago, the figure of Durga had been standing on it.

'This,' Feluda said, holding the lion's head, 'is the king of Africa, and the animal Durga rides. The Ganesh had been hidden inside the parted mouth of this lion. It was Captain Spark's belief that, after the immersion, it would float all the way to the sea and would be swallowed by a shark. Captain Spark himself would then kill the shark with a harpoon and rescue the little Ganesh. Isn't that right, Captain Spark?'

'Yes, absolutely,' Ruku replied.

'But Machchli Baba had other plans. He had decided to swim for a little while, so that people knew he was actually in the water. Then he was going to swim under water, return to Dashashwamedh unseen and hide behind a boat until the idol was immersed. Once the lion had been thrown into the river, it would have taken him only a few minutes to detach its head. Then he had instructions to go to a quiet spot between Munshi and Raja Ghat, where Maganlal would arrive in his barge and collect the loot.'

'But,' said Mr Ghoshal, frowning once more, 'the date of the Baba's departure had been decided by his devotees. How could he be sure that he would get to leave on this very day? Besides, how could either he or Maganlal have known that the Ganesh was inside the lion's mouth?'

'Very simple. Seven days before Bijaya Dashmi, he asked his followers to choose a number between one and ten. He knew most people would choose seven. So that gave him his date of departure. As for the Ganesh, Ruku might not have told many people where he had hidden it, but he did mention it to his friend Suraj. Didn't you, Ruku?'

Ruku nodded in silence. He looked puzzled.

Feluda sighed. 'Shaitan Singh, I fear, lived up to his name. Suraj, you see, is Maganlal's son. His full name is Suraj Meghraj. Maganlal and his men live in the house we had gone to. His family live in that red house near yours. It was Suraj who told his father where the Ganesh was hidden.'

'Traitor!' cried Ruku.

Ambika Babu spoke for the first time. 'You found the head of the lion. Where is the Ganesh?'

Feluda picked up the lion's head once more and put his hand in its mouth. When he brought it out, it was empty except for a sticky white substance that was smeared on a fingertip.

'Captain Spark found an amazingly simple way to make sure the Ganesh did not slip out,' Feluda said.

'Chiclet!' said Ruku.

'Yes, he used chewing gum. There are traces of the gum still to be found, as you can see. But the Ganesh is no longer here.'

There was an audible gasp of disappointment as everyone drew in their breath. Mr Ghoshal slapped his forehead. 'What are you saying, Mr Mitter? After all these revelations, how can you stand there and tell us the Ganesh isn't there?'

Feluda placed the lion's head back on the table.

'No, Umanath Babu,' he spoke calmly, 'I didn't ask you to gather here simply to pour cold water on all your hopes. The Ganesh hasn't vanished. But before I tell you where it is, I'd like to remind you of an unhappy event—the death of Shashi Babu.'

'But wasn't he killed by his son?' Mr Ghoshal interrupted. 'Did his son steal the Ganesh?'

'Wait, Mr Ghoshal, please let me finish. What I am now going to tell you remains to be proved. But I am sure of getting enough evidence.'

There was complete silence in the room. Lalmohan Babu had stopped laughing loudly, although a smile still lingered on his lips.

'Shashi Babu was one man who was most likely to have spotted the Ganesh inside the lion's mouth,' Feluda went on, 'especially when he was painting the lion's face, the day before Puja began. He was killed the same day.

'You weren't home that evening, if you remember. Trilochan told me you had all gone to the temple of Vishwanath.' Mr Ghoshal nodded.

'We learnt from the police,' Feluda said, 'that Shashi Babu had started feeling unwell by the time he finished his work. So he took some medicine from Vikas Babu and left immediately. Trilochan tells me that a few minutes later, Vikas Babu went out, too. May I ask him why he did so?'

Vikas Babu looked faintly annoyed. 'I don't see what that has to do with anything. However, since you ask, the answer is that I stepped out only for some fresh air. I walked to Harishchandra Ghat, where I ran into someone I know—Dr Ashok Datta. You can check with him, if you like.'

'No, I'm sure you're telling the truth. There was a special reason why you went to the ghat, but I'll come to that later. I now have another question for Ruku. Captain Spark, Suraj knew your secret. Did you also tell your assistant, Little Raxit?'

'He didn't believe me,' said Ruku.

'I know. That is why he opened the chest to see if what Ruku had told him was true. When he discovered that it was, he felt tempted to steal the Ganesh. But strangely enough, he didn't actually have to do anything himself. It fell into his hands the day Shashi Babu found it in the lion's mouth. Oh yes, the story of giving him a dose of medicine is true enough. But what Vikas Babu did not tell the police was that Shashi Babu had handed the figure of the Ganesh over to him since there was no one else in the house. But, even so, there was every chance that Shashi Babu would talk about it the next day. So he had to be silenced. Vikas Babu followed him, stopping on the way at the Sreedhar Variety Stores to buy a sharp knife. It couldn't have been difficult to catch up with an old, sick man and stab him in a dark alleyway. He didn't know, of course, that we would find Shashi Babu and he would try to tell us about the lion. So he coolly walked to Harishchandra Ghat and threw away the knife into the river.'

'Lies!' Vikas Babu shouted, very red in the face, his eyes bulging. 'It's nothing but a pack of lies! If I took the Ganesh, where is it now? Where did it go?'

'If we had waited for just a day longer, you would have sold it to

Maganlal. But because you couldn't go out of the house during the five days of Durga Puja, you had to hide it.'

'That's not true!'

'Mr Tiwari!' Feluda stretched out a hand. The inspector handed him another object.

It was Vikas Babu's transistor radio.

Feluda opened the compartment for batteries and slipped in a finger. A second later, on his palm lay a two-and-a-half inch long, diamond-studded, golden Ganesh.

Spat!

Ambika Ghoshal had taken off one of his huge slippers and thrown it at Vikas Sinha. It struck him on his cheek.

'Traitor! Traitor! Traitor!' Ruku shrieked.

We were walking back to the hotel, after a sumptuous meal with the Ghoshal family. Before we came away, Mr Ghoshal had thrust a thick white envelope into Feluda's hand, which was now nestling in his pocket.

Lalmohan Babu had stopped laughing. It was difficult to tell whether it was because the effects of *bhang* were wearing off, or whether it was the result produced by frequent stern looks from Feluda and sharp nudges from me.

However, when we stopped at a paan shop, he burst into a guffaw once again.

'What is the matter with you?' Feluda asked, surprised. 'Do you want to be sent to Ranchi? Or did this whole mysterious affair strike you simply as a joke?'

'No, no,' Lalmohan Babu replied, controlling himself with some difficulty. 'You don't know what happened. It really is funny. Mystery no. 63 in the adventure series—*The Bleeding Diamond* by Jatayu—was right there on the bookshelf in Ruku's room. Do you know what happens in the book? The hero hides a diamond in the statue of a crocodile to keep it safe from the villain. Just imagine, my friend, Ruku got the idea from my own book, and yet I failed to spot it. You came out as a hero once more!'

Feluda stared at Lalmohan Babu for a few moments. Then he said, 'No, Lalmohan Babu, that's not true. The mystery you created with your pen almost led to my retirement from my profession! So you are as much a hero as anyone else.'

Lalmohan Babu stuffed a huge paan into his mouth.

'You're quite right, Felu Babu,' he said with a complacent air. 'Jatayu is the greatest!'

The Bandits of Bombay

ONE

Lalmohan babu—alias Jatayu—arrived one day, clutching a box of sweets. That surprised me, since all he ever carried when he came to our house was an umbrella. Whenever he published a new book, he would carry it as a parcel—but that happened twice a year, no more. That day, what he held in his hand was a box from a new sweet shop in Mirzapur Street, called Kallol. It was a white cardboard box tied with a golden ribbon, priced at Rs 25. On two sides of the box, printed in blue, were the words 'Kallol's Five-mix Sweetmeats'. Inside, I knew, there were five compartments, each holding a different kind of sweet. In its centre was Kallol's own special creation—the 'diamonda'. It was a sandesh filled with syrup, shaped like a diamond and covered with silver foil.

Why was Lalmohan babu carrying such a box? And why was there such a triumphant smile on his face?

Feluda spoke as soon as Lalmohan babu placed the box on a table and took a seat. 'Good news from Bombay, I take it? Did you hear from them this morning?'

Lalmohan babu was taken aback by these questions, but the smile did not leave his face. Only his eyebrows rose higher. 'How did you guess, heh heh?'

'The siren at 9 o'clock rang an hour ago. Yet your watch is showing 3.15. It can only mean that when you wore it this morning, you were so excited that you didn't even glance at it. Did you forget to wind it? Or has the spring gone?'

Lalmohan babu said nothing about his watch. He simply tossed one end of his blue shawl over his shoulder, like an ancient Roman, and said, 'I'd asked for twenty-five. This morning my servant woke me with a telegram. Here it is.'

He took out a pink telegram from his pocket and read it out: '"Producer willing offer ten for bandits please cable consent." I sent my reply, "happily selling bandits for ten take blessings."'

'Ten thousand?' Even Feluda, who hardly ever loses his cool, was round-eyed. 'Your story sold for *ten thousand* ?'

Lalmohan babu gave a smooth, velvety smile. 'I haven't actually got the money. I mean, not yet. I'll be paid only when I go to Bombay.'

'You are going to Bombay?' Feluda still sounded amazed.

'Yes, and so are you two. At my expense. I couldn't have written that story without your help.'

What he said was perfectly true. Perhaps I should explain.

It was Jatayu's long-cherished dream that a film be made from one of his stories. He was naturally keen on a Hindi film, as that was far more likely to make money. So he had started writing a story that he thought might be suitable for a Hindi film. He knew a man called Pulak Ghoshal who worked in the Bombay film world. He was once Lalmohan babu's neighbour in Gorpar. Having worked as an assistant director in Tollygunj in Calcutta, he made a snap decision one day to go to Bombay. Now he was a successful director himself. Many of his films had already done very well at the box office.

Lalmohan babu's story got stuck after the third chapter. When he began to feel that he wasn't getting anywhere, he came to Feluda for advice. Feluda cast his eye over the unfinished story immediately, and said, 'It is good that you got stuck at an early stage. If you'd plodded on and finished it, it would have been a complete waste of time. Bombay would have rejected it.'

Lalmohan babu scratched his head. 'So what should I write that's going to be accepted? At first, I'd thought of watching a few current films, and then base my story on those. There were long queues everywhere I went. One day I had my pocket picked while I was standing in a queue. The second day, I spent more than an hour just to reach the ticket window, and then they said they had a full house, no tickets. I could see tickets being sold on the black market, but each was for twelve rupees. I could have bought one, but in the end I thought, what if I spend all that money and then get a headache? I might have had to take a pain killer when I came out. So I just went home.'

'Don't worry, I'll give you a formula,' Feluda reassured him. 'Double roles are very popular these days, aren't they?'

It turned out that Lalmohan babu didn't even know what a double role was.

'Sometimes, there are two heroes in a film, who look identical.'

'You mean twins?'

'Yes, they can be twins; or just two men who look similar, but are not related. They may look the same, but one of them is good, the other is evil. Or one is bold and strong, the other is meek and mild. Generally, that's what you'd find in a film. You could be a little different, and instead of having just one pair of twins, you could have two. Hero number one and villain number one could be the first pair; and hero number two and villain number two could be the second. At first, the audience need not be told about the second pair. It can be a secret. Then . . .'

Lalmohan babu interrupted him. 'Wouldn't that make things far too complicated?'

Feluda shook his head. 'You need enough material to last three hours. It's no longer fashionable to show a lot of violence, there are new rules about that. So you have to tell your story in a different way. You'll need an hour and a half to create a tangled web, and another hour and a half to straighten things out.'

'So all I need are these double roles?'

'No, there is more. Note it down.'

Lalmohan babu fished out a red notebook and a golden pencil from his pocket.

'Smuggling, you need smuggling,' Feluda went on, 'Gold, diamonds, ganja, charas—it doesn't matter what it is. Then you need at least five songs. One of them should be devotional, that will be quite useful. You will also need a couple of dances, and two or three chase sequences during which at least one expensive car should be shown rolling down a hill. Then you must have a fire. The hero has to have a girlfriend, she'll be the heroine; the villain must have a girlfriend, too, except that she will be called a vamp. What else will you need? A police officer! Yes, a police officer with a strong sense of duty; flash-back for the hero; comic relief; quick changes in scenes and events, so that your story doesn't get boring. Also, it will help if the story can take the major characters to the sea or into the hills because it's not good for film stars to stay cooped inside a studio for very long . . . Did you get all that?'

Lalmohan babu was still writing furiously. He nodded without pausing for a second.

'Last, but not the least—in fact, this is most important—you need a happy ending. However, if you can create tragic situations and jerk a few tears before the happy ending, it will work much better.'

Lalmohan babu went back that day with an aching hand. Over the next two months, his struggle to get his story completed led to the appearance of calluses on two of his fingers. Thank goodness Feluda did not have to leave Calcutta during those months. He was called in to help solve the mysterious murder of Kedar Sarkar, but he did not have to travel beyond Barrackpore to make enquiries. Lalmohan babu was thus able to call on us twice a week to consult Feluda. His novel, *The Bandits of Bombay,* was published a week before Durga Puja began. The story had all the ingredients of a Hindi film, but all within reasonable limits. If a film was made from that story, one thing was for sure. One wouldn't have to reach for pain killers after seeing it.

Lalmohan babu sent a copy of the manuscript to Pulak Ghoshal even before it came out as a book. About ten days ago, Mr Ghoshal had replied saying he liked the story very much and wanted to start work as soon as possible. He would write the screenplay himself, and the dialogue in Hindi would be written by Tribhuvan Gupte. Every word that Gupte wrote was said to be as sharp as a knife, it went and hit the audience straight in the heart. In reply to that letter, Lalmohan babu had demanded twenty-five thousand rupees for his story (without saying a word to Feluda). The telegram he just showed us was in response to his letter. Perhaps he had realized that twenty-five thousand was a bit excessive.

'Aaah!' said Lalmohan babu, sipping hot tea, his eyes half closed. 'Pulak told me they haven't changed the original story. Most of the details that I—sorry, we—wrote . . .'

Feluda raised a hand and stopped him. 'I'd feel happier if you didn't say "we". *You* wrote that story.'

'But . . .'

'No buts. Even Shakespeare took ideas from other people. But did anyone ever hear him say "our *Hamlet*"? Never. I may have suggested some of the ingredients, but you were the cook. I cannot cook like you. I simply haven't got your touch!'

Lalmohan babu grinned from ear to ear in gratitude. 'Thank you, sir. Anyway, he said there were no major changes made to the story. Only a minor one.'

Oh? And what's that?'

'It's the funniest thing. You'll call it telepathy, I'm sure. You see, I'd mentioned a high-rise building with forty-three floors. My smuggler, Dhundiram Dhurandhar, lives in a flat in that building. You always tell me to pay attention to detail, so I found a name for that building—Shivaji Castle. I thought the name of a Maharashtrian hero would be most appropriate, since all the action took place in Bombay. Pulak wrote saying there really is a tall building in Bombay with the same name. And guess what? The producer of the film lives there! What can you call it but telepathy?'

'Hm. What about the kung-fu? Are they keeping it or not?' Feluda asked.

We three had gone to see *Enter the Dragon*. Lalmohan babu had instantly decided that his story must have kung-fu in it. In reply to Feluda's question, he said, 'Of course they are. I asked them specially. Pulak says they are getting a fight-master from Madras to handle the kung-fu scenes. I believe he was trained in Hong Kong!'

'When does the shooting start?'

'I don't know. I'm going to write again to Pulak and get the date. Then I'll arrange our travel. How can we stay here in Calcutta when they start shooting our—I mean my—story?'

I bit into a 'diamonda'. I had had it before, but it had never tasted as delicious as it did that day.

TWO

Lalmohan babu returned the following Sunday. Feluda had decided, in the meantime, that he'd offer to meet half the expenses for our travel to Bombay. He had made a little money recently—not only from the cases he'd handled, but also from writing. In the last three months he had translated two books written in English (both were travelogues written by famous travellers in the nineteenth century) and been paid an advance. I had seen him write before in his free time. This was the first time he had done it seriously.

Lalmohan babu rejected his offer outright. 'Are you mad?' he asked. 'In the matter of writing, sir, you are my god and godfather. If I am willing to meet your expenses, it is only out of gratitude. Treat it as your fee!'

So saying, he took out two aeroplane tickets from his pocket and placed them on the table. 'The flight is at 10.45 on Tuesday morning. We have to check in an hour before that. I will meet you at the airport.'

'When is the shooting going to start?'

'Thursday. They're starting with the climax—that scene with the horse, a car and a train.'

Lalmohan babu had another piece of news for us. 'Yesterday, Feluda babu, something interesting happened in the evening. A film producer here in Calcutta turned up at my house. He has an office in Dharamtala, he said. He'd got my address from the publishers. Said he wanted to make a film from my *Bandits*! It seems no Bengali film has a chance, unless it shows the same things you see in Hindi films. I had to tell him my story was already sold, which seemed to disappoint

him no end. Mind you, he hadn't read the book himself, but had
heard about it from a nephew. He was surprised to hear I'd written it
without ever having visited Bombay. I didn't tell him I couldn't have
done it without Murray's Guide to India, and Felu Mitter's guidance.'

'Was he a Bengali?'

'Yes. Sanyal. He spoke with a slight accent, said he was brought
up in Jabalpur. And he was wearing some strong perfume—God, it
nearly burnt my nose! I didn't know a man could wear so much
perfume. Anyway, when he heard I was off to Bombay, he gave me
an address. Said it was his friend's. This friend is supposed to be
most helpful. I was free to contact him any time I wanted to.'

Although Calcutta can get quite cold in December, I'd heard that
Bombay would remain warm. So we didn't have to pack warm clothes,
and everything we needed fitted into two small suitcases.

On Tuesday, I woke to find everything hidden in thick fog. Our
neighbour's house across the road was barely visible. Oh God, would
our plane be able to take off on time? Strangely enough, by nine
o'clock the fog lifted and a dazzling sun came out. VIP Road, which
ran all the way to the airport, was usually more misty than the city-
centre; but today the mist was negligible.

The plane was due to leave in fifty minutes by the time we reached
the airport. Lalmohan babu was already there. He had even checked
in—I saw a boarding card peeping out of his breast pocket. 'I didn't
wait for you, please don't mind,' he said, 'There was such a long
queue, I thought if I didn't check in quickly, I might not get a window
seat. I'm in Row H. Who knows, you might get seats close to mine?'

'What's that packet you've got? Have you bought a book?' Feluda
wanted to know.

There was a brown packet tucked under Lalmohan babu's arm. I
had assumed it was one of his own books that he was carrying as a
present for someone in Bombay.

'No, no, I didn't buy it,' he told Feluda. 'Remember Sanyal? The
man I told you about? He came and gave it to me ten minutes ago.'

'A present for you?'

'No, sir. Someone will meet me at Bombay airport and collect it.
He's been given my name and description. Yes, it's a book and is
meant for a relative of Sanyal's in Bombay.' Then he smiled and
added, 'I say, can't you smell an adventure in all this?'

'That's a bit difficult, Lalmohan babu,' Feluda replied, 'as the smell of Bharat Chemical's Gulbahar scent has drowned everything else!'

I had got the smell as well. Mr Sanyal's perfume was so strong that even the packet had picked it up.

'You're quite right, heh heh!' laughed Lalmohan babu in agreement. 'Sometimes, I have heard, people pass on all kinds of things like this— I mean, stuff that's banned and illegal!'

'Yes, that's true. There's that large notice hanging outside the check-in counter, warning against the danger of accepting a packet from a stranger. But then, Mr Sanyal is technically not a stranger; and I see no reason to think that his parcel contains anything other than a book.'

We could not get adjacent seats on the plane. Lalmohan babu took the window seat three rows behind us. The flight was more or less eventless—except when the pilot, Captain Datta, began announcing that we were flying over Nagpur, I happened to turn around at that moment. Lalmohan babu had left his seat and was heading straight for the rear of the plane. An airhostess stopped him and pointed in the opposite direction. Lalmohan babu turned back, walked the entire length of the plane again, opened the door of the cockpit and came out instantly, looking profoundly embarrassed. Finally, he found the door to the toilet on his left.

On his way back to his seat, he stopped by my side and whispered into my ear: 'Take a good look at the fellow sitting next to me. Shouldn't be surprised if he turns out to be a hijacker.'

I turned my head once more and looked at the man. If Lalmohan babu wasn't absolutely desperate for an adventure, he would never have imagined his fellow passenger to be a hijacker. The man looked far too meek and mild.

When we landed at Santa Cruz, Lalmohan babu had already taken out the brown packet and was clutching it in his hand. We made our way to the domestic lounge and were looking around, when a voice suddenly said, 'Mr Ganguli?' We turned to our right to find a man in a dark red terylene shirt looking eagerly at a south Indian gentleman. It was he who had asked the question. The south Indian man looked faintly irritated, shook his head and went on his way. Lalmohan babu approached red shirt.

'I am Mr Ganguli and this is from Mr Sanyal,' he said in one breath.

Red shirt took the packet, inclined his head, said 'thank you' and left. Lalmohan babu, having done his duty, looked relieved and dusted his hands.

Our luggage emerged half an hour later. It was 1.20 when we collected it. By the time we reached the city, it would be nearly two o'clock. Pulak Ghoshal had sent a car to meet us, and told us its number. It turned out to be a mustard-coloured Standard. Its driver was both smart and cheerful. He could speak Hindi and English and didn't seem to mind at all that he'd been hired to drive three strangers from Calcutta. On the contrary, judging by the salute he gave Lalmohan babu, it appeared that he was quite gratified by his assignment. It was he who told us that we were booked at the Shalimar Hotel in the city. Pulak Ghoshal would meet us there at 5.30. In the meantime, we could keep the car and were free to go where we liked.

Feluda had read up on Bombay before our arrival, as was his wont. According to him, unless you learned something about a place before you went to visit it, you could never really get to know it fully. Just as a person can be identified not just by his appearance and character, but also by his personal history, so can a city. The appearance and character of Bombay were still unknown to Feluda, but he did know that our hotel was near Kemp's Corner.

We left the airport. As soon as our car left the highway and took a road to go to the city, Feluda spoke to the driver. 'See that taxi in front of us? MRP 3538. Follow it, please,' he said.

'Hey, what's going on?' Lalmohan babu asked.

'Simple curiosity about something,' Feluda replied.

Our car overtook a scooter and two Ambassadors and slipped behind the Fiat taxi Feluda had indicated. The passenger on its back seat was visible through the glass. It was the man in the red shirt.

My heart gave a tiny lurch. Nothing had happened, I didn't even know why Feluda wanted to follow that taxi; yet I felt a bit nervous, I suppose because the whole thing was so unexpected. Lalmohan babu said nothing more. He knew there was no point in asking Feluda to explain his behaviour. The real reason behind his action would be revealed at the right time.

Our driver drove on, keeping close to the taxi. We began taking in all the sights of a new city. One thing that struck all of us was the presence of large hoardings and posters of Hindi films on virtually every road. I couldn't remember having seen such a thing, in such large numbers, in any other city. Lalmohan babu craned his neck to read what was written on many of them. Then he said, 'There are so many names . . . but the writer of the story is hardly mentioned on these! Don't these people use writers?'

'Lalmohan babu,' Feluda told him, 'if you are expecting to make a name as a writer, then Bombay is not the right place for you. Stories aren't written, but manufactured here. It is a commodity, a consumer product, like any other. Who would know the name of the person who actually makes Lux soap, tell me? At the most, one might know the name of the company. You should simply be happy that you are being paid for your pains. Take your payment, and keep quiet. Forget about recognition.'

'I see . . .' Lalmohan babu sounded quite concerned. 'You mean Bengal will bring fame, and Bombay will produce fortune?'

'Exactly,' said Feluda.

By this time, we were passing through an area that Feluda said was called Mahalakshmi. Soon, we'd left it behind. Now the taxi we were following turned right. 'If you want to go to your hotel, sir, I should go straight on,' our driver told us.

'No, turn right,' Feluda instructed him.

We turned right, still following the same taxi. Only a couple of minutes later, it slipped through the front gate of a building. Feluda told our driver to stop outside the gate. The three of us got out. Almost at once, Lalmohan babu made a noise that sounded like a hiccup.

The reason was clear. We were standing before a high-rise building. High on its wall, written in large black letters, were the words: Shivaji Castle.

THREE

I was so taken aback by the sign that, for a few moments, I could not speak at all. 'This is Telepathy with a capital T!' Lalmohan babu exclaimed.

Feluda did not say anything. He wasn't just looking at the building, but was darting sharp glances all around. To the left were a number of similar tall buildings, each with at least twenty floors. The buildings to the right were older and lower in height. Through the gaps between some of those buildings, the sea was visible.

Our driver was looking at us with a puzzled air. Feluda told him to wait and went through the gate. Lalmohan babu and I stood outside, feeling a little foolish.

Feluda returned in about three minutes. 'Now let's go to Shalimar Hotel', he said to the driver.

We started another journey. Feluda lit a cigarette and said, 'It is very likely that your packet went to the seventeenth floor.'

'Oh my God, are you a magician? You managed to find out, in just three minutes, where that fellow went with the packet?' Lalmohan babu asked.

'There was no need to climb to the seventeenth floor to guess where he might have gone. There was a board over the lift on the ground floor. By the time I got there, it had already started climbing up. The board was flashing the numbers where it stopped. The last number that came on was seventeen. Now do you understand?'

Lalmohan babu sighed. 'Yes. What I don't understand is why I can't think of simple explanations.'

It took us only five minutes to reach our hotel. Feluda and I were given a double room on the fifth floor. Lalmohan babu's room—a single—was opposite ours. Our room overlooked the street below. Every time I looked out of the window, I could see an endless stream of traffic. Facing the window were two high-rises, through which I could catch glimpses of the sea. It was easy to tell what a lively, thriving city Bombay was even without stepping out of the room.

We were all feeling very hungry. So, after a quick wash, we went to the restaurant called Gulmarg on the second floor. As soon as our order was placed, Lalmohan babu asked the question that must have been trembling on his lips.

'So you, too, can smell an adventure, Felu babu?'

Feluda did not answer that question. Instead, he asked another.

'Did you notice what that man did after collecting the book from you?'

'Did? He just walked away, didn't he?'

'No. You saw him go, but didn't notice the finer details. He walked away from you, then stopped and fished out a few coins from his pocket.'

'Telephone!' I exclaimed.

'Well done, Topshe. I believe he then used a public telephone and rang someone in the city. I saw him again when we were waiting for our luggage.'

'Where did you see him?'

'Do you remember a car park just outside the terminal building? Visible from where we were standing?'

'Yes, yes!' I shouted. Lalmohan babu said nothing.

'That man got into a blue Ambassador. There was a driver. He tried to start the car, but even after five minutes, nothing happened. The man got out and shouted at the driver. I could not hear him, but could tell by the expression on his face and his gestures that he was most displeased. Eventually, he gave up and walked away from the car.'

'To get a taxi!' Lalmohan babu spoke this time.

'Exactly. So what does that tell you?'

'The man was in a hurry.'

'Good. Eyes and your brain—you need to keep these open. If you do, you'll find that it's possible to deduce certain facts really quite easily. So, you see, if I was trying to follow that taxi, it was for a reason.'

'Yes, but what exactly is on your mind?' Lalmohan babu asked, sitting up straight and placing his elbows on the table.

'Nothing. Nothing specific. I only have a doubt . . . a little doubt about something.'

After that, we began talking of other things and did not refer to the matter again.

Lalmohan babu joined us in our room at around five o'clock, after a short rest. We ordered tea, and were in the process of drinking it, when there was a knock on our door. The man who entered was most definitely no more than thirty-five but his thick, wavy hair had already turned amazingly grey.

'Hello, Laluda! How are you? Everything all right?' he asked.

Laluda! It had simply not occurred to me that anyone could possibly call Lalmohan babu 'Laluda'. So this was Pulak Ghoshal. Feluda had warned Lalmohan babu not to reveal his profession, so he was introduced merely as his friend. Mr Ghoshal looked at Feluda and suddenly shook his head most regretfully. 'You are Laluda's friend, one of our very own—and look, here we are, struggling to find a suitable hero. Mr Mitter, can you speak Hindi?'

Feluda grinned. 'No, sir. I cannot speak Hindi, and what is worse, I cannot act. But why are you still looking for a hero? I thought you'd found Arjun Mehrotra.'

'Yes, but Arjun has changed a lot, he's not the same person any more. Now he's learnt to make endless demands. I don't call these actors heroes, you know. They are all villains under the surface; never mind if they play heroes on the screen. The producers have spoilt them rotten. Anyway, I am here to invite you to the first day's shooting the day after tomorrow. The spot is about seventy miles from here. Your driver knows the place. Try to leave as early as you can. Mr Gore—my producer, I mean—isn't here. He's out visiting Delhi,

Calcutta and Madras to sell this film. But he told me to make sure you were well looked after.'

'Where is this spot?'

'Between Khandala and Lonavala. We'll shoot inside a train. If there aren't enough passengers, I'll ask you to sit in the compartment.'

'Oh, by the way,' said Lalmohan babu, 'We've seen Shivaji Castle.'

His words brought a frown on Mr Ghoshal's face immediately. 'Really? When?'

'On our way from the airport. Say, around two.'

'I see. That means it happened after two o'clock.'

'What happened?'

'A murder.'

'Wha-at!' All of us exclaimed, almost simultaneously. There is something so sinister about the word 'murder' that it made me shiver involuntarily.

'I learnt about it only half an hour ago,' Mr Ghoshal told us, 'I am a regular visitor to that building. That's where Mr Gore lives, on the twelfth floor. Now do you see why we had to change that name? But Mr Gore himself is a very nice man. Did you go inside?'

'I did,' Feluda said, 'only up to the lift. I didn't get into it.'

'Good heavens! The murder took place inside that lift. The body has not yet been identified. I believe he looks like a hooligan. A man called Tyagarajan lives on the third floor. Around three o'clock he pressed the button for the lift. It came down from upstairs. So Tyagarajan then tried getting into it, and saw what had happened. The fellow was stabbed in the stomach. Horrible affair!'

'Wasn't anyone else seen getting in and out of the lift around that time?' Feluda asked.

'No, there was no one out in the passage near the lift. But two drivers were waiting outside, they saw five or six people go into the building. One of them was wearing a red shirt, another one had a shoulder bag and was wearing a brown . . .'

Feluda raised a hand and stopped him. 'That second man was me. No need for further details.'

My heart skipped a beat. Was Feluda now going to get involved in a murder case?

'Anyway,' said Mr Ghoshal reassuringly, 'please don't worry about it. You, too, Laluda. So what if you've written in your story that a smuggler lives in Shivaji Castle? There's no apartment house in Bombay that doesn't have one or two smugglers living in it. All they've done so far is peel the top—it'll be a long time before they can get to the core. The entire city is run by smugglers.'

Feluda was looking rather grim. But his expression changed as we were joined by another man. When we heard another knock on the door, Mr Ghoshal rose from his chair saying 'That must be Victor', and opened the door. A man of medium height walked in. He had a body as lean and supple as a whip.

'Let me introduce you. Laluda, this is Victor Perumal, the kung-fu expert, trained in Hong Kong!'

Mr Perumal smiled and shook hands with everyone.

'He can speak a certain amount of English,' Mr Ghoshal added, 'and, of course, he can speak Hindi, though he comes from southern India. He doesn't just teach kung-fu, he's a marvellous stuntman. In fact, he's going to handle that scene where the hero's brother has to jump off a horse and into a moving train. Victor's going to be made up to look like the actor who plays the brother.'

There was something so frank and disarming about Victor's smile that I began to warm to him instantly. Besides, I have a lot of respect for stuntmen. Heroes get all the acclaim for performances given by proxy, but it is these stuntmen who risk their lives every day, for very little money. One has to admire them.

Victor Perumal said, 'Yes, I know kung-fu, and also mokka-iri.'

Mokka-iri? What was that? Even Feluda said he didn't know. It was useless asking Lalmohan babu as he reads chiefly what he writes himself, and little else.

Victor explained. Mokka-iri, he said, was a form of combat in which one had to balance one's body on one's hands and walk on them, with one's legs raised in the air. Apparently, it had been introduced in Hong Kong only six months earlier. Japan was its place of origin.

'Will your film include this mokka-iri?' asked Lalmohan babu, sounding a little apprehensive. Mr Ghoshal smiled and shook his head. 'No, no,' he said, 'Kung-fu is difficult enough to manage. Since early November we've been holding training sessions for eleven men, morning and evening. You only wrote about it, but we have to deal with the practical problems, Laluda. But the scene you'll see tomorrow won't have any kung-fu in it. It will have some dramatic stuff from stuntmen, though. We'll make a super film from your story, Laluda, don't you worry.'

After Victor and Mr Ghoshal had gone, Feluda went and opened all the windows. At once, our room was filled with the sound of traffic, although it wasn't loud enough on the fifth floor to be really disturbing. None of us was used to an airconditioner, so we didn't wish to have it on and keep the windows closed. The noise didn't matter. After all, it wasn't just the noise that was coming in through the open windows; so was fresh air.

Feluda returned to the sofa and said somewhat seriously, 'Lalmohan babu, that smell of adventure you were talking about is getting too strong for comfort. You shouldn't have agreed to deliver that packet. If I was with you at the time, I'd have told you not to.'

Lalmohan babu looked a bit crestfallen. 'What could I do? The fellow said he was still interested in my stories. He told me to reserve the next one for him. How could I refuse after that?'

'Usually,' Feluda said, 'if a passenger happens to be carrying a packet, the security officials at the airport open it and look inside. You must have struck them as completely harmless, so they didn't bother. If they had, God knows what they might have found. Who knows whether or not there is a link between that packet and the murder?'

Lalmohan babu cleared his throat. 'Yes, but how can a book . . .?' he began.

'Suppose it wasn't a book? Or something more than a book? In Mughal times kings sometimes carried poison in their rings. Surely you've heard about that? Now, if a ring was filled with poison, would you still call it just a ring? It would then also be a repository for poison, wouldn't it? Anyway, you've done your duty, so I don't think *you* are in any danger.'

'You think so?' A smile appeared on Lalmohan babu's face at last.

'Certainly. And, in any case, if you are in danger, so are we. We're tied together by the same thread, aren't we? If anyone pulls that thread, they'll get all three of us!'

Lalmohan babu sprang to his feet, kicked his left leg high in the air in the style of a kung-fu fighter, and said, 'Three cheers for the Three Musketeers! Hip-hip!'

Feluda and I joined in. 'Hurrah!' we said.

FOUR

We left the hotel at around six o'clock. All of us believed that unless one explored a city on foot, one couldn't get to know it at all. We had roamed similarly in Jodhpur, Varanasi, Delhi and Gangtok. Why shouldn't we do so in Bombay?

A little way away, to the right, was Kemp's Corner. We found an impressive flyover there. It was like a bridge, supported by massive pillars. Traffic ran both on it, and under it. We crossed the road under the bridge and went down Gibbs Road. Feluda pointed at a road on our right and said it went to the Hanging Gardens. The hill where these gardens were built was called Malabar Hill.

We had to walk another mile before we could reach the sea. We crossed the road, managing to avoid the rush hour traffic, and found ourselves standing by a stone wall. The top of the wall came up to my waist. Behind that wall roared the sea, its waves crashing against it.

The road on our left ran to the east, then curved and went towards the south, ending where rows of skyscrapers stood hazily in the setting sun. The arc that we could see was called Marine Drive.

'Never mind if there are smugglers here,' Lalmohan babu proclaimed, 'Look at that sea, and the hills . . . I must say Bombay is a champion city!'

We began walking by the stone wall towards Marine Drive. Cars were moving down the road to our left, looking like rows of ants. After a few minutes, Lalmohan babu made another remark.

'I suppose the Metropolitan Development Authority isn't quite so active here, is it? They don't keep digging up streets all the time?' he asked.

'Why? Are you saying that because there are no potholes?'

'Yes. I noticed it as soon as we left the airport. There I was, travelling in a car, but there were no jerks, no bumps. Amazing!'

I had spotted a crowded area by the sea. It looked a bit like the area around Shaheed Minar in Calcutta, on a Sunday. As we got closer, Feluda told me it was called Chowpatty. Apparently, it was always crowded. There were rows of stalls. Perhaps they were selling snacks like bhelpuri, chaat and ice-cream.

My guess turned out to be quite correct. It looked as if a huge mela was being held. Half the city of Bombay appeared to have turned up. Lalmohan babu offered to buy us bhelpuri. We agreed readily enough, as he was about to come into a lot of money, and could therefore well afford to pay. When packets of bhelpuri were handed to us, we left the crowded spot and moved away to sit on the beach. It was a quarter to seven according to my watch, but the sky was still glowing pink. Like us, several others were relaxing on the beach. Lalmohan babu finished eating, waved his hand in the air, began chanting a Sanskrit shloka, then stopped abruptly. A sheet of newspaper had escaped—possibly from one of the groups sitting nearby—and come flying towards him. Now it was stuck to his face, gagging him momentarily.

He pulled it free, looked at it briefly and had just said, '*Evening News* ', when Feluda snatched it from his hand.

'You saw the name of the paper, but didn't you see the headline?' Feluda asked.

All of us bent over the paper. 'Murder in Apartment Lift,' announced the headline. Below it was a photo of the murdered man. No, it was not the man in the red shirt.

According to the report, the murder took place between two and two-thirty. The murderer was still at large, but the police had begun their investigation. The murder victim was called Mangalram Sethi. He had been involved with the black market and smugglers for quite some time, and was wanted by the police. Signs of a struggle had been found inside the lift. And the only clue that had been found was a piece of paper, lying by the body. It had a name written on it. The name was . . .

'Arr-r-rr-r-ghh!'

A strange groan escaped from Lalmohan babu's throat. I flung my arms around him quickly, in case he fainted. There was plenty of reason to do so. The report ended by saying that the piece of paper found in the lift said, 'Mr Ganguli, dark, short, bald, moustache.'

As soon as he'd finished reading the report, Lalmohan babu grabbed the paper, whisked it away from Feluda's hand, tore it into several pieces and let the wind carry them away.

'Look what you've done! You've filled this wonderful, clean beach with garbage,' Feluda complained.

Lalmohan babu was still unable to speak. Now Feluda had to be stern. 'Do you seriously believe that the whole city can figure out from that description that it's talking about *you*?'

Lalmohan babu continued to look worried. Then he swallowed hard and finally found his tongue. 'But. . . but . . . you can see what it means, can't you? You can guess who's the murderer?'

Feluda stared fixedly at him for a few seconds, before saying slowly, 'Laluda, you have spent four years in my company. Even so, you haven't learnt to think calmly and rationally, have you?'

'Why, why—that red shirt—?'

'What about it? Even if we assume that it was the fellow in the red shirt who dropped that piece of paper, what does it prove? Who says that *he* is the murderer? Just think for a minute. Once he had met you and taken that packet from you, he had no further need to keep that piece of paper. So, when he found it in his pocket as he got into the lift, he threw it away, then and there. That's a perfectly logical and simple explanation. Is that so hard to believe?'

Lalmohan babu refused to be reassured. 'Never mind all that Felu babu,' he muttered, 'If my name and description have been found lying next to a corpse, I am most definitely going to be harassed. I can see it all happening. There is only one way out for me. Naturally, I cannot grow hair on my bald head. My height won't change; nor will my complexion. That only leaves my moustache. I am going to get rid of it tomorrow.'

'I see. And what do you think the people in our hotel are going to think? Do you suppose none of them reads the *Evening News* ? Most people—ninety per cent of them—will read any report that mentions a murder. That's human nature. If you suddenly shave your moustache off, everyone's eyes—and suspicion—will fall on you!'

By this time, the red sky had turned purple. When that faded to grey, and the evening star appeared through a chink in the clouds in the western sky, blinking alone in a brave attempt to vie with the thousands of glittering lights on Marine Drive, we rose from the sandy beach, dusted ourselves down and made our way back to the crowded stalls in Chowpatty. Then we walked over to the main road and caught a taxi back to the hotel.

We had to stop at the reception desk to collect our keys. I noticed that when he stretched his hand to take the key from the receptionist, Lalmohan babu kept his face firmly averted. But that did not help. Opposite the desk, seated in the lobby were seven people, some of them foreigners. Three of them were reading the *Evening Standard*. Its front page carried a report about the same murder, together with a picture of the victim. It seemed highly unlikely that the report in the *Standard* would make no mention of the short, bald, dark and moustachioed Mr Ganguli.

FIVE

In the end, Lalmohan babu did not shave off his moustache. When I asked him the following morning if he had slept well, he told me he hadn't because each time he began nodding off, it seemed to him as if his entire room was moving up and down like a lift, and he woke with a start.

Mr Ghoshal had called us the previous night and told us that he'd collect us at ten o'clock to take us to his studio. We finished our breakfast at eight, then went for a walk down Peddar Road, where we found a paan shop. We bought some paan filled with sweet masala, and returned to the hotel. As soon as we entered the lobby, we could all feel an air of suppressed excitement.

The reason was simple. The local police had decided to pay a visit to our hotel. A man in uniform, who looked like an inspector, was standing at the reception desk. One of the men behind the counter made a gesture as we approached. The inspector wheeled around and glanced at Lalmohan babu. Although the look in his eyes wasn't even remotely hostile, I heard a faint click beside me, which meant that Lalmohan babu's knees were knocking against each other.

The inspector came forward, a smile on his face. Feluda placed a hand on Lalmohan babu's shoulder and gave it a light squeeze, to let him know that there was nothing to worry about.

'I am Inspector Patwardhan from the CID. You are Mr Ganguli?'

'Ye-ye-yess.'

Patwardhan looked at Feluda. 'And you are—?'

Feluda took out one of his cards and handed it to Patwardhan. The inspector read it, then looked inquiringly at Feluda again. 'Mitter? Are you the same Mitter who helped save that statue in Ellora?'

Feluda gave his famous lopsided smile and nodded.

'Glad to meet you, sir,' Patwardhan said, offering his hand, 'you did a very good job there.'

Lalmohan babu could now relax a little. As Feluda's friend, his status had certainly improved. Nevertheless, he had to answer a number of questions. We went to the manager's room to have a chat.

Patwardhan told us that various fingerprints had been found on the body, but the police hadn't yet made any arrests. The man in the red shirt had been traced back to the airport. The police had tracked down the taxi he had used, but did not know who the man was. They believed the murder had been committed by the same man, and the piece of paper with Lalmohan babu's name on it had slipped out of his pocket. What Lalmohan babu told him simply confirmed this belief. Patwardhan said, 'It was clear that he had gone to the airport to meet a Mr Ganguli. We checked the passenger list of every plane that landed at Santa Cruz yesterday, until we found your name on the Calcutta flight. Then we made enquiries at all the hotels, and finally learned that a Mr L. Ganguli had checked in at the Shalimar.'

What Patwardhan really wanted to do, of course, was find out how Lalmohan babu was connected to the whole business, and why his name and description appeared on that piece of paper. Lalmohan babu explained about Mr Sanyal. 'Who is this Sanyal? How well do you know him?' asked Patwardhan.

Lalmohan babu told him what little he knew, but had to admit, when asked, that he did not have Sanyal's address.

Finally Inspector Patwardhan gave a little lecture, exactly as Feluda had done. 'This is how,' he said, 'innocent people are being used these days to transfer smuggled goods. We've learned that some valuable jewels have arrived in India from Kathmandu, including the famous naulakha necklace that once belonged to Nanasaheb.'

I knew of one Nanasaheb who had fought against the British during the sepoy mutiny of 1857. Was Patwardhan talking of the same man?

'It is my belief that the packet you were given contained some stolen object,' Patwardhan told us. 'Two gangs must be after the same thing. One sent it from Calcutta. Someone from the other gang, I suspect, learnt about its arrival and was hanging around Shivaji Castle. He attacked red shirt, and red shirt killed him.'

Lalmohan babu had assumed that he would either be hanged, or put behind bars for life, simply because the possible murderer was known to be carrying his name and description in his pocket. When all he got from the police was a piece of advice to be careful in future, Lalmohan babu's demeanour changed at once. He perked up and his eyes sparkled once more.

Mr Ghoshal arrived at eleven o'clock instead of ten. When we told him about our encounter with the police, he said, 'Yes, I was afraid of this. My heart sank the minute I read the evening papers yesterday. That piece of paper they found seemed to have every description that fits Laluda—yet the whole thing is a complete mystery to me!'

Lalmohan babu then told him about Mr Sanyal. 'Which Sanyal is this?' Mr Ghoshal asked, 'Is it Ahi Sanyal? Medium height, sunken eyes, cleft on his chin?'

'Don't know. Didn't see his chin, he had a beard. Perhaps he was clean shaven before.'

'I saw him two years ago. God knows if it was the same man. He worked in Bombay for a while, even produced a couple of films. As far as I can remember, both films were flops.'

'What was he like as a man?'

'I have no idea, but I never heard anyone say anything bad about him.'

'In that case, perhaps there was nothing wrong with that packet he gave me.'

'Look, Laluda, we are all told to be careful only because these days you often hear about cases of smuggling. But in the past, didn't we carry packets and parcels for other people? I mean, even people we didn't know that well? There were never any problems, were there?'

The four of us went in the same car that we had used the day before, and soon reached the studio in Mahalakshmi. As we were getting out, Mr Ghoshal said, 'We were running into problems with the railways over tomorrow's shooting. So Mr Gore had to be informed, and he came from Calcutta by the evening flight yesterday. Come with me, I will introduce you to him.'

'Will the shooting take place tomorrow?' Lalmohan babu asked a bit uncertainly.

'Of course. Most certainly. Don't worry about it—everything has been sorted out.'

We were taken to what looked like a workshop with a tin roof. It was used for shooting at times; but today, a kung-fu session was in progress. On a huge mattress, under Victor Perumal's guidance, a number of men were jumping, kicking and falling. About twelve feet away sat a man in a wicker chair. He was probably in his mid-forties.

'Let me introduce you,' said Mr Ghoshal. 'This is our producer, Mr Gore . . . and this is Mr Ganguli, the writer . . . and Mr Mitter, and . . . what is your name, dear boy?'

'Tapeshranjan Mitter.'

Mr Gore's cheeks looked like a pair of apples, in the centre of his head was a shiny bald patch, and his eyes were hazel. He had a sizeable paunch, too, but presumably that was a recent development. No one could possibly wear such tight clothes voluntarily. Mr Ghoshal disappeared as soon as the introductions were made, as he had a lot of things to attend to before the first day's shooting. 'I'll come back at one-thirty,' he said before leaving us, 'you will all have lunch with me.'

Mr Gore asked for extra chairs and was most hospitable. He took a chair next to Lalmohan babu and said in Bengali, '*Aapni elen bole aami khoob khushi holam.* (I am very pleased that you could come.)'

'I say, you speak fantastic Bengali!' Lalmohan babu enthused, going slightly over the top in his praise, possibly because of the money Gore was about to pay him.

'My father ran a business in Canning Street. I was a student in Don Bosco for three years. Then my father died, and I came to Bombay to live with my uncle. I've been here ever since. But this is my first venture in film-making,' Mr Gore told us.

Perhaps because he was impressed by Mr Gore's Bengali, Lalmohan babu told him all that had happened, starting from Sanyal's visit and ending with his chat with Inspector Patwardhan. Mr Gore clicked his tongue in sympathy and said, 'No one can be trusted these days, Mr Ganguli. You are an eminent writer; I am ashamed to think that *you* were used to cart smuggled goods!'

Feluda now joined the conversation.

'You live in Shivaji Castle, I hear?' he said.

'Yes. I've been there for the last couple of months. Horrible murder. I returned by the evening flight yesterday, and got home at about eleven. Even at that time there was a large crowd in the street. If there's a murder in a high-rise building, it's always a big problem.'

'Er . . . do you know who lives on the seventeenth floor?'

'Seventeenth . . . seventeenth . . .' Mr Gore failed to remember. 'I know someone who lives on the eighth floor—N.C. Mehta; and there's Dr Vazifdar on the second. My flat is on the twelfth floor.'

Feluda asked nothing more. In any case, Mr Gore seemed to want to leave. 'I have a lot of things to see to,' he said, 'Producing a film is a complicated business, you see. There are always problems?' From what we'd heard, the shooting planned for the next day was really going to be a complex affair. A train had been hired. It would start from Matheran and arrive at the level crossing between Khandala and Lonavala. Mr Gore had to go to Matheran to pay the railway company. Apparently, the train had an old-fashioned first-class compartment. Mr Gore would get into it and travel by the same train to the shooting spot. 'I'd be delighted if you came along and had lunch with me on the train,' he invited. 'Are you vegetarians?'

'No, no. Non-veg, non-veg!' said Lalmohan babu.

'What would you like? Chicken or mutton?'

'We had chicken yesterday. Let's have mutton tomorrow. What do you say, Felu babu?'

'As you wish,' Feluda replied.

Although Feluda was listening to Mr Gore's conversation with Lalmohan babu, his eyes were straying frequently to the group practising kung-fu. Victor Perumal's patience and perseverance were remarkable. It was clear that he wouldn't give up until every movement was perfect. One or two trainees were already performing extremely well.

Victor was also glancing at Feluda from time to time, possibly encouraged by the admiration in Feluda's eyes. When Mr Gore had gone, Victor beckoned Feluda and asked him to come closer. Feluda put out his cigarette and went over to Victor and his men.

'Come on, Mr Mitter. Try it. It's not so difficult!' said Victor.

The trainees moved away. Victor gave a slight jump, raising his right leg above his head before kicking it forward in a peculiar fashion. Had someone been standing in front of him, he would certainly have been hit and possibly knocked down. Feluda stepped onto the mattress, and jumped around a few times to get ready. Victor stood at a distance of about six feet, and said, 'Try and kick your leg towards me!'

What Victor did not know was that, after seeing *Enter the Dragon*, Feluda had spent about a month at home, kicking his legs high in the air, every now and then, exactly as he had seen it being done by kung-fu fighters. He had done it purely for fun, but it had given him a certain amount of experience.

'One - two - three!' shouted Victor. At once, Feluda's leg shot out horizontally, and Victor took a step back, falling on the mattress. I knew, however, that Feluda's leg had not made contact with Victor's body.

Over the next five minutes, everyone watched a kung-fu demonstration between Victor Perumal and Pradosh Mitter. I couldn't help looking from time to time at Victor's trainees, who had spent over six weeks learning how to jump, kick and fall. They knew how much effort it took to do all that. What was reassuring was that their faces registered more admiration than envy. When, at the end of those five minutes, the two participants shook hands and thumped each other on the back, their audience broke into spontaneous applause.

SIX

Around two o'clock, we walked into the Copper Chimney restaurant in Worli to have lunch with Pulak Ghoshal and Tribhuvan Gupte, the dialogue writer. The place was packed, but Mr Ghoshal had reserved a table for us.

'I say, Pulak,' Lalmohan babu asked, 'what is the name of your film?'

I, too, had wondered about the name, but hadn't found the chance to ask Mr Ghoshal, All I knew for sure was that the film was not going to be called *The Bandits of Bombay.*

'You cannot imagine, Laluda,' said Mr Ghoshal, 'the trouble we've had over the name. Whatever we chose had either already been used, or registered by some other party. You can ask Gupteji here how many sleepless nights he's spent, puzzling over an appropriate name. Only three days ago—suddenly, out of the blue—it came. A high-voltage spark!'

'High-voltage spark? Your film is called A High-Voltage Spark ?' Lalmohan babu asked in a low-voltage voice.

Mr Ghoshal burst out laughing, making those sitting at neighbouring tables turn their heads and stare. 'Are you mad, Laluda? You think a name like that would work? No, I was talking about a sudden flash of inspiration, a brain wave. It's *Jet Bahadur.*'

'Eh?'

'*Jet Bahadur.* You'll be able to see hoardings go up all over the city, even before you leave. You couldn't find a better name for your story. Just think. Action, speed, thrill. . . you'll find all three in the word "jet". Plus you've got "bahadur". We've sold the film—on all circuits—on the strength of that name and casting alone!'

Lalmohan babu had started to smile, but the joy on his face faded a little as he heard Mr Ghoshal's explanation. Perhaps he was thinking: name and casting? Did only those things matter? Did no one appreciate the story?

'Have you seen any of my previous films?' asked Mr Ghoshal. '*Teerandaj* is running at the Lotus. You could catch the evening show today. I will tell the manager, he will keep three tickets for you in the Royal Circle. It's a good film, it did a silver jubilee.'

None of us had seen any of his films. Lalmohan babu was naturally curious, so we accepted Mr Ghoshal's offer. If one didn't have friends in Bombay, the evenings sometimes became long and boring. The car would remain with us. It would take us to the Lotus whenever required.

While we were eating, one of the men from the restaurant came and said something to Mr Ghoshal. Judging by the warm smile on every waiter's face since we arrived, Mr Ghoshal was a frequent visitor here. Clearly, in a place like Bombay, a successful director was a welcome figure.

Mr Ghoshal turned quickly to Lalmohan babu. 'You're wanted on the telephone, Laluda.'

Lalmohan babu had justed lifted a spoonful of pulao. Thank goodness he hadn't yet put it in his mouth. If he had, he'd certainly have choked. As it happened, when he gave a start, a few grains of rice jumped out of the spoon and landed on the tablecloth; but there was no further damage.

'Mr Gore wants to speak to you,' Mr Ghoshal explained, 'He may have some good news for you.'

Lalmohan babu left, and returned a couple of minutes later. 'Mr Gore asked me to go to his house at four o'clock,' he told us, picking up his knife and fork, 'Looks like I'm about to come into some money—heh heh!'

That meant ten thousand rupees would make their way to Lalmohan babu's pocket by the evening. 'You're buying us lunch tomorrow!' Feluda told him, 'And a copper chimney won't do, let me tell you. We should look for a golden one!'

By the time we finished our meal of rumali roti, pulao, nargisi kofta and kulfi, and left the restaurant, it was a quarter to three. Mr Ghoshal and Mr Gupte returned to the studio. Some of the dialogue still remained to be written. Writing the dialogue always took time, Mr Ghoshal informed us, as every word had to shine and sparkle. Mr Gupte simply smiled, without removing the cigar from his mouth. I noticed that although he wrote all the dialogue in a film, he spoke very little himself.

We bought some paan and climbed back into the car. 'Shalimar?' asked our driver.

'It would be silly,' Feluda remarked, 'to return to Calcutta without having seen the Gateway to India. Please take us to the Taj Mahal Hotel.'

'Very well, sir,' the driver replied. He could tell we had all the time in the world, and were interested only in seeing the place. So he drove around the city and showed us Victoria Terminus, Flora Fountain, the television station and the Prince of Wales Museum, before reaching the Gateway to India at around half past three. We got out of the car.

Behind the Gateway was the Arabian Sea. I counted eleven ships in it, big and small. The road here was very wide. To the left, facing the Gateway, was a statue of Shivaji, astride his horse. To our left was the world-famous Taj Mahal Hotel. We could hardly leave without seeing it from inside. From the outside it was just awesome.

My head began reeling as we stepped into the cool lobby. Where had I come? I had never seen so many people from so many different communities. Arabs seemed to outnumber other foreign visitors. But why? When I asked Feluda, he said it was because they could not travel to Beirut. So they had all come to Bombay to have a holiday. Thanks to the oil in their country, money was not a problem for them.

We roamed in the lobby for about five minutes before returning to the car. By the time we finally reached Shivaji Castle and were pressing the button for the lift, it was two minutes past four.

We emerged on the twelfth floor. There were three doors on different sides. The one in the middle had a sign saying, 'G. Gore'. On our ringing the bell, a bearer wearing a uniform opened the door.

'Please come in!' he said. Obviously, we were expected.

As we stepped in, we heard Mr Gore's voice before he could be seen. 'Come in, come in!' his voice greeted us. Then we saw him coming down a narrow passage with a smile on his face. 'How was your lunch?'

'Very, very good!' Lalmohan babu replied.

Mr Gore's living room was amazing. It was so large that I think almost the entire ground floor of our house in Calcutta would have fitted into it. On one side was a row of windows through which one could watch the sea. All the furniture was expensive—each piece had probably cost two or three thousand rupees. Apart from those, there was wall-to-wall carpeting, paintings on the wall, and a chandelier hung from the ceiling. A huge bookcase took up one side of the room. The books in it looked so glossy that it seemed as if they had only just been bought.

Feluda and I took a settee with a soft, thickly padded seat. Lalmohan sat on a similarly padded chair. At once, a very large dog came into the room and stood in its centre, turning its head to look first at the chair, and then at the settee. Lalmohan babu turned visibly pale. Feluda stretched a hand and snapped his fingers. The dog went to him immediately. I learnt later that it was a Great Dane.

'Duke! Duke!'

The dog left Feluda and went towards a door. Mr Gore had waited until we were seated, then he had left us for a few moments. Now he returned to the room with an envelope in his hand, and sat on another chair by Lalmohan babu's side.

'I had meant to keep this ready for you,' he said to Lalmohan babu, 'but I had to take three trunk calls, so I didn't get the time.'

He offered the envelope to Lalmohan babu, who managed to steady his shaking hand and took it casually. Then he slipped his hand into it and took out a wad of hundred-rupee notes.

'Please count them,' Mr Gore advised.

'C-count them?'

'Of course. You must. There should be one hundred notes there.'

By the time Lalmohan babu finished counting, a silver tea service had been placed before us. One sip told me that it was the best quality Darjeeling tea.

'I haven't really learnt anything about you,' Mr Gore turned to Feluda.

'There's nothing to learn. I am Mr Ganguli's friend, that's all.'

'No, sir. That is not enough. You are no ordinary person. Your eyes, your voice, your height, walk, body—nothing is ordinary. If you don't want to tell me about yourself, that's fine. But if you say you are no more than Mr Ganguli's friend, I cannot believe that!'

Feluda smiled, sipped his tea and changed the subject. 'I see that you have a lot of books,' he said.

'Yes, but I do not read them. Those books are only for show. The Taraporewala Book Shop has a standing order . . . they send me a copy of every good book that comes out.'

'I can even see a Bengali book there!'

Goodness, how sharp Feluda's eyes were! Even from a distance he had spotted a solitary Bengali book amongst the rows of books in English.

Mr Gore laughed. 'Not only Bengali, Mr Mitter, I have books in Hindi, Marathi, Gujarati—everything. I know a man who can read Hindi, Bengali and Gujarati. He reads novels in all those languages, and makes synopses for me. I have even read the outline of Mr Ganguli's novel. You see, Mr Mitter, in order to make a film . . .'

The telephone began ringing, interrupting him. Mr Gore rose and walked over to answer a white telephone resting on a three-legged stool by the door.

'Hello . . . yes, hold on. A call for you, Mr Ganguli.'

Lalmohan babu gave another start. I hoped these frequent starts were not going to damage his heart.

'Is it Pulak?' he asked on his way to the telephone.

'No, sir. I don't know this person,' Mr Gore replied.

'Hello,' Lalmohan babu spoke into the receiver. Feluda cast him a sidelong glance.

'Hello . . . hello . . . ?'

Lalmohan babu looked at us in puzzlement. 'No one's speaking up!'

'The line must have got disconnected,' Mr Gore said.

Lalmohan babu shook his head. 'No, I can hear various sounds, but no one's saying anything.'

Now Feluda went and took the receiver from him. 'Hello, hello!' Then he, too, shook his head and said, 'Whoever it was just put the phone down!'

'How strange! Who could it have been?' Lalmohan babu exclaimed.

'Don't worry about it,' Mr Gore told us, 'That kind of thing happens all the time in Bombay.'

Feluda remained standing. We took our cue and rose. Lalmohan babu did not seem all that concerned about the mysterious phone call, possibly because of the ten thousand rupees nestling in his pocket.

'We're going to the Lotus to see one of Pulak's films this evening,' he remarked casually.

'Yes, you must. Pulak babu is a very good director. I am sure *Jet Bahadur* will also be a great box office success!'

Mr Gore came to the front door to see us out. 'Don't forget about lunch tomorrow. I hope you've got transport?'

We assured him that Mr Ghoshal had made all the arrangements. We would have a car at our disposal all day.

We emerged on the landing and pressed the button for the lift. 'Now you know how much money these people have!' Feluda said to Lalmohan babu.

'Yes. In fact, I've got some of it in my own pocket!'

'True, but that's peanuts. Even a hundred thousand rupees, to these people, is a laughably small amount. Did you notice that he didn't ask you to sign a receipt? That means your pocket is filled with his black money. You have taken your first step into the world of darkness!'

The lift came down from upstairs and stopped with a clang.

'Whatever you may say, Felu babu, if one has a lot of money in one's pocket, be it black or white . . .'

Lalmohan babu broke off. Feluda had just opened the door of the lift to get into it. A strong scent wafted out—it was the scent of Gulbahar. All of us could recognize it, Lalmohan babu in particular. It rendered him speechless.

We followed Feluda into the lift, our hearts beating faster. 'I am sure,' I couldn't help saying after a few moments, 'plenty of people in this country use Gulbahar. Mr Sanyal cannot be the only one!'

Instead of replying, Feluda pressed the button for the seventeenth floor. We climbed another five floors.

Like the others, this floor had three doors near the lift. The one on the left said, 'H. Hekroth'. 'A German name,' Feluda muttered. The door to our right said, 'N.C. Mansukhani'. He had to be a Sindhi. The door in the middle bore no name at all.

'That flat's empty,' said Lalmohan babu.

'Not necessarily,' Feluda replied, 'Not everyone uses a name-plate. In fact, I think someone does live in this flat.'

Lalmohan babu and I looked at him curiously.

'If a doorbell has not been used for some time, its switch should be dusty. But take a look at this one. Then take a look at the other two, and tell me if they are any different.'

I peered closely at the switch. Feluda was right. It was shining brightly, there was no trace of dust.

'Are you going to press it?' Lalmohan babu asked, his voice trembling a little.

Feluda did not ring the bell. What he did instead was even more puzzling. He threw himself down on the floor and began sniffing through the tiny gap between the door and the floor. I saw him inhale deeply a couple of times, after which he got back to his feet and said, 'Coffee. I could smell strong coffee.'

Then he did something else that was no less surprising. Instead of taking the lift, he took the stairs to climb down to the ground floor. He stopped at every floor on his way, and spent at least half-a-minute, looking around. God knows what he was looking for.

When we finally came out of the building, it was ten minutes past five.

We had been in Bombay for only a short while, but most undoubtedly, we had already got entangled in a complex mystery.

SEVEN

'If I asked you a few questions, would you mind?' Feluda asked Lalmohan babu. We had returned to our hotel from Shivaji Castle about ten minutes ago. The receptionist had informed us that while we were out, someone had rung Lalmohan babu, but didn't leave his name or a message.

'It must be Pulak, trying to get hold of me every now and then,' said Lalmohan babu. 'It cannot be anyone else.'

Now he turned to Feluda and said, 'If I could handle a police interrogation and come through with flying colours, why should I mind questions from you?'

'Very well. You don't know Sanyal's first name, do you?'

'No. I didn't get round to asking him.'

'Can you describe him? I want a full and clear description—not the slipshod type of description you use in your books!'

Lalmohan babu cleared his throat and frowned.

'His height would be . . . let's see . . .'

'Do you always take in a person's height before anything else?'

'Yes, if he is exceptionally shorter or taller than average . . .'

'Was Sanyal very short?'

'No.'

'Remarkably tall?'

'No.'

'Then let's not talk about his height right now. Tell me about his face.'

'I saw him late in the evening. And the light bulb in my living room isn't particularly strong, it's only forty watts.'

'Never mind. Tell me what you can remember.'

'A broad face. His eyes . . . ah . . . he was wearing glasses. Had a beard—pretty thick—and a moustache, attached to his beard . . .'

'You mean a French beard?'

'N-no, it was different, I think. It was joined to his sideburns as well.'

'All right, go on.'

'His hair . . . salt-and-pepper. Yes, that's what it was, and he had a right. . . no, no, a left parting.'

'Teeth?'

'Perfect. Didn't appear to be false teeth.'

'Voice?'

'Neither too deep, nor too thin. Sort of medium.'

'Height?'

'Told you. Medium.'

'Didn't he give you a phone number? Didn't he say it was his friend's number in Bombay, and this friend was a very helpful man?'

'Oh yes! I say, I'd forgotten all about it. I could have told the police, but even when that inspector was asking me all those questions, I clean forgot.'

'No matter, you can tell *me*.'

'Wait, let me see . . .!' Lalmohan babu opened his wallet and took out a blue, folded piece of paper. Feluda examined it carefully, as the writing was Sanyal's own. Then he put the paper away in his own wallet, and said to me, 'Topshe, could you please ask for that number—tell the operator it's 253418.'

I picked up the phone and spoke to the operator. Then I passed the phone to Feluda.

'Hello,' Feluda said, 'Could I speak to Mr Desai, please?'

How perfectly weird! It turned out that no one called Desai had ever used that number. The man who answered it was called Parekh, and he had been using that same number for ten years, he said.

'Lalmohan babu,' said Feluda replacing the receiver, 'forget about selling your next story to Sanyal. The man sounds decidedly fishy, and I think that packet he gave you is no less suspicious.'

Lalmohan babu scratched his head and sighed. 'To tell you the truth, Felu babu,' he muttered, 'for some funny reason, I didn't like the man, either!'

Feluda's voice took on a sharp edge. 'For some funny reason? I hate that expression. You should know the exact reason; don't dismiss it as "funny". Come on, try to explain. *Why* didn't you like Sanyal?'

Lalmohan babu didn't mind Feluda speaking to him sharply; he was quite used to it. In fact, he was the first to admit that his writing had improved chiefly because Feluda did not hesitate to point out his mistakes.

Now he sat up straight. 'First,' he said, 'the fellow did not look straight at me when he spoke. Second, he spoke in a low voice—as if he had come to discuss some secret plan. Where was the need to speak so softly? Third . . .'

Here his voice trailed away. Over the next few minutes, Lalmohan babu tried very hard to remember the third reason, but failed.

The evening show at the Lotus was going to start at six-thirty. So we left the hotel at six o'clock. Only Lalmohan babu and I got into the car, as Feluda said he had some work to do. His blue notebook had emerged from his bag; I didn't have to be told what 'work' was going to keep him busy.

The Lotus cinema was in Worli, so we had to go back there. Lalmohan babu was looking decidedly nervous. The film we were about to see would prove what kind of a director Mr Ghoshal was. 'Well,' he said to me, 'if three of his films have been successful—one after the other—then he can't be all that bad, can he? What do you think, Tapesh?'

What could I say? That was exactly what I was telling myself to find reassurance.

Mr Ghoshal had not forgotten to inform the manager. Three tickets had been reserved for us in the Royal Circle. However, as it was a repeat show, plenty of seats were empty in the main auditorium.

We realized, even before the intermission, that *Teerandaj* was the kind of film that would be liable to give one a severe headache. Lalmohan babu and I exchanged glances in the dark. I wanted to laugh, but at the same time, felt concerned each time I thought about the future of *Jet Bahadur*. What was Lalmohan babu going to do?

When the lights came on during the intermission, Lalmohan babu sighed. 'Pulak,' he said with a lot of feeling, 'you and I come from the same city, same area. Is *this* all you've learnt to do in so many years?' Then, after a pause, he turned to me and added, 'Pulak used to put on a play every year during Durga Puja. As far as I can recall, he failed his B. Com. Well, what else can you expect from such a character?'

We left the auditorium as soon as the lights dimmed again. I was afraid we might find either Pulak Ghoshal himself, or one of his men, outside in the lobby. But there was no one.

'If he asks me, I am going to say it was first-class,' Lalmohan babu decided. 'Frankly, Tapesh, I would have felt quite heartbroken, had I not received all those fresh, crisp notes from Gore!'

Our car was parked opposite the cinema. Lalmohan babu did not immediately make for the car. He walked over to a small grocery store instead, and bought a packet of savouries, two packets of biscuits, six oranges and a packet of lemon drops. 'Sometimes I get quite hungry in my hotel room. These will come in handy,' he confided.

We returned to the car, our hands laden with various packets. As soon as I opened the door, each of us received an enormous shock. The car was reeking with the scent of Gulbahar. It was certainly not there when we arrived here. It had appeared in the last one-and-a-half hours.

'My head is reeling, Tapesh. This is positively spooky, isn't it? I'm sure Sanyal has been murdered. And we're being haunted by his perfumed ghost!' Lalmohan babu exclaimed.

I asked the driver if he knew anything. He said he was in the car most of the time, but he did leave it—only for about five minutes—to watch a Hindi programme (*Phool Khile hain Gulshan Gulshan*) on TV at a shop nearby. Yes, he could smell the perfume too, but had no idea how it had got there. It was like magic, he thought.

We told Feluda about it as soon as we got back to the hotel. 'When the plot thickens, this kind of thing is bound to happen, Lalmohan babu! Or one can't call it a real mystery; and if it isn't a real mystery, then Felu Mitter cannot exercise his brain, can he?' said Feluda.

'But. . .'

'I know what you're going to ask me. No, I haven't worked out the whole plot. All I'm doing right now is trying to understand its nature.'

'It seems that you went out?' I put in, sounding most sleuth-like.

'Well done, Topshe. But I didn't have to leave the hotel to get it. The receptionist gave it to me.'

The object in question was an Indian Airlines time-table, which was lying by Feluda's side. 'I wanted to find out how many flights go to Calcutta from Kathmandu, and what time they arrive,' Feluda explained.

The mention of Kathmandu reminded me of something I wanted to ask Feluda.

'Inspector Patwardhan mentioned a Nanasaheb. Which Nanasaheb did he mean?'

'There is only one who is famous in Indian history.'

'The one who fought against the British during the mutiny?'

'Yes, but later he escaped and left India. He went all the way to Kathmandu, taking with him a lot of valuable jewels—including a necklace studded with diamonds and pearls. It was called the naulakha. Eventually, it went to Jung Bahadur of Nepal. In return, Jung Bahadur gave two villages to Nanasaheb's wife, Kashi Bai.'

'Has that famous necklace been stolen?'

'Yes, so it would seem from what Patwardhan said.'

'Oh my God, did I hand over that same necklace?' Lalmohan babu's voice rose with concern. He almost shouted.

'Just think about it. If you did, your name will be recorded in history, in letters of diamond!'

'But . . . but . . . in that case, it's gone where it was meant to go. Now it's for the police to make sure it doesn't leave the country. Why are *you* so worried? Do you wish to catch these smugglers yourself?'

Before Feluda could reply, the telephone began ringing. Lalmohan babu picked it up as he was standing close to it.

'Hello . . . yes, speaking!'

So the call was meant for him. Perhaps it was Pulak Ghoshal. No, it wasn't. It couldn't possibly be. Mr Ghoshal could never say anything that would make Lalmohan babu's mouth hang open like that, and his hand tremble so much. I saw him take the receiver away from his ear. Even the receiver was shaking.

Feluda took it away from him and placed it to his own ear. However, presumably because he couldn't hear anything, he replaced it almost immediately. 'Was it Sanyal?' he asked.

Lalmohan babu tried to nod, but clearly even that was difficult for him. Perhaps every muscle in his body had frozen.

'What did he say?'

'S-s-said,' Lalmohan babu gave himself a shake and made a valiant attempt to pull himself together, 'Said if I open my mouth, he'll r-r-rip open my st-stomach!'

'Okay, that's good.'

'Wh-what!' Lalmohan babu stared foolishly at Feluda. I, too, found Feluda's remark distinctly odd. Feluda explained quickly, 'It wasn't enough simply to have that strong perfume every now and then. I mean, it wasn't good enough as a clue. I couldn't be sure whether Sanyal himself had come to Bombay, or someone here was using that scent. Now I can be sure.'

'But why is he hounding me?' Lalmohan babu cried desperately.

'If I knew that, Lalmohan babu, there would be no mystery. If you want an answer to that question, you will have to be a little patient.'

EIGHT

Lalmohan babu simply toyed with his food that evening, saying he wasn't hungry at all. Feluda said it didn't matter as Lalmohan babu had eaten the most that afternoon at the Copper Chimney.

The previous night, we had all gone out together after dinner to buy paan. Tonight, Lalmohan babu refused to leave the hotel. 'Who wants to go out in the crowded streets? I bet Sanyal's men are watching the hotel. One of them will plunge his knife straight into me, if I am seen.'

In the end, Feluda went out alone. Lalmohan babu stayed put in our room with me, muttering constantly, 'Why on earth did I have to accept that packet?' After a while, he began blaming something else for his present predicament: 'Why did I have to write a story for a Hindi film?' Eventually, I heard him say, 'Why the hell did I ever start writing crime thrillers?'

Feluda returned in a few minutes and offered us the paan he'd bought. 'Will you be all right sleeping alone in your room?' he asked Lalmohan babu, who made no reply. 'Look,' Feluda said reassuringly, 'there's a tiny cubby-hole at the end of the passage. You've seen it, haven't you? A bell boy remains in that room, all the time. Besides, some of the hotel staff are on duty all night. This is not Shivaji Castle.'

A mention of Shivaji Castle made Lalmohan babu shiver once more. However, around ten o'clock he mustered enough courage to wish us good-night and return to his room.

I went to bed soon after he left. Pulak Ghoshal's film had caused me a great deal of strain—much more than travelling all over the city. Feluda, I knew, would remain awake. His notebook was lying on a bedside table. He had made several entries throughout the day. Perhaps now he'd make some more.

In the past, I had tried, at times, to make a note of the exact moment when I fell asleep. But I had failed every time. Tonight was no different. I have no idea when I fell asleep, but do remember the moment when I woke. Someone was banging on the door, *and* pressing the buzzer repeatedly. I sat up in bed. Feluda's bedside lamp was still on; my watch showed quarter to one. Feluda rose and opened the door. Lalmohan babu tumbled into the room.

He was panting, but did not appear to be frightened. When he spoke, his words were curious, but nothing that might cause alarm.

'A scandal!' he exclaimed. 'This is a positive scandal, I tell you!'

'Come in and sit down,' Feluda said.

'No, no, I'm too excited to sit down. Look, here's the famous necklace, the valuable jewels I was supposed to have handed over!'

What Lalmohan babu then held under Feluda's nose was a book. A famous book, written in English. I had seen a copy of it only recently, displayed in a shop window in Lansdowne Road. It was *Life Divine* by Sri Aurobindo.

Even Feluda could only gape. 'And look,' Lalmohan babu went on, 'the binding is faulty. After the first thirty pages, the next few pages are stuck together. If someone paid good money for this book, every penny has been wasted. How could a binder in Pondicherry do such a shoddy job?'

'But . . . if this is the original packet, what did you pass on to Mr Red Shirt the other day?'

'You're not going to believe this. Can you imagine what I did? I passed on one of my own books! Yes, *The Bandits of Bombay* ! You see, what I had sent Pulak was a copy of my manuscript. So I thought

I'd now give him a copy of the book, with my blessings and autograph. In fact, I have three more copies in my bag, each wrapped with brown paper. I know I have fans all over the country . . . thought I might meet a few in Bombay, so I brought extra copies. And it was one of those that I . . . ha ha ha!'

I had not seen Lalmohan babu so cheerful in a long time.

Feluda took the book from him, looked at it briefly and asked, 'But what about the threat from Sanyal? Didn't he threaten you on the phone? How does that fit in with this *Life Divine* ?'

Lalmohan babu refused to be daunted. 'Well, who knows if it was Sanyal in person? It isn't always possible to identify a voice on the telephone, is it? It could well have been some crackpot, trying to be funny. Anything is possible in Bombay. I mean, if a film like *Teerandaj* could run for more than twenty-five weeks . . . need I say more?'

'All right, but what about that perfume in the car?'

'That? I bet our driver was wearing it. He's a fashionable young man. Didn't you see his hairstyle? But when we began asking questions, he was embarrassed and wouldn't admit to using the scent.'

'Well then, every mystery is solved. You may relax now, and have a good night's sleep.'

'Yes, I certainly will. I had a headache when I went to bed, so I opened my bag to take out a pain killer. That's how I made this amazing discovery. Anyway, now that everything's cleared up, I am going to leave that book with you. Perhaps you should read up on spiritual matters, it can't do you any harm. Good night!'

Lalmohan babu left, and I went back to my own bed.

'Imagine being handed a copy of a book by Jatayu, when one was expecting *Life Divine*. Feluda, how do you suppose the fellow felt?'

'Furious,' Feluda replied, resting his head on his pillow. But he did not switch the light off. I felt quite amused to see that he put his blue notebook away, and began turning the pages of Sri Aurobindo's book.

It was at this moment, I think, that I fell asleep again.

NINE

The following day we were supposed to travel down the road to Pune to a level-crossing between Khandala and Lonavala. That was the spot where the final climactic scene was going to be shot. All

told, there were eleven 'action' scenes in the film. Pulak Ghoshal was
going to start with the last one.

The complete scene could not be shot in a single day. The whole
thing would take as many as five days. We had decided to watch the
shooting every day—that is, if we enjoyed the first day's experience.
The train would be available on all five days, for an hour between
one and two o'clock. But the horses meant for the group of bandits,
and a Lincoln Convertible meant for the hero, could be used any
time. The scene in question went like this:

The villain had replaced the real engine driver and was driving the
train. In one of its compartments the heroine and her uncle were
being held, their hands and feet tied. The hero was chasing the train
in a motor car. At the same time, the hero's twin—who had been
kidnapped by bandits when he was a baby, and had now become a
bandit himself—was riding with his entire gang to attack the train.
He would get close enough to the train to jump into it straight from
his horse. About the same time, the hero in his car would also catch
up with the train, and he would arrive on the scene to see the bandit
and the villain (pretending to be the engine driver) having a fight.
The villain would be killed. What would happen next? . . . All would
be revealed on the silver screen!

Apparently, three different versions of the final scene were going
to be shot. Then the director would decide which appeared the best
on the screen, and retain it, discarding the other two.

Mr Ghoshal dropped in briefly quite early in the morning. We told
him we were ready to go, and all arrangements were in hand. 'Laluda,'
he said, 'I can tell just by looking at you that you really enjoyed
watching *Teerandaj* !'

Lalmohan babu could be seen smiling to himself from time to time,
as he recalled the previous night's events. Mr Ghoshal had noticed
that smile and misunderstood the reason for it. Lalmohan babu
laughed loudly and said, 'Bravo, my boy—to think that a boy from
our Gorpar in Calcutta could achieve so much! You have shown
them all. . . ha ha!'

Since we were going to be out all day, Feluda told me to take all
the edible stuff in our hand luggage. We packed the oranges, biscuits
and sweets that Lalmohan babu had bought the day before and put
them in the car. Then Lalmohan babu deposited all his cash with the
hotel manager and took a receipt from him. 'Who knows,' he told us,
'whether a real bandit or two won't get mixed up with the actors?'

Feluda went out for a while—to buy cigarettes, he said. He had run out completely, and the place where we were going might not have a shop within miles. We left shortly after he got back. The car was still smelling of Gulbahar.

Thane station was about twenty-five kilometers from Bombay. The road made a right curve there, joined the national highway and went towards Pune. Khandala was eighty kilometers down that same road. The weather that morning was quite good. Broken clouds were flitting across the sky, driven by a strong breeze—and the sun was peering frequently through them, bathing the city with its light. Mr Ghoshal had already remarked on the weather. It was said to be 'ideal' for shooting outdoors. Lalmohan babu was pleased, not just with the weather, but with everything he could see. 'Now I needn't worry about going abroad!' he announced. 'Bombay is such a wonderful place, who wants to go to England? Have you seen the buses? Not one is overcrowded, not one has people hanging out of it. Oh, what tremendous civic sense these people have!'

It took us nearly an hour to reach Thane, at around a quarter past nine. As we had plenty of time on our hands we stopped at a tea stall and had masala tea. Our driver, Swaruplal, joined us.

Only a few minutes after we left Thane, I realized we were travelling alongside the hills of the Western Ghats. The railway track I had noticed before had disappeared. It had gone towards Kalyan to the north. From Kalyan, it would turn back and go south again, passing through Matheran before going to Pune. Our level crossing was situated somewhere in the middle of that particular stretch.

Our journey was eventless, except for Lalmohan babu choking on some orange pips at one point. Feluda remained silent throughout—it was impossible to tell from his face what he was thinking. I knew from experience that even when he lapsed into silence, it did not necessarily mean that he was worried about anything.

At around half past twelve, we passed through Khandala. Only a mile later, a large number of people came into view. It seemed as if a fair had sprung up by the roadside. As we got closer, I was struck by the number of vehicles I could see. Why should there be so many of them at a fair? Then I noticed something else—horses! Now I realized that the 'fair' was Mr Ghoshal's unit, gathered here to start shooting *Jet Bahadur*. There were at least a hundred people milling about; and there was a lot of equipment and other material . . . cameras, reflectors, lights, large durries . . . it was a huge affair.

Our driver slipped into a gap between an Ambassador and a bus, and parked the car there. Mr Ghoshal came forward to greet us as soon as we emerged. He was wearing a white cap, and from his neck hung an object that looked like binoculars.

'Good morning! Everything all right?' he asked.

We nodded. 'Listen,' he went on, 'I have a message from Mr Gore. He's gone to Matheran—I think to talk to some railway officials, and perhaps make some payments. He will make his own way here, either on the same train that we're going to use, or by car. You will be told the minute the train gets here. In any case, whether or not Mr Gore arrives on time, you three should get into the first-class compartment. Is that clear?'

'Perfectly,' said Feluda.

We met some of the other workers as we waited. I had no idea so many Bengalis worked in the Bombay film industry. It was hardly surprising that one of them should recognize Feluda. The cameraman, Dashu Ghosh, wrinkled his brows upon hearing Feluda's name. 'Mitter? Are you the detec—?'

'Yes,' Feluda said hurriedly, 'but please keep it to yourself.'

'Why? You are our pride. When that statue in Ellora—'

Feluda placed a finger on his lips. Dashu Ghosh lowered his voice, 'Are you here on a case?'

'No, no. I am here on holiday, with this friend of mine.'

Dashu Ghosh had lived in Bombay for twenty-one years. Even so, he read Bengali books regularly, and had read two or three books by Jatayu. There were two other cameramen working with him that day. They came from other parts of India. Two of the four assistants who worked with Mr Ghoshal were Bengalis. But among the actors, none came from Bengal. Apart from Arjun Mehrotra, there was Micky playing the villain. He was just Micky, without a surname. He was considered the best amongst villains who were on their way up in Bombay at the moment. It was said that he had signed contracts for thirty-seven films, but twenty-nine of those were being rewritten, simply to reduce the number of fights. Thank goodness *Jet Bahadur* had only four fights. If it had more, Mr Ghoshal and Mr Gore would have been in big trouble.

We learnt all this from the production manager, Sudarshan Das. He was from Orissa. Like Dashu Ghosh, he had been in Bombay for many years; but as soon as *Jet Bahadur* was completed, he planned to return to Cuttack and start directing Oriya films.

Feluda had walked over to another group. All the actors who were going to play the bandits were being made up and dressed for the big scene. Suddenly, I noticed one of those men chatting with Feluda.

Curious, I went forward and realized, as I heard his voice, that it was none other than the kung-fu master, Victor Perumal. He was made up to look like the hero's twin. It would be his job to jump from a galloping horse and land on the roof of the train. Then he would have to walk over as many as six coaches and enter the engine to fight with Micky, the villain, and kill him. That would be followed by a dramatic clash with the hero, who had been separated from his twin twenty years ago.

Lalmohan babu saw the elaborate arrangements and sank into silence. He really ought to have been pleased since all that action was centred around *his* story. He told me of his feelings: 'I feel kind of peculiar, Tapesh,' he explained. 'At times, it's giving me a sense of power, you see, to think that *I* wrote the story that's led to so much work, such complex arrangements, so much expense! Yet, sometimes, I feel a little guilty for causing a lot of headache to a lot of people. And I cannot forget that the writer gets no recognition here. How many people in this unit know Jatayu's name, tell me?'

I tried to comfort him. 'If the film is a success, everyone will learn your name!'

'I hope so!' Jatayu sighed.

The bandits who had finished their make-up were already on their horses, running around. All the horses were initially gathered under a large banyan tree. There were nine of them.

A minute later, a huge white Lincoln Convertible turned up, its tinted glass windows rolled up. It contained the hero and the villain. There was no need for the heroine that day, as the scenes in which she would appear, with her hands and feet tied, would be shot later in a studio. It was just as well, I thought. The two male stars caused enough sensation in the crowd. The presence of the heroine would only have made matters worse.

Sudarshan Das had given us some tea. We were in the process of returning the empty cups, when suddenly a raucous voice could be heard on a loudspeaker: 'The train is coming! Train's here! Everybody ready!'

TEN

An old-fashioned engine came into view, huffing and puffing, blowing thick black smoke. Behind it were eight coaches. It stopped at the level crossing at exactly five minutes to one.

Even from a distance, we could see that there was only one first-class compartment. Other coaches already had passengers in them—they had been planted there when the train left Matheran. There were men, women and children, both young and old. Mr Ghoshal became extremely busy as soon as the train arrived. We could see him rushing from one camera to another, from the hero to the villain, and from one assistant here to another assistant there. Even Lalmohan babu was forced to admit that it wasn't simply the producer's money that made a film.

Arjun Mehrotra—the hero—was ready. He was at the wheel of his car, wearing sunglasses. Beside him sat his make-up man, and two other men, possibly hangers-on. A jeep with an open top was ready, too. In it stood a camera on a tripod. Victor and his men had already departed with their horses. They would wait for a signal from the moving train, and then ride down a particular hill. Then they would be seen galloping alongside the train. I saw Micky go towards the engine, accompanied by one of Mr Ghoshal's assistants.

We didn't know what to do. There was no sign of Mr Gore. Was he on the train? There was no way to tell.

The crowd had dispersed by now, but no one had told us what to do. Lalmohan babu began to get restless. 'What's going on, Feluda babu? Have we been totally forgotten?' he asked.

'Well, we were told to get into a first-class compartment, and there is only one such coach. So we should get into it . . . but let's wait for two more minutes.'

Before those two minutes were up, the engine blew its whistle, and we heard Sudarshan Das call out to us: 'I say, gentlemen! This way!'

We ran towards the first class carriage, clutching our bags. Mr Das went with us up to the door to the carriage. 'I knew nothing of the arrangements,' he said. 'Someone just told me Mr Gore will arrive in half an hour. After the first shot, this train is going to return here.'

We got into the compartment, to be greeted by a large flask standing on a bench, together with four white cardboard boxes. The name of the Safari Restaurant was printed on every box. In other words, it was our lunch. I was surprised by Mr Gore's care and attention, in spite of his being so busy.

There was another whistle, then the train started with a jerk. All of us got ready to watch the activities outside. This was going to be a totally new experience, so I was feeling quite excited.

The train was now gathering speed. A road ran by the track on the right hand side. On our left, very soon, we'd see hills. The bandits would arrive from the left, and the hero from the right.

A little later, when the train was running faster, the jeep with the camera could be seen, travelling down the road. It was followed by the hero's car. Now the hero was alone, his companions had gone. The camera was facing him. Apart from the cameraman, there were three other men in the jeep. One of them was Mr Ghoshal's assistant. He was speaking through a microphone, instructing the hero: 'Look to your left!' and 'Now to your right!'

Mr Ghoshal himself was handling the second camera, which was placed inside one of the carriages. The third camera was on the roof of the last coach, towards the rear of the train.

The hero wasn't driving all that fast, which I found somewhat disappointing. But Feluda pointed out that, in the film, it would appear fast enough as the speed of the camera had been reduced to shoot this particular scene.

'Besides,' he added, 'that car isn't moving as slowly as you seem to think, because it's running to keep pace with our train; and the train is moving pretty fast, isn't it?'

True. I hadn't thought about that.

In a few minutes, the hero's car and the jeep passed our compartment and went further down the road. Since it was an old-fashioned carriage, there were no bars on the windows. I wanted to lean out and see how the remaining scene was being shot, but Feluda stopped me. 'How do you suppose you'd feel if you went to see *Jet Bahadur* at a cinema, and found yourself on the screen, leaning out of a train?'

I had to resist the temptation to poke my head out. Then I decided to get up and sit near a window on the opposite side. The scent of Gulbahar hit my nostrils as soon as I got to my feet.

Suddenly, I realized that Feluda was no longer by my side. He had sprung up and moved to the opposite end of the carriage. His eyes were fixed on the door to the bathroom, and his hand was in his jacket pocket.

'It's no use, Mr Mitter. Don't take out your gun—a revolver is already pointed at you!' said a voice.

The door on our left opened. A man entered and stood blocking the exit. In his hand was a revolver. Where had I seen him before? Oh, of course, this was Mr Red Shirt! But today he was wearing different clothes, and there was a vicious expression on his face that had been absent that day when we'd seen him at the airport. Looking at him now, I had no doubt in my mind that this man was a killer, and he would kill without the slightest qualm. His revolver was aimed straight at Feluda.

The door to the bathroom, which was ajar, opened fully and the whole compartment was filled with the scent of Gulbahar.

'San . . . San . . .' muttered Lalmohan babu, then his voice trailed away. His whole body seemed to have shrunk with fear.

'Yes, I am Sanyal,' said the stranger, 'and my real business is with you, Mr Ganguli. You have brought that packet here, haven't you? Open your bag and give it to me. I needn't tell you what's going to happen if you don't.'

'P-p-packet. . .?'

'Surely you know which packet I am talking about? I did not meet you at the airport that day in Calcutta just to hand you a copy of your own book, did I? Come on, give me the real packet.'

'You are mistaken. That packet is with me, not Mr Ganguli.'

The train was making such a lot of noise that everyone had to raise his voice to be heard; but Feluda spoke slowly and steadily. Even so, his words reached Sanyal's ears and his eyes lit up behind his glasses.

'You destroyed so many pages of *Life Divine*. Did that bring you any special gain?' Feluda was still speaking calmly, his words were measured.

'Nimmo,' Sanyal gave a sidelong glance at the hooligan and spoke harshly, 'finish this man off if he creates any trouble. Keep your hands raised, Mr Mitter.'

'Aren't you taking a very big risk?' Feluda asked. 'You will not release us, will you, even if you get what you want? You're going to finish us off, anyway. But what's going to happen to *you*, once the train comes to a stop? Have you thought about that?'

'That's easy,' Sanyal's face broke into an evil grin, 'No one knows me here. There are so many passengers on this train—you think I couldn't just disappear amongst them? Your corpses will lie here, and I will move to another compartment. It's that simple.'

Feluda and I had faced many tricky situations before and that had taught me not to lose my nerve easily. But, right at this moment, although I was trying very hard to stay calm, one thing kept making me break into a cold sweat. It was the figure of Nimmo. I had only read about such characters. The look in his eyes held pure malice. He had closed the door and was now leaning against it. The fine cotton embroidered shirt he was wearing was fluttering in the breeze; his right arm was shaking a little because of the train's movement, but the revolver was still pointed straight at Feluda.

Sanyal advanced slowly. My nostrils were burning with the scent. His eyes were fixed on Feluda's bag. It was an Air India bag, placed on a bench in front of Sanyal. Lalmohan babu was standing behind me, so I couldn't see the look on his face. But, in spite of the racket the train was making, I could hear him breathing heavily, wheezing like an asthma patient.

The train was speeding on its way. It meant that the shooting was going ahead as planned. Did Mr Gore have any idea just how badly he had messed things up?

Sanyal sat down, grabbed the bag and pressed its catch. It did not open. The bag was locked.

'Where's the key? Where is it?' Sanyal's entire face was distorted with impatient rage. 'Where the hell did you put it?'

'In my pocket,' Feluda replied coolly.

'Which pocket?'

'The right one.'

That was where Feluda kept his revolver. I knew it.

Sanyal rose to his feet, still looking livid. After a few uncertain moments, he suddenly turned to me. 'Come here!' he roared.

Feluda looked at me. I could tell he wanted me to do as I was told.

As I began moving towards Feluda, a different noise reached my ears. It wasn't just the noise of the train. I could hear galloping horses. Unbeknown to me, the train had reached the hills, which were now stretched on the left. By the time I could slip my hand into Feluda's pocket, the gang of bandits was moving swiftly down a hill, throwing up clouds of dust.

My fingers first found the revolver, then brushed against the key. 'Give it to him,' Feluda told me.

I passed the key to Sanyal. Feluda's hands were still raised.

Sanyal unlocked the bag. *Life Divine* was resting on top of everything else. Sanyal took it out.

There was the sound of hooves quite close to the window. Not one, but several horses had sped down the hill and were now galloping beside the track, keeping pace with the train.

Sanyal leafed through the pages quickly until he got to the point where many of the pages were stuck together. Then he did something most peculiar. Instead of turning the pages, he began scratching and clawing at them. At once, one of the pages tore, revealing a square 'hollow'. A certain section had been cut out from the centre of several pages to create that hollow.

Sanyal peered into it—and the expression on his face changed at once. It was really worth watching. God knows what he was expecting to find, but what the hollow contained were about eight cigarette stubs, a dozen used matches and a substantial quantity of ash.

'I hope you don't mind,' said Feluda, 'but I couldn't resist using that as an ash-tray.'

Now Sanyal shouted so loudly that I was sure the whole train could hear him.

'You think you can get away with this? Where's the real stuff?'

'What stuff?'

'You scoundrel! Don't you know what I'm talking about?'

'Of course. But I want to hear you spell it out.'

'*Where* is it?' Sanyal roared again.

'In my pocket.'

'Which pocket?'

'The left one.'

The bandits were now just outside the window. The hill was much closer. A lot of dust was coming in through the window.

'You there!'

I knew I would be ordered once more.

'Don't just stand there—get it from his pocket!'

I had to slip my hand into Feluda's left pocket this time. The object that I found was something the like of which I had never held in my hand before. It was a necklace strung with pearls and studded with diamonds. Such an amazing piece of jewellery was fit to be handled only by kings and emperors, I thought.

'Give it to me!' Sanyal's eyes were glinting once more, not with rage, but with greed and glee.

I stretched my hand towards him. Feluda kept his hands raised. Lalmohan babu was groaning. The bandits were . . .

CRASH!

Something heavy had made an impact against the carriage, making it shake a little. In the next instant, Nimmo was rolling on the floor. A pair of legs had slipped in through the window and kicked him hard. The gun in his hand went off, hit a light fixed to the ceiling and shattered it. In a flash, Feluda lowered his hands and took out his own revolver.

Then the door on the left opened again, and a man dressed as a bandit climbed into our carriage. He was known to all three of us. 'Thank you, Victor!' said Feluda.

ELEVEN

Sanyal flopped down on a bench. He was trembling once more—but with fear this time, not rage. He knew there could be no escape.

In the meantime, someone must have realized there was something wrong and pulled the cord, for the train came to an unexpected halt. It wouldn't have stopped unless the cord had been pulled.

Within seconds, we could hear a confused babel. Several voices were shouting the same name: 'Victor! Victor! Where have you gone, Victor?'

I could hear Mr Ghoshal's voice. Victor Perumal had messed things up. He was supposed to jump on the roof of the train. Instead of doing that, he had jumped into our compartment.

Feluda leant out of the door and called, 'Mr Ghoshal! Over here!'

Mr Ghoshal arrived, looking profoundly distressed and harassed. That was hardly surprising as any hold-up in shooting such a complex scene would be liable to cause heavy losses, perhaps to the tune of thirty thousand rupees.

'What's the matter with you, Victor? Have you gone completely mad?' he demanded.

'Mr Ghoshal,' said Feluda, 'if anyone in your film deserves to be called Jet Bahadur, it is Victor Perumal.'

'What's that supposed to mean?' Mr Ghoshal asked. He was now looking perplexed, but perplexity was still outweighed by annoyance.

'Besides,' Feluda went on, 'the role of that smuggler should have gone to this man here, not your actor called Paramesh Kapoor.'

'What rubbish are you talking, Mr Mitter? Who is this man?' Mr Ghoshal glanced at Sanyal.

By this time, two vehicles had appeared on the road. One was a police jeep, and the other was a police van. The jeep pulled up next to our compartment. Inspector Patwardhan climbed out of it.

In reply to Mr Ghoshal's question, Feluda walked up to Sanyal, grabbed his beard and moustache and yanked them off, before pulling off his wig and glasses.

'I would have been delighted,' Feluda remarked, 'if I could remove that scent from your body, Mr Gore. Sadly, that's something even Felu Mitter cannot do.'

'Laluda, who told you a film would remain incomplete if its producer was arrested?'

The question came from Mr Ghoshal. To tell the truth, Lalmohan babu hadn't spoken at all. He was simply sitting there, looking pensive and morose. Anyone could guess that he was worried about the future of *Jet Bahadur.*

'No one,' Mr Ghoshal continued, 'can stop our film. Gore might go to prison—or hell—or wherever—but don't you see, he wasn't the only producer in Bombay? There's Chuni Pancholi; he's been pestering me for over a year to make a film for him. I'll get things going again, you mark my words. Even before you leave Bombay, you'll see me shooting the film under a new banner.'

That day, however, all shooting had ground to a halt at half past one. Gore and Nimmo were arrested and handcuffed. Nanasaheb's naulakha necklace was in police custody.

Feluda had anticipated trouble during the first day's shooting. When he'd told us in the morning that he was going out to buy cigarettes, he had actually gone to speak to Patwardhan. Gore, apparently, had spent twelve years in Calcutta. He had been not just to Don Bosco, but also to St. Xavier's. Hence he could speak Bengali very well, although in Bombay he was heard speaking only Hindi and Marathi besides English.

We were sitting on the veranda of a dak bungalow in Khandala. It was a beautiful place and there was a decided nip in the air. People from Bombay often went to Khandala for a change of air, I had heard. We had already finished the food (naan and mutton do-pyaza) we'd found in those boxes, provided by the Safari Restaurant. It was now four-thirty, so we were having tea and pakoras.

Mr Ghoshal had joined us for a while, then moved to a different table where Arjun Mehrotra was seated. Mehrotra was looking a little crestfallen, perhaps because most undoubtedly, the real hero that day was Pradosh Mitter. Plenty of people from the unit—including Micky, the villain—had asked Feluda for his autograph.

There was a second hero, and unquestionably that was Victor Perumal. It turned out that Feluda had spoken to him before the shooting started. 'When you come riding down the hill and get close to the train,' he had said, 'keep an eye on the first-class compartment. If you see anything suspicious, come in through the door.' Victor had seen Feluda standing with his arms raised. That had told him instantly that help was required, and he had swung into action.

Strangely enough, even after a heroic act like that, Victor was quite unmoved. He was back with his men, practising kung-fu, in the little field opposite the bungalow, as if nothing had happened.

'The thing is, you see . . .' Lalmohan babu finally opened his mouth. But Feluda interrupted him. 'The thing is that you are still totally in the dark, is that it?'

Lalmohan babu smiled meekly and nodded.

'It shouldn't be difficult to throw light on everything. But, before I do that, you must be told about Gore, and understand how he functioned.

'The first thing to remember is that he was really a smuggler, though he was trying to pass himself off as a respectable film producer. He decided to make a film from your story. You wrote in that story that a smuggler lived in a building called Shivaji Castle. Naturally, that caused some concern. Gore wanted to find out how much you knew about the real occupants of Shivaji Castle, since he was one of them, and he was a smuggler. So he dressed as Sanyal and went to your house. But, having spoken to you, he realized that you were completely innocent and harmless, and your entire story was purely imaginary. The reference to Shivaji Castle was just a coincidence.

'Gore felt reassured, but then it occurred to him that he could use you to transfer the stolen necklace. So he hid it in a book, and tried to pass it to someone in his own gang—possibly someone who lived on the seventeenth floor in Shivaji Castle. If you were caught, you would blame Sanyal, not Gore. Isn't that right? So Gore could safely hide behind the figure of Sanyal.

'However, things went wrong. What you handed over to Gore's man was not a necklace worth five million, but one of your own books worth five rupees. Mr Red Shirt—or Nimmo, if you like— went to Shivaji Castle, and was taking that packet to a flat on the seventeenth floor, when he was attacked in the lift by a man from a rival group. Nimmo killed him and took the packet up, as instructed. Then, whoever opened it realized that the necklace wasn't in it. Gore was informed, and he returned at once. *He* knew what had happened. So he had to accomplish two things—one, he had to get the necklace back; and two, he had to get rid of us. Luckily for him, we hadn't handed the necklace over to the police. As soon as he'd met us, Gore realized that, somehow, Sanyal must reappear. If Sanyal had given you that packet, then only Sanyal could recover it from you. No one would then suspect Gore.'

'But that perfume . . .?'

'Wait, wait, I am coming to that. Using Gulbahar was just an example of Gore's cunning. He had prepared the ground in Calcutta. Whenever you would smell that perfume, you'd think of Sanyal, and automatically associate the two. You were convinced, weren't you, that Sanyal was following you everywhere in Bombay?'

'Yes.'

'Right. Now, just think back a little. That day, when we went to his flat, Gore left us in the living room and disappeared for a few minutes. It seemed as if he had gone to fetch your money. Isn't that right?'

'Yes.'

'It couldn't have been difficult, could it, to slip out in that time and sprinkle a few drops of that perfume in the lift? When I went to every floor from top to bottom, sniffed everywhere and still found no trace of that scent outside the lift, I knew at once that no one wearing it had used the lift. It was planted there deliberately. Similarly, when our car was parked outside the Lotus cinema, Gore could have asked one of his men to slip a hand through a window and spray a few drops on the seats. It was easy!'

Yes, everything seemed easy once Feluda had explained it. Lalmohan babu had clearly grasped the whole story by now, but even so, he did not look very happy. That surprised me. Why was there no smile on his face? Eventually, a question from Mr Ghoshal changed everything.

Tea was over, and the whole unit was getting ready to go back. The sun had disappeared behind the hills and now it was really quite cold. I felt myself shiver, and saw Mr Ghoshal striding towards us busily.

'Laluda, all the posters and hoardings for *Jet Bahadur* are going up on Friday. But there's something I need to know now,' he said.

'What is it?'

'How do you wish to be named? I mean, should we use your real name, or your pseudonym?'

'The "pseudo" *is* the real name, my friend!' replied Lalmohan babu with a huge grin. 'And it should be spelt J-a-t-a-y-u!'

The Mystery of the Walking Dead

ONE

'Didn't you once tell me you knew someone in Gosaipur?' Feluda asked Lalmohan Babu.

We—the Three Musketeers—had just visited the Victoria Memorial and come walking to the river. We were now sitting under the domes near Princep Ghat, enjoying the fresh breeze and munching daalmut. It was five o'clock in the evening.

'Yes,' Lalmohan Babu replied, 'Tulsi Babu. Tulsicharan Dasgupta. He used to teach mathematics and geography in my school. Now he's retired and lives in Gosaipur. He's asked me to visit him more than once. He loves my books. In fact, he writes for children himself. A couple of his stories were published in *Sandesh*. But why are you suddenly interested in Gosaipur?'

'Someone called Jeevanlal Mallik wrote to me from there. His father's called Shyamlal Mallik. I believe the Malliks were once the zamindars of Gosaipur.'

'What did Jeevanlal Mallik write?'

'He is worried about his father. He thinks someone is planning to kill him. If I can go and throw some light on the matter, he'll be very grateful and he'll pay me my fee.'

I knew the letter had arrived this morning, but had no idea about its contents. Now I remembered seeing Feluda looking thoughtful and smoking quietly after he had finished reading it.

'Why don't we all go?' Lalmohan Babu sounded quite enthusiastic. 'Look, we are both free at this moment, aren't we? Besides, I think we'll enjoy a visit to a small village after all the hectic travelling we have done in the past.'

'To be honest, I was thinking of going, too. Mr Mallik said he could not have me stay in his house—there is some problem, apparently. He's spoken to a relative who lives three miles away. I could stay with him, but then I'd have to travel in a rickshaw every day. It struck me that it might be simpler to stay somewhere within walking distance. That's why I thought of your friend.'

'My friend will be delighted, especially if he hears you are going to join me. He's a great admirer of yours.'

Lalmohan Babu wrote to his friend the next day, and Feluda answered Jeevanlal's letter. Tulsi Babu was so pleased that he wrote back instantly, saying that the Gosaipur Literary Society wanted to give a joint reception to Lalmohan Babu and Feluda. Lalmohan Babu was thrilled by the idea, but Feluda put his foot down. 'Leave me out of receptions, please,' he said firmly. 'No one must know who I really am and why I'm visiting Gosaipur. Please tell your friend not to tell anyone.'

Rather reluctantly, Lalmohan Babu passed the message on, adding that he was perfectly happy about the reception. With this event in mind, he even packed a blue embroidered kurta.

We had to take a train to Katwa Junction, and then a bus to get to Gosaipur, which was seven miles from Katwa. Tulsi Babu was going to wait for us at a provision store near the bus stop. His house was just ten minutes away.

On our way there, I saw a palanquin from the bus. This surprised me very much for I didn't know palanquins were still in use. Feluda and Lalmohan Babu were similarly taken aback.

'I wonder which century these people think they live in?' Lalmohan Babu exclaimed. 'I hope Gosaipur has electricity. I had no idea the area was so remote.'

The conductor of the bus knew where we wanted to get off. He stopped the bus before the provision store, shouting, 'Gosaipur! Go-o-sai-pu-u-r!' We thanked him and got down quickly.

The elderly gentleman who came forward to greet us with a smile had the word 'ex-schoolmaster' written all over him. In his hand was an ancient patched-up black umbrella, on his feet were brown canvas shoes, on his nose were perched his glasses and under his arm was a very old copy of the *National Geographic* magazine. He was wearing a kurta and a short dhoti. On being introduced to Feluda, he winked and said, 'I did what you said. I mean, I didn't tell anyone about you. You are only a tourist, you've lived in Canada for years, now you want to see an Indian village. I thought of this because it occurred to me that you might have to ask questions, or visit places unseen. A tourist can claim to be both curious and ignorant. No one's going to be offended by what you say or where you go.'

'Good. I hope you have books on Canada I can read?' Feluda asked with a smile.

'Don't worry about that,' Tulsi Babu grinned. Then he turned to Jatayu. 'For you, my friend, I have arranged a function on Friday. It's going to be a small informal affair—a couple of songs and dances, then you'll be presented with a citation, and there'll be speeches. The barrister, Suresh Chakladar, will preside. The citation is being written out by a young boy, but its contents—I mean the actual words—are mine, heh heh.'

'There was no need . . . you didn't have to . . .' Lalmohan Babu tried to look modest.

'We wanted to. It isn't every day that a celebrity deigns to visit us!'

'We saw a palanquin on the way,' Feluda said. 'Is that still used here as a mode of transport?'

Tulsi Babu stopped to prod a young calf with his umbrella to get it out of the way. Then he looked at Feluda and replied, 'Oh yes. If you want a palanquin, you'll get it here. But that isn't all. We specialize in providing all sorts of things from the past. Do you want guards in uniform, carrying spears and shields? You'll find them here. A man who spends his time getting hookahs ready? You'll find him here. A punkha-puller? Oil lamps? Yes, we've got those, too!'

'But you've got electric connections, haven't you?'

'Oh yes. Every house has electricity, except the one where it's most needed.'

'What do you mean?'

'The house where Mr Mallik lives.'

All of us stared at him in surprise.

'Shyamlal Mallik?' Feluda asked.

'Yes, sir. There's no other Mallik in Gosaipur. They used to be local zamindars. Shyamlal's father, Durlabh Singh, was an utterly ruthless man. People were terrified of him. Shyamlal himself did not stay a zamindar long, for by then the government had changed the laws regarding the zamindari system. However, he went to Calcutta, built a plastic factory and made a lot of money. Then, one day, he came home in the dark and tried to switch on the light. He did not know that there was a loose, exposed wire in the switchboard. He nearly got electrocuted! After spending a few weeks in a hospital, he handed over his business to his son, returned to Gosaipur and removed the electric connection to his house. If he had stopped there, it might have made some sense. But he decided to remove everything that was modern, or "Western". He gave up smoking cheroots, and went back to hookahs. He stopped using fountain pens, his toothbrush was replaced by neem twigs, every book in his house that was written in English was thrown out, as were all the medicines. Now he relies purely on ayurvedic stuff. The only man to benefit from all this was the local ayurvedic doctor, called Tarak Kaviraj.

And yes, Shyamlal's car has been sold as well. What he uses is a palanquin. There was an old palanquin in his house. He simply had it repaired and painted. He's appointed four bearers to carry it for him. There are many other things that he's started to do . . . you'll get to see everything for yourself, I am sure.'

'Yes, I probably shall. I am here because his son asked me to come.'

'I know his son is visiting him, but why did he want you here?'

'Are you aware that someone is planning to kill Shyamlal Mallik? Have you heard any rumours or gossip?'

Tulsi Babu appeared quite taken aback by this. 'Why, no! I've certainly heard nothing. But if someone wants to get rid of him, you shouldn't have to look very far to see who it is.'

'What do you mean?'

'The same man who wrote to you. He and his father don't get along at all. Mind you, I don't blame Jeevanlal. It can't be easy to deal with a father who has such perfectly weird ideas. After all, Jeevanlal has to stay in the same house when he visits. It's enough to drive one mad.'

We reached Tulsi Babu's house just before four o'clock. His wife had died a few years ago, and his sons worked in Calcutta. He had only one daughter, who was married. She lived in Azimganj. Tulsi Babu lived here alone, with a servant called Ganga. 'In a place like this,' he told us with a smile, 'one may live alone, but there's no chance of being lonely. My neighbours and other friends in the village drop in at all times. We look after one another very well.'

Ganga was told to make tea as soon as we arrived. Feluda had brought a packet of good quality tea. That was the only thing he was really fussy about. A few minutes later, Ganga served us tea on the front veranda, with plates of beaten-rice and coconut, a typical evening snack in rural Bengal.

There were two bedrooms on the ground floor, one of which was Tulsi Babu's. We were given a much bigger room on the first floor. Three beds had been placed in it. One of its doors opened on to a terrace.

'I told Jeevanlal I'd call on him at five-thirty,' Feluda said, sipping his tea, 'so I'll have to find his dark and dingy house.'

'I'll take you there myself, don't worry. Shyamlal's house is only five minutes from here. But I hope you'll come back soon? I am expecting a few people later in the evening. They want to talk to

Lalmohan Babu, and then I'd like to take you to see Atmaram Babu.'

'Atmaram Babu? Who's he?'

'That's what some people call him. His real name is Mriganka Bhattacharya. He can speak to the dead, get souls and spirits to visit him in seances . . . you know, that kind of thing. He's one of our local attractions. But I think he's really got a certain power. I don't laugh the whole thing off.'

I wanted to ask what had made him think so, but couldn't, for at this moment we saw the palanquin again. Tulsi Babu's veranda overlooked the main road. The palanquin was making its way to the village. As it got closer, Tulsi Babu said, 'Why, Jeevanlal appears to be in it!'

A man was peering out of the window. The bearers were carrying the palanquin in exactly the same style that one reads about, making a strange rhythmic noise. The noise stopped as they put the palanquin down. The man inside got out with some difficulty. Clad in trousers and a shirt, he looked terribly incongruous as he emerged.

'Mr Mitter?' he asked, looking at Feluda with a smile.

'Yes.'

'I am Jeevanlal Mallik.'

'Namaskar. This is my friend, Lalmohan Ganguli, and that's my cousin, Tapesh. You know Tulsi Babu, don't you?'

'Yes. Namaskar. Er . . . do you think you could come to my house?'

Lalmohan Babu stayed back to wait for his visitors. Feluda and I went with Jeevanlal Mallik. He left the road and began walking through a bamboo grove, possibly to take a short cut.

'I had to go to the station to make a phone call,' he said.

'Is that why you had to take the palanquin?'

Jeevanlal gave Feluda a sidelong glance. 'Did Tulsi Babu tell you everything about my father?'

'Yes, we learnt what an electric shock did to him.'

'Things were not so bad in the beginning. He simply did not want to have anything to do with electricity. That was understandable. But now . . . he's become absolutely impossible. You'll soon see what I mean.'

'Do you come here often?'

'Once every two months, to talk about business matters.'

'You mean your father still takes an interest in his business?'

'Oh no. But I don't want to give up. I keep trying to bring him back to normal.'

'Have you had any luck?'

'No, not so far.'

TWO

Mr Mallik's house was clearly quite old, but had been well maintained. It was large enough to be called a mansion, if not a palace. As we passed through the front gate, I saw a pond to our right. A number of trees behind the house suggested a garden. Only the compound wall did not appear to have been repaired for some time. It was broken in many places, showing gaps. Seedlings had grown through large cracks in it.

A guard stood at the gate, clutching a shield and a spear, looking as if he was dressed for a part in a historical play. A bearer, wearing an old-fashioned uniform and looking just as peculiar, gave us a smart salute at the front door. It was all done seriously, and certainly the atmosphere inside the house was far from lighthearted, but both men looked so comical that I almost burst out laughing.

We were taken into the living room. It had no furniture. A mattress, covered with a spotless sheet, was spread on the floor. We went and sat on it. There were a few pictures on the wall, of Hindu gods and goddesses and scenes from the *Ramayana*. There were bookshelves on the wall, but apart from half-a-dozen books in Bengali, they were empty.

'Would you like the fan? If so, I can ask Dashu to pull it for you,' Jeevanlal said.

I had not noticed it at first, but now I glanced up and saw the fan—two mats edged with large frills—hanging from an iron rod. The rod hung from two hooks fixed to the ceiling. A rope tied to the rod went outside to the veranda, through the wall over the door to our left. I had only read about such fans. The servant called Dashu presumably sat on the veranda and pulled the rope, so that the fan swung from side to side, creating a breeze. But it was an October evening. None of us needed a fan.

'Let me show you something. Can you tell me what this is?' said Jeevanlal, opening a cupboard and taking out a square piece of cloth. What made it special was that one corner was knotted around a small stone.

Feluda frowned, then swung the cloth a few times in the air.

'Topshe, stand up for a minute.'

I rose. Feluda stood a few feet away from me swinging the cloth once more. Then he threw it at me as though it was a fishing net. The end that was knotted around the stone wound itself round my neck instantly.

'Thugee!' I cried.

Feluda had told me about thugees. They were bandits who used to attack travellers in this fashion and then loot their possessions. One swift pull was usually enough to tighten the noose and kill their innocent victims.

Feluda nodded, took the cloth away and asked, 'Where did you get something like this?'

'Someone threw it into my father's room through an open window, in the middle of the night.'

'When?'

'A few days before I got here.'

'What were the guards doing?'

'Guards?' Jeevanlal laughed. 'They like dressing up to please their master, but that's as far as it goes. They are bone idle, each one of them. Besides, they know their master has become quite senile, and there's really no one to control them.'

'Who else lives here?'

'My grandmother. She is perfectly happy with these old-fashioned arrangements. Then there's Bholanath Babu. He is a sort of manager—in fact, he takes care of everything from shopping to running errands for my father, fetching the doctor if need be, going to the next town to get things we can't get in the village . . . everything. There is no one else except a cook, two guards and a bearer. They live here. The four bearers for the palanquin and the punkha-puller come from the village.'

'Where did Bholanath Babu originally come from?'

'He is from this village. His family were our tenants. His forefathers were farmers. But he went to school, and I believe was quite bright as a student. Now he's nearly sixty.'

'Is that your grandfather?' Feluda asked, pointing at a painting on the wall. It was the portrait of a man with an impressive moustache. I had not noticed it so far. He was sitting on a chair, holding a walking stick with a silver handle in one hand, the other resting on a marble table. The look in his eyes was cold and hard.

'Yes, that is Durlabh Singh Mallik.'

'The zamindar everyone was terrified of?'

'Yes, I am afraid so. He was devoid of compassion or mercy.'

A bearer brought two glasses and a cup on a saucer on a tray and placed the tray before us. Feluda glanced at the hot drink they contained and said, 'Does this mean your father still drinks tea?'

'No, no. That's coffee, and it's mine. I always bring a cup and a tin of Nescafé. He couldn't find other cups and saucers, so you've been given glasses. I hope you don't mind.'

'No, of course not. I have drunk coffee out of bronze glasses in south India.'

A loud tapping noise coming from upstairs made Feluda glance up. 'Does your father wear clogs?'

'Oh yes. Isn't that far more natural than wearing shoes?'

'Yes, I suppose so. Tell me, was it just this piece of cloth that made you think someone was planning to kill your father, or was there something else?'

In reply, Jeevanlal simply took out a piece of paper from his pocket and offered it to Feluda. Written on it in pencil with large, distinct letters, were the following words:

You have been given a death sentence to atone for your ancestor's sins. Be prepared to die.

'This came on 5 October, the day before I got here. It had been posted in Katwa, which doesn't really tell us anything, for anyone from Gosaipur could have gone there and posted it.'

'If you don't mind, can you tell us what "ancestor's sins" might mean?'

'Well, as I told you before, Mr Mitter, my grandfather treated his tenants very badly. I have no idea which particular crime has been referred to.'

'Why didn't you go to the police?'

'There were two reasons,' Jeevanlal said. 'One, people here would not recognize you. So, hopefully, whoever wrote that note would feel no need to be on his guard. Two, if I called the police, I would have been their prime suspect.'

Feluda and I both looked at him in surprise. Jeevanlal explained quickly, 'Everyone knows I have not been able to get on with my father ever since this change came over him. I still live in the city, I find it impossible to do without certain modern amenities. I admit what happened to my father gave him more than just a physical shock. It also caused him great mental trauma. What really happened was that he and I returned together one evening, and stepped into our living room, which was dark. My father groped for the switchboard and received a shock from a live wire. I ran out and switched the mains off in five seconds. But, for some reason, he got the impression that I did not act quickly enough. This happened five years ago. But since that incident, he has stopped trusting me. We have violent arguments sometimes. Once I lost my temper and threw a burning kerosene lamp on a mattress, which naturally caught fire . . . and then there was hell to pay. The news spread, and everyone started to think I disliked my father intensely. That's the reason why I did not call the police. Besides, I knew of your reputation, and how well you had handled your previous cases. So I thought you were the best person to turn to.'

We finished our coffee. The same bearer brought an oil lamp and put it down in a corner. 'Would you like to meet my father?' Jeevanlal asked.

'Yes, I ought to.'

We rose and made our way upstairs. The few lamps and lanterns the servants had lit had done nothing to illuminate the staircase. In fact, most of the house was in darkness. Jeevanlal took out a small torch from his pocket and said, 'Even this had to be smuggled in secretly. He hates torches.'

We found Shyamlal Mallik seated on a mattress, clutching the pipe of his hookah and leaning against a bolster. His face bore a marked resemblance to that of his father. If he grew a thick moustache, he would probably look stern like Durlabh Singh. When he spoke, I could tell that if he ever got angry and raised his voice, one might do well to stay away from him.

'You may go now,' he said in his deep voice. The person he addressed was sitting on one corner of the mattress. Jeevanlal introduced him as Tarak Kaviraj, the ayurvedic doctor. He got to his feet and greeted us, but left immediately.

'What the hell is a detective going to do?' asked Shyamlal Mallik as soon as Feluda had been introduced. He sounded extremely annoyed. 'Durlabh Singh's soul has already told me my enemy is in my own house. I have that written on a piece of paper. A departed soul can see it all . . . no one can hide the truth from it. What more can a detective from the city do for me?'

Jeevanlal looked profoundly startled. He obviously did not know anything about Durlabh Singh's soul.

'Did you go to Mriganka Bhattacharya's house?' he asked.

'No, why should I have gone to him?' his father barked. 'He came to me. I called him. I had to know who was trying to cause me such distress. Now I do.'

'When did he visit you?'

'The day before you came.'

'You did not tell me.'

Shyamlal Mallik made no reply. He began smoking.

'May we see what Durlabh Singh told you?' Feluda asked politely. Shyamlal Mallik stopped smoking and glared at him.

'How old are you?' he asked abruptly. Feluda told him.

'I am amazed,' the old man announced, 'by your impertinence. Do you really think you'd understand the spiritual significance of a departed soul writing a message? Is that something to be shown to all and sundry?'

'Please forgive me,' Feluda said gently. 'All I want to know is whether your dead father told you how you might get out of your present difficulties.'

'I could tell you what he said. There's no need to look at the writing. He simply said there was only one thing to be done: get rid of the enemy.'

For a few minutes, none of us could speak. Then Jeevanlal said slowly, 'You are asking me to go away?'

'When did I ever ask you to come here?'

Jeevanlal refused to give up. 'Baba,' he said, 'you have begun to trust Bholanath Babu much more than you trust me. Have you forgotten his family history? Durlabh Singh's men had gone and set fire to his house because his father had failed to pay the rent on time. And—'

'Fool!' Shyamlal Mallik shouted. 'Bholanath was only a small child at the time. Are you suggesting that he has waited almost sixty years to plan his revenge? How absurd can you get?'

At this point, we decided to leave. 'Let me take you back,' Jeevanlal offered. 'I don't think you can manage the short cut in the dark.' As we came out of the house, he added, 'I had no idea he would insult you like that. I am terribly sorry.'

'Don't be,' Feluda replied. 'The first thing a detective learns to grow is a thick skin. I am used to handling slights and insults. It is you I am more concerned about. You must realize one thing, Jeevan Babu. Suspicion is more likely to fall on you because that anonymous letter points at Bholanath.'

'But when that cloth and the note arrived, I was in Calcutta, Mr Mitter.'

'So what? How do I know you haven't got an accomplice here in Gosaipur?'

'Even you are turning against me?' Jeevanlal sounded deeply distressed.

'No. Right now, Jeevan Babu, I am not flinging accusations at anyone; nor am I making assumptions about anyone's innocence. But I must ask you something. What kind of a man is Bholanath Babu?'

After a moment's silence, Jeevanlal replied, 'Very reliable and trustworthy. I have to admit that. But that's no reason to suspect me, surely?' He sounded a little desperate.

Feluda raised a hand. 'Jeevan Babu,' he said soothingly, 'you must appreciate my position. I have to assess the whole situation objectively and impartially. You will simply have to be patient. Neither you nor I have a choice in the matter. We must wait until I learn the truth. The only thing I can promise you is that I will definitely protect whoever is innocent.'

Jeevanlal did not reply. It was impossible to see his face in the dark and tell whether Feluda's words had reassured him. Feluda asked him something else as we emerged from the bamboo grove. 'Does your father ever walk barefoot outside the house?'

'Outside the house? Never. Why, he doesn't take off his clogs even inside the house. Why do you ask?'

'I thought I saw traces of mud on his feet. And . . . doesn't he use a mosquito net?'

'Of course. Everyone here uses mosquito nets. They have to.'

'Perhaps you have not noticed it, but his face, neck and arms were covered with mosquito bites.'

'Really? No, I hadn't noticed. It's strange, because he certainly uses a net.'

'Then perhaps the net is torn. Could you please check?'

THREE

Tulsi Babu and Lalmohan Babu were waiting for us. I felt immensely relieved to see electric lights again.

'Can you imagine,' said Lalmohan Babu, 'even in this tiny village, I found as many as twenty people who had read more than fifty per cent of my books? Of course, many of them got them from the school library, but those who had bought a few copies had them signed by me.'

'Very good. I am very pleased to hear that, Lalmohan Babu.'

Tulsi Babu turned to Feluda, 'Let's go and call on Atmaram. We can see the Bat-kali temple tomorrow.'

'Bat-kali temple? What on earth is that?'

'Yet another local attraction. There is an old and abandoned Kali temple in the bamboo grove you just came through. It's two hundred years old. It must have once had a statue of Kali, but it's gone now. Dozens of bats live in it, which is why people call it the Bat-kali temple. When it was in use, it must have seen a lot of activity.'

'I see. By the way, does your Atmaram come from this village?'

'No, but he has been living here for some time. Two years ago, his special power came to light. Besides, he knows astrology and palmistry as well. People from Calcutta often come here to consult him.'

'Does he charge a fee?'

'Yes, he probably does. But I've never heard of him charging any of the locals. He holds seances on Mondays and Fridays. Today, we'll just go and meet him.'

'All right, let's go.'

I could see that, somehow, Mriganka Bhattacharya had become a part of Feluda's investigation. We left the house once more.

Although lights were on in every house in the vicinity, it was very dark outside, possibly because of the large number of big trees. The moon had not yet risen. Crickets and owls and jackals in the distance had started a regular concert, which made me think that, in a place like this, it was Shyamlal Mallik's palanquin and the flickering light from his oil lamps that fitted the atmosphere far better. Lalmohan Babu whispered into my ear, declaring that he had never seen a place so full of mystery and excitement. 'You know, Tapesh,' he said, 'I had thought of Guatemala as the place of action for my next novel; but now I think I will change it to Gosaipur.'

'Really?' Feluda laughed, having overheard this remark. 'But you haven't even seen the thugee's noose. Can you think of anything more exciting?'

'What are you talking about, Felu Babu?'

Feluda explained quickly. He also mentioned the anonymous note.

'If Mr Bhattacharya got Durlabh Singh's spirit to come and reveal the truth, you need not look any further, Mr Mitter,' Tulsi Babu remarked 'Shyamlal Mallik's enemy must be in his house.'

No one said anything after this, for we had reached Mr Bhattacharya's house. This house did not appear to have an electric connection, either. Perhaps souls found it easier to re-enter the earth if they could move in the faint and hazy light of lanterns.

Mriganka Bhattacharya turned out to be a man with an impressive appearance. It was impossible to guess his age. His hair had thinned, but not turned grey. His features were sharp, his skin smooth, except around his eyes and mouth. He was seated on a divan, facing three chairs and two benches. He clearly did not share Shyamlal Mallik's aversion to furniture. A young man of about twenty-five was sitting on one of the benches, leafing through an astrological magazine. We learnt later that he was Mr Bhattacharya's nephew, Nityanand. He helped his uncle in hailing spirits.

Tulsi Babu touched Mr Bhattacharya's feet quickly and said, 'These are my friends from Calcutta. I brought them here so that they could meet the man Gosaipur is so proud of.'

Mr Bhattacharya raised his eyes and looked at us. Then he glanced at the chairs. The three of us sat down. Tulsi Babu remained standing.

Mr Bhattacharya closed his eyes, sat erect, his legs crossed in the lotus position. A few moments later, he suddenly opened his eyes and said, 'Sixteen, three, thirteen. Which one of you has those initials?'

We stared at him, perfectly taken aback. Feluda was the first to speak, after a short pause. 'I do,' he said. 'My full name is Pradosh Chandra Mitter, and you are quite right. P, C, M, are the sixteenth, third and thirteenth letters from the alphabet.'

I felt considerably surprised by this. Tulsi Babu had certainly not mentioned our names. How did Mr Bhattacharya guess Feluda's initials? I saw Tulsi Babu cast an admiring glance at Mr

Bhattacharya. Then he asked, 'Can you guess his profession?'

By this time, another man—possibly a client—had entered the room. Feluda naturally did not want his profession disclosed before a stranger. So he said hurriedly, 'Oh, there's no need to do that.' Tulsi Babu realized his mistake and began to look embarrassed.

'I'll bring them back on Friday,' he said, changing the subject. 'We came today only to meet you.'

Mr Bhattacharya looked steadily at Feluda. 'You simply seek the truth, don't you? Stop worrying, sir, nobody will understand my meaning if I say that.'

We took our leave and left soon after this. 'He must have a very strong sixth sense,' Lalmohan Babu remarked as we began walking, 'and he can speak in riddles. Remarkable!'

Someone was coming from the opposite direction, carrying a lantern in one hand. It swung as he moved, making his shadow sweep the ground. Tulsi Babu raised the torch in his hand, shone it on the man's face and said, 'Off, to see Bhattacharya? You've started visiting him pretty frequently, haven't you?'

The man smiled, hesitated for a second, then went on his way without saying anything.

'That was Bholanath Babu,' Tulsi Babu informed us, 'Bhattacharya's latest devotee. I believe Bhattacharya went to his house once and spoke to a spirit. Whose, I couldn't say.'

Tulsi Babu's cook, Ganga, produced an excellent meal that night, including moong daal, three types of vegetables and egg curry. After dinner, our host regaled us with stories of his life as a schoolteacher. When we said good night to him and went to bed, it was only half past nine, though it seemed like midnight. We had brought our own bedding and mosquito nets. Feluda said he'd use Odomos and not bother with a net. I had noticed that he had plunged into silence since our return from Mr Bhattacharya's house. In the last couple of hours, he had opened his mouth only to praise Ganga's cooking. What was he thinking?

Lalmohan Babu lit a lantern and placed it by his bed. He needed the light, he said, to work on his speech for his reception. He didn't want to disturb us by keeping the main light on.

I couldn't go to sleep without asking Feluda something that was puzzling me very much.

'How did that man guess your initials, Feluda? And he knew about your profession, too!'

'Yes, those are questions I have been asking myself. I haven't got an answer yet, Topshe. Sometimes . . . some people do turn out to have extraordinary powers that cannot be rationally explained.'

FOUR

The next morning, we went for a long walk and explored the whole village. The local club, Jagarani, was rehearsing for a play. We were invited to watch the rehearsal. A lot of people were curious about life in Canada, so Feluda ended up giving a short lecture on the subject. Then we met the only mime artist of Gosaipur, called Benimadhav. He offered to visit us on Friday and show us what he could do. 'I can climb stairs without any props . . . I can show you what happens to a man caught in a storm . . . change the expression on my face— through six different steps—from sad to happy!'

In the evening, Tulsi Babu took us to a fair in the next village. By the time we returned, having enjoyed ourselves hugely, it was nearly six o'clock. The sun had set, but it wasn't dark yet. Feluda said he'd like to visit Jeevanlal Mallik. Tulsi Babu went home to wait for us.

Jeevanlal came out of his house even before we could reach the front door.

'I saw you coming from my bedroom window,' he explained.

'Has there been any new development?' Feluda asked.

'No.'

'May I look at your garden?'

'Of course.'

The 'garden' was not really a garden: that is to say, there were no flower beds or a lawn. It was simply a large, open area in which stood a number of tall trees. Feluda began inspecting it carefully. I had no idea what he was looking for. I saw him stop at one point and stare at the ground for a few minutes. After a while, a voice cried out from a balcony on the first floor: 'Who's there? What are you doing among the trees?'

It was Jeevanlal's grandmother. 'It's all right, Grandma!' he shouted back. 'It's only me, and my friends.'

'Oh. I keep seeing people roaming about in the garden. God knows what they do.'

'Can she see well?' Feluda asked.

'No, not very well; nor can she hear unless one shouts.'

'I don't suppose anyone looks after the garden?'

'No, not really. Bholanath Babu does what he can, but obviously that's not enough.'

'Do the guards keep an eye on it at night?'

'At night? You've got to be joking. No guard here would dream of staying awake to do their duty.'

'The front door is locked, surely?'

'Oh yes. That's Bholanath Babu's job. But when I am here, I lock the front door and keep the key with me.'

'I haven't yet met Bholanath Babu. Could you call him, please?'

Jeevanlal asked one of his bearers to call Bholanath Babu, and bring us some lemonade. We were sitting outside by the pond. The recent monsoon rains had filled it to its brim. It was now covered with *shaluk* flowers.

Bholanath Babu arrived in a couple of minutes. He was wearing a dhoti and a shirt, but his appearance was really no different from an ordinary farmer. I could easily picture him working in a field, tilling the land.

Feluda began talking with him. There was no noise anywhere except the faint strains of music from a distant transistor. Had that not been there, it would have been quite easy to pretend we had travelled back in time by more than a hundred years.

'Has Mriganka Bhattacharya visited this house just once?' Feluda asked.

'Recently, yes. Just once.'

'You mean he has visited Mr Mallik before?'

'Yes, a few times. I think the master had asked him to draw up his horoscope.'

'And did he?'

'I don't know.'

'What made him pay a visit recently? Who asked him to come?'

'The master did. Er . . . the doctor and I had both told him it might help.'

'You visit Mr Bhattacharya regularly, don't you?'

'Yes, sir.'

'Do you believe in his powers?'

Bholanath Babu bent his head. 'What can I say, sir? I had a daughter—Lakshmi, she was called. Beautiful like the goddess, and she had manners to match. But. . . when she was only eleven, she got cholera and . . . she died. I was devastated. Then Mr Bhattacharya came to me and said, "Do you want to hear from her how she is?"'

Bholanath Babu stopped, and wiped his eyes with one corner of his dhoti. Then, with an effort, he pulled himself together and went on, 'He then spoke to her. She came and she said she had found peace and was very happy where she was, so I must stop feeling sad. I mean, she didn't actually say all this, but the words were written on paper. I . . . from that day . . . I . . .' He choked again.

Feluda did not press him any more. 'Were you present when Mr Bhattacharya contacted the dead Durlabh Singh?' he asked, changing the subject.

'Yes, but I was not in the room. The master did not want his mother to find out, so he told me to stand at the door and watch out for her. In the room were Mr Bhattacharya, his nephew Nityanand and the master.'

'Did you hear anything at all?'

'I heard very little, sir, They were totally silent for the first ten minutes. Then, a jackal called in the distance, and I remember hearing the master's voice the same instant. He said, "Are you there? Has anyone come?" But I heard nothing else after that. When it was over, I took Mr Bhattacharya home.'

Feluda finished his lemonade and lit a Charminar. 'Durlabh Singh Mallik's men had set fire to your house. Do you remember that?'

After a brief pause, Bholanath Babu uttered two words: 'I do.'

'Don't you wish to take revenge? Have you never thought of settling old scores?'

I had heard Feluda ask such hard-hitting questions before. A lot depended, he had told me once, on how a person reacted to such questions.

Bholanath Babu shook his head mutely. Then he said, 'Never. The master may have changed in the last few years, but certainly I don't know anyone more kind, or more generous.'

Feluda had no further questions for him.

'May I go now, sir?' Bholanath Babu asked after a few seconds. 'I'd like to go to Mr Bhattacharya's house again, sir, if you don't mind.'

'Oh no, please go ahead. Thank you for your help.'

Bholanath Babu left. Jeevanlal started fidgeting.

'What is it, Jeevan Babu?' Feluda asked.

'Nothing. It's just that I'm curious about whether you have made any progress.' He was obviously worried about himself.

'Bholanath Babu struck me as a very good man,' Feluda replied. This seemed to upset Jeevanlal even more.

'You mean that I . . . ?' he began.

'No, no. I liked Bholanath Babu. That does not automatically mean that I dislike you. Look, to be honest, I still haven't reached any conclusions. I have a few doubts about certain things, but those aren't enough to build a case, particularly when I can't see how they can be linked to the main problem. I have to wait until something happens, something that might—' He was interrupted.

'Who's there? Jeevan, is that you?' shouted Jeevanlal's grandmother again. We could hear her only because it was so quiet.

Feluda rose instantly and began running towards the back of the garden. We followed him. Lalmohan Babu had been staring at the water and humming under his breath. He, too, broke off and joined us.

We found Feluda standing by a gap in the compound wall. A portion of it had crumbled away.

He was shining his torch on the wall.

'Did you see anyone?' Jeevanlal asked.

'Yes, but not closely enough to recognize him. He slipped out through that gap.'

We spent the next thirty minutes searching the grounds. Thousands of mosquitoes kept us company, as did as many crickets who kept up an incessant chorus. What we eventually found was immensely mystifying. At the far end, under what must have been the last tree, was a big hole in the ground. It had obviously been dug recently. Jeevanlal, who appeared as surprised as us, could not offer any explanation. 'Hidden treasure!' Lalmohan Babu declared. 'Someone just removed it.'

But Jeevanlal shook his head. 'No,' he said, 'Nobody in our family ever hid any treasure. I would have known if they had. I mean, there would have been stories and gossip.'

The comment Feluda made sounded just as mysterious. 'Jeevan Babu, didn't I say I was waiting for something to happen? I think it now has.'

We returned home after this. After dinner, Lalmohan Babu and I wanted an early night. He had ended up with cuts and bruises, for some of the plants in Jeevanlal's garden were thorny. After dabbing himself with Dettol, he declared he was ready for bed. So was I.

Feluda was the only one who didn't seem tired at all. He opened his notebook, applied Odomos all over his hands and feet and face, and settled down on his bed, leaning against a pillow. Tulsi Babu came in with a plate of paan. Lalmohan Babu started to yawn, but broke off as Feluda glanced at our host to ask him a question.

'Tell me, Tulsi Babu,' he said, 'if you told a good and honest man a way of cheating others, and that man then actually put that into practice, would you still call him good and honest?'

Tulsi Babu looked flustered. 'Good heavens, Mr Mitter, I am hopeless with puzzles and riddles. But since you ask, if the man is really good, surely he wouldn't stoop so low? And if he did . . . no, I would not call him good any more.'

'Ah. I am glad to see you and I agree on this.'

I was too tired to worry about why Feluda was making cryptic remarks. So I got into bed, but could not go to sleep. My mind was still buzzing with questions: Why did Shyamlal Mallik have mud on his feet? Who sent the anonymous note and that noose? Who did his mother see this evening in the garden? Who dug that hole and what did it contain? Why didn't Shyamlal want us to see the paper on which a spirit was supposed to have written?

God knows when I dropped off. When I opened my eyes, it was still dark. Then I realized I had been woken by a scream. It had probably come from Lalmohan Babu, for he was sitting up on his bed, having flung aside the mosquito net.

'What happened?' I asked.

'A dream . . . a nightmare! Oh God, it was terrible. Do you know what I saw? I was being given a reception and my own grandfather was there, putting a garland round my neck. "See, what an exciting garland I have given you!" he said. I looked and . . . and . . . saw that they weren't flowers, but tiny human heads, dripping with blood! Can you imagine it?'

'Why, Lalmohan Babu, why must you have such an awful dream at this beautiful moment when dawn is just breaking?' asked Feluda.

With a start, I realized Feluda was already up. I saw him coming in through the door that led to the terrace. He had obviously been doing his yoga.

'What am I to do, Felu Babu? It's all this talk of a reception and speaking to dead ancestors, and old Kali temples . . . all of those things got mixed up in my mind!'

There was no point in going back to bed. I rose and went out on the terrace quietly. Tulsi Babu might still be asleep. The moon was still shining, but its light had turned pale. I noticed a few stars, winking bravely, but they couldn't possibly last long. The eastern sky had just started to turn pink.

This morning I had decided to chew on a neem twig instead of using a toothbrush. It was far more healthy, Feluda had said. So I picked one from the pieces I had kept ready the previous night, and had just put it into my mouth, when someone arrived at the front door and began screaming loudly:

'Mr Mitter! Come quickly. Please, sir . . . Mr Mitter!'

We rushed down the stairs. It was Bholanath Babu. 'Last night. . .' he gasped as he saw us, 'we were attacked by burglars. They tied me up, and they tied and gagged the master. There were two of them. Everything the big chest contained . . . all the money . . . has gone. Only Jeevan Babu was spared somehow. He came and untied me, and told me to call you. Please, sir, you must come at once!'

FIVE

Shyamlal Mallik was not injured, but the two hours he had had to spend with his hands and feet tied had shaken him very deeply. He was sitting on the mattress in his room, staring blankly into space. 'If they had to tie me up like that, why didn't they kill me?' I heard him mutter. I wondered if he knew all his money was gone.

Feluda searched Shyamlal's room very thoroughly. Only the big chest had been opened. Everything else had been left undisturbed. The key to the chest used to be kept under his pillow. Bholanath Babu, who also slept on the first floor, was attacked in his sleep. Naturally, he had not been able to offer any resistance at all. The bearer had slept through it all, no one had gone anywhere near his room. One of the guards was away, and the other had been struck on his head by a heavy rod, which had left him unconscious for several hours. Jeevanlal's grandmother lived in the rear portion of the house. Fortunately, she knew nothing of what had happened.

We spent fifteen minutes talking to Bholanath Babu and the servants, but there was no sign of Jeevanlal. 'Did he go off to call the police?' Feluda asked.

'I don't know, sir,' Bholanath Babu faltered 'He sent me to your house and I saw him go out, but I haven't seen him since.'

Without a word, Feluda ran towards the stairs, with Lalmohan Babu and me behind him. We climbed down to the ground floor, crossed a courtyard and went into the garden through the back door. The sun had just risen, and there was a thin mist. The grass and the leaves were wet with the early morning dew. Crows and mynahs and some other birds I couldn't recognize had started going about their business.

We made our way through the garden, but had to stop in just a few minutes. Under a jackfruit tree lay the figure of a man. I recognized the blue shirt he was wearing, the white pyjamas and the chappals. It was Jeevanlal Mallik. Feluda strode forward quickly and looked down at him.

'My God!' he exclaimed in horror, stepping back.

'Felu Babu!' Lalmohan Babu called, pointing at an object lying a few feet away from the body.

'I know, I have seen it. Please don't touch it. That's what was used to kill Jeevanlal.'

It was a square piece of cloth, with a stone tied round one corner.

Bholanath Babu had followed us out and realized what had happened.

'I don't believe this!' he cried and looked as if he was about to faint.

'Please pull yourself together,' Feluda said to him, laying a hand on his shoulder. 'This is not the time to give way to despair. You must inform the police. If you like, Lalmohan Babu will go with you. Nobody must touch either the body or the weapon. This must have happened pretty recently. Perhaps the killer is still in the area. Go at once, but please make sure your master is not told about the murder.'

Feluda ran towards the compound wall, and stopped before the gap in it. Then we both slipped out of it and found ourselves facing the bamboo grove through which we had walked on our first night here. There were no houses within a hundred yards. We stepped into the bamboo grove. What was that structure, tucked away in a corner? Oh, it was probably the old Kali temple Tulsi Babu had mentioned.

A man was standing by the temple, looking at us. 'Why are you up so early?' he asked, coming forward. It was Tarak Kaviraj, the ayurvedic doctor.

'Haven't you heard?' Feluda asked.

'Heard what?'

'The old Mr Mallik—'

'What!'

'No, no, it's not what you think. Mr Mallik is fine, but his house was burgled last night and . . . his son has been killed. But the old man does not know that, so please don't tell him.'

Tarak Kaviraj hurried on. After a few moments, we decided to return. The culprit had clearly escaped.

We slipped back into the garden. What I saw next—or, rather, what I did not see—made me blink and wonder if I was dreaming. Could this really be true?

The ground under the jackfruit tree was empty. Jeevanlal's dead body had vanished, and so had the piece of cloth.

Lalmohan Babu was standing a few feet away, trembling visibly. He had to make an effort to speak: 'Bh-bholanath Babu and I went back to the house, but he s-said he'd go to the police station al-alone. I let him g-go, and then I walked this way to look for you, b-but th-then I s-saw . . .'

' . . . That the corpse had gone?'

'Y-yes.'

Feluda ran again, but in a different direction. This time, we made our way to the far end, where we had found the hole in the ground. Behind the garden, we now realized, was another large pond as well as a bigger gap in the wall. No doubt the body had been dragged out through the gap and thrown into the pond. The tree under which the hole had been dug, I noticed, was a mango tree.

We retraced our steps and went back into the house, using the staircase at the back to go up to the first floor.

'Jeevan! Jeevan!' we heard his grandmother call. 'Where's he got to, now? Didn't I just see him?'

We saw the old lady—clad in a white saree—come out of her room. Her heavily lined face looked sunken, her hair was cut very short and her eyes were hidden behind thick lenses. She must be at least eighty, I thought.

Feluda stepped forward to speak to her. 'Jeevanlal had to go out. Do you need anything? Perhaps I can get it for you?'

'Who are you?'

'I am a friend of his. My name is Pradosh.'

'I haven't seen you before, have I?'

'No. I arrived from the city only two days ago.'

'From Calcutta?'

'Yes. Can I get you anything? What did you want Jeevanlal for?'

The old lady suddenly seemed uncertain. She raised her face, looked around and said a little helplessly, 'I can't remember. What did I want him for? I can't remember anything any more.'

We left her mumbling to herself and made our way to Shyamlal's room. The doctor was with him, feeling his pulse. 'Where's Jeevan gone?' Shyamlal asked, his tone as helpless as his mother's. The doctor had obviously refrained from saying anything about the murder.

'Didn't you want him to go back to Calcutta?' Feluda asked.

'Back to Calcutta? You mean he left without telling me? How did he go? In a palanquin?'

'No. There's no way anyone can go all the way to Calcutta in a palanquin. You know that very well.'

'Are you mocking me?' Shyamlal sounded hurt.

'I am not the only one, Mr Mallik,' Feluda replied. 'The whole village makes fun of you. Surely you realize your present lifestyle is not doing any good to anyone, least of all yourself? If you had a guard with a gun, that would have been far more effective than one with an old and blunt spear. Tell me, isn't this kind of a shock as bad as the electric shock you received years ago? Trying to put the clock back doesn't achieve anything, Mr Mallik. You cannot bring back the times that have gone by. It's just not possible.'

I expected Shyamlal Mallik to flare up and order Feluda to get out at once. To my amazement, he didn't. In fact, he did not speak at all. All he did was sigh, and stare at the opposite wall.

SIX

'God, just look at my face!' Lalmohan Babu exclaimed, peering into his shaving mirror. Our faces looked just the same. We were all covered with mosquito bites.

'I should have warned you,' Tulsi Babu remarked. 'Mosquitoes are a big menace here. In fact, they are the only drawback of Gosaipur.'

'No,' Lalmohan Babu said, 'not the whole village, surely? I would say it's just that garden the Malliks own. That's where most of the mosquitoes breed, that's where they are the most vicious.'

We were back in our room after lunch. The police had arrived and started their investigation. Feluda had lapsed into silence once more. Perhaps Jeevanlal's murder was so totally unexpected that it had thrown all his calculations haywire. If Jeevanlal had been killed by burglars, the police were in a far better position to track them down. Feluda could hardly do anything on his own.

The inspector in charge—a man called Sudhakar Pramanik—had already talked to him. He had heard of Feluda, but did not seem to have a great deal of regard for him. He was particularly cross about the disappearance of the body.

'You amateur detectives simply do not believe in systems and methods, do you?' he said irritably 'I know your sort, I have had to work with private detectives before. If you had to leave the body, why didn't you get someone to guard it? Now we have to dredge the pond at the back. If that doesn't work, then we have to do the same to all the other ponds and lakes here . . . and there are eleven of them. It's all your fault, Mr Mitter. You really shouldn't have rushed off, leaving the body unattended.'

Feluda heard him in silence, without saying a word to defend himself. What he did say after a while irritated the inspector even more. 'Do you believe in ghosts?' Feluda asked. Inspector Pramanik stared at him, then shook his head and said, 'I had heard you took your work seriously. Now it's obvious that is not the case.'

'I had to ask you,' Feluda explained, 'because if you cannot catch the killer, I have to turn to Mr Bhattacharya. Perhaps he can contact Jeevanlal Mallik's spirit? Surely the spirit of the dead man will be able to reveal the truth?'

'Do you admit defeat, Mr Mitter? Are you giving up?'

'No. I cannot continue with my investigation . . . yes, I admit that . . . but if Mr Bhattacharya helps me, I can bring the culprit to justice. Of that I am certain.'

'Can you tell the difference between a dead man and a live one?'

'Mr Pramanik, I don't think I need answer all your questions, especially since I have no wish to join the police force. If I am talking of ghosts and spirits, it's only because my methods are quite different from yours.'

'Oh? Have you no reason to suspect Bholanath?'

'My only suspicion—no, my fear—is that you will arrest him immediately simply because you have heard his family history and you think he had a motive. If you do that, Inspector, you will be making a big mistake.'

The inspector laughed and stood up. 'Do you know what your problem is?' he said, clicking his tongue with annoyance. 'You see complications when there are none. This is a very simple case. Just think for a moment. Isn't it obvious whoever opened that chest knew where the key was kept? Had it been an ordinary burglar, surely he'd have broken it open? Bholanath took the money and was running away with it, when Jeevanlal caught up with him. Bholanath might not have planned to kill him, but was obliged to. Then he went off to call you, so that suspicion did not fall on him. He says he, too, was tied up, and Jeevanlal came and untied him. But can he prove it? How do we know he is not lying through his teeth?'

'Very well. But where did all that money go? What did Bholanath do with it?'

'We have to look for it, Mr Mitter. Once we find the body, we'll arrest Bholanath. He'll talk . . . oh yes, he'll tell us everything, never fear.'

I did not like to think of Bholanath Babu as the culprit, but what the inspector said made sense to me. What I could not understand was why Feluda was brushing it off. Just as the inspector began climbing down the stairs, he called after him, 'Jeevanlal's spirit will talk tonight in Mr Bhattacharya's house. You may learn a thing or two, if you come!'

Tulsi Babu was the only one who appeared more concerned with the reception the next day than with Jeevanlal's spirit. If the killer was not caught by then, the reception would have to be cancelled. Naturally, no one would be in the right mood for songs and speeches. Lalmohan Babu had accepted this, and was heard saying, 'I don't mind at all. After all, I sell murder mysteries, don't I? Here I've got a real murder, and a real mystery. If I can't have a reception, who cares?'

He said this, but couldn't get the idea of a reception out of his mind. I caught him, more than once, muttering lines from his speech and then quickly checking himself.

'Could you please tell Mr Bhattacharya that we'd be calling on him this evening?' Feluda said to Tulsi Babu. 'Tell him we cannot wait in a queue with his other clients. He must give us top priority.'

This time, Tulsi Babu realized that Feluda was absolutely serious about consulting Mr Bhattacharya. He looked very surprised.

'I have done all I could,' Feluda told him. 'Now I cannot proceed without Mr Bhattacharya's help.'

I thought again about what he had told me about keeping an open mind. There were dozens of occurrences every day, all over the world, that could not be explained by scientists. That did not necessarily mean they were all hoaxes. Only recently, I had read about a man called Uri Geller who could stare at steel forks and spoons and bend them simply through his will power. Well-known scientists had watched him, yet no one knew how he had done it. Perhaps Mriganka Bhattacharya was a man like Geller?

Tulsi Babu looked at his watch. 'It's half past five now,' he said. 'I think you and I should go together and make our request.'

'Very well,' Feluda said, getting to his feet. 'Why don't you two go for a walk?'

This struck me as a very good idea. Lalmohan Babu had mentioned how pleasant an October evening in Gosaipur could be, and I wanted to stretch my legs. So we left as soon as Feluda and Tulsi Babu went off to speak to Mr Bhattacharya.

SEVEN

Two days ago, the village had seemed a totally different place. Today, I felt strangely tense as we began walking away from the house. I simply could not stop thinking of the missing corpse. It could well be lying behind any of the bushes and shrubs we passed . . . no, no, I must not dwell on it, I told myself firmly.

We found the bamboo grove and turned into it. It was appreciably darker here, and the creepy feeling I was trying to overcome grew stronger. But at this moment, I saw the mime artist, Benimadhav, walking towards us. The sight of a third person helped me pull myself together. 'Hey, where are you off to?' he asked genially. 'I was going to your house. Didn't I tell you I'd come and show you my acting on Friday?'

'I know,' Lalmohan Babu replied, 'but after what happened, none of us are in the mood to watch a performance. I mean, who knew such an awful thing was going to happen? We're all worried and upset. You do understand, don't you?'

'Of course, of course. You're not going back to Calcutta immediately, are you?'

'No, we should be here for another three days.'

'Good. So where are you going now?'

'Nowhere in particular. Is there something we should see? You should be able to tell us!'

'Have you seen the Bat-kali temple? It was built in the seventeenth century. It's full of bats, but the outside walls still have some carvings left. Come with me, I'll show you.'

I did not tell him I had seen the temple this morning. At that moment, of course, I had not had the time to look at wall carvings.

We reached it in three minutes. I began to get goose pimples again. It would have been far better to have come here during the day. There was a banyan tree next to the temple. Its roots had grasped the roof, making it crack and crumble.

'This is where they used to have sacrifices, sir,' Benimadhav said, pointing at a spot near the trunk of the banyan tree.

'S-sacrifice?' Lalmohan Babu asked, his voice hushed.

'Yes, sir. Human sacrifices. Haven't you heard of Nedo *dakaat*, the famous bandit of Gosaipur? He used to worship Kali and hold sacrifices here. Why, you could write a whole book on him! Would you like to go inside? Have you got a torch?'

'In-inside? No, I don't think so. Didn't you say it was full of bats? Besides, we didn't bring a torch.'

'No, the bats will have gone out now, on their evening excursion . . . heh heh. If you wish to see them you'll have to come back—'

'No! We have no wish to see them, thank you.'

'All right. Look, I've lit a match. May I smoke a beedi?'

'Yes, certainly. Smoke as many as you like.'

Benimadhav lit his beedi, then held the match near the broken door. What I saw in its flickering light made my heart skip a beat. Lalmohan Babu had seen it, too.

'J-j-jee-jee-jee—' he stammered.

It was Jeevanlal's dead body. There could be no mistake. His blue shirt and white pyjamas were peeping out from behind a pillar inside the temple. I even caught a glimpse of his left arm. He had been wearing a watch this morning. Now the watch was gone.

'Look, someone left their clothes here!' exclaimed Benimadhav, and began to stride forward to retrieve the clothes, possibly with a view to returning them to their owner.

'D-don't!' Lalmohan Babu pulled him back urgently. 'Th-that's a dead body. We sh-should tell the p-police!'

At these words, the mime artist turned totally mute. Then he showed us just how gifted he was. We saw, in a flash, the expression on his face change from amazement to horror, in one single step; then he turned around and legged it, in absolute silence. We, too, decided not to spend another moment there, and came back home immediately, walking as fast as we could.

Feluda had already returned. He glanced at me briefly and said, 'Why do you look so pale? Get ready quickly. We have to be back in Mr Bhattacharya's house in fifteen minutes.'

Lalmohan Babu, I noticed, had regained his composure on seeing Feluda.

'Felu Babu,' he announced calmly, 'we made an important discovery. Jeevanlal's body is lying inside that old Kali temple. Are you going to tell the police, or will you let them go on looking for it?'

Lalmohan Babu had taken an instant dislike to the inspector. So he seemed all in favour of not doing anything to make it easier for him.

'Did you actually go into the temple?' Feluda asked.

'No; nor did we touch the body. But there can be no doubt about what we saw.'

'OK. I met the inspector just now. He'll probably be coming to Mr Bhattacharya's house. We can tell him when we see him.'

We left in ten minutes. Tulsi Babu said he'd have to go and see Mr Chakladar, just to warn him that the function he was supposed to preside over the next day might well be cancelled.

'You carry on, I'll join you later,' he said.

On our way to Mr Bhattacharya's house, Feluda told us how eager he had seemed to get in touch with Jeevanlal's spirit. He had offered to do this first, even though it meant making three other clients wait outside.

This evening, his room had a table instead of the divan. Five chairs had been arranged around it. On the table was an oil lamp. Mr Bhattacharya was sitting on one of the chairs. On his right was a writing pad and a pencil. Behind the table were two small stools and a bench. Nityanand was seated on the bench.

We took three chairs. The fourth remained empty for Tulsi Babu.

'Should we wait for Tulsicharan?' Mr Bhattacharya asked.

'Let's give him five minutes,' Feluda replied.

'Very well. I knew . . . you'd have to come to me,' Mr Bhattacharya's deep voice boomed out. 'I realized it that day, when I first set my eyes on you. I could tell you would not scoff at this highly specialized branch of science, for that's what it is. Only the ignorant, only those who know nothing about the different ways through which one may arrive at the truth, mock and laugh at my methods. A true believer in science—such as yourself—keeps an open mind. He does not ridicule.'

I began to feel a bit bored with all this talk of science and truth. Why didn't he start?

'You have all met Jeevanlal, and he has only just died,' he went on. 'For these two reasons, I expect today's session to be a success. His soul has not yet had the time to lose all its earthly bonds and escape into the other world. It is still lingering near us, waiting for our call. It knows it cannot refuse our invitation. I know we simply have to say the word, and it will be with us. It is immortal, and it is aware of not just the past and the present, but also the future. It will speak through me, it will reveal the truth on this sheet of paper, just as we . . .'

Feluda interrupted him. I failed to see how he could speak, for my own throat had started to feel parched, and I suspect Lalmohan Babu was feeling the same. There was a hypnotic quality in Mr Bhattacharya's voice that inspired awe.

'Everyone will want to see what you write,' Feluda said, 'but with the exception of myself, everybody is sitting opposite you. Will you mind if I read out what you write?'

'No, not at all. What do you want to ask the spirit?'

'Three things—who burgled the house, who killed Jeevanlal, and when he was killed.'

'Very well. You shall soon have the answers,' said Mr Bhattacharya.

EIGHT

Five minutes passed, but there was no sign of Tulsi Babu. Mr Bhattacharya decided to get to work.

'Please place your hands—palm downward—on the table. Your little fingers should touch those of your neighbour's.'

We placed our hands as instructed. A tapping noise started at once, caused by Lalmohan Babu's trembling fingers. He might have been playing a tabla. I saw him grit his teeth to steady his hands.

Mr Bhattacharya's eyes were closed, but his lips moved. He was reciting a Sanskrit *shloka*. A minute later, he stopped. There was a deathly silence in the room. The lamp flickered. Around its flame three insects hovered. Our shadows, large and trembling, fell on the walls, nearly touching the ceiling. I gave Feluda a sidelong glance. His jaw was set, and he was staring steadily at Mr Bhattacharya with a totally expressionless face. Mr Bhattacharya himself was sitting still as a statue. He had picked up the pencil, which was now poised over the blank sheet of paper.

Then his lips started to tremble. Beads of perspiration broke out on his forehead. Lalmohan Babu began playing the tabla again, perfectly involuntarily. I could see why. The atmosphere in the room was decidedly eerie. My heart beat as fast as Lalmohan Babu's fingers shook.

'Jeevanlal . . . Jeevanlal . . . Jeevanlal!' Mr Bhattacharya called softly. His lips barely moved.

'Are you there? Have you come?'

This time, to our amazement, the questions were spoken by a voice behind us. It was Nityanand. Now I realized what his role was. He spoke on behalf of his uncle. Perhaps Mr Bhattacharya found it impossible to speak at a time like this.

'Yes,' said Feluda. The word had been scribbled on the pad by Mr Bhattacharya. His eyes were still closed. I watched his hands carefully.

'Where are you?' asked Nityanand.

'Here, very close,' wrote Mr Bhattacharya. Feluda read the words out.

'We'd like to ask you a few questions. Can you answer them?'
'Yes.'

'Who stole the money from your father's chest?'
'I did.'

'Did you see your murderer?'
'Yes.'

'Did you recognize him?'
'Yes.'

'Who was it?'
'My father.'

But we didn't get to hear when the murder was committed, for Feluda stood up abruptly and said, 'That'll do.' Then he turned to me and said, 'Topshe, go and get that lantern from the passage outside. I can hardly see anything.' Considerably startled, I got up and fetched the lantern.

Feluda picked up the piece of paper Mr Bhattacharya had scribbled on, ran his eyes over the few words written and said, 'Mr Bhattacharya, your spirit may have left the earth, but it hasn't yet learnt the truth. There are discrepancies in his answers.'

Mr Bhattacharya glared at Feluda, looking as if he wanted to reduce him to a handful of dust, but Feluda remained quite unmoved. 'For instance,' he continued, 'he is being asked who opened the chest and took the money. He says, "I did", meaning Jeevanlal. But that chest was empty, Mr Bhattacharya. There was no money in it.'

As if by magic, the fury faded from Mr Bhattacharya's face. He began to look rather uncertain. Feluda went on, 'I can say this with some confidence because it was not Jeevanlal Mallik who opened that chest, but Pradosh Chander Mitter. Jeevanlal helped me do it by opening the front door for me in the middle of the night and telling me where the key was kept. He also helped me to tie up his father and Bholanath Babu. Anyway, instead of any money, what we found in the chest was this.' He slipped a hand into his pocket and brought out another piece of paper.

'The old Mr Mallik had refused to show it to me. But I needed it urgently as I had serious doubts about Mriganka Bhattacharya's intentions. My suspicions were aroused the minute I met him. He pretended to have guessed my name and profession by some supernatural means. The truth is that Tulsi Babu had already told him who I was and what I did. Am I right, Tulsi Babu?'

I realized with a start that Tulsi Babu had joined us, though I had not seen him arrive. He looked profoundly embarrassed and tried to explain: 'Y-yes, I am afraid . . . you see . . . I wanted you to get a good impression, so I . . .'

Feluda raised a hand to stop him. 'I don't blame you, Tulsi Babu. You don't pretend to be something you are not. But this man does. Anyway, when I realized Mr Bhattacharya was simply putting on an act to impress me, I was determined to get hold of the paper that Shyamlal Mallik wanted no one to see. There were a few doubts in my mind about Shyamlal, too, which I thought this piece of paper would help clarify.'

Mr Bhattacharya was now sweating profusely. Feluda held the paper closer to the lamp and said, 'Durlabh Singh's departed soul was supposed to have answered some questions. The questions were spoken, but it isn't difficult to guess what was asked. The written answers are good indicators. I shall now read out to you all the questions and the answers given. If I get any of it wrong, I hope Mr Bhattacharya will correct me.'

Mr Bhattacharya was breathing so fast that the flame flickered strongly. Feluda began reading, 'The first question was: "Who is my enemy?" Answer: "He is in your house." "Does he want me dead?" "No." "Then what does he want?" "Money." "How can I save my money from him?" "Don't keep it in your chest." "Where should I kept it?" "Bury it under the ground." Where?" "In your garden." "Where in the garden?" "At the far end—under the last mango tree—by the gap in the wall."'

Feluda put the paper back into his pocket. 'The traces of mud on his feet and the mosquito bites on his face had suggested that Shyamlal Mallik had spent some time out in the garden. Now I know why he had done that. He simply followed the instructions Mr Bhattacharya gave him, except that he thought they were given by his dead father. Mr Bhattacharya knew about the money Shyamlal possessed and had been planning to steal it for quite some time. But he knew it was impossible as long as the old and trusted Bholanath remained with his master. At first he tried to poison Shyamlal's mind against Bholanath. Sadly, that did not work. Then, miraculously, Mr Bhattacharya found a new opportunity. Shyamlal himself called him to his house and asked him to contact a spirit. Mr Bhattacharya seized this chance to kill two birds with one stone. He got Shyamlal to believe that someone in his own house had become his enemy, and he managed to get the money removed from the chest and placed at a spot which would be accessible to him. Shyamlal raised no objection to burying his money in the garden, for this was an ancient method of keeping things safe, which was perfectly acceptable to him, as Mr Bhattacharya knew it would be. So he put everything in a separate box and buried it under the last mango tree. Yesterday—

A sudden noise made him stop. Nityanand had suddenly sprung to his feet and leapt out of the door. But he could not get very far. A pair of strong arms caught him neatly and pushed him back into the room. Then their owner stepped in himself. It was Inspector Pramanik.

'We found the box, Mr Mitter,' he said, 'with everything intact. He had hidden it under some clothes in an old trunk. Constable!'

A constable stepped forward and placed a fairly large steel box on the table.

'Why, the lid's been broken!' Feluda exclaimed. Then he lifted it. The box was crammed with bundles of hundred-rupee notes. Never in my life had I seen so much cash.

'But . . . but . . . what about the murder?' Mr Bhattacharya cried desperately. 'I did not kill Jeevanlal!'

'No, I know you didn't,' Feluda spoke scathingly. 'I did. The murder was also my idea. What I did manage to kill and destroy, Mr Bhattacharya, was your greed, your deception and your cunning. Your career in fraud is over, for everyone in this village will soon learn what you achieved today. Tell me, have you ever heard of anyone speaking to the soul of the living? Come in, Jeevan Babu!'

As a collective gasp went up, Jeevanlal entered the room through the front door. A piercing scream tore through Mr Bhattacharya's lips, and he scrambled to his feet. The constable quickly put handcuffs on him.

Inspector Pramanik had only one complaint to make. 'Why did you make us dredge two lakes, Mr Mitter? We wasted such a lot of time!'

'No, no, please don't say that. It was necessary to pretend that Jeevanlal had really been killed, and that we were looking for his body. How else could we have exposed Bhattacharya so completely?'

It turned out that Feluda had planned the whole thing to the last detail. When he and I left the 'body' and Bholanath and Lalmohan Babu went back to the house, Jeevanlal had got up and slipped into an old store room in the house. His grandmother had seen him, but Feluda had managed to cover it up quickly. In the evening, he had stolen out to make his way to Mr Bhattacharya's house, so that he could hide among the bushes and come out at the right time; but, rather unfortunately, we were walking through the bamboo grove at the same time, which made him dive into the old temple and pretend to be a corpse once again.

After dinner that night, Tulsi Babu came up to Feluda and said a little ruefully, 'Are you cross with me, Mr Mitter?'

'Cross? Of course not. If anything, Tulsi Babu, I am most grateful to you. If you hadn't told that man my name, he wouldn't have dared to make up a puzzle about my initials, and I would have had no reason to wonder if his powers were genuine. You helped me a great deal.'

Jeevanlal Mallik turned up a few minutes later. 'My father is speaking to me again!' he said, beaming.

'What did he say?'

'When I went and touched his feet this evening, he spoke to me with an affection he hasn't shown for years. He even asked me how our business was doing, and seemed really interested. I could scarcely believe it!'

Lalmohan Babu was busy dealing with the head of a fish. Now he finished chewing and opened his mouth.

'Then . . . er . . . tomorrow? . . .' he asked tentatively, looking at Tulsi Babu.

'Oh yes. It's definitely going ahead. Everything's ready.'

'Very good. My speech is ready, too. Felu Babu, will you please cast an eye over it?'

The Secret of the Cemetery

ONE

Three days after Pulak Ghoshal's film completed twenty-five weeks in the Paradise cinema in Calcutta, a second-hand Mark 2 Ambassador drove up to our front door, blowing its horn and making a terrible racket. It was no ordinary horn. What it played, very loudly, was an entire set of musical notes.

Pulak Ghoshal was a film director in Bombay, and his film running at the Paradise was based on a story written by Lalmohan Babu. We knew Lalmohan Babu was thinking of buying a car to mark the occasion, but did not realize that it would happen so soon. Actually, he had done more than buy a car. He had also appointed a driver as he could not drive himself. He had no wish to learn to drive, either. In fact, he made that comment repeatedly, so much so that one day, Feluda was obliged to ask him, 'Why not?' Lalmohan Babu had then offered an explanation. Apparently, five years ago, he had started taking lessons, using a friend's car. After only two days, he had got into the car with a wonderful plot in his head. But, as he was switching to the second gear from the first, the car had given such an awful jerk that the plot for a new novel had flown straight out of his head, never to return.

'I still regret its loss, I tell you!' Lalmohan Babu sighed.

His driver—clad in a white shirt and khaki trousers—got out and opened the door for Lalmohan Babu, who tried to hop out onto the pavement, caught his feet in the trailing end of his dhoti and nearly lost his balance, but the smile on his face remained in place. Feluda, however, was looking serious. He opened his mouth only when all three of us were seated inside.

'Until you change that horrible horn to something more simple and civilized, your car cannot be allowed to enter our Rajani Sen Road,' Feluda told him.

Lalmohan Babu looked a bit rueful. 'Yes, I knew I was taking a risk. But when the fellow in the shop gave a demo . . . well, it was just too tempting. It's Japanese, you know.'

'It's ear-splitting and nerve-racking,' Feluda declared. 'I had no idea Hindi films would influence you so quickly. And the colour of your car is equally painful. Reminds me of south Indian films!'

'Please, Mr Mitter!' Lalmohan Babu pleaded, folding his hands, 'I will change that horn tomorrow, but allow me to keep the colour. I find that green most soothing.'

Feluda gave up and was about to order some tea, when Lalmohan Babu interrupted him. 'We can have tea later. Let's first go for a drive. I won't feel satisfied until I've given you and Master Tapesh a ride in my car. Where would you like to go?'

Feluda raised no objection. He thought for a moment and said, 'I would like Topshe to see Charnock's grave.'

'Charnock? Job Charnock?' asked Lalmohan Babu, pronouncing the first name as 'job'.

'No,' Feluda replied.

'No? Are there other Charnocks?'

'Yes, I'm sure there are, but only one Charnock founded the city of Calcutta.'

'Yes. That's who I . . . I mean . . .'

'His name was Job—pronounced Jobe. A job is work for which you are paid. Jobe is a man's name. Most people mispronounce the name. You should know better.'

Feluda's latest passion was old Calcutta. It started with a visit to Fancy Lane, where he had to go to investigate a murder. When he learnt that the word 'fancy' had come from the Indian word 'phansi', meaning death by hanging, and that two hundred years ago, Nanda Kumar had been hung in the same area, Feluda became deeply interested in the history of Calcutta. In the last three months, he had read endless books on the subject, looked at scores of pictures and studied dozens of maps. As a result, even I had gained some knowledge, chiefly by spending two afternoons at the Victoria Memorial.

According to Feluda, although Calcutta was a 'young' city compared to Delhi and Agra, its importance could not be undermined. It was true that Calcutta did not have a Taj Mahal, or a Qutab Minar, or the kind of forts one might see in Jodhpur and Jaisalmer, or even a famous alley like Vishwanath ki gali in Benaras.

'But just think, Topshe,' Feluda had said to me, 'one day, an Englishman was sitting by the Ganges in a place that was really a jungle, packed with flies, mosquitoes and snakes, and this man thought he'd build a city in the same place. And then, in no time, the jungle was cleared, buildings were built, roads were made, rows of gas lights appeared, horses galloped down those roads, palkis ran, and in a hundred years, the new place came to be known as the city of palaces. What that same city has now been reduced to does not matter. I am talking simply of history. Now, some people want to change the street signs, rename them and wipe out history. But is that right? Or, for that matter, is it possible? All right, admittedly, what the British did was purely for their own convenience. But if they hadn't, what would your Felu Mitter have done today? Try to picture the scene . . . your Feluda, Pradosh Chandra Mitter, private investigator . . . bent over a ledger, pushing a pen and working as a clerk in some zamindar's office, where the term "fingerprint" would simply mean a man's thumb impression on a document!'

We went to BBD Bagh, which was known as Dalhousie Square at one time, named after the same Lord Dalhousie who was once the Governor-General of India, well known for annexing Indian states and introducing the railways and the telegraph. Job Charnock's tomb—said to be the first brick structure built in Calcutta—was in the compound of the two-hundred-year-old St John's Church in BBD Bagh. Lalmohan Babu saw it and said, 'Thrilling!' But that might have been partly because of the dark, ominous clouds in the sky and the rumble of thunder. He stared at a marble plaque on the tomb and said, 'Look, it's not even "Job", it says "Jobus". Why is that?'

'Jobus is the Latin version of Job,' Feluda explained, 'can't you see whatever's inscribed on that plaque is in Latin?'

'No, sir. All I can see is that it's not English and it makes no sense to me. Why does it say D-O-M above his name?'

'It stands for Dominus Omnium Magister. It means God is the master of all things. Look at the words beneath. May I draw your attention to one in particular? Marmore. You know the Bengali word marmar, don't you? That and this "marmore" mean the same thing—marble. What is more interesting is that the word marmar hasn't come from Sanskrit. It is a Persian word. However, if you say marmar-saudh—meaning a marble column—that's really funny because "saudh" is a Sanskrit word. So we mix Persian and Sanskrit words quite happily in our own language without even realizing it. Take, for instance—'

Feluda could not complete his lecture for, even as he was speaking, a fierce dust storm started without the slightest warning. (Lalmohan Babu called it 'apocalyptic'.) I had never seen anything like it before. All of us ran blindly towards Lalmohan Babu's green Ambassador and scrambled into it. The driver, Hari, started it instantly and began speeding towards the Esplanade. For the first time, I saw Shaheed Minar totally obliterated by a sheet of dust. I couldn't guess the wind speed because all the windows were firmly shut. But I did see a long, thin wicker stand—the kind that chanachur-walas use—come spinning in the air from the direction of the maidan, strike against the top deck of a double-decker bus in front of us, and fly away the next instant towards Curzon Park.

As we approached Park Street, we realized that the trams weren't running because a tree had fallen across the tramline. Feluda had wanted to show us the old cemetery in Park Street, but the storm made him drop the idea. If we had gone, we might have witnessed a particular event which was reported in the press the following morning. During this catastrophic storm on 24 June (wind velocity 145 kilometres per hour), a tree was uprooted in the South Park Street cemetery. It seriously injured a middle-aged man called Narendra Nath Biswas. What was not explained in the press report was what Mr Biswas was doing in that ancient cemetery, so late in the evening.

TWO

The following morning was wet. It stopped raining only in the middle of the afternoon. Feluda had managed to get hold of an old map of Calcutta and Howrah, going back to 1932. After a meal of khichuri and omelettes, he stuffed a paan into his mouth, lit a Charminar, and unfolded the map. In order to look at it properly in our living room. we had to push all the furniture out of the way, and create enough space on the floor to fit the map. It measured 6'x6'.

Lalmohan Babu turned up as we were crawling all over it, inspecting old roads and streets, and Feluda was saying, 'Don't try looking for Rajani Sen Road. This whole area was a veritable jungle in those days!' I noticed that Lalmohan Babu was smartly dressed in dark blue trousers and a yellow bush shirt. 'Seventy-six trees came down yesterday during the storm,' he announced. 'And I've done what you told me to do. My car has a new horn which will not remind you of Hindi films, I assure you.'

We were not in a hurry to go out, so we waited until we'd had some tea. Then we set off in Lalmohan Babu's car and I could see for myself the devastation caused by the storm. I had seen the press report that mentioned the number of uprooted trees, but had been unable to believe it. Now I counted nineteen trees—in some places, a number of branches—lying on the ground by the time we reached Park Street. Three of them were in Southern Avenue alone. It was staggering, although many of the fallen branches had been cleared away.

As we reached the entrance to the Park Street cemetery (Feluda told us where we were going only when we reached Camac Street), I happened to glance at Lalmohan Babu. He appeared a bit subdued. Feluda looked enquiringly at him. 'In 1941,' Lalmohan Babu explained, 'I was in Ranchi. There I saw an Englishman being buried. When the coffin was lowered into the grave, and they threw clods of earth . . . ugh, the sound they made was terrible!'

'You won't have to hear that sound here,' Feluda assured him. 'There is no chance. In the last one hundred and twenty-five years, no one has been buried in this cemetery.'

The chowkidar's room was to the right of the entrance. Anyone was free to enter the cemetery during the day, so presumably the chowkidar had little to do. 'The only thing he must ensure,' Feluda said, 'is that no one makes off with a marble plaque. Genuine Italian marble would fetch a good price. Chowkidar!'

The man came out of his room. His appearance told us instantly that he hailed from Bihar. He was chewing tobacco; perhaps he had just put it in his mouth.

'Was a Bengali Babu injured here yesterday? Hit by a falling tree?'

'Yes, sir.'

'Can we see that spot?'

'Go down that path . . . right up to the end. Then if you turn left, you'll see it. The tree is still lying there.'

We went down the paved path he indicated—overgrown with grass—and walked through rows of tombs. They were all twelve or fourteen feet high. At some distance, to our right, was a tomb as high as a three-storeyed house. Feluda said it was probably the tomb of the scholar, William Jones. It was the tallest tomb in Calcutta.

Each tomb had either a white or a black marble plaque, with the dead person's date of birth, the date on which he died and some other facts. Some large plaques had brief details of the person's entire life. Most tombstones rose like columns. Their bases were broad, but they tapered off as they rose higher. 'These are spooks in burkhas!' proclaimed Lalmohan Babu. He was right in a way, except that these spooks were quite immobile. They were more like spooky guards, protecting the being that was buried underground, encased in a coffin.

'Do you know what these columns are called in English? Each is an obelisk,' Feluda told me. Lalmohan Babu repeated the word to himself about five times. I was darting quick looks at the plaques as I passed them by, reading aloud the names written on them: Jackson,

Watts, Wells, Larkin, Gibbons, Oldham . . .! Some tombs bore the same family name—obviously the people were all related to one another. The earliest date I had noticed so far was 28 July 1779, twelve years before the French Revolution.

When we reached the far end of the path, I realized how large the cemetery was. The sound of traffic going down Park Street had become quite faint. Feluda told me later that there were more than two thousand graves in that cemetery. Lalmohan Babu pointed at a block of apartments on Lower Circular Road, close to the cemetery, and declared that he would never live there, even if someone paid him a hundred thousand rupees to do so.

The uprooted 'tree' turned out to be a large, leafy branch from a huge mango tree. It had crashed to the ground, destroying a large part of a tomb in the process. Several smaller branches were also strewn about.

We walked towards the damaged tomb.

The column rising from it was shorter than the others, barely reaching Lalmohan Babu's shoulders. It was obvious that even before it was hit by the tree, it had been in a state of disrepair. The portion that had escaped being struck by the falling branch was cracked in several places. The plaster had worn off to expose the bricks within. The branch had also broken certain portions of the marble plaque. The broken pieces were scattered on the grass. The recent rains had turned the whole area wet and muddy, but the slush near this particular grave seemed worse than elsewhere in the cemetery. 'That's remarkable!' exclaimed Lalmohan Babu. 'The word "God" is still there on the plaque—I mean the portion that's still intact. Look!'

'Yes, and you can see the year under that line, can't you?' Feluda said.

'Oh yes. 185—the last digit is broken. That "God" must be to do with the master of all things.'

'You think so?' Feluda's question made me glance at him. He was frowning. 'You haven't looked carefully at the other plaques. Look at the next one.'

There was a large plaque on the next tomb. It said:

To the memory of
Capt P. O'Reilly, H. M. 44th Regt.
who died 25th May, 1823 aged 38 years

'The date appears just below the name, see? Most of the plaques follow the same pattern. Besides, did you see the word "God" on any other plaque?'

Feluda was right. I had already read the inscription on at least thirty different plaques, but not one mentioned God.

'You mean to say "God" was the dead man's name?' Lalmohan Babu wanted to know.

'No, I don't think anyone is ever called "God", although some Hindus may be called Ishwar or Bhagwan. Look at the plaque more closely. There is a sizeable gap to the left of the "G". That can only mean that there was no word or letter on that side. But there's no way of telling what followed the "d" because that portion is now lying on the grass. I think the first three letters of the dead man's surname were g, o and d, as in Godfrey or Goddard.'

'In that case, why don't we gather those pieces and arrange . . . '

Lalmohan Babu had started walking over to the broken branches and leaves that were lying on the ground. Just as he reached the tomb, he suddenly slipped and slid forward, as if he had stepped into a hole. Before he could fall, however, Feluda stretched out his long arms, caught him and put him back on solid ground. I was puzzled. How could there be a hole in that area? 'It does seem strange,' Feluda commented. 'I mean, what came down in the storm was a branch from a mango tree, right? So what are these other leaves doing here? They're not all mango leaves!'

Lalmohan Babu was already feeling a bit unhappy about being in a cemetery. And now this! He dusted himself down, muttered 'This is too much!' and stood with his back to us, possibly to regain his composure.

'Topshe, help me remove these leaves and smaller branches. Be careful!' said Feluda.

We cleared the area, taking great care to avoid the gaping hole in the ground. It became clear at once that, by the side of the grave, there was a ditch about two feet deep. Feluda might have guessed the truth, but I certainly could not figure out whether the ditch had always been there, or whether someone had dug it recently.

Feluda now turned his attention to the marble pieces lying on the ground. We collected twelve pieces and put them together, exactly as if we were assembling a jigsaw puzzle on the grass. The final picture looked like this:

Sacred to the memory of
THOMAS—WIN
Obt. 24th April—8, AET. 70—

'Godwin!' cried Feluda. 'The man was called Godwin. "Obt" is "obitus", meaning death. "AET" is "aetatis", meaning age. Now, the question is . . .'

'I say!'

A sudden shout from Lalmohan Babu startled me. As we turned towards him, he held up a dark, flat and square object. 'Do you think thirty-seven rupees will pay for dinner for three at the Blue Fox?'

'What have you found?'

Feluda and I went forward to join him, feeling intrigued.

In his left hand, Lalmohan Babu was clutching a black wallet. In his right hand were three ten, one five and a two-rupee note. The wallet and the money were both sodden. Lalmohan Babu had overcome his fear and now appeared quite cheerful. He knew he had found an important clue for Feluda.

Feluda took the wallet from him and took out everything from its various compartments. Four different things emerged:

(1) a bunch of visiting cards. The name 'N.M. Biswas' was printed on each, but there was no address or telephone number. 'That press report got it wrong. It showed his name as Narendra Nath! But it must be Narendra Mohan,' Feluda remarked.

(2) Two cuttings from old newspapers. The first mentioned that a cemetery had been built in Park Street; and the other reported the construction of the Ochterlony Monument—which was now called Shaheed Minar.

That meant that both cuttings were one hundred and fifty, or two hundred years old. 'How did Mr Biswas acquire such ancient reports? I am deeply curious,' Feluda observed.

(3) A cash-memo from the Oxford Book Company in Park Street, showing a transaction for Rs 12.50.

(4) A piece of plain white paper. Someone had scribbled a few lines on it with a ball-point pen. The words made no sense to me. The only thing I recognized was the name Victoria.

'I read an article on the Monument only the other day!' Lalmohan Babu exclaimed. 'As far as I can recall, the writer was called Biswas. Yes, that's right. Biswas!'

'Where did you find the article?'

'In a journal, either Lekhani or Vichitrapatra. I'll check when I get home.'

Lalmohan Babu's memory was not very reliable, so Feluda did not pursue the matter. He copied the words down in his own notebook, replaced the piece of paper in the wallet together with everything else, and put it in his pocket. He then spent five minutes searching the ground thoroughly around the damaged tomb. Two things that he found were also transferred to his pocket. One of them was a brown jacket button, and the other was a damp form-book, usually seen in the hands of people who go to horse races.

'Let's speak to the chowkidar, and then we must go home. It's getting cloudy again,' Feluda said.

'Will you return the wallet?' Lalmohan Babu asked.

'Of course. I must find out which hospital he was taken to. Then I'll visit him, possibly tomorrow.'

'And suppose the fellow is dead?'

'We can hardly make that assumption and grab his property. That would be unethical. Besides, all you can hope to buy in the Blue Fox with thirty-seven rupees is tea and sandwiches. So stop dreaming about dinner.'

We made an about turn and began walking back to the entrance, through rows of tombs. Feluda was quiet. He had lit a Charminar. Although he had cut down on smoking of late, if he smelt a mystery anywhere, almost unconsciously, he put a cigarette in his mouth.

We were halfway down the path, when Feluda stopped suddenly. I could not immediately see why. So I followed his gaze, and saw something that almost made me miss a heartbeat. I, too, stopped in my tracks.

In front of a tomb with a dome—the dead person's name on the plaque read 'Miss Margaret Templeton'—lying on the grass, on top of an old brick, was a cigarette, still burning. Only a quarter of it had been smoked. A thin ribbon of smoke was rising from it. There was no breeze—possibly because rain was imminent. That was why the smoke was visible.

Feluda picked up the cigarette and said, 'Gold Flake.' Lalmohan Babu said, 'Let's go home.' I said, 'Should I go and see if the fellow's still here?'

'If the fellow had any intention of remaining here, he would have waited with the cigarette in his hand; or he would have dropped it on the grass and stubbed it out with his foot. He would not have left it like this. No, he has clearly run away, and he was in a hurry to remove himself.'

We then proceeded on our way and found the chowkidar's room. But it was empty. A few minutes later, he emerged from behind a bush, walked slowly back to his room, and said, 'I've just got rid of a rat!'

So he had gone behind the bush to arrange a rat's funeral! Feluda went straight to business.

'Who was the first to find the injured man? I mean the one who was hit by that tree?' he asked.

The chowkidar admitted to being the first to find the man. He was not actually in the cemetery when the tree crashed. He had gone to Park Street to rescue one of his own shirts which had been blown away in that direction. He had found the injured man on his return. He knew the man by sight, as he had visited the cemetery a few times in the recent past.

'Did anyone else come here yesterday?'

'I don't know, Babu. When I went running to get my shirt, there was no one here.'

'But it's possible to hide behind these tombs, isn't it?'

The chowkidar acknowledged the possibility. I, too, was thinking what a wonderful place it would be to play hide-and-seek. Perhaps the best possible place in the entire city!

When he found Naren Biswas, the chowkidar had gone out into the street and spoken to a passing 'sahib'. From his description, it sounded as if he had found a priest from St Xavier's. It was this sahib who had called a taxi and arranged to send Mr Biswas to the hospital.

'Did you see anyone come in today? A little while ago?'

'A little while ago?'

'Yes.'

No, he had seen no one, for he was nowhere near the gate. He was behind that bush, performing the last rites for the dead rat. When the rat was disposed of, even then he could not return to his room immediately for he had to deal with a call of nature.

'Are you here at night?'

'Yes, Babu. But there is no need to guard this place at night because people are too scared to come here. At one time, the wall near Lower Circular Road was broken; but now, no, no one dares to come into the cemetery at night.'

'What's your name?'

'Baramdeo.'

'I see. Here you are!'

'Salaam, Babu!'

Feluda had thrust a two-rupee note into the chowkidar's hand. This simple act was to bear fruit in the course of time.

THREE

'Godwin . . .? Thomas Godwin?'

Six creases appeared on Uncle Sidhu's forehead.

I call Uncle Sidhu Mr Encyclopaedia. Feluda calls him Mr Photographic Memory. Both descriptions fit him very well. He does not forget anything that he reads, sees, or even hears—if he finds it sufficiently interesting. Feluda is obliged to consult him from time to time. That was what he was doing today.

Every morning, at dawn, Uncle Sidhu goes to the Lake for a walk. He walks for a couple of miles, and then returns home by half past six. He never misses his walk, even on days when it rains. All he does is grab an umbrella as he steps out. On his return, he sits on his divan, and remains seated there all day. He leaves that spot only to have his bath and eat his meals. Then he's back again. In front of him stands a desk, piled high with books, journals and newspapers. Uncle Sidhu never writes anything. Not letters, not his accounts, not even a list of his clothes when his dhobi takes them away to be washed. All he does is read. He doesn't have a telephone. If he needs to contact us, he sends a message through his servant, Janardan. We get his message in ten minutes.

Uncle Sidhu never married. Instead of a wife, he lives with his books. 'My wife, my child, my mother, father, brother, sister, doctor, master . . . everything in life that you can think of is here, amongst my books. Books are my family, my friends!' he claims. It is he who is partly responsible for Feluda's interest in old Calcutta. But Uncle Sidhu knows the history of the entire world, not just this city.

He sipped black tea and repeated the name 'Godwin' to himself. Then he said, 'Any mention of that name is likely to remind one of Shelley's father-in-law. But I can think of a Godwin who came to India. When did your Godwin die?'

'1858.'

'And when was he born?'

'1788.'

'Yes, it might well be the Godwin I'm thinking of. In 1858—or maybe it was 1859—an article appeared in the Calcutta Review. Thomas Godwin's daughter wrote it. Her name was Shirley. No . . . no, it was Charlotte. Yes, that's right. Charlotte Godwin. She'd written about her father. Yes, it's all coming back to me now . . . my word, it's an extraordinary story, my dear Felu! What Charlotte didn't mention was what happened to him in his old age, so I know nothing about that. But what he did when he first arrived in India . . . it would sound like a novel. You've been to Lucknow, haven't you?'

Feluda nodded. It was in Lucknow that he had solved the mystery of a stolen ring which had once belonged to Emperor Aurangzeb. That was the case that established him as a brilliant detective.

'So you know about Sadat Ali?' Uncle Sidhu went on.

'Yes.'

'At the time, Sadat Ali was the Nawab of Lucknow. The Sultanate in Delhi was all but over. It was Lucknow that could offer the glamour of courtly life. Sadat had been in Calcutta in his youth. He had known some Englishmen, learned something of their language, and adopted their ways in full measure. When Asaf-ud-Daula died, Wazir Ali became the Nawab of Lucknow. Sadat was then in Benaras, feeling morose. He had hoped to get the throne in Lucknow after Asaf. Wazir Ali, as it happened, was perfectly useless. The British couldn't stand him. In just four months, they put an end to his rule. Don't forget that at that time, the East India Company had a lot of influence in Lucknow. Every Nawab had to kowtow to them. So when they got rid of Wazir, they brought Sadat in and made him the new Nawab. Sadat was so pleased with the British that he gave them half of Awadh.

'The lanes of Lucknow crawled with British and other European men. The Nawab had English and Dutch officers in his army. Then there were European merchants, European doctors, painters, barbers, even schoolteachers. But there were some who had not come to do a specific job. Their only aim was to make money. They tried to impress the Nawab, and fleece him anyhow. In that category of men fell Thomas Godwin. He was a young man from England—his home was in Sussex, or Suffolk . . . or was it Surrey? I can't remember. Anyway, he heard about the Nawab's wealth and arrived in Lucknow. He was good-looking and well spoken. It did not take him long to please the British Resident, Mr Cherry. Cherry gave him a letter of introduction, and Godwin turned up in Sadat Ali's court. Sadat asked him what his speciality was. Thomas had heard that the Nawab was fond of European food, and Thomas was a good cook. So he said he was a master chef, he'd like to prepare a meal for the Nawab. 'Go ahead!' said Sadat. Thomas produced such an excellent meal that Sadat Ali immediately appointed him as a cook in the royal kitchen. Everywhere that the Nawab went, his entourage included a Muslim cook and Thomas Godwin.

'When the Governor-General came to Lucknow, Sadat would invite him to breakfast, knowing that he would benefit if the Governor-General was pleased with him. The only person he could depend on was Godwin. And if Thomas could please the Nawab with a new dish, he would be duly rewarded. Not just a couple of mohurs, mind you, we are talking here of a Nawab of Lucknow. His generosity matched his status. So you can imagine the kind of money Thomas Godwin made. If the money wasn't good, he would not have worked in a kitchen. He simply wasn't that kind of a man.

'Eventually, he left Lucknow and stepped out of the Nawab's domain. He came to Calcutta, and married a woman called Jane Maddock. She was the daughter of an army captain. Within three months, Godwin started his own restaurant—in the heart of Chowringhee, no less. He was still doing very well. But then the inevitable followed. After all, good times don't last for ever, do they?

'Godwin had developed a passion for gambling. When he was in Lucknow, he often put his money on cockfights, or even fights between partridges. He made a lot of money—but he lost as much. Now, in Calcutta, the same passion returned . . . His daughter did not say much more in her article. As far as I can remember, it was published only a few months after he died. So, obviously, Charlotte Godwin could not write at length about her own father's weaknesses, particularly at that age and time. Anyway, if you want to read that article, you will find it in the Asiatic Society. It will naturally give you many more details.'

Feluda and I both remained silent for a few moments after hearing such a fascinating story. It was Uncle Sidhu who broke the silence.

'But why this sudden interest in Thomas Godwin?' he asked.

'I shall soon explain,' Feluda replied. 'Before that, I need to know something else. Have you heard of a Narendra Biswas, who writes on old Calcutta?'

'Where does he write?'

'I don't know.'

'If he writes for some little known magazine, I don't think I'll have seen his articles. I've virtually stopped reading magazines—I mean, other than all my usual stuff. But why do you ask?'

Feluda quickly described the previous day's events. 'What I want to know,' he said, 'is why a man's wallet should be found at least twenty feet away, if that man is hit by a falling tree which makes him drop to the ground.'

'Hmm.'

Uncle Sidhu remained thoughtful for a few seconds. Then he said, 'Yesterday, the wind speed was ninety miles per hour. If that wallet was in the breast pocket of his shirt, it could well have dropped out of it when the man began running. The wind may have carried it further. That tree may have fallen on him even as he was running. Where's the mystery in that?'

'The man fell right next to Godwin's grave.'

'So what?'

'There was a hole near the grave, as if someone had started digging the ground.'

This time, Uncle Sidhu's eyes grew round. 'What! Grave-digging? That's grave news indeed. In fact, it's incredible. I've heard of new corpses being dug up and sold to medical colleges. That may bring in a certain amount of money. But what would anyone do with a two-hundred-year-old corpse? They'd only find a few bones. It would have neither archaeological significance nor any resale value! Are you sure this place had been recently dug up?'

'No, not entirely sure. The rain had wiped out any marks a spade would have left, but even so . . .'

Uncle Sidhu fell silent again. However, in the end, he shook his head and said, 'No, Felu, my boy. I think you're off on a wild goose chase. Haven't you got a real case to work on at the moment? Is that why you're trying to make one up, eh?'

Feluda gave his famous lopsided smile, but said nothing. Uncle Sidhu went on, 'If there was someone left here from the Godwin family, they might have been able to shed some light. But I don't suppose you'll find anyone. After all, not all English families were like the Barwells or the Tytlers, whose descendants remained in India until quite recently—right from the time of Clive!'

It was at this point that Feluda played his trump card.

'Thomas Godwin's family remained here for three generations after his death. I know that for a fact.'

'Really?' Uncle Sidhu sounded amazed. The truth was that, before going to Uncle Sidhu's house, we had spent an hour and a half that morning in another cemetery in Lower Circular Road. It had been built later than the one in Park Street, and was still in use.

'We saw Charlotte Godwin's grave,' Feluda said. 'She died in 1886, at the age of sixty-seven.'

'Was her surname shown as Godwin? That means she remained unmarried. Ah, she was a good writer!'

'Next to Charlotte was her brother, David's tomb. He died in 1874.' Feluda took out his notebook and began rattling out a list, 'He was the head assistant in Kidd & Co. in Kidderpore. Next to him lies his son, Lt. Col. Andrew Godwin, together with his wife, Emma. Andrew died in 1882. Their son, Charles, is buried beside them. He was a doctor, and he died in 1920.'

'Well done! Full marks for your meticulous research and perseverance.' Uncle Sidhu sounded really pleased. 'Now you must find out if anyone from their family is alive and living in Calcutta. Did you find the name Godwin in the telephone directory?'

'Just one. I rang the number. That Godwin has nothing to do with Thomas.'

'You might need to look a bit further. Who knows, there might be a link? Mind you, I have no idea how you'd ever be able to find it. But if you do, we might learn something more about this colourful character called Thomas Godwin. All this talk of grave-digging trikes me as pure nonsense. Anyway, good luck!'

FOUR

When we returned home, I waited patiently until the afternoon; after that, my patience ran out and I couldn't help asking Feluda, 'There was a piece of paper in Naren Biswas's wallet. What was written on it?'

Feluda had made some enquiries and learned that Mr Biswas had been admitted to Park Hospital. He had decided to go there in the evening and return Mr Biswas's belongings to him.

My question made Feluda open his own notebook and offer it to me. 'If you can make any sense of this, you're bound to win the Nobel Prize!'

I found the following words written on the ruled page of his notebook:

B/S 141 SNB for WG Victoria & P.C. (44?)

Re Victoria's letters try MN, OU, GAA, SJ, WN

To myself, I said silently, 'I've just missed the Nobel Prize!' Aloud, I said, 'It seems the man is interested in Queen Victoria, but I can't figure out what "Victoria & P.C." might mean.'

'P.C. might stand for Prince Consort. That would be Prince Albert.'

'Oh. But I can't understand anything else.'

'No? Surely you know the meaning of the words "for" and "try"?'

It was obvious from Feluda's mood that he hadn't had much luck with the words, either. To be honest, what Uncle Sidhu had said made sense. Perhaps Feluda was trying to find a mystery when there wasn't one. But, as soon as I thought that, I remembered the half-finished cigarette, and suddenly there was a sinking feeling in my stomach. Who had run away from the graveyard on seeing us? What was he doing there, anyway, on a wet and windy evening?

It had been agreed that Lalmohan Babu would collect us and take us to Park Hospital at four o'clock. He turned up on time, clutching a magazine. 'What did I tell you, sir? Look, here's a copy of Vichitrapatra, and here's that article by Naren Biswas. There's a picture of the Monument, but it's printed rather badly.'

'But . . . look, the writer is called Narendra Nath Biswas, not Narendra Mohan. Is it a different man?'

'No,' said Feluda, 'I think the problem is with those visiting cards. Maybe he had them printed at some small, inefficient press that printed "N.M. Biswas" instead of "N.N". I bet he didn't check the proof. We found those cuttings in his wallet, and now there's an article by Naren Biswas . . . surely it can't be dismissed as a coincidence?'

Feluda skimmed the article quickly, then dropped the magazine on a side table. 'His language isn't bad, but what he's said is nothing new. What we must find out is whether the writer is the same Naren Biswas as the one who was injured by that tree.'

Baba happened to know one of the doctors—Dr Shikdar—at Park Hospital. He had visited our house a couple of times, so he knew Feluda. Only five minutes after Feluda sent his card in, we were summoned into Dr Shikdar's office.

'What brings you here? A new case?'

People who know Feluda always ask him that question if he turns up anywhere unexpectedly, even if the reason for his visit has nothing to do with a case.

Feluda smiled. 'I'm here to return something to one of your patients.'

'Who?'

'Mr Biswas. Naren Biswas. The day before yesterday . . .'

'But he's left. Only a couple of hours ago. His brother came in his car to collect him. They've gone.'

'Really? But the papers said . . .'

'What did they say? That he was seriously wounded? Press reporters often exaggerate. If a whole tree fell on someone, naturally he wouldn't survive. What hit Mr Biswas was a relatively small branch. He needed treatment more for shock than actual physical injury. His right wrist was injured, and he needed a few stitches in his head, that's all.'

'Could you tell me something? Was it the same Naren Biswas who writes on old Calcutta?'

'Yes, the very same. Obviously, I was curious to know why he was in the cemetery, in the first place. So he said he was doing some research on old Calcutta. I told him he had found a good subject. The more one stays away from today's Calcutta, the better.'

'Did his injuries seem normal to you?'

'Ah. Now you're talking! That was a question worthy of a detective.'

Feluda failed to hide his embarrassment. 'No, I mean . . . did he say himself that a tree fell and . . .?'

'Look, a large part of a tree did come crashing down, didn't it? Surely there's no doubt about that? And the fellow was in the vicinity. Is there any reason to question that?'

'Did he think there was anything suspicious?'

'No, of course not. He said he actually saw and heard the tree cracking and coming down . . . naturally, it was not possible to guess exactly how far its branches were spread. But . . . yes, when he regained consciousness, he uttered the word "will" two or three times. I don't know if there's anything mysterious in that. I wouldn't have thought so, as that was the only time he mentioned a will. He said nothing about it afterwards.'

'Do you happen to know his full name?'

'Didn't that newspaper report mention it? Narendra Nath Biswas.'

'I have another question—please forgive me, I am taking up a lot of your time—do you remember what clothes he was wearing?'

'Certainly. A shirt and trousers. I even remember what colour they were—the shirt was white and the trousers were biscuit coloured.

Not Glaxo biscuits, mind you, but cream crackers . . . ha ha ha!'

After that, Feluda took Mr Biswas's address from Dr Shikdar and we left the hospital. Mr Biswas lived in New Alipore. We went there straightaway. Usually, it is not easy to find a house in New Alipore unless one knows its exact location, but it turned out that Lalmohan Babu's driver knew the streets of Calcutta very well. We did not have to spend more than three minutes looking for Mr Biswas's house.

The building had two storeys. It must have been built about twenty years ago. Outside the front gate, a black Ambassador was parked. The nameplate bore two names: N. Biswas and G. Biswas. We rang the bell. A servant opened the door.

'Is Naren Biswas at home?'

'He is unwell.'

'Isn't he up to receiving visitors at all? I need to see him. There's a little

'Who are you looking for?'

Someone standing behind the servant had asked the question. A man in his mid-forties stepped forward. He was clean shaven, his eyes were hazel. He was wearing a bush shirt over pyjamas, and a cotton shawl was wrapped around his shoulders.

'I'd like to return something that belongs to Mr Naren Biswas. It's his wallet. He dropped it in the Park Street cemetery.'

'Oh, I see. I am his brother. Please come in. Dada is in bed. He's still covered in bandages. He can talk, but an accident like that . . . I mean, it's a big shock, after all. . .!'

There was a bedroom behind the staircase going up to the first floor. Mr Biswas was in that room, lying in his bed. He appeared darker than his brother and sported a thick moustache. His head was covered by a bandage, but one didn't have to be told that, underneath the bandage, his head was quite bald.

He lowered the newspaper he was holding in his left hand, and bowed his head in greeting. A bandage was wrapped around his right wrist, so perhaps it was difficult for him to raise both hands in a proper namaskar. His brother left the room. I heard him call out to the servant and ask him to bring two more chairs. Naren Biswas's room had only one chair, placed in front of a desk, not far from the bed.

Feluda took out Mr Biswas's wallet and handed it to him.

'Oh. Thank you. Thank you very much. You went to so much trouble . . .!' he said.

'No, it was no trouble, I assure you,' Feluda said most politely. 'We just happened to be there, and this friend of mine found it, so . . .'

Mr Biswas opened the wallet with his left hand and briefly glanced into its compartments. Then he looked enquiringly at Feluda. 'Happened to be . . . in the cemetery?'

Feluda laughed. 'I was going to ask you the same thing. You are doing some work on Calcutta's history, aren't you?'

Mr Biswas sighed. 'Yes, so I was. But I've been adequately punished. I don't think the wind-god wants me to continue.'

'The article in Vichitrapatra . . .?'

'Yes, I wrote it. On the Monument? Yes, it's one of mine. I've written elsewhere as well. I had a job until last year. Now I'm retired. I have to keep myself occupied, don't I? I was once a student of history, you see. I've always been interested in that subject. When I was in college, one day I walked all the way from Bag Bazar to Dum Dum to look at Clive's house. Have you ever seen it? It was there until recently—a house built like a bungalow. Its front wall bore the East India Company's coat-of-arms.'

'Did you go to Presidency College?'

On the wall, above the desk, was a group photo. 'Presidency College, Alumni Association, 1953,' it said.

'It wasn't just I,' Mr Biswas informed us, 'my son, my brother, father, even grandfather went to Presidency. It's a family tradition. Now I am ashamed to admit that we won gold medals, both Girin and I.'

'Ashamed? Why should you be ashamed?'

'Well, that didn't get us anywhere, did it? What did we achieve in life? I held down a job, and Girin ran a business. That's all. No one knows us, our names mean nothing to people.'

Feluda had stepped closer to the photo to take a good look. Now his eyes travelled to the desk. A blue notebook was lying open. Only about ten lines had been written on the page, no more.

'Is your name Narendra Nath, or Narendra Mohan?' Feluda asked.

'. . . sorry?'

Perhaps Mr Biswas had become a little preoccupied. Feluda had to repeat his question. That made Mr Biswas smile and look faintly surprised. 'As far as I know, it's Narendra Nath. Why, do you have reason to believe that's not my name?'

'Your visiting card says N. M. Biswas.'

'Oh, that? That's a printer's error. When I give one of those cards to anyone, I always change the "M" to "N". I could have got some new cards printed, but never got round to it. To tell you the truth, I don't really need a card. I put a few in my wallet only because, of late, I've been visiting museums, and sometimes I have to meet some of their officials. By the way, are you going to write about that old cemetery? I hope not! I could never compete with a young rival like you.'

'No, I don't write,' Feluda said as he rose to take his leave, 'I'm happy simply to learn. Incidentally, I have a request. While you're doing your research, if you come across any mention of a family called Godwin, could you please let me know? It would really help me.'

'Godwin?'

'Yes. Thomas Godwin was buried in the Park Street cemetery. In fact, the same tree that injured you also damaged Godwin's tomb.'

'Really?'

'Five more Godwins were buried in the other cemetery in Lower Circular Road.'

'Very well, if I find anything, I'll certainly let you know. But I need your address to do that.'

Feluda handed him one of his cards.

'Private investigator?' Mr Biswas sounded considerably taken aback. 'Is that what you do for a living?'

'Yes.'

'I see. I'd heard that there were private detectives in Calcutta. This is the first time I've actually met one!'

FIVE

'Why didn't you ask him about Victoria?' I said to Feluda, on our way to Chowringhee. We were in Lalmohan Babu's car, and he was determined to take us to the Blue Fox for tea and sandwiches. Who knew a visit to that restaurant would change everything?

Feluda replied, 'Well, I don't think Mr Biswas would have been pleased to learn that I had gone through his papers and read those words. They may not be a secret code or anything dramatic like that, but certainly abbreviations had been used for personal reference. It could well be that they weren't meant to be seen by anyone else.'

'Yes, there is that.'

Lalmohan Babu was looking a bit withdrawn. Feluda hadn't failed to notice it. 'What's the matter?' he asked, 'why do your eyes look so distant?'

Lalmohan Babu sighed. 'I had thought up a wonderful plot for Pulak. It was bound to be another successful film—but he wrote today saying that in Hindi films these days, thrill and fighting are not drawing enough crowds. Everyone wants a devotional theme. The trend started after Jai Santoshi Ma became so successful. Just imagine!'

'So what? Where's your problem? Haven't you got any feelings for God and religion?'

Lalmohan Babu did not find it necessary to make a reply. He simply made a face, said, 'Hell! Hell!' and fell silent. The reason for that was not Pulak Ghoshal's letter, but what we could see on our left. Our car had, by now, passed Birla Planetarium and entered Chowringhee. A veritable mountain of earth was hiding the maidan from sight. Of late, Lalmohan Babu had started referring to the underground railway as 'hell rail'.

The car kept hitting potholes, one after another. Each time that happened, Lalmohan Babu shuddered. 'The springs in my car aren't really as bad as you might think,' he offered eventually. 'When we go down Red Road—and that's totally without potholes—you'll see that the car is not to be blamed for these jerks.'

'No, we shouldn't complain. At least we're on a paved road. Two hundred years ago, these roads were like country lanes, not one was paved. Can you imagine that?'

'There were no Ambassadors running on the roads then. And the roads were not so crowded.'

'No. There weren't quite so many people, but what could be seen in large numbers were scavenger birds.'

'Scavenger birds?'

'Yes. They were as common in those days as crows and sparrows are today. They were big birds, about four and a half feet high. They went about pecking at all the rubbish they could find in the streets. If they saw a corpse floating down the Ganges, they would perch themselves on it and get a free ride down the river.'

'Oh, that's awful! It must have been all quite wild and barbaric. How terrible.'

'Yet, in the same city, where those birds roamed, there was the house of the Governor-General, St John's Church, the Park Street Cemetery, theatres in Theatre Road, and a lot of other buildings where the British lived. That area was known as White Town. Native

Indians were not allowed to live there. North Calcutta was known as Black Town.'

'Oh, that makes my blood boil!' Lalmohan Babu declared.

As we turned into Park Street, Feluda asked the driver to stop before we could reach the Blue Fox. 'I have to check something at that bookshop,' he explained.

Lalmohan Babu was not interested in Oxford Book Company, as they did not sell his books. 'Long live the shops in College Street and Black Bookshop in Ballygunj,' he told us.

Feluda went into the shop, glanced briefly at the shelves, then went and stood at a counter. Rows of stationery were displayed on it—red and blue notebooks, files, diaries, engagement pads. Feluda picked up a blue notebook and looked at its price. Rs 12.50. We had seen an identical notebook on Naren Biswas's desk.

'May I help you?' A shop assistant came forward.

'Would you have a collection of Queen Victoria's letters?' Feluda asked.

'Queen Victoria? No, sir. But if you can let us know the name of the publisher, we can get it for you. If it's either Macmillan or Oxford University, we can ask their Calcutta office.'

Feluda thought for a moment. Then he said, 'All right. I'll get back to you.'

We came out on Park Street again. Our car was now parked in front of the Blue Fox. We began walking towards the restaurant.

'Stop!' Feluda said, taking out his own notebook from his pocket. 'I can't read if I have to keep walking in this crowd.'

A few seconds later, he shut the notebook and resumed walking. 'Did you find anything?' I asked.

'Let's first go and sit down,' Feluda replied.

When we were finally seated, Lalmohan Babu told us why he had chosen that restaurant. It was only because he liked the name 'Blue Fox', he said. He'd never been there before; in fact, he'd never eaten at any restaurant in Park Street. 'Look,' he said, 'I live in Gorpar. My publishers are in College Street. Where is the opportunity—or the need—for me to come and eat somewhere in this area?'

When the waiter had taken our order for tea and sandwiches, Feluda took out his notebook again and placed it on the table. Then he opened it and said, 'The first line continues to mystify me. But I think I've worked out the second line. All these letters stand for names of foreign publishers.'

'Which letters?' I asked.

'MM, OU, GAU, SJ and WN are Macmillan, Oxford University Press, George Allen and Unwin, Sidgewick and Jackson, Weidenfeld and Nicholson.'

'Good heavens!' Lalmohan Babu exclaimed. 'How did you manage to rattle off so many foreign names without stumbling even once? God bless your tongue!'

'It's obvious that Mr Biswas had either already written, or was going to write to these publishers about a collection of Queen Victoria's letters. But he needn't have gone to such trouble. It would have been far simpler to go to the British Council or the National Library and ask them to help. He might have been able to read some of the letters straightaway.'

Feluda put the notebook back in his pocket in order to make room on the table for our sandwiches. Then he lit a Charminar. Lalmohan Babu began humming a western tune, marking time with his fingers. Then he stopped and said, 'Let's go out somewhere. I mean, out of town. Every time we do that, you get a case to work on, and I get wonderful plots. But where can we go? It would have to be somewhere rough and wild. Not anywhere on the plains—nowhere that is green, soggy, lazy and quiet. What we need is a . . .'

Our sandwiches arrived at this moment, so Lalmohan Babu could not finish his sentence. We were all quite hungry. Lalmohan Babu bit into a huge sandwich, chewed three times, and stopped abruptly. Then I saw his eyes widen as he muttered, 'God be praised! God be praised!' As a result, little pieces of bread shot out of his mouth and fell on the table.

What had happened was this: Feluda and I were facing the street outside. Lalmohan Babu was looking into the restaurant. At the back, there was a low platform. Clearly, a live band played there in the evenings. On the platform stood a signboard. It was this board that had so amazed Lalmohan Babu. It bore the name of the band. Underneath were the words: Guitar—Chris Godwin.

Feluda snapped his fingers to call a waiter.

'Do you have live music at night?'

'Yes, sir.'

'May I speak to your manager?'

It was his intention to get hold of Chris Godwin's address, and he had already made up a story. When the manager came to our table, Feluda said, 'There's a wedding in Mr Mansukhani's house in

Ballygunj Park. They're looking for a band. I've heard so much about the one that plays in your restaurant. Do you think they'll agree to play at a wedding?'

'Why not? That's how they make a living!'

'Does Chris Godwin lead the band? Could you please give me his address?'

The manager wrote the address on a piece of paper and gave it to Feluda. It said: 14/1 Ripon Lane.

On any other day, we would have taken much longer to finish our food and chat for a while afterwards. Today, we spent very little time. Feluda only ate one sandwich. He was not hungry any more, he said. Lalmohan Babu worked at enormous speed and gobbled the two remaining sandwiches on Feluda's plate as well as the three on his own. 'Why waste good food when we're going to pay for all of it?' he said as he finished.

My heart sank as we approached 14/1 Ripon Lane. I hadn't been able to forget the stories of opulence of Sadat Ali's court. The exterior of the house in Ripon Lane was so ugly and uninviting that the contrast struck me as horrific. Feluda said I should not feel surprised. In four or five generations, a wealthy and affluent family could sink to abject poverty; there was no end to the hardships they might have to suffer. The houses in the street were not small—each had three or four floors. But I just didn't feel like stepping into any of them. Lalmohan Babu said it was obvious to him that every house was haunted. Feluda decided to speak to a paan-wala outside 14/1, just to make sure we had come to the right place.

'Does anyone called Godwin live in this house?'

'Goodin sahib? Which one? The one who plays music?'

'Yes, but is there another one?'

'There's the old man. Markis sahib. Markis Goodin.'

'Which floor. . .?'

'Second. There's Arkis sahib on the third.'

'Arkis and Markis? Are they brothers?' Lalmohan Babu wanted to know.

'No, babu. Arkis sahib is Arkis sahib. Markis is Goodin . . . go to the second floor. You'll find him.'

Feluda left the discussion on Arkis and Markis and walked into the building. We followed him.

I was right. The interior of the building was no better than its exterior. Since it was an evening in June, it was still bright outside at half-past six; but near the staircase, it was pitch dark. Undaunted, Feluda quickly began climbing the stairs. He has a special gift—he can see in the dark, far better than most people. Lalmohan Babu clutched the railing and proceeded with considerable difficulty. 'Cat burglars I had heard of,' he muttered. 'This is the first time I have seen a cat detective!'

The second floor was surprisingly quiet. All that we could hear— very faintly—was music, possibly being played on a radio. There was a door where the stairs ended, behind which was a balcony. A certain amount of daylight was coming in through the door. The pattern on the mosaic floor was visible in that light. To our left was a room, but it was empty and dark. Further down, there was another room. The light in it was on and falling across the threshold into the passage outside. A black cat was sitting curled up where the light fell, looking straight at us. Above us, from the third floor, came the sound of a man's voice. Then I thought I heard someone cough rather chestily.

'Let's go home!' Lalmohan Babu urged. 'This is the cemetery of Ripon Lane!'

Feluda went towards the second room.

'Anyone home?' he called.

For a few seconds, there was silence. Then someone said, 'Who is it?'

Feluda hesitated before speaking again. The same voice rang out, this time with a hint of impatience. 'Come in! I can't get out.'

'You want to go in? Or should we just leave?'

Feluda ignored Lalmohan Babu's question and crossed the threshold. He was like a kite. We were only his tail. He went; we followed, zigzagging on the way.

'Come in!' the voice commanded.

SIX

The three of us stepped in. It was a medium-sized living room. Opposite the door was an old sofa, torn in three places, its coir stuffing exposed through the gaps. A table with a marble top was placed in front of the sofa. At least, once upon a time it must have looked like marble. To our left was an ancient book case, which contained about fifteen ancient books. On top of this case sat a brass vase with a bunch of dusty plastic flowers in it. It was impossible to guess their colours. A framed picture hung on the wall, but the glass had such a thick layer of dust on it that the picture had become quite indistinct. It might have been the picture of a horse, or it might have been a train.

A Philips radio—possibly older than Feluda—stood on another table next to the sofa. Strangely enough, it still worked, for that faint music was coming from it. Now, a thin, pale hand, with rather prominent veins, reached out and turned a knob to switch it off. The owner of that hand was seated on the sofa, gazing steadily at us. On his lap was a cushion. His left leg was resting on a stool. It was evident from the colour of his skin that one of his ancestors must have been British. The few strands of his hair that had not yet turned grey were blond. It was difficult to see the colour of his eyes, as the bulb that hung from the ceiling was probably no more than twenty-five watts.

'I suffer from gout, so I can't move,' explained the man. 'I have to take the help of my servant, and that idiot slips away whenever he can.'

Feluda introduced us, and got straight down to business. If the other man was annoyed by our sudden arrival, he did not show it.

'We have come only for some information. Are you a descendant of Thomas Godwin, who came to India in the early nineteenth century?'

The man raised his eyes and looked directly at Feluda. Now I could see that his eyes were faded blue. He stared hard for a few seconds, then he said, 'Now, how the hell do you know about my great-great-grandfather?'

'So my assumption is correct?'

'Yes, but there's more. In fact, I have got something that once belonged to Thomas Godwin. At least, that's what my grandmother told me. One hundred and fifty years . . . oh hell!'

'Why, what's wrong?'

'That scoundrel, Arakis—cheat, bloody fraud! He took it from me only last night. Said he'd return it today. They're going to have their meeting this evening. It's Thursday, isn't it? Right. You'll hear all kinds of strange noises from upstairs. Give it a few more minutes, then it'll start.'

The room seemed darker than before. Was it because I was feeling quite confused? Or because night had fallen? No, there was a rumble of thunder. The sky had become overcast. No wonder the room had grown darker.

Feluda was seated in an armless chair, facing Mr Godwin. Lalmohan Babu had taken an easy chair by his side, but did not appear to be at his ease. He was restless and kept shifting in his chair, which probably meant that it was infested by bugs. Feluda was staring straight at Mr Godwin. Even without uttering a word, he seemed to be saying, 'You can tell me whatever you want. I am here to listen.'

'It's an ivory casket,' said Mr Godwin, 'and there are a few things in it. Two old pipes, a silver snuff box, a pair of spectacles, and a parcel wrapped with silk. Perhaps it contains a book—I have never bothered to look. We had plenty of other antiques. My son—that vagabond—has sold everything. He dropped out of college, began smoking ganja, and then started removing various things from this house. I don't know why he didn't take the casket. Perhaps he would have, but his luck changed, so he didn't really have to. He's formed a music group. We live on what he earns, if you can call this living. But who am I to talk, or blame my son? Much of it was my own fault. I have heard that Thomas Godwin lost his possessions in gambling. I had the same problem.'

Mr Godwin stopped. He was breathing hard, possibly because he had talked at such length. Then he winced. His gout was clearly bothering him. But he resumed talking:

'When I was a young man, once I went to England. My uncle was a cashier with the Midland Bank in London. Three months—that's all I could take. I couldn't bear the cold. I couldn't stand the food. I was used only to Indian food. So I returned to Calcutta. Then I got married. My wife died ten years ago. Now I only have Christopher. I see him—maybe just once every day. Sometimes not even that. He stays in his room when he's at home, and strums his guitar. Yes, he plays well.'

A peculiar noise had started above our heads. Tap, tap, tap, tap. Tap, tap. It would stop from time to time, then start again. The shadows began moving, because with the noise, the light hanging from the ceiling had started to sway. Now I was feeling as frightened as Lalmohan Babu. I had never been to such a house, or seen such a room; nor had I heard such tales from anyone. What on earth was going on upstairs?

Mr Godwin did not bother to look up. 'It's that table,' he told us simply, 'it's jumping. Four frauds are sitting around it. They claim it's been possessed by the soul of some dead person, that's why it's jumping.'

'Who are they?'

'Cronies of Arakis. Society for Spook Studies. Two Jews, one Parsee, and Arakis. They tried to rope me in, but I refused. One day, in front of Arakis, I had mentioned something about Thomas Godwin. So he said he could arrange a conversation with him. I said, certainly not! Sooner or later, I am going to meet him, anyway. Then, yesterday, Arakis said . . .'

Mr Godwin stopped. The table was jumping again.

'But why did he take that casket from you?'

'Yes, I'm coming to that. He said they could contact Thomas Godwin's soul even without my presence. All they needed was some object that had once belonged to him. Judging by that noise, they've succeeded.'

Tap, tap, tap . . . the table jumped again.

'Is this whole business carried out in the dark?' Feluda wanted to know.

'Every fraudulent business is carried out in the dark,' Mr Godwin replied, his voice heavy with sarcasm.

'Could we go upstairs?'

Lalmohan Babu heard these words, and promptly grabbed the arms of his chair to indicate his disapproval. Mr Godwin's reply seemed to reassure him.

'They won't let you go into that room,' Mr Godwin said. 'That privilege is for members only. Arakis has a servant; he guards the entrance. But, of course, if someone wants their help in contacting a spirit, then he's allowed in. Twenty rupees in advance, and another hundred if the spirit turns up.'

'I see . . .'

Feluda rose. 'Thank you, Mr Godwin. You've been most helpful. Thank you very much. Sorry if we disturbed you.'

'Good night.'

Mr Godwin's pale, thin arm reached out once more towards the radio.

We came out on the landing. What Feluda did next took me completely by surprise. It was too dark to see the expression on Lalmohan Babu's face and gauge his reaction. Instead of going down, Feluda began climbing the stairs to the next floor.

'What are you doing, Felu Babu? Those stairs go up, not down!' Lalmohan Babu exclaimed hurriedly.

'Come on, don't be afraid!' came the answer.

We found Mr Arakis's servant at the door, clad in a lungi.

'Are you looking for someone?' he asked.

'We are here,' Feluda said, 'only to help you.' I saw that he had taken out a five-rupee note and was offering it to the man, who looked quite taken aback. Feluda went a little closer and whispered into his ear: 'Just tell me if that room is locked, from all sides—I mean the one where your master is sitting with his friends.'

Perhaps the magic of money had started to work. The man told us there were two doors. The one facing the passage was locked, but the other opened into the bedroom. That door was open.

'You don't have to do anything,' Feluda went on. 'Just show us where the bedroom is. If you don't, there will be trouble. We are from the police. This gentleman here is an inspector.'

Lalmohan Babu quickly stood on his toes and added two inches to his height. There was a light on this landing. Feluda thrust the note into the servant's hand, which automatically closed around it.

'Come with me. But . . .'

'No buts. We are after one of those friends of your master, so we've got to talk to him. You or Mr Arakis won't come to any harm, I promise you.'

'Follow me, please.'

The bedroom was dark, as was the next room on the other side of the open communicating door. We made our way to it. All was silent. But, only a little while ago, we had heard the table jump three times. It was clear that the group holding the seance was waiting with bated breath for the arrival of Thomas Godwin's spirit. Lalmohan Babu was gasping so loudly and painfully that I felt afraid it might alert the group to our presence. Feluda had probably moved closer to the door. A smell of kerosene was coming from somewhere. A cat meowed. Perhaps it was that black cat on the floor below.

'Tho-mas Godwin! Tho-o-mas Godwin!'

The name was called out twice in a voice that was hoarse and distorted. It sounded like a groan. Obviously, that was how they invited a spirit.

'Are you with us? Are you with us?'

No answer. No sound. Half a minute passed. Then the same question was repeated, this time more urgently:

'Thomas Godwin . . . are you with us?'

'Ye-es! Ye-es!'

Next to me, I could feel a leg shaking violently. No, not the leg of a table, but that of a man. To be precise, it was Lalmohan Babu's knee.

'Yes. I have come. I am here!'

Although the voice said 'here', it sounded as if it was speaking from quite far.

The group resumed asking questions. 'Are you happy? Are you in peace?'

'No-o-o!' came the answer.

'Why are you unhappy?'

Silence fell again. Mr Arakis and his friends waited for nearly a whole minute before repeating the question: 'Why are you unhappy?'

'I . . . I . . . want . . . I want . . . I want my . . . my casket!'

This remark was followed by some strange happenings. Someone let out a bloodcurdling scream from the next room—a scream born out of pure terror—and, the next instant, someone pulled hard at my sleeve. A voice whispered in my ear: 'Come on, Topshe!'

The guard outside was so perplexed to see us rush out that he did nothing to either stop us or follow us down the stairs. A minute later, we had left Ripon Lane behind us and were moving towards our car parked on Royd Street.

'That,' Lalmohan Babu declared, 'was a special show. If anyone showed a similar thing in a film, it would crash all box-office records!'

The reason for this praise was simple. Feluda was now clutching an ivory casket, given to Thomas Godwin by Nawab Sadat Ali.

SEVEN

The following morning, Feluda himself summoned me to his room. After Lalmohan Babu had dropped us the previous night, Feluda had had a shower and finished his dinner within half an hour. Then he had gone straight to his room and shut the door. I had not been able to sleep very well. It was clear that we had got embroiled in a bizarre mystery. It was like being lost in a maze . . . something perhaps even more complex than the Bhoolbhulaia in Lucknow. I had no idea where to turn; my only hope was Feluda. But did Feluda know the way out of the maze?

I found him seated on his bed. In front of him was Thomas Godwin's casket. Its contents were strewn over the bed. There were two white pipes that could be filled with tobacco—but they looked different from any pipe I had seen before; a snuff box; a pair of spectacles set in a gold frame; and four red leather-bound notebooks.

Each had the word 'diary' inscribed on the cover in gold letters. The piece of silk in which they had been wrapped was lying on one side, together with the blue ribbon with which the parcel had been tied. Feluda offered me one of the notebooks, saying, 'Turn the first page— be careful!'

'Why, this is Charlotte Godwin's diary!'

'Yes. These are all her diaries, from 1858 to 1862. Her writing is as clear and lucid as her language. It took me all night to read the whole thing. Imagine, this priceless object was lying in a dark corner in Ripon Lane! Incredible.'

I stared at the first page, not daring to turn it, for I could see that each page was fragile and brittle.

'Arakis opened that diary,' said Feluda.

'How do you know?'

'If you turn a page quickly and carelessly, the top right-hand corner tends to break. Look!' Feluda gave a quick demonstration. 'Besides,' he went on, 'here, look at this ribbon. It is quite worn in some places, as it had remained tied and knotted for more than a hundred years. But look, apart from those worn bits, the ribbon is crushed and twisted in places. That's because a new knot had been tied. Whoever untied it did not bother to knot it in exactly the same place. If he had, it would have been more difficult to be sure.'

'Why do you have a black stain on your finger?' I asked. I had noticed it as soon as I entered Feluda's room.

'This is another clue, but I'll explain it later. It came from that snuff box.'

'What did the diaries tell you?' I asked breathlessly.

'They speak of the last few years of Thomas Godwin's life. He was penniless by that time, and cantankerous. One of his sons was dead, and he neither loved nor trusted his other son, David. In fact, he trusted no one, not even Charlotte. Yet Charlotte loved him, prayed for him and took care of him as best she could. He had gambled everything away. Charlotte earned a little money by sewing for the local English ladies, and making carpets. Godwin had sold most of the expensive gifts he had received from the Nawab. All he had left were three items—that casket, the snuff box which he had allowed Charlotte to have, and the third was the first gift Sadat Ali had given him.'

'Did he give that to Charlotte?'

'No, he gave it to no one. He told his daughter before he died that it should be buried together with his body. Charlotte fulfilled his last wish, and found much comfort from that.'

'What was that object?'

'Charlotte calls it "Father's precious Perigal repeater".'

'Eh? What on earth is that?'

'That,' said Feluda, 'is where even your Feluda has drawn a blank. According to my dictionary, a repeater can be a gun—like a pistol—or a watch. Perigal might be the name of the manufacturer. Even Uncle Sidhu isn't sure. I went to his house early this morning, before you got up. Now I must speak to Vikas Chakravarty and see if he can throw some light on this matter.'

Vikas Chakravarty worked in Park Auction House in Park Street. Feluda knew him well. They had got to know each other when Feluda's investigations had taken him to the auction house, in connection with a case. He had had to pay more than one visit.

'I passed that shop only the other day. There were a lot of old clocks and watches displayed in the window. I have a strong feeling Godwin's repeater was a clock, not a gun.'

Feluda then proceeded to tell me more about what he had read in Charlotte Godwin's diary. Apparently, Charlotte had mentioned a niece. She had referred to her as 'my dear clever niece'. This niece had done something to offend her grandfather, Thomas. But Thomas forgave her before he died, and gave her his blessings.

Charlotte had also talked about her brothers, David and John. We had seen David's grave in the cemetery in Lower Circular Road, John had returned to England and killed himself there. Charlotte did not know why.

Lalmohan Babu turned up a little later. 'Until yesterday,' he told us, 'I was in a dilemma. Pulak had told me to write a new story for his next film—one with a devotional theme. So I couldn't decide whether to stay at home and start writing, or stick with you and see how this case develops. After what happened yesterday, I have no doubt left. Thrill is better than religion. By the way, did you find anything in that casket?'

'Yes. I found diaries nearly one hundred and twenty-five years old. They told me that, if Thomas Godwin's grave was dug up, one might find a Perigal repeater.'

'Peter? What Peter?'

'Let's go out. How much petrol have you got?'

'Ten litres. Filled my car only this morning.'

'Good. We have a lot of travelling to do.'

Feluda frowned as we stepped into Park Auction House.

'Mr Mitter! How are you? Do come in. This must be my lucky day. Are you here on a new case?' Mr Chakravarty came forward to greet us. He was plump, his cheeks bulging with paan. Something in his appearance immediately made me think he was from north Calcutta.

'I can see that you've had quite a lot of luck,' Feluda remarked. 'I saw about eight clocks—big and small—in your window quite recently. Have you sold them all?'

'Clocks? You want a clock? What kind? A wall clock, or an alarm clock?'

Feluda was still looking around. I knew instinctively that Mr Chakravarty was not the kind of person who would know anything about a clock with a long and difficult name. Feluda asked him, anyway.

'Repeater? That's probably some sort of an alarm clock,' he replied, 'but I've no idea what Perigal might mean. But don't worry, I know someone who knows a lot about clocks. I've heard that he has two hundred and fifty clocks in his house. He's completely mad about clocks.'

'Really? Who is he?'

'Mr Choudhury. Mahadev Choudhury.'

'A Bengali?'

'Yes, but I think he was brought up somewhere in western India, or perhaps the north. His spoken Bengali is not that good. In fact, he speaks English most of the time. He's a very clever man. I believe he was in Bombay before he came here. He's been buying whatever he can lay his hands on, as long as it's an antique. Those clocks that you saw here before are now all in his house. He really is quite knowledgeable. Why don't you go and talk to him? He put an ad in the papers. Didn't you see it?'

'What advertisement?'

'If anyone has an antique clock for sale, he should get in touch with Mr Choudhury.'

'So he must be extremely wealthy!'

'Yes, sir. He owns cloth mills, cinemas, tea gardens, jute mills, race horses, business in imports and exports . . . just name it!'

'Do you know where he lives?'

'Yes. He has a house in Alipore Park in Calcutta, and another one in the country, by the Ganges. I believe his cotton mill is somewhere nearby. He's probably in Calcutta at the moment, but I suggest you go and see him in the evening. Right now he'll be in his office . . . Wait, let me go and get you his address.'

We took Mahadev Choudhury's address, and left the auction house. 'Why don't you,' said Feluda, 'drop me at the Esplanade reading room of the National Library, and go back to the Park Street cemetery? See if there's anything to report?'

'Rep-p-port?' Lalmohan Babu's voice suddenly sounded unsteady.

'Yes. All you need to do is take another look at Godwin's tomb. Today you'll find that area quite dry; it hasn't rained in the last couple of days, has it? Have a look around, then come back and collect me. We'll have lunch somewhere. There won't be time to go back home for lunch . . . we have a lot to do today. Don't forget we must also return to Ripon Lane.'

Feluda had brought Mr Godwin's casket—wrapped with brown paper—and was carrying it under his arm.

'In broad daylight, of course, there's no reason to feel afraid,' Lalmohan Babu observed. 'It's only after dark that a visit to a cemetery is . . . er . . . difficult!'

'You wouldn't be afraid of spooks and spirits—any time of the day—if your mind wasn't crammed with superstitions!' said Feluda.

Our car got held up for a while in a traffic jam on the way to the reading room. While we were waiting for the jam to clear, Lalmohan Babu said, 'This clock, or watch, or whatever you're looking for . . . might it be a pocket watch?'

'I don't know. I mean, not yet.'

'If it's an old pocket watch, I have one of those.'

'Whose was it?'

'My grandfather's. I have three things that were once his. A watch, a walking stick and a turban. The late Pyaricharan Gangopadhyay. I say, where did the name "Pyaricharan" come from, do you think?'

'Nowhere. It was always here, in this country. You are a writer, and you don't know the meaning of "Pyari"? It's another name for Radha, that's all.'

'Thank you, sir. Anyway, I'd like to give you that watch.'

Feluda looked quite taken aback. 'To me? Why?'

'Well, I wanted to give you something—you know, to show my appreciation. After all, you made such a significant contribution to the success of my Hindi film. And this car is a result of that. Now, if you look at this watch, who knows, you might find that it's a Peripeter, or whatever.'

'No, that isn't likely. But I am very grateful for your offer. Your watch will be very well looked after, I promise you. I cannot, of course, use it every day—not if it's so old and goes back to the nineteenth century. But certainly I am going to wind it regularly. Does it still work?'

'Beautifully.'

By the time Lalmohan Babu and I reached the cemetery, having dropped Feluda at the reading room, it was almost twelve o'clock. When we finished our business there, we'd pick him up and go to Nizam's for mutton rolls. That was Feluda's plan, and it would be his treat. But, before we went for lunch, we would have to go back to Ripon Lane to return that casket.

Park Street had far less traffic running on it now. The cemetery was therefore quiet. We entered through the main gate and looked for Baramdeo, the chowkidar. He was nowhere in sight, and did not emerge even when we called out to him. Perhaps he had disappeared behind a bush to cremate another dead rat.

We went down the path that cut across the cemetery. Although both Feluda and I made fun of Lalmohan Babu's fears, and Feluda dismissed them as mere superstition, I had to admit that there was something creepy in the air. It wasn't just the tombs, but the abundance of trees and bushes and undergrowth. They added to the generally eerie atmosphere. Nevertheless, Lalmohan Babu's responses seemed a trifle exaggerated. It was, after all, broad daylight and I failed to see why he was so afraid. He proceeded slowly, looking at the tombstones out of the corner of his eye, and muttering constantly, as if he was chanting a mantra. What was he saying? I had to strain my ears to catch the words. They were certainly worth hearing.

'Please, Mr Palmer, please, Mr Hamilton, and you, too, Miss Smith; please don't break our necks, please let us get on with our work. You've given so much, taken so much, taught us so much, even beaten the hell out of us . . . Mr Campbell, Mr Adam, and—I say, I can't even pronounce your name!—but anyway, I beg of you, all of you, if you're no more than handfuls of dust, do stay that way . . . dust to dust, dust. . . dust. . .!'

I could contain myself no more. 'What are you going on about? What's all this about dust?' I asked.

'Dear Tapesh, I read about all this as a child. Dust thou art, to dust returnest. All these people have been reduced to dust.'

'In that case, what's there to be afraid of?'

'That's what a poet wrote. Poets aren't always correct in what they write, are they?'

We turned left. The fallen tree was still lying on the ground, and the ground was now dry. But there was rather a lot of earth spread around Thomas Godwin's grave.

'Dust . . . dust . . . dust . . .!'

Lalmohan Babu continued to chant that word like a robot—perhaps in order to gather courage—and moved towards Godwin's tomb. Then he stopped, gasped, said 'Sk-sk-skel-skel-skel-!' and promptly keeled over, like a felled tree, landing on top of the mound of earth.

Quite close to the spot where he had fallen was a chasm. The earth had been dug quite deep. In the centre of that chasm, still half-buried in the ground, was a human skull.

EIGHT

I had to shake Lalmohan Babu at least ten times before he opened his eyes. Had he not come round, I would have really been in trouble since I'd never found myself in a similar situation before. Finally Lalmohan Babu picked himself up, dusted himself down, and announced that, when frightened, writers had a tendency to faint more easily than others, as their imagination was more powerful than other people's.

'What your cousin said about superstition is complete nonsense. I have no such . . . er . . . problem!' he told me.

We did not waste another second, and left the cemetery at once to collect Feluda. He had finished his work in the reading room. Even if he hadn't, I knew that after hearing our story, he would drop everything and go back to the cemetery with us. He saw how the grave had been dug up, thereby exposing the skull. Then he searched the area around the tomb most thoroughly—but found nothing except a spade. It was lying only ten feet from the grave.

This time, we met Baramdeo. He said he had gone to pass on some urgent message to his nephew in his paan shop, just round the corner on Lower Circular Road. He knew nothing about the grave being dug up. It was his belief that whoever was responsible had entered the cemetery the previous night by climbing over the wall. Feluda then asked him to lend a hand, and refilled the yawning hole with earth and fallen leaves. Before we left, Feluda told Baramdeo not to mention the matter to anyone else.

From Park Street, we went straight to Ripon Lane.

There was a slight delay as we got to 14/1 and were about to go up the stairs. A young man was climbing down, a long leather case in his hand—a guitar case. He appeared to be in his mid-twenties, and looked very much like other young men who are seen around Park Street, particularly in the evenings. There is therefore no need for further description. This man had to be Chris Godwin. He would not return to Ripon Lane until late at night, after he finished playing at the Blue Fox.

When he had gone, we made our way upstairs. The first floor was not as silent as it had been before. Raised voices reached our ears from Mr Godwin's living room. We recognized one of them. The other was probably Mr Arakis's. The first voice was scolding and threatening. The second was whining and denying all allegations. Both were frequently using the word 'casket'.

Feluda walked down the passage, and knocked on the door At once, three words shot out like bullet's: 'Who is it?'

We stepped into the room. The second gentleman's skin was pale, with a yellowish tinge to it, and covered with freckles. His head was bald and he had two gold teeth. He was perhaps in his mid-sixties. Feluda went straight to Mr Godwin and unwrapped the parcel in his hands. 'I just could not resist taking it away yesterday. It will help me a lot in my research,' he said.

Mr Godwin simply stared for a few seconds, then burst out laughing.

'So you fooled them, you fooled them! Those morons! Cheats, frauds, swindlers!' Then he looked at the other man and continued, biting sarcasm in his voice, 'Tom Godwin's spirit walked off with that casket, did it? Is he Tom Godwin's spirit? This gentleman? What do you think? Look, this is Mr Arakis, my neighbour from upstairs. The same man whose table prances around every Thursday, and ruins the entire evening for me.'

Mr Arakis was gaping stupidly at the casket. Then he glanced at Feluda in silence, and shifted the same foolish gaze to the door. He began moving towards it, but had to stop. Feluda had called out his name.

'Mr Arakis!'

The man looked at Feluda. 'I think one of the items in that casket is still with you,' Feluda said calmly.

'Certainly not!' Arakis thundered. 'Besides, how would you know anything about it? Marcus, open that box and see if anything is missing.'

So Mr Godwin's first name was Marcus. That explained the mystery of Arkis-Markis.

Marcus Godwin opened the casket and went through its contents. Then he said, with a somewhat embarrassed air, 'Why, Mr Mitter, everything appears quite intact!'

'Could you please take out that snuff box? Charlotte Godwin described it in her diary, and said it was studded with emeralds, rubies and sapphires.'

Mr Godwin took out the box and peered at it.

'Can you see now that it's a cheap, new snuff box, simply painted black? Mr Arakis tried to make it look like an antique!'

Within five minutes, Mr Arakis fetched the real thing from his flat upstairs. 'I swear upon God,' said Mr Godwin, 'if I hear your table making any noise next Thursday, I will inform the police!' Mr Arakis slunk out of the room like a thief, his face dark with embarrassment.

'Thank you, Mr Mitter,' said Mr Godwin, sighing with relief.

'Have you any idea how valuable Charlotte Godwin's diaries are?'

'No. I didn't even know that the casket contained such diaries. To tell you the truth, Mr Mitter, I am not even remotely curious about my forefathers. In fact, I am no longer curious about anything. I am simply waiting for death. The only thing I can call my own is that cat. In the past I used to visit a friend to play poker. Now, thanks to my gout, even that has come to an end.'

'In that case, perhaps there's no point in asking you a few questions.'

'What questions?'

'Your great-grandfather was called David, wasn't he, and he was buried in the cemetery on Lower Circular Road?'

'Yes.'

'Did David have a brother or sister?'

'Don't know. One of my ancestors killed himself. I can't remember if he was David's brother.'

'Was David's son—your grandfather, that is—called Andrew?'

'Yes, he was in the army.'

'Charlotte talks of a niece. She was either your grandfather's sister, or . . .'

'My grandfather was an only child.'

'Then it must be a cousin.'

'I couldn't tell you anything about cousins. My memory has become quite weak. Besides, families in our community do not live together.

We tend to go our own way, so we scatter and disperse—unlike your Bengali joint families!'

We were sitting at Nizam's, opposite Society cinema. Over a plate of mutton rolls, Feluda asked Lalmohan Babu, 'What did you think of Naren Biswas? I mean, as a person?'

Lalmohan Babu finished chewing, swallowed and said, 'Why, he seemed quite a nice man! There was something rather impressive in his appearance, I thought.'

'Yes, that's what I had thought as well, at first.'

'You don't think so any more?'

'No, but it must be said that one flaw doesn't—or shouldn't—ruin a man's entire personality. Nevertheless, he did commit a serious crime.'

Lalmohan Babu and I stopped eating.

'Remember those press cuttings in his wallet? Today, I saw for myself that they were removed with a blade from a hundred-and-fifty, or maybe two-hundred-year-old newspaper, preserved with great care in the National Library's reading room. I think a man ought to be jailed for such a crime!'

I tried to imagine Naren Biswas in the reading room, holding his breath and secretly cutting out those reports, dodging the eyes of the library officials . . . but failed to picture the scene. It is truly impossible to guess, just by looking at a man, what he may be capable of doing.

'This is a kind of ailment,' Feluda continued. 'Some people get a hideous pleasure from committing such crimes successfully, without being caught. They think they are more clever than anyone else, and feel very pleased with themselves. It's all very sad.'

Having finished the mutton rolls, we ordered lassi. Feluda asked for the bill at the same time. It was half-past two. We had to kill another three hours before we could visit Mr Choudhury, the one who was said to be crazy about clocks. I knew Feluda would not give up until the matter of the Perigal repeater was cleared up.

'Tell me,' said Lalmohan Babu, 'did those scavenger birds in ancient Calcutta sit on parapets and call, in the hope of getting some food?'

We were sitting close to a window facing the street. A crow was sitting on the parapet over it, cawing loudly. Hence Lalmohan Babu's question.

'No, I don't think so,' Feluda replied, 'but they certainly used to sit on compound walls and railings. There is enough evidence of that in old pictures drawn at the time.'

'I don't even know what those birds looked like!'

'We could go to the zoo; that's one way to find out. Or we could go via Corporation Street. The municipal building has its crest on the front wall. There's a picture of a scavenger bird in it. I can show it to you.'

'Do you still call it Corporation Street?' Lalmohan Babu asked with a smile.

'Oh sorry. It's got a new name, hasn't it? I meant Suren Banerjee . . .'.

Feluda stopped. The look in his eyes had changed. He fished out his notebook from his pocket and took a quick look. Then he began to fidget as the waiter had not yet brought our bill. 'Waiter!' Feluda called impatiently, which was rather unusual for him.

When the bill had been finally brought and paid, we got back to the car at once. Feluda told the driver where to go. As soon as we reached Suren Banerjee Road, Feluda began looking at the number of each building. Not all of them had a number clearly displayed— an unfortunate feature of houses in Calcutta. 'Keep going,' he told the driver, 'Topshe, if you can spot 141, tell me immediately.'

Suddenly, I remembered something. 141 SNB. Surendra Nath Banerjee. My heart began beating faster.

'Look! There's 141.'

The car stopped. There was a sign outside the building. 'Bourne & Shepherd,' it said. BS! We had found it.

Lalmohan Babu and I went in with Feluda. There was a lift to go upstairs. As we emerged, we found ourselves in a reception area on the first floor. One of the staff came forward to greet us. Feluda hesitated a little before he asked a question. Whatever he said was bound to sound foolish.

'Er . . . do you have any pictures of Victoria?' he said finally.

'The Victoria Memorial?'

'No, Queen Victoria.'

'I'm afraid not. We've got pictures of only those who came to India. There's Edward VIII, when he was the Prince of Wales, and George V, the Delhi Durbar . . .'

'Their photos are still available?'

'Yes, but there's no ready-made print. We have the negatives, so prints can be made from those if anyone places an order. We've got all the negatives of photos taken since 1854.'

'What! 1854?'

'Bourne & Shepherd is the world's second oldest photographic studio.'

'But that means you've got thousands and thousands of negatives!'

'Yes. If you come with me, sir, I can show you everything. See that photo hanging on the wall? It was taken from the top of the Monument in 1880.'

I hadn't noticed it so far, but now my eyes went straight to it. The photo probably measured 1' x 5'. It showed Calcutta as she had appeared almost a hundred years ago from the Monument. There was Dalhousie Square, the Esplanade, and then it stretched northward, offering an unbroken view. The church spires rose over every other building. Not a single highrise was anywhere in sight. It was a quiet and peaceful city, there could be no doubt about that.

We were then taken to the room where the negatives were kept. My eyes nearly popped out. Shelves rose almost from the floor to the ceiling. Each was crammed with square brown boxes, bearing the date and description of their contents.

Feluda inspected the shelves and peered closely at some of the dates. Then he glanced at his watch and said, 'Why don't you two go for a walk? You can come back in an hour. I have some work to do here.'

We went back to the lift. 'Your cousin's wish is my command,' said Lalmohan Babu, 'I could never say no to him. He has such a tremendous personality! Anyway, let's go to Frank Ross.'

We left the car parked in Suren Banerjee Road and walked down Chowringhee towards the Grand Hotel. I had no idea why Lalmohan Babu wanted to go to a chemist, nor did I need to know. Our only aim was to kill time.

We proceeded through the crowded streets, trying to avoid bumping into others. After a while, Lalmohan Babu asked, 'Do you have any idea what your cousin is thinking?'

I was forced to admit that I was completely in the dark. All I could guess was that someone other than Feluda had read Charlotte Godwin's diaries and that was somehow linked with Thomas Godwin's grave being dug up.

'Do you know that a skeleton can remain intact even two hundred years after the body is buried?' Lalmohan Babu asked me.

His question reminded me of a story Feluda had told me about Job Charnock's tomb. I repeated it to Lalmohan Babu. Two hundred

years after Charnock's death, a priest at St John's Church suddenly
grew suspicious about what lay underground. Had Charnock really
been buried there, or had someone simply erected a tombstone? His
doubts began to worry him so much that the priest had the grave dug
up. At first, his men dug four feet, and found nothing. Then they dug
deeper, and another couple of feet lower, the arm of a skeleton slipped
out. The priest quickly had the grave refilled.

We entered Frank Ross. Lalmohan Babu walked up to the counter.
Just as he had started to say, 'One Forhans for the gums, family size,'
I spotted a man coming into the shop, and recognized him. It was
Naren Biswas's brother, Girin Biswas. He did not recognize us
immediately. I saw him glance at us two or three times before a smile
appeared on his face. In his hands was a large parcel. The words
Hong Kong Dry Cleaners were printed on it. 'Hello!' he said. 'I've
come to buy some medicines for my brother.'

'How is he?' Lalmohan Babu asked.

'Better, thank you. Oh, by the way, that other gentleman who was
with you that day . . . I believe he is the detective, Pradosh Mitter?
My brother told me. I had heard his name. In fact, I was thinking . . . '
Girin Biswas stopped. He was frowning, and seemed a bit preoccupied.
Then he said, 'When is he usually at home?'

'That's difficult to say,' I replied, 'but you will find our number in
the telephone directory. You can give him a call before you come to
our house.'

'Hmm. I wanted to . . . never mind, I will ring him. Tell Mr Mitter
I will come and see him, if need be . . . heh heh!'

We returned his 'heh heh!' politely, and left the shop.

Then we went round New Market, looking at all the shops, and
came out on Moti Sheel Street to go back to Suren Banerjee Road.
Feluda was waiting by the car near Bourne & Shepherd's. He had
finished his work sooner than he'd expected.

I told him about our meeting with Girin Biswas. 'Really?' Feluda
raised an eyebrow. 'What did he say?'

I knew it wouldn't do to be vague, so I told Feluda in detail about
our conversation. I even mentioned the parcel from the drycleaners.
Feluda heard me in silence.

'Did you get your work done? All went well, I hope?' Lalmohan
Babu asked.

'Oh yes, first class. That place is a veritable goldmine. And I rang
Mr Choudhury from the shop. His voice was as smooth as velvet.
He's returned home and we now have a firm appointment.'

NINE

I had heard chiming clocks before, but as soon as we stepped into Mahadev Choudhury's house at six o'clock, various clocks began striking the hour. The sound that came from one clock after another was quite extraordinary. I had never heard anything like it.

'Oh my God!' exclaimed Lalmohan Babu. 'Are we slipping through the gates of heaven? What an incredible reception!'

We could not meet Mr Choudhury straightaway. One of his employees took us to a small office and told us we would have to wait, as Mr Choudhury was busy. There were two fancy clocks even in that small room—one on the wall, and the other on a bookshelf.

When the last chime had died away, a somewhat eerie silence gripped the whole house. It was a huge, modern building. The marble floor shone so brightly that, if I looked down, I could see my own face reflected in it.

After a few moments, I became aware of a voice. It was coming from somewhere within the house. Feluda said it was Mahadev Choudhury's, though it was difficult to tell whether or not it could be termed as velvety. However, when it suddenly rose and began shouting, all traces of velvet disappeared.

Mahadev Choudhury was scolding someone furiously. The three of us held our breath and were more or less forced to eavesdrop. The second person was still speaking gently, so we could not hear what he was saying. But soon, Choudhury's voice boomed out again: 'I never pay an advance in matters like this, but I paid you because you insisted. And now you're telling me you've already spent that money? Honestly, I don't believe a word you're saying. Besides, why should I have to pay such a lot of money for such a small job? I don't understand at all! But . . . all right, I'll pay. I want that stuff within two days. No excuses this time. Is that clear?'

Complete silence followed these remarks. Then we heard footsteps, which seemed to be going towards the front door. A minute later, Mr Choudhury's employee came back. 'Please follow me,' he said.

Mr Choudhury's appearance—from head to toe—was truly like velvet. Even at six in the evening, his cheeks were smooth and shiny. 'I bet he shaves twice a day!' I thought to myself. Lalmohan Babu told us later, 'If a fly had gone and sat on his cheek, it would have slipped off!'

The huge living room we were in was as shiny and polished as its owner. There was not even a speck of dust anywhere, and its nooks and corners certainly seemed free of ants and cockroaches.

Mr Choudhury raised a gold cigarette holder to his lips, inhaled and glanced at Feluda. 'Well? Have you brought that clock?' he asked.

We were all startled by the question. 'Clock? What clock?' Feluda said.

'Didn't you say you wanted to see me regarding a clock? I thought you had seen my ad in the papers and that's why you were calling.'

'Forgive me, Mr Choudhury,' Feluda told him, 'I did not see your advertisement. I need some information. It may be related to a clock. I was told you know a lot about the subject, so I . . .'

Creases appeared on the velvety surface. Mr Choudhury shifted in his chair, looking faintly irritated. 'I haven't got a lot of time, Mr Mitter. I am about to leave town. Please try to be brief.'

'What is a Perigal repeater? That's all I want to know.'

The velvet suddenly turned to stone. The cigarette-holder was poised a couple of inches from his mouth. Mr Choudhury's eyes were still, fixed unblinkingly on Feluda.

'Where did you find that name?'

'In a nineteenth-century English novel.'

There were times when Feluda did not hesitate to lie, if it helped in getting results. I had seen him do it before. 'I know that a repeater can be either a gun or a clock. I saw that in a dictionary. But no one can tell me anything about Perigal.'

Mr Choudhury was still staring at Feluda. When he spoke, the velvet in his voice had taken on a sharp edge. 'If you come across an unfamiliar word, Mr Mitter, do you always visit complete strangers just to learn its meaning?'

'Yes, if need be.'

I thought Mr Choudhury would want to know what the pressing need was in this particular case. But, instead of asking such a question, he continued to stare at Feluda. The remark he made a few seconds later made my heart race faster, thudding loudly in my ears, matching the loud ticking of the clock kept on a side table.

'You are a detective, aren't you?'

I had to marvel at Feluda's steady nerve. There was a delay of about five seconds before his reply came. But when he spoke, his own voice sounded perfectly smooth. 'I see that you are well informed!'

'I have to be, Mr Mitter. I have people who gather information and pass it on to me.'

'You seem to have forgotten the question I just asked you. Perhaps you don't know the answer. If you do know it, but do not wish to tell me, I will take your leave. There's no point in wasting your time any further.'

'Sit down, Mr Mitter!'

Feluda had risen to his feet, hence that command. I glanced quickly at Lalmohan Babu. He looked as if he had no strength left in his body, and would need assistance to get up.

'Sit down, please,' said Mr Choudhury

Feluda sat down.

'A repeater is a gun,' Mahadev Choudhury informed us. 'However, if you add "Perigal" to it, it becomes a watch. A pocket watch. Francis Perigal. An Englishman. Towards the end of the eighteenth century, there were few watchmakers in the world as skilled as Perigal. Two hundred years ago, the best watches were made in England, not Switzlerland.'

'How much would a Perigal repeater be worth today?'

'You could never afford to buy such a watch, Mr Mitter.'

'Yes, I know.'

'I could.'

'I know that, too.'

'Then why do you wish to know its price?'

'Simple curiosity.'

'Idle curiosity. It's useless.'

Mr Choudhury took one last puff from his cigarette, took it out of its holder and stubbed it out in a glass ashtray. Then he stood up.

'You have got the information you wanted. You may leave now. There is only one Perigal repeater in Calcutta. I am going to get it, not you . . . Pyarelal!'

The same man returned, who had met us on arrival. As we were leaving the room, the smooth, velvety voice spoke once more: 'I have a different kind of repeater, Mr Mitter. The sound it makes isn't as melodious as a clock.'

'That man appears to be the hero of this story!' remarked Lalmohan Babu.

We were on our way back from Alipore Park. The windows of the car had been rolled up, as it was raining again. The rain had started as soon as we reached Judges Court Road.

Feluda did not reply. He was staring out of the window. Lalmohan Babu could never remain silent for long. He began speaking again. 'Perhaps I should call him a villain rather than a hero. But you have often told me that, in a crime investigation, no one is above suspicion. Anyone can be a villain. So I didn't use that word. Mind you, I'm not quite sure why I should be suspicious. A grave has been dug up—but is that a criminal act?'

Still Feluda said nothing. Lalmohan Babu became a little impatient. 'What's the matter with you, Felu Babu? Are you giving up? If you do, what's going to happen to us? To start with, that man's behaviour was such . . . such . . . that it froze my limbs! And then there were all those clocks, chiming away. Now you're not saying a word, the weather's foul, there are potholes in the roads . . .!'

Feluda opened his mouth at last. 'You are quite wrong, Mr Ganguli. I haven't given up. If you found a way out of a complex maze, would you give up?'

'You've found a way out?'

'Yes, but I still don't know what lies at the other end. Nothing is simple and straightforward. We shall have to proceed, and tackle all the twists and turns, before we get to the end.'

It continued to drizzle even after we reached home. Lalmohan Babu left with a promise to return early the following morning. 'I don't think you can do without my help, Felu Babu,' he said. 'Just think how much time you'd waste if you had to travel in buses!'

Earlier in the day, when we were having lunch, I had noticed Feluda scribbling something in his notebook. I went to his room after dinner, and discovered what it was. I had to talk to him, anyway, as I was feeling quite concerned about him. Having seen and heard Mahadev Choudhury, I had reason to feel worried. Every time I recalled his face, my heart gave a tiny jump. It hardly mattered what Lalmohan Babu called him—hero or villain. To me, he was a dreadful character. His appearance might be smooth as velvet. But on the inside, he seemed as rough and prickly as a cactus bush in a desert.

Feluda, however, did not appear concerned at all. He was staring hard at a diagram in his notebook. When I entered his room, he offered it to me, saying, 'Look at this tree and its branches!' This is what it looked like:

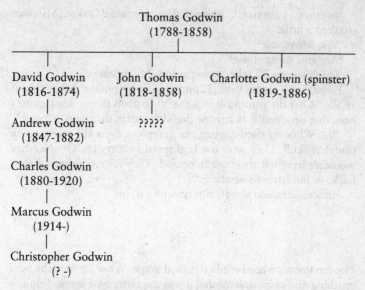

Thomas Godwin
(1788-1858)

David Godwin (1816-1874) — Andrew Godwin (1847-1882) — Charles Godwin (1880-1920) — Marcus Godwin (1914-) — Christopher Godwin (? -)

John Godwin (1818-1858) — ?????

Charlotte Godwin (spinster) (1819-1886)

'Doesn't it look kind of empty on the right hand side?' Feluda asked.

'But of course it would. Charlotte did not marry, did she?'

'No, it's not Charlotte I'm thinking of. Her case is pretty straightforward. The problem is with the man called John. That particular branch is hidden from sight. But I've seen something from the reverse. If I could see it properly, that might throw some light on this matter. Tomorrow morning, perhaps.'

Feluda was talking in riddles again. It was typical of him. I knew he would not explain anything even if I asked him.

The rain had stopped while we were talking. Suddenly, to my surprise, Feluda sprang to his feet.

'Are you going out?' I asked.

'Yes, sir.'

'What! Where?'

'I have to be on duty.'

'Duty?'

'Yes, I am keeping guard tonight.'

Suddenly I realized Feluda had taken out his hunting boots. Every time I see those boots, I break into goose-pimples as they are linked with each of Feluda's past adventures. Tonight, if he was planning to visit the cemetery, those boots would make the most suitable footwear.

'Are you . . . are you . . . going to the graveyard?' I asked. My voice croaked a little.

'Yes, where else?'

'Are you going alone?'

'Don't worry. I'll take a companion. My repeater.'

Feluda took out his Colt .32 and put it in his pocket. I didn't like it at all. 'What do you think is going to happen there? That grave's been dug up already. If anyone found a watch, they took it away.'

'No. Whoever tried digging the grave ran away the minute they saw that skull. They were too frightened to carry on. Or else, they wouldn't have left their spade behind. They'd have either taken it back, or hidden it somewhere.'

Such an idea had simply not occurred to me.

TEN

Heaven knows when Feluda returned home. When I got up the next morning and came downstairs, it was a quarter past seven. Feluda's door was shut. Perhaps he was still asleep. After all, he hadn't slept for two nights in a row.

He opened his door at nine. He'd had a shower and shaved. There was not even a trace of tiredness on his face. When he saw me, he simply shook his thumb to indicate that nothing had happened during the night at the cemetery.

Lalmohan Babu arrived at half-past nine.

'See if you like it!' he said.

As promised, he had brought his grandfather's watch. It was a silver watch, attached to a silver chain.

'It's beautiful!' exclaimed Feluda, taking the watch from Lalmohan Babu. 'At one time, Cooke-Kelvey as watchmakers were quite well known.'

'But it's not what you're after, is it?' Lalmohan Babu asked, a hint of regret in his voice. 'This watch was made in Calcutta.'

'Yes, but do you really want to give it to me?'

'With my blessings and my compliments. I am older than you by three and a half years, so you shouldn't object to my blessings!'

'Thank you.'

Feluda wrapped the watch in his handkerchief and put it in his pocket. Then he took a step towards the telephone, but before he could get to it, someone rattled the knocker on our door.

I opened it to find Girin Biswas standing outside. He had dropped a hint the day before, but I had not really expected him to turn up—and so soon, at that. He was dressed to go to work, wearing a suit and carrying a briefcase in his hand.

'Please don't mind my barging in like this,' he said, 'I tried calling your number, but just couldn't get through. I must have spent at least ten minutes dialling!' Mr Biswas sounded a bit nervous and agitated.

'No, why should I mind.' It's a miracle if a telephone works, isn't it? What brings you here?'

Mr Biswas sat on a chair. Lalmohan Babu and I went back to the divan, and Feluda took the settee.

'I couldn't decide who to turn to,' Mr Biswas remarked, wiping his damp forehead with a handkerchief. 'I haven't got a lot of faith in the police, frankly speaking. Since you happened to visit us. . .'

'What is the problem?'

Mr Biswas cleared his throat. Then he said, 'My brother was not hit by a tree.'

The next few moments passed in silence. Feluda finally broke it by saying, 'No? What exactly happened?'

'He was struck deliberately. That blow to his head was an attempt to kill him.'

Calmly, Feluda took out his packet of Charminar and offered it to Mr Biswas, who declined politely. Feluda then took one out for himself, and said, 'But your brother seems convinced that it was a tree.'

'That's because he would rather die than name his son.'

'His own son?'

'Prashanta. His elder son. The younger one is in England.'

'What does Prashanta do?'

'It would be easier to tell you what he does not do. He's involved in every possible illegal activity. He changed over the last three or four years. My sister-in-law—Prashanta's mother, that is—died in 1970. About a month ago, my brother got fed up with Prashanta's behaviour and threatened to cut him out of his will. He said he'd leave all his property to his other son, Sushanta.'

'I see. Prashanta lives in the same house as you, I take it?'

'He could—certainly he has the right to live with us, and there's even a room meant for his use. But he doesn't. It's difficult to tell where he does live. He's part of a gang. Low-down criminals, each one of them. I think he would have killed his father that day if that terrible storm hadn't started.'

'What does your brother have to say about all this?'

'He insists it was a tree. He just doesn't want to believe that his son might be responsible for his injury. But I have to say this. Prashanta may be my nephew, but if you don't do something to stop him, he'll try to kill again.'

'If Naren Biswas makes a new will, his son will gain nothing by killing him, surely?'

'No, but a financial gain can't always be the only motive. He might just get furious and lose his head. People kill so often to take revenge and settle scores, don't they? Besides, my brother won't change his will. He cannot think straight. You have no idea, Mr Mitter, how far parental love can go.

'I was at home all this while, but today I have to go out of town for a few days. That's in connection with my business. So I came to you. Now if you will kindly . . .'

'Mr Biswas,' Feluda flicked the ash from his cigarette into an ashtray, 'I am very sorry to tell you that I'm already involved in a different case. Certainly your brother should receive some form of protection, but if he continues to insist that he was hit by a tree, no police force on earth can do anything to help him.'

Girin Biswas left. Until his arrival, we had all been feeling quite cheerful as the sun had come out after many grey and wet days. Girin Biswas had managed to spoil our mood.

'How very strange!' Feluda remarked when he'd gone, and finally made the phone call he was about to make when Mr Biswas arrived.

'Hello, Suhrid? This is Felu.'

Suhrid Sengupta and Feluda were classmates in college.

'Listen. Once I saw a copy of the Presidency College magazine in your house. It was a special issue, to mark its centenary. I think it belonged to your brother. Published possibly in 1955. Do you think he might still have it? . . . Oh good. Can you leave it with your servant before you go to work? I'll drop by at around half-past ten and collect it. All right? Thanks a lot.'

We finished our tea and left. Feluda had three ports of call—Naren Biswas, Bourne & Shepherd, and the Park Street cemetery. I was surprised to hear him mention Naren Biswas. 'That's because,' Feluda explained, 'I can't really dismiss what his brother just told us. So I ought to visit Mr Biswas once more. You two needn't go to the cemetery afterwards, but I think I'll ask you to come along for tonight's vigil. You must see and feel the atmosphere there, in the middle of the night. Or you'll miss an extraordinary experience.'

'Jai Santoshi Ma!' said Lalmohan Babu. A little later, he added, 'Tell me, can't one make Son of Santoshi, like Son of Tarzan?' That could only mean that he was still thinking of Pulak Ghoshal's offer.

Naren Biswas was physically a lot better. He told us he was no longer in pain, and his bandage would come off in a few days. Nevertheless, he did not look very happy. In fact, he looked decidedly morose and depressed.

'I'd like to ask you a few questions,' Feluda said, 'I won't take long.'

Mr Biswas cast a suspicious glance at him and asked, 'If you don't mind my asking, are you conducting an investigation? I know you are a detective, so . . .'

'Yes, you are quite right. It will help me a lot if you don't try to hide the truth.'

Mr Biswas closed his eyes, as if he was trying to deal with some inner pain. Perhaps he had guessed that it would not be easy for him to answer Feluda's questions.

'When you regained consciousness in the hospital,' Feluda began, 'you mentioned a will.'

Mr Biswas did not open his eyes.

'Why did you do that?'

This time, Naren Biswas opened his eyes. His lips moved and trembled a little, before he spoke. 'I am not obliged to answer your question, am I?'

'No, of course not.'

'In that case, I won't.'

Feluda remained silent. So did we. Mr Biswas looked away.

'Very well,' Feluda said after a few moments, 'let me ask you something else.'

'I reserve the right to remain silent.'

'Yes, you certainly have that right.'

'Well?'

'Who is Victoria?'

'Victoria?'

'Er . . . I have to make a confession here. I looked at the contents of your wallet. There was a piece of paper . . .'

'Ah . . . ha ha ha!' To our amazement, Mr Biswas suddenly burst out laughing. 'That's a very old story. I'd almost forgotten all about it. You see, when I was still working, one of my colleagues was an

Anglo-Indian. His name was Norton, Jimmy Norton. He once told me he had several letters in his house, all written by his grandmother. I never saw them. Apparently, his grandmother was in Behrampore at the time of the mutiny—she was only about seven. The letters were written much later, but she referred to her childhood experiences. Since there's some interest these days in such matters, and books are being written, I'd told Norton that I'd let him have the addresses of a few foreign publishers. Norton himself knew nothing about such things. Wait, let me get hold of that piece of paper.'

Mr Biswas stretched an arm to open the top drawer of a table and took out his wallet. There he found the slip of paper.

'Here, look! Bourne & Shepherd. I wanted to tell Jimmy to find out from Bourne & Shepherd if they had any old photos of his grandmother. And the rest are the initials of various publishers. I never got the chance to pass this piece of paper to Jimmy Norton. He went down with jaundice, and was off sick for six weeks. After that he left his job.'

Feluda rose to his feet. 'Thank you, Mr Biswas, that will be all. There's just one thing, though, that I think is most regrettable.'

'What is it?'

'In future, if you work in a library, please do not tear or cut anything out of an old book or magazine. That's my only request. Goodbye.'

We left the room. Mr Biswas could not bring himself to look anyone in the eye.

From Naren Biswas, we went to Feluda's friend, Suhrid Sengupta's house in Beni Nandan Street. His servant handed a huge tome to Feluda. It was the special centenary issue of the Presidency College magazine. On the way to Bourne & Shepherd, Feluda went through the magazine very carefully and, for some reason I failed to fathom, said, 'Just imagine!' at least three times.

It took Feluda only ten minutes to finish his business at Bourne & Shepherd. He came out carrying a large red envelope. Obviously, it contained an enlarged photograph, or perhaps there was more than one photo in it.

'Whose photo is that?' Lalmohan Babu asked.

'Mutiny,' Feluda replied. Lalmohan Babu and I exchanged glances. Feluda's reply clearly meant that the photo—or photos—were not meant for the public.

'Let's go to the cemetery,' Feluda said, 'but you two don't have to go in with me. I'll just check if everything is all right.'

Lalmohan Babu's driver parked the car in front of the cemetery. As Feluda passed through its gate, I saw the chowkidar, Baramdeo, give him a smart salute.

Feluda returned in a few minutes and got back into the car. 'Okay,' he said. It was decided then that we would go back to the cemetery that night, at half-past ten.

Something told me that we were very close to the final act in our play.

ELEVEN

Feluda and I had travelled to so many different places trying to solve mysteries—Sikkim, Lucknow, Rajasthan, Simla, Varanasi—and had had plenty of adventures everywhere. But I had no idea that this time, we would get involved in such a bloodcurdling experience without even stepping out of Calcutta.

Lalmohan Babu called the final day a 'black-letter day', but changed it later to 'a black-letter night'. I had to agree, when he asked me, that we had never been in such a fix before.

Lalmohan Babu was always punctual, but ever since he'd acquired a car, he'd become more strict about punctuality. That night, when he returned to our house, he knocked smartly on our door instead of rattling the knocker. Feluda and I had had our dinner and were ready. I was wearing my own hunting boots. Mine had been bought only the year before; Feluda's were eleven years old. Perhaps they were not in very good condition because I saw him fiddling with a sole and making repairs. Now he was limping a little. Perhaps he should have gone to a cobbler. Surely it wouldn't do to hobble if the night ahead was likely to be full of danger?

We got to our feet as soon as we heard the knock on the door. Feluda had a brown leather shoulder bag. A portion of the red envelope from Bourne & Shepherd was peeping out of it. He had instructed us to wear dark clothes. Lalmohan Babu was wearing a black suit.

He walked into our living room, saying, 'You wouldn't believe what modern medicine can do. My doctor told me about a nerve-soothing pill—it's got two "x"-s in its name! At his suggestion I took one after dinner, and already I feel charged and ready to take on the world. Dear Tapesh, come what may, we'll fight to the end, won't we?' He had no idea who he was supposed to fight, nor had I.

Feluda decided that our car should be parked at some distance from the main gate of the cemetery. 'If its colour matched your dark clothes, I wouldn't have worried,' he said. The driver, Hari, was told to stop the car even before we reached the crossing at Rawdon Street after passing St Xavier's. 'You two go ahead,' Feluda said, 'I have to leave some instructions with Hari.'

We left the car and walked on. God knows what Feluda's instructions were, but it was clear from Hari's general demeanour that he was most intrigued by our activities, and perfectly willing to join in.

Feluda came back in a few minutes. 'You are very lucky to have found such a good driver,' he told Lalmohan Babu. 'He seems most reliable. I'm quite relieved, now that I've asked him to handle certain responsibilities.'

'What responsibilities?'

'Nothing, really, if all goes well here. If it doesn't, a lot will depend on Hari.'

Feluda refused to say any more.

The large iron gate was standing open. How come? 'Normally, at this time of night, it would be closed,' Feluda whispered back when I asked him. 'But tonight there's a special arrangement. There are pieces of glass fixed to the edge of the compound wall, you see. Climbing over it would have been risky. But where's Baramdeo?'

A light flickered in the chowkidar's room, but it didn't look as if anyone was in there. We searched the area around the room, and found no one. In the faint light that came from Park Street, I could see a frown on Feluda's face. It meant that the chowkidar should have been in his room. That was the arrangement Feluda had made with him.

We decided not to waste any more time, and walked on, but not right down the central path this time. Feluda took a few steps, then turned left. We began moving through the host of tombstones. There was a strong breeze. Ribbons of clouds were flitting across the sky. A pale half-moon was peeping out fleetingly through them. When it did, the names on the marble plaques became visible just for a few moments, then they were gone. When we finally stepped behind a large tomb, the moon came out again, and I saw the name, Samuel Cuthbert Thornhill. This tombstone was not a long, tapering obelisk. There was something like a platform, surrounded by pillars which were covered by a dome. Three people could easily hide behind it. It was totally dark—the light from the main road did not reach that spot. However, if I looked to my right, I could see a portion of the gate through all the other tombstones.

Feluda spoke, possibly because he was reasonably sure there was no one in the cemetery except ourselves. But he kept his voice low. 'Could you please sprinkle this around?' he asked Lalmohan Babu, offering him a bottle with a stopper. He had taken it out of his shoulder bag.

'Sp-sprinkle?'

'Yes, it's carbolic acid. Should keep snakes at bay.'

Lalmohan Babu did as he was told, and returned a minute later. 'Well, that's a relief! Even a nerve-soothing pill couldn't take away my fear of snakes,' he remarked.

'What about your fear of ghosts? Has that gone?'

'Totally.'

Frogs were croaking nearby. Crickets were chirping. One of them seemed to have set up its home right next to Thornhill's grave. Scattered clouds were still flitting by. Perhaps some of them were thicker than the others, which was why the darkness all around us was growing deeper every now and then. As a result, the tombstones were all dissolving into one black mass. Then, as the moon slipped out, they separated from one another and became dimly visible again.

Feluda took out a packet of chewing gum, and offered it to us before putting some in his own mouth.

The sound of traffic was growing less. I counted the seconds, and realized that for nearly half a minute, I had heard nothing but the frogs, the crickets, and leaves rustling in sudden gusts of wind.

'Midnight!' whispered Lalmohan Babu.

Why midnight? Only a couple of minutes ago, I had looked at my watch in the moonlight. It was then twenty-five minutes past eleven.

'Why do you say it's midnight when it's not?' I had to ask.

'Oh, I said that only because . . . because midnight has a special . . . er . . . something, doesn't it?'

'What something?'

'Midnight in the graveyard, you see? That's special. I read it somewhere.'

'You mean that's when spooks come out?'

Instead of making a reply, Lalmohan Babu made a funny sound that ended in a hiss. A faint noise by my side told me that Feluda had struck a march, but had kept the flame hidden behind his hand. Then he lit a cigarette, inhaled and blew some smoke out, without removing his hand.

The clouds were getting thicker. The sound of traffic had stopped completely. The wind, too, was silent. Every noise, every sound had vanished. The crickets and the frogs had gone to sleep. My body felt cold, my throat was parched. I tried licking my lips, but they remained dry.

An owl hooted loudly. Lalmohan Babu promptly clapped his hands over his ears. Slowly, Feluda rose to his feet.

A car had stopped somewhere close by. It was impossible to tell exactly where it might be parked, but my instinct told me that the sound had come not from Park Street, but from Rawdon Street to the west. There was no gate facing Rawdon Street. There was only the compound wall, with pieces of broken glass fixed to its edge. I heard a car door slam.

Our eyes remained glued to the gate. Lalmohan Babu opened his mouth to speak, but Feluda stretched out an arm and gave his shoulder a light squeeze to stop him. No one came through the gate.

Perhaps there was some perfectly reasonable explanation why the car had suddenly arrived in the middle of the night. There were so many houses and residential apartments in the area. Perhaps someone had simply returned home after a late night show. I hoped fervently that that was the case. Then we need not worry about the car at all.

Feluda, however, was standing straight, his tense back flattened against the wall. Facing him was a pillar. Everything was pitch dark. No one could see us. But how were we going to see them? If they were here?

A minute later, I realized that there was no need to see anything. We did not have to use our eyes. Our ears told us what was happening.

Thud . . . thud . . . thud . . . thud!

Someone was digging the ground. The sound continued for some time. We listened with bated breath.

Thud . . . thud . . .!

It stopped. Now we could see a light. Through the gap between two distant obelisks, a dim light had travelled and fallen on the grass. It was not still, but moving, swaying, playing on the grass. It was clearly coming from a torch.

Suddenly, it disappeared.

'They climbed over the wall!' Feluda spoke through clenched teeth. 'I'll follow them!' he added. He was now waiting to hear the car restart.

A whole minute passed. Then another. And another.

'Strange!' remarked Feluda.

There was no noise, either from Rawdon Street or Park Street.

The car that had arrived was still parked at the same spot. What was going on?

Two more minutes passed. The clouds parted again. The moon reappeared. No one was in sight.

'Hold this, Topshe!' Feluda passed me his shoulder bag and stepped onto the grass. Then he began moving in the direction where we had seen the torchlight. There was no reason to worry about him—he had his Colt .32 in his pocket. Very soon, it was going to roar and shatter the silence of this cemetery.

But . . . Feluda was still limping. One of his boots was clearly bothering him. The limp was slight, but it was there. God knows why he had to try and repair his boot himself.

We waited. Where was the roar from Feluda's revolver? The silence continued.

'Mistake!' Lalmohan Babu spoke hoarsely. 'Your cousin made an awful mistake!'

I hissed like a snake to stop him from speaking further. Feluda had disappeared in the dark. I simply could not tell what was going on behind all those tombstones. What was that? A noise of some kind? No, I must have imagined it.

A clock struck the hour. Midnight. Where could the clock be? St Paul's? The wind was coming from that direction. Sometimes, if the wind blew from the west, from our house in Ballygunj we could hear lions roar in the Alipore zoo.

Oh. There was a car starting.

Another door slammed. Then it revved its engine, and drove off.

We could wait no longer. I wasn't afraid, but I certainly felt anxious.

The two of us got to our feet. Lalmohan Babu was muttering something, but I decided not to pay him any attention. There was no time for that.

We began walking as fast as we could, feeling our way through the tombstones. We passed one that said 'Mary Ellis'. Lalmohan Babu was clutching the back of my shirt. The grass under our feet was still wet, still cold.

The next plaque I could see said 'John Martin'. Then came Cynthia Collette. Captain Evans. That was followed by an obelisk. On a black marble plaque . . .

Crunch!

I had stepped on something. I removed my foot and looked down. The moon had come out again. I picked up the object.

It was a packet of Charminar, and it wasn't empty. There were quite a few cigarettes left in it. Each had been squashed.

Feluda!

I cannot tell what happened next. All I remember is a slight pressure on my mouth, and a smothered scream from Lalmohan Babu.

TWELVE

When I came round, the first thing I thought was that I was lying on the beach in Puri. It was only by the sea that one could hope to feel such a strong breeze. My ears felt cold, as did my nose. My hair was blowing in the wind.

But where was the sea? The water? Sand? Roaring waves? There was a sound . . . but it was certainly not the sea. I was in the back seat of a car, being driven in the dark, down an empty road. On my right was Lalmohan Babu. A complete stranger was sitting on my left. I had never seen the man before. The driver was wearing a turban. There was another man sitting next to him. No one was talking.

As soon as I raised my head, the man on my left looked at me. He looked a bit like a crook. But he didn't say anything. Why should he? We were unarmed, and offered him no threat. Feluda had a weapon. He was not in this car. I had no idea where he might be.

He had handed me his bag. Where was it?

There it was, behind my head, in the space in front of the rear windscreen. Its strap touched my cheek.

'Midnight!' said Lalmohan Babu. I gave him a sidelong glance. His eyes were still closed.

'Midnight! Ma! Jai Ma, Ma Santoshi! . . . Midnight . . .!'

'Shut up!' threatened the man on my left.

My eyes grew heavy again. Everything went dark once more. The sound of the car faded away.

When I opened my eyes again, I expected to find myself in a temple. No, not a temple. It had to be a church. These bells were not made of brass. They were ringing a foreign melody.

But it was neither a temple nor a church. It was, in fact, someone's drawing room. A chandelier was hanging from the ceiling, but it hadn't been lit. There wasn't a great deal of light in the room. All it had was a table lamp kept by the side of a settee with velvet upholstery.

I was sitting on another settee, also covered with velvet. No, not sitting. Reclining. By my side was Lalmohan Babu. His eyes were still closed. Feluda was seated in a chair on the other side. His face looked grim. The right side of his forehead was bruised and swollen. On our left stood a man, who we knew as Pyarelal. In his hand was a revolver, a Colt .32. Presumably, it was Feluda's.

There were three other men standing in the room. All were looking at us, but saying nothing. Perhaps the man who would do all the talking hadn't yet arrived. The largest settee in the room—upholstered in black velvet—was still empty. Maybe it was waiting for someone. Probably Mr Choudhury. But this was not the smart modern house in Alipore. It was a very old house. The ceiling appeared to be about thirty feet high. Its beams were all made of iron. The door was so enormous that a horse could have passed through it.

There was more. Clocks. Some were standing upright, others were hanging on the wall. One of the standing clocks was as high as a man of medium height, or maybe even higher than that. It was these clocks that had chimed a little while ago. It was two o'clock in the morning.

I had caught Feluda's eyes only once. The look in them said, 'Don't worry. I'm here to deal with things.' I had learnt to read Feluda's face. So I was feeling somewhat reassured.

'Good morning, Mr Mitter!'

It took me a few seconds to find the man who had spoken those words. He had come in through a door directly behind the lamp. His voice still had a velvety texture. In fact, it sounded smoother than before. There was reason for that. Now it was he who had the upper hand, not Feluda.

'What's that? Have you searched it thoroughly, Pyarelal?' he asked, looking at Feluda's shoulder bag. Somehow, it had made its way back to Feluda.

Pyarelal informed his master that the bag contained nothing but papers, a notebook and pictures. They had found a bottle, but it had been removed.

'I'm sorry you had to be dragged here, Mr Mitter, please don't mind,' Mr Choudhury said, oozing charm. 'Since you were so interested in that Perigal repeater, I thought you might be pleased to be present when it came into my hands. Balwant, have you finished cleaning the watch?'

One of the men nodded and told him that they were nearly done with the cleaning, it would soon be brought into the room.

'It has been lying in a grave for two hundred years,' Mr Choudhury continued, 'William did not tell me at first. All he told me was that he had a Perigal, but he was taking a very long time to bring it. Then, when I put pressure on him, he admitted that it was buried underground, hence the delay. As it was buried with a corpse, I told my men to dust and clean it properly before they brought it to me. I even told them to wipe it with Dettol.'

Feluda was looking straight at Mr Choudhury. It was impossible to tell from his face what he was thinking. Lalmohan Babu and I had been chloroformed. Feluda had been hit on the head and knocked unconscious.

'How did you learn about this particular watch, Mr Mitter?'

'From a diary written by someone in the nineteenth century. It was the daughter of the man who owned the watch.'

'A diary? Not a letter?'

'No. It was a diary.'

Mr Choudhury had taken out a packet of foreign cigarettes, together with a gold lighter and holder.

'Don't you know William?' he asked, inserting a cigarette into his holder.

'No, I don't know anyone called William.'

A flame appeared at the end of Mr Choudhury's Dunhill lighter.

'So what you read in that diary was enough to make you greedy?'

'Greedy? No, Mr Choudhury, only you have a monopoly on greed.'

A shadow appeared on Mr Choudhury's velvety face. The cigarette-holder, clutched between two fingers, was trembling a little.

'Mind how you speak to me, Mr Mitter!'

'I never mind how I speak to anyone, when I speak the truth. All I wanted to do was make sure that the watch did not leave Godwin's grave. If a man like you could lay . . .'

Feluda could not complete his sentence. A man had come into the room, carrying an object placed on a silk handkerchief. As soon as Mr Choudhury picked it up, Lalmohan Babu—sitting next to me—began groaning and spluttering.

'M-m-my-my-my-!'

He had just opened his eyes and seen the object in Mr Choudhury's hand. It was something with which Lalmohan Babu was thoroughly familiar.

It is impossible to describe what happened to Mr Choudhury. Once Feluda had told me that the seven major musical notes bore a relationship to the seven colours of a rainbow, but I had no idea that a man's face could change colour so quickly and pass through so many shades. Nor had I ever heard anyone's voice strike a different pitch every second.

The expletives that poured out of his mouth were difficult to hear, impossible to repeat. Feluda, however, remained perfectly unperturbed. I could tell the whole thing was his doing. When he had visited the cemetery in the afternoon, he must have done it then. But did that mean that the real watch did not exist at all?

Like a mad man, Mr Choudhury flung the Cooke-Kelvey watch on an empty chair by his side. 'Call William!' he roared, 'and give me that revolver!'

Pyarelal handed the revolver to Mr Choudhury and left the room. Mr Choudhury muttered 'Scoundrel!' and 'Swindler!' a couple of times. Then he got to his feet and began pacing impatiently.

Pyarelal returned in a few moments through the door at the back. With him was another man with long hair going down to his shoulders, and a moustache that drooped down to his chin. He was wearing trousers, a shirt and a cotton jacket.

'What is this watch that you've dug up?' Mr Choudhury thundered. He was sitting on the sofa once more, still clutching the revolver, his eyes still fixed on Feluda's face.

'I've brought you exactly what I found, Mr Choudhury,' pleaded the new arrival. 'How could I hope to cheat an expert like you?'

'What about that letter? Did it tell a lie?' Mr Choudhury's voice shook the entire room.

'How should I know, Mr Choudhury? That was the only thing we could depend on. Look, here it is.'

The man took out an old letter and offered it to Mr Choudhury. The latter took it, glanced at it briefly, then threw it away irritably. Feluda burst out laughing in the same instant. It was laughter born from pure amusement. I hadn't heard him laugh so merrily for a long time.

'What's there to laugh about, Mr Mitter?' Mahadev Choudhury shouted. Feluda controlled himself with an effort and replied, 'I am laughing because all your dramatic arrangements have come to nothing!'

Mr Choudhury rose with the gun in his hand and walked silently over to Feluda. The thick carpet on the floor stifled his footsteps. 'So you think my drama is over, do you? How do I know the real watch is not with you? You visited the cemetery so many times. Even this evening, you were there long before William. If you have got that watch, do you think I'll let you leave without taking it from you? You may have hidden it somewhere, but you will have to take it out yourself, and hand it over to me. Do you understand, Mr Mitter? Even if there is no watch, even if that letter is full of lies, why do you think I will spare you? Your habit of poking your nose into everything is most inconvenient for me. So don't think the drama is over. No, Mr Mitter. It has only just begun!'

When Feluda spoke, his voice held a note that I could recognize instantly. He always uses it when a case reaches its climax. Lalmohan Babu says it reminds him of the sound made by Tibetan horns.

'You are making a mistake, Mr Choudhury,' he said. 'The drama is now in my hands, not yours. I will direct it from now on. I will judge who is a bigger criminal—you, or that man called William . . .!'

Suddenly, complete chaos broke out in the room. William gave a giant leap, knocked down Pyarelal who was standing in front of him, and rushed towards the exit. Mr Choudhury fired his gun, but missed him by a couple of feet. The bullet hit the dial of a standing clock and shattered it completely. To everyone's surprise, the damaged clock immediately began chiming.

Two of the other men ran to catch William, but they could not go very far. Blocking their way was a group of armed men. They stopped everyone and entered the room, pushing William back into it. None of us had to be told that the man leading the group was a police inspector. Behind him were five constables and, peeping over their shoulders, was the eager and curious face of Lalmohan Babu's driver, Hari Datta.

'Shabash, Mr Datta!' said Feluda.

'You are Felu Mitter, aren't you?' the inspector asked, looking at Feluda. 'What on earth is going on here? I know Mr Choudhury, but who is this man who was trying to get away?'

Before answering the question, Feluda strode over to Mr Choudhury and retrieved his own revolver from him. Choudhury was obviously so completely taken aback that he did nothing to protest.

'Thank you, Mr Choudhury,' said Feluda. 'Kindly go back to the sofa. You will find it easier from there to watch the final scene in this drama. Besides, black velvet suits you so well! And Mr William—', Feluda's eyes turned away from Choudhury, 'in that wig and false moustache, you are looking exactly like your great-grandfather. Will you please take them off?'

One of the constables pulled at William's hair and moustache. Both came off easily, and we saw—to our absolute amazement—that the man standing in the place of William was Naren Biswas's brother, Girin Biswas.

'Now, tell me, Mr Biswas,' said Feluda, 'what is your full name?'

'Why, don't you know my name already?'

'You appear to have two names. Together, they make up your full name, don't they? You are called William Girindranath Biswas. Isn't that right? At least, that is how you are described in the list of gold medallists in the Presidency College magazine. And your brother is called Michael Narendranath Biswas. The "M" on his visiting card stands for "Michael", does it not? Since you generally use your Bengali names, your brother printed "N. M." on his card rather than "M. N.". Am I right?'

Girin Biswas remained silent. Feluda was obviously right.

'What does your brother call you?'

'Why? What's it to you?'

'Very well. If you won't tell anyone, I shall. He calls you "Will". When he regained consciousness in the hospital, it was your name that he mentioned twice. Isn't that so?'

Feluda took out a large red envelope from his bag. A photograph emerged from it. 'Look at these people, Mr Biswas. See if you know who they are. Perhaps you don't have this photo in your house. But there was a copy at Bourne & Shepherd.'

The photo showed a couple. Presumably, it was taken soon after their wedding. The man looked amazingly like Girin Biswas. The woman was clearly British.

'Do you know these people?' Feluda went on, 'the gentleman is Parvati Charan—P.C. Biswas, your great- grandfather. It is obvious from his clothes that he had become a Christian. The lady is Thomas Godwin's granddaughter, Victoria. It was she who wrote that letter. In fact, she had her photo taken even before she was married. Bourne & Shepherd have a copy of that, too. Victoria fell in love with your great-grandfather, a native Christian. So she fell out of favour with her own grandfather, Thomas Godwin. However, before he died, he forgave Victoria and gave her his blessings. A year later, Victoria and Parvati Charan were married.

'What this means is that Tom Godwin's name is linked with not one, but two families in Calcutta—one in Ripon Lane, and the other in New Alipore. What is more intriguing is that both families had old documents that mentioned Tom's watch. One was the letter from Victoria; the other was Thomas Godwin's daughter, Charlotte's diary.'

How extraordinary! Truth was really stranger than fiction. It turned out that a bundle of letters written by Victoria was lying in an old trunk in Naren Biswas's house. It had remained there for decades, but no one had bothered to read the letters. When Naren Biswas began to read up on the history of Calcutta, he came across the bundle one day and read every letter. That was how he learned about the Perigal repeater and told his brother, Girin.

All these details emerged slowly, as Feluda continued to shoot a volley of questions at Girin Biswas. Mr Biswas began to wilt visibly, but Feluda hadn't finished. Rather abruptly, he asked, 'Are you in the habit of going to the races, Mr Biswas?'

Mr Choudhury spoke before Girin Biswas could say anything. 'He took an advance from me!' he barked. 'And then he lost that money in the races, didn't he? Now he brings me a Cooke-Kelvey watch. Useless fellow!'

Feluda ignored Mr Choudhury. 'That means you inherited one of Tom's traits. Is that why you were prepared to take such an enormous risk?'

Girin Biswas made a spirited reply. 'Mr Mitter, there's one thing you seem to be forgetting. Anyone can bury his property in a grave. But, a hundred years after its burial, no one can make a personal claim on it. That watch is no longer Tom Godwin's property.'

'I am aware of that. The watch now belongs to the state. Even you cannot claim ownership. The truth is, you see, you didn't just try to steal from the cemetery. You did something else. That is also a criminal offence.'

'What offence?' Girin Biswas shot back defiantly.

Feluda took out a tiny object from his pocket. 'Let me see. Did this button come off the jacket you are wearing? Didn't you have it cleaned at Hong Kong Laundry only the other day?'

Feluda compared the little button in his hand with the others on Mr Biswas's jacket. 'Yes, it's a perfect match!' he declared.

'So what does that prove? That I went to the cemetery? Of course I did. I'm not denying it.'

'If I said this jacket wasn't your own, but your brother's, would you deny that?'

'What! You are talking complete nonsense, Mr Mitter!'

'No. If anyone is talking nonsense, it is you. You came to our house yesterday, and told us a pack of lies. Now you're doing it again. The jacket that you're wearing belongs to your brother. He was wearing it when he visited the cemetery just before the storm. He found Godwin's grave being dug up, and saw you there. He tried to stop you. You struck his head—with a heavy stick, or something like that. Naren Biswas lost consciousness. You would probably have killed him, but at that moment, the storm began. You tried to run away. The tree . . .'

Girin Biswas interrupted Feluda. 'Are you saying that my brother is a liar? Didn't he say himself that a branch broke and . . .?'

It was impossible to stop Feluda. He went on speaking, ' . . . the tree lost a branch. It broke and fell on your back. You were not wearing a jacket. So you took your brother's jacket and put it on to cover your bruises. That was when that button came off, and your brother's wallet slipped out of a pocket. From your own trouser pocket, a form-book for the latest race . . .'

Mr Biswas tried to make for the door again, but failed. This time, Feluda himself caught him and took his jacket off. Under his shirt, a bandage was clearly visible.

'Your brother told several lies to protect you, didn't he? He cares for you very deeply. Perhaps too much.'

Feluda picked up the watch made by Cooke-Kelvey, and the letter written by Victoria. Then he thrust them into his bag, and turned to Mr Choudhury, who was looking perfectly dumbstruck. 'Tonight, I missed the chance to hear all your clocks strike the midnight hour. But who knows, I might yet get the chance—one day!'

Lalmohan Babu could be aroused only after our third attempt. I had no idea that he had fainted again and missed the most crucial scene in the drama.

'The Mahadev Choudhurys of this world are very difficult to keep down. Even the police can't do anything. A man like him is like a Hitler. He can buy people off whenever he wants,' said Feluda.

We were now sitting by the Ganges. This particular ghat was only five minutes from Mr Choudhury's country manor. The eastern sky had started to brighten—the sun was about to rise. Heaven knew what would have happened to us if Hari Datta hadn't meticulously followed every instruction Feluda had given him. ('What would have happened? Death!' declared Lalmohan Babu.)

He had chased the car into which we had been bundled, and then gone straight to the police. Only a man with a steady nerve and a remarkable sense of responsibility could have handled such a task. Lalmohan Babu sipped tea from an earthen pot that Hari had fetched from somewhere, and said, 'So now you've seen all the good a new car can do!'

'Yes, undoubtedly,' Feluda replied. 'We have made several demands on your car in the last three days. When we get back to the city, I need to visit two more places. After that, I promise not to use your car—at least for a few days!'

'Two places? Where do you want to go?'

'First, to see Naren Biswas. We need to tell him what's happened, and return Victoria's letter to him.'

'And the second place?'

'The South Park Street Cemetery.'

'Ag-ag-again?'

'Do you have any idea how carefully I had to take every step? I couldn't even fight properly with those men because of this!'

Feluda removed the hunting boot from his left foot. Then he slipped a hand into it and took out a false sole, under which was a little compartment. In it, wrapped carefully in cotton wool, was an amazing object that was still undamaged except for a broken dial, in spite of all the turmoil that had swept over it.

'Don't we have to put it back where it belongs?'

Dangling from Feluda's fingers was the first reward bestowed by Nawab Sadat Ali on Thomas Godwin for his excellent cooking—a repeater pocket watch made by one of the best watchmakers in England, Francis Perigal. For two hundred years, it had lain buried underground beside the skeleton of its owner. Even so, as it caught the first rays of the rising sun, it glittered and dazzled our eyes.

The Curse of the Goddess

ONE

Lalmohan Babu looked up from his book and said, 'Rammohan Roy's grandson owned a circus. Did you know that?'

Feluda was leaning back, his face covered with a handkerchief. He shook his head.

Our car had been standing, for the last ten minutes, behind a huge lorry which was loaded with bales of straw. Not only was it blocking our way, but was emitting such thick black smoke that we were all getting choked. Our driver had blown his horn several times, but to no avail. I was tired of being able to see nothing but the painting of a setting sun and flowers on the back of the lorry, and all that a lorry usually said: 'Ta Ta', 'Horn Please', 'Goodbye' and 'Thank You'. Equally bored and tired, Lalmohan Babu had started to read a book called *The Circus in Bengal*. His next book was going to be set in a circus, so he had taken Feluda's advice and decided to do a bit of reading on the subject. As a matter of fact, we had stopped in Ranchi earlier in the day and seen posters advertising The Great Majestic Circus. It was supposed to have reached Hazaribagh which was where we were going. If we happened to be free one evening, we had decided to go and see the circus.

Winter had only just started. All of us wanted a short break. Lalmohan Babu's latest book—*The Vampire of Vancouver*—had been released last month and sold two thousand copies in three weeks, which naturally pleased him no end. Feluda had objected to the title of the book, pointing out that Vancouver was a huge modern city, a most unlikely place for vampires. For once, Lalmohan Babu had overruled Feluda's objection, saying that he had been through the atlas of the world, and Vancouver had struck him as the most appropriate name.

Feluda, too, was free for the moment. He had solved a case in Bihar last September. His client, Sarveshwar Sahai, had been so pleased with Feluda's work that he had invited us to his house in Hazaribagh. He did not live there permanently. It remained empty for most of the time. There was a chowkidar, whose wife did the cooking. We could stay there for ten days. All we would have to pay for would be the food.

The offer seemed too good to miss. We decided to go by road in Lalmohan Babu's new Ambassador. 'Let's see how it performs on a long run,' he said. We might have gone via Asansol and Dhanbad, but chose to go through Kharagpur and Ranchi instead. Feluda drove the car until we got to Kharagpur, then the driver took over. We reached Ranchi in the evening and stayed overnight at the Amber Hotel. This morning, we had left Ranchi at nine o'clock, hoping to reach Hazaribagh by a quarter past ten. But, thanks to the lorry, we were definitely going to be delayed.

After another five minutes of honking, the lorry finally moved and allowed us to pass. Much relieved, we took deep breaths as our car emerged in the open. The road was lined with tail trees, many of which had weaver birds' nests. If I looked out of the window, I could see a range of hills in the distance. Small hillocks stood by the side of the road. We passed these every now and then. Lalmohan Babu saw all this and muttered 'Beautiful! Beautiful!' a couple of times. Then he began humming a Tagore song, looking more comical than ever. He was totally tone-deaf as well, and inevitably chose songs that were quite inappropriate. For instance, on this cool November morning, he had started a song that spoke of the new joys of spring. He had once explained his problem to me. Apparently, he felt like bursting into song the minute he left Calcutta and came into closer contact with nature; however, his stock of songs being rather limited, he couldn't always think of a suitable one.

But there was one thing for which I had to thank him. In the last twenty-four hours, he had told me a lot of things about the circus in Bengal that I did not know. A hundred years ago, it was circuses owned by Bengalis that were famous all over the country. The best known among these was Professor Priyanath Bose's The Great Bengal Circus. There were American, Russian, German and French artists, in addition to Indian. Even women used to take part. An American called Gus Burns used to work with a tiger. Unfortunately, when Professor Bose died, there was no one to take charge. His circus went out of business, as did many others in Bengal.

'This Great Majestic in Hazaribagh . . . where does that come from, I wonder?' Lalmohan Babu asked.

'It has to be south India,' Feluda answered. 'They seem to have a monopoly in that line now.'

'How good is their trapeze? That's what I'd like to know!'

In this new book he was planning to write, trapeze was going to play an important role. One of the artistes was going to grab the arm of another while swinging in mid-air and give him a lethal injection. His hero, Prakhar Rudra, was going to have to learn a few tricks from trapeze artistes to be able to catch the culprit. When Lalmohan Babu revealed these details to us, Feluda remarked dryly, 'Thank goodness there is at least one thing left for your hero to learn!'

We saw the second Ambassador soon after passing a post that said '72 kms'. It was standing by the side of the road with its bonnet up. Its driver was bending over it, only partially visible from the road. Another gentleman was waving frantically at us. Lalmohan Babu's driver put his foot on the brake.

'Er . . . are you going to Hazaribagh?' the man asked. He was probably around forty, had a clear complexion and wore glasses.

'Yes, we are,' Feluda replied.

'My car . . . the problem seems to be serious, you see. So I wonder if . . . ?'

'You may come with us, if you like.'

'So kind of you. I'll try and get a mechanic and bring him back in a taxi. Can't see what else I can do.'

'Do you have any luggage?'

'Only a small suitcase, but I can take it with me later. It shouldn't take me more than forty-five minutes to return.'

'Come on then.'

The man explained to his driver what he had decided to do, then climbed into our car and said 'So kind of you' again. Then he told us a great deal about himself, even without being asked. His name was Pritindra Chowdhury. His father, Mahesh Chowdhury, was once an advocate in Ranchi. He had retired ten years ago and moved to Hazaribagh. Everyone there knew him well.

'Do you live in Calcutta?' Feluda asked him.

'Yes. I am in electronics. Have you heard of Indovision?'

I remembered having seen advertisements for a new television by the name. Mr Chowdhury worked for its manufacturers.

'My father turns seventy tomorrow,' he went on. 'I have an elder brother. He has already reached Hazaribagh, and so have my wife and daughter. I was away in Delhi, you see, so I very nearly did not make it. But my father sent me a telegram saying "Must come", so here I am. Could you please stop the car for a minute?'

The car stopped. Mr Chowdhury took out a small cassette recorder from his shoulder bag and disappeared among the trees. He returned in a couple of minutes and said, 'I heard a flycatcher. It was still there, luckily. It is something of an obsession for me—I mean, this business of recording bird calls. So kind of you.'

The last words were meant to convey his thanks for stopping the car. Strangely, although he told us so much about himself, he didn't seem interested in us at all.

We dropped him outside Eureka Automobiles in the main part of Hazaribagh. He said 'So kind of you' yet again and got out. Then he suddenly turned around and asked, 'Oh, by the way, where will you be staying?'

Feluda had to raise his voice to make himself heard, for a lot of people were gathered nearby, talking excitedly about something. We learnt the reason for such excitement a little later.

'I can't give you directions, for this is our first visit to Hazaribagh. All I can tell you is that the house belongs to a Mr Sahai, and it isn't far from the District Board rest house.'

'Oh, then it can't be more than seven minutes from our house. Do you have a telephone?'

'Yes—742.'

'Good.'

'My name is Mitter. P.C. Mitter.'

'I see. I didn't even ask your name. Sorry.'

We said goodbye and went on our way. 'He's probably tense about introducing a new product,' Feluda observed.

'Eccentric,' Lalmohan Babu proclaimed briefly.

The District Board rest house was not difficult to find. Mr Sahai's house stood only a few houses away. Our car stopped and tooted outside the gate over which hung colourful branches of bougainvillaea. A short, middle-aged man emerged immediately and opened the gate. Then he stood aside and gave us a salute. We drove up a long driveway and finally stopped before a bungalow. The man who had opened the gate came running to take our luggage. It turned out that he was the chowkidar, Bulakiprasad.

I realized how quiet everything was when we got out of the car. The bungalow was surrounded by a huge compound (Lalmohan Babu took one look at it and said, 'At least three acres!'). On one side was a garden with pretty flowerbeds. On the other side stood quite a few large trees. I could recognize mango and tamarind amongst them. Beyond the compound wall, in the far distance, were the Kanari Hills, about two miles away.

The house seemed ideal for three people. Three steps led to a veranda, behind which were three rooms. The one in the middle was the living room, the other two were bedrooms. Lalmohan Babu chose the one that faced west since he thought it would give him a good view of the sunset every evening.

We had only just begun unpacking, when Bulakiprasad came in with three cups of tea on a tray, and said something that made us drop everything and stare at him.

'When you go out, sir,' he said, 'please take great care.'

'Why? Are there pickpockets about?' Lalmohan Babu asked.

'No, sir. A tiger from the Great Majestic Circus has run away.'

What! What on earth was the man talking about?

Bulakiprasad did not hesitate to give us all the details. A huge tiger had escaped from its cage only that morning. He didn't know how that had happened, but the entire town was in a state of panic. The star attraction of the circus was this tiger. I remembered the painting of a tiger on all the posters I had seen in Ranchi. Feluda had even noticed the name of its trainer. 'A Marathi man,' he said, 'his name is Karandikar.'

Lalmohan Babu remained silent for a few moments after hearing this news. Then he said, 'This has to be telepathy. Would you believe it, I had been wondering if I could include something like this in my book? I mean, a tiger escaping from a circus is such a thrilling event, isn't it? But you, Felu Babu, must remain totally incongito. If they realize you are a detective, they'll get you to track the animal down, mark my words!'

Feluda and I were both so taken aback by what we had just heard that neither of us bothered to point out that the word was actually 'incognito'. He need not have feared, however. Feluda never disclosed his profession to anyone without a good reason.

Bulakiprasad also told us that, in the past, the circus used to be held in a park called Curzon Park which was in the middle of the town. But this year, for some reason, they had gone to an open area at one end of the town, beyond which stretched a forest. The tiger only had to cross the main road to go into it. There were small Adivasi villages in the forest, so it could quite easily feed on their domestic animals.

None of us had imagined we'd hear something so sensational within minutes of our arrival in Hazaribagh. But it seemed a great pity that we couldn't walk in the streets without having to watch out for a wild animal. Lalmohan Babu suggested after we had finished our tea that it might be a good idea to visit the circus in the afternoon to find out what exactly had happened.

'When you say visit the circus, do you mean going to the show?' Feluda asked.

'No, not really. I was actually thinking of meeting the owner. He'd be able to tell us everything, surely?'

'Yes. But, in order to do that, Mr Jatayu, you most definitely need the assistance of Felu Mitter.'

TWO

Bulakiprasad's wife made arahar daal and chicken curry for lunch. We did full justice to it, and then left in the car. Feluda was clearly as curious as Lalmohan Babu about the escaped tiger. He rang the local police station before we left. He had had to work with the police in Bihar on his last case, and Sarveshwar Sahai's name was well known in Hazaribagh. The inspector who answered the phone—Inspector Raut—recognized Feluda's name as soon as he had introduced himself and explained why he was calling. We did need help from the police to see the owner of the circus, under the present circumstances. 'One of our men is posted outside the main entrance,' Inspector Raut said. 'He will let you in.' Feluda told him he wanted to go there purely out of curiosity, not to start an investigation.

On our way to the circus, we saw groups of men gathered around street corners, still talking animatedly. Near a big crossing, someone was actually beating a drum and shouting words of caution. Feluda stopped at a small stall to buy a packet of cigarettes. The stallholder told him the tiger had been seen near a village called Dahiri to the north of Hazaribagh, but there were no reports of any damage.

My heart suddenly lifted at the sight of the tents as we got closer to the circus. It reminded me of all the circuses Feluda had taken me to when I was a small child. The blue-and-white striped tent of The Great Majestic Circus was very neat and tidy, which meant they were true professionals and knew their trade well. A yellow flag fluttered on top of the tent, and rows of bunting had been carefully arranged between the compound fence and the main entrance. Hundreds of people were jostling outside near the ticket counters. The show was going to go on even without the tiger. Various other posters showed what else the circus had to offer. The artist who had drawn them did not appear to be particularly gifted, but what he had managed was enough to arouse both curiosity and excitement.

The constable on duty had been told about us. He gave Feluda a smart salute, and let us in immediately. 'Mr Kutti—that's the owner—has been informed, sir. He's waiting for you in his room,' the constable said.

Behind the tent was an open space. It ended where a partition made with corrugated tin sheets began. Mr Kutti's caravan stood just behind the partition. Like the tent, it was tidy and well maintained. There were rows of windows on both sides. Curtains with attractive patterns hung at these, through which the sun came in and formed patches on the furniture. Mr Kutti rose as he saw us arrive and shook our hands. Then he gestured towards a mini sofa. He seemed to be around fifty, although his hair had turned totally white. When he smiled, his teeth gleamed in the semi-darkness of the caravan. They were clearly his own, not dentures.

Feluda explained, as soon as we were seated, that he had decided to call not because he had anything to do with the police, but because he had heard a lot about the Great Majestic and wanted to see their show. 'It's such a pity we can't see your best item!' he exclaimed. Then he introduced Lalmohan Babu as a famous writer who was interested in the circus and wanted to write a book about it.

Mr Kutti nodded. 'Before I joined a circus, I spent six years in Calcutta working for a shipping company,' he told us. 'I like Bengalis. They seem to understand and appreciate the true spirit of the circus. Please don't be disappointed just because our tiger is missing. There are quite a lot of other things to be seen. We had a special show yesterday. Many well-known personalities were invited. I am inviting you now, you are welcome to any of our shows.'

'Thank you,' Lalmohan Babu spoke unexpectedly. 'How did it happen? I mean, the tiger . . . ?'

'It's all very unfortunate, Mr Ganguli,' said Mr Kutti, 'the door of the cage was not fastened properly. The tiger pushed it open. Even so, it might not have got out in the open, but someone had removed a portion of the partition to make a short-cut and then forgotten to replace it. So the tiger slipped out through the gap. I have taken steps to find out who was responsible, and make sure it does not happen again.'

'Didn't a tiger once escape like this in Bombay?' Feluda asked.

'Yes, from the National Circus. It actually got out in the streets of Bombay, but the ringmaster caught it before it could get very far.'

Mr Kutti told us something else about the escaped tiger. Apparently, it had been spotted by at least fifty different people. There had been reports from various sources. A lady had seen it enter her courtyard and promptly fallen into a swoon. Why and how the tiger had left her unharmed was not known. Then there was a Nepali man who had seen the tiger cross a road. He himself happened to be driving a scooter at the time. Startled by the sight, he had driven straight into a lamp-post and was now in a hospital with three broken ribs.

'Surely you have a ringmaster?' Lalmohan Babu asked.

'Yes, Karandikar. But he hasn't been too well for sometime. He is nearly forty, you see. He gets a pain in his neck every now and then, but goes on to perform despite that. I have told him a million times to see a doctor, but he won't listen. So, about a month ago, I got another trainer, called Chandran. He's from Kerala and is very good in his work. It is he who acts as the ringmaster when Karandikar feels unwell.'

'Who performed with the tiger at the special show yesterday?' Feluda wanted to know.

'Karandikar. He seemed fine. There is one special item which only he can do. Chandran has never tried it. Karandikar puts his hands into the tiger's mouth, opens it wide, then puts his head in it. Unfortunately, something went wrong yesterday. He tried twice, but the tiger refused to open its mouth. Instead of trying again, Karandikar simply gave up and finished his show. There was some applause, but many people booed and jeered at him.'

'Didn't you do anything about it?'

'Of course. He's been with me for seventeen years, but I had to speak to him very sternly last night. Now he's saying he will leave the circus. That would be most unfortunate, both for him and for us. He can easily perform for at least another three years, I think. His work with the Great Majestic has made him quite well known.'

'Hasn't anyone from your team gone to look for the tiger?'

'Karandikar should have gone, but he flatly refused to have anything to do with a search party. So I sent Chandran with people from the Forest Department.'

'Could we see Karandikar?' Lalmohan Babu asked rather boldly.

'You could try, but there's no guarantee he'll agree to see you. He's extremely moody. I'll ask my bearer, Murugesh, to take you to his tent.'

Murugesh was standing outside. He came with us as we thanked Mr Kutti and left his caravan.

The ringmaster's tent was divided into two sections. One half of it acted as a living room. The other was clearly where he slept. Much to our surprise, he came out of this 'bedroom' as soon as he was informed of our arrival. One look at him told me why a tiger obeyed his command. I had rarely seen anyone who looked so strong physically. He was as tall as Feluda, but his body was much more muscular. A jet-black moustache on a fair skin gave him an added air of strength and power. His eyes seemed distant, but sometimes they glowed with emotion as he spoke. He told us he could speak Marathi, Tamil and Malayalam, in addition to English and Hindi. Feluda decided to speak to him in English.

The first thing Mr Karandikar asked was whether we had been sent by a newspaper. Perhaps the notebook and pencil in Lalmohan Babu's hands prompted this question. Feluda had to choose his words carefully before making a reply. 'Suppose we were newspaper reporters. Would that make any difference? I mean, would you object to talking to the press?' Feluda asked.

'Oh no. On the contrary. I'd be glad to talk to them. People must be told that if the tiger escaped from his cage, it was certainly not the fault of his old trainer. The owner of this circus must take all responsibility. A tiger does not obey two different trainers. It can respond to only one. Sultan had started to get irritable soon after the other trainer arrived. I had explained this to Mr Kutti, but he didn't pay any attention to me. Now I hope he's happy with the result.'

'Why didn't you go to look for your tiger?'

'Why should I? Let them find him again!' he said, sounding deeply hurt.

Lalmohan Babu whispered something into Feluda's ear. This meant he wanted to ask Mr Karandikar something, but was afraid to. Feluda translated quickly.

'Would you go if the others fail, or if your presence becomes absolutely necessary for some reason?'

'Why, yes! If I hear anyone is thinking of killing my Sultan, I'll certainly go and try to save him. I look upon him as family—no, I think he's even closer to me than a family member.'

I, too, wanted to ask him something. As it turned out, I didn't have to. Feluda spoke before me.

'Did a tiger ever scratch your face?'

'Yes, but it wasn't Sultan. I used to work for The Golden Circus before I joined the Great Majestic. It was one of their tigers. It clawed my face; one of my cheeks and my nose were badly injured.' He than took his shirt off. We were amazed to see endless scars on his body. Heaven knows how many times he had been mauled.

Before we left, Feluda asked him one last question. 'Will you continue to stay here?'

'I don't know. A small tent in a circus has been my home for more than seventeen years. Now . . . I may well have to look for something different. Who knows?'

Lalmohan Babu wanted to see all the other animals. He had already spoken to Mr Kutti about it. When we left Mr Karandikar, Murugesh took us to where the animals were kept. There were two other tigers, a large bear, a hippopotamus, three elephants and six horses. Sultan's cage stood on one side. There was something rather eerie about its emptiness.

By the time we got back home, it was five o'clock. Bulakiprasad came in with the tea a little later, and told us that someone from Mr Chowdhury's house had called in our absence. He would call again later, he had said.

Pritindra Chowdhury arrived at half past six. The sun had set by this time, and the temperature had dropped appreciably. We had all slipped on our woollen pullovers.

'You didn't tell me you were a detective!' Pritin Babu said most unexpectedly. 'When I told my father about you, he said he knew you were coming. Your client, Mr Sahai, knows him, you see. He had happened to mention your visit. I am here now to invite you to our picnic tomorrow. Baba would like all of you to come.'

'A picnic?' Lalmohan Babu raised his eyebrows.

'Didn't I tell you? It's Baba's birthday tomorrow, so we are all going to Rajrappa for a picnic. We'll have lunch there. If you came to our house in your car at around nine o'clock, we could all leave together. Our house is called Kailash. It's not far from here, I'll tell you how to find it. And,' he added, 'if you came a little earlier than nine, you'd be able to see my father's collection of butterflies and rocks.'

Rajrappa was fifty miles from Hazaribagh. It had a waterfall and an old Kali temple called the temple of Chhinnamasta. It was well known for its scenic beauty. We had heard of it before and had, in fact, planned to go there ourselves during our stay.

'But . . .' Lalmohan Babu began doubtfully, 'haven't you heard about the tiger?'

'Yes, of course,' Pritin Babu laughed, 'but there's no cause for alarm. My brother is a crack shot. He'll be taking his gun with him. Besides, the tiger is supposed to have gone to the north. Rajrappa is to the south of Hazaribagh, near Ramgarh. You may relax.'

Feluda thanked him and said we would arrive at his house at eight-thirty. Pritin Babu gave us the necessary directions and left.

'Why is the house called Kailash, I wonder?' Lalmohan Babu asked.'

'Possibly because its owner is called Mahesh,' Feluda replied. 'Mahesh is another name for Shiva, isn't it? Since Shiva lives in Mount Kailash, Mahesh Chowdhury decided to call his house by the same name.'

It was now pitch dark outside. But we did not switch the lights on since the moon had risen and we wanted to sit by its light on the veranda. For some strange reason, Lalmohan Babu was muttering the word 'Chhinnamasta' under his breath, over and over. Then he suddenly stopped at 'Chhin—' because Feluda had raised a hand.

We sat in silence for a few seconds. There was no noise outside except the steady din made by crickets. Then, from the far distance, came a different noise. It froze my blood, for I had heard it before. It was the roar of a tiger. We heard it three times.

Sultan was calling from somewhere. Only an experienced shikari could tell how far he was, and from which direction he was calling.

THREE

I had thought the news of an escaped tiger would be the highlight of our stay. But who knew something else would happen, and Feluda would get inextricably linked with it? I will not be able to forget Mahesh Chowdhury's birthday on 23 November for a long time to come. And the memory of the scenes in Rajrappa, particularly the temple of Chhinnamasta, standing against its strangely beautiful dry and rocky background, will always stay alive in my memory.

But I must go back to the previous evening. The roar of the tiger made Lalmohan Babu go rather pale. However, just as I was about to suggest he should sleep in our room, he announced that he was fine, but could he please have the big torch with five cells? The reason for this was that he had heard somewhere a tiger would retreat if a bright light shone in its eyes for more then a few seconds. 'Mind you,' he said before going to his own room, 'if the tiger roared outside my window, I'm not sure if I'd have the nerve to open it and shine the torch in its face. But Bulakiprasad tells me he has a weapon, and he's not afraid of wild animals.'

Luckily, even if the tiger did pay us a visit in the middle of the night, it decided not to roar; so all was well.

We reached Kailash the following morning on the dot of eight-thirty. Lalmohan Babu took one look at the house and said, 'The Shiva who lives in this Kailash must be an English one!' Feluda and I had to agree with him. It might have been built only ten years ago, but its appearance was that of a house built fifty years ago during British times.

A chowkidar opened the gate for us. We passed through and parked in one corner of the compound. There were three cars. Pritin Babu's black Ambassador, a white Fiat and an old yellow Pontiac.

'Look, Felu Babu, I have found a clue!' Lalmohan Babu exclaimed. He had found a piece of paper near the edge of the lawn. Like Mr Sahai's house, Kailash had a garden on one side.

'How can you find a clue when there's no mystery?' Feluda laughed.

'I know, but just look at what's written on it. Doesn't it seem sort of mysterious?'

It was a leaf torn from a child's exercise book. A few letters from the alphabet were written on it. There was no mystery in it at all. Whoever had written it seemed to be rather fond of the letter 'X'. It said:

XLNC
XL
XPDNC
NME
OICURMT

Feluda put it in his pocket with a smile.

A very old Muslim bearer was standing near the portico. He said 'Salaam, huzoor', and took us inside. A familiar voice had already reached our ears. We saw Pritindra Chowdhury as soon as we stepped into the drawing room. He came forward to greet us warmly: 'Oh, do come in. So kind of you to come!'

We returned his greeting, then stood still, staring at the walls. Instead of framed paintings, they were covered by framed butterflies. Each frame had eight of them, carefully pinned and beautifully displayed. There were eight such frames, which made a total of sixty-four butterflies, each with its wings spread, looking as though they were ready to take flight. The whole room seemed to glow with their bright colours.

The collector himself was seated on a sofa. He rose with a smile when he saw us enter the room. In his youth, he must have been both good looking and physically strong. He was still tall, and held himself straight. His complexion was very fair, he was clean-shaven and dressed in a fine dhoti, a silk kurta and a heavily embroidered Kashmiri shawl. On his nose were perched rimless glasses.

Pritin Babu only knew Feluda's name, so Lalmohan Babu and I had to be introduced by Feluda. Before Mahesh Chowdhury could say anything, Lalmohan Babu piped up, 'Happy birthday to you, sir!'

Mr Chowdhury laughed. 'Thank you, thank you! I don't see why an old man like me should celebrate his birthday, but this whole thing was arranged by my daughter-in-law. Look, she even made me dress up. But I am very glad you were able to come. Hope you didn't find it difficult to find our K dash eyelash?'

Lalmohan Babu and I stared dumbly at him. But Feluda raised his eyebrows only for a fleeting second before saying, 'No, sir, we found it quite easily.'

'Good. I knew you'd get my meaning. You must be used to dealing with codes and ciphers. However, your friends are still looking puzzled.'

Feluda had to take out his small notebook and pen and write the code down to explain. 'K—eyelash,' he wrote. 'Now say the words quickly,' he said with a smile. Lalmohan Babu promptly started saying 'K eyelash, K eyelash' rapidly, breaking off suddenly to say, 'Oh, oh, I see. It does sound like Kailash, doesn't it?'

I had to laugh. Then I saw a little girl of about five, who was sitting on the floor in the middle of the room with a doll in her lap. In her hand was a pair of tweezers. She kept pinching the doll's forehead with it, possibly to pretend that she was tweezing its eyebrows.

'That's my granddaughter,' Mr Chowdhury said. 'She's a double-bee.'

'I see. You mean she is called Bibi?' Feluda asked. This time, even I could figure out double-bee could only mean BB. Feluda and I often played word games at home, so this wasn't difficult.

'Yes. I like playing with words,' Mahesh Chowdhury explained.

'Let me get my brother,' said Pritin Babu and left the room. We sat down. Mr Chowdhury was smiling a little, looking straight at Feluda. Feluda returned his look without the slightest trace of embarrassment, and smiled in return.

'Well, well, well!' Mr Chowdhury said finally. 'Sarveshwar Sahai praised you a lot. So when I heard you were here, I told Trey to call you. My life is full of mysteries, Mr Mitter. Let's see if you can solve any.'

'Trey? Do you mean your third son?'

'Right again.'

'I like word games, too.'

'Very good. My oldest son—I call him Ace—can occasionally understand my meaning when I speak in codes, but Trey is quite hopeless. Anyway, how long have you been working as a detective?'

'About eight years.'

'I see. What about Mr Ganguli? What does he do?'

'He writes murder mysteries, under the pseudonym of Jatayu.'

'Really? What a fine combination! One creates mysteries, the other destroys them.'

'I can see your collection of rocks and butterflies,' Feluda remarked, 'but is there anything else you used to collect?'

The rocks and stones were displayed in a glass case that stood in a corner. I had no idea stones could be of so many different types and colours. But what did Feluda mean? Mr Chowdhury looked quite taken aback and asked, 'Why do you ask about other collections? What else could I have collected?'

'Those tweezers young Bibi is using appear to be quite old.'

'Brilliant! Brilliant!' Mr Chowdhury exclaimed. 'What sharp eyes you've got! But you are absolutely right. I used to collect stamps, and those were my tweezers. Even now, I sometimes look at the Gibbons catalogue. Philately was my first passion in life. When I used to practise as a lawyer, one of my clients called Dorabjee gave me his own stamp album to show me how grateful he was. He must have lost his interest in stamps by then, or certainly he would not have given it away like that. It had quite a few rare and valuable stamps.'

I felt quite excited to hear this. I had started to collect stamps myself, and knew that Feluda, as a young boy, used to do the same.

'May we see that album?' Feluda asked.

'Pardon?' Mr Chowdhury said after a few moments of silence. He had suddenly grown a little preoccupied. Then he seemed to pull himself together.

'The album?' he said. 'No, I'm afraid I cannot show it to you. It's lost.'

'Lost?'

'Yes. Didn't I just tell you my life was full of mysteries? Mysteries . . . or you may even call them tragedies. But let's not talk about it on a fine day like this . . . Come on, Ace, let me introduce you!

Pritin Babu had returned with his brother. He was much older, but there was a marked resemblance between the two brothers. 'Ace' was a handsome man, if just a little overweight.

'Trey could probably tell you a lot about mikes,' Mr Chowdhury said. 'Ace can only talk about mica. He has a business that deals with mica His real name is Arunendra. His office is in Calcutta, but his work often brings him to Hazaribagh.'

'Namaskar,' Feluda said, 'you are Ace and Pritin Babu is Trey. Is that Deuce?' He was looking at a photograph in a silver frame. It was a family group photo, taken at least twenty-five years ago. Mahesh Chowdhury and his wife were standing with two young boys. A third much smaller boy was in his wife's arms. The younger of the two boys standing had to be Deuce.

'Yes, you are right,' Mr Chowdhury replied, 'but you might never get the chance to meet him, for he has vanished.'

Ace—Arun Babu—explained quickly: 'He was called Biren. He left home at the age of nineteen to go to England, and did not return.'

'We don't know that for certain, do we?' Mr Chowdhury sounded doubtful.

'If he did, Baba, surely you'd have heard about it?'

'Who knows? He didn't write me a single line in the last ten years!' Mr Chowdhury's voice sounded pained.

No one spoke after this. The atmosphere suddenly seemed to have become rather serious. Perhaps Mr Chowdhury realized this. He stood up, and said cheerfully, 'Come on, let me show you around.

Akhil and Shankar haven't arrived yet, have they? So we have a little time.'

'You don't have to get up, Baba,' Arun Chowdhury said. 'I can take them upstairs.'

'No, sir. This is my house; I planned it and I had it built. I will, therefore, show it to my visitors.'

We followed him upstairs. There were three bedrooms, and a lovely wide veranda that overlooked the street on the north side. The Kanari Hills were dimly visible in the distance. Mr Chowdhury's bedroom was in the middle. The other two were occupied at the moment. Arun Babu was in one, and Pritin Babu was in the other with his wife and daughter. There was a guest room on the ground floor, we were told. Mahesh Chowdhury's friend, Akhil Chakravarty, was staying in it.

I noticed more butterflies and rocks in Mr Chowdhury's bedroom. A bookshelf in a corner contained rows of notebooks, almost identical in appearance. Mr Chowdhury caught Feluda looking at these and said they were his diaries. He had kept diaries regularly over a period of forty years. On a bedside table was another small framed photograph of a man, but not of anyone from the family. Lalmohan Babu recognized him instantly.

'Ah, it's Muktananda, isn't it?'

'Yes. My friend Akhil gave it to me,' Mr Chowdhury replied. Then he turned to Feluda and added, 'He has three continents to back him up.'

'Correct!' Lalmohan Babu sounded quite excited. 'He is a famous Tantric sadhu. Asia, Europe and America—he has followers everywhere.'

'How do you know so much about him? Are you a devotee yourself?'

'Oh no. But one of my neighbours is. He told me about his guru.'

There was nothing more to see on the first floor. As we began climbing down, I heard a car arrive. The two men Mr Chowdhury was waiting for soon made an appearance. One of them was of about the same age as Mahesh Chowdhury. He was wearing an ordinary dhoti and kurta and had a plain dark brown shawl wrapped around his shoulders. It was obvious that he had never had anything to do with the complex world of the law; nor did he seem even slightly westernized in any way. The other man was much younger, probably under forty. He had a smart and intelligent air.

He came forward quickly and touched Mr Chowdhury's feet as soon as he saw him. The older gentleman was carrying a box of sweets. He passed it to Pritin Babu and said, 'Look, Mahesh, please listen to me. Drop the idea of a picnic. The time's not auspicious at all, and then there's that tiger to be considered. What if he decides to visit the temple of Chhinnamasta?'

Mr Chowdhury turned to us. 'Please allow me to introduce you. This man here who cannot stop seeing danger and pitfalls everywhere is a very old friend, Akhil Bandhu Chakravarty. He used to be a schoolteacher. Now he dabbles in astrology and ayurveda. And this is Shankarlal Misra. I am exceedingly fond of this young man. You might say I look upon him as a sort of replacement for my missing son.'

We greeted one another, and then everyone began to get ready to leave. Akhil Chakravarty tried one last time: 'So nobody's going to heed my warning?'

'No, my dear,' Mr Chowdhury replied. 'I hear the tiger is called Sultan. That means he's a Muslim. He's not likely to want to visit a Hindu temple, never fear. Oh, by the way, Mr Mitter, do go and see the circus, if you can. We were invited the day before yesterday. I went with little Bibi and her mother. I had no idea that Indian circus had made such progress. The items with the tiger, particularly, were most impressive.'

'But didn't something go wrong towards the end?'

'Yes, but that wasn't the ringmaster's fault. Even animals have moods, don't they? The tiger was not in the right mood, that's all. After all, it's a living being, not a machine that will run each time you press a button.'

'Yes, but see what the animal's mood has done,' Arun Babu remarked. 'There's panic everywhere. That tiger ought to be killed. This would never have happened if it was a foreign circus.'

His father smiled dryly, 'Yes, your hands must be itching to pick up your gun. Anyone would think you were the president of the Wildlife Destruction Society!'

We met another person before leaving for Rajrappa. It was Pritin Chowdhury's wife, Neelima Devi. Like the rest of her family, she was very good looking.

FOUR

Rajrappa was eighty kilometres from Hazaribagh. We had to take a left turn when we reached Ramgarh, which took us through a place called Gola. Beyond Gola was the Bhera river. All cars had to be left here, and the river had to be crossed on foot. Rajrappa lay on the other side, only a short walk away.

Shankarlal Misra did not have a car, so he travelled with us. Two bearers had also joined the group. One of them was the old Noor Muhammad, who had been with Mr Chowdhury since he started working as a lawyer. The other was the tall and hefty Jagat Singh, who was carrying Arun Chowdhury's rifle and cartridges.

Mr Misra proved to be very friendly and easy to talk to. From what he told us about himself, it seemed there was a mystery in his life as well. His father, Deendayal Misra, used to work as Mahesh Chowdhury's chowkidar. Thirty-five years ago, when Shankar was only four, Deendayal suddenly went missing one day. Two days later, a woodcutter found his body in a forest nearly eight miles away. He had been killed by a wild animal. No one knew why he had gone to the forest. There was an old Shiva temple there, but Deendayal had never been known to visit it.

Mahesh Chowdhury took pity on Deendayal's child. He brought him to his house, and began to bring him up like his own son. In time, Shankar proved to be a very bright student. He won scholarships and finished his graduation from Ranchi University. Then he opened a bookshop called Shankar Book Store in Ranchi. Recently, he had opened a branch in Hazaribagh. He travelled frequently between the two cities.

This mention of books prompted Lalmohan Babu to ask, 'What kind of books do you keep in your shop?'

'All kinds,' Mr Misra replied, smiling, 'including crime thrillers. We have often sold your books.'

After a few moments, Feluda asked, 'Mahesh Chowdhury's second son must have been the same age as yourself. Is that right?'

'Who, Biren? He was younger than me, but only by a few months. We went to school together, and were in the same class. All three brothers went to Calcutta for higher studies, but Biren was never really interested in them. He was always restless, fond of adventures. I was not surprised when he left home at nineteen.'

'Does his father believe in tantrics and holy men?'

'He didn't earlier. But he has changed a lot over the years. I didn't see it myself, but I've heard that he used to have an extremely violent temper. He may not actually visit holy men, but today . . . I believe the reason for going to Rajrappa is that temple of Chhinnamasta.'

'Why do you say that?'

'He doesn't talk about it, but I have gone to Rajrappa with him before, more than once. I've seen how the look on his face changes when he visits the temple.'

'Could this be linked to something in his past?'

'I don't know. I know very little about his past. Don't forget I was only his chowkidar's son, never really one of the family.'

At around ten-thirty, three cars stopped by the side of the Bhera river. Ours was the last, just behind Pritin Chowdhury's car. We saw him get out, tape recorder in hand, and disappear among the trees on our left. Mahesh Chowdhury was in the first car. He got out, and came towards us. 'Let's have a cup of coffee before going across,' he said. 'Rajrappa isn't far from here. There's no point in hurrying.'

We walked towards the river. There wasn't much water in it now, but after the monsoon it often became knee-deep, which made it difficult to cross. Even now, it was flowing with considerable force, rushing over a great many rocks of various sizes and different colours, polishing and smoothing their surface, as if it was in a great hurry to jump into the great Damodar. Rajrappa stood at the point where the Bhera met the Damodar.

Neelima Devi opened a flask and began pouring coffee into paper cups. We went and helped ourselves. Pritin Babu was the only one missing. Perhaps he had had to go deeper into the wood to record bird calls. A variety of birds were chirping in the trees.

I looked at and tried to make a study of every new character I had met since my arrival. Feluda had taught me to do this, although his own eyes caught details that I inevitably missed.

The youngest in our group had placed her doll on a flat stone and was talking to it: 'Sit quietly, or I'll throw you into the river. You wouldn't like that, would you?'

Arun Babu finished his coffee, threw the cup away, then disappeared behind a bush. The faint smoke that rose a little later told me that he didn't smoke in his father's presence.

Mahesh Chowdhury was standing quietly by the river, staring at its gushing water. His hands were clasped behind his back.

Feluda had picked up two small stones and was striking one

against the other to see if they were flint, when Akhil Chakravarty walked up to him and said, 'Do you know what sign you were born under?'

'Yes, sir. Aquarius. Is that good or bad for a detective?'

Neelima Devi picked up a wild yellow flower and stuck it into her hair. Then she looked at Lalmohan Babu and said something which made him throw back his head and laugh. But, only a second later, he stopped abruptly, gasped and jumped aside. Neelima Devi's laughter broke out this time. 'That was only a harmless chameleon!' she said. 'Don't tell me you are afraid of them?'

I looked around for Shankarlal, but saw that he had already crossed the river and was talking to a man in saffron clothes, on the other side. A busload of visitors had crossed over a few minutes ago. The saffron-clad sadhu must have been one of them.

We finished our coffee, and Pritin Babu returned. It was now time to wade through the river. Everyone lifted their clothes by a couple of inches. Little Bibi decided to ride on Noor Muhammad's back, and I saw Lalmohan Babu stop, close his eyes and mutter something before stepping on to a stone. He nearly lost his balance at least three times before he got to the other side. Then, landing safely on the dry ground, he said, 'Hey, who knew that was going to be so easy?'

There were more trees here, though not enough to call it a wood. Nevertheless, from the way Lalmohan Babu kept casting nervous glances over his shoulder, I knew that he had not forgotten about the tiger. We turned a corner in a few minutes, and stopped. It was as if a curtain had been lifted to reveal Rajrappa. Lalmohan Babu said, 'Waah!' so loudly that two little birds flew away.

He had every reason to say that. I could see both rivers from where we stood. On our left was the smaller river, the Bhera, and to our right, down below, flowed the Damodar. There was a waterfall, not yet visible, but I could hear it. Huge rocks stood out from the water, looking like giant turtles. The forest began at a distance, beyond which stood the hills in a faint, bluish line. It was a truly charming sight.

The temple was only twenty yards away. It was obviously quite old, but parts of it had been restored recently. Only a few days ago, we were told, a buffalo had been killed here for Kali Puja. 'I bet once they used to have human sacrifices!' Lalmohan Babu muttered into my ear. He might well have been right.

None of the passengers who had come by bus seemed interested in the scenery. All of them had gathered before the temple. Shankarlal was right about Mahesh Chowdhury. I saw him stand still at the door of the temple and stare inside. He spent nearly a minute there, although it was so dark inside that the statue was almost invisible. Then he moved away, and slowly followed the others.

The waterfall came into view in a few minutes. The two bearers began spreading a durrie on the sand.

'This is an unexpected bonus, isn't it?' Lalmohan Babu said. 'Who knew we'd be invited to a picnic on the second day of our visit?'

'This is only the beginning,' Feluda observed.

'Really?'

'Have you ever played chess?'

'Good God, no!'

'If you had, you'd have understood my meaning. When a game of chess comes to a close, and only a few pieces are left on the board, something like an electric current flows between the two players. Neither of them moves, but they can feel it with every nerve in their body. All the members of the Chowdhury family remind me of these pieces. What I still don't know is who is black and who is white—or who's the king, and if there's a bishop.'

We chose a spot between the temple and the place where the main picnic was being arranged, and sat down under a peepul tree. It was not yet eleven o'clock. Everyone was relaxed and roaming around lazily. Bibi was sitting on the sand, and Akhil Chakravarty was talking to her, explaining something with different gestures. Neelima Devi was sitting on the durrie. I saw her take out a paperback from her bag. It was probably a detective novel. Pritin Babu was walking aimlessly; then he sat down on a small mound and began inserting a new cassette into his recorder. Arun Babu took his gun from Jagat Singh, and Mahesh Chowdhury picked up a stone from the ground, only to throw it away again.

'Shankarlal is not around,' Lalmohan Babu commented.

'Yes, he is, but at some distance. Look!'

I followed Feluda's gaze and saw that Shankarlal was standing under a tree behind the temple, still chatting with the sadhu.

'Somewhat suspicious, isn't it?' Lalmohan Babu asked. I looked at Feluda to see if he agreed, but before he could say anything, Arun Chowdhury walked over to us, gun in hand.

'Is that adequate for a tiger?' Feluda asked him.

'That tiger from the circus is not going to come here,' Arun Babu laughed. 'I have killed sambar with this gun, but usually I only kill birds. This is a twenty-two.'

'Yes, so I see.'

'Do you hunt?'

'Only criminals.'

'Do you work for an agency? Or are you private?'

Feluda handed him one of his cards with 'Pradosh C. Mitter, Private Investigator' written on it.

'Thanks,' said Arun Chowdhury. 'I may need it one day, who knows?'

Then he moved away.

I saw Feluda clutching the same piece of paper we had found near the lawn in Kailash. This surprised me, for I hadn't seen him taking it out.

'Why this sudden interest in letters from the alphabet?' Lalmohan Babu wanted to know.

'Look carefully. These aren't just letters from the alphabet. These are words, proper words.'

'Nonsense! If they are, it must be some strange foreign language.'

'Not at all. These are ordinary English words, and you know them very well. Try reading them out.'

Lalmohan Babu leant across to read the letters.

'Eks El En See,' he read, 'Eks El. Eks Pee Dee . . . oh, I see! The first word is "excellency", isn't it? One has to read it quickly. And the second word is "excel". Then it's "expediency", and the last word is "enemy". But what's this beginning with an O?'

'OICURMT,' I read quickly. 'That's "oh I see you are empty".'

'Good. How clever!' Lalmohan Babu beamed.

With a grin, Feluda turned the paper over. More words and figures were written oh it:

UR
2 good
2 me
2 be
4 got
—
10
—

'Read it,' he said to Lalmohan Babu, who seemed to have got the hang of things and was enjoying it hugely.

'You are too good to me to be four-got-ten? I see, that should read "forgotten". Yes, that's right.'

'OK, now look at the other words. Topshe, try and work it out.'

I looked carefully. There were two columns, one showing words, and the other possibly their meaning:

Revolution	to love ruin
Telegraph	great help
Astronomers	no more stars
Festival	evil fast
Funeral	real fun

'Anagrams?' I asked.

'Yes. The last three are called "antigrams", for they give you the opposite meaning to the real one. I mean, "funeral" could hardly be called "real fun", yet if you rearrange the letters . . .'

'. . . Where did you find that?' asked a voice. Mahesh Chowdhury was standing near us, smiling.

'It was lying near your garden,' Feluda replied.

'I was just . . . trying to find some amusement.'

'Yes, I had guessed as much.'

All of us began rising, but Mr Chowdhury said, 'Please don't!' and sat down beside us.

'Let me show you another piece of paper,' he said. He wasn't smiling any more. He took out his wallet, then extracted an old folded card from it. It was a picture postcard, showing the city of Zurich including the lake.

'This was the last postcard sent by my second son,' he said gravely. On the other side of the postcard there was no message at all. All that was written was his name and address.

'That's what he had started to do,' Mr Chowdhury explained. 'He sent postcards just to let me know where he was. He was never much of a letter writer, anyway. His earlier postcards seldom had more than a couple of lines.'

He took the card back from Feluda and put it back in his wallet.

'Did you ever learn what kind of work your son Biren did in England?' Feluda asked.

'No. He wasn't the type to do an ordinary job. He was a rebel, totally different from most young men. And he had a hero. Another Bengali, who left home a hundred years ago and went to England, working as crew on a ship. Eventually, he ended up in Brazil—or was it Mexico?—and joined its army. He became a colonel and greatly impressed everyone by his valour and courage.'

'Do you mean Suresh Biswas?' Feluda asked. Lalmohan Babu, too, had recognized the name. His eyes gleamed.

'Yes, yes,' he said hurriedly, 'Colonel Suresh Biswas. He died in Brazil.'

'Right,' Mahesh Chowdhury went on. 'My son Biren had read the story of his life. He wanted to be like him, and have as many adventures. I did not try to stop him, for I knew I couldn't. So, one day, he vanished. Two months later, I got his first letter from Europe. He didn't always write from England, you know. He had seemed to travel all over Europe . . . Holland, Sweden, Germany, Austria. He never told me what he was doing. His short letters simply meant that he was alive. I was very sorry he had left me without a word; at the same time, I couldn't help feeling proud to think that he had made it entirely on his own. Then . . . after 1967, he stopped writing altogether.'

Mahesh Chowdhury stopped, looking sadly at the distant hills. 'I know he will never come back to me,' he sighed. 'I will never know any peace. I have been cursed.'

'What? Since when did you start to believe in curses?'

This was another voice, and it was speaking lightly. We turned to find we had been joined by Akhil Chakravarty.

'You only looked at my horoscope, Akhil,' Mahesh Chowdhury complained. 'You didn't bother to consider me as a man.'

'Rubbish. A man and his horoscope are linked together. Didn't I tell you in 1942 a big change would come over you? Have you forgotten that?' He turned to Feluda. 'Would you believe me, Mr Mitter, if I told you this amiable old man that you see today had once pushed his car off a cliff in a fit of rage, just because its engine had died on the way from Ranchi to Netarhat?'

Mr Chowdhury rose slowly to his feet. 'People change as they grow older. One doesn't need to be an astrologer to see that,' he said shortly and walked away, possibly to look for stones.

Akhil Chakravarty took his place. He seemed to be in the mood to tell stories. 'Mahesh is an extraordinary character,' he began. 'I used to be his neighbour. We came from two different worlds. I was only a schoolteacher, and he was a rising star in his profession. I worked for a while as his sons' private tutor and got to know him well. He didn't believe in conventional medicine. If any of his children was unwell, he used to come to me for ayurvedic herbs. Never did he let me feel that we belonged to two different social classes. He treated my son with the same affection that he treated his own. He was devoid of snobbery.'

'What does your son do?'

'Who, Adheer? He's an engineer. He went to IIT Kharagpur, and then to Dusseldorf. He spent ten years there, but he returned home and . . .'

The sound of an explosion made him stop.

'Uncle's gun!' Bibi shouted. 'Uncle's killed a partridge. We'll have it for dinner!'

'Let me go and find Mahesh,' Akhil Chakravarty said, getting up. 'At his age, he shouldn't go looking for stones. Heaven forbid, but if he slipped and fell near the water, his birthday would . . .' he moved away.

'It doesn't feel like a picnic at all!' said Neelima Devi. She had put her book away and come over to join us. 'Why has everyone disappeared?'

'Don't worry,' Feluda reassured her. 'They'll all turn up when they're hungry and it's time to eat.'

'Probably. In the meantime, why don't we play a game?'

'Cards?' asked Lalmohan Babu. 'But all I can play is Screw.'

'No, I'm afraid I didn't bring any cards,' Neelima Devi said. 'It will have to be something we can play orally.'

'Let's try water-earth-sky. Lalmohan Babu could join us quite easily,' Feluda suggested.

'How do you play that?'

'It's very simple, really. Suppose I look at you and say "water!" or "earth!" or "sky!"—and then start counting up to ten. You have to think of a creature that can be found in it, within those ten seconds.'

'Is this a very difficult game?'

'Try it,' Neelima Devi smiled. 'Let me ask you the first one.'

'OK.' Lalmohan Babu took a deep breath, and sat crosslegged, holding himself straight. Neelima Devi looked at him in silence for a few moments. The she suddenly shouted, 'Sky! One, two, three, four . . .'

'Er . . . er . . . er . . .'

' . . . five, six, seven . . .'

'Bafrosh!'

Feluda was the first to break the amazed silence that followed this perfectly weird remark.

'What, pray, is a bafrosh? A creature of the sky in a different planet, perhaps?'

'N-n-no. You see, I had thought of a balloon, a frog and a shark. But I mixed them all up!'

'A balloon? You think a balloon qualifies as a living creature?'

'Why not? Every living being needs oxygen. So does a balloon.'

'Really? Well, I must confess I did not know that. I've heard of hot air balloons, hydrogen and helium balloons, even balloons that fly with gas made from coal, but this is the first time anyone mentioned oxygen. Perhaps you'd like to . . .'

Neelima Devi raised a hand to stop further argument. As things turned out, she need not have bothered. Something happened at this moment that automatically put a stop to all arguments.

It was Pritin Babu.

A long time ago, Feluda had shown me a painting by Leonardo da Vinci, which showed a man who had both fear and sadness etched in every line on his face. Pritin Babu's face wore the same expression.

He emerged from behind a bush, took a few unsteady steps, then sat down quickly, trembling visibly. Neelima Devi got up and ran towards her husband, but Feluda had reached him already. Pritin Babu had to swallow a few times before he made an effort to speak.

'B-b-b-baba,' he managed finally, pointing at the direction from which he had come.

FIVE

By the time Mahesh Chowdhury was brought home, it was half past two. He was still unconscious. Judging by the injury on his head, he had been standing when he fell. The doctor who examined him said it was a heart attack. His heart was not particularly strong, anyway. The attack might have been caused by a sudden shock. His overall condition was critical; the doctor could not hold out much hope for a recovery.

He was found lying in an area behind a large boulder. We could see the boulder from where we sat, but not what lay behind it. None of us had seen him go there. Pritin Babu, who had climbed up a slope to go into the trees on the top of a hill, found him on his way back, as he came out in the open and looked down. At first, he had thought his father had died. That was why he had rushed to us, looking deathly pale. Feluda felt Mr Chowdhury's pulse and said he was still alive. His head had struck against a stone the size of a brick. A pool of blood lay around it. Like everyone else, I felt dazed, but couldn't help noticing two pretty yellow butterflies fluttering around the unconscious man.

A minute later, we were joined first by Arun Babu, and then Akhil Chakravarty. Shankarlal was the last to arrive. He broke down immediately as he realized what had happened. There could be no doubt about his attachment and devotion to the old man.

It was clearly impossible for us to pick him up and carry him across the river. His two sons left at once to go back and get an ambulance. It took them more than two hours to return with a medical team, and another hour to move their father away in the ambulance. All of us returned to Kailash and remained there for a while. Since no one had had any lunch, Neelima Devi served the food that had been packed for the picnic: parathas, aloo-dum and kababs. Once she had got over the initial shock, she had regained her composure fully. I had to admire her.

Little Bibi was the only one who didn't understand the seriousness of the situation. She kept saying her Dadu had simply had a dizzy spell, and would soon be playing with her again. We waited in the drawing room. Arun Babu remained upstairs with his father, and Pritin Chowdhury came and joined us every now and then. Shankarlal was sitting still like a statue. He hadn't spoken a single word since we left Rajrappa. Akhil Chakravarty was saying the same thing over and over: 'I told him not to go out today, but he didn't listen to me!'

We left at around four o'clock. 'We'll come back tomorrow,' Feluda told Pritin Babu. 'Please do let us know if we can do anything to help.'

'Thank you.'

On reaching our own house, each of us had a quick wash before going and sitting on the front veranda. I was still feeling dazed. Feluda wasn't speaking much, which meant he was thinking hard. I knew he wouldn't like being disturbed, but there was something I felt I had to ask him. 'I heard the doctor say Mr Chowdhury's heart attack might have been caused by a sudden shock. How could he have received a shock in Rajrappa, Feluda?'

'Good question. That is what I've been thinking. Of course, we don't know that for a fact.'

'So all we need to do is wait until Mr Chowdhury gets better. Then the whole thing will become clear,' Lalmohan Babu remarked.

'Yes. But will he get better?' Feluda sounded doubtful.

He was clearly curious about Mahesh Chowdhury. While we were waiting in the drawing room, I saw him looking closely at the books and every other object in the room. He did this very discreetly, but I knew he was making a mental note of everything he saw. The group photograph of all the Chowdhurys seemed to intrigue him the most. He spent at least five minutes looking at it closely.

Drums were beating in a distant village. It suddenly made me think of the escaped tiger. Obviously, it had not been captured, or Bulakiprasad would have told us.

It was now quite chilly outside. Lalmohan Babu pulled his cap tighter and said, 'It's significant, isn't it?' Perhaps he had expected one of us to ask him what he meant by that; but when we didn't, he expanded further, 'When Mr Chowdhury suffered this heart attack, we were with Neelima Devi and that little girl was playing with her doll. But we know nothing of the movements of the others, do we?'

'Yes, we do,' Feluda replied. 'Arun Babu was trying to kill birds, Pritin Babu was recording bird calls, Akhil Chakravarty was looking for his friend, Shankarlal was chatting with a sadhu, and the two bearers were sitting under a cotton tree, smoking beedis.'

'Yes, I saw them. But what about the others? They were all out of sight. How do we know they're telling the truth?'

'There is absolutely no reason to think they are not. I don't know them well, and I'm not prepared to start by treating them with suspicion.'

'OK, you're right, Felu Babu.'

But Lalmohan Babu had more to tell. It came a few hours later, while we were at dinner. I saw him give a sudden start, slap his forehead and say, 'Oh no, no!'

'Whatever is the matter, Lalmohan Babu?' Feluda asked.

'I forgot to tell you something—something very important. I found another clue, a terrific one this time. As we got close to the spot where the body—sorry, I mean Mr Chowdhury—was lying, I stumbled against an object. It was Pritin Chowdhury's tape recorder.'

'Have you got it with you?'

'No. I thought I'd pick it up later and give it back to him. But with all the hue and cry and everything, I totally forgot. When we were returning, however, I did remember, but by then it had gone!'

'Maybe Pritin Babu himself had picked it up?'

'No. He most definitely did not go anywhere near it. Besides, it was lying under a bush. I wouldn't have seen it myself if my foot hadn't actually struck against it.'

Feluda started to make a comment, but was stopped by the phone ringing.

It was Arun Babu. Feluda spoke briefly, put the phone down, and turned to us.

'We must go back to Kailash. Mr Chowdhury has regained consciousness, and is asking for me.'

It took us only a minute to reach their house by car. Everyone was gathered around his bed, with the exception of Bibi. Mr Chowdhury was lying in his bed with a dressing on his head, his hands folded and resting on his chest, his eyes half closed. His lips parted in a faint smile as he saw Feluda. Then he slowly raised his right hand and straightened his index finger.

'A j-j-j-' he tried to speak.

'A job for me?' Feluda asked anxiously.

Mr Chowdhury gave a slight nod. Then he raised his middle finger as well.

'We . . . we . . .' he folded his fingers and raised his thumb, shaking it.

With an effort, he then moved his head and looked at the bedside table. Muktananda's photograph rested on it. As he tried to stretch his arm towards it, Arun Babu picked it up and offered it to him. Instead of taking it, Mr Chowdhury looked at Feluda. Arun Babu passed the photo to Feluda without a word. Mr Chowdhury sighed and raised two fingers again. He tried to speak once more, but no words came.

After a while, he gave up trying and just stared in silence.

SIX

We had returned to our room. The passport-size photograph of

Muktananda was now with Feluda. I could not imagine why Mr Chowdhury had given it to him and told him he had a job. Lalmohan Babu, however, ventured to hazard a guess.

'I think he asked you to become a follower of Muktananda,' he observed.

'Then why did he raise two fingers?'

'Maybe he meant . . . as a follower of Muktananda, your skills at your job would double themselves? Mind you,' Lalmohan Babu added sadly, 'I cannot figure out why he then shook his thumb at you!'

Early in the morning, Akhil Chakravarty rang us to say that Mahesh Chowdhury had breathed his last two hours after we had left his house the previous night.

By the time the funeral was over, it was past eleven o'clock. On our way back from the cremation ground, Lalmohan Babu asked, 'Where do you want to go now, Felu Babu? To Kailash, or back home?'

'I don't think we should spend any more time in Kailash, just at this moment. They are bound to receive a lot of visitors. I won't get any work done.'

'What work do you mean?'

'Gathering information.'

After lunch, Feluda took out his blue notebook and began scribbling in it. When he finished, he let us see what he had written:

1. Mahesh Chowdhury: Born 23 November 1907; died 24 November 1977 (Natural causes? Heart attack? Shock?). Fond of riddles, stamps, butterflies, rocks. A valuable stamp album given by Dorabjee—lost (how?). Attached to second son. What about his feelings towards the other two? Deep affection towards Shankarlal. No snobbery. Violent temper in the past; drinking. A changed man in later years, amiable. Why a curse?
2. His wife: Dead. When?
3. First son: Arunendra. Born (approx.) 1936. Deals with mica. Travels between Calcutta and Hazaribagh. Fond of shooting. Doesn't talk much.
4. Second son: Birendra. Born (approx.) 1939. Very bright, a rebel. Left home at nineteen. Admired Col. Suresh Biswas. Wrote to father until 1967. Alive? Dead? Father thought he had returned

5. Third son: Pritindra. Younger than Arunendra by at least nine years (basis: family photo), i.e. born (approx.) 1945. Electronics. Bird calls. Talks a lot, chiefly about himself. Left tape recorder in Rajrappa.
6. Pritin's wife: Neelima. Age twenty-five/twenty-six. Intelligent, smart, collected.
7. Akhil Chakravarty: Age (approx.) seventy. Ex-schoolteacher. Mahesh's friend. Astrology, ayurveda.
8. Shankarlal Misra: Born (approx.) 1939. Same age as Biren. Mahesh's chowkidar Deendayal's son. Deendayal died in 1943. Question: why did he go into the forest? Mahesh raised Shankarlal. Owner of bookshop. Griefstricken by Mahesh's death.
9. Noor Muhammad: Age between seventy and eighty. Serving Mahesh for over forty years.

Feluda was right in thinking there might be a lot of visitors. When we arrived at Kailash long after lunch, we were told the last of them had just left. Mr Chowdhury's two sons and Akhil Chakravarty were in the drawing room. Pritin Babu seemed more restless than ever. He was sitting in a corner, fidgeting and cracking his knuckles. Akhil Babu was sighing and shaking his head from time to time. Only Arun Chowdhury seemed calm and composed. Feluda addressed him directly.

'Are you going to be here for a few days?' he asked.

'Why do you ask?'

'I need your help. Your father gave me a job to do, although he was in no condition to explain the details. What I want to know is this: did any of you understand his meaning?'

Arun Babu smiled slightly. 'Few of us could understand his meaning even when Baba was alive and well. A serious man in many ways, there was a childish streak in him, which you probably saw for yourself. I don't think there is any need to pay too much attention to his last words.'

'But his last words did not strike me as totally without meaning.'

'No?'

'No. But obviously, I could not understand the significance of each little gesture. For instance,' he turned to Akhil Chakravarty, 'I do not know why he wanted me to have that photograph. Perhaps you can help me there? Didn't you give it to him?'

Akhil Chakravarty smiled sadly. 'Yes, I did. Muktananda once came to Ranchi, and I went to see him. He struck me as a genuine person, so I said to Mahesh: "You have never believed in sadhus and gurus, but if you keep a photo of this one with you, it cannot do any harm. He is worshipped in three continents, his influence can only do you good." But I had no idea he had kept it in his bedroom. I never went into his bedroom until yesterday.'

'Do you know anything about it?' Feluda asked Arun Babu, who shook his head.

'No, I'm afraid not,' he said. 'In fact, I didn't even know he had such a photograph. I saw it yesterday for the first time.'

'I don't know anything either,' Pritin Babu piped up before anyone asked him.

'Very well. But may I request you to give me two things? They would help me a great deal.'

'What are they?'

'The first thing I'd like are the letters and postcards your brother Biren sent your father.'

'Biren's letters?' Arun Babu sounded very surprised. 'What do you need those for?'

'I believe your father wanted me to give that photo to his second son.'

'How strange! What made you think that?'

'Well, your father asked you to pass the photo to me, and then raised two fingers. All of you saw that. It could be that he meant to say "deuce". Isn't that what he called Biren? I could be wrong, of course, but I must proceed—at least for the present—on that assumption.'

'But how will you find Biren?'

'Suppose Mr Chowdhury was right? Suppose he has returned?'

Arun Babu forgot himself for a moment and burst out laughing.

'Mr Mitter, do you know how many times in the last five years my father claimed to have actually seen Biren? He wanted to believe he had returned. If he had, wouldn't he have got in touch? Besides, how could anyone expect to recognize him after twenty years, if they saw him from a distance? Particularly an old man like my father, with failing eyesight?'

'Please don't get me wrong, Arun Babu. I am not saying he came back. That was a suggestion made by your father. However, even if he is living abroad, I still have to fulfil my responsibility. I must try to find out where he is and arrange to send him the photo.'

Arun Babu seemed to relent a little.

'Very well, Mr Mitter,' he said. 'I will separate Biren's letters from my father's correspondence and give them to you.'

'Thank you. The other thing I want are Mr Chowdhury's diaries. I'd like to see them, if you don't mind.'

I had expected Arun Babu to object to this, but surprisingly, he did not.

'You're welcome,' he said. 'My father's diaries are no secret. But you are going to be disappointed.'

'Why?'

'I doubt if anyone ever kept diaries that could be as dry, mundane and boring as my father's. You won't find anything except the most ordinary record of his daily life.'

'I don't mind. I am perfectly willing to risk being disappointed.'

'All right, so be it. You may take the diaries right now, if you like. I will let you have the letters tomorrow.'

We thanked him and came out a little later, all three of us carrying heavy packets wrapped with newspapers. There were seven of these, each containing Mahesh Chowdhury's diaries. Feluda would get very little sleep tonight, I thought, for the total number of diaries was forty and he had promised to return them the next day.

As we emerged out of the house and reached the driveway, we saw Bibi roaming in the garden, playing with her doll. She appeared to be looking for a flower to put in her doll's hair. She turned her head to face us, and spoke unexpectedly.

'Dadu didn't tell me!' she complained.

'What didn't he tell you?' Feluda asked her.

'What he was looking for.'

'When?'

'The day before yesterday, and the day before that, and the day before that.'

'Three days?'

'I saw him looking, but I asked him only one day.'

'What did you say?'

'I said: "What have you lost, Dadu?" because he was in his room, and he was moving his books and all the papers on his table and everything else, and he wouldn't play with me . . . so I asked.'

'What did he say?'

'He said . . . a pier, that which opens and . . . and that which shuts.'

'What utter nonsense!' Lalmohan Babu muttered under his breath.

Feluda ignored him. 'Did he tell you anything else?'

'No. No, he said he'd explain later, and he'd tell me everything . . . but he didn't. He died.'

Bibi had found a flower for her doll. She lost interest in us, and turned to go back inside. We came away.

SEVEN

Since Feluda was now going to start reading the diaries, Lalmohan Babu and I decided to go for a drive soon after a cup of tea at four o'clock.

'If we go towards the main town, we might get to hear the latest on Sultan,' Lalmohan Babu told me. 'Your cousin may have found a mystery related to Mahesh Chowdhury's death, but I think an escaped tiger is much more interesting.'

We didn't have far to go to get news of the tiger. We had to stop for petrol at a local station, where we saw another group of men gathered round someone who was speaking very rapidly. He raised a hand and pawed the air, so there was no doubt that he was talking of the tiger. Lalmohan Babu got out of the car and went forward to make enquiries. This wasn't easy, for his Hindi was not particularly good. However, what we eventually managed to learn was this:

To the east of Hazaribagh was a forest, near the town of Vishnugarh. Sultan's new trainer, Chandran, and a shikari from the Forest Department, had found Sultan there. Apparently, it had looked for a while that the tiger was willing to be captured, but he had then changed his mind and run away again after clawing Chandran. The shikari had shot at him, but no one knew whether the tiger was hurt. Chandran was in a hospital, but his injuries were not serious.

'Do you know anything about Kandarikar?' Lalmohan Babu asked his informant. I felt obliged to correct him. 'It is Karandikar, Lalmohan Babu, not Kandarikar. He's the old trainer.'

'No, I don't know anything about him,' the man replied, 'but I do believe the circus isn't doing so well since the main show with the tiger is off.'

We were both curious to know how Mr Karandikar had reacted to the news of Sultan being shot at, so we went from the petrol station straight to the Great Majestic.

Normally, if Feluda accompanies us, Lalmohan Babu keeps to the background. Today, however, he walked up smartly to the man outside the main entrance and said, 'Put me through to Mr Kutti, please.' God knows what the man thought of this strange request, but he let us in without a word. Perhaps he had recognized us from our first visit.

We found Mr Kutti in his caravan, but what he told us sounded like another mysterious riddle. Karandikar had disappeared the previous night.

'The audience has been demanding to see the tiger,' Mr Kutti said. 'I went and personally apologized to Karandikar. I promised him I wouldn't allow anyone else to train the tiger, if it could be captured. Even so, he left without telling a soul. He used to go off occasionally, but he always came back in a few hours. This time . . . I don't think he's coming back.'

There didn't seem to be anything else to say. We thanked Mr Kutti and left the circus. Lalmohan Babu said as we came out, 'Now we'll never get to see Sultan being captured, Tapesh. We simply won't get another chance.'

I, too, felt sad and depressed. So we decided to go for a long drive instead of returning home. Debating over whether to go towards the Kanari Hills in the north, or Ramgarh to the south, we eventually tossed for it and got Ramgarh.

'There are hills there, didn't you see them that day? They're just as beautiful,' Lalmohan Babu remarked.

I agreed with him, and we set off in the direction of Ramgarh. Neither of us had any idea of what lay in store.

Things began to go wrong as we passed a signpost that said '11 kms'. To start with, Lalmohan Babu's car—which he had bought only six months ago—hiccuped three times, slowed down and then died altogether. His driver got out to investigate. He was our only hope, for Lalmohan Babu knew nothing of cars and engines. 'If I can move about without knowing how many bones and what muscles I have in my legs, where is the need to worry about how my car moves on its four wheels?' he had once said to me.

We climbed out of the car and went and sat on a culvert. The sun was about to set, and the time was 5.20 p.m. There were dark patches of clouds in the sky, behind which the sun happened to be hiding at the moment. It peeped out for just a second a little later, only to call it a day almost at once.

'I think I've fixed it, sir!' the driver called. 'I am ready when you are.'

We rose, and I looked at my watch. It said 5.33 p.m. It is important to mention the time, for it was at this precise moment that we saw Sultan.

I might have described the event in a much more dramatic fashion, but Feluda has always told me not to use cliches and other hackneyed phrases just to create an effect. 'Keep your descriptions brief and simple,' he tells me often, 'and you will see how effective that can be.' I shall therefore try to relate what happened as briefly as possible.

I had seen a tiger in the wild before, about which I have written in *The Royal Bengal Mystery*. On that occasion, we were accompanied by several other armed men, including Feluda; and Lalmohan Babu and I were sitting on a treetop, out of harm's way. Now, we were standing by the side of an open road that was lined by trees and woodland. There were bound to be wild bears in the wood, and it was quickly getting dark. Worst of all, Feluda was not with us.

The tiger came out of the trees to our right and appeared on the road, barely fifty yards away. All three of us saw it together, for each one turned into a statue. The driver had stretched out an arm to open a door. He stood still with an outstretched arm. Lalmohan Babu had leant forward slightly to blow his nose. He remained in that position, clutching his handkerchief. I was in the process of dusting my jeans. My hands remained stuck at my waist.

The tiger, at first, did not see us. It began to cross the road, took four steps, then suddenly stopped and turned its head to look at us.

My legs began shaking and a hammering started in my chest. Yet, I could not move my eyes away from the tiger. Out of the corner of my eye, I could vaguely see the outline of Lalmohan Babu's body getting lower and lower, which could only mean that his legs were going numb and were unable to support the weight of his body. Then my vision began to blur. The figure of the tiger became hazy, and its stripes suddenly started to vibrate.

It is impossible to say how Song Sultan stared at us. The time seemed endless. Lalmohan Babu likes to call it eight to ten minutes, but I think it was eight to ten seconds. Even so, it was a long time.

Once he had finished looking at us, Sultan simply turned his head away, crossed over to the other side and made for the wood. We saw him gradually disappear among the tall trees.

Strangely enough, we remained rooted to the spot for nearly a whole minute even after Sultan had gone (Lalmohan Babu said fifteen minutes). Then we uttered only three words before getting back into the car. The driver said, 'Sir!'; I said 'Coming!'; and Lalmohan Babu said 'G-go!' Fortunately, it turned out that the driver's nerves were strong and steady. He began to drive with admirable equanimity. Apparently, when he used to work in Jamshedpur before, he had once seen a tiger by the roadside.

We returned home to find Feluda still deeply engrossed in Mr Chowdhury's diaries. I knew Lalmohan Babu was dying to tell him about our experience, so I said nothing. Instead of coming straight to the point, he decided to create a preamble. First, he began humming a tune, then remarked casually, 'Tell me Tapesh, tigers have padded feet, don't they?'

'Yes, so I've heard,' I replied, hiding a smile.

'It must be true, for we didn't hear its footsteps, did we? And we were only a few feet away!'

Sadly, this great build-up to his story had no effect on Feluda. He didn't even look at us. All he did was put one diary away, pick up another and say, 'If you have seen the tiger, you should tell the Forest Department immediately about the exact spot and the time it was seen.'

'The time was 5.33 and the place was near a culvert close to the "11 kms" signpost on the road to Ramgarh.'

'Good. There's a directory in the living room. The Forest Department's office will be closed at this hour, but you can look up the residential number of the Chief Forest Officer and inform him. I'm sure he'll appreciate it.'

Lalmohan Babu licked his lips. 'You are asking me to ring the officer?'

'Yes. You saw the tiger, I didn't.'

'That's true. So what should I tell him? "The tiger which escaped from the circus . . ."?'

'Yes, that's right. Go on.'

I found the number in the directory. Perhaps I should have made the phone call as well, for Lalmohan Babu picked up the phone, coughed twice and said, 'Er . . . the circus that escaped from the

Great Majestic tiger . . . oh sorry!'

Luckily, Feluda had heard him from the next room. He rushed in, snatched the receiver from his hand and passed on the information himself.

EIGHT

Bulakiprasad brought us tea in our room. He had already told Feluda about the attempt made to catch Sultan, and Chandran being injured in the process. It was Feluda's belief that no one but Karandikar could catch the tiger alive.

Lalmohan Babu took a long, noisy sip from his cup and asked, 'Did you find anything interesting in those diaries? Or was Arun Babu right?'

'You tell me.' Feluda opened a diary and pushed it towards Lalmohan Babu.

'Self elected president of club—meeting on 8.4.46,' he read aloud. 'Tea party at Brig. Sudarshan's, and, on a different page—Trial for new suit at Shakur's . . . why, Felu Babu, you think any of this stuff has any relevance?'

'Topshe, have a look and tell me what you think.'

I had been leaning over Lalmohan Babu's shoulder. Now I picked the diary up.

'Bring it closer to the light,' Feluda ordered. I went forward and put it directly under a table lamp. A shiver of excitement ran down my spine.

The diary was fairly large in size. The main entries had been made in ink, but on the top of the page, over the printed date, something had been scribbled with a hard pencil. The words were barely legible.

'Why, this seems to be a message of some kind!' I exclaimed.

'Read it out.'

'Conveyance destroyed because of two.'

Good heavens, more puzzles?' Lalmohan Babu gave a start.

'Yes. Now look at this. This is the first diary, going back to 1938.'

On the very first page, Mr Chowdhury had written: 'Shambhu is ruled by two and five.'

'Who is Shambhu?' Lalmohan Babu asked, surprised.

'Shambhu is another name for Shiva, like Mahesh. Mr

Chowdhury referred to himself in his diaries by using various names for Shiva.'

'All right, but what's this about "two and five"?'

'Do you know about the six deadly sins that Hindus believe in?'

'The six *ripus*? Yes, yes. They are . . . let me see . . . *kaam, krodh, lobh, maud, moha, matsarya.*'

'Yes, but not in that order. The correct order is *kaam, krodh, lobh, moha, maud, matsarya.* What do they mean?'

'Lust, wrath, greed, attachment, drinking, envy.'

'Right. So two and five are wrath and drinking.'

'I see, I see. That's easy, isn't it?'

'Yes. Now if you look at the message Topshe read out, you'll get his meaning.'

I had, in fact, already worked it out. 'Conveyance destroyed because of two. Could that mean car destroyed because of wrath? Because of his temper?' I offered.

'Shabaash. But there's more. I have not yet been able to understand what the second message means, and that involves these same six numbers.'

Feluda had marked the pages where coded messages appeared. He opened one of these and showed it to us. '2+5=X', it said.

'X is an unknown quantity, isn't it?' Lalmohan Babu asked. 'Why don't you just ignore it? Why are you assuming every strange message has a significant meaning?'

'If a man writes a code on just twenty occasions in a whole year—and don't forget he writes in that diary three hundred and sixty-five times—then I must assume every code has a special meaning. I just have to work harder to find out what it is, that's all.'

'Isn't there anything else in the diary that might help?'

'No, but there's another message ten days after he wrote 2+5=X. Look!' I read the message Feluda pointed out: 'Old friend—herbal hair oil. Calms two.'

'A hair oil that might help him control his temper? This one's easy, Felu Babu. Only, I can't make out why he calls it an old friend. Maybe he'd been using it for a long time?'

'No. You didn't pay attention to the "dash" after the word "friend". It can only mean an old friend is in some way related to the oil.'

'Akhil Chakravarty! He knows about ayurvedic herbs, doesn't he? He must have given the oil to his friend!' I exclaimed.

'Very good, Topshe. Now read these other messages.'

There were two. The first said, 'Getting rid of five from today.' That meant he gave up drinking. But, only a month later, he wrote: 'Bholanath goes back to five. Five helps forget.'

'The question is, what did he want to forget so desperately?' Feluda muttered. Lalmohan Babu looked at me, I scratched my head. Now it was obvious why Mr Chowdhury had said his life was full of mysteries. Feluda opened another diary and showed us one more message. 'I am as feather today. I took charge of SM. SM will be my salvation.'

'SM is Shankarlal Misra, surely?' I said. 'But why is he as a feather?'

'I think that simply means "light as a feather",' Feluda replied. 'He was happy and possibly relieved by something. Maybe a load had been lifted from his mind. Taking charge of young Shankarlal clearly had a lot to do with it.'

Feluda rose and began pacing. I sat staring at the diaries. If Mahesh Chowdhury had lived a little longer, he and Feluda would have got on very well. Feluda was just as interested in word games and riddles. Lalmohan Babu was sitting quietly, frowning thoughtfully. After a while, he said, 'Why don't you have a chat with Akhil Chakravarty? He knew him pretty closely, didn't he? He made his horoscope, gave him ayurvedic medicines . . . surely he'll be able to tell you a lot more about the man than his diaries?

Feluda stopped pacing and lit a Charminar. 'I was trying to get to know the man myself, through his thoughts. Those few messages written with a pencil have kept him alive.'

'Did you find anything about his sons? Did he mention any of them?'

'There isn't much in the first fifteen years. But later—' Feluda broke off. A car had arrived outside. It stopped and tooted at the gate.

We came out on the veranda to find Arun Babu getting out of his Fiat. In his hand was a small packet.

'I was on my way to see Mr Singh—he's our Forest Officer,' he explained. 'Since your house was on the way, I thought I'd stop by and give you Biren's letters. They can hardly be called letters, mind you, but you wanted to see them, so . . .' he shrugged.

'I'm very sorry if I have caused you any trouble. You must have a lot on your plate,' Feluda said.

'No, no, it's no trouble at all. Frankly, I cannot imagine what Baba might have tried to say. See if you can figure out his meaning. I hardly knew my father, you see. My visits to Hazaribagh have always been short. I used to come here frequently in the past to go on shikar, but now big game has been banned. However, I may get a chance tomorrow. Let's see.'

'What do you mean?'

'That's the reason why I am going to see Mr Singh. I believe the tiger has been spotted near Ramgarh. One of its trainers is lying in hospital, and the other has disappeared. I've already spoken to Mr Singh. "If you must have the tiger killed," I said, "let me do the job." It's already been shot at. If it was injured, it's now a most dangerous beast.'

I opened my mouth to say the tiger hadn't appeared to be injured, but shut it at a glance from Feluda.

'I am taking my .315 with me,' Arun Babu continued. 'There's panic everywhere. I believe it attacked a herd of goats in a village. I don't think being killed in a forest is in any way worse than growing old in a cage in a circus. Anyway, you can come tomorrow, if you're interested. We'll leave early in the morning.'

'OK. Let's see how far I can get with this other job I am trying to tackle. My going with you would have to depend on that. Oh, by the way . . .

Arun Babu had turned to go. At Feluda's words, he turned back again.

'It was you who fired the shot that day at the picnic, wasn't it?' Feluda asked.

Arun Babu laughed. 'I see what you mean. You must be wondering what happened. I fired a shot, but didn't produce a dead bird. Your detective's mind finds that suspicious, doesn't it? The truth is, Mr Mitter, I missed it. It was a partridge. Sometimes even the best of shikaris miss their targets.'

NINE

The letters sent by Biren Chowdhury told us nothing. They were all postcards, most of which had nothing but Mahesh Chowdhury's name and address on them. The few that had hastily scribbled messages had been signed 'Deuce'.

Bulakiprasad served dinner at nine o'clock. Feluda came to the dining table with some of the diaries and his notebook. There were a few more coded messages that he hadn't yet been able to solve, he told us. I saw Feluda write these down in his notebook, using his left hand as easily as he used his right. Halfway through the meal, Lalmohan Babu said, 'Look, Felu Babu, do stop writing; or you won't be able to do any justice to this terrific lamb curry.'

'I am busy with monkeys, Lalmohan Babu, so please don't disturb me by talking of lambs.'

Feluda was frowning deeply, but a smile played around his lips. I had to ask him to explain. He read out a line from a diary:

'Great generosity by the worshipper of fire. The nine jewels, according to the monkeys, value two thousand Shylock's demands.'

Lalmohan Babu swallowed quickly. 'There's a loony bin in Ranchi, isn't there?' he asked. 'I've heard the people of Ranchi are all a bit . . . you know, not quite normal!'

Feluda ignored this remark. 'Parsees worship fire,' he commented, 'but the rest of the message doesn't make any sense at all.'

'Shylock . . . isn't that from *The Merchant of Venice?*' I asked.

'Yes. That's what makes me wonder. What did Shylock demand, Topshe?'

'A pound of flesh?'

'Correct. But that doesn't help, does it?'

'Felu Babu, please give it a rest,' Lalmohan Babu pleaded, 'at least while you're eating!'

Perhaps Feluda was really tired. So he put away the diaries and his notebook, and said he'd like to go for a walk after dinner with both of us.

The moon had just risen when we set out. It still had a yellow glow. But there were patches of clouds as well, which made Lalmohan Babu say, 'I think the moonlight's going to be shortlived.' Gusts of wind came from the west, bringing with them the faint sounds of a circus band.

A right turn soon brought Kailash into view. We could see the house through a row of eucalyptus trees. A window on the first floor was open, and the light was on. Someone was moving restlessly in the room. Feluda stopped. So did we. Whose room could it be? The moving figure came and stood at the window. It was Neelima Devi. Then she moved away again and began pacing once more. Why was she so agitated?

We began walking once more. Kailash disappeared from sight. Each house we passed had a large compound. A radio was on somewhere. We could hear snatches of the local news. Lalmohan Babu cleared his throat and had begun humming another unsuitable Tagore song ('In the rice fields today, do the sun and shadows play hide-and-seek'), when my eyes fell on the figure of a man coming from the opposite direction. He was wearing a blue pullover.

I recognized him as he got closer. 'Namaskar,' said Shankarlal Misra. 'I was going to call at your house.' He seemed to have recovered somewhat, but had not yet regained his normal cheerful looks.

'Is anything the matter?' Feluda asked politely.

'I . . . I would like to make a request.'

'A request?'

'Yes. Please, Mr Mitter, stop making enquiries. Drop your investigation.'

I was quite taken aback by such a request, but Feluda spoke calmly.

'Why would you like me to do that, Mr Misra?'

'It won't do anyone any good.'

After a short pause, Feluda smiled lightly. 'Suppose I told you it would do me some good? I cannot rest in peace if there are doubts in my mind. I have to settle them, Mr Misra. Besides, someone spoke to me from his deathbed and asked me to do something for him. How can I leave that task undone? I am sorry, Mr Misra, but I have to continue with my investigation. As a matter of fact, I need your help. Different people may say different things about Mahesh Chowdhury, but you had very deep respect for him, didn't you?'

'Of course.' Mr Misra's reply came a few seconds later, possibly because he couldn't immediately accept what Feluda had said to him. Then he added more firmly, 'I certainly did. But . . .' his voice changed, 'should one allow that respect, all those feelings, to be destroyed by one single blow? All that had built up over a number of years . . . should one let it go, just like that?'

'Is that what you were doing?'

'Yes. Yes, I nearly allowed that to happen. But then I realized my mistake. I will not let anything destroy my beliefs. I have decided that, and now I have found peace.'

'May I then expect you to help me?'

'Certainly. How may I help you?' Mr Misra sounded almost like his old self. He met Feluda's eyes directly.

'I would like to know how Mahesh Chowdhury felt about his other two sons. No one but you can give me an impartial assessment.'

'I can only tell you what I felt. I don't think Mr Chowdhury had any affection left for anyone except Biren. Arun and Pritin had both disappointed him.'

'Why?'

'I don't know the precise details, for I've never been very close to either of them. But Arun had started to gamble. Mr Chowdhury himself told me one day; not directly, but in his own peculiar style. He said, "I would have been pleased if Arun was good. But I worry because he's better. I believe he visits the equine communities quite often." It took me a while, but eventually I figured out that "better" meant one who lays bets and the "equine communities" simply meant horse races.'

'I see. But why should Pritin have disappointed him? Surely he's doing quite well in electronics?'

'Electronics?' Mr Misra sounded perfectly amazed. 'Is that what he told you?'

'Why? Doesn't he have anything to do with Indovision?'

Mr Misra burst out laughing. 'Good God, no! Pritin has a very ordinary job in a small private firm, which he managed to get only because his father-in-law knew the right people. Pritin is a good man, basically, but is extremely impractical and impulsive. Luckily for him, his wife is the only daughter of a wealthy father. That car you saw him using belongs to his father-in-law. He came here later than his wife and daughter because he had problems getting leave.'

It was our turn to be astounded.

'But,' Mr Misra added, 'his passion for birds and bird calls is absolutely genuine.'

'I have one more question.'

'Yes?'

'You were seen talking to a man dressed as a sadhu when we went to Rajrappa. Was that Biren?'

Mr Misra was naturally taken aback by such a question, but he recovered quickly. The reply he made sounded rather cryptic. 'You are so clever, Mr Mitter, I'm sure you'll soon unravel every mystery.'

'There is a special reason for asking this question. If indeed that man is Biren, I have got something that his father wanted him to have. I must hand it over to him. Can you arrange a meeting?'

'I will try my best to make sure Mr Chowdhury's last wish is fulfilled, I promise to try . . . but I cannot tell you anything more.'

Mr Misra turned abruptly, and went back in the same direction from which he had come.

I hadn't realized how far we'd walked. Feluda looked at his watch and said, 'Ten-thirty.' We decided to go back. When we reached Kailash, the whole house was in darkness. The sky was now overcast, the moon had disappeared and the distant band was silent. Purely out of the blue, Feluda broke the silence by shouting one word: 'Monkeys!' Lalmohan Babu automatically turned his head and asked, 'Where?'

'In that diary,' Feluda explained quickly. 'Sorry if I startled you, but I've just realized what he meant by it. What a brilliant mind that man had! I'd totally forgotten about those monkeys that produce catalogues.'

'Felu Babu, why are you doing this to me? Monkeys was bad enough, but now you want monkeys that produce catalogues? What catalogues?'

'Gibbons! Gibbons! Gibbons!' Feluda shouted impatiently.

Of course! Gibbons was a species of monkey. I knew that, but could never have made the connection.

'He would have made a lot of money,' Feluda said.

'Who?'

'The thief who stole the stamp album.'

Lalmohan Babu remained in our room until midnight to watch Feluda solve more puzzles. He had to call Arun Babu at eleven o'clock to get the answer to one of them. On 18 October 1951, Mr Chowdhury had written, 'He passes away.' Arun Babu told Feluda that was the day his mother had died, and she was called Heronmoyee. That explained who 'He' was.

A few entries made in 1958 said, 'Be foolish', 'Be stubborn', 'Be determined'. These sounded like mottoes, but 'Be' in this case could only mean 'B', i.e. Biren.

One page in 1975 said, 'A is ruled by three.' He was obviously referring to the six deadly sins, and 'A' meant Arun. His father thought he was greedy.

The last entry had been made the day before he died. All it said was, 'Come back. Hope, return.' The following pages were all blank.

By the time we finished with the diaries, it was one o'clock. I went to bed, but Feluda began reading the book on the circus in Bengal that Lalmohan Babu had lent him. It had been agreed long ago that Feluda would read it after Lalmohan Babu, and would pass it to me when he had finished.

I heard him speaking just as my eyes began to feel heavy.

'When there's a murder, the police place a mark over the spot where the body is found. Do you know what it is?'

'X marks the spot?' I said sleepily.

'Exactly. X marks the spot.'

I fell asleep almost immediately, and had a rather awful dream. A huge figure of Kali was standing before me, her arms and legs spread like the letter 'X'. But she wasn't looking at me. She was staring at Arun Babu, and saying, 'Three rules you, three rules you, three rules you!'

Then, suddenly her face dissolved and it became Lalmohan Babu's face. He was grinning from ear to ear and saying, 'Three thousand copies sold in one month . . . Kalmohan Bengali, that's my name!'

Then I woke with a start. A noise at the door had woken me. This was followed by the sound of two men struggling with each other. It was raining outside.

I reached out automatically and pressed the switch of the bedside lamp. Nothing happened. I had forgotten Bihar, like Calcutta, had frequent power cuts.

Something fell on the floor with a thud. 'Get your torch, Topshe,' said Feluda's voice, 'I dropped mine.'

I groped in the dark and eventually found my torch, but not before I had knocked over a glass of water and broken it.

Feluda was standing near the door, his face flushed with helpless rage.

'Who was it, Feluda? He got away, didn't he?'

'Yes. I didn't see his face, but he was large and hefty. I think I know why he had been sent here.'

'Why?'

'To steal.'

'Did he take anything?'

'No, but he would have taken something very valuable, if I wasn't a light sleeper.'

'Something valuable? But we haven't got anything valuable, have we?'

Feluda did not answer me. 'One thing is now quite clear, Topshe,' he said slowly. 'I am not the only one who was been able to work out the meaning of Mahesh Chowdhury's riddles. But for this other man, it is a bit too late.'

TEN

When Lalmohan Babu heard about the thief the next day, he said, 'I told you to keep your door locked, didn't I? There have always been petty thieves in these areas!'

'You keep your door locked for fear of the tiger, Lalmohan Babu, not because of possible theft. Come on, admit it.'

'All right, but it's better to be safe than sorry, isn't it? A locked door would protect you from both a thief and a ferocious animal . . . Bulakiprasad, where's our breakfast?'

'Why are you in such a hurry this morning?'

'Why, aren't we going to watch the capture of Sultan?'

'Who's going to catch him? Karandikar has vanished, hasn't he?'

'Yes, but he's still bound to be around somewhere, and I bet he's heard of plans to kill his tiger. He won't be able to stay away, Felu Babu, mark my words. Just think what a thrilling event we might get to watch! Oh, we mustn't miss this chance. I don't understand how you can take this so calmly.'

We finished breakfast by eight o'clock and got ready to go to Kailash to return the diaries and the letters. Akhil Chakravarty turned up unexpectedly.

'One of your neighbours is a homoeopath, and a friend of mine,' he explained. 'I was going to see him, but I thought I'd just drop in to say hello, since your house was on the way.'

'Good. Please have a seat. Tell me,' Feluda said, 'did the herbal oil help in controlling your friend's temper?'

'Good heavens, did Mahesh mention that in his diary?'

'Yes, amongst other things.'

'I see. To tell you the truth, what really helped Mahesh was his own will power. I saw how difficult it was for him to give up drinking, but he did it. It wasn't simply because of a herbal oil or anything like that.'

'Since you mention the word "will", can you tell us if he made one?'

'I don't know the details, but I do know that Mahesh changed his first will.'

'I think his second son, Biren, was dropped from the second will.'

'What makes you say that? Did he mention this in his diary?'

'No. He told me just before he died. Do you remember his gestures? He raised two fingers, then he said "we . . . we . . . " and then he shook his thumb. He couldn't quite manage to say "will". If the two fingers indicated "Deuce", then the rest of the message could only mean that Deuce had not been left anything in his will.'

'Brilliant! And you're quite right. Biren had a share in the first will Mahesh made. But when he stopped writing, Mahesh waited for five years before changing it, cutting him out altogether. He was deeply hurt by Biren's silence.'

'If Biren came back, do you think Mahesh Chowdhury would have changed his will a second time?'

'Undoubtedly. I am sure of it.'

Feluda paused for a second before asking his next question.

'Did you ever think Biren might have become a sadhu?'

'Look, it was I who drew up Biren's horoscope. I knew he would leave home quite early in life. So the possibility of his renouncing the whole world and becoming a sadhu cannot be ruled out.'

'One last question. That day, in Rajrappa, you said you were going to look for your friend. But you arrived on the scene long after we had found Mr Chowdhury. Did you get lost? It's not a very large or complex area, is it?'

'I knew you'd ask me that,' Akhil Chakravarty smiled. 'You're right, of course. It's not a complex area, but you must have noticed how the main path parts in two directions. I would have found Mahesh easily enough if I had turned left. But I turned right instead. Do you know why? It was only because my childhood memories suddenly came back. Fifty-five years ago, I had visited the same spot and carved my initials and the date on a rock. I remembered that and felt an irresistible urge to go and see if it was still there. And it was, as were the figures I had carved: ABC, 15.5.23. If you don't believe me, you can go and see it for yourself.'

We reached Kailash to discover that Arun Babu had already left. Old Noor Muhammad told us Pritin Babu was at home, and went off to inform him. He came down to see us in a few moments.

We handed him the packets of diaries and the letters and were about to leave, when someone else entered the drawing room, it was Neelima Devi. I noticed her husband going pale as she came in.

'There is something you ought to know, Mr Mitter,' she said. 'My husband should tell you himself, but he doesn't want to.'

Pritin Babu looked at her appealingly, but Neelima Devi didn't even glance at him. 'When he found my father-in-law that day,' she went on, 'my husband dropped his tape recorder. I found it and put it in my bag. I think you'll find it useful. Here it is.'

Pritin Babu tried once more to stop his wife, but failed.

'Thank you,' Feluda said and took the small, flat recorder from Neelima Devi. Then he put it in his pocket.

Pritin Babu looked as if he was about to break down.

I had a feeling Feluda was as interested in watching the capture of the tiger as Lalmohan Babu and myself. The instructions he gave our driver upon leaving Kailash proved that I was right.

Lalmohan Babu's enthusiasm, however, now seemed to be mixed with a degree of anxiety.

'Arun Chowdhury has a number of guns. Why didn't you ask for one, Felu Babu?' he said after a while. 'What good will your Colt .32 do if we see the tiger?'

'Well, if a fly came and sat on the tiger, my revolver would be quite adequate to destroy it, Lalmohan Babu, I assure you.'

Then Feluda lapsed into silence, holding the recorder close to his ear and listening intently. He did not tell us what he heard, and we knew better than to ask him.

Last night's rain had left the earth wet and muddy in many places. As we got closer to a crossing, it became clear that a car and other vehicles had turned left from here, for there were fresh tyre marks going towards the forest. We made a left turn, too, and followed these marks. A mile later, we saw three different vehicles standing next to a banyan tree: a jeep from the Forest Department, Arun Babu's Fiat and a huge truck from the circus that had the tiger's cage in it. Five or six men were sitting under the tree. They told us a team had already gone into the forest to look for the tiger, and pointed us in the right direction. I recognized one of the men, having seen him at the circus before. Feluda asked him if Sultan's trainer had gone with the others. He said the new trainer, Chandran, was with them, but there was still no sign of Karandikar.

We got out of the car and began walking. I had no idea what lay in store, but knew that Arun Babu had a gun, and the shikari from the Forest Department was undoubtedly similarly armed. There was therefore little fear of the tiger being allowed to attack anyone. Lalmohan Babu looked a little disappointed, presumably because Chandran was there instead of Karandikar.

Faint footprints on the damp ground guided us. There were not many trees in this part of the forest, so movement was fairly easy. A peacock cried out a couple of times, which could well be a warning to other animals that a tiger was in the vicinity.

Ten minutes later, we heard a different noise. It was decidedly the tiger, but it wasn't actually roaring. It sounded more like a growl, as though the tiger was irritated by something.

We walked on and, only a few minutes later, through the gap between two trees, our eyes fell on a strange sight. I call it strange because I never thought I'd see something like this outside the arena of a circus.

Three men stood in a row a few feet away from where we had stopped. Two of them had guns. The one in Arun Chowdhury's hands was raised and pointed at some object in front of him.

What they were facing was an open area, a bit like a circus ring. A man was standing in the middle of this ring, a long whip in his right hand and a torn branch in his left. Judging by the dressed wound on his left shoulder, he was the new trainer, Chandran.

Chandran had his back to us. He was moving forward slowly and with extreme caution, cracking his whip every now and then. The animal he was approaching was one we had met already. It was Sultan, last seen on the road to Ramgarh.

Four other men were standing at a little distance. Two of them were holding a heavy chain, which would no doubt be put around Sultan's neck, if he allowed himself to be captured. What was most amazing was Sultan's behaviour. He clearly did not wish to be caught, but—at the same time—was making no attempts to run away. His eyes seemed to convey not anger or ferocity, but annoyance and a great deal of contempt. The low growl he kept up indicated the same thing.

Chandran was getting closer every minute, but he did not seem too sure of himself. Perhaps he could not forget that the same animal had attacked him already. I cast a quick look at Arun Babu. From the way he was holding his gun, I had no doubt that he would fire at once if Sultan showed the slightest sign of aggression. Feluda was standing before me, a little to the left; and Lalmohan Babu was by my side. His mouth was hanging so wide open that he didn't look as if he'd ever be able to close it. He told me afterwards that the memory of everything he had seen in circuses before had been totally wiped out by the show we witnessed in the forest.

When Chandran came within five yards, Sultan suddenly stiffened and began to crouch. At the same instant, Feluda leapt and reached Arun Babu, stretching a hand to change the position of his gun. Its point now faced the ground.

'Sultan!'

A deep voice boomed out. We had been joined by another man. Feluda had obviously seen him arrive and decided to act before it was too late.

'Sultan! Sultan!'

The voice became softer, and the tone much more gentle. The man stepped forward and entered the stage. It was Karandikar. In his hand was another whip, but he was not cracking it. He moved closer, calling Sultan softly in a low voice, as if he was a pet dog or a cat.

Chandran looked absolutely amazed, and stepped back. Arun Babu lowered his hands. The officer from the Forest Department gaped, very much like Lalmohan Babu. There were eleven men present in the forest to witness what followed in the next few minutes. With incredible tenderness and dexterity, Sultan's old trainer calmed him down, put the chain around his neck and then walked him over to where the truck stood with his cage. The men waiting outside quickly opened its door and placed a high stool before it. Mr Karandikar cracked his whip just once and said, 'Up!' Without further ado, Sultan ran, jumped on the stool and into the cage. The men locked the door instantly.

We had followed Mr Karandikar and were standing at a distance. He turned to face us as soon as the tiger was safely back in his cage. Then he gave us a salute, and made his way to a taxi waiting near the other cars. Without a word or a glance at anyone else, he got into it and drove off.

'Brilliant!' exclaimed Arun Chowdhury. Turning to Feluda, he added, 'Thanks.'

ELEVEN

All of us returned to Kailash. With Arun Babu's permission, Feluda rang someone, though I couldn't tell who it was. Then he joined us in the drawing room. Neelima Devi sent us tea. Pritin Babu was taking her and Bibi back to Calcutta the very next day, we were told. On hearing about Sultan's capture, Akhil Chakravarty said, 'Oh, I wish I had gone with you!'

'I think tomorrow I'll go back, too,' said Arun Babu, 'unless you need me here for your investigation.'

'No, that won't be necessary. I've finished my investigation and even arranged to fulfil your father's last wish.'

Arun Babu gave Feluda a startled look over the rim of his cup.

'You mean you know where Biren is?' he asked, very surprised.

'Yes. Your father was right.'

'Meaning?'

'Biren is here.'

'In Hazaribagh?'

'In Hazaribagh.'

'I find that . . . amazing!' Arun Babu said, his tone implying that he also found it impossible to believe.

'Yes, that's understandable,' Feluda said. 'But isn't that something you yourself had started to believe?'

Arun Babu put his cup down on the table and stared directly at Feluda.

'Not only that,' Feluda went on calmly, 'you were afraid that your father might make a new will and leave you out of it, giving your share to Biren.'

No one spoke for a few seconds. The atmosphere in the room suddenly became charged. Lalmohan Babu, who was sitting next to me, grabbed a cushion and clutched it tightly. Pritin Babu sat in a chair, supporting his head with one hand. Arun Chowdhury slowly rose to his feet. His eyes had turned red and a vein throbbed at his temple.

'Listen, Mr Mitter,' he roared, 'you may be a famous detective, but I am not going to let you sit there and throw totally baseless accusations at me. Jagat Singh!

His bearer slipped into the room through an open door.

'Stop! If you take another step, I will shoot you,' Feluda threatened coldly, holding his revolver. 'Jagat Singh, it was you who stole into our room, wasn't it? I managed to take off a fair amount of your hair. And I know who sent you there, with what purpose.'

Jagat Singh froze. Arun Babu sat down again, his whole body shaking with rage.

'Wh-what are you trying to say?' he demanded.

'Listen very carefully. You knew your father was thinking of changing his will. You didn't want him to find and destroy the old one. So you hid his key. Bibi saw him looking for it, and he even told her what he was looking for: "a pier . . . that which opens and that which shuts". By a "pier" he meant a "quay". Bearing in mind that he liked to play with the sound of words, I realized that the "quay" was really a "key", something which could be used to open and shut an object. Presumably, the will was kept in a locked drawer. But even after stealing the key, you weren't satisfied, were you? So, that day in Rajrappa, you seized your chance and played your trump card. You knew it would come as an enormous shock to your father, which might well be enough to kill him. If that happened, you would no longer have anything to worry about.'

'You are mad. You're just raving. You don't know what you're saying, Mr Mitter.'

'I do, I can assure you; and I can produce witnesses. There are three of them, although none of them might wish to admit what they have seen and heard. Your own brother, Akhil Chakravarty and Shankarlal . . . they all know.'

'Well then, Mr Mitter, if your witnesses won't talk, I think you are wasting your time, don't you? How are you going to prove your case?'

'Very simply. There is a fourth witness who will not hesitate at all in revealing the truth.'

Suddenly, the room was filled with strange noises. Where were they coming from? There were birds calling from somewhere, and a waterfall gushed in the background.

Feluda quietly placed a small black object on a table. It was Pritin Chowdhury's tape recorder.

'What your brother accidentally saw and heard that day made him drop his recorder near a bush. His wife saw it and picked it up. There is much more on that tape besides the chirping of birds.'

Arun Babu swallowed. His heightened colour had started to recede. In just a few minutes, he turned quite pale. Feluda kept his revolver raised and pointed at him. The tape recorder continued to run. Now there were voices, rising over the sound of the water.

'Baba, what makes you think Biren has come back?' asked Arun Babu's voice.

'If an old man likes to believe his missing son has returned, why should that bother you?' Mahesh Chowdhury asked.

'You must forget Biren. He will never come back. I know that. It simply isn't possible.'

'How can you say that? Who are you to tell me what to believe? You have no right—'

'I have every right. I don't want you to do something wrong and unfair, just because of your stupid belief.'

'What is wrong and unfair?'

'I will not let you deprive me of what is rightfully mine!'

'What are you taking about?'

'You know very well. You changed your will once, thinking Biren was not going to come back. Now you're planning to . . .'

'What I am planning is my business. I was going to change my will, in any case,' Mahesh Chowdhury had raised his voice, sounding angry, as though his old violent temper was about to burst through. 'How can you expect to be mentioned in my will at all?' he went on. 'You are dishonest, you are a gambler, you are a thief! You took Dorabjee's stamp album from my safe—'

Arun Babu's voice cut him short, 'And what about you? If I am a thief, what are you? You think I don't know about Deendayal? Your screaming and shouting woke me that night. I saw everything through a chink in the curtain. I've kept my mouth shut for thirty-five years, but I know exactly what happened. You hit Deendayal on the head with a heavy brass statue of Buddha. Can you deny that? Deendayal died. Then you got Noor Muhammad and your driver to take his body . . .'

He broke off. Something heavy fell with a thud, and then there was nothing except the birds and the waterfall. Feluda switched the recorder off and returned it to Pritin Babu.

There was absolute silence in the room. Everyone was looking tense, with the only exception of Feluda. He put his revolver back in his pocket. 'What your father did was utterly wrong,' he said. 'There can be no doubt about that. But he realized it, and for thirty-five years he suffered in silence, trying to make amends in whatever way he could. Still he didn't find any peace. From the day Deendayal died, Mahesh Chowdhury began to think he was cursed and one day he would be punished for his sins. What he did not know was that the final blow would come from his own son.'

Arun Babu sat very still staring at the floor. When he spoke his voice sounded faint, as though he was speaking from a long way away.

'There was a dog,' he said slowly. 'An Irish setter. Baba was very fond of it. For some reason, the dog did not like Deendayal. One day, it tried to bite him, so Deendayal got very cross and hit it with a heavy stick. The dog was injured. That night, Baba returned quite late from a party and found that his dog was not waiting for him in his room, as it did every day. Noor Mohammad had to tell him what had happened. Baba called Deendayal, and in a fit of rage . . . when he lost his temper, you see, Baba used to become a different man altogether.'

We rose with Feluda to take our leave. Akhil Chakravarty also got to his feet.

'Could you come with us for a minute?' Feluda asked him. 'There's something I'd like you to do. It won't take long.'

'Very well,' Akhil Chakravarty replied. 'With Mahesh gone, there's nothing left for me to do here, anyway. I have all the time in the world.'

TWELVE

Akhil Chakravarty began talking to us in the car. 'I did go off in a different direction,' he said, 'but I didn't go far. In fact, I could hear every word from where I stood near the rock with my initials on it. I used to ask Mahesh why he grew preoccupied at times and sank into silence. He used to laugh and tell me to look at his horoscope to find out. It is amazing, isn't it, that such an important event in his life remained a secret, even from me? Perhaps it's my own fault, I failed to study his stars properly.'

As our car drew up outside our gate, I realized who Feluda had called from Kailash. Shankarlal Misra was waiting for us.

'Mission successful?' Feluda asked him, getting out of the car.

'Yes,' Mr Misra replied. 'Biren has come to meet you.'

We walked into the living room to find the same sadhu from

Rajrappa sitting on a sofa. He rose as he saw us and said, 'Namaskar.' Clad in long saffron robes, he was tall and well built, his thick matted hair almost reaching his waist. An equally thick beard covered most of his face.

'He agreed to come only when I told him about his father's last wish,' Mr Misra said. 'He has got nothing against his father.'

'No,' agreed Biren, 'but then, I don't feel any love or attachment for him, either. Shankar tried very hard to bring me back. He thought if I saw my father and other members of my family, even from a distance, I might wish to come back. That is the reason why I was in Rajrappa that day. But I realized after seeing my family that that was not going to make any difference at all. I had ceased to care for them. My father was a complex man, but he was the only one who seemed to have understood me. So, in the beginning, I used to write to him. But later . . .'

'But those letters were not sent from abroad, were they? I don't think you ever left the country!' Feluda said coolly.

We gasped, but Biren Chowdhury simply stared at Feluda with an expressionless face. Then, unexpectedly, he smiled. 'Shankar had told me how clever you were. I was only testing you,' he laughed.

'Very well. Now you may take off your disguise,' Feluda suggested. 'It may be enough to fool the whole town of Hazaribagh, but you don't fool me.'

Biren Chowdhury continued to laugh as he took off his wig and his false beard. I gave another gasp as his face was revealed. Lalmohan Babu clutched at my sleeve and whispered, 'Kan-kan-kan—' He had got the name wrong again, but I was too astounded to correct him. Mr Karandikar looked at us and nodded.

Akhil Chakravarty broke the silence. 'What do you mean, Mr Mitter? Biren never went abroad? Well then, his letters—?'

'It is possible to send letters from abroad, Mr Chakravarty, if one has a friend like your son.'

'My son? What's he got to do with anything?'

'Mr Mitter's right,' Biren Chowdhury—or should I call him Mr Karandikar?—replied, 'Adheer was in Dusseldorf, wasn't he? I wrote to him and got him to send me several European postcards. Then I used to write Baba's name and address on them, sometimes adding a line or two, put them in envelopes and send them back to Adheer. He would then arrange to have them posted from various parts of Europe. He travelled a lot himself. But when he returned to

India, naturally I had to stop.'

'How extraordinary! Why did you have to be so secretive?'

'There was a reason,' Feluda said. 'I would like Mr Karandikar to confirm if my guess is correct.'

'Yes?'

'You were much impressed and inspired by the life of Colonel Suresh Biswas, and you wanted to be like him. I knew Colonel Biswas had left home as a young man and made his way to England and Brazil, but what I didn't know was that he was the first Bengali who had learnt to train tigers to perform in a circus. I read about this last night in a book called *The Circus in Bengal*. One of the items for which he became famous was parting the tiger's mouth and placing his head in it.'

Lalmohan Babu opened his mouth to speak once more.

'Sh-sh-sh-sh—' he began.

'What is it, Lalmohan Babu? Would you like us to be quiet?'

'N-n-no. Sh-shame on me, Felu Babu, shame on me! I read that book before you, and yet I failed to pick that up. I must be crazy, I must be blind, I must be . . .'

'All right, all right, you can blame yourself later. Now please let me finish.'

Lalmohan Babu simmered down. Feluda went on, 'Biren Chowdhury wanted to work with wild animals, like his hero. But an educated young man from a well-known family is not expected to join a circus as a trainer of tigers, is he? Mahesh Chowdhury might have been different from most men, but even he would not have approved. Biren knew that, and so he decided to indulge in a little deception. Am I right?'

'Absolutely,' Biren Chowdhury replied.

'What is most astonishing is that Mahesh Chowdhury could recognize his son even after so many years when he went to the circus on the first day. Arun Babu failed to do that, although he saw you from only a few feet away. You had to have plastic surgery done on your nose, didn't you, when you were attacked by a tiger? That's why you even look different from the old photo in your father's house.'

'Ah, that explains it!' Akhil Chakravarty exclaimed. 'I did wonder why everyone was calling him Biren, and yet I could not recognize him at all.'

'Anyway,' Feluda said, 'I must now tell you why I really wanted you to come here.'

He took out the photo of Muktananda from his pocket. Then he turned to Biren Chowdhury again. 'You are probably unaware that your father made a new will when he became convinced that you would never return. He left your name out of it. However, he didn't want you to be deprived altogether. So he left you this photograph.'

Feluda turned the photo over and took it out of its frame. A small folded cellophane envelope slipped out. There were a few tiny square, colourful pieces of paper in it.

'There are nine rare and valuable stamps here, which come from three different continents,' Feluda explained. 'Mr Chowdhury was afraid his album might be stolen, so he removed the most precious stamps and hid them here. According to the prices mentioned in the Gibbons catalogue twenty-five years ago, the total value of these was two thousand pounds.'

'How do you know that?'

'There was a message in your father's diary. He referred to these nine stamps as the "nine jewels", and Gibbons as "monkeys". Then he said they were worth "two thousand Shylock's demands". Tapesh reminded me that Shylock had demanded a pound of flesh. That's how I got the word "pounds". But now, I think, these jewels would fetch a lot more.'

Biren Chowdhury took the envelope from Feluda and stared at it. Then he said, 'I am only a ringmaster, Mr Mitter. I spend my life like a nomad, travelling all the time. What shall I do with something like this? Where shall I keep it? It will be such a liability! Mr Mitter, what am I going to do?'

'I can understand your problem,' Feluda replied. 'Tell you what, why don't you leave them with me? I know a few stamp dealers in Calcutta. I will speak to them and see that you get the best possible price. Then I will send you the money. Is that all right? Could you trust me, do you think?'

'Oh, absolutely.'

'Very well. But I shall need to have your address.'

'The Great Majestic Circus,' Biren Chowdhury replied. 'Kutti has realized he cannot do without me. I am going to be with them for some time. In fact, Sultan and I will be performing tonight. Please do come and watch us, all of you.'

We went to find Biren Karandikar after the show that evening to thank him and to say goodbye. He and his tiger had enthralled the audience by working together with perfect understanding and coordination. The idea of seeing him backstage was Lalmohan Babu's. It soon became clear why he was so keen.

'I am going to write a new novel,' he told him. 'The main action will take place in a circus and the ringmaster will have a very important role. May I please use the name "Karandikar" in my novel? I quite like it.'

'Of course,' Biren Chowdhury laughed. 'It is not my real name, so you may use it wherever you want!'

We thanked him and came away.

'So you changed your mind about the injection?' Feluda asked Lalmohan Babu as we emerged out of the big tent.

'Certainly not. The tiger will now be given an injection. Its second trainer is going to be the villain. He'll give the injection to make the tiger drowsy, so it doesn't perform well and the ringmaster gets the blame.'

'I see. What about the trapeze?'

'The trapeze?' Lalmohan Babu gave a derisive snort. 'The trapeze is nothing. Who wants it now?'